THE COMPLETE PERFECT SERIES

LINDSEY POWELL

Content copyright © Lindsey Powell 2021
Cover design by Lindsey Powell & Wicked Dreams Publishing 2021

All rights reserved. No part of this book may be reproduced or utilised in any form, or by any electronic or mechanical means, without the prior written permission of the author.

The characters and events portrayed in this book are fictional. Any similarities to other fictional workings, or real persons (living or dead), names, places, and companies is purely coincidental and not intended by the author.

The right of Lindsey Powell to be identified as the author of this work has been asserted by her in accordance with the Copyright, Designs and Patents act 1988.

A CIP record of this book is available from the British Library.

Except for the original material written by the author, all mention of films, television shows and songs, song titles, and lyrics mentioned in The Complete Perfect Series are the property of the songwriters and copyright holders.

BOOKS BY LINDSEY POWELL

The Perfect Series
Perfect Stranger

Perfect Memories

Perfect Disaster

Perfect Beginnings

The Complete Perfect Series

Part of Me Series
Part of Me

Part of You

Part of Us

The Control Duet
Losing Control

Taking Control

Stand-alone novels
Fixation

Take Me

Checkmate

A Valentine Christmas

PERFECT STRANGER

CHAPTER ONE

This is it.

This is how I am going to die.

I would never have imagined my life ending in this way. The fear coursing through my entire body only moments ago has now been replaced by a feeling of shock.

My body trembles as I acknowledge an agonising pain in my left side. Everything is becoming hazy, making it difficult for me to register exactly what is happening to me.

Time seems to stop as I try to focus on my surroundings. Unfortunately, I can't seem to divert my focus from the immense pain that is spreading through me like wildfire.

My head throbs from where it smashed against the floor when I fell only seconds ago. I dazedly manage to lift my head slightly, so that I can look to my left side where the pain is all consuming.

It's difficult lifting my head up off of the floor as all I want to do is give in to the darkness that beckons to me. It takes all of my remaining energy to move, and when I look down, I see shiny metal sticking into my side.

My mouth starts to fill with saliva and I desperately swallow it down, willing myself not to vomit. The red substance seeping out of my side is starting to saturate my clothes.

My blood.

Lots of my blood.

I try to call out, but my mouth doesn't want to cooperate. I let my head fall back to the floor and my eyes begin to feel heavy. I fight the urge to close them, but the darkness seems so inviting.

Images flash through my mind rapidly. So many images and memories, and so little time in which to process them all.

In the distance I can hear some sort of commotion. An evil laugh brings back the element of fear and then there's the sound of footsteps beside me. I hear a voice shout, "NOOO," which alerts me to who's voice it is. The voice shouting brings me comfort. Such a beautiful voice.

I let go of the fear and let my eyes flutter shut. A pair of arms feel like they are enveloping me. Strong arms that hold me in their embrace. It brings a warmth that I wasn't expecting to this moment. I try to open my eyes once more to look at what I know will be the most handsome face I have ever seen, but all of my energy has left me.

I stop fighting against the urge to sleep and I let the darkness slowly seep in. The images return and flicker through my mind, until they stop at one particular moment of my past.

Full lips grazed my cheek softly as he leant in to whisper, "Spend the night with me."

A statement, not a question. His words made my insides melt. My knees felt like they were going to buckle beneath me. Excitement raced through my core. Butterflies fluttered wildly in my stomach.

His heated breath on my skin was enticing. He smelt incredible. His voice deep with smooth undertones, luring me to accompany him.

Sparks jolted through my body as his hand found a resting place at the bottom of my back. A delicious tingling ran through me and arousal radiated from my body.

The memory fades and the image of caramel coloured eyes fills my brain. The eyes of my perfect stranger. The mere sight leaves me gasping for my final few breaths. Through the fogginess I am abruptly pulled back to reality for a few seconds by three simple words.

"I love you."

That beautiful and comforting voice is lulling me into a secure feeling.

With the images and memories now gone, those final words imprint on my last waking moment.

I finally give in.

Darkness has consumed me.

CHAPTER TWO

THREE WEEKS EARLIER

"STACEY! What the bloody hell is taking you so long?" Charles bellows up the stairs, his voice making me cringe.

"I'm coming. Will you keep your voice down!" I shout back to Charles.

"Well for goodness sake's, get a move on. We need to leave in the next five minutes." I can hear the irritation in his voice. He is such an impatient man. How I ever thought that I was in love with him I will never know.

Charles is my boyfriend and we have been together for nearly three years. I used to think that I was quite lucky to have caught his eye. His short blond hair and dark green eyes were what first attracted me to him. I am a sucker for nice eyes.

His athletic body wasn't bad to look at either. Don't get me wrong, he wasn't what you would call ripped, but he certainly wasn't lacking in the abs department. To be fair, Charles still has a good physique as he likes to take care of himself.

When we first started dating he was kind and charming. He would take me out for dinner and to the movies, and we had a fairly decent sex life. Not outstanding but satisfying enough.

He seemed to want to look after me, and I craved that feeling. It was a feeling I had craved ever since my Nan had passed away. My Nan was my rock and she looked after me from a young age.

I was nine years old when my parents were taken from me. They died in a horrific car crash, and a little piece of me died along with my parents on that day. The two most precious people in my life were taken in such a brutal way. The crash wasn't even their fault, it was caused by some drunk-driver who obviously couldn't resist the urge to drive rather than walk.

My Nan instantly became my legal guardian. She embraced her role and made me feel loved and cared for. I worshipped her. She took me in, an angry little nine-year-old girl, and made me into the woman I am today. Well, the woman I was before Charles came along.

I think that if she were around today, she would be disappointed by my life choices at this moment in time. I try not to think about that too much though.

My Nan died three and a half years ago after a long battle with cancer. I was devastated. There isn't a day that goes by that I don't miss her, and of course my parents. I was twenty-five when my Nan died. She never met Charles. I don't know what she would have thought about him, but I can take a good guess that she would have seen right through his nice guy act from the start.

Charles came into my life six months after my Nan's death. I am not close to many people, so at a time when I was vulnerable, Charles managed to get through to me.

My best friend Lydia has never liked him. She says that she has had his card marked since the day I introduced her to him. I never let her dislike of him phase me though. He wanted to care for me and that was all I wanted at the time. How ridiculously naïve of me. I should have listened to Lydia.

"STACEY! COME ON!" Charles bellows again, breaking me from my thoughts.

I roll my eyes, quickly finish applying my lip-gloss and take one last look at myself in the full-length mirror.

I am wearing the most gorgeous red, floor length, lace dress with killer red stiletto heels. The fabric of the dress hugs my body in all the right places and gives me just the right amount of cleavage due to the slight plunge from the neckline. I look classy, and of course the dress has been pre-approved by Charles. He is such a control freak.

I have my long brunette hair loosely curled and swept to one side, where I have placed a clip so that it flows down my right shoulder. I have kept my make-up to simple nude shades as I don't want to distract from the dress. I have small silver-hooped earrings in, and a plain silver bracelet on my left wrist. The bracelet has sentimental value as my Nan gave it to me for my twenty-first birthday.

Pleased with my appearance, I quickly make my way down the stairs to find Charles waiting by the front door with his car keys in his hand, tapping his foot and glaring in my direction.

"Finally! Why do you always insist on making us late for everything?"

"We're not late. If I was to come down the stairs looking slightly dishevelled then you would moan that I embarrass you, and we can't have your colleagues seeing us as less than perfect now, can we?" The sarcasm drips from each word that I speak.

Whilst muttering under his breath, Charles passes me my coat and ushers me out of the front door and towards his car. His brand new, flashy sports car that he purchased this morning. We couldn't possibly be seen in my car, the boring bog standard three-door run-about. Heaven forbid that people see us arriving in any vehicle that's isn't classed as 'posh' by Charles' standards.

Once in the car, we sit in silence and my mind starts to wander. How did things become so bad between us? How have we lost the respect that we used to have for one another? Maybe he has never respected me, and it is only since living together that I have noticed?

I took the plunge and moved in with him six months ago. Charles had been pestering me for a few months, prior to me giving in, about living with him.

He made me an offer that I couldn't refuse, and I agreed to share his home. The offer was one in which I would be able to become a full-time writer. My dream is to become a published author and Charles used this reason to finally get me to say yes. He told me that I could give up work and that he would look after me.

Now, up until that point I had never been a kept woman, but I am so passionate about my writing that I had to seriously consider his proposal. At the time I was working at The Den and I had been there for five years.

The Den is a club that is the place to go on any night of the week. It was where I first met Lydia. I loved my bar job, but it was never my lifelong dream.

I took a few days to think about what Charles had offered, and I concluded that if I was ever going to devote my time to becoming a full-time writer then this was my chance. I told Charles that I would move in with him and he seemed delighted, leading me to think that I had made the right choice. How wrong could I have been? Very, as it turns out. I handed in my notice at The Den and moved in with Charles a few days later.

Within two weeks of moving in with him, Charles started to show his true colours. Granted, I had seen some of his bad traits on occasion, but doesn't everyone have bad points? Maybe I was just too ignorant to see those traits executed to their full extent beforehand? He was only ever badly behaved in relation to his business, and even that wasn't very often. His bad behaviour had never been directed at me.

If I ever questioned him about the way in which he was acting, he would always have a perfectly good reason as to why he acted in this manner. All I wanted was to be loved and cared for, and I fell for his excuses every time.

I saw Charles as the closest thing to family that I had. What an idiot I truly was.

The first week of living with him was good. In fact, it was so good that I was kicking myself for not moving in when he had asked me the first time. He made me dinner every night, bought me flowers and generally made me feel special. I bragged to Lydia about how great he was being, and generally made her feel sick with my renewed affection for him.

I should have kept my mouth shut because week two brought with it the real Charles Montpellior. He became an absolute nightmare, and he still is to this day.

I remember it clearly, the day that it all changed.

It was a Monday evening and the start of my second week of living with

Charles. I was quietly sat in the lounge, watching the evening soaps on the television when Charles walked in with a folder tucked under his arm.

I didn't take much notice as he brought work home with him all the time. He is the owner of J & M Accounting. However, on this particular Monday evening, Charles picked up the television remote and turned the television off. I looked at him, appalled that I was unable to watch the rest of my programme. He sat down in the chair opposite me and I was about to ask him what he was doing, but the look on his face stopped me. His serious expression had me sitting up to attention.

"Now that you have been here for a week, I feel I need to set some ground rules," he said. *Ground rules?*

I must have looked confused because he quickly carried on talking. "I have a list of things here that I would like you to adhere to. I feel it is only fair seeing as you no longer work."

His expression was so serious that I almost wanted to laugh. I didn't though. His comment about me not working stung a little. I wanted to argue back that it was his idea for me to stop working, but he continued with his little speech.

"In this folder, you will find lists of what I find acceptable. If you could read this tonight, then from tomorrow you can start to follow these routines and rules."

It wasn't a question; it was an order.

Charles placed the folder on the coffee table between us and then stood up. "I will be in my study if you need to discuss anything." With that, Charles strode out of the room.

I looked at the folder as if it were going to bite me. What on earth did he mean by routines?

I sighed, picked up the folder and opened it to the first page. There were ten pages in total, each one detailing what he expected of me. There was a cleaning rota, a shopping list, a weekly allowance budget for myself, and a schedule of when I would be required to attend functions with Charles.

At first, I honestly thought that he must have been playing some sort of joke. I said as much to him, only to be greeted with a scowl. It was the following morning and onwards that I realised that I had made a mistake.

I had just turned twenty-eight, and here I was being instructed on how to live my life. I managed to follow the routines and lists for the first few weeks, and then I thought I would mix it up a bit. I don't mean drastically, I just mean that instead of cooking lasagne on the Wednesday I decided to cook it on the Monday. This did not go down well with Charles and resulted in him having a complete hissy fit at me.

I can only compare his tantrum to that of a two-year-old toddler. It was ridiculous for a grown man to be acting this way. I recall the poisonous words he spoke to me. You would have thought that I had threatened to castrate him with the way that he went on.

Charles then sulked about the lasagne incident, or lasagne-gate as I call it, for the next week. Yes, a whole fucking week.

I told Lydia, and my friend Martin, about his behaviour and neither of them were surprised. In fact, I had to stop Lydia from marching round to our house and giving him what for. She's extremely feisty and protective of her friends.

Martin on the other hand has to be careful, seeing as he works for Charles as an event planner. Martin has been a witness to many of Charles' outbursts. He's also been on the receiving end of a few of them too.

Martin has worked for Charles for the last three years. We got chatting at an event two years ago and we have maintained a friendship ever since. A secret friendship that is, as Charles would never approve of me befriending his staff.

Martin has such an infectious personality, and I adore him. It is hard to meet up with him though as every time I go out I am asked numerous questions by Charles about where I have been and who I have been with. After six months, I suppose I have gotten used to the interrogating.

So, here I am, playing the dutiful girlfriend and making sure that others think Charles and I have the perfect life. Hell, I have gotten so good at putting on a show that I could probably pursue a career in acting.

Whilst I have perfected my outer shell, on the inside I am in turmoil. I am bored. Bored of being his arm candy, bored of having my life planned out for me, and bored of having no chemistry whatsoever, sexually or otherwise.

I'm sure no one would really blame me for losing my sexual appetite though. We have sex once a month, on a designated night of Charles' choice. Although, we have given that a miss for the last two months, much to my relief.

I crave the feeling of intimacy and love. I fantasize about having the types of orgasms and sexual trysts that you read about in romance novels, or that you see in the movies. I love to read and often have my nose in a book. However, it is not just the story that grips me, it is also the escape a good book gives me. It's like a time out from my real life. I can almost imagine that I am the heroine in a novel, and that I am the one who is being seduced by the man that worships her on a daily basis.

My mind often wanders back to the only one-night stand that I have ever had. It was the night before I moved in with Charles, and my last shift working at The Den. I know I shouldn't have done it, but this guy was so mesmerising. That night was one of the best nights of my life. God, how pathetic does that sound? I didn't even ask what the guy's name was, I just knew that I needed to be with him and give my body to him. And by God did he take it. Even now my body hums at the mere memory of him.

"And for God's sake, don't say or do anything stupid. Last time you made a fool of yourself as well as a fool of me." Charles once again interrupts my thoughts. His voice holds nothing but anger and disgust.

"Charles, I didn't do anything wrong." I sigh, bored. We must have had this conversation about a hundred times. He is like a broken record.

"Oh please, your dancing was atrocious. I had to excuse your behaviour for weeks afterwards." He actually screws his face up as he speaks.

"If I am such an embarrassment to you then why the hell are you taking me to this event?" I ask, exasperated. Anyone would think that I had done a bloody strip tease for the entire room with the way he goes on about it.

"People will expect you to be there. It will look bad if you don't accompany me. I don't need people asking me questions about where else you might be. I don't have time to make excuses for you."

Charles leaves no room for any more discussion on this topic. I can't be bothered to respond anyway. I am deflated. I feel beaten down by him. The situation that I am in is beyond dire.

The truth is that Charles has merely become a means to an end for me, and he has been for a while now. If I leave Charles, then I won't be able to continue being a full-time writer. Selfish I know, but this is what it comes down to.

I should have kept a few of my shifts at The Den, but no, I stupidly thought that he might just want to see me succeed in my writing career. I now see that he just wanted me to become his personal skivvy.

He always hated me working at The Den. Charles maintains that he hated all of the male attention that I received, and before I moved in with him I genuinely believed that was the reason. Now however, I realise that Charles wanted me at his beck and call. It was also not a 'posh' enough job for his girlfriend to have. I mean, in Charles' mind, the thought of saying that he lived with a barmaid must have been so beneath him.

I miss my independence, and I suppose he thinks that he can treat me how he wants now that he controls all of my finances.

Three years of my life have been dedicated to this relationship, obviously not taking into account my one night of dalliance. I think it took moving in with Charles to see that we really aren't a good match.

I like to take each day as it comes and enjoy life, but Charles is incapable of that. I personally think his bad traits all come from his mother. Oh my, he is a mummy's boy in every sense. I really don't like his mother, and the feeling is mutual.

Charles is an only child, born into a rich family. His mother, Margaret, always lets him have his own way. Charles and his mother share the worst trait of all, being a snob.

Margaret has always been very vocal about how Charles deserves to be with someone better than me. These types of comments used to hurt me, but I just ignore them now. Over time, I guess you just learn to grow a thicker skin to hateful words.

His father, James, was the complete opposite. He was such a lovely man. He died two years ago from cancer. Bloody cancer seems to take all the good people away from me… well, either that or a car crash. James dying is how Charles acquired fifty percent ownership of J & M Accounting, and the company is known in various countries around the world.

Charles does work hard to make sure that the company is running to a high standard, but would it kill him to take one day off? Apparently so, according to him. We haven't had one whole day together, by ourselves, for over a year.

When I had my own job, and I didn't live with him, I suppose we managed to make time for one another. Something we stopped doing and took for granted, or at least Charles did anyway. Charles' money is far too important to him nowadays to pay any attention to his girlfriend, also known as the live-in maid.

I seriously need to rethink what I am doing. I don't know how much longer I can put up with his behaviour. I never pictured myself being with a man like this. I am nearly at my breaking point.

The drive to the Bowden Hall takes about twenty minutes, and that is where tonight's event will be held. We regularly attend functions here and its beauty never ceases to amaze me.

The vast grounds are spectacular with luscious green grass that is always maintained to the highest standard. It never looks like anyone has set foot on it. The gardens go on for miles, with beautiful flowers lining the driveway all the way up to the stunning building that is the Bowden Hall.

The building has big sash windows and eighty rooms in total which are all decorated with the finest antiques and painted in the richest colours. Golds, reds and greens are the main colours throughout. It makes you feel like you have entered a building out of a fairy-tale.

We pull up to the front doors and the valet comes straight over, standing to attention by the car, waiting for us to get out so that he can go and park it at the rear of the building.

Charles gets out, not bothering to walk around and open my door for me. I emerge from the car and walk around to take my place by Charles' side. I know the drill.

"Now, darling, make sure that you smile and generally adore me," Charles says, smirking. God, you would think that he was fifty-odd instead of being twenty-nine years old with the way that he talks. I could quite happily slap him, but instead I plaster a fake smile on my face as we walk up the steps and enter the building.

The entrance hall is vast with an impressive cascading staircase leading to the first floor. The butler stood by the door greets us politely as we walk past him. To the left of us is the Great Ballroom which is the room that tonight's event is taking place in.

There are four other rooms on the ground floor, but Charles always insists on using the Great Ballroom for events. I presume it is because it is the biggest and most lavish room of them all.

As we enter, I admire once again how stunning the décor is. From the gold-plated trim to the crystal chandeliers that hang above us. The lighting of the room is soft and intimate, ready for the dinner and dance that is about to begin. I take a flute of champagne from a passing waiter's tray.

"That's right, on the booze already," Charles snarls in my ear.

"Oh shut up, Charles. It's a party. There are drinks all around. Now lighten up," I say sweetly, keeping the smile plastered on my face as I speak. I can see that he wants to retaliate, but Martin is walking over to us, so Charles kisses my cheek instead. Keeping up appearances is in full swing.

"Ah, Martin," Charles says. "Wonderful party so far, eh?" Ugh, I think I am going to throw up. What an idiot.

"Oh, yes. It has been a pleasure planning this event, sir," Martin responds, ever the dutiful employee. Martin then turns to me and takes my hand. "Looking as beautiful as ever, Miss Stacey." He places a kiss on the back of my hand which makes me smile.

Martin does a good job of acting like we are just acquaintances at these events. I give him my most dazzling grin. His partner Clayton is also just as charming. They make a wonderful couple.

Martin has toned down his look for this evening's event. Normally he would be wearing some sort of fluorescent coloured clothing, but tonight he dons a simple black tuxedo and white shirt combo. His black hair is swept to one side and gelled to within an inch of its life. His blue eyes sparkle, and his goatee has been neatly trimmed. He looks very handsome and nowhere near his thirty years.

"Why thank you, Martin. You don't scrub up too badly yourself," I say to him. Martin chuckles and excuses himself to go and promote his party planning skills to the other guests. Can't say I blame him for wanting to get away from Charles as soon as he can. Seeing him at work five days a week is bad enough but having to pander to him on a Saturday night must be torture.

"I wish you wouldn't talk like that to my employees. You sound so common," says Charles. I feel anger course through my body. I cannot listen to this man for a moment longer.

"Well, I hope this is common enough for you; fuck off, Charles," I respond and turn on my heel, leaving him so that I can go and find someone more interesting to talk to. Although, that is a challenge in itself seeing as nearly everyone here is probably just as stuck up as Charles is.

I can feel my blood boiling at how much of a dick Charles is being. I walk through the throngs of people, smiling politely and saying the odd hello here and there.

As I approach the back of the ballroom, my eyes rest on a gentleman with his back to me. I stop walking and admire his stance, which even from the back is commanding.

For some reason my body begins to react to him. There is a humming radiating through me, and the hairs on my body stand to attention. Goosebumps cover my entire being and I shiver as the man starts to turn around.

I feel the breath leave my lungs and butterflies make an appearance in my stomach as his eyes lock with mine. His caramel coloured eyes, so beautiful that I could get lost in them. His silky, jet black hair is styled to perfection, and his lips look so soft and kissable. The slight stubble on his chin gives him a handsome, rugged look.

I can't believe that I am looking at him.

I squeeze my eyes shut.

I must be dreaming.

But when I open my eyes, he is still there. He is standing a few feet away from me, looking like a God.

This can't be happening.

My sex clenches with excitement as I continue to look into his eyes.

Time stops.

I never thought I would ever see him again.

My one-night stand.

My perfect stranger.

CHAPTER THREE

I stand on the spot for what feels like hours, but in reality, must only be a few seconds. I cannot move. My feet feel like they are glued to the floor, and my mouth has gone completely dry.

He is talking to someone else, but his eyes never leave mine. His gorgeous, penetrating eyes. It has been six months since I had my wild night with this man. I truly thought that I would never see him again, but here he is, in the flesh, at my pompous boyfriend's event. I have never seen him at any events that Charles has thrown before.

I feel someone pulling on my arm and I get the sudden urge to swat them away like I would an annoying fly buzzing around me. I blink a few times and manage to avert my eyes from my handsome stranger, only to come face to face with Margaret. I can't help but roll my eyes. Of all the people in this room who may want to speak to me, it has to be her. She looks angry, and I know that I am about to face her acidic tongue.

"What do you think you are doing, young lady? How dare you walk off from my son like that. You are making yourself look ridiculous and not to mention childish. You are lucky to be classed as his girlfriend, Stacey. Now, go back and treat him with the respect that he deserves." She hisses each and every word at me like a ticked off snake, and her pudgy face is screwed up in distaste.

I guess a simple hello wouldn't have sufficed.

The years have not been kind to Margaret Montpellior. Her hair is completely grey and is pulled back into a tight bun. There are multiple crow's feet around her eyes, and her double chin wobbles as she shakes her head at me. Margaret is only a short woman, but she doesn't shy away from anyone who pisses her, or her son, off. Her nose is wrinkled at me in disgust, and I feel something shift inside me. I can no longer bite my tongue.

"Excuse me, Marge," she hates it when I call her that, "I really don't appreciate being spoken to like that. After all, you wouldn't want me to make a scene now, would you?"

The look of shock and disbelief on her face is priceless. I can't deal with her right now.

"I am not going to stand here and argue with you. Just tell Charles that I am going to get some fresh air, and when I am ready I will be back to carry on our sham of a relationship." I don't wait for her to respond, turning and walking towards the entrance hall.

I can't believe I spoke to her like that. I can normally keep a lid on my emotions, but something has happened to my brain to mouth function. The look on her face is one that I will forever keep logged in my memory. I feel a smirk creep across my face, and I do nothing to try and hide it.

Seeing my stranger has clearly thrown me.

I quickly make my way through the guests who are still entering the ballroom and head out to the front gardens, keeping my head down to avoid eye contact with anyone. I am not in the mood to make idle chit-chat right now.

I walk into the first garden and find a secluded area behind one of the glorious rose bushes. The scent that radiates from the flowers is heavenly.

I sit on a dainty little white bench which looks onto a pond that is filled with koi carp fish. No one can see me sat here, behind the rose bush. I sit and watch the fish happily swimming about. What with Charles, Margaret, and my stranger all in the same room, my brain is in overload.

I close my eyes and let out a sigh and am instantly frozen in place when I hear, "Surely it's not that bad to run into me?"

Oh my God, that voice, so smooth.

It's him.

My stranger.

Shit.

I seem to have lost the ability to speak.

I take in a deep breath and open my eyes. I turn my body in the direction of his voice and I raise my head, so I can look at his caramel pools.

"I didn't think I was so scary that you had to run off," he says whilst suppressing a smile.

My gaze settles on his mouth and my tongue darts out to moisten my dry lips. My mind is screaming at me, *get your shit together, Stacey!*

Oh God, what do I do?

My body reacts to him in much the same way as it did when I saw him in the ballroom. The humming is racing through me, and I have to clench my sex as it starts to stir. He is just watching me, waiting for me to respond. I clear my throat and manage to get my voice to work.

"Well, not scary as such, but maybe a bit underdressed for the occasion," I say with a hint of sarcasm in my tone.

Of course he doesn't look the slightest bit underdressed, but it was the first thing I could think of to say. I am totally out of my depth. I need to remain calm and not allow myself to panic.

"I don't think I did too badly," he says, holding his arms out either side of him so I can get a look at his full form. Even with his tuxedo on I can see that his body is well cared for. Hell, I can remember his body being like a work of art.

He slowly turns around and my eyes fixate on his pert behind. My, my, my, he really is breath taking. It's a good job that I am sitting down, otherwise I think my knees would have given way by now. His black tuxedo is complete with a bow-tie and he looks good enough to eat. Looking very smart in his ensemble he manages to ooze a cool-yet-casual vibe.

"Judging by the look on your face, I would say you agree," he says, smiling.

Shit, now I just look pathetic and am probably a few seconds away from having drool running down my chin. I am struggling to form words, which is something I have never really struggled with before. *Think, Stacey, think.*

"Okay, so you do look very handsome in your tuxedo, but then so do the other men in this place." *Oh yeah, great move, Stace. Making yourself sound like a tart who eyes up other men is the way to go with this. Genius. You should have just kept your mouth shut.*

"Have a wandering eye do we, Miss…"

"Paris. Stacey Paris."

I hold my hand out for him to shake, praying silently that he doesn't notice that I am quivering. He steps closer and takes hold of my hand. I feel sparks shoot through my body as our skin connects. My eyes go wide as I stare into his eyes.

He lifts my hand, bends down, and places a kiss on the back of it. I draw in a long, shaky breath and squeeze my legs together. *How can he have this effect on me? I barely know the guy.*

I clear my throat. "And you are?" I enquire.

"Jake Waters."

"Jake Waters," I repeat. I know that name. *Why do I know that name?* I cast my mind back to a conversation I overheard Charles having a few weeks ago, and it suddenly dawns on me. "Jake Waters? As in Jake Waters who owns the company Waters Industries?"

"The very same," he replies.

Fuck.

I didn't realise that was who he is. Well, why would I when all I did was fall for his charms in a bar and spend the night with him in a moment of madness without even asking his name.

He frowns at me. "Why do you look like you have just seen a ghost?" I realise that he is still holding my hand, and I abruptly pull my hand away before jumping up off the bench.

"Uh, I have to go. It was nice to meet you, *again*," I say as I dash past him and head back to the entrance of the Bowden Hall.

I walk as quickly as my stilettos will allow me to. He looked taken aback by my reply, but I can't let myself get into a proper conversation with him. My heartbeat is pounding, and I feel dizzy with the realisation of who I have slept with. Charles will flip his lid if he ever finds out.

Jake Waters owns one of the largest companies in the world, and it ranges in all types of business from accountants to construction. The guy is a multi-millionaire and he's only thirty-three years old.

Jake also happens to be the rival accountant company for Charles' firm. Oh, and Charles just happens to hate Jake's guts.

I try to calm my breathing and stop myself from shaking. The last thing I need is Charles noticing my current state and asking me a hundred and one questions.

I stand outside the Great Ballroom and take long, deep breaths.

When I have managed to regain some composure, I enter the ballroom. The guests are all sat down and are being served their starters. I scan the room, looking for Charles and spot him at a table, right in the middle. I steadily walk towards him, although he seems to be far too engrossed in conversation to notice where I am.

"I'm sorry that I took so long," I say to Charles as I take my seat beside him. "I just needed to clear my head."

Charles looks at me for a few seconds and then returns to his conversation with another guest at the table. He doesn't even speak to me. I am mortified. How dare he make me feel so worthless.

I quickly look at the other guests sat around the table and hope that none of them just witnessed Charles humiliating me. Most of the diners are immersed in their own discussions, but Martin, who is sat opposite me, is looking directly at me. I give him a weak smile which he returns with a frown. I just shake my head at him and avert my gaze.

I quietly start to pick at my duck starter. I would much rather be eating a burger to be honest. All this rich food makes me feel a bit sick.

Putting my fork down, I feel goose-bumps cascade over my body as I see Jake walk across the room and sit at the table next to me. He is staring at me and I can almost feel his eyes undressing me. The heat gathering between my legs would suggest that I like the thought of him undressing me.

Shit, I need to get a hold on my body's reactions to him.

I watch as Jake picks up his glass and raises it in my direction. I quickly look away.

So, not only have I got my feelings to contend with, but now Jake will be able to see that I am here with Charles.

The last thing I want is to become a pawn between the two of them. For all I know, Jake may decide to hold me to ransom over the fact that we slept together. I'm really hoping that Jake keeps his mouth shut about what happened between us. I dread to think how Charles and his precious mother would react if they were ever to learn the truth.

CHAPTER FOUR

Charles acts like an ignorant ass throughout the entire meal. I also have to endure Margaret staring daggers at me the whole time with her beady little eyes. On top of that I have to keep my eyes from wandering over to where Jake is sat. This really does go down as the most uncomfortable event that I have ever attended.

Once the dessert has been cleared away, we are all asked to move to one end of the room so that the staff can quickly clear the tables away for the dancing part of the evening to begin. I am relieved that the meal is over.

As I stand up, Charles grabs hold of my hand and leads me to a corner of the room.

"Why did you speak to Mummy the way you did earlier?" He is not happy one little bit. It makes me cringe that he calls her mummy.

I roll my eyes as I sense a storm brewing, and I don't mean the mother nature kind. God, Charles and his mum are like a tag team; piss one of them off and the other one comes at you too. I don't stand a chance against the both of them.

"She was going on at me and I snapped. I came here to support you, but all I seem to get is grief, and to be quite honest, I'm bloody sick of it," I say quietly. As much as I would love to embarrass Charles in front of all these people, I really don't need them knowing that my love life is a sham.

"Well, have a little more respect next time," he hisses at me. I smile at him through gritted teeth and turn away.

I spot Jake leaning against the wall just along from us. He is talking to Martin. I wish I could go over there and just be near him, but I know that I can't. I turn back towards Charles and dutifully stay by his side whilst the ballroom is prepared.

After about fifteen minutes the ballroom is ready, and the band are all set up to play. They start off by playing some jazz music which has a great vibe. I feel my body start to sway in time to the beat.

"Do you want to dance, Charles?" I ask him, even though I know that he will say no.

"No thanks. There are people that I need to speak to." With that he walks off and starts chatting to some young blond woman. I don't feel remotely jealous. I do however feel rejected. I know that we're not in a great place and haven't been for some time, but a little attention wouldn't go amiss. I could cry through sheer frustration at my situation. My head is all over the place.

"I'll dance with you."

I look to the side of me to see that Jake is still leant against the wall, but somehow without me noticing, he has managed to sneak right up next to me.

"I don't think that's a good idea," I tell him.

"Come on, one dance won't hurt. I promise I'll let you lead," he says with a smirk and I feel a smile creep across my lips. Why the hell shouldn't I dance with him? My boyfriend certainly isn't interested in doing so.

"You have a beautiful smile." I can feel the blush on my cheeks from Jake's compliment. Thank goodness the lighting is dim in here.

I give into the temptation and grab Jake's hand, pulling him onto the dance floor. The band finishes playing their jazz number and start to play a slower song. Maybe dancing to this isn't the best idea, what with it being a much slower pace.

I am about to make an excuse when Jake takes both my hands and places them on his shoulders. He then puts both of his hands on my hips, causing my adrenaline to sky rocket.

I am frozen in time and butterflies start doing somersaults in my stomach. I am aware of everything he is doing. Nothing and no one else exists in this moment as we start to dance to the music.

He leads, I follow, and we dance in silence for the first half of the song. Jake is staring into my eyes which makes this moment seem significant, for reasons that I can't comprehend.

I know that if Charles can see me then he will be furious, but I really don't care. I will deal with the fallout later.

"So, Stacey," Jakes says, breaking the silence between us. "Why did you run off from me?"

"Oh, I knew that the food was being served at any moment, so I thought it best that I get back," I reply.

Jake chuckles quietly and leans towards me, putting his lips right by my ear. "I don't mean tonight, Stacey. I meant when we had our first encounter together all those months ago."

Oh God.

I feel my heartbeat quicken and my sex starts to stir. I am positive that I look the colour of a beetroot right now. I am a little shocked that he even remembered me. Then again, I never forgot him. I'm not quite sure what to tell him, so I simply stick to the truth.

"We met in a bar, we went back to yours and had sex. Then, when the morning came, I left. That's how it works, isn't it?" I manage to make myself sound cheap from my brutal description. It was so much more than sex, but how am I meant to say that to him? I am doing a fantastic job of impressing people tonight. Not.

"I suppose it is. I wouldn't know though, it's not something that I would usually do," Jake says with a wink.

"Me either," I say a little too loudly.

A couple dancing near us looks over and I manage to smile politely at them. I feel my defences rise at Jake's comment. He probably thinks that I am just some floozy who will jump into bed with anyone. I can hardly blame him for thinking that I suppose, but I am still going to put him right on the matter.

"That was the one and only time that I have been crazy enough to go home with a stranger and have a one-night stand. Don't think that I make a habit of it, buddy."

"Whoa, calm down. I didn't mean it to sound like that. I just wondered why you left whilst I was asleep. I didn't mean anything by it, I promise." Jake stares into my eyes and I know that he is telling me the absolute truth. Why do I feel like this around him?

"Okay. Sorry," I say, my anger slowly ebbing away. I should really think before I react sometimes. I suppose I am just so used to Charles putting me down that I expect every guy to do the same thing.

"I didn't think that you would want me there the morning after, so I left. It was only meant to be a one-night thing. I have a boyfriend," I say coyly.

"Ah, you mean the ever-charming Charles Montpellior." Jake's voice is laced with sarcasm.

"Uh, yeah. I guess you figured that out, huh?" *Now you just sound fucking stupid, Stacey. Of course he figured it out.*

"Yeah." Jake chuckles. "Were you guys together when you slept with me?" I avert my eyes from Jake in shame at his question. I can't bear to admit that I cheated on Charles. "I'll take that as a yes."

"I know it looks bad. I know what I did was terrible, but I just needed to clear some stuff in my head and I needed to be wild, just once." I try to explain my scandalous behaviour. "I never intended to come back to yours, it just happened."

"So coming back to mine was a mistake then?"

"God no." *For fuck's sake, Stace, tone it down and make yourself sound less eager.* "I meant to say that you were not a mistake, but I just needed one night out of my reality. One night where I did something for me. Just one night where I did something wild and enjoyed it."

Jake is smiling, and I am now aware that we are slow dancing to a completely different pace of song. We must look ridiculous.

"So, I was your wild something?" Jake asks.

"Yeah, you could say that. Sort of like my perfect stranger."

Oh Christ, did I really just say that out loud? I need to stop embarrassing myself and get the hell out of here.

I break away from Jake and stand a few feet back from him. I feel flustered and need to regain my composure, which I am not going to achieve by being near him.

Jake puts his hands in his trouser pockets and I ache from the loss of contact.
"Thanks for the dance, Jake, but I really need to go and find Charles now."
With that I walk off of the dance floor and go in search of Charles.
I can feel Jake's eyes on me, burning into my back as I walk away.

CHAPTER FIVE

I find Charles sat at the bar with the same young blond woman that he was talking to earlier. He doesn't appear to be aware of Jake and I dancing together just now. Thank goodness for that.

I roll my eyes at the sight of the woman hanging on his every word and I go and interrupt their conversation. I stand just behind Charles and tap him on the shoulder.

"I don't mean to interrupt, but I would like to go home now, please," I tell him. Charles turns around and scowls at me.

"What? We can't possibly leave yet, darling. We need to mingle some more. Would you like a drink?" Charles looks and sounds utterly pissed off that I have intruded on him talking to this blond woman.

Whoever she is, she sits there with her legs crossed in front of her and the slit of her dress reveals the top of her thigh. Her make-up appears to have been applied with a trowel, and her breasts look like they are trying to make a bid for freedom from her low-cut dress. Christ, it barely covers her nipples.

She is twiddling a lock of her long blond hair around her finger, an obvious sign that she is flirting with Charles. She smiles at me, but I can sense that she would rather I just disappear. This woman clearly doesn't care that I am Charles' girlfriend. I sigh and turn my attention back to Charles.

"I don't want a drink, I want to go home," I say a little more forcefully.

"We're not going anywhere yet, so just stop being so rude," Charles says before turning away from me and continuing his conversation with the blond.

That's it.

That is the final straw.

I have had it with him.

I whirl around on my heels and march towards the entrance hall, where I ask the butler if he would kindly call me a taxi. He says that he will, and he goes off to fulfil my request.

I am so mad at Charles right now. He has done nothing but humiliate me and make me look stupid all evening.

I can feel my blood pressure rising, and I can't wait to get out of this place and put tonight behind me.

I stand by the front doors and tap my foot impatiently as I wait for the butler to confirm he has ordered me a taxi.

Whilst I am waiting, I can sense Jake approaching me. I look in his direction as he exits the Great Ballroom.

Oh God, he is so handsome.

His eyes are fixed on me as he comes closer. He reaches me and runs his eyes up and down my body, making me feel as if I am stood naked before him. I feel a blush creep up my neck and reach my cheeks.

"Going somewhere?" he asks me.

"Not that it is any of your business, but yes, I am going home. I am just waiting for my taxi to arrive." My tone comes across as rude and I don't mean it to be, but I also don't want him to see the effect that he has on me. Plus, I'm still really pissed at the way Charles has treated me tonight.

"Uh, Miss?" The butler interrupts us, diverting my attention from Jake. "Your taxi will be here in the next fifteen minutes."

"Thank you," I politely answer. The butler nods his head and goes to resume his position, stood opposite Jake and I, by the front doors.

"I can give you a ride, if you like?" Jake says, seemingly unaffected by my rudeness towards him only seconds ago. It takes me a moment to control my shock at his suggestion.

"Um, that's really not necessary."

"Look, I know it will be difficult to keep your hands off of me, but surely it beats waiting around for a taxi?" Jake says, trying to make a joke of it.

I feel a slight grin start to tug at my lips at his playful nature. I would love him to give me a ride, but it's dangerous territory, isn't it?

I think back to how Charles has treated me this evening and decide that I should live a little.

"Oh, go on then," I reply, not taking more than a few seconds to make up my mind.

His mouth breaks into a grin and he holds his arm out to me. I link my arm through his and as we walk out of the Bowden Hall, I apologise to the butler and tell him that I will no longer be needing the taxi he has ordered for me.

If the butler is annoyed, he doesn't show it. He just simply nods his head and bids us goodnight. Jake leads me to a sleek, black limo waiting out the front.

"This is yours?" I ask him, astonished. Jake laughs and signals for the driver to wait in the car.

"It sure is."

Jake opens the door and gestures for me to get in. The look on my face must say it all. I thought that Charles had plenty of money, but Jake is clearly in a different league. Charles has never had a limo escort us anywhere. The thought is actually quite surprising seeing as Charles is obsessed with flaunting his wealth.

I enter the limo and sit back into one of the glorious leather seats. It is so soft, and my ass literally sinks into it. I hope it doesn't leave a massive dent when I get up.

"So, where is it we are going to, Stacey?" Jake asks as he enters the limo and sits opposite me.

I am very conscious of the fact that our legs are inches apart. The thought of brushing my leg against him is enough to make me want to jump his bones.

I shake my head and try to concentrate on calming my nerves, which are rapidly becoming overwhelming. What was I thinking? Getting into a limo with Jake was not a good move. The images of our one-night stand come flooding back to me. His mouth, his touch, his body, his...

"Stacey?" Jake's brow is furrowed as he gives me a questioning look.

Shit, I must have zoned out for too long.

I clear my throat, which has gone dry. I manage to relay my address to him and there is a distinct quiver in my voice. The thought of returning home isn't exactly filling me with pleasure right now. Going home and later being confronted by Charles fills me with dread.

"I don't know about you, but all that fancy food doesn't exactly do it for me. Want to grab a burger and fries on the way to yours?" Jake asks as he hands me a glass of champagne that he has just poured.

Champagne in a limo is not how I thought I would be escorted home tonight. I take the glass off of him and gratefully take a sip, enjoying the bubbles making their way down my throat.

"Now that sounds like a brilliant idea. You really are perfect, aren't you?" And there I go again. My brain really needs to engage with my mouth before I speak.

I take a few more gulps of the champagne, hoping that the alcohol will enable me to speak to Jake without making myself sound like a complete fool. Although, I am pretty sure it is having the opposite effect.

Jake laughs and instructs the driver, through an intercom in the side of the door, to go to the nearest burger place. We travel in silence as I continue to drink my champagne until the glass is empty.

I feel Jake's eyes on me the whole time, but I keep my gaze averted. If I look into his eyes, then I know that I am going to say or do something stupid.

Feeling awkward, I am glad when we reach the burger place. I go to get out of the limo, but Jake stops me. He asks me what I want and then he exits the car, leaving me alone.

I look around and realise that the driver must still be sat in the front. I am way out of my comfort zone here. For all I know, Jake could be a complete psychopath. For some reason though, I just know that he isn't.

I eye the champagne bottle which is by the side of Jake's seat and I quickly pour myself another glass. I am just finishing off the last drop when the limo door opens, and Jake climbs in, burger bags in hand.

"Voila. Cheeseburger and fries, madam," Jake says in a French accent. I stifle a giggle.

"Why thank you, kind sir." I smile and Jake gestures for me to eat my food.

I unwrap the burger and try to be as lady-like as I can whilst eating it, but is it really possible? Burgers are one of the messiest foods to eat in front of a man. Especially a man that is a virtual stranger but is someone who makes your stomach do somersaults every time he looks at you. I decide to just take small bites, this will at least stop me from getting burger sauce all around my mouth.

Jake finishes his food whilst I have barely eaten half of mine. I should have just ordered some fries and left it at that. My appetite wains as Jake speaks to the driver through the intercom.

"Hey, Eric, do you mind just driving around for a while please?"

"No problem," I hear Eric say.

"Why are we driving around for a bit?" I ask Jake as I take another minuscule bite of my burger and then put it back into the bag it arrived in.

"I want to get to know you a little better before you leave me again." Jake's eyes almost burn with intensity. I try to remain calm and just focus on keeping this conversation casual.

"Oh." I feel breathless.

What could he possibly want to know about me?

Only one way to find out.

"Okay, what do you want to know?" I have managed to make myself sound normal, and by normal, I mean that there is no wobble in my voice betraying how nervous I am. *Excellent, Stacey, nice and relaxed.* I give myself a mental clap.

"I want to know what I have to do to get another night with you?" Jake says, his voice low. His eyes have a wicked glint in them, and all of a sudden, I feel like I am his prey.

Oh shit, calm and relaxed has deserted me.

"Excuse me?" I say breathlessly. The wobble in my voice is back. I was not prepared for a question like that. What happened to simple questions like what's your favourite colour?

"You heard me, Stacey. I remember everything that happened the night we slept together. You are not a woman that is easily forgot." I gasp at his honesty, and I can feel that I am losing myself in those beautiful caramel eyes of his.

My panties are becoming wet with my need for this man, and time seems to stop as Jake's hand touches my thigh, making my whole body vibrate.

As his fingers gently stroke the top of my thigh, I close my eyes as I try to wrestle with my emotions.

My body is screaming at me to give into my urges, but my head is trying to make me realise what my actions could result in. I am torn. Seeing as I have made no attempt to stop Jake, his hands continue their exploration of my body.

He slowly trails his hands up either side of my ribcage, stopping when he reaches beside my breasts. I let out a soft sigh, and I can feel his breath getting closer to my face.

"Look at me, Stacey," he says in a low voice.

I slowly open my eyes and stare at his facial features. He has just the right amount of stubble to make him look even more desirable than he is already. His skin is flawless and lightly tanned. I know that if he kisses me then I won't be able to stop myself from giving in to him.

His lips are millimetres away from mine.

All it would take is for me to lean forward slightly for our lips to connect.

As I battle with myself about whether to kiss him or not, Jake smiles, and then moves his lips to my neck.

I place my hands on his chest, feeling his hard body beneath my palms. He showers my neck with light kisses before tracing along my jaw line with his tongue. It feels so good.

My hands travel down from his chest, and I am just about to untuck his shirt so that I can run my hands over his body when my phone starts to ring, jolting me out of our embrace.

"Fuck," I say, a lot louder than I intended to.

I quickly push Jake away from me and grab my clutch-bag. I find my phone and see that it is Charles ringing me. I am not even tempted to answer it and I let the call go to voicemail. I think it is safe to say that reality has just imploded on whatever planet I thought that I was on only seconds ago.

"Jake, I really need to be getting home now."

"Are you sure?" Jake asks.

He is sat opposite me again with his arms resting on his knees so that he is leaning forwards. He looks at me with a slight frown and his head tilted to one side. I feel as though he is trying to reach into my soul.

"Yes, I'm sure. I'm going to be in enough trouble tonight without adding anything else to the list." I can't look at him as I speak, and Jake doesn't argue with me.

Out of the corner of my eye, I see him push the button on the intercom. He instructs Eric that our drive is over and that we need to go to my address.

I straighten out my dress and just stare out of the window for the journey home. I must look like a complete slut, what with the one-night stand and now this limo scenario. I mentally kick myself for getting into this type of situation.

Jake doesn't attempt to speak to me, which I am grateful for. I fear that if he did then I would just make a fool of myself.

It only takes ten minutes to reach my house and I ask Jake to pull up a couple of doors away, so that Charles doesn't see me arrive home in a limo.

"Thank you for the food and the ride home, Jake," I say, still refusing to look at him.

"No problem. It wasn't quite the ride I had in mind, but there is always next time."

My head snaps up to look at him and our eyes lock. I must look dumbfounded as I try to find words, but nothing to say comes to my mind. Instead I pick up my bag, quickly exit the limo and briskly walk to my front door.

What did he mean next time?

There can be no next time.

The limo doesn't drive past my house until I am walking in my front door. I shut the door and slump against it, trying to regain my composure. I have had to try and regain that a lot tonight.

I almost expected Charles to be waiting by the door, tapping his foot, but it turns out that he isn't even home yet.

Once I feel like I can walk without my legs giving way, I make my way upstairs to the bedroom. I carefully take off my dress and get into my comfy pyjama bottoms and vest top. I then take off my make-up and tie my hair into a ponytail before climbing into bed.

I would rather be asleep before Charles gets home. At least that way the argument we are most definitely going to have can be postponed until tomorrow morning.

I glance at my phone and see that Charles actually left me a voicemail when he phoned me, whilst I was with Jake. I reluctantly listen to the message, only to find out that he isn't coming home tonight. He's staying at mummy dearests for the night.

Relief surges through me.

I place my phone on the bedside table and close my eyes. I can feel the smile pulling at my lips as I imagine the things that Mr Jake Waters would have done to me in that limo before I succumb to sleep.

CHAPTER SIX

I don't wake up until ten o'clock the following morning. I am normally an early riser, but I must have needed the sleep.

I slowly get out of bed and go to take a shower. I let the warm water cascade over me as I pleasure myself following last night's events with Jake. I have so much pent up sexual frustration that it is the only thing I can do right now to help relieve some of it. Images of Jake running through my head means that it doesn't take me long to reach my climax. Even in my mind Jake manages to make me feel things I have never felt before.

Once satisfied, I get out of the shower, dry myself and throw on some skinny jeans and a white vest top. I don't bother with any make-up. It's not like I am going to see anyone that is worth putting it on for. Lydia has always told me that I don't need make-up, she says that I am a natural beauty. In fact, she is more complimentary of my looks than my boyfriend is.

I grimace at the thought of facing Charles at some point today. He hasn't returned home yet, and I am dreading the tantrum that he is bound to have the minute he walks through the door. I push any thoughts of him to the back of my mind and pick up my laptop.

It is a glorious sunny day outside and I decide to walk to the local coffee shop for my morning caffeine hit. I will attempt to do some more writing to escape the thoughts of my current reality. I put on my white sandals and grab my handbag on the way out of the front door. It is only a short walk from my house to the coffee shop.

I love being able to do things like this without having to worry about work. I am very lucky to be able to do such things, but that luck comes at a high price; being with Charles. The coffee shop, called Danish, that I go to is a regular haunt of mine.

When I enter, I see that Bonnie is working today. She is a lovely girl, still at college and very happy-go-lucky. She has a petite frame and the longest dark brown hair that I have ever seen. It literally goes below her butt and that's when it is tied up. God knows how long it is when it's down loose.

She sees me walk in and instantly signals for me to sit down and says she will bring over my usual order of black coffee and a fresh croissant. I smile at her and sit at my favourite table in the corner, right next to the window. There are only a few other customers in here at the moment so it's nice and quiet. I put my laptop on the table and settle down in my seat, it's time to get myself into writing mode. Bonnie comes over once I have set my laptop up and places my food and drink by the side of it.

"Hey, Stace," she greets me. "How was the party last night?"

I happened to be in here the other day and I mentioned to Bonnie that I was going to a function last night. I suppose function automatically translates as a party in her eyes.

"Ugh, not great." I can feel my face pull into a grimace.

"Oh dear, that bad, huh?"

"Afraid so. I'm going to need several cups of coffee to keep me writing this morning."

"Well, I'm here until three this afternoon, so I'll make sure that your cup is filled if I see that it's empty."

"Thanks, Bonnie."

I gratefully smile at her as she bounces off to deal with another customer. I stare at the few pages that I have written in the last few weeks as I eat my croissant. So far, I have written half of the book, but if I want to leave Charles and get my life in order then I really need to get a move on and finish it.

I may think that the writing is the hard part, but once I am finished, I have the job of obtaining a publishing deal. I am hoping that it won't take long to do that, but it is a tough market out there. I have read countless interviews of authors who were rejected more than a few times before being given their big break. I try not to dwell too much on this though. I need to believe in myself and hope that an agent or publisher will see something special in my novel.

Before I know it, I have devoured my croissant like it is going out of fashion, and I am about to start typing when I sense someone standing in front of my table. I look up and am shocked to see that it is Charles.

"Oh. Hi," I say, thrown by his sudden appearance.

"Hi."

"What are you doing here?" I try not to sound too annoyed at his arrival, but I don't think I manage it.

"When I got home and saw that you weren't there I figured you would either be here or at Lydia's place. Lucky for me it's not the latter." I don't fail to notice the sarcasm in his tone at the mention of Lydia. His feelings for Lydia are the same as hers are for him. They hate each other. "So, I thought I would grab a coffee, and if you were here then I would see what you were up to. I feel bad that we didn't get to spend much time together last night. Give me a sec and then we can catch up. Would you like another coffee?"

Well, this is new. He has never come here before to spend time with me.

I politely decline his offer of coffee and watch him as he goes to order his.

He's wearing black khaki shorts, a loose white T-shirt and sandals. His hair is damp, so I presume that he hasn't long got out of the shower. As I watch him I feel empty. No emotions are present. He returns moments later, and I shut my laptop lid as I just stare at him with a puzzled expression on my face. He sits opposite me, looks at me and sighs.

"Stacey, I'm sorry for the way I treated you last night. It was wrong of me to ignore you. I should have been a better boyfriend. Please accept my apology?" he says.

My eyes are wide, and my mouth has dropped open. I must look shell-shocked. I open and close my mouth like a fish for a few seconds before I can find any words to reply to him.

"Okay," I say slowly as I feel my eyes narrowing with suspicion. "What's up, Charles? Something is wrong for you to come and find me and apologise. Don't get me wrong, it's very nice to hear an apology, but it's just not the norm. Help me out here because I'm a little confused."

I can see he is struggling to respond, but I need to know what has gotten into him. I lean back in my chair and fold my arms across my chest, waiting for him to answer.

"I just feel that I should treat you a bit better, that's all." He has a guilty look on his face. Charles doesn't do guilt, so this is a whole new experience for me.

"And that's it? You just feel that you should treat me better?" I am not convinced in the slightest that this is the reason he has come to find me, and he knows it. I see his breathing begin to quicken and he looks so uncomfortable that it is making me uncomfortable. He starts to squirm in his seat.

"Stacey, you know that I love you, don't you?" He looks into my eyes and I realise that I'm not sure I care enough to hear what he has to say. Maybe I need to make more of an effort too? I don't fail to notice that his declaration of love does nothing for me. There's not even a spark of emotion igniting within. This is also the first declaration of love that I have had from him in months.

My suspicions are heightening by the minute. I need to see where he is going with this.

"Okay, Charles. If that is all that is really bothering you, then we can go home and talk things out." I decide to play along for now. I will eventually find out what the real issue is here. Charles will crack under my interrogation; I am sure of it.

"I would like that. As long as I don't distract you from your writing. Why don't you come home in a couple of hours and I can cook us a nice lunch, and we can talk then?" he suggests. Wow, he is really pulling out all the stops.

"Okay. Sounds good." I force a smile on my face as he leans over and kisses me on the cheek before leaving the coffee shop. I still feel perplexed by the way he is acting.

I sit with my third cup of coffee and go over the conversation Charles and I just had. Whilst he was here I noticed some signs that he was nervous, but due to my shock, I guess I didn't process them at the time. But now that I replay it, he was very fidgety and perspiring ever so slightly.

Something is wrong. This doesn't feel right, and it doesn't sit well with me.

Shit, what if he chucks me out? I will have nowhere to live and no income. Oh my God, that has to be it. He's being nice to throw me off the scent. There is no way it can be anything else.

I quickly shut down my laptop and leave the money for what I have consumed on the table before saying a rushed goodbye to Bonnie. I need to go and speak to Lydia. Maybe she can help me figure out what Charles is up to?

After gathering up my things I walk to the front door, only to collide with someone.

"Shit," I say as I feel my laptop slip from my grasp. Lucky for me the person that I have collided with manages to catch my laptop before it hits the ground. I let out a sigh of relief and divert my gaze away from the laptop.

Oh God, of all the people I could have bumped into, it had to be him. Jake Waters. My heart does a little flutter and I stare at him, flabbergasted.

What the hell is he doing here?

I seem to have lost the ability to speak and I just stare at him like some lust filled teenager, trying to calm the hormones that are raging through my body. I suddenly feel very self-conscious of my plain appearance.

"In a rush, Miss Paris?" Jake's smooth tones make my knees weak.

"Uh, yeah," I say breathlessly. *Pull yourself together, woman, he's just a guy. An extremely hot guy that you happen to be attracted to, but still just a guy none the less.* "Sorry, I didn't mean to bump into you. I guess I should pay more attention in future." I avert my gaze from his as I struggle to get my breathing under control.

"Well I have to say, of all the people who could have bumped into me, I am pleased that it was you." *Oh, Christ, does he have to be so charming?* I giggle like a school girl. "So, I guess you don't have time to get a cup of coffee with me?"

Jake looks at me with those smouldering eyes and all I want to do is give in and spend some time in his presence, but my brain decides to wake up and reminds me that I have to go and see Lydia.

"I'm afraid not, I need to be somewhere. Maybe another time?" I instantly regret the words as soon as I say them. Another time? What am I thinking? I can't be within five feet of the guy without my brain going into meltdown.

"Shame. But I will hold you to that 'another time,' Miss Paris." Jake flashes his megawatt smile at me, and it takes all of my willpower not to change my mind.

"Nice to see you, Jake," I say as I step around him and start to walk away.

"You too," I hear Jake say behind me.

I resist the urge to turn around, but I know that he is watching me. I can feel it in every fibre of my being. It isn't until I get around the corner that I let out the breath that I have been holding.

CHAPTER SEVEN

I rush to Lydia's flat which is about a five-minute walk away from Danish. It's good that she lives so close.

I fly up the stairs, knock on her door and wait for her to answer. I tap my foot impatiently whilst I wait. Lydia answers the door a minute later looking like she had a very good night indeed, judging by the sight of her.

Her long, auburn hair is all in disarray and her clothes look like they have just been thrown on her body in a hurry. I can't fail to notice the great big grin across her face and the twinkle in her emerald green eyes. I'm guessing her boyfriend Donnie has given her a night to remember.

Ugh, Donnie. He makes my skin crawl, but he seems to make Lydia happy, so I keep my opinions to myself. The last thing I want to do is fall out with Lydia over my feelings of her choice of boyfriend.

"Hey, babes," she says cheerfully. "Come on in and make me a coffee. You can have one yourself if you like." Yep, typical Lydia, she makes me feel at home instantly, always so welcoming and full of life. That's why I love her so much.

We have been best friends for the last five years after meeting at The Den. She is the one who hired me, and she is still running the place now, which hardly surprises me as she is great at her job.

I go through to her little kitchen, put my laptop and handbag down, and click the kettle on. I presume Lydia went back to her bedroom as there is no sign of her. I shout out, "I presume Donnie wants a cup as well?"

"Yes please, Stace," Donnie's voice says, making me jump. My back was to the doorway of the kitchen and I didn't hear him approach.

I turn and see that he is leant against the door frame, wearing only a pair of jogging bottoms which are hung loosely on his hips.

"Christ, you scared the shit out of me. Go and make yourself guest appropriate, would you?" He just laughs at me and ignores my request as per usual.

Donnie has no qualms about letting visitors see him in half of his clothes. Actually, if it was up to him, he would probably walk around naked, but I think Lydia puts a stop to that when there is company present.

"You mean you want me to hide my body and deprive you of the privilege of seeing this?" Donnie says as he points towards his body.

I roll my eyes and try not to be sick as I make the drinks. I hand Donnie his mug and he saunters away like a slithering snake. I shudder, pick up mine and Lydia's drinks and make my way through to the lounge to wait for her. I'm surprised Lydia can put up with Donnie's massive ego.

Donnie doesn't come back and join me in the lounge which is a relief. However, just in case he changes his mind and comes in, I choose to sit in the armchair rather than on the sofa, that way he won't be able to sit by me.

He may look relatively good with his olive skin, shaved head, brown eyes and muscly physique, but he really is a slime-ball and Lydia just can't see it. He must be fucking awesome in bed for her to stay with him.

Lydia waltzes in a few minutes later looking a little less dishevelled.

"Good night then, huh?" I ask her.

"Fucking fabulous, babes," she says as she takes her seat opposite me on the sofa and picks up her cup of coffee. "So, what's up?"

"Why would anything be up?"

"Because you look a little pale and I can just sense these things you know. Call it best friends' intuition." Damn her. She's right. She always knows when something is wrong with me. I sigh and fill her in on what happened with Charles last night and this morning.

"Oh dear, that doesn't sound too good. Very out of character for him, isn't it? Or maybe he really has just realised that he's got a good thing with you? It may have taken him three years to finally see this, but hey, miracles do happen," Lydia ponders sarcastically.

I raise one eyebrow at her and she rolls her eyes. "Don't look at me like that, missy. He treats you like shit and you know it." I sigh at her, but she continues to speak. "Look, I know I'm not his biggest fan, but come on, babes, you are gorgeous and have a great personality to match. He would be a fool to lose you."

"I don't know, Lyd. I think something has happened and he's going to chuck me out of the house. Maybe it's because I snapped at his mother at the event last night? Or maybe it's because he actually did see me dancing with Jake? Or maybe—" I am cut off abruptly by Lydia.

"Whoa, whoa, whoa... wait just a minute. Who is Jake?" Lydia enquires.

"Oh, um, you remember the guy I went home with from The Den, the night before I moved in with Charles?"

"Oh, good grief, how could I ever forget him? What a gorgeous hunk of man he was."

"Yeah, him, that's Jake." I then proceed to fill her in on what happened at the

Bowden Hall and about what happened afterwards in the limo. I relay all of the information to her quickly so that she can't interrupt me whilst I am in full flow.

"Well, that's just fan-fucking-tastic, Stace," she screeches at me when I have finished speaking. "But I don't understand why you pushed Jake off of you?"

Her reaction is what I was expecting. Lydia does not believe that Charles is who I am meant to be with for the rest of my life.

"Because, Lydia, I don't want to be known as a cheat. Not only that, but I gave up my job and my independence to live with Charles as I thought that he was going to be my happy ending. It hurts that the more I stay with him, the more I realise that isn't the case. I just need to focus on writing my book and I need to forget about Jake," I reply.

She looks at me with a little sadness in her eyes and I just shrug my shoulders. I may not love Charles anymore, but it still stings that things haven't worked out the way I hoped that they would.

"Actually, the first thing I need to do is go home and see what Charles has to say." I stand and go to the kitchen to get my handbag and laptop.

"Good luck, babes," Lydia calls out to me. "And you know that if you need to you are always welcome to stay here."

"Thanks, Lyd," I say, as I poke my head back around the lounge doorway. "I'll call you later."

I leave her flat and decide not to shout bye to Donnie as I go as he usually tries to hug me when I leave which makes me cringe. I wish Lydia would see sense as she's far too good for him.

I stroll back home slowly as I prepare myself for what I am going to walk into when I get there.

CHAPTER EIGHT

I walk in the front door and the house smells divine. The scent of roast lamb wafts down the hallway, and my stomach grumbles in appreciation.

I walk through the lounge to go to the dining room, and I hear Charles faffing about in the kitchen. Wow, he has really gone to town. The dining table is set, there is soft music playing, candles are lit on the table and the curtains are drawn. The silver ware is making an unexpected appearance, and a bottle of wine sits in a cooler at the end of the table.

I call out to Charles to let him know that I am back.

"Oh, okay. If you could sit in the dining room, darling, I will bring the food through. Help yourself to a glass of wine whilst you are waiting," Charles replies.

What the fuck is wrong with him? This is not the actions of someone who is going to kick me out of the house, surely?

I put my laptop and handbag on a little table in the corner of the room, and I busy myself by pouring some wine for both of us before taking a seat and waiting to see how all of this plays out.

Charles enters the room a few moments later carrying a plate with roast lamb on it and my mouth starts to water. He then goes back to the kitchen and returns to the dining room with all the accompaniments that he has made to go with the lamb. After placing everything on the table, he sits opposite me.

"Would you like me to serve?" he asks.

"No, no, I can manage, thanks." I sound confused. He must pick up on it as he just sits and stares at me.

This is so out of character for him.

I put some lamb on my plate, trying to ignore Charles' fixed gaze, but it only takes me about thirty seconds before I decide that I cannot sit through a whole meal and deal with his weird behaviour.

"Charles, what the hell is going on? Forgive me for coming across as unappreciative, but you never do anything like this for me, and you certainly don't spend your time staring at me over the dinner table. I don't understand what is with the dramatic change in you?" I look at him and wait for a response.

Minutes of tension and silence passes by, and then all of a sudden, Charles starts to cry.

Oh shit, why is he crying? This must be serious.

The only other time I have seen him shed any tears was at his father's funeral. I am unsure whether to comfort him or just stay where I am.

I opt for the latter.

"Charles, what the hell is the matter with you? What's happened?" I sound panicky, and to be honest, I need him to talk to me as he is starting to make me feel nervous. My appetite quickly disappears, and I wait as Charles tries to calm himself down.

After a minute or so he takes a sip of wine and inhales a few deep breaths. The urge to tell him to hurry up and speak is so strong, but I manage to keep my mouth shut. All the while, my mind is racing as I try to figure out what the problem is.

"Stacey, I am so sorry... I need to tell you something," he says in a shaky voice.

"Well, come on then, out with it." I can't help but show the impatience in my voice. He's really panicking me now.

"You know I told you that I stayed at Mummy's last night?" I just nod my head at him. I daren't speak for fear that he will go all quiet on me again. "Well... I didn't... I didn't stay there. I'm so sorry, darling, I don't know what came over me." He starts blubbing again.

"Okay," I say warily. "So, where did you stay?"

I start to feel very uncomfortable.

"I went home with Claire, the woman I was talking to. I was so drunk, and you had left, and I really don't know what came over me," he rambles quickly.

It takes me a few seconds to process his words. He spoke so fast that I am almost convinced that I misheard him.

As I stare at the lamb on my plate, which now looks very unappealing, I replay his words in my head. I haven't misheard anything. His behaviour at Danish and the treating me better is just his way of trying to deal with his guilt.

"Please talk to me, darling. I need to know what you are thinking," he pleads with me.

I lift my eyes from my plate of lamb and look at him. He looks panicked.

"The blond woman?" I ask.

"Yes."

"So, you went home with this Claire woman and fucked her.... then you come home to me and cook a lovely dinner and break out the fancy plates, which is meant to achieve what exactly? Forgiveness?" My tone is flat in my reply.

"I just... I just thought that I would do something nice, so you would be able to see how sorry I am." His reply is pathetic. He really is an ass. He would have been better off letting me live in ignorant bliss. I mean, we haven't had sex for weeks now, so I really couldn't give a toss that he slept with someone else. I would be a hypocrite to start shouting and bawling at him. Lucky for me he is unaware about my past dalliance.

The first thought that springs to mind is where the hell am I going to live? And what am I going to do for work seeing as I can no longer continue to live here now that he has dropped this bombshell.

Jeez, I'm not even fazed by the concept of not being with Charles.

Surely, I should feel some sort of jealousy or anger? I don't though. All I feel at the moment is a mixture of panic and relief. Panic at having to find somewhere else to live with no money, and relief that it's finally over. No longer will I have to play the part of the doting girlfriend. No longer will I have to listen to his mother's snide remarks.

Maybe I can finally start to feel good about myself again?

Charles speaks, interrupting my thoughts. "You're not going to leave me, are you? I don't want this to break us, Stacey."

I don't mean to, but I actually laugh in his face. "Oh, come on, Charles, we have been on the rocks for a long time. These last few months especially have solidified just how different we both are."

"But... But—" I cut him off before he can say anymore.

"I'm going to get some of my things together and go and stay at Lydia's. I can't stay here, Charles. We're not good for each other. We just don't fit anymore, and to be honest, I'm not sure if we ever did."

He tries to speak again but I just hold my hands up to stop him. "Don't worry about sleeping with Claire. She is probably a much better fit for you than I ever was."

With that, I stand up, drain my glass of wine, and go upstairs to pack my bag.

As I pack my essentials the sense of relief washes over me again. My dreams of becoming a writer may be put on hold, but I am finally free. Free of his critique and free to do whatever the hell I want. I will no longer have to adhere to the weekly meal plan, or to his insistence that I accompany him to all of his boring events. And the best part is that he will have to be the one to tell people why I left him.

I smile and head back to the dining room to retrieve my handbag and laptop. Charles is still sat at the table looking gobsmacked.

"Goodbye, Charles. I will collect the rest of my stuff in a few days." He doesn't answer me.

I turn and feel almost serene as I leave the house.

I decide to walk to Lydia's instead of taking my car, I can pick it up when I collect the rest of my stuff. I need a walk to clear my head a bit. It's at times like these that I really do wish that I had some family to turn to. I miss having the security of a family to support me in times of need. I should count myself lucky that I met Lydia, because without her, I don't know where I would go right now. She is like the sister that I never had.

I slowly walk, processing all that has happened. It's been an emotional twenty-four hours, that's for sure, and I reach Lydia's flat in a daze. I knock on her door for the second time today and try not to cringe as Donnie answers, wearing only a towel around his waist.

Jeez, does this guy not know where his clothes are?

"Hey, pretty lady," he drools at me.

"Uh, hi. Can I come in?" I ask as politely as possible.

"Sure." He steps back from the door slightly to let me in. "Lydia is in the lounge recovering from our last sex session."

Ugh, why does he feel the need to announce this to me?

"Going somewhere?" he asks me as his eyes rest on the holdall that I have in my hand.

"Not exactly." I would rather speak to Lydia first before saying anything to Donnie about needing a place to stay. "I'll just go through and see Lyd. Perhaps you could try and wear some clothes whilst I'm here?" Donnie chuckles to himself as I walk through to the lounge. Lydia is led on the sofa watching some crappy day time television.

"Hey, Lyd."

"Crikey, Stace, are you trying to give me a heart attack?" Lydia exclaims as she springs up to a sitting position and holds her hand over her heart for effect. "Don't sneak up on me like that."

"Sorry, I thought that you would have heard me talking to Donnie," I say through my laughter.

"It's not bloody funny," she says with a smirk. Her eyes soon notice the holdall in my hand. "Things didn't go well with Charles then?"

I flop down on the sofa next to her and tell her all about what happened when I got back home. Although, I shouldn't think of it as my home anymore because it isn't.

She doesn't say anything until I have finished updating her, but when she speaks all she says is, "About bloody time you left that douche bag."

"I should have guessed that you would be happy."

"Oh, Stace, I'm not happy that you have split up—"

"Really?" I interrupt her and give her a knowing look.

"Okay, maybe I am a little happy, but it's only because I know you deserve better than to be treated like someone's maid. I just want you to be happy and I know that you weren't." She has a point. I haven't been truly happy for a long time.

"Can I stay here with you for a few days? I just need to get myself sorted."

"Of course you can stay here, and you can stay for as long as you want."

"Thanks, Lyd. I don't know what I would do without you."

I am so grateful to this girl. I'm sure Martin would have helped me, but Lydia is always the first person that I turn to. Plus, if Charles were to find out that I was staying with Martin then I know that he would make Martin's life difficult at work.

"Now I have the task of finding a job." As I finish speaking, I can almost see the cogs turning in Lydia's head.

"Why don't you come back and work at The Den? You know what you're doing, and who better to have as your boss than your best friend, *again?* What do you say? It will be like old times."

"Really? You don't think that everyone would be pissed off if I came back?" I feel myself perk up a little at the prospect of finding work so quickly.

"Don't be so bloody stupid. Everyone loved you working there. I will take a look at the shifts when I go in tomorrow and see what I can do," she says with a wink. "As for tonight, get your glad rags on because we are going out to celebrate."

"Oh no, I really don't feel like going out," I tell her. I don't know why I bother though, once Lydia has her mind set on doing something there really is no way that she will take no for an answer.

"Bollocks. You're coming out with me and that's final. It's been so long since we went out, not to mention that I get to see single Stacey in action." I roll my eyes at her. I'm really not looking to catch another guy's attention tonight. I think I should just concentrate on myself for a while. "The spare bedroom is all yours, babes. Make yourself at home."

"Thanks, Lyd," I reply with a smile.

I take my few belongings into the spare bedroom, shutting the door behind me. The room is small with a single bed, wardrobe, chest of drawers and a bedside table. I don't mind it being small though, it makes the room feel cosy. Lydia has decorated it in a pastel yellow colour, which brings a warm vibe to the room.

I leave my bags at the end of the bed and set up my laptop on the bedside table. I decide to do some writing to occupy my mind. I get myself settled on the bed and proceed to write for as long as I can before Lydia demands that I stop, so that I can get ready for our impromptu night out.

I have only been writing for ten minutes when I hear my phone ringing in my handbag. I retrieve my phone and am unsurprised to see that Charles is trying to phone me. I don't even consider answering his call. I put my phone on silent and ignore his attempt to speak to me. Even if I did answer, there would be nothing that he could say to convince me to go back to him. I am just glad that he never found out about Jake. I know Charles, and I know that he would have used it as ammunition to help his current situation.

Surely, he must agree that we no longer fit together? I can't imagine that he was truly happy with me. Maybe he just liked having me around to be at his beck and call? If Charles had been the one to end things with me, then I am in no doubt that he would never have contacted me again.

Maybe his ego has been hurt at how I left him without batting an eyelid? I silently curse myself that it took him admitting that he slept with someone else in order for me to finally leave. In retrospect, I have used him as much as he may have used me.

I make a promise to myself right now that I will never again let myself stay in an unhealthy relationship.

Life is too short to be unhappy.

CHAPTER NINE

A couple of hours pass by and I have managed to write another two thousand words of my novel. I am pleased with my progress, especially with all the moaning and groaning that I have heard from the bedroom next door. Lydia and Donnie are literally at it like rabbits. I am surprised that Donnie can go so many times. Maybe that's why Lydia sticks with him?

I save my work and shut down my laptop. There is a knock on my bedroom door and Lydia enters my room.

"Hey, babes. We need to start getting ready to go out." Lydia looks every bit as dishevelled as she did when I first came to see her this morning.

"Was just thinking the same thing. You have finally finished shagging then?"

"Yes thanks." A stupid grin crosses Lydia's face. "Now, get your ass in the shower and get ready. It's already seven o'clock and we need to get the drinking started. Help yourself to anything in my wardrobe as I presume you didn't pack any going out clothes in your rush to get away from the douche bag."

I chuckle. "Thanks, Lyd. Are you sure you're not too tired to go out? I mean, it sounds like you have been having quite the workout this afternoon?" I raise one eyebrow at her.

"Number one, I am never too tired to go out. Number two, you shouldn't be eavesdropping. And number three, get a bloody move on."

Lydia exits my bedroom before I can respond, shutting the door behind her. I shake my head as I get off of the bed and head to the bathroom to get ready.

Unfortunately for me, Donnie is stood in the bathroom doorway. I have to physically stop myself from rolling my eyes at him.

"So, wild night out tonight then, huh? Lydia told me about you and Charles. So sorry to hear that by the way," Donnie says.

Yeah, the sarcasm dripping from your words makes you sound so sincere. Ugh, this guy gives me the creeps.

"Maybe you might be up for some extra special fun later?" He winks at me, and I am too shocked by his suggestion to respond, but my face must say it all. "Calm down, I'm only messing about." Donnie laughs.

I'm not convinced that he is just joking though. I think that if I said yes to his little proposal then he would be more than willing to cheat on Lydia. What a slime-ball. I push past him and lock myself in the bathroom. With him around, living here may be harder than I thought. I turn on the shower and let the water warm up as I try to erase Donnie's words from my mind. The guy really needs to get a better sense of humour if he calls remarks like that a joke.

I get undressed and step into the shower. I take my time, letting the warm water cascade over my body as I replay the day's events in my head.

When I woke up this morning I did not expect any of this to have happened. I feel happy and elated that I have my freedom back, I may possibly have a job, I have the bestest friend ever, and I'm going out tonight to let loose and enjoy myself.

Surely nothing else could possibly go wrong?

I hear Lydia's voice which breaks through my thoughts. "Stacey! Get your butt out of the shower and get ready! I've got the drinks waiting."

I drag myself out of the shower, dry myself and wrap the towel around me before dashing to Lydia's bedroom to choose an outfit. I mentally curse myself for not having chosen an outfit before having a shower. The last thing I want is for Donnie to see me in just a towel, but luckily for me, he must be in the lounge or kitchen.

I have a rifle through Lydia's wardrobe and come across a pair of small black tailored shorts, which I team with a black sparkly vest top. Charles would never have approved of this outfit, but I love it.

I hurry back to my bedroom and put the outfit on and opt for minimal make-up, applying beige eyeshadow, a touch of mascara, eyeliner and some clear lip gloss. Perfect. I dry my hair and add in some soft waves and put on a pair of Lydia's black stilettos; luckily, we are the same size in clothes and shoes.

I take a look at myself in the hall way mirror and I love the way that I look. The outfit makes me feel sexy and confident. Pleased with my appearance, I head to the lounge where I can hear Lydia and Donnie talking, and as I enter, Donnie wolf whistles.

"Looking good, Stacey," he leers at me, and his eyes roam over my body. It makes me feel uncomfortable and I contemplate changing into something less revealing, but then I change my mind. I shouldn't let this jackass stop me from feeling good about myself.

Lydia is sat next to him on the sofa. I wonder if she feels as uncomfortable about his comment as I do? It doesn't appear so as she doesn't seem to bat an eyelid.

"He's right, girl. You will be fighting the men off of you." Lydia picks a glass up off of the coffee table and hands it to me.

"I'm not going for the men, Lyd; I've only just broken up with Charles." I take the glass from her and take a sip. Gin, lemonade and lime. Delicious.

"So?" Lydia replies. "You should enjoy some attention now that you are finally rid of him. No one is saying that you need to jump straight into another relationship, just live a little."

Donnie nods in agreement with her whilst still leering at me. I look away from him and admire my best friends outfit choice. Lydia looks beautiful in her hot pink, strapless jump suit and white stilettos. She has never been one to shy away into the crowd.

I notice that Donnie is dressed up too, and this can only mean that he is coming with us. Oh great, I will be playing the part of a gooseberry for most of the night whilst they play tonsil-tennis with each other. I can't help feeling a little disappointed that it isn't just Lydia and I going out.

The three of us sit chatting and drinking for the next hour. My acting skills are really improving as I manage to speak to Donnie without cringing. When we are ready to leave, I go back to my room to grab my phone off of the bedside table. I notice that I have three missed calls and a text message. They are all from Charles. He hasn't left any voicemails. I open the text message and begin to read.

> *Stacey, please will you talk to me. I'm so sorry for what I have done, but you can't leave me! What will people think? We can sort this out, just come back and talk to me.*
> *Charles x.*

And in that one message it shows me the real reason that he's sorry. He's worried about how it will look to everyone else. I scoff and decide not to take my phone out. I switch it off and place it back on the bedside table. I don't want to have my night ruined by receiving anymore messages from him.

I grab my little black handbag, put my money inside, take one last look at myself in the mirror and I am ready to go.

The three of us leave the flat and walk to The Den. I can tell that Lydia is half-cut already by the slurring of her words and the gentle way in which she sways as we walk.

Ten minutes later and we arrive at our destination. We enter the bar area and I see that Susie is working tonight. As I approach her, she screams loudly and comes running over to me to give me a hug.

"Hey, hun. I've missed seeing you," she shouts into my ear drum, nearly deafening me. "Where have you been hiding?"

"Hey, Susie," I say whilst giggling. "I haven't been hiding, but I am now free and single, and I am ready to party my ass off."

"Well say no more then. Let me fix you one of my special cocktails." She heads back behind the bar with a wink. For such a small, petite woman, Susie is very loud. She looks cute with her blond hair cropped into a pixie style haircut.

Lydia and Donnie join me at the bar as Susie is bringing me my drink. She quickly goes and whips them up the same. The drink is divine and tastes of raspberries more than anything else. I moan my approval and signal for her to make me another one. I drain the second drink as quickly as the first and grab Lydia's hand to go and dance. I literally pull her off of the bar stool that she is sat on and drag her behind me.

"Whoa, calm down, babes. You nearly pulled my arm out of its socket," Lydia says.

"Sorry. I just feel so alive and I need my dancing partner to help me out," I reply.

We dance for what feels like ages. There are a few guys I have to tell to back off as I don't want their attention. Tonight is all about celebrating new beginnings and leaving the past behind.

Eventually, Donnie joins us on the dance floor and I excuse myself to go to the toilet. I feel his eyes watching me as I walk away, and it makes my skin crawl.

I finish up in the toilets and decide that I will get myself another of Susie's amazing cocktails before doing anymore dancing. As I exit the toilets, Donnie is waiting outside for me. I instantly panic that something is wrong with Lydia.

"Is everything okay, Don? Where's Lydia?" I ask, worried.

"Everything's fine, Lydia's getting some more drinks at the bar. I thought that I would come and make sure you were alright."

"I'm fine. Why wouldn't I be?" I may be a little bit drunk but I'm perfectly capable of getting to the toilet and back by myself.

Donnie closes the space between us and grabs my arm. Before I have the chance to say anything, he leads me down a small corridor next to the toilets.

"Donnie, what the fuck are you doing?" I shout at him.

"Shhhh," he says as he pushes me up against the wall and places his finger over my lips. I feel panic start to overtake all of my senses. "I have been waiting to get you alone all night. You look sexy as hell, and I know you want me just as much as I want you."

What the fuck? Has he gone insane?

This guy really does think that he is God's gift to women. His hand grips my waist and the other is playing with a ringlet of my hair. I try to calm my breathing.

"Donnie, I don't know what's going on here, but I have no interest in you in that way. You are with Lydia and I tolerate you for *her* sake. If it were up to me, she would have kicked your ass to the curb a long time ago." I speak as confidently as I can, but the nerves in my voice betray me.

I stare straight at him as I try to prise his hand from my waist. The more I try to prise his fingers off of me, the tighter his grip gets. "Donnie, get your hands off of me. I'm not interested."

"You always have been a fucking tease, Stacey." His tone has changed to one of anger.

He pins me to the wall with his body, stops playing with my hair, and holds my hands above my head with one of his. I feel the other hand leave my waist and start to stroke the top of my thigh. I try to wriggle free, but he is just too strong for me. My eyes widen, and I can feel the onset of tears as I desperately try not to show him that I am frightened.

"Donnie, please get off of me. I don't want this," I plead with him, but he's not listening. Fear envelopes me as I feel his hand shift and he grazes the inside of my thigh with his fingers.

Oh my God, he's going to assault me. He's going to assault me here, in The Den.

No one knows that he has brought me down this corridor, and with the music loud, no one will be able to hear me scream.

I continue to try and jerk him away from me, but he just pushes his body into me so much that I almost feel like I can't breathe. I am trapped. I can feel my stomach churning, my heartbeat is racing, and I am desperately trying to figure out how to get myself out of this situation and away from this man.

"Donnie, get the fuck off of me, NOW!" I scream at him again and again, but he's still not stopping. I feel like I might pass out at any moment.

As his hand moves upwards and brushes my sex, I suddenly hear a voice.

"Get the fuck off of her, *now*."

Oh my God, someone has come to save me. Thank fuck for that.

A feeling of recognition rushes through me at the voice that has spoken.

I feel Donnie's grip on my hands loosen slightly. His other hand moves back to my waist, and his grip there is still firm. He turns his head in the direction of the voice at the same time as I do.

Jake is standing there with his fists balled at his sides, and he looks all shades of pissed off. I feel immense relief at seeing him standing there and I can see the menace in his eyes, which are fixated on Donnie.

"And what are you gonna do about it?" Donnie goads.

"You don't want to find out, believe me. Now get your filthy hands off of her and I'll let you walk out of here with your face still in one piece." Jake's voice is like ice.

Donnie looks back to me and smirks.

"She wants this just as much as I do, mate. Now, why don't you piss off and leave us to it?" Donnie says as he looks back to Jake.

My eyes plead with Jake to stay where he is. Jake however is keeping his gaze on Donnie. I hold my breath as I will Donnie to let go of me.

"I'm going nowhere. Now. Let. Her. Go." He pronounces each word slowly, and I almost whimper at Jake's answer.

He's not going anywhere. He's going to help me.

"For fuck's sake," Donnie says as he lets go of me and turns to face Jake.

My legs give way and I collapse onto the floor as the tears that I have been holding back start to fall from my eyes. I move myself along the floor and as far back from Donnie as I can.

I see Donnie move towards Jake, but he's not quick enough. Jake launches himself and punches Donnie in the face. Donnie falls to the ground where Jake proceeds to punch him in the face, repeatedly.

Donnie is shouting at Jake to get off of him, but it's like Jake has completely lost it. I need to do something and quick, before Jake puts Donnie in a coma, or worse.

"Jake!" I shout. "Jake, please don't. He's not worth it. Please stop." I sob as the tears continue to fall.

My voice has an impact as Jake looks at me. He has Donnie pinned to the floor, his arm across Donnie's neck.

"Please Jake," I whisper as a last attempt to get him to let go of Donnie.

He registers my words, although how he hears me over the background music, I'm not quite sure. Jake takes his eyes off of me and looks back to Donnie.

"If you ever go near Stacey again, I will kill you. Understand?" Jake's voice is laced with venom. Donnie just nods his head. He looks petrified. "And if you ever tell anyone what I did to you, your pathetic existence won't be worth living. Understand?" Again Donnie just nods.

Blood covers Donnie's face, but I don't feel sorry for him. How could I ever feel sorry for someone like him? I dread to think about how far Donnie would have gone if Jake hadn't shown up when he did.

Jake stands up, releasing his grip on Donnie and picks me up in his arms as if I weigh nothing more than the weight of a feather. Jake carries me past Donnie and out into the main room of The Den. I bury my face in Jake's chest so that no one can see that I have been crying. The last thing I need is Lydia or Susie spotting me and asking questions about what's wrong.

We walk through the main room undetected, and straight out of the front doors. It is only when the fresh air hits me that I turn my head to see where Jake is taking me.

I see Jake's limo parked across the road from The Den. There is a man leant against it, and I assume it is Eric as I didn't actually see what he looked like the last time I was with Jake. When he sees us approaching he opens the door and Jake slides me in first, climbing in after me.

I sit on the plush leather seats, but I feel no comfort this time. I feel numb.

As Eric gets back into the driver's seat, Jake puts his arms around me and pulls me onto his lap. I can feel my body shaking and my tears keep flowing.

"It's okay, baby, I've got you. No one will hurt you again." Jake speaks softly as he places a kiss on the top of my head. His words make me feel safe and I cling to him. I don't want him to let go of me.

I don't ask where we are going, and I don't really care either. I am far too dazed to concentrate on anything but the feel of Jake's arms holding me.

This was supposed to be my night, my new beginning, and my celebration.

Now it just feels like my world is ending.

CHAPTER TEN

I manage to stop crying as the limo pulls to a stop. Jake gently slides me off of his lap and tilts my chin up to look at him.

"It's okay. You're safe. I'm going to look after you." He cups my face in both of his hands and gently wipes my cheeks with his thumbs, wiping away the remainder of the last of my tears. The act is so unexpected that I almost start crying again from how gentle he is being with me.

I don't have the energy to argue with him about letting him look after me, so I let him take my hand and lead me out of the limo.

Jake turns to Eric, who is stood beside the limo. "Thanks, Eric. Take the day off tomorrow. I will be working from home."

"Yes, sir," Eric replies. Eric is an older guy with greying hair, but he is huge. He must be in his fifties, and his shirt can barely contain his muscles. He has to be at least six foot in height, if not more. "Goodnight to you both."

I manage a feeble smile to acknowledge him. My eyes wander from Eric to the impressive building in front of us. It is massive. From the outside there appears to be three floors. The house is detached and is surrounded by a six-foot-high red brick wall. Flowers line the steps up to the front door, and hanging baskets show an array of colourful flowers. We are stood on a large gravel covered drive way. I look behind me and see that Eric has returned to the limo and is reversing back out onto the road.

"Where am I?" I ask.

"You're staying at mine tonight," Jake says in a firm tone.

I fall silent as I let him lead me up the few steps to the front door. Once Jake has opened the front door, he takes me down a long, spacious hallway and only stops when we reach a door at the very end.

He opens the door and leads me into the biggest kitchen that I have ever seen.

Beautiful oak cabinets line the back wall of the room, and the black granite worktops sparkle as if they are brand new. For all I know, they could be brand new.

There is a kitchen island in the middle of the room with two bar stools on one side. To the right of me there are a set of impressive French doors. I don't know what the doors lead out to as it is pitch black outside, so I can't see anything.

To my left is a stunning black aga and more granite worktops housing different kitchen equipment. I turn slightly and see that behind me is an American sized fridge. It must cost a fortune to fill it up with food. I feel like I have walked into a show home.

Jake clears his throat which draws my attention back to him. My eyes connect with his and he gestures for me to take a seat on one of the bar stools. I oblige as I suddenly feel very tired.

As I sit, I think about how this room alone is bigger than Lydia's entire flat.

Oh my God! Lydia!

She has no idea what her boyfriend has done to me tonight.

"Jake, I need to see my friend Lydia. I need to speak to her. I can't let Donnie get to her first." The last thing I need is Donnie telling her some cock and bull story that he has concocted. Saying his name leaves a bitter taste in my mouth. I start to feel panicky that she may be left alone with him at some point.

"Oh God, what if he tries to hurt her too?" My mind is in overdrive now. I feel sick at the thought.

"Don't worry, I have asked someone to get a message to her to let her know that you are safe," he says as he hands me a glass of water. I gratefully take a sip as my mouth is so dry.

"How the hell have you managed that? And how do you know who Lydia is?" He's been with me since it all happened, and I can't recall him talking to anyone.

"It doesn't matter how. The important thing is she knows that you are safe. I just want to make sure that you are okay. Don't worry, she will get home safely. I promise." I don't quite know what to say. He seems to have taken care of everything.

"Thank you. I appreciate you helping me back there. God knows how far he would have gone if..." I shudder as I recall Donnie's hands touching my body.

"Don't think about that now. I think it's best that you get some sleep. We can sort everything out when you are rested." Jake takes my hand. "Come, I will show you the guest bedroom."

I hop off of the bar stool, following him back into the hallway and up a set of stairs. We go up one flight of stairs and then we continue up a second flight before we reach a long corridor. There are only two doors, one on each side of the corridor.

Jake takes me into the room on the right, and I enter a large and very plush looking bedroom. The bed is gigantic; I've never seen anything like it. You could probably fit half a dozen full grown adults in it and still have some room left. Jake tells me that the door to the left of the room leads to an ensuite, and the door on the right leads to a walk-in wardrobe and a dressing room. A big flat screen television is on the wall at the end of the bed with a beautiful decorative fireplace underneath.

My jaw drops open at how vast and luxurious the room is. The bed looks very inviting, and all I want to do is disappear beneath the covers. I feel a little shaky and presume that the adrenaline and shock from what happened has started to subside a little.

"My bedroom is across the hall if you need me. There are some pyjamas in the ensuite but, uh, they are a pair of mine. I don't have anything else, but I figured that you may like to wear something comfortable to sleep in," Jake says.

"That's great, thanks." He is being so sweet. "Are you sure I'm not imposing on you?" I ask, hoping that he won't say yes. To be honest, I wouldn't feel safe going back to Lydia's tonight.

"Of course not. Treat it as you would your own bedroom, and please try to get some rest." Jake kisses my forehead and then leaves the bedroom, shutting the door on his way out.

I wrap my arms around myself and scan the room again. It's like I'm stood in a room out of a catalogue. It is beautiful.

I head to the walk-in wardrobe, open the doors, and take a look inside. The rails are all empty except for the pair of pyjamas that Jake said that I could wear. To the left of the rails there is a dressing table that has nothing but a hairdryer on it. I take the pyjamas and head in the opposite direction of the room to the ensuite.

I come to a standstill in the ensuite as I see that there is a walk-in shower taking up a quarter of the space, a big oval-shaped bath tub in the middle of the room, and a toilet and two sinks at the other end.

Wow, this guy really knows how to design a guest room. All I need is a kitchen and I'm set!

I quickly strip myself of the clothes I am wearing, which I throw into a bin in the corner of the room. I will replace them for Lydia. I just can't bear to look at them.

I turn on the shower and wait for the water to heat up, which takes all of a few seconds. There is shampoo, conditioner and body wash on a small shelf to the left of the shower head. The urge to scrub my body is overwhelming. The feel of Donnie's hands on my body makes me retch. I scrub and scrub my skin until it becomes too sore to scrub anymore.

I turn off the shower and dry myself on a mammoth sized towel. The towel is warm as it has been hanging on a heated rail just outside of the shower cubicle. I pull on the pyjama top and put the matching bottoms on. The bottoms are too big, but I tuck the top into them to help keep them up as best as I can. I head to the sink to see if I can find a toothbrush, so I can freshen my mouth.

I look in the mirror above the sink and see that I really do look bloody awful. My face is pale, and I look like I have aged about ten years. I sigh as I contemplate my reflection and then let my eyes wander to a cabinet just to the right of the mirror, which I open to find everything that I could possibly need. It's vanity heaven in here.

I find a toothbrush as well as a hairbrush and hair ties on the bottom shelf, all still in their packaging. I undo the packaging for the toothbrush and clean my teeth before using the hairbrush to brush my hair and tie it into a ponytail as my mind drifts off to how Lydia is. I hope that she is okay. I can't lose her, she's my best friend. I just hope she believes me when I tell her what happened.

I sigh, putting the hairbrush back in the cabinet before I exit the ensuite and climb into the bed, sinking into the mattress.

As I lie there I torture myself by replaying the events of what happened tonight over and over again, until eventually sleep takes over.

CHAPTER ELEVEN

I wake up to be greeted with a pounding headache. I sit up in bed, and for a few moments I wonder where the hell I am. Then I remember how Jake brought me to his place.

The horrendous events of last night flood my brain and I have to run to the bathroom as I feel the bile rising in my throat. Once I finish emptying the remaining contents of my stomach, I brush my teeth and wash my face. I still look pale, but that's hardly surprising really.

I decide to head downstairs and see if I can find Jake. I notice that it is only just gone eight in the morning. At least I have managed to get a few hours' sleep, even though it doesn't feel like it.

I leave my room and go to the stairs, only to hear Jake's voice coming from the floor below. I freeze and decide to listen. I know that I shouldn't be eavesdropping, but I don't want to interrupt anything.

"What part aren't you getting? I don't want you back and I never will. Now please stop phoning me Caitlin before I take out a restraining order." Jake goes quiet and I presume that he is done with his conversation.

I wonder who this Caitlin woman is whilst I descend the stairs. Then again, it's not really any of my business. Jake is just being kind to me after witnessing what happened last night. I just need to be grateful for his help and not read too much into his actions.

I walk down the stairs and see that Jake isn't in the hallway, meaning he must be in one of the rooms. I continue to head down to the kitchen so that I don't disturb him. I reach the kitchen and decide a coffee needs to be my first port of call, and I busy myself trying to find a cup. When I have located one, about four cupboards later, I spot the coffee machine on the far left worktop. I press the button for an Americano and let the machine do its work.

As the coffee filters into the cup, I breath in the aroma of the coffee beans. It smells divine.

Once the machine has finished, I take my cup and move to the sink to add a touch of cold water so that I can drink it straight away. I take my first sip, lean against the granite worktop and close my eyes at how delicious the coffee tastes.

I let out a small moan of approval and almost drop the cup when I hear, "Morning. Glad to see you're making yourself at home."

My eyes fly open and my heart hammers inside my chest.

"Christ you scared me," I say as I put my hand over my beating heart.

"Sorry, I didn't mean to scare you," Jake replies. He smirks as he says it though, so I would say he is more amused by my reaction than he is sorry.

"It's okay. Um, I just needed some coffee. I hope that's okay?" Shit, maybe I should have asked him if it was okay first? What if he thinks that he won't be able to get rid of me now? The last thing that I would want him to think is that I would outstay my welcome.

"Relax, it's fine." His playful tone makes me smile and butterflies start to dance around my stomach. "Nice pyjamas by the way," he says with a mischievous look in his eyes.

"Oh, uh, yeah. Thanks for letting me use them." I smile at him shyly.

"Would you like some breakfast?" he asks me.

"Oh no, I'm good with just the coffee thanks."

"No, you need to eat. I whip up a mean omelette, or there are fresh pastries in the box on the side." He points to where the box is sitting. I really don't feel like eating anything, but I don't want to be appear rude, so I go over to the box and take out a croissant. I take the first bite and it tastes good. Really good. In fact, it's so delicious that it doesn't take me long to finish eating it.

"Taste good?" Jake asks as he picks out a pain au chocolate for himself.

"Delicious. Thank you." I sit on one of the bar stools and sip my coffee. Jake sits beside me and finishes off his food. He looks divine in his white tank top and grey jogging bottoms with his hair all in disarray. His caramel coloured eyes burn into mine. His very presence overwhelms me.

"How are you feeling this morning?" he asks, concern etched all over his face.

"To be honest, I don't really know. I just need to speak to Lydia and see how she is." She is one of the only constants in my life and I really don't want to lose her friendship.

"She will be here at two o'clock to speak to you," Jake says as if it's no big deal.

I nearly spit out the mouthful of coffee that I have just taken. "Pardon?"

"She's coming here at two. I had a message sent to her this morning and I have arranged for Eric to pick her up to come and see you." He looks completely unfazed. I on the other hand probably look ridiculous with the faces I am pulling.

"Hold on. How did you know where to find her?"

"Now that is something that I can't share with you. Top secret I'm afraid." He winks at me and his playful tone is back, but I am a little freaked out.

"No, seriously, how do you know where she lives?" I need to know that he isn't some deranged stalker.

"I had a friend escort her home from The Den last night to make sure she got home safely. Actually, I think the friend ended up staying the night with her if the squealing in the background was anything to go by." Jake looks a little uncomfortable at the thought.

I can't help but burst out laughing. Jake's eyes go wide as he watches me giggling hysterically.

"I'm sorry, it's just your face is such a picture."

"I'm glad that I amuse you," he smiles.

Once I have managed to calm down from my laughing fit, I open my mouth to ask him if Lydia knows anything about last night, but before I can do so he cuts me off.

"She doesn't know anything about what happened."

How did he know I was going to ask that?

"What are you, a mind reader?"

"No, just good at reading people." He stares at me intently. I break the gaze and get up from my stool to get myself another coffee. "It's not anyone else's place to tell her what happened."

"Thank you," I say as I smile at his thoughtfulness for a second before a dark thought suddenly crosses my mind. "Hey, wait a minute. You beat the shit out of Donnie, aren't you worried that he will report you?" I ask. I start to worry what repercussions Jake may face for helping me.

"Not worried in the slightest. You will not be hearing from him again and neither will I. And if he has any sense then he won't be bothering Lydia again either," Jake informs me.

Fuck, did he do something else to him?

Jake sees the look on my face and instantly shuts down my thoughts. "Stop worrying. It's a guy thing. He just knows not to come near you ever again and that's all you need to know."

Once again, he appears completely unfazed.

"Well... Okay then." I can't think of any other response. I lean against the worktop and stare into my coffee, trying to look for answers.

Why did Donnie do it? Why didn't I see it coming?

"Stop worrying," Jake says. He walks over to me and takes my coffee cup from my hands, places it on the worktop behind me and puts his arms around me. I automatically put my arms around his waist. "And stop over thinking. Everything is going to be fine." His words bring me comfort, and the feel of his arms enveloping me puts my body at ease.

We stand like that for some time, in silence. I am enjoying the closeness too much to think about how strange it is that we are embracing like we have been lovers for years. It should feel strange, hugging a virtual stranger, but it doesn't. In the very little time that I have known Jake, I can honestly say that I have never viewed him as a stranger. He almost feels like home to me.

I try to distract from my thoughts of Jake, and I begin to ponder over what may happen when Lydia comes over. What if she doesn't believe me?

My eyes flick up to the clock on the wall. It's quarter past nine, I have plenty of time to get ready for Lydia to arrive. I may just take a long, hot bath and wear my comfortable clothes.

Clothes... Shit!

I pull away from Jake as I realise that I have no clothes to wear.

"Um, Jake. I have no clothes to wear... For when Lydia gets here," I say shyly, pulling my head back to look at him.

"That's not a problem with me," he says with a wink. I playfully smack him on the chest and he laughs. "Don't worry, I have someone collecting your things from Charles' house as we speak."

"WHAT?" I shout as I break my hands from around his waist and lean back. His arms drop to his sides, and he looks a little uncomfortable at my outburst.

"Uh, I hope that isn't a problem. I just thought that you may need your personal items whilst you are here."

"Jake, I appreciate the gesture but it's a bit much. I would have made do with these pyjama bottoms and one of your clean T-shirts. Oh my God, Charles is going to flip when he finds out where I am. I really don't need the grief from him right now." I am exasperated. What Jake is doing for me is too much. I mean, bringing me back to his and looking after me is one thing, then making sure I see Lydia is another, but getting my stuff from my ex-boyfriend's house is insane. That's a lot for some guy, that I hardly know, to do for me.

What reason does he have for doing this? My mind starts to race.

Oh God, what have I gotten myself into by staying here? How does he even know that my stuff is still at Charles' house?

"I quite like the thought of you in one of my T-shirts," Jake says, trying to lighten my mood. I roll my eyes and give a little groan. "I just thought that I was helping. I would like you to feel comfortable whilst you are here. I thought having your own things would help do that. Plus, Charles has no reason to know I sent the guys who are collecting your things. For all he knows they could be friends of yours." Jake looks a little offended and I instantly feel guilty.

"Oh God, Jake, I didn't mean to sound so ungrateful. It's just all so overwhelming. The last twenty-four hours have been crazy. My head is all over the place and I don't know how to process everything."

"I know. That's why I wanted to make things easier for you." He seems so genuine and my gut is telling me to trust and believe him.

"Thank you," I say, giving him a little smile.

"No problem." He flashes me his heart stopping grin and my knees feel weak. How does he have this effect over me? After what happened last night though, I am so glad that Jake isn't trying to make a move on me. He may be hot, but my confidence has been severely shaken.

The doorbell rings, making me jump. Jake leaves the kitchen to go and answer the door. I finish my coffee before following him, and the sight before me is a little more than I expected. There are boxes everywhere. It literally looks like all of my stuff has been brought here.

Shit, I assumed he meant that he was having a few items of clothes collected for me, not my entire life!

"Um, Jake?" He turns around to look at me. "Why is it that every item I appear to own is sitting in boxes, in your hallway?"

"I told you that I was having your stuff collected."

"Yes, but I thought you meant a few clothes, I didn't realise you meant everything that I own." I am gobsmacked.

"Well, this way you have no need to go back to Charles' to collect your belongings. Except for your car. Charles is adamant that he can't find the keys. We can go and get it in the next day or two." Jake doesn't bat an eyelid at how insane all of this is. He shakes hands with the guys who have delivered my stuff and closes the door as they leave.

"I will take all of this up to the guest room for you," he says, gesturing to the boxes.

"Whoa, hold on a minute, mister." Jake gives me a puzzled look. "How long do you think I am staying for?"

"As long as you need to," he replies. Well fuck me, he's only gone and moved me in.

"I don't think that's appropriate, Jake. We hardly know each other. I am so grateful to you for everything you have done so far, but I can't live here." Doesn't he see how ridiculous this is?

"Look, before you start getting worried, I am happy for you to stay here." I go to speak, but he raises his finger to stop me as he continues to talk. "I want to help you, Stacey. There is no ulterior motive here. I hope that by now you have realised that I am not some raving lunatic. You may come and go as you please, and you may use the house as you would your own place. I am out most of the time due to my work commitments, so you may as well take advantage of the situation. I feel like we have a connection, and I would like to pursue that."

My eyebrows raise, and Jake quickly corrects his wording. "I mean, I feel that we are starting to become friends, and that thought makes me happy." I feel myself start to soften at his words.

"I don't let many people into my life, Stacey. I have trusted people before and they have let me down, but when I do sense a connection with someone, I like to explore that connection."

"But... But... But I don't have a job, and I wouldn't be able to contribute to the bills or anything." *Oh my God, am I actually considering this?*

"Does it look like that bothers me?"

"Well it bothers me. I don't want people to think that I am using you for your money." *Yep, looks like I am considering this crazy idea.*

"I don't give a fuck what other people think," Jake says, and his tone tells me that I should just drop this conversation, but I can't.

"I don't know, Jake. It's all so rushed and sudden. This is a big decision, and like

I said before, we hardly know each other. I'm also meant to be staying with Lydia." Although, depending on how this afternoon goes, I may not be able to stay with her anyway.

"Well, you have the option to stay here if you need to," Jake responds.

We stand in the hallway, staring at each other. This is just more information to process in my overloaded brain. I don't have the energy to talk this out right now.

"I'll think about it." This is the only answer that I can give right now.

"Okay then. You think about it and I will start to take these boxes to your room," Jake says. I don't fail to notice how it has gone from the "guest room" to "your room." "Oh, and just for the record, it doesn't feel like we hardly know each other. Not to me anyway."

With that, Jake starts to move my boxes from the hallway as I look on in disbelief. Living here with Jake Waters would be luxurious, I have no doubt about that, but can I really do that? Could me living here actually work?

My life has gone from zero miles per hour to one hundred in a very short space of time. Mid thought, I pick up one of the smaller boxes and start to take it up the stairs. I am halfway up when Jake startles me, making me drop the box I was holding. I hope there was nothing valuable in there as it could well be broken now.

"What do you think you are doing?" he asks me. I am about to respond, but Jake cuts me off before I can reply. "Don't even think about lifting anything else up here, the boxes are way too heavy."

"Jake, I'm perfectly fine to bring some stuff up here." I roll my eyes at him.

"It's not up for discussion. If you want to help then I would love another cup of coffee, black with one sugar."

"Is this what it would be like if I lived here? Will I be allowed to do anything?" I mock.

"Of course you will. But if it involves carrying heavy items then that is my job, not yours. Now, where are we on that cup of coffee?"

I salute Jake as he continues up the stairs, chuckling to himself.

"Coming right up, sir," I respond playfully before I return to the kitchen.

Maybe I could get used to being looked after like this...

CHAPTER TWELVE

I take a quick shower, so much for a long bath, and spend the next hour looking through my boxes, trying to find what clothes to wear. I opt for some black leggings, pink vest top and my favourite jumper which is off the shoulder and baggy, meaning it is comfy. I dry my hair and style it into a side plait that hangs loosely over my shoulder. I don't bother applying make-up. I'm not in the mood to be all dolled up right now. My eyes still look a little puffy from last night, but I don't care about covering it up. I think that seeing Lydia is only going to spark more emotion, so make-up would be a waste of time.

I hear the doorbell ring and I head out of the bedroom and downstairs to see if it is Lydia. Jake has already answered the door and is chatting with a guy who has his arm around Lydia's shoulders.

So that must be who escorted Lydia home.

He is tall with an athletic build, green eyes and short blond, cropped hair. Lydia looks up and sees me coming down the stairs. As I reach the bottom, she comes over and pulls me into a massive bear hug. I am shaking when she hugs me, but she doesn't seem to notice.

"So, you dirty stop out, this is where you got to, huh? I wondered where the hell you had disappeared to, until this nice young gentleman came and told me," she says as she points to the guy talking to Jake.

"Uh, yeah. It's a long story," I reply.

"I bet it is, and I want to hear every little detail." Lydia doesn't even bother to keep her voice quiet. Jake stops talking to his friend and stares at me as I try to stop myself from crumbling here on the spot. I am struggling to find words.

"Why don't you ladies go through to the lounge, just on the right, through that door. You can talk more privately in there," Jake suggests, nodding at the relevant door. I mouth my thanks to him. He smiles back, and my heart does a little flutter. "Come on, Paul, let's leave them to it and go grab a beer."

"Cool," says the guy, who I now know is called Paul. The guys walk off in the direction of the kitchen as Lydia and I head to the lounge. I haven't seen the lounge yet, so I have no idea what it looks like.

I open the door and look around the room. It is beautiful, but not as big as I expected it to be. The fact that the lounge is small means it gives it a cosy and warm vibe. The colour scheme is lovely, and the floor is covered in a rich cream carpet that is so plush my feet sink into it.

The walls are painted cream but there is a feature wall that is painted in a glorious gold colour. Fresh flowers sit in a vase on the ornate mantelpiece, and a gigantic television literally covers one of the walls opposite the seating area.

The seating area consists of a cream coloured corner sofa and a little coffee table in front of it. Jake really does have great taste when it comes to decorating a house. Each room I have seen so far has been stunning.

"Fucking hell, Stace, you hit the jackpot when you met him," Lydia says as she strides in and takes a seat on the sofa. "Oh God, this is like bliss on your butt cheeks." I giggle at her comment and go and sit next to her, taking her hand in mine.

"Stace?" her face looks puzzled. "What's going on?"

I take a deep breath and try to calm my nerves. "Lyd, I need to tell you something, and I need you to let me get to the end of this before you say anything."

"Come on, Stacey, out with it. You're scaring me."

"Something happened to me at The Den last night. I wish I didn't have to tell you this, but..." I take another deep breath before carrying on. Lydia is staring at me with wide eyes. I need to get this over with.

"Donnie tried to assault me."

Lydia doesn't move a muscle. She seems to have frozen at my words.

"He was waiting for me outside the toilets when I came out. I started to panic as I thought that something had happened to you, for him to be waiting for me." I fight back the tears that are threatening to break through my strength.

"After assuring me that you were okay, he grabbed me and led me down the corridor next to the toilets. He shoved me against the wall. I couldn't move, Lydia, he had me pinned. I tried to fight him off, but he was too strong. He touched me, and I was screaming at him to get off of me, but he wasn't listening. If it wasn't for Jake showing up when he did, I think he would have..." my voice breaks, and I can't bring myself to finish the sentence.

Tears start to sting the backs of my eyes, but I need to keep talking. "I'm so sorry, Lyd. I never thought that I would ever have to tell you anything like this. I know this must be a shock..."

Lydia scoffs and I look at her in surprise.

"Donnie wouldn't do that to me, what are you talking about?" Lydia removes her hand from mine, stands up and starts to pace the room.

"He did, and I wish to God that he hadn't. It breaks me to have to tell you this.

You are my best friend, Lyd. I need to know that you have understood what I have just told you." Lydia stops pacing and turns to face me.

"Oh, I understand. I understand perfectly." There is a tone to her voice that she has never used with me before. "What I don't understand though is why you didn't tell me last night? Why didn't you come straight to me and tell me?" She looks hurt.

"I'm sorry, Lyd. I was a mess. Jake had to physically carry me out of the place and I had no idea that he was bringing me here. I was scared, and he made me feel safe."

"Oh, I bet he did." Lydia's voice is laced with sarcasm.

"It's not like that, Lydia." I feel defensive at her insinuation. "Jake has been nothing but kind, and he doesn't expect anything in return."

"But *I* am your best friend. You should have been able to come to *me*," Lydia says, raising her voice. I knew this wouldn't exactly be a happy conversation, but I did expect her to show some concern. I start to feel anger rise within me.

"You *are* my best friend, but Donnie is the guy that you have been shagging for the last three months. How would I have been able to tell you? He would have made sure that I wouldn't have had the opportunity to."

"You could have at least tried, but instead you let some guy that you barely know bring you to his place. Is this why Donnie ditched me at The Den? Is this why Jake's friend took me home?" I can't answer her, but then I don't really think I need to. I think the answers to those questions are fairly obvious after what I have just told her.

"I need to get out of here. I can't be near you right now." Lydia turns to leave the room and panic surges through me.

"Lyd, please don't go. We need to talk about this." I jump up off of the sofa and follow her into the hallway. Lydia doesn't stop, and she doesn't turn around. All I can do is watch as she walks out of the front door, slamming it behind her.

I let myself sink to the floor as I watch my best friend walk out of my life. I replay the conversation with Lydia back in my head, and I try to figure out if I could have handled it better. I don't think there is a right way that I could have told her. There is no way that I could have kept it from her, she needed to know the truth about what happened. Not telling her was never an option.

I slowly stand on shaky legs and go to the mirror in the hallway. I look at my reflection and I don't recognise the person staring back at me. I look pale and my eyes have lost any sparkle that they may have held before. My whole body starts to shake uncontrollably, and sheer exhaustion takes over. I'm so tired. I can't face seeing Jake at the moment, so I head for the guest bedroom, needing to be alone with my thoughts.

I walk in a daze until I reach the bed and curl up into a ball with my back to the door as I close my eyes. Emotions are rife within me and I don't know how to dissect all that I am feeling. I hate Donnie for what he has done. I despise men who make women feel powerless. I feel used, I feel angry, and I feel lost. I am lost. I have no home, no job, no family, and it looks like I have lost my best friend.

Everything is whirring around in my head so quickly that I don't notice that Jake has entered the room until he sits behind me on the bed. He doesn't say anything, and I don't turn to look at him.

I feel his weight shift as he lies down behind me and puts his arm around me. He just holds me, and I let my tears silently fall. I don't attempt to move away from him because his touch brings me comfort.

I am hurting, and right now I will take any little bit of comfort that I can get.

CHAPTER THIRTEEN

I open my eyes to a darkened room. I must have fallen asleep. I feel behind me, but Jake isn't there.

I turn over, reach for the bedside lamp and turn it on. The time on the alarm clock shows it's just before quarter to four in the morning. I have been asleep for about twelve hours and I feel groggy as I head to the ensuite and use the facilities. I choose to avoid looking at myself in the mirror. I already know that I must look awful without having to see it. My mouth feels dry, so I decide to head downstairs to get a drink.

I quietly tip-toe along the hallway and down the first flight of stairs as I don't want to make any noise. I presume Jake is asleep and I don't want to wake him. I only make it to the first floor though, when I hear voices coming from further along the hall way.

Voices at this time of night?

I freeze and turn my head in the direction of the noise. The voices are faint as they appear to be in one of the rooms, so I tip-toe along the hallway a bit in order to hear what is being said.

"What the fuck is wrong with you, Jake?" a woman's voice says. Whoever she is, she sounds agitated.

"Nothing is wrong with me." I hear him sigh. "I just don't want you here. Now, please will you leave."

"I'm not going anywhere until you explain why you are doing this to me. I love you, Jake, and we are good together. Why won't you just accept that?" The woman now sounds desperate. I suck in a breath of air as I wait to see what Jake's response will be.

"For Christ's sake, Caitlin, we are not good together. I don't know how else I can sugar coat this, so I'm just going to be blunt. You are crazy. The only reason I indulged you for so long is because I didn't want you completely losing it. I don't love you, and I never have." This doesn't sound like the Jake that I have come to know, and I know I shouldn't be listening, but I can't just walk away now.

"Jake, baby, please don't do this to us. I am not crazy. I just love you so much." The woman, whom I now know is called Caitlin, starts to cry.

"Oh for fuck's sake, Caitlin, don't you think that turning up at my home at three in the morning is just a little bit strange? I don't want to hurt you, but you are just so infuriating. I am telling you that nothing is going to happen with us anymore, and it never will again. I made a massive mistake by ever sleeping with you in the first place." He sounds mad.

Shit, is this the real Jake?

I barely know the guy. What if the nice Jake is all an act?

I quietly move back along the hall way and up the stairs to return to my bedroom as I don't want to listen to any more of their conversation. My heart is racing as I try to figure out what to do next. I need to leave here. The way he spoke to that woman was horrendous. I definitely won't be able to go back to sleep now. I reach my room and sit on the bed, my mind racing with what options I have. *Who am I kidding, I have no options.*

My thoughts are quickly interrupted by the sound of something smashing downstairs.

Oh my God, what the hell was that? Do I go and see? Do I pretend that I am still asleep?

My feet seem to make the decision for me as I stand up off of the bed and head back out into the hallway. This may be one of the worst decisions ever, but I need to see what's happened.

I hear the front door slam shut as I reach the first floor before I hear a grunt coming from one of the rooms.

I gingerly walk down the hall way and reach the door that is open slightly. It's Jake's office by the looks of it. My heart is beating wildly as I push the door open fully.

As the door opens, Jake comes into view. He's stood clutching his arm, which is covered in blood. My eyes go wide, and my mouth drops open at the sight.

"Oh, fuck." I can't help the words escaping from my mouth. Jake looks up at me and I can see fear in his eyes. I quickly rush over to him to take a look at the damage to his arm. There is a large slash mark going down his forearm, and a broken vase lays scattered all over the floor.

"What the hell happened in here, Jake?" I ask, panic evident in my tone.

"I just knocked the vase and cut myself," Jake answers through gritted teeth.

Really? This is the best excuse that he can come up with?

"That's bullshit, and you know it." However, I don't have time to quiz him on the matter right now. "Wait here. I'll go and grab some towels and then I'm taking you to the hospital."

I don't give Jake time to respond as I race out of his office and upstairs to my bedroom. I grab a couple of the plush white towels and race back to Jake as quickly as I can. He is sat in his office chair and is on the phone talking to someone. I don't ask questions, I just go and wrap the wound as best as I can with the towels to try and stop the blood flow.

He says to whoever is on the phone that he will be waiting outside and then he gets up, walks past me, and heads for the hallway.

"Um, Jake? Where the bloody hell are you going?" I stand with my hands on my hips and wait for him to answer me.

"To the hospital. Eric is on his way to take me." He doesn't even turn around to look at me.

I scurry after him. I manage to overtake him in the hallway and I stand in front of him so that he has to stop walking. He looks at me and I can see a range of emotions flicker through his eyes.

"Now just you hang on. Don't think for one minute that I am not coming with you," I say defiantly.

"You don't need to do that. It's late and Eric will wait for me."

"Jake Waters, I am coming with you whether you like it or not. I will only sit here worrying about whether you are okay otherwise." I fold my arms across my chest and just stand there.

There is no way that I am staying here by myself. I prepare for him to try and fob me off, but to my astonishment, he doesn't.

"Thank you," is all he says as he offers up a weak smile. I nod my head, turn around and race downstairs to get my shoes on. I help Jake with his shoes once he reaches the bottom of the stairs, and I put a jacket around him.

I open the front door and step outside to see that Eric is already waiting on the driveway. Jake takes some door keys off of the hooks by the door and goes to lock the house up. I grab the keys off of him as I point to the limo. He walks off muttering as I lock the door. I catch up to him and follow him into the limo.

Jake has now gone pale and is perspiring. I hold his hand, of his uninjured arm, as we make our way to the hospital.

It doesn't take long for Eric to reach the hospital, and together Eric and I help Jake out of the limo. We get Jake to the reception desk and the receptionist instantly gets Jake sat in a wheelchair. A doctor comes racing over a few seconds later and then we are on the move.

We head past a few doors before the doctor enters a big spacious room, complete with bed, sofa and television. It is only now that I realise that we are in a private hospital rather than the NHS one.

Of course, he's a millionaire, why would he not pay a fortune for healthcare?

I go to exit the room with Eric when Jake grabs my arm with his good hand.

"Stay with me," he says in a quiet voice. His eyes are pleading with me, but it doesn't take me more than a second to make my decision. I smile and gently shake my arm from his grasp before taking a seat on the sofa. He smiles at me and the doctor tells Jake to sit on the bed.

I remain silent as the doctor examines Jake and says he will need to have some shards of glass removed from his arm, and then he will need a few stitches.

Jake lets out a groan as the doctor leaves the room to retrieve the required equipment.

"How are you feeling?" I ask him as I walk over and stand by the side of the bed.

"Scared," Jake answers.

"Scared?"

Jake sighs. "I hate needles." I can't help but giggle at him. "What's so funny?" he says, raising one eyebrow and looking at me quizzically.

"You mean to tell me that a big, strong man like you has a fear of little, tiny needles?" I can't stop laughing.

"Oh, I'm glad you find this so funny," he says. He may not sound too thrilled, but I can see his eyes light up as he watches me.

"I'm sorry. I just wasn't expecting you to be scared of something like that."

"It's my only weakness, I swear." He manages a tiny smile, but it soon evaporates as he grimaces from the pain in his arm.

The doctor returns, so I once again take my seat on the sofa. Once the doctor is satisfied that he has removed all of the glass, he cleans the wound, which I can tell is causing Jake immense pain if his facial expressions and use of foul language are anything to go by.

I jump up and go over to hold his good hand. Jake squeezes my hand slightly which I take to mean as a thank you. The doctor then stitches Jake's arm and bandages the wound.

"You will need to rest, Jake. The wound isn't as bad as it looks, but you need to make sure you don't do anything to aggravate the healing process. I will see you in two days' time. I will book you an appointment and forward you the details," the doctor says before standing up.

Jake and I both thank him for his help. He smiles, nods and then exits the room.

"You heard the doc, you have to rest," I reiterate to Jake.

"I don't do resting. I have a company to run." He does not look pleased. Jake doesn't seem like the type of guy to follow orders.

"Well, it's lucky for you that I will be on hand to help then, isn't it?" Jake frowns and I give him a smirk before walking towards the door. "Come on then, scaredy cat. Let's get you home and away from any sight of needles."

"Ha ha, very funny," he replies. I can hear the amusement in his voice as he follows me out of the room and out of the hospital to the limo.

CHAPTER FOURTEEN

We arrive back at the house as the early morning workers make their daily commute. I leave Jake talking to Eric as I go and unlock the front door. I walk straight into the kitchen where I grab Jake a glass of water and decide to make some toast as well, seeing as neither of us has had anything to eat.

Jake appears a few moments later and watches me from the kitchen doorway.

"What?" I ask him.

"Nothing," he replies.

"Well, in that case, get your butt up to bed and I will bring this up to you," I say as I point in the direction of the stairs. Jake stands to attention and salutes me before marching off up the stairs. He really does make me smile.

I busy myself getting the toast ready and then I find a tray to carry it all upstairs on. I decide against making any coffee as I am hoping that I will be able to have a little nap, and with caffeine in my system there would be no way I would be able to rest.

As I make my way up the stairs, I cast my mind back to the conversation Jake was having with the mysterious Caitlin woman in his office. I just can't understand why Jake spoke to her like that. I am yet to see a bad side to him, and I don't want to think badly of him because he has helped me so much in the last couple of days.

God, is that all it's been? Two days?

It feels like I have been here so much longer with all that has happened so far. I don't know how much more shock I can take. I still haven't really had much time to process the whole Donnie situation, but maybe that's a good thing. Keeping busy is better than dwelling on it. I wish I could call Lydia though. I feel saddened as I think of how she walked out on me, and how I haven't heard from her since. I shake my head as I reach Jake's bedroom. I can think about that another time. Right now, Jake needs my attention.

The door to his bedroom is open, but I don't feel comfortable just walking in. I can see Jake's bed, which is even bigger than the one that I have been sleeping in. How is that even possible?

I spot a sofa which runs along the length of the window on the back wall, and the décor is very simple. Cream walls and black furnishings. Very manly. Jake comes into view, emerging from a doorway in his room and striding across his bedroom. He is wearing just a black pair of silk boxer shorts. My God, he is perfection. I admire his physique as he sits on the bed and looks at me standing in the doorway.

"Are you coming in?" he asks, a smirk visible on his lips.

"Uh, I didn't feel right just walking in without asking," I say, feeling stupid. I start shuffling on the spot due to nerves creeping in at the thought of going into his bedroom.

"Don't be silly. You're welcome in my bedroom any time," he says as he winks at me, and I feel myself swoon.

Get a bloody grip, Stacey, I tell myself. *The guy has just come home from the hospital. He is your friend and nothing more.*

I casually stroll over to the bed and put the toast and glass of water on his bedside table. I motion for Jake to get into his bed and lie down. He does, and I turn and walk from the room without saying a word. I quickly go to my bedroom across the hall and retrieve the soft blanket that lies across the end of my bed as well as a pillow. I go back to Jake's room and head for the sofa.

"Stace." Jake says my name to get my attention. "What are you doing?" He looks puzzled as I put the pillow on the sofa and get myself settled under the blanket. I sink into the sofa and my body is instantly grateful for the pure softness that is enveloping my body. I stifle a groan at how comfortable it is.

"What does it look like I'm doing?" I answer sarcastically. He remains silent and I grin. "I am staying in here with you just in case you need anything. Is that a problem, Mr Waters?"

"There really is no need. I haven't lost a limb. I've just cut my arm."

"Don't argue with me because you won't win. Now, eat your toast and then get some rest. I don't know about you, but after the events of the last few days, I'm exhausted." Forgetting about needing to eat any toast myself, I close my eyes and hope that he will take the hint.

I hear Jake chuckle to himself as I curl up on my side and get some much-needed rest.

CHAPTER FIFTEEN

I am awoken by the sound of banging downstairs. I groggily look over to Jake's bed, but he is fast asleep. *That's weird. Maybe it's Eric?*

Whoever it is, they are making quite a racket for me to be able to hear it up here on the second floor. I drag my body off of the sofa and head downstairs to see what all the noise is about. As I get closer to the ground floor, it appears that the noise is coming from the kitchen.

I walk along the ground floor hall way and enter the kitchen to see a blond-haired woman banging pots around. The kitchen is an absolute mess with food and crockery scattered everywhere.

What the fuck is going on?

The woman has her back to me, so it isn't until I speak that she realises that I am here.

"What the hell are you doing?" I ask the strange woman. She spins around and fixes me with a deadly stare. Her dark brown eyes burn into me and make me feel uncomfortable. Her face is screwed up and she looks pissed off. I can only assume that she is annoyed at my unexpected interruption.

"I'm cooking. What the fuck has it got to do with you?" she snarls at me.

Thank goodness that she is on the other side of the kitchen island because she looks positively evil. I stay in the kitchen doorway to keep my distance from her. For all I know, this woman is a complete psycho.

"Um, should you be here?" I am more than confused as to what is going on.

"Of course I should. I am making Jake a meal. Who the hell are you and what are you doing here?" The venom in her voice is obvious. This woman lacks some serious manners.

"I don't think that's important, but I do think that you should leave," I say firmly. I start to feel extremely wary around her.

"I'm not going anywhere." And just like that it appears that we are in a stand-off. I really don't have the energy for all of this. So much for all the shocks being over and done with.

"Jake needs to rest, and he isn't up to visitors at the moment. Why don't you come back another time?" A change of tactic may work? At least I am hoping that it will.

"Who are you?" she asks again, her eyebrows draw together and her eyes narrow.

I sigh. "I'm a friend of Jake's. I'm looking after him seeing as he has had a bit of an accident."

She scoffs. "Accident? Is that what he told you?"

Ah, the penny drops. This must be Caitlin. Oh Christ, that's all I need to deal with, Jake's scorned ex or whatever the hell she is to him.

"There is no reason for him to lie to me." Of course I am not going to admit to her that Jake has tried to pass off the vase incident as a mere case of his own clumsiness. Caitlin smirks.

"You're one of those tramps he likes to screw, aren't you?" I am gobsmacked at her question.

Before I can form words to answer her, she continues to speak. "For your information, Jake did not have an accident. He was going to throw the vase at me, so I grabbed it off of him and hit his arm with it."

My mind processes her words. Surely this woman isn't telling the truth? From what I know of Jake, I am certain that he wouldn't physically hurt any woman. Then again, maybe I am a poor judge of character? She watches for my reaction, and I don't know how I manage it, but I don't move an inch, not even a facial twitch.

"Why don't you run along home and I will continue to tend to Jake's *needs*." Ugh, this woman is repulsive. I am way too tired to deal with this bullshit, so I decide to play her at her own game.

"Listen here, Caitlin." Her eyes go wide as I say her name. "I think you need to get the fuck out of this house before this situation gets out of hand. Jake has told me all about you, and you are not welcome here. If you don't leave then I will be forced to call the police, which I'm sure is the last thing you want."

Caitlin just stares at me, but I never break away from her gaze. After a few long, tense minutes it seems that she has come to her senses as she grabs her bag and walks towards me. I step back to let her pass. She stops, inches from me and looks me up and down.

I feel my defences rise at her sinister stare. Adrenaline pumps through my system as I realise that this situation could get more heated than it is already. After an unbearably awkward few seconds, she simply smirks, shakes her head, turns away and starts walking to the front door.

She opens the front door and stops, still with her back to me. "Don't think that this is the last you will be hearing from me, bitch."

My heart hammers against my chest as she slams the door behind her. I run to it and lock it, leaning my back against the door as I take a few deep breaths.

Fuck, she was rather scary.

In one way, I am proud that I stood up to her, but in another way, I think how stupid I was to confront her. I shakily walk back to the kitchen, feeling deflated as I look at all of the mess she has made. I better clean all of this up before Jake sees it. At least doing this will keep my mind occupied for a while. My life really has become bizarre over the past few days. And now, with this Caitlin issue, it seems that there is more to Mr Waters than meets the eye.

I spend the next half an hour chucking the food Caitlin was making into the bin and washing everything that she appears to have touched. I am half way through the mess when Jake enters the kitchen.

"Having a Gordon Ramsey moment, are we?" he asks with a smile, unaware of the conflict that happened in here not so long ago.

"I wasn't, but some woman called Caitlin was." I wait and watch his reaction. He visibly recoils at the mention of her name. I decide now is the time to ask about her, before he has the chance to change the topic. "Who is she, Jake?"

"She's not important." His jaw clenches as he looks at his arm.

"Are we really going to do this?" I ask.

"Do what?"

"Skirt around the subject. I know that she was here last night, and I know her version of events, so why not just tell me your side of the story?" It may not be my place, but if I am staying here then I need to know the truth.

Jake runs his hands through his hair and takes a seat at the kitchen island.

"I need scotch for a conversation like this but seeing as I'm on medication, would you mind making me a coffee?" he asks.

I turn and pick one of the clean cups off of the draining board and make Jake his coffee. I make one for myself at the same time, seeing as I haven't had chance to before now. I walk around the kitchen island and sit on the stool next to Jake. Jake sips his coffee and I wait patiently for him to start talking.

After what feels like an eternity he finally starts to speak.

"I have known Caitlin for three years. She came to work for me as my PA. She had been working with me for over two years when I stupidly decided to mix business with pleasure. I slept with her on and off for a few months, but I was never in a relationship with her. I suppose you could say that I led her to believe that we were a couple because, to be honest, I never told her otherwise."

I say nothing as I want to hear where he is going with this.

"I stopped sleeping with her after I spent the night with you, six months ago. I just couldn't do it anymore. It felt wrong after being with you."

Well, knock me down with a feather, I wasn't expecting that. I decide not to comment as I don't really want to bring attention to the fact that we had a one-night stand together, especially as we are starting to form a friendship.

"She took it well at first, but things soon changed. She became erratic and wouldn't leave me alone. I had to fire her as my PA as she kept messing up my meetings and making me look bad. After I fired her, she said that she was pregnant." I gasp at this piece of news as it comes as a shock.

Jake puts his head in his hands. "I didn't want to have a child with her, but I thought that I should step up and take responsibility for my actions. It was coming up to the first scan and I had arranged to meet her at the hospital. Only, she wasn't at the hospital when I got there, and with a bit of persuasion I found out that they didn't even have her on their records.

"She lied about the pregnancy. She believed that I wouldn't turn up to the scan, and she thought that she would get away with the lie for a bit longer. I then told her I wanted nothing more to do with her, but her behaviour just keeps getting more and more crazy. She tries to follow my every move. Then last night she showed up here as you are already aware. She got angry with me, and that's when she smashed the vase and cut my arm."

I sit there and take in everything that he has just told me. My gut feeling tells me to trust him, and to trust what he is saying.

"So, what you're saying is, on top of everything else going on I now have to worry about some lunatic ex of yours that now knows I am staying here? Wow, this has been quite a week, and it's not even over with yet." My life has turned into some kind of soap opera.

"I'm sorry, but I didn't think you would ever have the misfortune of meeting her."

"I understand why you never said anything. I mean, I've only been here a few days, why the hell would you tell me? Not to mention that we still hardly know each other. I will say though, if I am going to be staying here until I get myself sorted, then you need to update me on things like this. It would be nice to have a heads up. That way, at least I can try and prepare myself for altercations like the one I had with her an hour ago."

"I'm sorry." Jake looks genuinely apologetic, then his face suddenly lights up. "Did I just hear you say that you are going to stay here?" His eyebrows are raised in anticipation. It seems like he really does want me to stay here.

"Yes, Jake. Who else is going to look after you? Besides Caitlin of course." I smile at my comment. I need to try and make the best of this situation.

"Not funny, Stace."

"Sorry, just trying to lighten the mood." I get up from the stool and continue with tidying the kitchen.

"Are you really okay with what I just told you?" Jake seems surprised.

"Hey, it could be worse. So you have a psycho ex, big deal. Everyone has baggage." I shrug my shoulders as I put the last of the pans away. "Besides, life is full of struggles, it's just how you deal with them that matters." I lean on the island and look into Jake's eyes. Something passes between us, but I can't pin point what it is.

"You're incredible, you know that?" I feel myself blush at Jake's words, but I just want to keep the mood light.

"I do try," I tease. "How about I cook us some food and you can go and pick out a movie for us to watch?"

In my opinion there are no other words needed on the Caitlin matter. He has told me all that I need to know, and for that I am grateful. It just shows that he must trust me enough for him to tell me. I hear Jake's stomach grumble at the mention of food.

"That would be great," he says. I smile at him and I take pleasure in being able to look after him. He gets up from the stool and is about to exit the kitchen when a question pops into my head.

"Just one more thing," I say. Jake turns around and looks at me. "How did she even get in here? Does she have a key?"

Oh God, please don't say she has a bloody key.

Jake sighs and looks just as confused as I must do. "No, she most certainly does not have a key. I can only think that I must have forgotten to lock the patio doors last night."

"Hmmm. Maybe we need to be more vigilant about locking doors from now on then?"

"Agreed."

"Don't worry, I locked the front door when she left. I will go and lock the patio doors whilst you go and put your feet up."

"Yes, ma'am," Jake replies in a cocky manner. He salutes, and I laugh at his playfulness. I shoo him away and am overcome with a sense that maybe, just maybe, I was meant to meet Jake for a reason. He really does seem to have a way of making me feel at ease, even with all the crazy going on around me.

Psycho ex's aside, I feel very lucky to have had the fortune of meeting him.

My perfect stranger most certainly is keeping me on my toes.

CHAPTER SIXTEEN

"I am so full," I whine as my stomach hurts from eating too much food.

"That was delicious," Jake says as he lies back on the sofa. I cooked us a mixture of Indian dishes which, I have to agree, were very tasty.

I ask Jake to pause the film we're watching as I get up and take all of the plates and dishes into the kitchen. I pile them all on the side as I don't have the inclination to even place them in the dishwasher right now. There are some left over samosa's and onion bhaji's, so I find a container to put them in and I place them in the fridge.

I pour myself a glass of wine from the bottle that Jake opened for me to have with my food, and I head back to the lounge. Jake is on soft drinks due to the medication he is taking for the pain in his arm.

"You know, Jake," I start to say as I sit down next to him and cover myself with the blanket he is hogging. "I don't think you could have picked a more inappropriate film than this."

"What do you mean? It's a good thriller."

"You choose a film about a woman who makes her ex's life hell, and yet we have had your crazy ex here twice in the last twenty-four hours. Are you missing her already?" I tease him. The irony is uncanny. I also think that the wine is making me a little bit more loose-lipped than I normally am.

"Oh God, Stace, please don't joke about that." He's pulling the most ridiculous faces at the thought. I laugh hysterically.

"If someone had told me last week that all these different things were going to happen to me, then I would have thought that they were on drugs."

"I know. It's been a bit of a rollercoaster," Jake replies.

I place my wine glass on the coffee table and turn to look at him. I need him to know how much I appreciate what he has done for me, and I feel now is the time to say it.

"Jake, I am so grateful to you for helping me at The Den the other night. You will never know how relieved I was to see you standing there. And I just wanted to say that what you have done for me since then is more than I deserve. I am indebted to you, and I will pay you back one day, somehow... I'm just not sure how yet." Tears prick the backs of my eyes.

"I haven't had anyone look after me this way in such a long time. I have no family left, and it's nice to feel protected by someone. I'm really glad that I can class you as a friend."

Jake's gaze penetrates into my eyes. I now feel a little bit silly for being so open with him, but I needed him to know.

Jake cups my cheek with his good hand. "It's no problem. It's nice to have someone to look after."

It is taking all of my willpower not to lean in and kiss him. My body is humming with need for him, but I can't let myself give in.

I clear my throat and excuse myself to go to the bathroom, choosing to run upstairs and use the one in my bedroom, just to get some space. The moment we just shared was intense, and I don't want to lose Jake as a friend by doing something stupid.

I pace up and down the bathroom, trying to push away all of the emotions that I am feeling. This would be the point where I would phone Lydia and she would probably tell me to stop acting like a muppet and enjoy myself. I miss her.

I go to the sink and splash some water on my face. It's in this moment that it suddenly dawns on me that I don't have my phone with me.

Shit, I can't believe that I have gone all this time with no phone and I have only just realised.

And I haven't thought about my laptop either. Mind you, with everything that's been going on, I'm surprised that I even remember my own name.

I dry my face as there is a knock on the bathroom door.

"Stace, is everything okay?" Jake asks, concern evident in his tone of voice.

Come on, Stace. Don't let him see that he is affecting you. He's just your friend.

"Yeah, I'm fine. I'll be out in a minute." I give myself a check in the mirror. My cheeks are a little flushed, but apart from that I look okay.

I take a deep breath and open the bathroom door. Jake is standing there, looking like some sort of God. He may only be wearing jogging bottoms and a T-shirt, but my-oh-my, he looks good enough to devour.

I watch him as he rakes his eyes over my body. I may only be wearing some leggings and an oversized shirt, but Jake manages to make me feel as sexy as hell from his gaze. The heat that emanates from him nearly floors me.

I take in another deep breath and am about to ask him to kindly move out of the way when he surges towards me, grabs me at my waist and places his lips on mine. He picks me up and I automatically wrap my legs around his waist, and our kiss becomes more desperate. He walks us towards the sink unit and sits me on top of the counter. I keep my legs wrapped around him, enjoying the feel of his body so close.

As the urgency of our kiss continues, I run my hands through his hair and hear him let out a quiet moan. What this man does to me is remarkable. The electricity between us is so powerful it's almost frightening.

Jake continues to explore my mouth with his tongue as his hands tighten their grip on my waist. My sex is already wet with my need for him. I move my hands to the bottom of his T-shirt and lift the hem slightly so that I can feel his skin beneath my fingertips, but that is the moment when Jake abruptly stops the kissing and touching.

My legs break from around his waist as he backs away from me with wide eyes. I frantically search his face for answers, but I find none. We are both breathing heavy and the sound is deafening in the otherwise silent room. It's almost as if Jake's shutters have come down and he has blocked out all emotions.

"I can't do this."

Those are the only words he speaks as I look at him, dumbfounded. I watch as he practically runs from the bathroom, and I sit, shell-shocked, on the sink.

What the hell just happened?
Why did he leave?
Did I do something wrong?
Am I a bad kisser?

I have a million different questions going around in my head, and I have no answers to any of them. I suddenly feel raw and exposed. It is a stark contrast to the heat and passion I felt only seconds ago.

My body reacts to the rejection. I feel cold and unwanted, not to mention stupid. I shouldn't have let him kiss me. I shouldn't have given in to my urges. Now the friendship Jake and I were building has been shattered into a million pieces. We have just begun getting to know each other, and now it is ruined.

The hurt that I am feeling right now is indescribable.

Pain sears through me as hopes for Jake to be a part of my life have been dashed.

CHAPTER SEVENTEEN

I am barely aware of what I am doing until I am half way down the road and walking in the direction of Lydia's flat. I know we left things on bad terms, but I need to see her right now. I really hope we can put aside our differences. I need to talk to her, and I really need to be away from Jake. I don't know where he went after the bathroom incident, but I didn't see him again.

It starts to rain and all I have on is the same clothes that I left the house in. I didn't even think to grab a jacket. All I thought about was getting my shoes on and getting the hell out of there. Marvellous, I now get to look like a drowned rat as I walk along the pavement.

I fold my arms across my chest and quicken my pace. It only takes me twenty minutes and I am stood in front of Lydia's front door. It's late, so I hope that she is still awake.

I summon up all of my courage and I knock on her door. It takes a few moments but eventually Lydia answers, gasping when she sees me.

"Hi," I say shyly. I don't know what else to say. I would normally just walk in, but I wait to see if she invites me in this time.

"Uh, hi. I wasn't expecting to see you?" Lydia asks a question rather than just making a statement.

"I just um, I just..."

I just what? Got rejected by the guy that I am developing feelings for? How pathetic would that sound?

I search for words, but nothing comes. Instead I just stand there, looking at the floor, feeling like an utter fool.

"You better come in. You must be freezing." Lydia ushers me inside. "Let me go and grab you a towel. Your clothes are still in the spare bedroom if you want to go and get changed."

"Oh. Thanks, Lyd." I gratefully smile at her. She goes off to get me a towel and I head to the spare bedroom. I don't fail to notice that Lydia didn't refer to it as my room, so I'm guessing that she is still angry with me.

I enter the room, and everything is exactly as I left it a few days ago, nothing has been moved. Lydia comes back with a towel and says that she will go and make us a hot drink. I quickly dry myself and get changed into some jogging bottoms and a black jumper.

I look at my phone which is still on the bedside table and pick it up to try and turn it on to see if anyone has called, but there is no charge left in it. Bloody typical.

I place the phone in the pocket of my jogging bottoms. I will just have to check for any messages another time.

I go through to the lounge where Lydia is sitting on the sofa with a mug of hot chocolate in her hands, and she points to my mug on the coffee table. I feel awkward, something that I have never felt in Lydia's presence before. She gestures for me to sit down next to her. I oblige as I pick up my mug. I take a sip and am grateful for the warm chocolate that heats my insides.

"So, how have you been?" I ask her. I figure this is the best way to try and break the tension between us.

"Not great actually." Her reply is solemn. Silence engulfs the room and makes it feel smaller somehow. Shit, I should have thought of something else to ask. I mentally curse myself for making things seem more uncomfortable.

"Listen, Lyd—" I am cut off before I can continue.

"No. I need to talk first." Lydia holds her hands up as she speaks.

I purse my lips together and dread what she may be about to say.

"I'm sorry that I ran out and left you the other day. I just wasn't expecting to be told something like that. I needed to be on my own and just think things through. I guess it was the shock that made me react like that.

"When I came back here, I found Donnie sitting in the kitchen, drinking a cup of coffee. His face was a mess. He acted like nothing was wrong to start with. Anyway, I tricked him to see if he would tell me the truth, but he didn't." Lydia takes a deep breath and pushes her hair away from her face.

"Deep down, I knew that you would never lie about something like that. I knew that I had made a huge mistake by ever letting him into my life. As he was talking, he made my skin crawl. After he gave some piss-poor excuse about being attacked by some random group of men, I let him have it. I shouted at him until I could shout no more. Not for what he had done to me, but for what he had put you through." Lydia takes a pause and I can see her eyes glaze over. I feel utter relief wash over me that Lydia believes me.

"I told him that I never wanted to see him again, and if I ever did, then I would tell everyone about what he had done. I also said I would notify everyone of the fact that he has a small penis, just for good measure." I feel a smile pull at my lips when she says the last bit.

"I have been trying to call you ever since that day, but your phone has just been going to voicemail. I thought that you didn't want to talk to me."

"Oh God, that's not the case at all." I pull my phone out of my pocket and show her that it has no battery. "I left the phone here, Lyd. It's been in the spare bedroom the whole time. That's why I never got your calls."

"Oh." There are a few beats of silence before Lydia speaks again. "So, do you forgive me?" she asks tentatively.

"There is nothing to forgive you for. I'm just glad that Donnie hasn't come between us."

With that, we both stand up and give each other a hug. Tears start to fall down my cheeks as I feel a piece of my life slot back into place. Thank goodness for that. I really thought that we weren't going to be able to patch things up.

Lydia pulls away first and wipes tears from her own face. "Now, enough of this crying lark. We have wasted too much time talking about that asshole Donnie already. What we should be talking about is that hunk of a man that you have been staying with."

I am so glad that Lydia doesn't want to talk about Donnie anymore. He is the last person I want to be thinking about. However, the subject of Jake isn't exactly a happy one at the moment either.

"Oh, Lyd, it's all such a mess." New tears emerge, only this time they are laced with sadness rather than joy.

"Oh, fuck. Start from the beginning," Lydia says. "We have all night if needs be. I'm not at work tomorrow and, of course, you can stay here. That's if you want to?" She seems unsure about whether I will or not.

"That would be great. Thank you."

She smiles at me and I get myself comfortable on the sofa as I proceed to explain to Lydia about all the events that have happened over the last few days. Lydia listens patiently as I pour my heart out to her. I can't shake off the sense of feeling naïve and stupid. I shouldn't have let my guard down with Jake. I knew that he was too good to be true.

When Caitlin showed up, I should have just got the hell out of there. I can see that Lydia wants to give her honest opinion, but when I look at the clock it says that it is three in the morning. Where did the time go?

I feel exhausted, so we both decide to pick up this conversation again when we have got some much-needed rest. I give Lydia a hug goodnight before plodding to the spare bedroom. I daren't call it my bedroom again yet, just in case something else happens to kick me in the teeth. I keep my jogging bottoms and jumper on, and I climb into bed. As soon as my head hits the pillow, sleep consumes me.

CHAPTER EIGHTEEN

I wake up to the sound of Lydia crashing into the spare bedroom. I jolt upright in bed and look over to see that she has fallen over and landed on her ass. I break out into a fit of laughter at the sight of her. I have missed her antics over the last few days.

"Shit, Stace. He's here! He's here!" she says breathlessly.

"Who's here?" I ask, the laughter dying on my lips as I start to panic that Donnie has shown up. The fear in my voice is evident, and my heart starts to beat a little faster.

"Jake."

"WHAT?" I shout.

"Shhh, he will hear you."

"Lyd, I'm pretty sure that the entire apartment block heard you fall over just now." I smile at her.

I also experience a flutter in my stomach at the thought of Jake being near.

"He's standing outside the front door. Do you want to see him?" she enquires.

I ponder her question for a few moments. One half of me would love to see him, but the other half of me is still hurt by his rejection. I need to remain sensible in my choice.

"No. I don't want to see him. If he asks, just tell him that you haven't seen me." I need to stay strong, for my own sake more than anything.

"No worries, babes. Lydia to the rescue." She jumps to her feet and bounds out of the bedroom, shutting the door behind her on the way out.

I feel nerves start to kick in and those damn butterflies are dancing around frantically inside me. I feel my body hum as I know that he is near. I daren't move from the bed for fear of making any noise. He can't know that I am here.

I stay sat in my upright position as I listen to their muffled voices. I am dying to go and use the toilet, but I desperately hold it in. After ten minutes, I hear the front door shut and Lydia comes back into the spare bedroom, taking a seat at the end of the bed. I look at her, waiting for her to speak.

After a few seconds she still hasn't spoken, and I can be patient no longer.

"Well?" I ask her.

"He came to apologise for his behaviour. I don't think he believed me when I said that I hadn't seen you. He asked if he could take you to dinner, to explain things to you."

"Like hell am I going to dinner with him." I can't believe the nerve of the guy.

Does he think that by taking me for some fancy dinner that it will soften the blow of his rejection? Not bloody likely!

"He did look really sorry, Stace. He doesn't look like he has slept either. Even so, he still looks dangerously fuckable." Lydia has a dreamy look on her face and I can't help but laugh at her. "Maybe you should talk to him and tell him how you really feel?"

"No. I don't want to." I sigh. I will have to face him at some point considering that he has the majority of my possessions at his house. I'm just not ready to face him today.

"There is no way that I am telling that man anything. I need to forget about Jake Waters. Actually, I need to just forget about men full stop for a while. Plus, I want to spend the day chilling with my bestie. What do you say? Wine and chick flicks?"

"Sounds like a plan to me. What a gripping life we do lead," Lydia says whilst she gives me a cynical look. I know that I am not fooling her with saying that I need to forget about Jake, but I am trying my hardest to.

"Hey, I will take boring and predictable over the last few days any time."

"I think on this occasion I have to agree with you. I will nip out and get some wine, and I'll pick up some nibbles too." Lydia stands and goes to walk out of the room, but she pauses at the door and turns back to face me. "Just promise me that you will think about speaking to Jake. I know you don't want to do it right now, but you might change your mind in a few days. He seems genuine." She then bounces out of the room before I can reply. I choose to ignore what she just said. I need to focus on myself for a bit.

I get out of bed and go to the bathroom to relieve myself now that Jake has gone. Lydia calls out that she is leaving and that she will be back as quick as possible. I finish up in the bathroom and go to the kitchen to put the kettle on. Whilst waiting for the kettle I go back to the spare bedroom to find my phone charger, only to find Jake sat on the end of the bed.

I give a high-pitched shriek at the shock of him being in here. My heart is racing, and it takes all my energy to try and remain calm.

"What the hell are you doing here?" My shock is quickly overtaken by anger.

He looks at me with dark bags under his eyes. Lydia was right, he doesn't look like he has slept. I have to agree with her on the still looking dangerously fuckable part too.

I push any sexual thoughts out of my mind so as not to cloud my judgement.

"How dare you barge in here. Who do you think you are?" I rage.

Jake may not be the kind of guy to take orders from people, but actually entering a property without permission is pushing the boundaries ever-so-slightly.

"Stacey, I came to say that I am sorry for how I handled things last night. It was wrong of me to push you away like that. I can't imagine how you must have felt."

"You can't? Well, let me give you a hint, shall I? Hurt, confused, rejected, do I need to go on?" I am so angry. How dare he invade my space and privacy like this.

"No, I get it. I didn't want to hurt you. I wanted to explain stuff to you over dinner, but a part of me knew that you wouldn't agree to that. I knew that Lydia was covering for you by saying that she hadn't seen you. I had to find a way of speaking to you, Stace." He sounds desperate, but in my irate state I couldn't care less.

"So you just come in here uninvited? Do you respect anyone's privacy, Jake?"

"Of course I do, but like I said, I needed to speak to you."

"I don't want to hear what you have to say." I'm being stubborn. Of course I want to hear what he has to say, but I don't want to make it easy for him.

"In that case, I think that it's best that you don't stay with me anymore." His tone turns cold and flat. I wasn't expecting that to be his next line at all. Anger flares up within me again.

"Oh, you don't? And I suppose you thought that by taking me to dinner that you would have done your best to break this news to me gently?" Sarcasm drips from my voice. "Well, let me make this easy for you. I wouldn't come back to yours if you paid me. I will collect my stuff as soon as possible." I can hear myself speaking and I don't like what I hear. This isn't me. This is just pent up anger over this whole situation.

"It's okay, I'll have all your stuff sent over here for you. There's no need for you to come to the house." He doesn't look at me as he speaks.

If I thought that I couldn't hurt anymore, I was wrong. It is like a stabbing to my heart. What did I do to make him behave this way towards me? Maybe his psycho ex *was* right about how things went down with them the other night? Maybe he is the one who is lying?

"Fine. Now, please will you leave. I have nothing more to say to you." I look away from him and stare out of the window.

I can't bear to watch him walk out of here knowing that I won't see or speak to him again.

I hear him stand and walk to the bedroom door.

"Goodbye, Stacey," are his final words to me. I don't answer him. I couldn't answer him even if I wanted to. My throat feels like it has closed up. My life just keeps going wrong. I don't understand what I did to deserve this.

I feel my heart breaking, but I don't understand why it hurts so much.

CHAPTER NINETEEN

Lydia comes back to find me curled up on the sofa with my duvet wrapped around me, and used tissues strewn about the place.

"Christ, Stace, what happened to you? I wasn't gone that long, was I?"

"I saw Jake," I say sadly as more tears threaten to emerge.

"I'll go open the wine," Lydia says, and she goes into the kitchen without saying another word.

All I seem to have done this week is cry. I'm surprised that I have any tears left.

Lydia returns with two large glasses of rose wine and makes me sit up so that she can sit next to me. Lydia gets snuggled under my duvet with her drink and I inform her of what happened when I found Jake in the bedroom. There isn't much to tell though, so it doesn't take long for me to relay it all to her.

"Shit. I thought he had left when I told him that you weren't here. I thought I was convincing. There was no sign of him when I went out. The sneaky sod must have been waiting along the corridor," she says, almost as if she is just clarifying her own thoughts out loud.

"Why do I feel like this, Lyd? I've never had feelings like this before, not even with Charles in our earlier days." I am desperate for answers, but nothing is coming to me. Whatever the reason is for me feeling like this, I sure as hell don't like it, and I don't know how to deal with it.

"Far be it for me to point out the obvious, Stace, but I think you have developed feelings for this guy that are a lot stronger than you may have realised."

"Don't be ridiculous. I've only known him for a few days."

"So? Who's to say how long it takes to fall for someone. It can happen in an instant," Lydia says, ever the romantic even after her failed relationships. I think about her words, but I can't admit to myself just how much I like him.

I drain my wine glass and get up off of the sofa to go and pour myself another one. The doorbell rings whilst I'm mid-pour. I put the wine bottle down with a sigh and I go to answer the door. Surely nothing else can go wrong today?

I open the door to find two men standing there. I have never seen these guys before in my life.

"Stacey Paris?" the tall, bald one asks me. He looks rather menacing and I feel the hairs on the back of my neck prickle.

"Uh, yeah, that's me." My eyes turn to look at the shorter man. He is far stockier than the tall one but looks just as hard-faced.

Who the hell are these guys? And how do they know my name?

"We have your belongings from Mr Waters. We will start to bring the stuff up." Neither of them says anything else and they both turn around and head back down the stairs to, I presume, get all of my belongings. These guys certainly get to the point quickly. And Jake certainly isn't wasting any time in making sure that I am out of his life.

Lydia appears in the lounge doorway, breaking me from my thoughts.

"Who is it now? It's like Piccadilly Circus in here today," Lydia exclaims.

"It's my stuff from Jake's. Some guys are dropping it off."

"Seriously?" She looks just as flabbergasted as I feel. "Ugh, what an asshole. He didn't hang around, did he?" Lydia's words near enough echo my thoughts from a moment ago.

"Better to get it done and out of the way I suppose," I say to her with a shrug of my shoulders. If Jake doesn't want me in his life, then that's his loss.

The two guys return, carrying a large box each. I direct them to the spare bedroom and tell them to pile as much in there as they possibly can. Of course the bedroom won't be big enough for everything, so Lydia says that the rest can go in her bedroom for now.

It doesn't take long for the meaty looking men to bring my stuff up, and when they have finished, I thank them and close the door as they leave.

"More wine, Lydia. I've got a lot of sorting out to do."

"I'm on it, babes," Lydia says before she disappears into the kitchen.

I survey the boxes before me; my whole life packed in them. What a truly pathetic sight it is.

I start going through the boxes in my room first, so that I can make room for the ones that are residing in Lydia's bedroom. Most of the boxes are full of clothes and I start making three separate piles; one for charity, one for rubbish, and one for the stuff that I am going to keep.

I am halfway through the first box when Lydia returns with the wine. I gratefully take my glass off of her and take a long sip.

She watches me for a few moments before she speaks. "Hey, why don't you come to The Den with me tomorrow? We could sort out some shifts for you?"

To say that I am surprised at her suggestion is an understatement, and I almost spit my mouthful of wine at her.

"I don't know, Lyd. The Den doesn't exactly hold the greatest of memories for me at this moment in time." I shudder as a picture of Donnie forms in my mind. I shake my head to try and rid myself of the image.

"I know that, but it would be nice to have you working with me again. The offer is still there." Lydia smiles affectionately. "Plus, you shouldn't let that low-life bastard Donnie stop you from going somewhere that you love to go. The security team know never to let him in again too, so he would have to be a miracle worker to get in."

At least Lydia understands why I am reluctant to return there. I know that she is trying to help, but I need to be confident enough to return to The Den, and right now, I don't feel confident at all. I need to shut down Lydia's attempts at trying to get me to go there, without dismissing the idea completely.

"I will seriously think about it... I just need a bit more time. Thanks though, Lyd, I do appreciate the offer." It's all I can say to keep her suggestions to a minimum. Once Lydia forms an idea in her head, there is no stopping her until she has achieved the result that she wants.

"It's the least I can do," she says before she starts to help me unpack the boxes and sort each item into their relevant pile. There is no more talk of The Den, which I am relieved about, and it takes us a couple of hours to clear all of the boxes. We have even managed to sort the ones in Lydia's room too.

During the unpacking process we have managed to polish off the remainder of the bottle of wine, and we are just starting on the second bottle. I stand in the bedroom doorway and look at all of our hard work. *My* bedroom may look a little cluttered, but at least I have all of my stuff here. I'm feeling brave enough to consider it my bedroom again now. I don't think Lydia will be kicking me out. I was stupid to think that she would do that in the first place. Shock can do crazy things to your mind.

I decide that I will get rid of all the rubbish tomorrow and then I will take the other stuff to the charity shop. All the unwanted items are currently lining the hall way, so I need to get rid of it all as soon as possible. At least that will give me something to do tomorrow.

I decide to have an early night as I am physically and mentally exhausted, and I'm sure that the wine has helped me to feel even more tired. I say goodnight to Lydia and drag my weary body to my bedroom.

As I get into bed, I realise that I still haven't switched my phone on, so I get back out of bed with a groan to locate my phone charger. After a few minutes, I find the charger underneath my bed; it must have got shoved there during the sorting out process. I plug the charger into the plug socket by the bedside table and then attach my phone.

After a few minutes there is enough charge in the phone for me to be able to turn it on, and I settle back into bed and wait to see what messages are going to come through. I have a few missed calls from Lydia, which I can see are the ones I missed whilst I was staying at Jake's. I also have a text from Susie, a text from Martin, ten missed calls from Charles, and a couple of messages from him too.

I open Susie's message first. She is just texting to see how I am. I tap out a quick reply to her and then proceed to open Martin's message. He wants to catch up over coffee, which I am more than happy to do. I have missed his infectious personality.

I then open the first of Charles' messages. The first one, and the following three, all consist of him grovelling to save himself from embarrassment. I roll my eyes at each one.

However, the final message from him really makes me take notice and pisses me off immensely.

> *Stacey. I now understand that you probably don't want to speak to me. I have taken the liberty of having your car impounded as it was a nuisance. I apologise, but I needed the space.*
> *Regards, Charles.*

Oh great. That's just what I needed. An impounded car. Fucking fantastic!

The message was sent two days ago, so there will already be costs racking up from the impound lot. He really is such a selfish asshole. He has done this out of spite because I won't go back to him. How I ever stayed with him for so long, I really don't know. Although, if I had just have stayed with Charles, then none of the events of the last few days would have occurred.

Maybe this is all karma for me cheating on Charles all those months ago?

I resist the urge to text back a shitty reply. I don't need to stoop to his level, and I definitely don't need to give him the satisfaction of knowing that he has pissed me off. I need to be the bigger person here.

I put my phone on the bedside table and lie down.

I just stare at the ceiling and try to keep calm, and I decide that, as of tomorrow, I need to take charge of my life and sort myself out once and for all.

CHAPTER TWENTY

I am up and dressed before Lydia even emerges from her bedroom. I have had enough of being made to feel like shit. Today is a new day, and I am going to take charge. Luckily, I have no hangover, which is surprising with the amount of wine I drank last night.

I make myself a cup of coffee and take it through to the lounge. I sit on the sofa and put the morning news on, although it is more for background noise than for me to watch. In my mind I have my whole day planned out. Firstly, I will go and get my car from the impound lot. Secondly, I will use my car to take all of the rubbish to the tip. And thirdly, I will take the rest to the charity shop.

The fourth and final thing on my list to do is the most nerve wracking as it involves going to The Den. Lydia is right, I shouldn't let what happened with Donnie stop me from going there. So, on that basis, I will meet Lydia back here to go with her when I have finished everything else on my to-do list.

I need to get back to being strong and independent, and I can't do that if I am living in fear.

Lydia walks into the lounge as I am finishing my coffee and flops down next to me on the sofa.

"What are you doing up so early?" she asks me whilst still yawning. "Are you feeling okay after yesterday?" She looks a little concerned at my complete turnaround.

"I'm fine, Lyd. I need to stop wallowing and make stuff happen." I stand up and take my cup into the kitchen, then go to my bedroom to grab my handbag before returning to the lounge.

"What time are you going to The Den?" I ask Lydia.

"About eleven-ish. Why?"

"I will be back before you leave. Bye, Lyd." I don't give her chance to ask any more questions as I turn and head for the front door, so that I can start walking to the impound lot. It takes me a while to get there, but I enjoy the peace. It's a relief not to have to discuss Jake with Lydia.

When I arrive at the impound lot, I go to a little port-a-cabin that is situated in front of two big steel gates. An old man is sat in there, and he looks bored shitless. He sees me approaching and makes himself look busy.

"Hi," I say. "My car was brought here the other day and I would like to pick it up please."

The old man asks me some details about which car, and I tell him all of the necessary information. He taps the information into a computer and then goes to a cupboard on the back wall, selecting the relevant keys for my car.

"That will be four hundred and fifty pounds to pay." The old guy doesn't bat an eyelid at the amount of money that he has asked me for.

"What?" I bellow at him.

"Four hundred and fifty pounds. That's the price to get your car back."

"But, how is it so much money?" I am astounded that it could cost this much.

"Two hundred and fifty pounds' collection fee and then one hundred pounds per day for keeping it here." He remains unfazed. He must have to deal with people asking him this question all of the time.

"That's outrageous." The words are out of my mouth before I can stop them. Charles is such a prick. If he thinks that making me pay hundreds of pounds to get my car back is going to make me go back to him, then he is sadly mistaken. I bet in his small mind he thinks that I am going to ask him to bail me out. No fucking chance.

With determination to outwit Charles, I hand over my card and begrudgingly make the payment. The old guy then takes me through a small gate, to the side of the big metal ones, to where my car is. I sarcastically thank him, and he heads back to his little cabin to open the gates, so that I can drive out.

I drive my car back to Lydia's, still seething about how much it cost. I arrive back at the flat, park the car, and literally stomp all the way up to the front door. I then have to wait for Lydia to let me in.

"Jeez, you don't look quite as happy as you did when you left," Lydia comments as she opens the door.

"I have just had to pay four hundred and fifty quid to get my car back," I tell her as I march into the flat. She stares at me with a blank expression on her face, probably wondering why the hell I have had to pay money for my car. I quickly fill her in. "Fucking Charles had it impounded at the lot. He is such a selfish prick." I am surprised that there isn't steam coming out of my ears, that's how ticked off I am.

"Oh my God. What a dick." Lydia shuts the door and I am pleased to hear that she agrees with me. Although, I don't think she would ever agree with Charles, but that's beside the point.

"Yeah, well, it's done now. I can't change it."

Charles has occupied more than enough of my thoughts in the last half an hour.

To keep myself busy and on schedule, I start to pick up some of the stuff that is sitting in the hallway. Time to go and do the tip run.

"Where are you going now?" Lydia asks.

"Tip run, and then I'm taking the rest to the charity shop."

"You're on a mission this morning, aren't you?"

"Yeah. Best to keep busy," I say as I exit the flat with the bags that I have picked up.

It only takes a couple more trips and all of the rubbish is in my car. There is still plenty of room left, so I load up the charity stuff as well. At least I can do it all in one trip now rather than coming back here for the charity stuff.

I shout to Lydia that I am leaving, and she comes running from her bedroom.

"Here you go," she says as she hands me a key. "Keep this. It's your home too now, and you'll want to be able to get in if I'm not here." Lydia smiles and I take the key from her and I feel my mood lighten significantly.

"Thanks, Lyd." My eyes start to fill at the realisation that I have somewhere that I feel I can call my 'home.' I hastily blink back tears and give Lydia a quick hug. "I know I said I would be back before you left for The Den, but I will meet you there, if that's okay?"

"Sure thing, babes. Have fun."

Have fun? She must be taking the piss. There is nothing fun about a tip run.

I return to the car and drive to the tip, humming along to the radio as I go. After emptying the car of the rubbish, I take the rest of the stuff to the charity shop.

By the time I am done it is only half past ten. Lydia won't be at work yet, so I decide to take a quick trip to Danish to appease my caffeine needs. I park the car just outside the coffee shop, and when I walk in, I see that Bonnie is working. I take my usual seat and she brings over some coffee.

"Hey, girl, where have you been hiding? Haven't seen you for a few days," Bonnie says.

"Well, to cut a long story short, Charles and I broke up, so I've just been busy sorting some stuff out." I don't want her to know just how eventful my life has been in the past week, so I keep it simple.

"Oh, I'm sorry to hear that. This coffee is on the house." She smiles and goes to serve another customer.

I sit quietly, drinking my coffee. It's nice to be out and about and doing something normal.

I look out of the window and watch all the workers and shoppers rushing around. I like people watching from time to time.

I notice an elderly couple sat on one of the benches across the road from the coffee shop. They look so cute together. They are holding hands and they seem to be sat in comfortable silence. The man gives the woman a kiss on her cheek, and she smiles at him. I can see how much they love each other. It radiates from every fibre of their being. I want to have that with someone one day. Grow old and grey with them, and still be completely in love with them. Being content, happy and secure is something I yearn for.

I finish my coffee and am about to stand up when I notice Jake coming out of the estate agents, just behind the elderly couple. He's with a woman. I sit back in my seat and take in every detail that I can.

The woman has jet-black hair that is short and spiky, her lips are full and accentuated by her deep-red lipstick, and her eyes sparkle as she seems to hang on Jake's every word. He is laughing at something she is saying. My heart feels like it's being stabbed, repeatedly.

I should look away, but I can't.

I savour every bit of him. His silky hair, his athletic build, how good he looks in his suit, his tanned skin and his gorgeous caramel eyes. I miss those eyes. They brought me so much warmth when I was scared.

I watch them both until Jake's limo pulls up and Eric gets out of the driver's seat to open the door for them. The woman slides in first and then Jake follows.

I wait until they have driven off before I emerge from the coffee shop. I feel like running back to Lydia's and spending the rest of the day curled up under my duvet, but I won't do that. I need to stick to my plan and go to The Den.

To hell with Jake bloody Waters. If he can be happy and forget, then so can I.

CHAPTER TWENTY-ONE

I park my car at the back of The Den, in the private parking space. As I am walking around to the front of the building, I see Lydia talking to some guy by the front doors. When I get closer, I see that the guy in question is Paul, Jake's friend.

Oh God, really? It could have been any other guy in the world, but no, it has to be someone who is connected to Jake.

I can see that Lydia is flirting as she is playing with her hair and looking generally dopey-eyed.

"Hey, Lyd," I say as I walk up behind Paul. Paul turns around and grins at me. "Nice to see you again, Paul," I say as I shake his outstretched hand. There is no point in being rude to him, he has done nothing wrong.

"Hey," he says casually.

"Hey, babes. Paul has just come to see if I want to go out with him tonight." Lydia is beaming. "He's taking me to the big fancy restaurant on the other side of town." She can hardly contain her excitement and I don't want to appear grouchy, so I join in with her enthusiasm.

"You mean Claringtons?" I ask her.

"Yeah." Lydia seems so excited, and I can't say that I blame her. Claringtons is one of the most upscale restaurants in the area.

"That's great. I hear the food is amazing." I plaster a big grin on my face. I want my friend to see that I am pleased for her.

I excuse myself whilst they finish their 'moment' and I wait inside the front doors of The Den. I don't want to venture any further without Lydia by me. The memories will be too much. She comes through the door seconds later, with the dopey look still on her face.

Lydia lets me know that John, one of the security guys, is in the main room. She locks the front door behind her and motions for me to go on in. I greet John as we enter the main room. He gives us a nod and carries on with some paperwork he has set up at the bar. John is big and burly and does not look like someone that I would want to piss off.

Lydia goes ahead of me and I follow her into her office. Her office is like a hive of bright colours. There is no coordination, it's just bright. The yellow walls make me want to put sunglasses on as they are verging on a neon shade. Lydia sits at her desk and I take the seat opposite her on the other side.

"Oh my God, Stace, Paul is so hot. I can't believe that he just showed up like that to ask me out."

"I'm pleased for you, Lyd. You deserve to be spoilt." I mean it, I really do, but I can't help feeling a little disappointed that my love life has spiralled out of control.

Her smile disappears as she asks me her next question. "Oh, Stace, are you okay with all of this?"

"All of what?" I try to appear like I don't know what she is talking about.

"About Paul taking me out."

"Why wouldn't I be?" I ask innocently, although I know what she is getting at. I am going to have to pull out some amazing acting skills to convince her that I am okay with the thought of possibly seeing Jake if things work out between her and Paul.

"Come on, Stace. Paul is Jake's friend and I don't want to go out with him if it makes you feel awkward."

"Don't be silly," I reply. I am not letting my feelings for Jake stop Lydia from meeting someone who could be perfect for her. "You go and enjoy yourself. I'm looking forward to hearing all of the details when you get back." I am astounded that I can make myself sound so happy. Inside I am breaking, but I will not spoil my friend's chance of happiness. If things work out for them, I will just have to overcome my feelings for Jake. I force myself not to roll my eyes at my ridiculous thought. Put my feelings to one side? How the bloody hell am I meant to do that? I only have to look at the guy and my knees go weak.

"Great. Now that we have got that out of the way, when are you coming back to work?" I'm glad that my acting skills over the Paul issue have paid off, but my eyes widen at her suggestion of work. I thought that she was going to let me think about it. "Don't look at me like that. I will make sure that you are safe working here, Stace. You were brilliant when you worked here before, and you can be again. What do you say?"

I am not overly keen on the idea and Lydia seems to pick up on this from my silence. "What if I make sure that we have the same shifts together for the next few weeks, to ease you back in? And, if you start to feel unsafe or threatened, then you can leave at any time."

"I don't know, Lyd. I told you that I need time to think about it."

"Oh come on, babes, you said that last night." She pouts at me to try and soften me up. "I also need someone to work with me on Saturday night, and I'm really hoping that it will be you. You are much more fun than the bloody agency staff I have to use."

"No pressure then," I reply sarcastically. I need to change the subject. "I'm going to go and grab a drink. Do you want one?"

"Yes please, babes," Lydia answers as she fires up her computer. "Just a diet coke though. I need to keep a clear head." I nod and leave her office to go back to the main room.

I look around the place that I used to love so much. There is no sign of John in the main room, but his paperwork is still on the bar counter.

I busy myself pouring mine and Lydia's drinks and I place them on the bar. Before I realise what I am doing, I find myself walking towards the ladies' toilets. My feet come to a stop as I stand and look down the corridor where Donnie attacked me, and flashbacks start to appear.

His hands on my body.

His breath on my face.

His words come back to taunt me.

"You always have been a fucking tease, Stacey... She wants this just as much as I do."

I close my eyes and try to push the memories away. Anger surges through me, and my body starts to tremble as I fight the urge to run.

I open my eyes and slowly walk down the corridor, stopping at the exact spot where he had me pinned against the wall. My breathing quickens, and I tell myself that he isn't here. No one is here to get me.

I collect my thoughts as I realise that the anger I am feeling has replaced any fear that I had. That bastard shouldn't be allowed to taint my memories of this place. Adrenaline pulses through me as I march back to the bar, pick up mine and Lydia's drinks, and head back to her office.

"Count me in," I say, startling Lydia.

"Pardon?" She looks at me confused.

"Count me in for Saturday night. I'll be damned if I'm going to let that wanker stop me from doing a job that I enjoy."

Lydia starts bouncing up and down on her seat and claps her hands together before standing up and coming over to hug me. I hold the drinks out either side of me, so I don't spill any.

"That's fab, babes. It will be just like old times."

I feel a new emotion flow through my body. I am ready to battle my demons. Donnie is the first one that I need to get rid of, and I think that by revisiting the scene in which he assaulted me, I am halfway there.

Once I have battled that demon, I need to concentrate on battling my feelings for Jake.

CHAPTER TWENTY-TWO

Lydia and I arrive back at the flat at six o'clock. Paul is picking her up for their date at eight, so I know that the next two hours will consist of watching Lydia trying on her entire wardrobe whilst I tell her that she looks great in every outfit. She really does have some fabulous clothes. I am so glad that we are the same size, meaning that I can always borrow them to wear.

Whilst Lydia has a shower, I go to my bedroom and put my pyjamas on. I intend to be a complete slob this evening. I laze around on the sofa watching re-runs of Friends as I wait for Lydia's fashion show to begin. The second episode of Friends comes on when Lydia sweeps into the room, carrying several outfits. Let the fashion show commence.

It takes her an hour to choose the outfit that she is happy with and she looks gorgeous in a dark blue halter-neck jumpsuit.

"You look amazing," I say to her. Her auburn hair has been styled in delicate waves, her make-up is perfect, and her shoes are to die for. Silver heels that sparkle, and they are Lydia's most prized fashion possession. These shoes only ever come out for special occasions, so I know that she is seriously trying to impress Paul. She finishes the outfit off with a silver clutch bag.

"Are you sure that it isn't too much?" she asks me.

"Honey, you are going to Claringtons, nothing is too much. Plus, you are going to be the most gorgeous person in the whole restaurant."

"I'm a little nervous, you know," she replies. This is very unlike Lydia. She is normally extremely confident when it comes to men. "I really like Paul. He makes me feel different."

"That's probably because he treats you with respect, Lyd. I can tell that he really likes you too. It's obvious from the way he looks at you." The doorbell rings and I think Lydia is going to have a panic attack from the look on her face. "Go to the bathroom and calm down. I'll go and let him in."

Lydia runs off to the bathroom and I go and answer the door. Paul stands there looking very handsome in a black shirt, black tie and charcoal grey suit.

"Hey, Paul, come on in. Lydia will be ready in a minute."

"Thanks." He looks on edge. Maybe he is nervous too?

"Would you like a drink whilst you wait?" I ask him.

"No, I'm good thanks." We stand awkwardly in the hallway, waiting for Lydia to appear. I try to think of something to say but words evade me. I have never been one for idle chit-chat.

Lydia emerges from the bathroom a few moments later, and the look on Paul's face is priceless.

"Wow. You look beautiful," he says as he walks up to her and places a kiss on her cheek. Lydia's cheeks blush as she thanks him.

"Okay, let's get going," she says to Paul. Paul takes Lydia's hand and leads her out of the flat. On her way out, Lydia turns and blows me a kiss.

"Have fun, guys," I shout after them. I close the front door and head to the kitchen for a take away menu and decide to order in pizza. I phone my order through to my favourite pizza place and order my usual; a barbecue chicken pizza. After I've done that, I settle back on the sofa to see what films are showing and see that Magic Mike is on, so I decide to ogle Channing Tatum for the next hour or so.

Twenty minutes later there is a knock at the door. Thank God for that, I'm bloody starving. My stomach grumbles as I grab my purse from my bedroom before going to the front door. I am busy fumbling with my purse to pay the delivery guy as the door opens, but when I look up, I see that Jake is standing there and he is holding my pizza.

I feel like the wind has been knocked out of me. I can feel my heart rate accelerating.

We just stand and stare at each other. I try to calm my breathing and appear unaffected by him standing there, but I am a complete wreck at the unexpected sight of him.

"Um, Jake, why are you delivering my pizza?" I ask.

"I'm not really delivering it as such. I just... I just..." He can't seem to find the words that he needs to say. It is now that I notice that some of Jake's confidence seems to have left him. He looks uncomfortable and is fidgeting slightly from foot to foot.

"You better come in," I say as I back away from the door to let him pass. Jake strides through the door and I close it behind him. I smell his aftershave as he walks past, and it does things to my insides. I realise at this point that I look like shit. My hair is chucked up into a ponytail and I am wearing my oversized pyjamas.

Crap, this is why you should always be prepared, I tell myself.

Although, I never thought that I would need to be prepared for Jake to show up on my doorstep, so I can forgive myself for this faux pas.

"Um, would you like a drink?" I ask him. I figure I need to say something in order to break the ice between us, and a drink is the only thing that comes to mind right now.

"That would be great, thanks. Just a cold drink will be fine." I see his shoulders relax a little at my offer of a drink.

"Go on through to the lounge and I will be there in a sec." I go to the kitchen, place my purse on the side, grab two glasses and a bottle of diet coke. My hands are shaking slightly from the shock of seeing him.

What could he possibly want?

I go to the lounge and set the glasses down on the coffee table. I manage to pour the drinks without spilling them everywhere, and then I take a seat on the sofa. I put my hands between my knees so that Jake can't see that I am shaking. Jake has chosen to sit in the armchair that is situated opposite the sofa. That's good. Distance is good. Jake's eyes bore into mine, but he makes no move to start a conversation. It looks like I am going to have to be the one to get the ball rolling.

"What are you doing here, Jake?"

"I just wanted to see how you were doing." He looks at me with sadness in his eyes.

"Oh." A wave of disappointment goes through me. What was I hoping he would say? Was I hoping that he would grab me and make love to me as if nothing had happened?

Stop it, Stacey, this is no time to be having those kinds of thoughts.

I clear my throat and answer him. "I'm good thanks. Why wouldn't I be?"

"It's just... With the way that I treated you yesterday, I thought—"

"You thought what?" I cut him off. "That I would be a wreck? That I would be crying all over the place?" My defences rise at his presumption that I would be a mess without him in my life.

"No, I wasn't thinking that at all." Jake looks panicked. "I just don't feel that I was very fair to you. I never should have acted the way that I did. I shouldn't have treated you like that after the way things were left at my place."

My mind quickly wanders back to both of us in the bathroom. His kisses, his eyes, his body. I feel my sex clench at the mere thought of it. I need to know why he rejected me after he initiated the kiss between us, and I decide to voice the issue that has been bugging me since that night.

"Why did you push me away, Jake?" I need to be strong. I need to hear his explanation. Jake runs his hands through his hair and looks at the floor.

"Things are not easy for me, Stacey. I have never had a connection with a woman like I have with you," he starts, and I notice that I am holding my breath. I slowly exhale as I listen to his words. "I know that it sounds crazy, but it's how I feel. I pushed you away because I am scared of hurting you, and I really wanted to keep you as a friend. If things were to go further with us, then I'm afraid that you would end up hating me."

Jake takes a sip of his drink before he carries on. "Although, I made you hate me anyway." He looks deep into my eyes at this point, and I feel like he is looking inside my soul. My heart is pounding, and adrenaline is surging through me.

"I don't hate you, Jake." He looks shocked and his eyes go wide. "You have hurt me, but I don't hate you."

"Why not? I acted like a complete asshole."

"Yes you did," I agree with him. "I just think that we got carried away with our emotions that night. What with what happened with Donnie and Caitlin, I just think that we were looking for some kind of comfort. I don't think that it meant any more than that." I am lying my ass off, but I hope that I can convince him otherwise.

"Really? That's what you think?" He sounds dubious and I nod my head at him.

"I understand that you don't trust many people. It's obviously a difficult thing for you to put your trust in others. But at some point, Jake, you need to let go of that fear and stop pushing people away. I think our connection is strong because we are meant to be in each other's lives. We are meant to be friends. And friends mess up and then they forgive each other. That's just how it works." I smile at him and I see him physically relax in the chair.

"You mean, we can still be friends after what I did?" He looks at me like I am speaking a foreign language and he doesn't quite understand what I am saying.

"Of course we can. You kind of did me a favour actually, because it made Lydia and I sort everything out."

"Glad to be of service." We both burst out laughing. I am not angry with him anymore. Now that he has explained himself, I understand why he did it. If only he had told me that to start with.

I may not have known him for very long, but it's almost like there was a small void in my life without him. I may have feelings for this guy, but I would rather have him as a friend than as nothing at all.

"Want some pizza?" I ask as I open the box. The tenseness of the last ten minutes has dissipated.

"I thought you would never ask."

CHAPTER TWENTY-THREE

I make Jake watch the whole of Magic Mike as punishment for being an ass. Needless to say, he isn't too pleased with the idea, but he's being a good sport about it. It's the least he can do. I think it's hysterical, especially when the actors start stripping off.

"How's your arm now?" I ask him as the film comes to an end.

"It's better. I had it looked at today and the bandage can hopefully come off in the next couple of days. The doctor seems to think that there will be minimal scarring."

"That's good news. Well, apart from the scarring part. Caitlin sure wanted to leave her mark on you, didn't she?"

"Yeah, well, it's my own fault for getting involved with her in a non-professional manner."

"No it's not. Just because you don't want to be with her doesn't give her the right to go all psycho on you. You mustn't blame yourself for her poor mental health." He can't possibly think that her behaviour can be excused? I look horrified at the thought, but he just hits me with his stunning smile. "Why are you smiling about it?"

"I'm not smiling about that. I'm smiling at you."

"Me?" I have no idea where he is going with this.

"Yeah, you. Even with me behaving like a bastard towards you, you're still willing to see the good in me. No one has ever been like that towards me before." My heart goes out to him. How can people not see the good in him?

"What can I say? I'm a sucker for nice eyes and a bit of charm." My tone is playful, and he laughs at my statement. This feels nice, and it feels right. "So, I start work again on Saturday night."

"Where are you working?" Jake asks me.

"At The Den with Lyd."

"Seriously? Is that a good idea with what happened there?" Jake looks concerned by this turn of events.

"It's fine. I went there today with Lydia whilst she was catching up on some paperwork. I found myself standing and looking down the corridor where Donnie assaulted me. I didn't feel any fear, I just felt so angry. I used to love working there before I moved in with Charles. I don't want to let what happened with Donnie take that away from me. I've got some great memories of that place, and I don't want one bad night to taint it." I don't want Jake to try and put me off of the idea of going back to work there. I have made up my mind and I'm going to stick to it.

"If you're sure, then I'm pleased for you. Just be careful though, Stace. There are still guys out there that won't care about your personal space."

"I'll be fine. Plus, security know not to let Donnie in ever again and I'm sure Lydia will have them keeping tabs on me to start with. I'm not going to let it break me, Jake. I also need a job and working with Lyd again will be awesome."

"Any trouble and I want you to tell me. I mean it." Jake looks and sounds deadly serious. His intense gaze is a little bit arousing. I feel a strange sense of comfort knowing that he is worried about me. It's crazy how we have got past our falling out like it never happened.

"Okay." I smile at him and he grins back at me like a Cheshire cat. A worried looking Cheshire cat that is. "So what—" I am cut off by the sound of the front door opening and I hear Lydia giggling.

"Sounds like they had a good time," I say to Jake. Lydia and Paul walk into the lounge with massive smiles on their faces. When Lydia clocks Jake, her mouth drops open.

"Oh, hey, guys," she says. She surveys the scene and studies us both in turn. "Am I sensing something going on here?" I need to shut down her over-active imagination, and quick.

"If you are sensing that Jake came by to apologise and then we ate pizza and watched a film, then you would be correct."

"Oh right. Sooooo, you two are all good now?" Lydia sounds a little wary and is looking at me for an answer.

"Yeah, we're fine, Lyd. Jake knows that he was a complete idiot for the way he acted."

"Hey!" Jake feigns a look of hurt and I roll my eyes at him.

"What? It's the truth," I say, smiling.

"Yeah, I have to agree with Stacey on this one, Jake," Lydia chimes in.

"Okay, I think that's enough for one night," Jake says as he stands up. "I think it's time for this idiot to leave." He's being playful, and I love it. I stand up as Jake walks to the lounge doorway. "Are you staying Paul?"

"Uh…" Paul looks dumbfounded at Jake's question.

"We're just gonna have a night-cap before Paul goes home," Lydia says, coming to Paul's rescue. I resist the urge to laugh and Jake smirks, giving me a wink.

"Well, enjoy your night-cap, guys. Do you want to see me out, Stace?"

"Sure." I get up off of the sofa and follow Jake to the front door. He opens it and then turns around and gives me a hug. I stiffen to start with, but I soon relax as his body presses against mine. What I wouldn't give to be in the same situation as Lydia and Paul right now.

"Thank you for forgiving me," Jake whispers in my ear.

"You still need to make it up to me, Waters. Magic Mike and a pizza just doesn't cut it," I whisper back jokingly. Jake stands back and releases me.

"Hmm, I will have to think about that one. Goodnight, Stace."

"Night, Jake."

I close the front door behind Jake as he leaves, and I lean against it. I collect my thoughts for a few moments before I go to tell Lydia that I am going to bed. I reach the lounge doorway and see Paul and Lydia kissing on the sofa, so I decide to just go to my bedroom without disturbing them. I get into bed with a smile on my face.

Today has been a productive day. I have my car back, I have a job, and I have Jake back in my life.

For the first time in nearly a week, I go to sleep feeling content.

CHAPTER TWENTY-FOUR

I wake up feeling as fresh as a daisy. I had a great night's sleep. Today is Saturday and I have my first shift back at The Den tonight. I am up, showered and dressed when Lydia comes walking into the kitchen.

"Good morning," I chirp at her. The smile she has on her face makes it look like she slept with a hanger in her mouth.

"Morning, babes."

"I take it last night ended well then?" As if I even need her to answer that.

"Shhh, keep your voice down. Paul's still in my bedroom."

"You minx," I tease her. "Is Paul staying for breakfast?"

"I don't know. He's still asleep."

"Well, just in case, how about I go out and pick us up some fresh pastries?"

"That sounds divine. Make mine a cream cheese bagel please." Lydia is practically drooling at the mouth.

I finish my cup of coffee and go to put my shoes on. Today I have opted to wear my skinny jeans, black vest top, black blazer and black kitten heels. Wearing a blazer makes me feel confident and kinda sexy. I've left my hair loose and wavy. I grab my sunglasses, purse and phone and I head out of the front door.

I arrive at Danish a few minutes later, and order some croissants and bagels, as well as some full-fat lattes. Bonnie isn't working today, so I take a seat and people watch whilst I am waiting for the food and drinks. It is a gorgeous morning. The sun is shining, and it seems to make my mood even brighter.

I am called to collect the food when it's ready, leave the coffee shop and go back towards the flat. I hear my phone beep to notify me that I have a text message. I stop walking and balance all of the food and drinks in one hand, so that I can retrieve my phone from my back pocket. I see that I have a message from a number that I don't recognise. I unlock the phone and read what it says.

Good morning, Miss Paris. You are looking well this morning x x x

I glance around me, but I don't see anyone.

Who the hell is this from?

They obviously know who I am, and whoever it is, they have my phone number and they can clearly see me right now. Panic grips me. I furiously look around again, trying to see any signs of the person it could be, when suddenly, someone taps me on my shoulder from behind. I shriek, drop the drinks and food on the floor and spin around.

Standing there, looking a little shocked at my reaction, is Jake. All at once I feel fear, anger and stupidity.

"What the hell were you doing, Jake? You scared the shit out of me!" I shriek at him. He looks dumbfounded, his mouth opening and closing like a fish.

As I start to calm down a little and the anger fades away, I suddenly start to laugh hysterically. I laugh so much that my sides begin to ache from it. Jake just watches me, and he looks even more shocked than he did before. I bet to him, and anyone else that might be watching, I look like a lunatic. This thought, of course, makes me laugh even harder.

"Uh, Stace? Are you okay?" Jake sounds nervous, which I guess anyone would do when their friend seems to have lost the plot.

"Yeah. Yeah, I'm okay. Just, don't ever do that to me again," I say once I have calmed down enough to form a sentence. I take off my sunglasses and wipe tears from my eyes. I then playfully smack Jake on the chest.

"Hey! There's no need for that."

"Oh, I think there is, Mr Waters. I presume that this message is from you?" I thrust my phone in front of his face with the offending text message on the screen, so that he can read it.

"Guilty." He holds his hands up in admission. "I didn't expect you to react like that though."

"It was just the look on your face. Priceless." I look down to the spilled drinks and the food strewn over the pavement. "Well, you have just ruined breakfast for the happy couple."

"Lydia and Paul?" he asks me. I nod to clarify that I am indeed talking about Lydia and Paul. "Oh shit, I'm sorry. I'll go and buy some more to replace them."

"No, don't worry about it. They're probably far too busy in the bedroom again to be honest."

"Things went well last night for them then?"

"I would say so, yes." I feel happy for Lydia, she deserves to be with someone who is going to treat her right. There is however still a little part of me that wishes that I was being made to feel like that right now. I missed out on so much whilst I wasted my time staying with Charles.

"Well, if they are going to be busy for a while, why don't I take you for breakfast? I have a meeting to get to in about an hour, but we have time to grab something, if you want to?" Jake says. I pick up the food and drinks from the floor and dump them in the nearest bin.

"Well, when you put it like that, how can a girl refuse?" I let my playfulness take over. "Come on, Mr Waters, but you're buying." Jake holds his arm out for me to link my arm through. I oblige and instantly feel the warmth that radiates from his body. It makes me feel safe. "How did you get my phone number anyway? I don't recall ever giving it to you."

"I have my ways, Miss Paris." Jake winks at me.

Why do his words not faze me in the slightest? To be honest, I don't even really care how he got my number, I'm just glad that he has it.

We end up going into Danish. The waitress looks at me a little oddly as I was only in here about ten minutes ago. I order a black coffee and a pain au chocolate and Jake then places his order.

"So, what's your meeting about today?" I ask him. I want to get to know as much as I can about him, even if that does involve discussing his schedule for the day.

"It's actually not the best meeting to be going to in the world. I have to fire someone today."

"Oh no, why?" I never comprehended that Jake would be the one to have to fire staff.

"Well, this is off the record obviously, but this person has been leaking information to another company. And not just any company, but one I am trying to acquire." Jake seems a tad timid saying the last part. My brain twigs straight away.

"You mean Charles' company, don't you?"

"Um... Yeah." He looks very uncomfortable discussing this.

"It's okay, you don't have to look so worried. I have no loyalties to that man at all. But, I feel I should tell you that he's never going to sell his company to you. He told me when we were together. Charles and his mother are not your biggest fans." I don't feel bad about telling Jake this information. He should know if he is wasting his time, which I think that he is.

"Hmm, there are ways and means of persuasion. I just haven't found out what Charles' is yet." Jake then tells me the tactics that he has used so far, and I have to say that I'm a little unimpressed that he hasn't done his homework of Charles better.

My lips start to twitch as I realise that I can actually help Jake with this matter. The question is though, even after everything Charles did to me, can I really help Jake out? It doesn't take me long to reach my decision.

"I'm a little disappointed, Waters," I tease.

"How so?" He looks intrigued.

"Well, a man of your intellect, I would have thought that you would have found out what makes Charles tick by now."

"Tick?"

"Yeah. What buttons you have to push in order to get what you want."

"Oh no, I don't want you to give me advice, Stace." Our waitress brings over our orders, interrupting our conversation. We politely thank her whilst she drools over Jake. When she walks away, our conversation continues.

"Why the hell not?" I reply, referring to his last statement.

"Because I don't want to get you involved in this. He's your ex-boyfriend, and I don't want you to feel uncomfortable by divulging anything. I would never ask that of you." I feel touched that he wants to keep me out of it, but I want to help him with this.

"Look, we're friends, and friends help each other out. There's nothing more to it than that." Apart from maybe a little satisfaction on my part that Charles will finally get his comeuppance, but I'm not going to admit that.

"Really? Nothing more to it?"

"Nope." He doesn't look convinced by my answer at all. "Look, I'm not about to divulge any big secrets as I don't know half of what Charles gets up to. The only thing I am going to say to you is, Charles' reputation and status is more important to him than anything. Maybe you need to dig a bit deeper into what prompted me to leave Charles." I leave it at that and I see Jake wrestling with himself over whether he should leave the conversation there or ask me more questions.

"And that's it?" he asks incredulously.

"Yep." I take a bite of my food and pick up my coffee. "One of two things will happen. You will either use this new information to help you to acquire the company, or it will tarnish Charles' reputation so much that you will acquire some of his business. Either way seems somewhat of a bonus, don't you think?"

Jake leans back in his chair and I can see him processing what I have said. He starts to smirk, and I return that with a cheeky grin.

"I like the way you think, Miss Paris," Jake says, making me feel a little bit smug. After what Charles put me through, he deserves a little pay back.

CHAPTER TWENTY-FIVE

Jake walks me back to the flat after we have finished in Danish. I feel a little sad that he has to go. I've enjoyed our time together.

"Want to come in and wait for your ride?" I ask him.

"No, it's okay. Eric will be here any minute now."

"Oh, okay." I try not to sound too disappointed. "Well, I best go in and explain to the happy couple what happened to their first lot of breakfast, and why it has taken so long for me to return." Jake replaced the food and drinks that he made me drop earlier on, even though I told him not to worry about it.

"Tell them that I will make it up to them sometime," Jake says. With that, his limo pulls up alongside the curb and Jake gestures for Eric to remain in the driver's seat. "So, I'll see you soon?"

"Sure. Now, go and kick ass at your meeting," I reply. I bet he looks hot as hell when he's in boss mode.

He smiles at me and I turn to walk to the flat.

"Hey, Stace," Jake shouts at me, making me turn back around to face him. "Good luck with your shift tonight. You're gonna do great." I just smile at him as he gets into the limo. Eric catches my eye, and I can see him smiling. I wonder what he's so happy about? He nods in my direction and I give him a wave.

I watch as the limo pulls away and I know that Jake is watching me from inside, even if I can't see through the blacked-out windows that conceal him. I can just feel it. My insides do a little flutter, but they quickly disappear as I see a blond woman stood across the road, peering out from behind a tree. A feeling of familiarity washes over me.

Oh my God, it's Caitlin! What the hell is she doing?

I feel a sense of unease creep over me. I close my eyes and re-open them a few seconds later to discover that she has disappeared. I scan the street and all over the other side of the road, but there is no sign of her. I shake my head. I must be seeing things.

I do another check before turning to enter the block of flats. I feel a little shaky and wonder if I should phone Jake and tell him?

No, Stacey, don't be stupid. You're just seeing things. There is no need to worry over this.

I reach the flat and unlock the front door. As soon as I have shut the door, I hear Lydia's voice shout to me. "Where the bloody hell have you been? We're starving."

I walk in the direction of her voice, and I see her and Paul sat at the kitchen table.

"Sorry, guys," I say as I put their bag of food and tray of drinks down on the table. "You'll have to ask Jake why I was delayed." I smirk at them both and go to my bedroom without explaining any further. Without knowing the full story, they will be able to come to their own conclusions about why I was gone for so long. I know that Lydia will have so many different scenarios running through her head about what may have happened. I shouldn't leave her in suspense, but it doesn't hurt to keep some things a mystery.

Jake and I may only have gone for a bit of breakfast, but to me it was the best breakfast that I have ever had. Just being near him makes me feel special. How he has this effect on me, I will never know.

My bubble is quickly burst as the image of Caitlin stood across the road pops into my mind. It can't have been her. Why the hell would she be stood across the road, peeking out from behind a tree? I am definitely seeing things. I must be.

I shake my head and turn on my laptop. I take off my shoes and blazer and make myself comfy on the bed. I need to spend some time working on my novel and decide to re-read what I have done so far to distract me from my over-active imagination. I need to get back into my writing groove and get my novel finished.

Before I know it, two hours have passed, and I have added another couple of chapters. Feeling pleased with myself, I take a bathroom break and get myself a drink. I glance at the clock and see that I have three hours before I need to be at work.

I can hear Lydia and Paul in the bedroom.

Jeez, how are they able to keep going? They have been holed up in there near enough all day. Actually, I don't think that I want that question answering.

I go back to my bedroom and rifle through my clothes to pick out an outfit to wear tonight. I settle for black skinny jeans, a white sleeveless shirt and black boots. I don't want to flash too much flesh, I still feel a bit wary about being too revealing, so a shirt is perfect. I go to take a shower as Paul emerges from Lydia's bedroom.

"Oh, uh... Hi, Stace," he says awkwardly as he runs one hand through his hair.

"Hi, Paul. You guys finished in there yet?"

His cheeks suddenly turn a rather bright shade of red. "Um... Yeah... I'm... I'm just leaving actually."

"Well, okay then. Enjoy the rest of your day."

Paul scurries off, puts his shoes on and leaves the flat. I chuckle to myself at his flustered behaviour and continue to the bathroom to take a shower.

By the time I have showered, dressed and finished sprucing myself up, I look confident and assured. I have tied my hair up into a ponytail and I have only applied minimal make-up. I don't want to attract any unnecessary attention, so I figure that remaining low-key is best. I put everything that I need in my handbag and watch some television in the lounge until Lydia is ready to leave.

Thoughts of Caitlin return to my mind as I am sat there waiting.

How would she have known where to look for Jake? She can't have been following him, surely? She must be really messed up to act in the way that she does. Maybe she doesn't realise that she's behaving like a loony?

I shake my head as the questions come thick and fast.

Stacey, you were just seeing things. Of course Caitlin wasn't there. It's either your mind or your eyes playing tricks. There is no need to be worried about this.

I convince myself once again that I was imagining things and push any thoughts of Caitlin to the back of my mind. It is now quarter past six and we need to be at work by seven. I go to see what Lydia is doing and to tell her to get a move on.

I open Lydia's bedroom door and see that she is putting her make-up on.

"Are you nearly ready to go?" I ask her. Lydia finishes applying her red lipstick and pouts in the mirror.

"Ready when you are, babes."

"Finally," I exclaim.

I just want to get to work and get started. I feel a little anxious and I need to keep myself busy. Eventually we arrive at the bar, at quarter to seven. In all honesty, I did think we were going to get here later than that seeing as Lydia was a tad behind schedule, so it's not too bad.

Lydia and I go and put our handbags in her office and then I follow her to the bar area. I stand behind the counter and instantly feel at home. The bar acts as a barrier, so it kind of makes me feel protected to a certain extent. The place isn't busy yet but give it another hour and I know that it will be four people deep at the bar.

I grab myself a bottle of water out of the fridge, and Lydia quickly updates me on anything that has changed since I left six months ago. I listen intently, determination coursing through me that I am going to do a good job tonight.

An hour and a half into my shift and I have no time to think about anything other than cocktails. It seems Lydia forgot to mention to me that I would be chief cocktail maker.

After making what feels like my thousandth cocktail of the night, I need a break. I pass cocktail duties to a girl named Penelope, and I go to collect some glasses from the various tables around the room.

I watch some of the people as they dance together. They all look so carefree. Either that or the alcohol has well and truly taken effect on them. I pick up as many glasses as I can carry, and I start to walk back to the bar. As I am walking, I feel someone pinch my bum. Rage instantly courses through my entire body. I literally dump the empty glasses on the nearest table and whirl around to see who the culprit is.

I come face-to-face with some young lad, who can't be a day over the age of twenty-one. He is grinning at me and sweating profusely.

Ugh, is this really attractive to anyone?

"Hey there, gorgeous. How about we have a little bump and grind?" He slurs each and every word. I resist the urge to slap him around the face for his inappropriate touching.

"No thanks," I reply in a pissed off voice. "And can I just say that, for future reference, if you ever touch my ass again, I'll pound *your* ass into the ground."

The guy looks seriously shocked, even in his inebriated state. It's almost like he is trying to decide whether he imagined what I said, or if I did actually say it.

"Are you having some trouble understanding what I said?"

"N... Nnn... No," he replies, putting his hands up as he starts to back away.

Who do these men think they are? It's almost like they think they have a green light to touch a woman wherever and whenever they want to.

I stand straighter and turn to the table that I placed the glasses on. I pick the glasses up and smile to myself as I carry them to the bar.

See, that wasn't so bad was it, Stace? You handled that really well. You threatened to beat up a teeny-bopper but hey, it worked.

My conscious starts to make me feel bad for being quite so short with the guy. I shrug off the nagging voice and see that I am due my twenty-minute break. I tell the other bar staff that I am going to Lydia's office for a time-out. I pour myself a soft drink and take it with me.

When I open Lydia's office door, the smell of Chinese food hits me. As the room comes into full view, I see Lydia has some company. Paul and Jake are sat there, eating from Chinese take-away cartons.

"Can anyone join this private party? Or is it invite only?" I ask. My mouth starts to water from the aroma of the food. Well, I presume it's from the food, it could of course be the sight of Jake sat there. He looks good in his suit trousers and white shirt which has the top two buttons undone. *My, my, my, very tasty.*

"Nah, we can allow you to gate-crash," Lydia's answer interrupts my thoughts.

"Well, jeez, thanks so much," I reply sarcastically. I sit on the empty chair, which is next to Jake, and I take the spring roll that he is about to eat out of his hand.

"Hey," Jake says.

"What?" I say innocently as I take a bite of the spring roll. Jake smiles.

"Don't worry, we didn't forget about you. Your food is in this bag," he says as he lifts a bag from the desk and hands it to me. I lick my lips and take a carton out of the bag. I delve straight into the carton to see that it is chicken chow mein. "Wow, someone is hungry."

"Yeah, I'm starving. I didn't eat before I came to work, and I've been busting my butt out there." The others all stare at me in amazement. "What?" I say once I have swallowed my mouthful of food.

"You know, for someone with such a cute little figure, you sure can eat, Stace." Lydia gawps at me as I shove noodles into my mouth. The food may not be piping hot, but it still satisfies my taste buds.

"Oh shut up. Anyway, what are you all doing in here? And Lydia, do you realise how busy it is out there? I really don't think that the other bar staff can cope."

"The staff will be fine, they do it all the time. The customers aren't going to leave as they are all too pissed to go anywhere else by now. And as for what we are doing, we are eating Chinese food. Isn't that obvious?"

"Oh, ha ha, very funny," I reply, sarcasm once again taking over my tone.

"Actually, I wanted to drop by and see Lyd, so I text her and Jake just so happened to be with me. We thought that we would grab some food on the way," Paul says.

"Uh huh," I reply. He's a really bad liar. I decide to bite the bullet and voice why I think they are really here. Well, why Jake is here anyway. "So, no one has come here to check up on how I'm coping then?" I direct my question at Jake. He averts his eyes away from me, confirming what I suspected. "I thought so. You guys really need to think of better excuses. And I'm doing fine by the way."

"I know, I saw you tell that guy that you would put him on his ass," Jake chuckles. I stare open-mouthed at him. "Remind me never to pinch your ass," he teases.

"How the hell did you know that?" I ask.

"Oh, I was coming back from the toilets when I saw the confrontation happen. I must say, I'm impressed. I don't think that he will be bothering you again."

Lydia and Paul burst out laughing and I can't help but smile. Warmth courses through my body from the people sat in this room.

This is how my life should be.

A life full of laughter, love and friendship.

CHAPTER TWENTY-SIX

I wake up on Sunday morning and my feet are throbbing. Wearing high-heeled boots for my first shift back at The Den was not my best idea. I forgot how excruciating the pain can be.

I get out of bed and make my way to the bathroom. After using the facilities and splashing some cold water on my face, I head to the kitchen to make some strong coffee. It is only nine in the morning, meaning that I have only had four hours' sleep. I make my coffee and go back to my bedroom to lie down on the bed. I smile to myself as I settle back under my quilt. My first shift back was brilliant. It has boosted my confidence significantly. It was also kind of sweet that Jake came to check up on me, but I'm not going to tell him that.

My phone buzzes to notify me that I have received a text message.

Good morning, sunshine. I hope that you are well rested, because we are going out for the day. Be ready for 11am. I will have Eric pick you up in the limo. Jake

What the hell? Why is he taking me out? Actually, I don't care why, but it would be nice to have some sort of clue as to what he has planned. I text back.

Morning, Mr Waters. And where might we be going? Stace x

It only takes a few seconds for him to reply.

Don't ask questions. All will be revealed

soon...
Jake x

So much for trying to get information out of him.

I jump back out of bed, take a few sips of coffee and then rush into the bathroom, where I shower at the speed of lightening. When I return to my room, I am faced with choosing what outfit to wear. With no idea of where Jake is taking me, I choose something simple. I put on my white sun-dress and team it with my sandals and white cardigan. I leave my hair to dry in waves and I apply some mascara and lip gloss.

The whole time my mind is conjuring up different ideas of what Jake might have planned. I wonder if he does this kind of thing with all of his friends?

Don't read too much into it, Stace. He has made his feelings clear about just being friends.

I take one more look at myself in the mirror and then I go and knock on Lydia's bedroom door, so that I can tell her that I am going out. I enter before being told to and am confronted by the vision of her and Paul in a very compromising position.

"Ahhhh," I shriek. They both stare in my direction and I quickly shut the door. I squeeze my eyes shut and try to erase what I just saw. "Sorry, guys," I yell so they can hear me. "I'll... Um... I'll leave you to it."

Shit, I was not expecting to see Paul's bare ass at this time on a Sunday morning. Actually, I never thought I would see Paul's bare ass at all. How awkward! I didn't even realise that he had stayed the night. I thought that he was just seeing Lydia to the front door for a goodnight kiss. I was so exhausted last night that as soon as I got in, I got changed into my pyjamas and went straight to sleep. Hence why I didn't hear a thing.

I sit on the sofa in the lounge and clock watch until it gets to eleven o'clock. The doorbell rings at the exact time stated in Jake's message. I grab my bag and answer the door to see Eric standing there, dressed in a smart suit.

"Miss Stacey." He smiles. "Mr Waters is waiting for you. Please follow me to the limo." I shut the front door behind me and do as he asks. I resist the urge to laugh at his tone. He sounds so serious.

"Eric, there really is no need to be so formal around me," I tell him, but I get the feeling that my comment falls on deaf ears. Eric strikes me as very old school when it comes to manners and etiquette. "Where am I being taken to?"

"I'm afraid I can't tell you that, Miss Stacey. Top secret." He winks at me as he answers.

"Uh huh." I get into the limo and pull my phone out of my bag.

Jake, are you going to tell me what's
going on? I'm not a great fan of
surprises.
Stace x

I hit the send button and wait for a reply. I get nothing back which irritates me. I'm not used to people surprising me. The usual surprises I tend to get are generally bad ones. This better be good.

I sit in the limo with my arms folded, waiting to see where I am going. Eventually, Eric pulls up in front of a clothes shop. And not just any clothes shop. It just so happens that we are in front of the most expensive clothes shop in the county. I gawp as Eric opens the limo door for me. I step out and my eyes instantly find the gorgeous outfits that are on display in the window.

"Here we are, Miss Stacey. Jake is waiting inside for you." I open and close my mouth a few times before I can speak.

"Uh, thanks," I say. Eric nods his head and then returns to the limo. I watch as he drives away and then I turn back to look at the big gold-plated front doors of the clothes shop. I have never set foot in here before.

What the hell has Jake brought me here for? Why a clothes shop? I thought guys hated shopping?

I approach the building and a doorman, who I hadn't noticed before, opens one of the doors for me.

"Good morning," the doorman says.

"Uh, morning." I smile sheepishly and walk through the door.

As I enter, I instantly feel underdressed. The women are in designer outfits, and the men are all in designer suits. Even the few children that are in here are immaculately dressed. Not a pair of trainers in sight. I look down at my clothes and gulp. My high street sun-dress just doesn't cut it in here.

I get a few snotty looks as I wander around the ground floor, trying to find Jake. A woman approaches me as I get half way through the store, and I think that she is coming to tell me that I am in the wrong place.

"Are you Miss Paris?" she asks me.

"Yes." I look at her name tag which says "Gloria."

"Please follow me. Mr Waters is waiting for you on floor five." Gloria then turns, and I obediently follow her. She doesn't give off a very friendly vibe and it makes me feel uncomfortable.

I survey the clothes as we walk to the lifts and each item I see is more exquisite than the last. I bet the price tags are pretty too.

When we get to the lifts, Gloria presses the button and we wait. When the lift arrives, I get in, but Gloria remains where she is.

"Remember floor number five is where you will find Mr Waters," Gloria says. I press the number five button and when I look up Gloria has disappeared. Thankfully, I am in the lift on my own, so there are no eyes judging my choice of attire.

I take a few deep breaths as I try to calm myself. My heart is beating a little faster than usual and I think it's a mixture of excitement at what Jake might have planned, and also a touch of nerves as I feel so out of place.

The lift doors ping open when I reach floor five, and I step out to see some of the most gorgeous dresses that I have ever set my sights on. However, none of them are as gorgeous as the man approaching me. Jake is wearing a navy blue suit and white shirt with open collar. He looks incredible. He smiles at me and I almost melt. As he reaches me, he gives me a hug.

"Hi. Are you okay?" he asks.

"Not really, Jake... I am dressed completely wrong. You could have given me a clue as to what to wear. The looks that I got off of some of the people shopping when I entered were looks of complete disgust. What the hell am I doing here?"

"You look beautiful. There is nothing wrong with what you are wearing." Jake gives my body a quick perusal and I feel my sex begin to stir. His gaze makes my body feel alive. I need to keep myself in check. We're friends and nothing more.

"Oh, and I brought you here to ask you a favour," Jake says. He appears to have finished looking at my outfit and seems ready to get to the point of this outing. I raise my eyebrows in question. "I have an event to attend this evening, and I was hoping that you would accompany me. If you say yes, then I want you to pick out one of these dresses as a thank you for coming with me." My mouth drops open. He wants to buy me one of these dresses? Wow, I wasn't expecting that.

"And what if I say no?" I decide to tease him for a moment. It's the least he deserves after not warning me about what to wear here.

"Well, then I guess I will just have to try and change your mind." I swear I see a mischievous glint in his eye, but I choose to ignore it. I can't let myself think that anything is going to happen between us.

"Hmm, now that could be interesting," I reply. I appear thoughtful for a few moments before giving him my decision. "Of course I will go with you, but you don't need to buy me one of these dresses, they are so expensive. I can't let you spend that kind of money on me."

"Why not? You would be doing me a favour and for that, I would like to get you something. In this case, the something is a dress."

"But—"

"No buts. If you don't want to choose a dress then that's fine, I'll just have one picked out for you." Jake smirks as I scowl at the sneaky sod. Either way it looks like I am getting a new dress from here. Seeing as he hasn't given me much choice, I might as well take a look around myself.

"What's the event for?" I ask.

"It's just some corporate thing that I need to attend."

"Oooo, sounds so exciting," I mirror his unexcited tone and Jake laughs.

"This is why you will be perfect as my plus one. You are just as excited by the thought as I am."

Now it's my turn to laugh. "You drive a hard bargain, Mr Waters," I tease.

"I'm sure the dresses did most of the persuading for me." He smirks. "Now, go and have a look around and see what catches your eye. Don't take any notice of the price tag either." He gives me a stern look, and I almost feel like I am being told off. "I will be waiting at the chairs outside the changing rooms." Jake then turns and leaves me standing like a lost lamb in the aisle.

I slowly start to walk around and study the dresses on display. How am I meant to know which dresses to try on? They are all so gorgeous. As I continue to look lost, an older lady approaches me.

"Can I be of help, dear?" she asks. She has white hair which has been tied back into a neat bun, and she has a kind face. Very different from Gloria's overall vibe.

"Oh, I'm just looking around. I'm not exactly sure where to start though, everything is so beautiful."

"Would you like me to help you? My name's Edele and I am one of the personal assistants here." She smiles at me and holds her hand out for me to shake.

"That would be great, thank you."

Thirty minutes pass by and Edele has helped me choose ten dresses to try on. Edele actually picked out most of them. She clearly knows what she is doing as I like each and every one of them.

I pass Jake as I walk into the changing rooms and give him a smile. He is busy talking on his mobile phone, but he still smiles back at me.

I enter a changing cubicle which is massive, and even has a plush armchair in the corner. Mirrors adorn each wall of the cubicle and the lighting is subtle. It is a vast difference from the harsh, bright lights of the high street changing rooms.

"If you need any help getting into any of the dresses then there is a bell you can press, just by the mirror there," Edele says as she points to the button. "I will only be outside the changing rooms anyway."

I thank her, and she draws a deep, purple velvet curtain across the cubicle so that I have some privacy. I eye each dress and pick the first one that I want to try on. It is a floor length, halter-neck, red dress. It is lovely, but it isn't really fitting my figure the way in which I would like it to. I take the dress off and try on a further three before deciding that those aren't right either.

I want a dress that is going to blow Jake's mind. Just because we are friends doesn't mean that I can't make myself look as good as possible around him.

The fifth dress I decide to try on is one of the dresses that I picked out myself. It is gorgeous. It is a floor length, strapless navy blue, silk gown with a thigh high slit. It is simple and made of the softest material. I slip it on, do up the side zip and gasp as I look at myself in the mirror. The dress hugs my body in all the right places, and it compliments my blue eyes.

I press the button to call Edele in to see what her opinion is, drawing back the curtain and waiting for her. She appears seconds later and gasps when she sees me.

"Oh my, that dress is perfect. It fits you like a glove, and it looks like it was made for you," she says.

"Thanks, Edele. I like this one too." I am so pleased to hear that Edele agrees with me about how good the dress looks. Of course she may be working on commission, but I don't let that thought cloud my judgement of her. I twirl around and survey myself in the mirrors once more. "I don't think that I need to try on any of the other dresses. This is the one that I want."

"Well then, my dear, this one it shall be. It is stunning. I will have it boxed up for you once you have changed out of it," Edele says.

"Okay." I pull the curtain back across the changing room and I carefully take the dress off. I put my white sun-dress back on and open the curtain to hand Edele the navy blue dress. "Um, could you not let Mr Waters see it, please? He's the guy sat in the chair out the front. I would like to keep the dress a surprise until I wear it."

"Of course. If I may say so, he isn't going to know what's hit him when he sees you in this." Edele takes the dress and I smile at her compliment. Edele then exits the changing rooms, and I slip my sandals back on, leaving the other dresses where they are.

I exit the changing rooms to see that Jake is now tapping away on his iPad. He looks up at me as I approach him.

"Have you chosen a dress?" he asks, looking to my hands and finding them empty.

"I sure have," I say grinning.

"Well, that didn't take as long as I thought it was going to. Where is it?"

"Edele is packing it for me."

"Do I not get to see it?"

"Nope. You will just have to wait until tonight." I feel a little bit of excitement at the suspense of making him wait.

"That's not fair." He pouts playfully.

"You surprised me with a shopping trip, and now I get to surprise you with what dress I have chosen." I can't wait for him to see it. I hope it does the trick and accomplishes blowing Jake's mind.

"You're a tease, Miss Paris."

I wink at him. "That's what makes our friendship so special."

CHAPTER TWENTY-SEVEN

Eric picks up Jake and I from the clothes shop and drives us back to the flat. I thank Jake for the shopping trip and say goodbye. I don't invite him in as I need to prepare myself for tonight.

I practically jump from the limo when Eric opens the door. He hands me the box with my dress in, and I near enough run to the block of flats and up the stairs. I can't wait to show Lydia my dress for tonight and I excitedly unlock the front door. I chuck my bag down and go through to the lounge. Lydia is dozing on the sofa, but I have to wake her.

"Lyd, wake up. I have to show you this amazing dress that I just got." She opens her eyes and groggily sits up.

"Calm down, Stace. I'm exhausted," Lydia moans whilst yawning.

"Hardly surprising." I raise my eyebrows as I speak. Lydia smiles as I thrust the box, with my dress in, in her face. Her eyes go wide at the name of the clothes shop sprawled across the front.

"Holy shit."

"I know."

"Well, come on then, what are you waiting for? Let me see, let me see." I knew her enthusiasm would reach its peak once she had realised where I had been. I place the box on the coffee table and undo it, carefully taking the dress out and holding it up so that Lydia can see. Her mouth drops open.

"Oh wow, that is beautiful. Did you buy this?" she asks me. Lydia knows her fashion, so she probably has a good idea of how much this dress is likely to have cost.

"Nope. Jake bought it for me. It's to wear to some corporate event tonight. He asked me to go with him, and he said that the dress was a thank you for doing him a favour by accompanying him." I can't stop smiling.

Lydia gets up off of the sofa and feels the fabric. "Oh my, that is so soft. It's a gorgeous dress, babes. So, are you and Jake still maintaining that you are just friends?" She looks at me skeptically.

"Yes." Lydia cocks one of her eyebrows at me. "Honestly, Lyd, he asked me *because* we are friends."

"Uh huh." I know that she isn't convinced. Hell, I don't even know if I am convinced. "Well, I wish I had friends that bought me dresses like this."

I roll my eyes at her. I don't want to let myself hope that Jake and I can become more.

"Anyway, is it possible that you could help me with my hair later? I was thinking of having a classy up-do."

"Absolutely. What time are you leaving here?" Lydia's eyes sparkle with excitement.

"Jake will be picking me up at seven o'clock."

"That only gives us a couple of hours. We better get started now."

"Can I grab a cup of coffee first?"

"No! You haven't got any time to waste. Now, go and get your butt in the shower so that we can get started," Lydia demands. I salute at her whilst she claps her hands together. She loves to help with things like this. I don't argue with her as I need to make sure that I look my absolute best for tonight.

I go and hang the dress up in my bedroom before going to the bathroom. Whilst I am in the shower, I make sure that I am hair free in all the right places, just in case. Who's to say that I won't meet someone at the event tonight? I am totally kidding myself, my eyes will only be for Jake, but it doesn't hurt to be prepared.

I wrap a towel around my body and exit the bathroom. On entering the lounge, I find that Lydia has set up a make-shift beauty salon. One of the kitchen chairs has been placed in the middle of the room, the coffee table is covered with hair necessities, and a vast range of make-up occupies the remaining space.

Lydia hands me a glass of wine and gestures for me to sit on the chair. I smile at her and take a sip. Lydia goes out of the room as I take my seat and wait to see what she is doing. She returns a few moments later with even more hair products.

"Christ, Lyd, I don't want to look like a poodle," I tease her.

"Shut up and let the magic happen." She takes a sip of her wine and then, somehow, she finds an empty spot on the coffee table to place her glass on.

I close my eyes as Lydia works her magic, and after what feels like hours of drying, curling and adding God knows what products to my hair, she has finally finished. "That's it. I'm done. Go and take a look."

I get up and head for the mirror hanging in the hallway. I don't know what I am expecting to see, but my hair looks awesome. Lydia has put it into a classy up-do like I wanted, and she has left a few loose curls hanging down, so that they frame my face in just the right places. I run back to the lounge and give Lydia a bear hug.

"Easy, you don't want to spoil your hair," she says in-between laughing at me. "Now, what are you thinking of doing make-up wise?"

"I thought that I would just do some eye shadow, mascara and lip gloss."

"Oh jeez, it's a good job that you have me here." Lydia sighs and manoeuvres me back onto the chair. She starts selecting various make-up items from the table and then stands in front of me. "Now, close your eyes and don't open them until I say so."

"Yes ma'am," I say with a smirk.

I feel various brushes touch my face, but I have no idea what I am going to look like. I'm not one for wearing much make-up at the best of times, so I have no idea what to expect.

By the time Lydia says that I can open my eyes, it is quarter to seven. I hope that I look okay as I don't have the time to re-do anything.

I get up from the chair and go back to the hallway mirror. As I stare at my reflection, I can't quite believe what I'm seeing. Lydia has used the subtlest grey eyeshadow, and my eyelashes look longer and thicker than normal. She has highlighted my cheekbones and coated my lips in a nude coloured lip-gloss. I stare, open-mouthed at her handiwork before looking to the lounge door and seeing that Lydia is leaning against the door frame.

"You like?" she asks me.

"I love it. Thank you." I go to hug her again, but she stops me by holding her hands up in front of her.

"You only have ten minutes to get yourself into that dress and get your shoes on. We can save the hugging and general worshipping of me until later." I smile at her as I quickly go to my bedroom to put the dress on.

I grab my grey stilettos from their hiding place and put those on too. I decide not to take a clutch bag with me, I don't need to take a phone or anything, so I don't need to bother carrying a bag. I forgo wearing a jacket because I don't want to cover the dress up.

I walk out of my bedroom and Lydia gasps.

"Wow, Stace, you are going to knock all those people dead tonight."

I look at myself in the mirror and see that I look like a different person. I feel like some sort of princess in my dress. I do a slow twirl, surveying myself from all angles, when there is a knock at the door which makes me jump.

"Shit! He's here, he's here," I say, starting to panic.

"Calm down, babes. You're all ready to go. I can't wait to see the look on his face when you open the door." I scowl at her as I know that she is convinced that there is something going on with Jake and me.

"Knock it off, Lyd. We're just friends."

"Yeah, yeah. You keep telling yourself that." I ignore her comment and go to answer the door.

As I open it, I can smell Jake's aftershave. God, he smells divine. Jake is looking at the floor when I open the door, and he slowly lifts his head, his eyes raking over my body, and when he meets my gaze, I almost orgasm.

Butterflies start to dance in my belly and my breathing becomes shallow. Jake appears to be lost for words, so he just smiles at me. A genuine, heartfelt smile. He looks absolutely gorgeous in his black tuxedo.

"Hi, Jake," I manage to say.

Jake clears his throat before he answers. "Stacey." He nods his head as he says my name. "Are you ready to go?" I can't mistake the heat lurking in his gaze.

"I sure am," I reply, sounding much more confident than I feel. I turn around to Lyd who is standing there with a goofy grin plastered on her face. "Don't forget to leave the door on the catch," I say to her.

"Okay. Have fun, guys. Don't do anything that I wouldn't do," I hear her shout as the front door closes behind me. We walk out to the limo and Jake places his hand at the small of my back.

He leans in and whispers in my ear. "You look incredible." I feel his breath on my cheek and it makes me shiver with delight.

"You don't look so bad yourself." I look at him and we mirror each other's smiles. As we reach the limo, Eric opens the door for us to get in.

"Miss Stacey," he says in greeting. "You look beautiful this evening."

"Thanks, Eric." I enter the limo and Jake follows me, taking the seat beside me. We set off and there is complete silence between us. I can feel tension mounting and I start to feel slightly awkward as Jake just gazes out of the window. I fiddle with my hands the whole time.

The limo pulls to a stop a short while later, and I feel a sense of unease.

Maybe Jake doesn't like my dress?

Maybe he thinks that it's too much?

Maybe I shouldn't have come to this event with him?

As I ponder these questions in my head, Eric opens the door for us to exit the limo. I take a deep breath and follow Jake out. I look around and can't see anywhere that looks like there is an event going on.

"I will give you a call when we are ready to leave," I hear Jake say to Eric in the background. I then feel his hand take mine and he leads me to the building situated in front of us. It's just an office block. This is a strange place to hold an event.

As we enter the lobby, it becomes clear to me that this is Jake's offices. The giant letters behind the reception desk are a big giveaway seeing as they say WATERS INDUSTRIES.

Oh great, I have got all dressed up just to come to Jake's offices.

Jake leads me to the lift at the far end of the reception area. He presses the button to call the lift and we wait. We are the only ones waiting and it seems to take an age for the lift doors to open. We enter the lift and Jake presses the button for the top floor. The doors close, and I decide that I have had enough of the tension between us.

"Jake is something wrong?" I ask. He turns and faces me.

"No, nothing is wrong. Should there be?"

"It's just that, you have hardly said two words to me since you picked me up. Have I done something to upset you? Did I pick the wrong dress?"

"God no. You picked the perfect dress, trust me. And you certainly haven't done anything to upset me. I'm sorry, I'm just thinking about tonight. I hate having to schmooze with people that have no personal regard to my life. To be honest, I can't stand most of the people coming, but business is business."

"Oh, right. Okay then." I can't think of anything else to say to that.

I turn to face the lift doors and wait for us to reach the relevant floor. We finally reach floor number thirty-two and the lift doors open. Jake still has hold of my hand and he leads us into the huge open-plan room.

There is classical music playing and there appears to be about a hundred people chatting amongst little groups. The whole space has been decorated to reflect an intimate vibe, but to be honest, I think it looks a little tacky. I instantly think of Martin and of how he would have made this place look so much better. I must give him a call and arrange to meet him for a catch up.

"Show time," Jake says, breaking my thoughts. I can tell that he doesn't want to be here by the tone of his voice.

As a few people start to notice Jake, they begin to come over to him. I am casually pushed aside by the people, mostly women, who want to get his attention. Jake didn't mention that all of these people were going to be assholes with no manners.

I leave him to it and walk over to the bar area that has been set up. I order a glass of white wine and take a sip when it is delivered to me. I am quite happily sipping my wine when I see a familiar face emerge from the throngs of people.

Oh fucking great. This is all I need.

"Well, well, well. Look who it is," says Charles sarcastically.

"Hello, Charles." I am completely caught off guard. Jake never mentioned that Charles would be here. I don't even pretend to make my greeting sound genuine.

Charles is wearing a dull grey suit with tweed patches at the elbows. He looks awful. How I ever slept with this guy is baffling.

"So, what brings you here?" he says as his eyes peruse my body. I involuntarily shiver from his gaze, but not in a good way. The guy still knows how to make me cringe.

"I came with Jake." I can see Charles' face change instantly from smug to shocked.

"You... You came with who?" he stutters.

"Jake. Jake Waters." It actually feels good to shock him.

"So, it was you who gave him information on me then?"

"What?"

"You told him about why we split up, didn't you?" Charles' face starts to go a little red.

"I most certainly did not." I actually didn't tell him the reason, I just hinted that he should look into it, but I'm not about to tell Charles that.

"You lying bitch. It must have been you." Charles looks infuriated and I'm starting to get the impression that he is going to turn into the volatile asshole that I used to live with.

"Charles, I never told Jake why we split up. If Jake found out, then he found out another way." Charles is going to believe what he likes, but I feel like I need to stand my ground.

"Rubbish. You have betrayed me. Why on earth would you come here with him, knowing that I was going to be here?"

"I didn't know that you were going to be here, actually. Believe it or not, Charles, I don't plan my life around your every move anymore." This guy really does think that he is a God. "And for your information, I came with Jake because we are *friends*."

"Pfft," Charles scoffs. "Well, did you know that your *friend* has taken half of my clients? Your *friend* is trying to put me out of business, all because I won't let him buy my company. You really think he made friends with you on the off chance, and that he has no ulterior motive? He is simply using you to get to me."

"Is that so?" God, he really is an egotistical pig.

"Yeah. He couldn't give a shit about you, and you have fallen for his charm, hook line and sinker. You really are fucking stupid, aren't you?" Charles snarls at me.

I feel anger start to rise within me.

Who the hell does he think he is, talking to me like this?

I need to keep my cool, but it is proving difficult right now.

"You can think and say what you like, Charles. I have no interest in pandering to your paranoia. Jake and I don't even talk about you. You are irrelevant to my life, and you have been for quite some time." There is so much more that I could say to Charles at this point, but I don't want to be the one to cause an unnecessary scene. I don't need to have an argument with him. Charles is part of my past, and I intend for him to stay that way.

"You are a nasty piece of work, Stacey Paris. What the hell did I ever see in you? I gave you everything and you just threw it back in my face. You are just a user and—" Charles doesn't get to finish his sentence because Jake has grabbed his arm and spun him around.

"I suggest you leave, *now*," Jake says as he looks at Charles like he is a parasite. Other guests are starting to look over, but I don't think Jake cares about that.

"I'm not going anywhere. I was invited here by your company, remember? I am just telling Stacey some home truths. It's not my problem if she doesn't like hearing them."

"Okay, let me make this clear to you, Charles. You were never supposed to be invited, but I guess your name was left on one of the mailing lists. That's the only reason you got an invite. And don't worry, I will be having a word with the person who sent the invites out. Maybe they will come to you for a job when I'm finished with them."

"Secondly, you do not get to speak to Stacey like that. She is here as a special guest of mine and if you disrespect her, then you disrespect me. Thirdly, I suggest that you put your drink down and get the hell out of here, before I throw you out myself." Jake's stance is intimidating, and Charles physically shrinks back in shock.

Charles turns to the bar, and with shaky hands he puts his glass down. He doesn't look at me again, and he turns back to Jake and excuses himself. Charles then heads for the lift and Jake watches him until the lift doors shut, erasing Charles from our sight.

I think that Charles made a very wise decision to get out of here when Jake told him to. I have seen Jake in action when someone pisses him off, and it's not pleasant for the person on the receiving end.

Jake's gaze locks with mine and I mouth a "thank you" to him. He comes closer to me so that he can whisper in my ear.

"Give me half an hour and then we're out of here."

"Okay," I reply. I watch him as he strides across the room and starts chatting to a couple of older guys. I feel so aroused by his protectiveness of me, and I suddenly find myself swamped by people wanting to talk to me about Jake's little display with Charles. I try to avoid answering their questions and opt for polite chit-chat instead. However, I'm not really listening to what any of them are saying. I am too busy studying Jake.

I feel a flutter as our eyes connect across the room. His are filled with heat, and I'm sure that mine reflect that feeling too. He looks up and down my body and then points to the lift. I look at him a little confused and he again just points to the lift. I make my excuses to the cling-on that is trying to ask questions about Jake, and I walk over to the lift. I press the button to call it and I wait for the doors to open.

I enter the lift when it's ready and Jake comes bounding in just as the doors are beginning to close. He stops in front of me, and then without warning, he pushes me against the side. My heart is racing, and I can feel the heat from his body. My sex is crying out for him. He leans closer to my face, but I stop him from getting any closer by placing my hand on his chest. I need to make sure that he isn't going to run away this time.

"Are you sure about this, Jake? I don't want a repeat of last time." Even though my body craves this man's touch, I am wary. Understandable, seeing as he freaked out after our last kiss.

My heart is pounding as I wait for him to answer me. I am willing him with every fibre of my being to say that he is sure about this. About us.

He looks intently at me and studies my face before he answers.

"I was a fool last time, I can't fight it anymore. I want you, Stacey. I need you."

His words undo me.

It's all I need to hear.

I put my hands behind his neck and bring his face closer to mine. As we are about to kiss, the lift stops, and the doors begin to open. We jump apart, and a group of four people get in and stand in front of us. Damn them. Just as things were about to get physical, we get interrupted.

The sexual tension in this lift is unbearable. I need to get out of here, I need to feel Jake's hands on me again.

The lift seems to take forever to reach the ground floor and when it finally does, Jake puts his arm around my waist and guides us to the exit. His limo is already outside, waiting at the curb for us. Eric greets us and holds the door open for us to get in.

I can barely contain my excitement at the thought of what might happen.

Jake sits opposite me and simply says four words that are like music to my ears. "Your place or mine?"

"Yours."

CHAPTER TWENTY-EIGHT

We get back to Jake's house and barely make it through the front door before his lips find mine. Our kiss starts out soft but quickly becomes frenzied. It's like we can't get enough of each other. All the pent-up frustration of the last few weeks have come to a head.

Jake puts his hands on my ass and lifts me up, so that I am straddling his torso. Thank God I picked a dress with a thigh high split. Although, if I had chosen a dress that was going to rip, I don't think I would even care at this moment in time.

He carries me up the two flights of stairs, our lips never leaving one another, and he takes me into his bedroom. He lies me down on the bed and then breaks our kiss. I let out a little moan at the loss of contact.

Jake stares down at me and begins to speak.

"You are so beautiful," he whispers. He strokes my cheek as I lean my face into his hand. He stands up and takes his suit jacket off. I quickly sit up and stop his hands as he reaches the top button of his shirt.

"Let me," I say in my most seductive voice.

He lets his hands fall to his sides as I begin to undo his buttons, slowly. When I am done, I stand up and slide the shirt down his arms. The material falls to the floor and I place my hands on his chest. His muscles ripple and it takes all of my willpower not to hurry things along.

I want to savour every moment of this.

My hands make their way down to his trousers and I unbuckle them. They fall to the floor and Jake steps out of them before kicking them to one side. My hands find the rim of his boxers, but he steps back, halting my progress.

"You have too many layers on. Let's even things out and remove this dress." He takes hold of hands and moves my arms, so I am holding them above my head. He finds the side zip and slowly undoes it before pushing the material of the dress down my body, until it is pooling at my feet.

I stand there with just a pair of white lace knickers on, and my shoes.

Jake nods approvingly. "You are breath taking."

I feel my legs quiver at his sensual words. I can't speak. A part of me is subconsciously waiting for him to run again. I hope that he doesn't. I don't think that I could bare it if he walked away a second time.

His hands skim up the sides of my body until he reaches my breasts, and he gently caresses them as he leans down to kiss my neck. I close my eyes and put all thoughts of him running away to the back of my mind. I feel his lips trail across my skin until they reach my right nipple. He gently licks and sucks which heightens how turned on I am right now. I can't think straight.

Jake proceeds to do the same to the other nipple before he finds my lips again. We kiss, and his hands travel back down my body until his fingers hook into the sides of my knickers. Before I know what is happening, Jake has ripped the lace from my body and thrown the knickers onto the floor. He then pushes me back onto the bed and lifts one of my legs into the air so that he can take my shoe off. He repeats the same manoeuvre with the other leg before swiftly removing his boxers and climbing on top of me.

"I'm going to make you scream my name, Stacey." I gasp at his words and stroke his back with my nails, enjoying the feel of goose-bumps on his skin.

Jake continues his delicious torture by kissing a trail all the way down my body, finally reaching my most intimate place. He pushes my legs apart, so that I am spread before him. He gently parts me and softly blows on my clit before licking it with his tongue. As he starts to swirl his tongue around in circles, I feel my insides start to tighten, bringing me closer to orgasm.

He pushes his fingers inside me and I am done for. I scream out his name as he continues to pleasure me until I have ridden out my orgasm. He makes his way back up my body and smirks. I feel his erection pushing against my opening. No words are needed as he slowly enters me. The feel of him inside me is like pure bliss.

My fingers grip his strong arms as he starts off with a slow rhythm. He returns his mouth to my nipples and gently bites them, and I grip his arms harder as I urge him to go faster. His speed picks up pace and I start to pant as I can feel another orgasm approaching.

Another one? Well, this is new.

Never in my life have I come more than once during a sexual encounter before.

"Look at me," Jake says. My eyelids are heavy, but I manage to open them fully so that I can look at him. His eyes capture me, his caramel pools sparking various emotions within me. Jake continues to increase his speed and I know that I can't hold on much longer.

"Jake, I'm nearly there," I say breathlessly. This seems to spur him on even more. His lips crash onto mine and I moan into his mouth.

Whilst he continues to pound into me, he moves one of his hands and places his thumb on my clit. He then moves his thumb in small circles and I break our kiss to shout out his name again.

I can feel that he is getting close as his breathing has changed. I tighten all of my muscles, gripping around him to heighten our combined pleasure.

"Come now, Stacey," Jake says on a growl. I obey and let myself be taken into oblivion by him as he finds his release at the same time.

We both cry out until our orgasms are complete.

Jake collapses on top of me as we both try to regain our breath.

"I have been waiting for that for so long," Jake says, his face buried into my neck.

I lie there, feeling more than satisfied. I remember how he made me feel all those months ago when he was just some one-night stand, but those feelings are nothing compared to what I am experiencing right now.

This man is perfect.

Emotion threatens to overtake me as I try to divert my thoughts from how strongly I feel for him. This moment is one that I will never forget, and I will certainly accompany him to more events in the future if this is how they all end.

CHAPTER TWENTY-NINE

I wake up to find that I am alone in Jake's bed. I immediately sit up, covering myself with the duvet and strain my ears in order to hear any noises. I don't hear anything.

Shit, what have I done? Jake is obviously regretting what happened last night, otherwise he would be here. Oh no, Stacey, you bloody idiot. You were friends with him, but you couldn't just leave it at that, could you?

I am silently cursing myself at how stupid I have been to give into my feelings for him. I hang my head and wonder how on earth I am going to prepare myself for the rejection all over again.

Why did you have to cross the line and sleep with him?

Now I will have definitely lost him as a friend, as well as anything else.

As I am about to climb out of the bed, Jake walks into the room, whistling to himself. Oh my. He is standing there, holding a tray with what appears to be breakfast food, in just his boxers. My eyes drink in his magnificent form.

He smiles and walks over to the bed. "I have made some breakfast in the form of coffee and toast. I hope that this is to madam's satisfaction?" He's in a playful mood. Thank God for that.

"Well, one can't have smoked salmon every day," I tease back. We both laugh and relief rushes through me.

He's still here. He hasn't run off.

Jake places the tray at the end of the bed, then climbs in next to me, leans over and kisses me passionately. I return the kiss and feel my sex start to awaken. He slowly pulls back, breaking our connection too quickly for my liking.

"Good morning, Miss Paris."

"Good morning yourself."

"I think that breakfast can wait a while," he says, making me feel excited all over again.

He moves the breakfast tray from the bed and onto the floor. He then moves the duvet off of me and pulls me on top of him. He settles back on the bed, so that his back is leaning against the head board. I grin and move my lips, so they connect with his skin. I start by kissing down his neck, and I keep going until I am level with his boxers. I gesture for Jake to lift his ass so that I can remove them. He obliges, and I quickly get the material out of my way. Without any warning, I take him fully into my mouth.

"Holy shit," he says as he grips the headboard above him with both hands. I move up and down his length and swirl my tongue across the tip. Jake's moaning turns me on even more. I've never enjoyed this activity before, but now, I can't get enough. I grab his balls with my hand and gently massage, feeling his legs stiffen as I do.

"Fuck, Stace," is all I hear before I feel him release his load into my mouth. I drink every drop and then kiss my way back up his body. "Well," he says, a little out of breath. "That is something that I could wake up to every morning."

"Play your cards right, Jake, and it might just happen." I appear to have turned into a kinky bitch in the space of a few hours.

Jake flips me on my back, so that he is on top of me and enters me hard, without any warning. I let out a yelp at the sudden intrusion, but it is an intrusion that is most welcome. He pumps into me, bringing me to orgasm quickly, and he follows a few strokes later.

Jake climbs off of me and turns me, so that I am lying on my side, facing away from him. He then settles behind me and pulls me into his arms. I love the feel of him wrapped around me and I nuzzle into him as much as I possibly can.

"Mmm," he mumbles as he nibbles gently on my ear lobe. "Now that is a great start to the day."

I giggle, but it is brought to an abrupt halt by the realisation that we haven't used a condom.

Oh my God, how could I have been so careless? And how did I not realise this before now?

"Jake, we haven't used a condom," I say, panic evident in my voice.

"Are you on the pill?" Jake inquires.

"Well, yes but—"

"Then there's nothing to worry about. I had a health check just before I last slept with you, and I haven't been with anyone since. I'm all clean," Jake states confidently. *Phew, well, there's a relief.* "How about you?"

"I was checked after Charles and I split up. All clean."

"Well then, there really is nothing to worry about." I relax against his chest. It isn't exactly the most romantic conversation that I have ever had, but I feel better knowing that he has been checked out.

I feel so safe, here in his arms, and in his bed. This must be what heaven feels like. I am definitely floating on cloud nine this morning.

"Would you like some coffee now?" Jake asks me.

"Yes please."

Jake sits up, picks up the breakfast tray and places it on the bed. I make myself comfy by leaning against the head board, mirroring Jake's position. He hands me a cup of coffee and I gratefully take a sip. The coffee is just as delicious as I remember it, even if it is only lukewarm. Jake picks up a piece of cold toast and takes a bite. He screws his face up and puts the toast back on the plate.

"Ugh," he says as I laugh at him. He looks so cute with his face all screwed up. "I'm going to go and pick us up some proper breakfast. Would madam like to order anything in particular?"

"Surprise me."

"I thought you didn't like surprises?" He lifts one eyebrow in question.

"I don't as a rule. But your surprises have all been good so far, so I figure I can change my mind." Jake gives me a quick kiss and gets out of bed. He puts on a pair of jeans and a T-shirt but fails to put any boxers on.

"I won't be long. Don't move." He points his finger at me and I salute. I hear him leave the house a few moments later. I do move as I need to use the bathroom, and when I have finished, I return to the bed. I'm so happy right now.

I replay the events of last night when Jake's phone ringing breaks through my thoughts. He obviously forgot to take it with him. I reach for his phone, which is on the bedside table, and see that Caitlin is calling him. I put the phone back down in disgust.

Why is she still ringing him? Hasn't she gotten the message yet?

I decide to try and not let her get to me. I don't want anything or anyone to spoil this moment of happiness.

I lie down and doze until I hear Jake return. He runs into the bedroom a few moments later and launches himself onto the bed. I scream as I think that he is going to smash into me. He manages to miss, but he quickly crawls over me and pins me to the bed.

"Did you move?" he asks, playfully.

"Only to use the bathroom," I reply.

"Hmm, I'll let you off on that one. Breakfast time." Jake gets back off of the bed and goes to the bedroom door. I now see that he dropped a brown paper bag before launching himself at me. He comes back over and starts pulling food trays out of the bag. My stomach starts to grumble in anticipation of the great smelling food. I pick up one of the food trays and see that it is full of scrambled egg. I start to eat some, and Jake's phone starts to ring again. Jake picks it up, sighs and cuts the call off.

"You okay?" I ask him. I don't want to look like I am prying into his life. I want him to tell me because he wants to.

"Yeah. It's just Caitlin. She keeps bothering me." Good start, he has been honest with me. "She just doesn't want to leave me alone. I'm consulting a solicitor about her next week."

I stop eating the eggs and turn to look at him. "Seriously?"

"Yeah. This shit has been going on for too long. Caitlin needs help, but she won't listen. The only thing I can do now is take legal action."

Well, I wasn't expecting that answer, but I am pleased that he is going to be taking action to stop her from contacting him. I finish my eggs and eat a couple of strips of crispy bacon before admitting defeat over being able to eat anything else. Jake's phone rings another three times before he decides to switch it off. I can sense how irritated he is, so I suggest taking a shower to try to distract him. My idea works as he carries me to the ensuite and we re-explore each other's bodies in the giant walk-in shower.

CHAPTER THIRTY

"Fuck," is all I hear Jake say from the bedroom before I hear him run into the hallway and down the stairs. I am getting dried after a steamy shower, so I have no idea what Jake is swearing at. I stand there, stunned by his outburst. I don't have to put my dress back on from last night as I have found a pair of leggings that are mine from when I was staying here before. Luckily for me they were missed during the packing up of my belongings. I borrow one of Jake's shirts which is huge on me, and I button it up to just above my breasts. I run a hairbrush through my hair and go down the stairs to see what is wrong.

I get to the kitchen and can hear voices coming from outside. I walk to the huge patio doors, which look onto the garden, and see Caitlin.

Really? Does this girl have nothing better to do with her time?

I stop myself from walking outside, just in case Jake doesn't want me to interrupt their conversation and hide behind the curtain, so I can listen.

"Jake, why are you doing this to me? I need you. Can't you see that I need you? Is it that slut that you had here the other week? Is she the reason that we're not together? I'll take her out if you need me to?" *Oh fuck me, this girl really is a lunatic.* I stand frozen on the spot.

"You need to watch your mouth right now," Jake says, and he sounds mad. "Get the fuck off of my property, Caitlin. I don't want you here."

"Jake, we can work this out. Come on, we're good together." Caitlin is pleading, and it sounds desperate. I feel a little sad for her that her life has come to this.

"I'm going to see a solicitor next week to get you out of my life. You need help Caitlin. You're not well."

"No," I hear Caitlin start to sob. "Please, Jake, don't do this. I love you."

"Well, I don't love you. How many more times do I need to tell you that? You just refuse to listen to me. I have tried being nice about this, but you are leaving me no choice but to go down the legal route." I can hear him getting exasperated, so I decide to go and see if I can help.

This may be one of my stupidest ideas yet, but I feel I need to do something. My legs start to move, and I approach Jake and Caitlin with slight caution. Jake's eyes go wide when he sees me. Caitlin has her back to me, so she hasn't noticed me yet. I get up behind her and tap her on her shoulder. She whirls around, and her eyes narrow at the sight of me. Before she can say anything, and before I can lose my nerve, I start to speak.

"I have already called the police, so if you don't want to be arrested then I suggest that you leave. Right now." I wait for her to hurl abuse at me. The seconds tick by slowly, but she doesn't say anything. Instead, she turns around and walks away.

I watch as she gets to the back gate and slams it shut behind her. Well, that was far easier than I thought it would be. I was expecting her to have a full scale fit about me being here.

I look to Jake who is staring open mouthed at me. "You're welcome," I say as I head back inside, appearing far more confident than I feel.

"Are you insane?" Jake asks me as he follows behind me.

"No. I just thought that you needed a little bit of help to get rid of her."

"Oh, Stacey," Jake says, running his hands through his hair. "What have you done?"

"I've gotten rid of her, that's what I've done. You clearly weren't having any luck in doing so." I feel my defences start to kick in.

"She is messed up, and I don't want her anywhere near you." Jake walks to me and puts his arms around my waist. I put my hands on his shoulders and I place a light kiss on his lips.

"Stop worrying. She's gone. End of story."

"I don't want you caught up in this." He sounds genuinely worried.

"The sooner you see your solicitor, the better it will be."

"Yeah, I know. I'm going to call him and move the appointment up to tomorrow. I also need to get some security installed here."

"What, like cameras?"

"Yes, babe, cameras. And whatever else I think I might need." Jake smiles at me and I melt against his body. "Fancy going out for some dinner?" He changes the topic and I am grateful to not have to discuss Caitlin anymore.

"Sure, but I can't wear your shirt out."

"I think you look sexy in my shirt. Makes me feel like you're mine," Jake growls.

"Yours? I'm not your property, Mr Waters."

"I know that, but it feels like you belong to me. Like we were meant to be together." Jake kisses me roughly and I lose myself in his embrace. I can feel his hard length through his jeans. *How the hell can he be ready to go again?* I pull back and look at him questioningly.

"Seriously? Again?" I ask. Jake gives me a cocky grin.

"You know, we haven't christened the kitchen yet," Jake says in his seductive tone.

He picks me up and places me on the kitchen island, so that I am sitting on the edge. "Now, you were saying something about not being able to wear this shirt. How about we remedy that and get rid of it?" Jake doesn't wait for my answer. He doesn't even undo the buttons. He just rips the shirt open, causing me to gasp in shock.

He pulls the shirt off of my arms and caresses my breasts. I lean into his touch and close my eyes. His touch feels so good. His lips cover mine, and his tongue delves into my mouth. I can't help but let out a small moan.

Jake lifts me up slightly, and I make quick work of pulling my leggings below my ass. Jake pulls back from me and removes my leggings completely. He looks a bit shocked as he realises that I'm not wearing any knickers. He gives me a lop-sided smile and I feel my cheeks blush.

"Very sexy," he says as he manoeuvres me so that I am lying flat on the kitchen island. The cold surface makes me draw in a breath and goose-bumps cover my body.

Jake moves his head between my legs and lets his tongue sweep over my highly sensitive clit. He moves his tongue in circles and my hands reach down to caress the back of his head. I can't get enough of him. I whimper as I feel myself approaching climax. I moan his name softly and he applies more pressure with his tongue, taking me closer to my undoing. Just as I am building to my climax, Jake pulls away and quickly undoes his jeans, freeing his erection. He pushes into me and places one thumb on my clit. I am quickly transported to another world as his punishing rhythm makes me start to tremble.

The shudders rack my body as I build back up to my release. I can hear Jake's breathing change to signal that he is close to finding his peak. I cry out as I feel myself free falling through my orgasm. Jake reaches his seconds later and I feel his juices pump into me. Jake slowly brings us down from our climaxes and I lie there, once again in a state of complete bliss.

He pulls out of me and pulls his jeans up but leaves them undone. I lazily sit up on the counter and retrieve his shirt to put on. Even though the buttons are broken, I can still wrap it around me.

"At this rate, we're never going to make it to dinner," I say. Jake pulls me off of the island and I wrap my legs around him as he carries me up to the bedroom and heads for his ensuite.

"Another shower?" he asks me.

"If you insist."

CHAPTER THIRTY-ONE

I finally make it back to Lydia's at six o'clock. I am exhausted as I climb the stairs, but my time spent with Jake was worth every second.

I open the front door, which is on the latch, and Jake follows behind me. Lydia comes marching into the hallway.

"Where the bloody hell have you been?" She glares at me. "I have been trying to get hold of you all bloody day."

"Sorry, Lyd. I left my phone here, remember?" I feel like I am about to be told off by a parent with the look she is giving me.

"You could have called me from another phone, you know?" She folds her arms across her chest and starts to tap her foot.

"I've, uh, been a little preoccupied."

"Too preoccupied to use a phone?"

"Uh..." I'm not quite sure what to say to her. I'm not used to Lydia reprimanding me for not phoning her. Lydia looks from me to Jake and her lips start to twitch.

"Oh, I see. You two finally came to your senses and got it on then?" She smirks, and I feel my cheeks flush. I hear Jake chuckle as I mentally scold my best friend for being so out spoken.

"Uh, you could say that. Anyway, I've just come to get changed and then we're heading out to dinner," I tell her. I turn and grab Jake's hand and I pull him into my bedroom. I shut the door behind me so that we can have a bit of privacy from Lydia's intense gaze. "I'm sorry about that. Lydia can be a bit—"

"Forward." Jake finishes my sentence for me.

"Yeah, you could say that." I grab some clean clothes and tell Jake that I am nipping to the bathroom to freshen up. I tell him to help himself to a drink if he wants one and I go to the bathroom.

I have a quick wash and I put on my skinny jeans and a hot pink sleeveless shirt. I quickly run a brush through my hair and brush my teeth. I apply minimal make-up and then go back to my bedroom. Jake isn't in here, so I presume he decided to get a drink. I take a quick look at my phone to see if I have any messages. I have missed calls from Lydia, and a message from Charles. I inwardly groan as I open the message to read it.

> *Stacey, I can't believe that you are friends with that man. He will hurt you. I know that he will. You have no idea who you have gotten yourself involved with. All I ask is that you keep your mouth shut about my personal business.*
> *Charles.*

I scoff at his message. He has got a bloody nerve. Charles obviously still thinks that he has the right to tell me what to do. I put my phone, purse and keys in my little black handbag, put my back sandals on, and I go to find Jake. He is sat at the kitchen table with Lydia. Oh God, I dread to think what kind of questions she has been asking him.

"Hey, are you ready to go to dinner?" I ask him.

"Sure. You look lovely," Jake replies.

"Thanks." I tell Lydia that I will be back at the flat after dinner. I grab my flat key on the way out and we walk to Jake's car. "So, where are we going to eat?" I ask as I climb into the passenger seat of Jake's BMW X5.

"I thought that we could go to a little American diner that I know of. It's nothing fancy, but the food is delicious."

"Sounds good to me." I'm not one for posh restaurants anyway. I like to feel comfortable, not judged by other diners. I am so hungry though that I don't think I would care if it was just a portion of chips from the local chippy. After all of the sex today, I completely forgot about eating anything after breakfast. Although Jake mentioned going to get food earlier, we got a bit carried away, and food was the last thing on either of our minds.

We arrive at the diner and wait to be seated. The waitress soon comes over and leads us to a booth at the rear of the diner. The smells all around me make my stomach grumble. I peruse the menu and decide to order a bowl of chilli with cheese fries. I figure that with all the working out Jake and I have done today, I can afford to eat the calories.

The waitress comes back to our table and takes our order. Jake orders a foot-long hot dog and fries. I only order a diet coke to drink as I want to keep a clear head. I want to remember everything about this day and drinking alcohol may distort my view of it. Jake and I chat about nothing in particular until the waitress has returned with our drinks. When she leaves, the conversation turns more serious.

"So," Jake says. "What are your plans for next weekend?"

"No idea. I need to go to The Den tomorrow and see what shifts Lydia has put me down for. I can't really plan anything until I have done that. Why?" I ask curiously.

"I thought that we could go away for the weekend. Somewhere where we won't be interrupted." Jake raises his eyebrows and I instantly know what he is getting at.

"Oh," is all I can say. *He wants to take me away?* This reaction to us hooking up is so different to what happened the other week. I am thrown by his suggestion and I don't really know what to say to him.

Jake starts to look a little worried when I don't say anything else. Our food arrives, letting me ponder his suggestion for a little bit longer. "Listen, Jake, what happened between us last night and today has been wonderful, but don't you think that it might be rushing things by going away together? I mean, it was only a short while ago that you told me that you only wanted to be friends." I hope he understands why I have some reservations about the idea.

"I get that, but I wasn't in the right head space then."

"It wasn't that long ago, Jake, and you seem to have done a complete one eighty on me. It's a pretty quick turnaround." I say as I pop a cheese fry in my mouth.

"I know what it must look like to you, but I was scared before. My feelings were so strong that I didn't know how to act around you." Jake grabs my hand across the table and penetrates me with his gaze. "I know that I hurt you before, and I can't apologise enough for that. I just... I've never felt this way before. I was trying to fight it because we haven't known each other that long, but I can't. I don't want to fight it.

"This is all new to me, Stace, but I love the way that you make me feel. I love the way that we are when we are together. I just want to prove to you that I mean every word that I say."

Wow. I am speechless. He feels as strongly as I do by the sounds of it.

"I don't want to come across as being too pushy, but why wait? Why should we take things slow? At the risk of sounding even more soppy, I feel like we were meant to find each other, Stace."

Fuck me. I am blown away by his honesty and I feel tears prick the backs of my eyes. I always thought that 'love at first sight' was a load of rubbish, but the way I feel about Jake has shown me that the saying can be true. I clear my throat and give him a smile.

"Let me see what shifts I am working and then we can see if we can plan something," I reply. Jake smiles and it makes my heart melt a little.

"Great. Now, eat up, you're going to need to keep your strength up." I feel my sex clench and a shiver runs up and down my spine. I have a feeling that I will be having trouble walking tomorrow if we keep this up.

The rest of the meal goes smoothly, and the conversation is so easy and comfortable. I could literally talk to Jake about anything. I don't feel that he is going to judge me in the slightest. We wrap up our meal and I decline the offer of a pudding. I am way too full after eating most of my chilli and cheese fries. Jake refuses to let me pay anything for the meal. I try to argue with him, but his stern glare soon makes me give up trying.

When he has paid, we leave the diner and Jake takes my hand as we walk back to his car. I have never felt so content with a man before. As we approach Jake's car, a flash of blond hair catches my eye across the road. I stop walking and scan the other side of the road. There is nothing. No one in sight. *That's weird. I could have sworn that someone was there.*

I feel a chill go through me as my mind once again tries to convince me that it was Caitlin. I feel Jake tugging on my hand and I look up at him. I force a smile on my face as I don't want Jake to think that I am going mad.

"What's wrong?" he asks me.

"Nothing."

"Really? Then why do you look like you have just seen a ghost?" I rack my brains for an excuse as to why I'm being so paranoid.

"It's nothing, honestly. I just feel really tired all of a sudden."

"Tired, huh?" Jake doesn't believe me, but I don't want to give him cause to worry.

"It's hardly surprising really is it?"

"Hmm." Jake takes me into his arms and places a light kiss on my lips. "Well, if that's all it is then we better get you back home." I kiss him again and then we resume walking to his car.

Jake opens the passenger door for me and I slide in, grateful for the safety of the car. I look back to where I thought I saw Caitlin, but again there is no one there.

I need to get a grip.

Jake climbs into the driver's seat and we are soon on the way to the flat. I remain quiet on the drive back, my mind in overdrive. When we pull up to the flat, Jake exits the car and comes around to let me out of the passenger side.

"Why thank you, kind sir," I tease, hoping to make up for my skittish behaviour just moments ago.

"No problem." Jake pulls me into his embrace.

"I've had a great time, Jake." I reach up and lightly kiss him on the lips.

"Me too. And don't forget to let me know what shifts you are working next weekend."

"I won't." I don't want to leave him, but I have to go and get some much-needed rest. I also have to answer the many questions that Lydia will be asking me when I step through the front door. "Goodnight, Jake."

"Night, babe." Jake gives me a slow, lingering kiss, making me want to do all sorts of things to him. I push the thoughts to the back of my mind, assuring myself that there will be another time to fulfil what I have in mind. I moan as Jake brings the kiss to an end. I smile at him and then break away from his embrace and head towards the flat. I practically run up the stairs and reach the flat in record time. I unlock the front door and walk in.

"Lyd, are you here?" I call out.

"In the lounge, babes," she answers. I close the front door and walk to the lounge. I am pleased to see that Lydia is on her own, meaning that I won't have to answer any questions in front of anyone else. "So, are you going to fill me in now?" I'm not even sat down and she's already waiting for the details.

"Are you sure that you want to hear this now?" I tease. "I mean, it's getting late and you do have work tomorrow."

"Oh no you don't. I have been waiting for you to get back so that you can tell me what the hell is going on. Now, spill, Paris." I laugh at her. Sometimes it's fun to wind her up a little.

I settle myself into the chair and I tell Lydia most of what has happened so far. She gasps in various places, and I know that she is loving this. I don't go into too much detail about the sex. I want to keep some things to myself. I also leave out the part about Caitlin. I don't want Lydia to think that I am being a paranoid mess.

"It sounds like by Charles being an asshole, it gave Jake the push that he needed," Lydia ponders.

"Hmm, maybe. I don't really care what pushed him though, I have had the best sex ever, so I'm not complaining." I can't stop the smile from creeping across my face as I think back to each and every sexual encounter between Jake and I over the last twenty-four hours.

"Oh, you dirty bitch," Lydia jokes. "On a more serious note though, I'm happy for you, Stace. It's about time that you had some fun."

"I think so too. Anyway, I am absolutely exhausted, I need to go and get some sleep." I stand up and go to give Lydia a hug goodnight. I use the bathroom and then go to my bedroom. I get into my comfy pyjamas and get myself into bed.

I lie awake for a while and just replay things from the last few days in my head. I never thought that I would ever be this happy. There is only one niggle in the back of my mind, and that is Caitlin. I am positive that she was there tonight. I can't shake off the feeling that she is doing this to mess with my head. She could potentially make things very difficult for Jake and me.

I just hope that we are strong enough not to let her come between us.

CHAPTER THIRTY-TWO

My alarm goes off at eight, and I get up, showered and dressed, and see that Lydia has already made a pot of coffee which is sitting on the kitchen table. There is no sign of Lydia though. I pour myself a drink as she comes waltzing into the kitchen.

"Morning, babes," she chirps at me.

"Morning, Lyd. You're cheerful this morning. Care to share?" Lydia normally hates early mornings, so I know that something has cheered her up.

"Paul's taking me to lunch today." She beams at me.

"Things are going good with you two, aren't they?"

"They really are. I can't believe how well though. I keep waiting for something to go wrong, but in the meantime, I figure I should just enjoy myself."

"Oh, Lydia, don't be so cynical. I think Paul really likes you, and you guys are good together." I wish that she wouldn't be so down on her self-worth. I'm also shocked as she has never been so nervous around another guy.

"I could say the same for you and Jake," Lydia replies. I just grin at her.

I finish my cup of coffee and then we both head off to go to The Den. When we get there, we enter through the back door. Lydia locks it behind us as there will be no one else in here until later on tonight. Lydia just needs to print off the rota and put it on the notice board for the staff to see. I only accompanied her so that I could see my shifts. I need to let Jake know about the weekend as soon as possible.

"Bugger," I say to myself as I see that I am working Friday and Saturday night next week.

"What's wrong?" Lydia asks in the background.

"Oh, I just, uh, broke a finger nail," I lie. I don't want to sound ungrateful and start moaning to her about what I am working. She was good enough to re-employ me, so the least I can do is work the shifts that she has given me. Lydia doesn't seem to catch on to my big fat lie. I take my phone out of my pocket and send a text to Jake.

> *Morning, handsome, I'm afraid that I am working Friday and Saturday night next week. Maybe we can take a rein check on going away?*
> *Stace x*

Within seconds my phone buzzes to notify me that Jake has replied.

> *Hmm, is there no way that you can switch your shifts?*
> *Jake x*

I sigh and text back my response.

> *I would rather not, seeing as I have only just started working here again. I'm sorry. We can go another time.*
> *Stace x*

I don't get a reply which makes me inwardly panic that I have pissed Jake off. I say my goodbyes to Lydia and leave her at The Den to get on with some paperwork before she meets Paul.

I decide to go to Danish and treat myself to one of their caramel latte's. I arrive there, but I can't sit in my usual seat as it is already occupied. The woman occupying the table has her back to me. Whoever she is she has long blond hair which makes my hackles rise. As she turns around, she confirms what I already know. It's Caitlin.

Shit, what is she doing here? I've never seen her in here before.

I now know that I haven't been imagining seeing her in different places. Caitlin has been following Jake and me. I quickly change my order to a take away latte, I don't want to sit in here and drink it now.

As soon as my latte is ready, I pay the money and then get the hell out of there. I feel a bit pissed off that due to Caitlin being there I feel that I have to leave. I turn in the direction of the flat and start walking. I get only a few paces ahead when I hear my name.

"Stacey Paris." I turn around and see that Caitlin is marching towards me. I roll my eyes and think of how to get out of this situation, and fast.

Bollocks, I really don't need this kind of hassle.

"So, I finally got you on your own. You tend to hide behind other people," she says as she stops in front of me. I straighten my stance and kick into defence mode.

"I haven't been hiding behind anyone," I reply in a firm tone.

What is this woman on about? She is nuts.

She starts to laugh, and I begin to feel uneasy.

"You should be hiding." She narrows her eyes at me as she speaks. I don't want to show any fear at her words, but I'm sure the whole street can hear the pounding of my heart.

"What do you want, Caitlin?" I am proud of how even I manage to make my voice sound. The last thing that I want to do is let her see that, physically, she is scaring me.

"I want you to leave Jake alone." This time it appears that it's my turn to laugh at her ridiculous request.

"He doesn't want you, Caitlin. What part of that don't you understand?"

"That's only because you're hanging around. Do yourself a favour and tell him that you are no longer interested in him, before things get really nasty." With that she grins wickedly, turns on her heel and marches off in the opposite direction.

I watch until she goes out of sight. I feel so shaken and I need to get somewhere safe. I manage to turn and power-walk back to the flat. I keep checking behind me to make sure that she isn't following me.

I reach the flat block and run up the stairs to the front door, unlocking it and slamming it shut behind me, making sure it is locked. I walk on shaky legs to the lounge and sit down on the sofa. I put the latte that I am still carrying, but have no desire to drink anymore, on the coffee table. I try to calm my racing heart and regulate my breathing whilst telling myself over and over again that she is just trying to scare me into leaving Jake alone. Well, she succeeded in the scaring me part, not so much in the leaving Jake alone though.

I pull my phone out of my bag and send Jake a message. I think he ought to know what just happened.

> *Hi, Jake. I don't mean to bother you, but I just had a bit of a run in with Caitlin. She told me to stay away from you. She seriously needs help. Call me when you're free. Stacey x*

I put my phone down on the coffee table and just stare at the blank television screen. It takes me a little while to completely calm down, but once I do, I switch the television on and settle myself back on the sofa. I have no plans for tonight, which isn't a bad thing. I think I would be a bit jumpy if I had to go out anywhere.

I flick through the television channels and try to find something decent to watch when a knock at the door interrupts me. I feel cautious as I go to answer it, but then I reprimand myself for being so silly. I shouldn't feel afraid to open my own front door. I think that I would feel better about things if I had spoken to Jake, but he still hasn't responded to my message. Whoever is on the other side of the door knocks again.

I take a deep breath, unlock the door and open it to see who it is. I am greeted by the sight of Jake in all his handsome beauty. A feeling of relief rushes through me, and before I know what is happening, Jake has taken me in his arms and is hugging me tightly.

"I just got your message. I'm sorry I didn't see it sooner, I've been stuck in meetings since this morning. Are you okay?" Jake says as he continues to keep me close to his body.

"Yeah, I'm fine. You don't need to worry about me." I try to appear calm about the situation. I breath in his scent as I nuzzle close.

"Of course I'm worried. Where the hell did she see you anyway?"

"I went to The Den with Lydia, which you already know about, and after that I went to Danish to get a drink. She was sitting at my usual table when I got there. I suspected it was her, but it wasn't until she turned around that I knew for sure. Anyway, when I saw it was her, I left." I pull back from Jake so that I can close the front door. I don't need any of the neighbours hearing about my life. I lock the door again, even though Jake is here. It just makes me feel a little better to have it locked. "When I left, she came after me to confront me about you. Basically she told me to leave you alone, and if I didn't, then things would get really nasty." Jake's face goes a little pale.

"Christ, Stace. That's it, you're coming to stay with me. I want to make sure that she can't get to you again." I laugh at him, thinking that he may be overreacting slightly. Jake doesn't join in with my laughter. He looks deadly serious.

"Jake, I'm not going anywhere. I live here and I'm not going to let some jealous ex of yours force me out of my home. She's just making idle threats because she wants you back." I don't know who I am trying to convince more, Jake or myself.

"Well, if you're not going to come to mine then I'm staying here the night," Jake says.

"Are you now?" I raise my eyebrows at him teasingly.

"That's not going to be a problem is it, Miss Paris?" Jake asks as he closes the gap between us.

Before I can answer he pushes me against the door and kisses me. My knees weaken, and I give myself to him. I have missed his lips all day, so I intend to savour the feel of them. Jake pulls me away from the door whilst keeping his lips connected to mine and carries me to my bedroom. Shutting the door behind us, he throws me onto the bed and I squeal as he pounces over me.

"I just want to keep you safe." My heart melts and I place a finger to his lips so that he stays quiet.

"I don't want to talk about that now. I just want you. All of you, inside me." I don't want to think about anything other than what we are about to do to one another.

Jake growls with appreciation. We both take our clothes off as quickly as possible and he slowly enters me.

We only manage to make love once before I fall asleep in his warm and safe embrace.

CHAPTER THIRTY-THREE

I wake up to the feel of Jake's lips on my neck. I smile and turn so that I am facing him.

"Hey, babe," he says in the sexiest voice.

"Hey, yourself." I give him a gentle kiss on the lips. "What time is it?"

"It's six o'clock in the morning."

"What?" I have been asleep since we had sex yesterday. "I've been asleep for ages."

"You obviously needed the rest."

"Did you stay here the whole time?" I ask him.

"Yeah. I didn't want to disturb you by moving." He is so sweet. I sit up and stretch my arms.

"I can't believe that I was out for so long." I yawn and get out of the bed. I need to pee, so I tell Jake that I am going to use the bathroom. I walk into the hallway after using the bathroom, and I can hear whispers coming from Lydia's bedroom, which means that she has company with her. I'm guessing that her lunch date yesterday with Paul went well. I smile and go back to my bedroom to see that Jake is putting his clothes on.

"What are you doing?" I ask him.

"I'm getting dressed, obviously," Jake says, smirking at me.

"Very funny. What I mean is, why are you getting dressed so early?" I already feel like I miss him, and he hasn't gone yet. The feelings I am having are crazy. I have never had to deal with such strong emotions before.

"I have to go back to mine and pick up some notes for a meeting that I have this morning. I wish that I didn't have to go, but I'm meeting with my solicitor."

"About Caitlin?" I ask, hopeful that he is going to see what route he can go down to keep her away.

"Yes."

"Well then, you need to get going. The sooner the situation with her is dealt with, the better it will be for both of us."

"I know. I don't want you to worry whilst I'm gone. I would take you with me, but you don't need to hear the details of what I need to say." Jake looks a bit worried by telling me this.

Ugh, if he's talking about how he used her for sex then no, I would rather remain oblivious than hear all the details.

"That's fine. I'm just going to chill here until I go to work later. I won't be leaving the flat until then." I'm hoping this information will put his mind at rest about the possibility of another run in with Caitlin.

"I will send Eric to pick you up and take you. No arguments." I sense from his tone that even if I try to argue I wouldn't win, so I just walk over to him and hug him.

"Okay." To be honest, it feels nice that he is looking out for me. I haven't felt this cared for in a long time. Jake kisses the tip of my nose.

"If I finish up with work on time then I will come over to The Den later."

"I will look forward to it." I take Jake's hand and lead him to the front door.

"Any signs of trouble and you are to contact me straight away."

"Mmm. I like this macho side of you, Mr Waters," I purr at him.

"You keep talking in that sexy voice and I won't make my meeting." I grin and bat Jake away, opening the front door for him.

"Go," I order him as I point out of the front door. Jake just looks at me and smirks. "Jake Waters, will you get your butt out of here, so you can make your meeting."

"I quite like this dominant side of you," he replies. I roll my eyes and chuckle as I kiss him goodbye.

"Good luck."

"Bye, babe." My heart does a little flutter and I close the door as Jake disappears down the stairs. I lock the door and go back to my bedroom. I put on some clean clothes and turn my laptop on. It's about time that I did some more writing.

Whilst I am waiting for the laptop to load, I go and make a pot of coffee and take it to my room with me. I settle on my bed and put my headphones in, so that I am not disturbed by any noises that Lydia and her guest may want to make.

I break for some lunch at one o'clock. Lydia is yet to emerge from her bedroom as far as I am aware. When I took my headphones out, I heard someone leave the flat, but I don't know if Lydia left with them. She usually tells me if she is going out, so I presume that she is still in bed. Before going to make myself a sandwich, I go to Lydia's bedroom. I knock on her bedroom door, but she doesn't call me in.

"Lyd?" I say loudly, so that if she in there she can hear me. There is no answer, but I can hear someone in there. Concerned, I open the door slightly and peak round. Lydia comes into view and she is on her own. She's on the bed, sobbing. I push the door open and walk over to her.

"Lyd, whatever is the matter?" I say as I take a seat by her on the bed. My cheerful mood is suddenly plighted by the sight of my best friend crying.

"Oh, Stace, I've been so bloody stupid," she blubbers at me. Lydia doesn't cry very often, so I know that something bad has happened.

"Well, why don't you tell me what's bothering you? It may make you feel better to talk about whatever it is?" I try to sooth her.

"Promise you won't judge me?" she says.

"Hey, I'm your best friend. Of course I won't judge you."

"Okay." Lydia takes a deep breath and then slowly breathes it out. "Paul and I got into a fight last night. We were at The Den and he didn't like the fact that some guy was trying to chat me up. I was working, so I could hardly tell the guy to go and fuck himself, could I? Plus, it's part of the job sometimes. I didn't feel that he was over-stepping any boundaries, so I wasn't really bothered by it.

"Anyway, this led to us arguing and Paul stormed out. I was so mad at him that when my shift ended, I started drinking with the guy that was trying to chat me up." A new wave of tears pours from her eyes, stopping her from continuing to speak. I let her regain some composure and then I gently prompt her to continue. "I can't even remember the guy's name, Stace. I was so drunk. All I remember is that he walked me home, and then one thing led to another, and..." Lydia can't seem to finish her sentence, and it dawns on me that Lydia slept with this guy, whoever he is.

"You had sex with him, didn't you?" I ask her. I already know the answer, but a part of me needs her to confirm it. Lydia just nods her head at me and then hangs it in shame. "Oh, Lyd."

I pull her into a hug as I try to comfort her without words. Nothing I say would be able to ease the guilt that she is obviously feeling right now.

"I'm so stupid. I was just so mad at Paul, and this guy was giving me attention. I don't know what to do, Stace. Do I tell Paul?" She pleads with me to give her the answers that she desperately needs, but I can't.

"That's up to you, Lyd. I can't decide that for you. You need to do whatever feels right for you." It's the only advice that I can give her. I feel my heart break for my best friend. I hope that if she decides to tell Paul then he can find it in himself to forgive her. "I'm going to go and get us some nibbles and then we can just laze around all afternoon watching movies. How does that sound?"

"Sounds good." Lydia sniffles into her pillow. I leave her to go and look in the kitchen to see what we have in the cupboards. I am disappointed to see that we don't have anything decent at all. Great, now I am going to have to go out when I promised Jake that I wouldn't. The shop is only five minutes away, if I run then I can be back here in no time. It is pointless taking my car as there is no parking by the shop.

With my best friend needing me to be there for her, I put on my trainers, grab my purse and keys, and leave the flat. I run all the way there and am gasping for breath by the time I enter the shop. My heart is racing as adrenaline spikes through me.

I pick up a basket and quickly go down the relevant aisles for the things that I need to buy. Crisps, chocolate, popcorn and diet coke. I decide against a bottle of wine. I don't really think getting drunk is the best idea under the circumstances. I also pick up a couple of pizzas for later on. I promptly head to the till and pay for my items.

I scurry out of the shop with my bags and run as fast as I can back to the flat. I have my keys ready as I reach the front door. *See, nothing to worry about, Stacey. No sign that Caitlin is following you.*

I enter the flat and lock the door behind me before taking the bags of food to the kitchen and unpacking them. I put the pizzas in the fridge and take everything else into the lounge with me. I call to Lydia to get her butt to the lounge. She walks in a few seconds later and is still crying. I point to the sofa where she flops down and curls into a ball. I go and grab her duvet and bring it into the lounge for us to snuggle under.

I decide to put on an action movie rather than a romantic chick flick. With the current state of Lydia, I don't think she needs to see happy couples on the screen, even if it isn't real life. I get settled beside Lydia, flick the television on and we stay like that for the next couple of hours as Lydia tries to come to terms with what she has done.

CHAPTER THIRTY-FOUR

Eric picks me up at half past six to take me to work. Lydia is asleep on the sofa when I leave. I am worried about her, but I feel that I should look after things at The Den so that she has one less thing to worry about at the moment. She should have been at work with me tonight, but I told her that Susie and I would manage. It's a Tuesday night and they are not generally too busy. I arrive at The Den and exit the limo.

"Thanks for the ride, Eric," I say as he stands by the limo, holding the door for me.

"No problem, Miss Stacey. I will be waiting out here for you when you finish your shift."

"There really is no need. It will be late and I'm sure you need to be getting home." I don't want to put Eric out any more than I have already.

"I insist," he says firmly. I think it is a bit unfair of Jake to ask him to pick me up, but I know that he won't disobey Jake's orders.

"Fine. I finish at eleven-thirty."

"I will be waiting outside, Miss Paris." Eric goes around the car and back to the driver's side. He is about to get in when I stop him.

"Hey, Eric?" I say.

"Yes?"

"When you speak to Mr Waters, tell him to give you a pay rise," I tease. Eric laughs and waves at me as I turn to walk into The Den. As I walk into the main room, I can see that there are only a couple of tables occupied. I wave to Susie who is behind the bar already, and I go to Lydia's office to put my handbag safe. As I enter her office, my mobile phone starts to ring. I take it out of my pocket and see that it is Jake calling me. A smile instantly emerges on my face.

"Well hello, handsome," I purr down the phone.

"What the hell do you think you are playing at?" Jake says in a pissed off tone.

"I beg your pardon?" My tone changes from playful to defensive.

"You told me that you wouldn't leave the flat today, so I will repeat my question. What the hell do you think you are playing at?" He sounds so mad.

"Jake, calm down. I only went out for a few minutes. Lydia was really upset, so I went to pick up a few bits and bobs to try and cheer her up. The shop wasn't far, and I ran there and back. Nothing happened, I am fine. It's all okay." I try to soothe him with my words.

"I don't give a fuck if you think that it is okay. Don't you understand that Caitlin is a psycho? You need to keep yourself safe, Stacey. Why didn't you just order some food in?" My words have had no effect on him whatsoever. Bugger.

"I don't particularly like your tone of voice, Jake. My best friend needed me, and I was helping her. God knows she has helped me enough times. If you want to be childish about this, then you carry on. I don't have time to listen to you have a tantrum. I have to go. I need to start work." With that I hang up the phone.

Who the fuck does he think he is talking to me like that? How dare he! I am so pissed off with him. I put my phone in my handbag and leave it on Lydia's desk.

I exit her office and go behind the bar to start serving some customers. I need to take my mind off of the conversation I have just had with Jake.

The first hour goes slowly, but as soon as eighty-thirty hits the place is packed. I had completely forgotten that there was some sort of student celebration going on tonight. It is just Susie and I and we are overwhelmed with all of the customers. I quickly try to call some of the other staff, but there is no response from any of them.

What the bloody hell am I meant to do? I can't call in any agency staff as I don't have the relevant details to hand, and I certainly can't go to Lydia's office and leave Susie on her own whilst I look for them. Susie and I try to work as quick as we can, so that we can keep all the customers happy.

Everything seems to be going okay until a group of four lads decide to try and cause trouble. They start shouting about the slow service and I can feel my anger rising. They just so happen to be at my end of the bar as well. Bloody typical. I listen to their taunts for another five minutes, and then I decide that I have had enough. I march over to them and look at each of them in turn. They must only be eighteen, and they clearly can't handle their drink. I politely ask them to calm down or they will be removed from the premises. It appears though that my words have no effect on them. If anything, it seems to spur them on to act like even bigger assholes.

One of the lads decides to try and act like a hero and lets himself behind the bar. He starts trying to pull his own pint and I look to see if security has noticed. They haven't. Looks like it's going to be up to me to do something for the time being.

"What the hell do you think you are doing?" I ask the young lad.

"Getting myself a fucking drink." He is slurring and has obviously had far too much alcohol already.

"Get back on the other side of the bar, now," I say in a slightly raised voice.

"What, so you can make us wait even longer? No chance, love." That's it. I've had enough. I grab the pint glass out of his hand and throw the drink that he has managed to pour all over him. "HEY! Why the fuck did you do that?" he asks, looking a little shocked. His mates are all laughing in the background.

"Get out from behind my bar, NOW," I shout. I hear Susie radio through to security, who still haven't noticed, and within seconds the young lad is removed from the bar. "Take his friends too," I tell security. They march the group of lads out and I continue to serve the other customers. Some of the customers waiting, who were near the group of guys, start to clap. I am shaking from the adrenaline rush of confronting the pissed-up youngster.

Who the hell do some of these guys think that they are? I don't have much time to reflect on it though as it is just too busy. The rest of my shift flies by, but thankfully goes more smoothly. Susie and I don't get a chance to take a break, so by the time we finish at eleven-thirty, we are both knackered.

"I'm sorry it was just the two of us tonight, Susie." I feel bad that I couldn't manage to get anyone else to come in to help.

"No worries. It's all over now. Although, I am glad that I'm not in tomorrow. I am exhausted."

"Yeah, me too." We walk out of The Den and I see Jake's limo parked right out the front. I give Susie a hug goodbye and tell her to enjoy her day off tomorrow.

Eric is standing by the limo with the door open for me.

"Miss Stacey." He nods as I get into the car. I just wave at him as I am too tired to speak. I sit down and squeal as I see that Jake is sat on the opposite side to me.

"Jeez, Jake, you nearly gave me a heart attack," I say to him. His face does not look amused.

"So, are we going to talk about earlier?" Jake gets straight to the point.

"Jake, I'm really tired and there is nothing more I can say to you." I sigh.

"I don't think that you are taking this situation with Caitlin seriously."

"Oh, I am," I snap. "I just don't see why I should have to be cooped up when you're the one who fucked her and made her paranoid." I am tired, and what I have just said has come out wrong. I didn't mean to sound so harsh.

"So, that's how you really feel, huh? You think that I made her crazy?" Jake's eyes pierce into mine.

"No, I didn't mean it like that. I just meant that I am not staying under lock and key because of her. I can handle her, Jake. I managed to survive the last run in with her. I don't want to live in fear." I try to reason with him, but it doesn't seem to be working.

"I don't want you under lock and key, Stacey, I just want you safe, and until she has been dealt with, you are not. You are at risk."

"She wants you, Jake, not me."

"Exactly. She wants me, and she will do whatever it takes to get me. The quickest way to get to me is to eliminate you." I can't quite process what he is telling me. It all sounds like too much. *Eliminate me?* I can feel a headache coming on and all I want to do is go home to bed.

"Jake, can we discuss this tomorrow? Talking about this subject when I'm tired really isn't the best time." I lay my head back against the seat and close my eyes.

"If you would just come and stay with me then I wouldn't need to worry about you quite so much." I open my eyes and look at him. He is looking out of the window, so I ease myself off of the seat and go and sit in his lap. I place my hand on his face and turn his head so that he is looking at me.

"Jake, I know that this must be difficult for you. I know that she is trying to hound every aspect of your life, but I can't come and stay with you. We have only just started seeing each other seriously and look what happened the last time that I stayed at yours." Jake goes to speak, but I silence him by placing my finger over his mouth. "Even if that wasn't enough of a reason, I need to be there for Lydia right now. She's having a hard time at the moment and I need to stay with her." My finger is still on his mouth and he opens his lips and sucks my finger, all the while looking into my eyes. My body shudders as I feel my sexual awareness heighten. I pull my finger out and place my lips on his. I kiss him softly and run my hands through his hair. His hands are wrapped around my waist. We are locked together like this until we pull to a stop outside the flat.

"I just… I don't want anything to happen to you," Jake whispers to me, breaking our kiss. I lean my forehead against his.

"Nothing is going to happen to me. I would invite you in to stay, but I don't think that Lydia needs to see a happy couple right now. I will call you tomorrow morning."

"You better, the minute you wake up." I giggle as Jake nibbles my ear lobe. I slowly move myself off of him as the limo door opens, meaning that Eric is stood waiting. I step out of the limo and Jake follows me. "I'm walking you to your front door."

"Don't be ridiculous. I will be fine."

"I'm walking you to the door, end of." I roll my eyes at him and say goodbye to Eric as we walk to the flat. We reach the front door and I turn to give Jake a hug. He squeezes me and kisses my forehead. "What's wrong with Lydia anyway?" he enquires.

"Women's troubles." I am not telling Jake anything. Paul doesn't even know what has happened, and I don't want him to find out from Jake.

"Say no more," Jake says. He releases me, and I unlock the front door. A thought suddenly occurs to me and I turn back around so that I am facing Jake.

"How did you know that I had gone to the shop earlier?" I ask. I am interested to know the answer.

"Eric was driving in the neighbourhood and he saw you."

"And why was Eric in the neighbourhood?" I think that I already know the answer, but I would like to hear what response he is going to give.

"He was just passing through." Jake shrugs his shoulders.

"Uh huh." I know that Eric wasn't just merely 'passing through,' but I don't want to argue about it tonight. I will tackle the subject another time. "Goodnight, handsome."

"Night, babe." He stays where he is until I have closed the front door. I really wish that he could have stayed here. I could do with releasing some sexual tension. I sigh.

Never mind, there is always tomorrow.

CHAPTER THIRTY-FIVE

I wake up at ten o'clock the following morning. I stretch out in bed before grabbing my phone off of the bedside table. I have one text message from Martin.

Hey, girlfriend! I haven't seen you in forever!
Let's hook up for coffee ASAP! Much love,
Martin xxx.

I love Martin. He's an awesome person with such an infectious nature. I quickly text back that I can meet him in an hour at Danish. I feel really bad that I have neglected mine and Martin's friendship for a while. Martin is easy going, so I am hoping that he will understand why my mind has been so preoccupied, once I fill him in on all the details of what's been going on.

I go and check on Lydia before I get dressed. She is asleep in bed, so I don't disturb her. I heard her crying at some point during the night, so I figure that she must be exhausted. I go back to my bedroom, put some clothes on, and I leave a note for Lydia on the kitchen table. I let her know where I am going, and if she needs me to come back then I have my phone with me.

I put my essentials in my handbag and leave the flat. I decide to phone Jake on my way to meet Martin. He answers after a couple of rings.

"Good morning, gorgeous," he says. His voice is so sexy.

"Morning, handsome." My face breaks out into a smile and I can feel a slight blush creeping across my cheeks. "How are you on this fine morning?"

"I'm great. You?"

"I'm fantastic. I'm just letting you know that I am on my way to meet a friend for coffee."

"You're what?" His voice rises a couple of notches. "Please tell me that you called Eric and asked him to take you?" I can hear the strain in his voice and I feel a little bad that I am making him worry like this.

"Uh... No."

"Stacey, why do you not listen to me?" Frustration creeps into his tone and I imagine him sat at his desk, well, some kind of desk seeing as I have no clue what his personal office actually looks like, rubbing his temples to try to soothe some stress.

"Jake, calm down." I need to get him to understand that I need normality in my life. I don't want to abide by Caitlin's crazy rules. "I am talking to you on the phone, and I will be at the coffee shop in two minutes. Please don't be mad at me. I don't want to argue with you," I say. I hear Jake let out a sigh. "I will make it up to you later."

"Oh yeah? And just how are you going to do that?" he enquires.

"You'll see. I would divulge the details, but I wouldn't want you getting all hot and bothered whilst you are at work." I love teasing him. "I've got to go, babe, I'm at the coffee shop and my friend is waiting. Talk to you later."

"Okay. But promise me that you will call Eric the minute that you need to go home," he insists. I choose to appease him on this matter seeing as he has probably, very nearly, had a heart attack over me walking on my own for a few minutes.

"Yes, I will call Eric. Bye, handsome." I hang up the phone and am enveloped in Martin's arms.

"Baby girl, it's so good to see you," Martin says as he squeezes me tight.

"You too stranger."

"And whose fault is that?" Martin releases me and raises his eyebrows at me.

"Okay, okay. I've been a bad friend, but just you wait until you hear why."

"I'm all ears, baby doll. Why are we still standing out here? Let's get inside, get some coffee, and get gossiping." I laugh and lead the way into Danish.

My usual table is free, so we sit there and then order some drinks. It is nice and quiet in here, and there is no sign of a certain blond-haired psycho. I relax and start to tell an excited Martin all about my life over the last couple of weeks. It takes me a couple of hours to tell him everything. We get through three coffee's and a couple of calorie-induced slices of cake. I don't hear anything from Lydia, so I assume that she must still be resting. I don't text her as I don't want to disturb her when she needs her sleep. I don't tell Martin about Lydia. It's not my place to tell anyone about what she is going through.

When Martin is satisfied that he has been updated sufficiently on my life, we leave Danish and head to the nearest clothes shop. I need to purchase some sexy office attire in order to surprise Jake. Martin helps me find exactly what I need and makes me try it on, so that he can see the full effect.

"Hot damn, girl, he is going to be blown away when he sees you in this get up. Hell, if I were straight, I would do you." I giggle and smack Martin playfully on the arm.

"You're terrible."

"I just tell it like it is." Martin is always straight to the point and I love that about him.

I get changed back into my original clothes and go to pay for the items that I am purchasing. When we exit the shop, I call Eric and ask him to collect me. I have sneakily called Jake's office to make sure that he has a free appointment this afternoon. Luckily for me he did. I then secured an appointment with him under the name of Miss Green. I only have a thirty-minute slot as Jake has other meetings to attend, and I am hoping that my visit to his office will be very memorable for the both of us.

Eric pulls up outside the clothes shop a few minutes after I have called him. Jake must have given him a clue as to where I was for him to arrive this quickly.

"Well, this is my ride," I say to Martin as I point at the limo. His jaw drops open.

"You are so taking me in that one day," Martin says. I laugh and give him a hug goodbye.

"I promise I won't leave it so long for us to catch up next time."

"You better not." Martin winks at me and I disappear into the limo.

"Hi, Eric," I say as I sit back in the seat.

"Miss Stacey." Eric nods. "Back to your flat?" he asks me.

"Actually, no. I need you to take me to Jake's offices, but it has to be a secret. I have a little surprise for him." I put on as much charm as possible and I see Eric smirking in the rear-view mirror.

"What's the surprise?" Eric asks.

"Um..." I feel my cheeks go red. I don't want to divulge my plans to Eric. I avoid eye contact with him and start to squirm in my seat, when Eric starts to laugh.

"It's okay, Miss Stacey. From the look on your face, I'm guessing that whatever you are planning is for Jake and Jake only."

"Exactly," I reply. "Do you mind if I put the partition up? I... I need to get changed." I feel embarrassed at having to ask.

"Sure." As I press the button for the partition to close, I see that Eric is still smiling. I feel a little uncomfortable that I have to get changed with Eric driving, but the partition is completely blacked out, so there is no chance that he will see anything. I don't think he would look anyway to be honest. He seems like an old-fashioned gentleman, and I get the impression that he is just happy to see Jake happy. Or that's what I like to think anyway.

I quickly pull the clothes that I have bought out of the shopping bags, and I start to get changed. I have to say though that putting on a skin-tight pencil skirt in a car is quite challenging. The skirt has a slit up the back which stops just below my ass. I put on stockings and suspenders and a tight-fitting white shirt. I finish the look off with a tight blazer, red lipstick, and I put my hair up into a high ponytail.

As I am putting on the black stilettos that I purchased, we pull up outside Jake's offices. I quickly put on the long coat that I bought in order to hide my outfit from anyone else's eyes. I would be mortified if anyone other than Jake got a look at my outfit. Eric opens the limo door for me and I thank him. I go to pick up the bags with my original clothes in, but Eric stops me.

"It's okay, Miss Stacey. You can leave that in here."

"Oh, okay. Thank you." I smile and give Eric a wave as I head inside the office building. Walking through the lobby, I get a few appreciative looks off of some men, but I ignore them and walk to the lifts. I select the relevant floor for Jake's office and am relieved that I am alone in the lift to go over my plan.

The doors ping open moments later and I step out. To the left is a desk with an older lady sat behind it. She looks up at me and smiles. She introduces herself as Valerie and asks me if she can help. I inform her that I have an appointment under the name of Miss Green, which she checks on her computer. She then gestures for me to take a seat in the waiting area which is a cosy collection of plush chairs just outside of Jake's office. I hear her telephone through to Jake, and then she is telling me to go on through. I nod, take a deep breath, and I walk to the doors of his office, opening them and walking in.

Jake doesn't look up, so I close the door behind me and lock it. His head snaps up at the sound of the lock.

"Good afternoon, Mr Waters," I say, putting on the sexiest voice that I possibly can. My hands start to undo the long coat that I am wearing, and Jake's eyes go wide as I let the coat drop to the floor. I walk forward, slowly, until I reach the front of his desk. I want to laugh at the fact that his mouth has dropped open slightly, but I manage to suppress it. He eventually clears his throat and manages to speak.

"Please take a seat, Miss *Green*." He motions for me to sit in the chair which is just behind me.

"Why thank you." I sit down, cross my legs and provocatively sit back in the chair. Jake smirks.

"Would you like a drink?"

"I don't have time for a drink, I'm afraid. I am a very busy woman and I have other things that I need to attend to."

"Is that so?" He raises one eyebrow at me.

"It is indeed. So, shall I get to the point of why I asked for this meeting?"

"Please do," Jake says, never taking his eyes off of mine. He then sits back in his chair and awaits my answer.

"Well, I was hoping that you would provide me with a service that is going to satisfy my needs," I purr at him. Where this inner vixen is coming from I have no idea, but it is doing exactly what I want it to. Jake's eyes look hungry. Hungry for me. I resist the urge to do a little jig in excitement.

"I'm sure that we could come to some sort of arrangement. What did you have in mind?" Jake asks, licking his lips.

I slowly stand up and walk over to a sofa that is to the right of his desk. The sofa is plush, as is everything else that Jake owns.

"I think that we should get a bit more comfortable over here, don't you?" I say as I sit down and pat the sofa next to me. Jake stands and starts to stalk his way over to me. My heart does a little flutter at the mere sight of him. His stance is dominating, and it is such a turn on.

I take off my blazer and throw it on the floor. My hands then start to undo the buttons on my shirt, and I let out a low groan as Jake gets closer. I bite my lip in anticipation of his hands touching me.

Jake takes off his suit jacket and then, before I know what is happening, he pounces on me. I squeal in delight and relish the feel of his hard body on top of mine. His lips devour me, and I run my hands through his hair. Jake kisses me passionately, and it is as if no one else exists. Jake pulls back from me slightly as we both try to catch our breath.

"I must say, Miss Green, I think this meeting is going extremely well." I don't get a chance to answer as Jake's lips find mine again.

Who knew that a bit of role play could be so much fun?

CHAPTER THIRTY-SIX

The next few days pass by in a blur and before I know it, it is Saturday. I have spent most of my time covering shifts for Lydia as she is still not in a good way. I have told her to speak to Paul, but she just says that she can't do it. She seems to think that avoiding him is the best answer. All I can do is be there for her and support her as best as I can. Working the extra hours hasn't been too bad seeing as Jake had to out of town to attend to some urgent business two days ago. I have missed seeing him, but he is due back tomorrow evening and I can't wait.

I have spoken to him on the phone, but it's not the same as having him here in person. I miss everything about him. His touch, his smell, his eyes, his laugh. I find myself daydreaming about him during every spare moment I get. Things have progressed between us so quickly, in such a short amount of time. Every fibre of my being craves him.

I know that I am in love with Jake. I haven't told him that yet as I don't want to get ahead of myself, but I do. If things don't work out with us, I know that I am going to be left heartbroken.

Before Jake left, he made me promise that I would call Eric if I needed to go anywhere. I don't like bothering Eric, but I also need to keep Jake from worrying about me whilst he is away. The sooner Caitlin leaves us alone, the better. I haven't seen any trace of her for a few days now. Maybe she has finally seen that she isn't going to get her own way? I am sure that some other woman would have run a mile when Caitlin threatened them, but not me. I don't see why she should be able to dictate who Jake has in his life. And she sure as hell doesn't get a say in who I choose to be with.

My shift at The Den tonight starts at five o'clock. I am starting earlier than normal due to needing to do some of Lydia's paperwork for her. It's a good job that not much has changed since I worked at The Den the first time, meaning that I understand what paperwork needs to be filled in and filed.

I make myself a cup of coffee and also make one for Lydia. I take it through to her bedroom and leave it on the bedside table for her. She is asleep which is all that she seems to be doing lately. I quietly leave the room, go back to the kitchen to get my coffee, and then I set up camp in the lounge with my laptop. I have the urge to do some more writing. I just want to finish the first draft so that I can then start editing my novel. I am so pleased with what I have written so far.

I settle down and begin to type. The day flies by as I do nothing but write and drink coffee. Lydia doesn't emerge from her room at all. Nothing distracts me all day, and by four o'clock I have to force myself to stop writing, save my work, and turn off my laptop so that I can get ready for work. I put my laptop back in my bedroom and then go and take a quick shower.

I have forty-five minutes until Eric will be here to pick me up. I dry myself and dress in my usual skinny jeans which I team with a black vest top, black cardigan, and black sandals. I have come to realise that flats are the best type of shoes to wear for work, especially with all the extra hours that I have been doing. Plus, there is less risk of me falling on my ass whilst carrying a tray of glasses.

I tie my hair back into a loose ponytail, apply some mascara and lip gloss, and then I am ready to go. Lydia still hasn't come out of her room, so I poke my head around the door to see if she is still asleep. She's awake but is just staring blankly at the television in the corner of her room.

"I'm going to work now, Lyd," I say. Lydia just waves her hand, not even moving her head to look at me. I close the door and let out a soft sigh. I need to get her out of this funk that she is in. I also need to get her to leave the flat before she develops some kind of cabin fever. I hate seeing her so upset, even if it is for something that she has brought on herself.

I grab my keys and handbag and head out of the front door. Eric is waiting outside for me, just as I knew that he would be. It has to be said that Eric is extremely punctual. I wouldn't be surprised if he had been waiting here for a while beforehand.

"Good evening, Eric." I smile at him in greeting.

"Miss Stacey." His usual greeting to me is paired with a nod of his head.

I enter the limo and sink into the luxurious seats for the short ride to The Den. I am the first one to arrive as the rest of the staff won't be in until six. We would normally be open all day today, but due to staff shortages I had to put a sign up saying that we were closed for a couple of hours this afternoon. I could have used agency staff, but they aren't that great and there wouldn't have been any regular staff to come in and do the shift with them. I hope that I made the right choice.

Eric says that he will be waiting for me when my shift finishes at two in the morning as I exit the limo. I politely thank him and unlock the front door of The Den so that I can go inside. I lock the door behind me as I will be in the office, and I won't be able to hear if anyone comes in. Plus, I don't fancy the idea of random customers coming in here when I am on my own.

I pour myself a glass of diet coke and walk into Lydia's office so that I can get started. It takes me half an hour to go over the rota for the following week. I pencil Lydia in, but I have managed to sort the shifts so that if she is still unable to work then I can fill in whilst also leaving myself a break in-between shifts. I print off the rota and stick it onto the staff notice board which is just by Lydia's office door.

As I am tidying up the desk, there is a knock on the office door. I freeze. My mind races as to who could be knocking on the door. Also, more importantly, it has to be someone else who has a set of keys.

Who the hell could it be?

I stand, looking at the door, trying to decide what to do. I become fidgety and very aware that I could be in danger.

Shit, what should I do?

I grab my phone and type out a quick message to Lydia.

> *Lyd, just remind me, does anyone else have keys to The Den? xx*

I get a short reply back a few seconds later.

> *Only the owner, but he never comes down. Why? xxx*

I fire off a quick reply, telling her not to worry as I try to calm my nerves.

Maybe it is the owner? But if it is, then why would he knock on the door?

Whoever is on the other side knocks again, making me jump. I need to remain calm. Everything is going to be fine.

I slowly walk over to the door and place my hand on the door handle. It feels like my heart is going to burst out of my chest. I close my eyes and take a couple of deep breaths.

I open my eyes at the same time as I open the door, and the sight before me is not one that I am pleased to see. It's Caitlin.

Fuck. What is she doing here? More importantly, how did she get in here in the first place?

I stand as confidently as I can and straighten my back. Her eyes glare at me, but I will not look away. I am a strong woman and I need to show her that I mean business. She looks awful. Her blond hair is all in disarray, and her eyes look wild. She is dressed in jogging bottoms, a T-shirt and trainers. It's almost as if she has given up on taking care of herself.

I wonder if she is high?

"What are you doing here, Caitlin?" I sound a hell of a lot more confident than I feel.

"I thought that we should have another little chat." She walks towards me and brushes me out of the way, so that she can enter the office. I stumble slightly, but I soon regain my balance. I am a little taken aback by her brazen manner, but I shouldn't be. She has so far proved that she doesn't care how her actions are perceived.

She takes a seat on the small sofa and crosses her legs. She really does think that she is something special. I would love to give her a slap and wipe that evil grin off of her face. I make myself move, and I sit on Lydia's office chair, behind her desk.

I need to act as casual as possible, so I lean back in the chair and wait to see how this scenario is going to play out. When a few minutes' pass by and Caitlin still hasn't said anything, I decide to get the ball rolling.

"So, what is it that we need to talk about, Caitlin? And you had better make it quick as I have staff arriving soon."

"Well, considering what I said to you the last time we spoke has had no influence on your decisions whatsoever, I thought that I should make my intentions much clearer." She leans forward, but keeps her legs crossed.

"What do you mean by that?" I ask her, urging her to get to the point. I want to get her out of here as quickly as possible.

"When I told you to stay away from Jake, I thought that I had made myself clear, but it turns out that I didn't do a very good job of showing just how serious I was about it. So, I am here to reiterate that message." I can't help but roll my eyes at her.

"Listen, Caitlin, I have had enough of this. I understood you perfectly the last time, I just chose to ignore your empty threat. You have absolutely no right to dictate what Jake and I do. You two are finished. You really need to accept that in order to move on with your life." She doesn't move a muscle.

"I understand that he hurt you and he is sorry that he ever did that. I can't begin to imagine what you are going through. I am not a horrible person, Caitlin, and I do have compassion for you, but the time has come for you to take a good look at yourself. You need to move on, Caitlin, and start living your life." I sound so calm and collected. I mentally clap for myself as I realise that I could be handling this situation completely differently.

"You don't understand anything," Caitlin screams at me. "You have no idea what Jake and I have been through. You don't understand anything. *You* are the reason that we aren't together, which means that I need to remove you from this situation."

Fuck, calm Stacey is no more. Remove? What is she talking about?

My heart starts to pump faster, and I can feel adrenaline surge through me.

"What do you mean by, 'I need to be removed?'" I manage to keep my voice steady as I speak. Caitlin's lips turn up into a smirk, and she lowers her eyes. I follow where she has lowered her eyes to. Her hand reaches inside the pocket of her jogging bottoms, and she pulls out a knife.

Holy shit! I need to get the hell out of here!

"Caitlin, what the fuck are you doing with that?" I ask as I point a shaky finger at the knife that is clutched in her hand.

"I thought that this may be a little bit more persuasive than just words." I lower my hand and try to rack my brains for a way to diffuse this situation. I pray to God that the bar staff show up early. "It certainly seems to be having the desired effect."

Caitlin gets up off of the sofa and stalks towards the desk. I push myself back on the chair until I hit the wall. I don't move that far back as the office isn't very big. Caitlin stands in front of the desk, so there is still a barrier between us.

Oh God, I need to keep her talking. Just until someone else arrives, and then I can alert them to what is happening.

"Caitlin, I think you need to put the knife away. We can just talk about things. I will listen this time. Just put the knife away before things get out of hand," I say in a shaky voice. I can no longer hide my fear from her. She is a crazy bitch and I curse myself silently for getting involved in the issues that she has with Jake. She doesn't move. She just stands there with the knife in front of her, and her eyes are glaring at me. "Caitlin... Please? You need to think this through."

"Oh, I have thought it through. I have thought about how nothing would satisfy me more than ruining that pretty little face of yours." I gulp loudly at Caitlin's words. "Maybe if you didn't look like that, then Jake would come back to me."

I can feel myself start to sweat. I look to the door and then back at Caitlin. I can't get out of here unless I run right past her.

Fuck, fuck, fuck.

I try to calm my breathing, and I can feel the blood pounding in my ears. I can't even phone anybody because, like an idiot, I left my phone on the bloody desk when Caitlin got up and walked over. If I try to grab it then she will be able to reach me.

Before I have time to think about anything else, Caitlin lunges over the desk. I let out a loud shriek and force my legs to make me move from the chair. Caitlin has obviously misjudged my position as she lands on the floor, just to the left of my chair.

As she makes contact with the floor, I run.

If the situation wasn't so scary, I think that I would be laughing at her attempt to lunge over the desk. As she is sprawled on the floor, I realise that this is my chance.

This is my chance to escape.

I run around the desk as fast as I can, and head for the door. I just think that I am about to make it safely out of the door, when Caitlin grabs my foot. I yell and fall to the ground, smacking my head on the floor in the process. I block out the pain from hitting my head and I furiously kick at Caitlin. She manages to dodge each kick, but I don't stop. She still has a knife in her hand, and there is a chance that I will kick her and put a stop to her psychotic plan.

I don't want to know what the end game is, but I have a fairly good idea of what she may have planned to do. I need to get away from her. I need to get her off of me.

I try to struggle but she still has a vice like grip on my foot. I am screaming to alert anybody to my whereabouts.

Why has no one else arrived here yet? Surely someone should be here by now?

As I try to scramble away, I hear Caitlin let out an evil cackle. I feel her release my foot and I am about to get up when I feel a sharp, piercing pain in my side.

Ouch, that fucking hurts.

I continue to scream as tears spring to my eyes.

I can still hear Caitlin laughing in the background.

Things start to go hazy and I stop screaming. I don't have the energy to keep screaming.

I groggily lift my head and look down my body to see the knife stuck in my side. Caitlin's hand is clasped firmly around the handle. My eyes shift to Caitlin, and all I see is her laughing like a deranged psycho.

It feels like I am led here for hours, but in reality, it must only be a few seconds.

Time has seemed to slow down in my foggy state.

Images start to flicker through my mind as I start to lose consciousness.

I hear footsteps and see that two figures have entered the room. They are soon lifting Caitlin off of me. *Maybe I am hallucinating?* I don't take any notice of who the figures are until I hear one of them shout.

"NOOO."

It's Jake. It's his voice.

I try my hardest to speak to him, but I can't. My mouth won't work. I can feel myself losing the fight to stay awake. The darkness is calling to me, and it seems so inviting.

My eyes are fluttering as I feel myself being pulled into someone's arms. I try to open my eyelids, but it's no good. I am far too sleepy. The darkness looks too good to resist.

As I give into the urge to go to sleep, I hear Jake speak.

"Stacey, baby, open your eyes. Please."

I can hear him pleading with me, but no matter how hard I try, I can't open my eyes. I can still hear Caitlin's laugh echoing in the distance, and I want nothing more than for that noise to disappear.

As her laughing eventually fades away, I hear Jake speak one last time.

"I love you," are the last words that I hear before the darkness engulfs me.

PERFECT MEMORIES

CHAPTER ONE

JAKE

The last twenty-four hours of my life have been like I am living in a nightmare.

Except that, it's not a nightmare.

What has happened is all too real.

I have been sat in this hospital since last night. The night when the psychotic Caitlin, stabbed my current girlfriend, Stacey. Now, Stacey lies in a hospital bed, hooked up to all sorts of machines. Her skin is pale, her hair is messy, and her features are tired looking. But, to me, she is still the most beautiful woman that I have ever seen.

She is in here because of me. Because of my past.

The guilt that I am feeling is indescribable. If I had just left 'us' as a one-night-stand all those months ago, then she wouldn't be in this hospital bed and she wouldn't be fighting for her life. If I had stayed away from her, then she would have been safe. Safe from Caitlin, and safe from me.

I have been selfish by bringing her into my world and involving her in my past. I will make Caitlin pay for this. She will pay dearly. I will make sure she gets sent to prison for a long time, even if it's the last thing that I do.

No one hurts Stacey.

She is just an innocent victim in all of this.

I stare at her lifeless form on the bed and I realise how crazy it is that I have fallen for this woman so hard, and so fast. She was made for me. Everything about her compliments me. Everything about her is perfect. Perfect for me. That is why I couldn't stay away from her. If only I had had the fortune of meeting her years ago, then none of this would have happened.

As I sit by her hospital bed, I gently hold her hand in mine. She has such soft skin and delicate, petite hands. As I turn her hand over and stroke her palm, I find myself talking to her.

"Stacey, I know that you can hear me. I am so sorry for what has happened. It's all my fault. I will make this up to you. I will spend the rest of my life making it up to you."

I drop my head onto the bed and squeeze my eyes shut. I will not show that I am weak by crying right now. I will not let the tears and the anger take over.

I need to remain strong.

I take a few deep breaths and lift my head back up to look at her. She had to go into surgery as soon as the ambulance got here. Her operation went well, and luckily, Caitlin failed to hit any vital organs when she stabbed her. The image of Stacey's blood on the floor, and Caitlin leant over her, laughing like a maniac, is something that I will never be able to erase from my mind. I thought that Stacey was dead as I took her in my arms and her body went limp. I cradled her until the ambulance arrived. I told her that I loved her for the first time. I don't know if she heard me, but I can only hope that she did. She needed to know. *I* needed her to know how I felt about her. It wasn't how I had imagined telling her, but then I never imagined that Caitlin would actually stab her either.

I knew Caitlin was unhinged, but I suppose I didn't really think that she would hurt anyone physically, other than me. I know that I tried to keep Stacey safe by having Eric take her places, but that was only to keep her away from Caitlin's nasty mouth. Stacey didn't need to hear any more details of what Caitlin did to me. I dread to think of what the ending would have been if I hadn't come back from my business trip early.

How long would Stacey have been left bleeding to death?

Would Caitlin have stabbed her again?

Would Caitlin have been caught?

The thoughts make me shudder. What a bloody fool I have been.

The door to Stacey's private room opens, interrupting my dark thoughts. Eric walks in and closes the door behind him.

"How's she doing, boss?" Eric asks. Concern is etched all over his face. Eric stayed here all night with me.

"Still the same. Her vitals are good though, so I am told. It's just a case of waiting for her to wake up."

She has to wake up.

I can't bear the thought of losing her.

"Why don't you go and take a walk and get yourself a coffee. I will stay with Stacey."

"I don't want to leave her," I snap at Eric. I have known Eric for a long time, and he has been my confidant for the last eight years. He is one of the few people that I trust. I know that he is trying to help, but I feel irritated by the fact that he is suggesting that I leave this room.

"Look, Jake, I can only imagine what you must be feeling right now, but you need to get out of this room. Get your ass up and go and get a coffee and maybe something to eat. You have been in here since Stacey came out of the operating theatre. Go and stretch your legs and clear your head." Eric doesn't often take a stern tone with me, but on this occasion, he does. I scoff and turn to look at him.

"Are you ordering me around?" *Who does he think he is?*

"Damn right I am." Eric stands there with his hands in his trouser pockets, looking defiant. A part of me wants to challenge him, but I know that he is right. I need to take a few moments to try and gather my thoughts. And I really could do with a coffee. I sigh and reluctantly stand up, but before I leave, I bend down and place a gentle kiss on Stacey's cheek.

"If anything happens—"

"Then I will phone you." Eric finishes my sentence for me.

I head to the door and mumble a thank you as I leave. The walk down to the cafeteria seems to take forever. My mind is scrambled. So many questions are circling around my head, and I have no answers to any of them. It's so fucking frustrating.

I wait in a queue to order my coffee, and I ignore the idea of eating any food. I think that if I were to put any food in my mouth, then I would throw it back up again.

When it is finally my turn to order, I ask for a triple shot americano. I need a good hit of caffeine in my system. I wait whilst the barista seems to take hours making the damn coffee.

Surely it doesn't take this long? Maybe the barista is new and needs better bloody training?

I feel my phone start to vibrate in my pocket and I pull it out to see that Eric is calling me. Panic and fear grip me at his name displayed on the screen. I answer the call and my heart is going crazy as adrenaline spikes through me at whatever news he may have.

"Eric?" I say, my tone impatient.

"Get back here now." The urgency in his voice has me bolting out of the cafeteria without my coffee. I hear the barista calling after me, but I couldn't give a fuck about my drink right now. I knew that I shouldn't have left Stacey's room.

Why do I seem to keep making bad choices?

I sprint to the lifts, but of course, every single fucking one of them is either full or it's on its way up to the top of the hospital.

"Bollocks." I can't wait for one to come back down, so instead, I head for the stairs and I start to sprint up the ten flights, so that I can get to Stacey's room.

CHAPTER TWO

STACEY

The fog is starting to lift.

I can hear a tapping noise. The sound is unbearable.

My head is pounding. My eyes remain closed. Trying to open them is too much effort. My eyelids are far too heavy.

I want to move, but it is like my body is paralysed.

I have no idea what is going on and I start to feel panicky.

Why won't my eyes open?

Why won't my head stop throbbing?

What is that tapping noise?

What the hell is going on?

Am I dead?

The questions stop as the fog starts to come down again, and I feel myself drifting off into the darkness, to the sounds of machines beeping…

JAKE

I finally reach floor ten and I race to Stacey's room.

I run like I have never run before.

My heart is pounding, and my mouth is dry.

I reach the door to her hospital room and swing it open. Eric is stood by the back wall with wide eyes. There are two nurses and a doctor hovering over Stacey.

"What's happened?" I demand.

The doctor and nurses ignore me as they carry on with whatever they are doing. Eric places his hand on my arm and moves me, so that I am standing by him, against the back wall. I watch helplessly as the doctor and nurses continue their work.

"Eric," I whisper, trying to remain as calm as possible. "What the fuck happened?"

"I don't know, Jake. One minute she was fine, and then the next, the machines started beeping and the doctor and nurses came in. They ushered me out of the way, and they haven't said a word to me since."

I grit my teeth at his words. If he hadn't sent me away, then I would have been in here with her. I would have been able to see what happened with my own eyes.

I take a few deep breaths to calm myself and I focus my attention on the doctor. I watch and wait, for what feels like forever, for the hospital staff to finish what they are doing. I can feel the tension radiating from my body, and my hands ball into fists at my sides.

Eventually, the doctor dismisses the nurses and turns to face me.

"Mr Waters?" he asks.

I step forward. "Yes?"

"Miss Paris is fine now, but her body went into shock. This is not uncommon in patients that have had a head trauma. I have completed the necessary checks and I am confident that Stacey will wake up soon. It's still just a case of waiting at the moment."

At the doctor's words, I let out the breath that I have been holding.

"So, she will be okay?" I ask, desperately hoping for the answer to be yes.

"I can't guarantee anything, Mr Waters. Head injuries can be complex, but her progress is good. I have no reason to think that Miss Paris won't make a full recovery. But, like I said, I can't guarantee it." The doctor doesn't seem to be too worried which eases my tension, slightly.

"Thank you, doctor."

"I will be back in an hour to do another check." With that, the doctor leaves the room.

I go to Stacey's side, and I resume my place in the chair, beside her bed.

"She's a tough cookie, Jake. She will pull through this," Eric says. I feel anger rise within me at the sound of his voice.

"Why did you make me leave the room? I should have been here with her." My voice is louder than I intend it to be. I can hear the venom in my tone, and I don't like that Eric is the one I am using it on. This isn't his fault, I know that, but I need to take out my frustrations on someone. Apart from Stacey, he is the closest person to me.

"You needed a break. It is unfortunate that something happened whilst you were gone. Don't take this out on me, Jake. This is down to Caitlin and, partly, you."

I turn to Eric, my eyes wide. I can't believe that he has just said that. I know that it's true but hearing it from someone else just shows what everyone will think.

What if Stacey thinks that too? What if she wants nothing more to do with me?

"Don't you think that I already fucking know that?" I rise from the chair and go to stand in front of Eric. He doesn't move. "I know that it is my fault that Stacey is in this mess. I don't need reminding of that fact." I feel sick. "Just get the hell out of here."

I can no longer contain my rage at hearing his words.

I have never fallen out with Eric, and he has always been there for me. But, right now, I don't want him here.

"Don't be stupid, Jake." There is a warning tone in his voice. I am going too far, but I still can't stop.

"Fuck off, Eric." My voice is menacing. Eric shakes his head, and just when I think that he is about to leave, a voice breaks the tension between us.

"Stop shouting. My head hurts."

Eric and I both turn and look at Stacey. Her eyes are open.

Her eyes are fucking open.

She's awake.

Her eyes roam around the room and then they settle and focus on me. I walk to her side and I hear Eric say that he will go and get the doctor.

I stare at her.

Shock renders me speechless.

I must be day-dreaming?

I close my eyes and re-open them to see that she is still staring at me.

A small smile forms on my lips.

She really is awake.

CHAPTER THREE

STACEY

What is going on?
   Who is this man in my room?
   Where the hell am I?

I stare at the man who is stood by my bed. Even in my lethargic state, I can see that he is incredibly handsome. His jet-black hair, chiselled features, and those gorgeous coloured eyes are stunning. He is just staring at me. His eyes are glistening, and his smile is infectious. He takes my hand in his, and his warmth radiates into me.

"Who are you?" I manage to ask him, even though my voice is croaky. My throat feels so dry and I desperately need a drink. His smile instantly fades, and he looks devastated.

What did I say that was so wrong?

I feel a frown form on my face from the confusion that I am feeling. He seems to be struggling for words as his mouth opens and then closes again.

I am about to speak again, when the door to my room opens, stopping me from saying anything. I see a doctor walk in, followed by the older guy who was in here a few minutes ago.

"Ah, Miss Paris, you are back with us. That's fantastic. I am Doctor Reynolds, and I have been treating you whilst you have been in here." Doctor Reynolds stands at the end of my bed, picks up a clipboard, and starts flipping through some of the pages attached to it. "If you don't mind, I just need to do some checks as a formality."

"Uh, sure. Can I have a drink of water first? My mouth is so dry." Doctor

Reynolds nods, and the guy with the gorgeous coloured eyes quickly pours me some water and brings the plastic cup to my lips.

I don't look at him as I drink. I can't bear to see the devastation on his face.

I wonder what's wrong with him?

I lay my head back down on the pillow to indicate that I have finished drinking. I still keep my eyes averted as I thank him for the drink.

Doctor Reynolds begins whatever checks he needs to do, and I realise how uncomfortable I feel with these two strange men watching me.

"Um, Doctor Reynolds?" I say, getting the doctor's attention. "I don't mean to be rude, but could this be done in private? Without an audience?" The doctor looks at me and then looks at Jake with a puzzled expression on his face.

"You don't want them in here with you?" he asks.

"No. Thank you." I keep my reply short and my eyes fixed on the doctor. He looks to the two men and politely asks them if they could wait outside. I can feel the younger guy staring at me, but I still don't look at him.

Doctor Reynolds repeats his request for them to leave. A few seconds later, I hear the sound of the door opening and then the sound of it closing, and I let out the breath that I have been holding.

"Can I just ask why you didn't want them in here with you?" Doctor Reynolds asks me.

"Why would I want two men that I don't even know, gawping at me? Are they trainee doctors or something?" I figure that this could be possible for the younger guy, but the older one I'm not so sure about.

Doctor Reynolds stares at me and I feel like I am asking the wrong questions somehow. He then shines a torch in each of my eyes and starts to ask me a series of questions.

"What's your full name?" he asks.

"Stacey Marie Paris."

"How old are you?"

"Twenty-Eight."

"What's your birth date?"

"September the ninth, nineteen-ninety."

These are pretty straight forward questions. Would he not already have this information on the clipboard?

"Where do you live?"

"Copperfield Drive."

Doctor Reynolds flips to a second page on my chart and studies it. "Well, you got them all correct, except for the last one. You do not live at Copperfield Drive."

"Of course I do. Where else would I be living?" There must be some mistake with my paperwork.

"Miss Paris, you live at Mason Terrace." I remain quiet and wonder why on earth the doctor is saying that I live at Mason Terrace.

"That can't be right, doctor. That is where my friend Lydia lives. I live at Copperfield Drive. I live there with my boyfriend, Charles."

Doctor Reynolds looks uncertain and he excuses himself from the room. "I will be back in a few moments. I just need to check something."

He disappears out of the door and shuts it behind him.

I lie there, trying to work out why my notes would say that I live at Lydia's. My head is pounding, and I can't think straight. I lift my arms to rub my temples and I feel a sharp pain go through my side.

Ouch. What the hell is that?

I lower the blanket that is covering my body, and I lift up my nightdress. On my side is a big white dressing.

What the bloody hell is that doing there?

What has been going on?

I rack my brains, trying to think about what might have happened to me, but I am at a loss.

The last memory that I have is of Charles and I going to a function at the Bowden Hall. I close my eyes and picture us driving up to the magnificent building. I can see myself getting out of the car, and then it all just goes blank. I lie there, puzzled.

What the hell is wrong with me? And where the hell is Charles? Why isn't he here with me? Maybe he is getting a drink? Yes, that must be it. He wouldn't leave me in here on my own. He will be able to explain all of this to me.

I feel a slight bit of relief at this thought.

However, until Charles decides to make an appearance, I am still none the wiser.

I feel my breathing start to quicken, so I take some deep breaths to try and regulate it. As I stare at the wall in front of me, I feel despondent. Almost as if I don't belong.

I can hear the mumbling of voices outside my door, and I wonder if the doctor is talking to the two strange men that were in here when I woke up. I listen for a few more minutes, but I can't make out any words, and my eyelids start to feel heavy. With nothing in the room to keep me distracted, I close my eyes, and I slowly feel myself start to drift off to sleep.

CHAPTER FOUR

STACEY

When I open my eyes, there is no doctor in the room. There is however, the guy with the beautiful eyes.

He is sat in the chair next to my bed. He is staring at me and gives me a soft smile as our eyes lock. I groggily point to the glass of water that sits on the table, beside my bed. The guy picks up the glass and helps me have a drink and waits patiently for me to finish before placing the glass back on the table.

"Thank you," I say. It only comes out as a whisper, but he acknowledges that he has heard me.

"No problem," he replies. His voice is husky. His eyes look tired.

I wonder why he is still here?

"I don't mean to be rude, but... Who are you?" I have to ask him the question again, seeing as I didn't get an answer earlier. He has been here both times that I have woken up. There is obviously some reason that he is here, and I need to know what that reason is.

He takes a deep breath before answering.

"You really don't remember?" he asks. I shake my head at him and he looks defeated. "Maybe I should call the doctor to come and talk to you?"

"No, please, can't you just tell me? I mean, there is a reason that you are here. It would be nice if you would tell me why." There is silence for the next few moments. I try not to show impatience as this guy is clearly struggling with something. He runs his hands through his hair and lets out a puff of air. His eyes then lock with mine and I feel like he is reaching into my soul.

"Stacey, my name is Jake. Jake Waters. I have been here with you the whole time because I am your boyfriend. We are together." My eyes go wide at his words.

Is this guy on drugs?
He can't be my boyfriend, I'm with Charles.
"I beg your pardon?" The disbelief is evident in my voice.
"We are together, Stacey."
"No... No, that's not right. I am with Charles. Charles is my boyfriend."
This has got to be some kind of joke? And not a very funny one at that.
"No, he isn't. You left Charles because he slept with another woman whilst you were still together. We became a couple not long after. Things progressed quickly between us." His eyes are searching mine for some kind of recognition, but I am at a complete loss. "I understand this must be confusing, but there is something else that I need to tell you."

He takes in a deep breath and lets it out before continuing. "It's my fault that you are in here. I am the reason that you ended up in hospital." He looks ashamed as he says these words and panic starts to course through my body.

I am in here because of him?
Christ, what the hell did he do to me?
"What do you mean? How am I in here because of you?" I don't know how to process this information.
Surely if he were a danger to me, he wouldn't be allowed in here?
"I... Um... I..." He clears his throat and takes a sip of my water. I am a little taken aback by his familiarity. "My ex did this to you. She couldn't stand the thought of us being together, so she got you on your own and stabbed you. That's why your side is bandaged."
What the fuck?
Is this guy for real?
"I'm so sorry, Stacey. I was away on a business trip and I came back early to surprise you. That's when I found you, lying on the floor, and then you lost consciousness."

I literally cannot speak.
This can't be true? Surely, I would remember something like that happening to me?
My eyes wander to my side, which is covered by the blanket. I try my hardest to remember what happened, but nothing is coming to me.
"Please say something, Stacey." This Jake guy is pleading with me, and I can see the hurt in his eyes.
Am I causing that look?
This is all so weird.
"None of this makes any sense," I say as I shake my head. "I don't remember any of that happening." I feel tired all of a sudden. This information is too much. "How am I meant to know if you are telling me the truth or not?" My head starts to throb.

"I promise you that I would never lie to you. Please, Stace, you have to remember me." His eyes look so sad that it almost makes me want to cry for him. I wish that I could believe this guy, but I'm not sure if I do. I'm too weak to deal with this right now. I need some space.

"I want you to leave. I don't know you, and I have no idea why you are saying all of these things." I keep my tone firm. I don't want to sound harsh, but I just want to be left alone.

He looks absolutely gutted. "You *do* know me. You can't just forget our time together."

"I don't know you," I repeat. "I have no idea what you are talking about."

"Just try to remember, *please*." He sounds desperate.

"Just go." I expect him to try and change my mind, but he doesn't. He just stands and goes over to the door.

He opens the door but turns back to face me. "What we have is special, Stacey. I am going to help you remember me, and I'm going to help you remember us."

He then walks out, closing the door behind him.

I stare after him, racking my brains, trying to place everything that he told me, but it still doesn't make any sense.

I have never felt so confused in all my life.

I'm sure that I would remember that guy.

He's far too handsome to forget.

CHAPTER FIVE

STACEY

Doctor Reynolds comes around a few hours after Jake has left. I haven't been able to sleep. I feel restless, and the information that Jake told me just keeps going around and around in my head. It's like his voice is repeating everything on a continual loop.

After the doctor has done all of the relevant checks on me, he sits in the chair beside my bed.

"Miss Paris, I need to inform you about what happened to you during your time in here and just before."

"Okay." I am eager to see if he can help shed any light on my current situation.

"I presume that you have spoken to Mr Waters? The man who was in here when you first woke up," he says for clarification, so I know who he is talking about.

"Yes. I spoke with him earlier. He came up with some elaborate story about how his jealous ex stabbed me. I mean, I don't even know the guy, so why would his ex stab me?" I give a little chuckle at how ridiculous it all sounds. I expect the doctor to laugh with me, but he doesn't, and I quickly become silent at the serious expression on his face.

"Well, Mr Waters has told you the truth. I don't know the personal ins and outs of the situation between you two, but you were stabbed." I look straight at the doctor with wide eyes.

"No, doctor, that can't be right. I would remember that happening to me."

Surely doctors aren't allowed to mislead their patients?

"Miss Paris, you have some form of amnesia. Your memory has been completely erased of the last few weeks of your life. You hit your head during the altercation that you were involved in, but I am hopeful that you will regain your memory. It is just a question of when.

"I'm afraid that I can't say any more about your head injury as the brain is a very complex part of the body. As for the operation that you underwent when you were first admitted, for your side, I'm pleased to say that there will be minimal scarring of the area and no vital organs were hit." Doctor Reynolds seems pleased with this diagnosis, but I am not. *Amnesia?* "Are there any questions that you may have for me?"

"Um…" I don't quite know what to say. I open and close my mouth a few times, but no sound comes out. My mind has gone blank of anything to ask.

"I can see that you are a little overwhelmed by what I have told you." I nod at him. "In that case, I am going to go so that you can get some rest. The nurses will be doing various routine checks with you, but I will be back first thing tomorrow morning, to see if there is any change."

"Thank you, doctor," I answer robotically.

"My pleasure, Miss Paris." Doctor Reynolds then gets up and leaves my room.

I feel like I have the entire weight of the world on my shoulders.

So, if the stabbing is true, then it must be true that I left Charles? It would certainly explain why Charles hasn't been here. And if that's true, then it must be true that Jake is my boyfriend.

How could I forget something like that?

It's a lot to get my head around.

I lie, staring at the ceiling and Jake's face pops into my brain. Everything that I have learned so far would certainly explain the crestfallen look on Jake's face when I said that I couldn't remember who he was.

I feel a tear roll down my cheek and I wipe it away with my hand. I almost feel like I have lost a piece of myself. Another tear rolls down my cheek, but this time I don't wipe it away. I close my eyes and let the tears fall.

JAKE

"She doesn't fucking remember me, Lydia." I am fuming. I know that this isn't Lydia's fault, and it isn't even Stacey's, but I need to talk to the one person that is closest to Stacey, and that is Lydia.

"Calm down, Jake. I understand that you are frustrated, but this is just temporary." Lydia is trying to appease me.

"What if it's not, Lyd? What if she never remembers me?"

This thought has been going around my head since I left the hospital. Each time I think about it, it's like a dagger going straight into my heart. Lydia is the first person that I have voiced this concern to.

"Don't be ridiculous. Of course she will remember you. This is not forever. You will get her back. It may take a little while, but she *will* remember." Lydia's words don't make me feel any better. I know that she is trying to put my mind at ease, but it's not working.

"When are you going to see her?"

"First thing tomorrow morning."

"Can you please talk to her, Lyd? Get her to try and remember me." I am clutching at straws here, but I don't care.

"I don't think that's how it works, but I will try and talk to her. There is no quick fix here, Jake. You're just going to have to be patient with her, and let's hope that her memory comes back quickly."

"Thank you." I sigh. "Call me as soon as you have seen her." I don't want to talk any more.

"Yes, sir," Lydia replies. I hear the line click off and I throw my phone onto the sofa.

I go to the kitchen and pour myself a glass of scotch. I need a drink after today. I return to the lounge and sit on the sofa.

How can this be happening?

I finally find her again, after our night together all those months ago, and then Caitlin destroys it all.

Caitlin has taken the one person that I love away from me. The bitch succeeded in her revenge, and she needs to pay for what she has done.

My mind whirrs as I sit back and close my eyes. I need to get Stacey to remember. I need to try and make her see that she belongs with me.

A thought suddenly occurs to me, which makes me sit bolt upright. If she doesn't remember the last few weeks, then she won't remember what happened with Donnie.

This is all so fucked up.

I drain my glass and go back to the kitchen to get the whole bottle of scotch and carry the bottle up to my bedroom. I stop in my bedroom doorway, my eyes drawn to the bed.

My mind conjures up the image of Stacey led there.

I can picture the want in her eyes at the thought of my touch.

I can feel her excitement from the anticipation of what I am about to do to her.

I imagine her arms around me, and her fingers running through my hair.

I shake my head in frustration and go and sit on the edge of the bed before taking a swig from the bottle that I am holding.

I can smell her scent in this room. It is driving me crazy that she doesn't want me with her at the hospital. It almost broke me when she told me to leave.

Stop being such a pussy, Waters.

I need to quiet all the questions in my head.

I need my mind to go blank.

I take some more swigs of scotch.

I drink and drink until I can drink no more.

The questions never go, and it isn't until sleep claims me that I can finally forget, even if it will only be for a few hours.

CHAPTER SIX

STACEY

God, I hate hospitals.

I have been awake since six this morning, listening to everything going on outside of my room. The nurses' bells have been going off every five minutes. The sound of feet rushing down the corridor and the shouting by other patients is enough to put me off ever coming back here again.

I just want to go home. Although, I'm not exactly sure where home is right now.

The sound of the seconds ticking by on the clock draws my attention to the hands going around and around in monotonous circles.

There is a knock on the door at quarter past nine and I could almost jump for joy that someone is coming to relieve my boredom. The door opens and Lydia bursts in. I almost squeal with delight at the sight of her. She looks immaculate. Her hair is shining, and she is like a burst of colour in her yellow sun-dress. She is beaming at me and I grin at her like a Cheshire cat. I am so pleased to see a friendly face.

More importantly, a face that I recognise and know.

"Babes! It's so good to see you." Lydia rushes over to me, dumps her bag on the floor, and gives me a gentle hug.

"It's good to see you too, Lyd. This place is driving me insane. It's so depressing being stuck in here. I need to get out."

"Not until the doctor says so you don't." I poke my tongue out at her and she laughs. "Speaking of doctors, are there any fit ones here?" I laugh at her question. This feels so normal. Lydia really is like a breath of fresh air.

"Nope. Not unless you're into the older man."

"Hell, if they are older and look like George Clooney, then I'm game."

"Lydia, you are terrible," I say whilst laughing. "Unfortunately, there are no George Clooney lookalikes."

"Shame." Lydia pouts at my answer. "So, how are you feeling anyway?"

"Confused. I don't understand—" I am interrupted by the door opening. Doctor Reynolds walks in and I stop speaking. I can chat to Lydia when he has gone.

"Good morning, ladies," he greets both of us. "How are you feeling today, Stacey?" he asks me with a smile on his face. It's the kind of smile that relaxes you and puts you at ease.

"I'm okay, just a bit tired. I had a restless night."

"Hmm." Doctor Reynolds checks my vitals. "Do you still have any pain in your head?"

"It's not as bad as yesterday. It's more of a dull ache today."

"Well, that is to be expected. As long as the pain is lessening, that is all that matters." Doctor Reynolds picks up a clipboard from the end of my bed and begins jotting something down on the paper.

Lydia and I sit quietly, waiting for him to speak again. It takes a few minutes for him to make some notes and then he pops the clipboard away again. "I must say that if your vitals keep improving this quickly, then you may be able to go home in the next few days."

"That's fantastic," Lydia exclaims, and I smile at her.

"Have there been any improvements with your memory since yesterday at all?" Doctor Reynolds asks.

"No. I still can't remember anything." I feel so frustrated with myself. Lydia looks at me sympathetically.

Huh, I would have thought that she would look shocked at the doctor asking me this question, seeing as I haven't seen her until now.

"It's still early days. Don't try to push yourself too hard. These things take time. The nurse will be round this afternoon to help you get out of bed and move around. That is if you feel up to it?" says Doctor Reynolds, interrupting my thoughts.

"Yes, I am definitely ready to get out of this bed," I answer, eagerly. I feel like I have been stuck in here for weeks.

"Fantastic. Well, don't forget that in the meantime, you still need your rest." He looks to Lydia and she gives him her most innocent look.

"I promise that I won't stay too long," Lydia says, which seems to satisfy the doctor.

"Okay, ladies. I will see you tomorrow, Stacey. I will be operating all day, so the nurses will be on hand if you need anything."

"Thank you, doctor." He smiles and then leaves the room.

I turn to Lydia and am desperate to talk about something else other than why I am in here, or why my brain has decided to forget the last few weeks of my life.

"So, Lyd. How's things with you? How's it going with Donnie?" The colour drains from Lydia's face at my question.

Shit, what did I say that has made her look like that at me?

"Um... You don't remember what Donnie did?" Lydia's voice is quiet. I look at her and my expression must be blank. She takes a deep breath and continues to speak. "He's gone, Stace. He turned out to be an asshole, so he's gone."

"What did he do?" Last I remember, Lydia was crazy about him.

"I don't really want to talk about that right now." Lydia looks to the floor and I am a little shocked that she doesn't want to tell me. We tell each other everything.

"Oh, okay." I decide to let it go for now. "I must say though, I am so glad that you got rid of him. He gave me the creeps."

"Anyway," Lydia says, clearly wanting to change the subject. "Tell me, what is the last memory that you have?"

"Hang on," I say, my suspicious gaze narrowing on her. "Why aren't you the least bit shocked that I am having a memory loss issue? I mean, this is the first time that you are visiting me, so I haven't been able to tell you."

"Uh..."

"Lydia?" I say in a questioning tone.

Lydia rolls her eyes and takes a deep sigh. "Jake told me."

"Jake? As in, the guy that was here when I woke up? That Jake?"

"Yes."

"So, I have no idea who he really is, and you two are discussing me behind my back?"

"It's not like that, Stace," Lydia insists. "Jake is worried about you, even more so now that you don't remember him."

"Oh jeez, I feel so sorry for him," I say sarcastically.

"Don't be like that."

"I'm sorry," I say with a sigh. "I just don't want you discussing me with someone that I don't even know."

"But, you do know him."

"No I don't," I reply a little more forcefully than before.

"Okay, point taken," Lydia says as she holds her hands up in surrender. "Are you going to tell me about your last memory now that you have finished berating me?" Lydia asks cockily, clearly wanting to change the subject.

"I hardly think berating you is the appropriate term. Questioning you is more like it."

"Hmm. Well, I feel like I have been suitably told off, so please, back to the memory stuff, if you don't mind?"

I giggle at her response and decide to appease her curious mind. "My last memory is going to the Bowden Hall with Charles for one of his events for work. I remember getting out of the car when we arrived, and then it just goes blank."

"And you have no recollection of anything after that? Nothing at all?" I shake my head at her. "Nothing remotely familiar about Jake?" I roll my eyes at her question.

What is the big deal about this Jake guy?

"I thought that we were done talking about Jake?" I ask her.

"We are. I just thought that I would double check," she replies with a sweet smile plastered on her face.

"You don't fool me, Lydia. I have known you far too long."

"I have no idea what you are talking about," Lydia answers, feigning ignorance.

"Uh huh," I reply, not convinced by her act in the slightest. "On a more serious note though, I need you to fill me in on what I have forgotten. I only have Jake's version to go on, and I don't know what to believe right now. I know that you won't lie to me."

"Of course I can, babes. But, before I start, I just need to say that, Jake wouldn't lie to you either."

"And how can you be sure of that?" I raise an eyebrow quizzically.

"Because, he isn't like that." Lydia pulls the chair closer to my bed and puts her feet up on my mattress. She makes herself comfortable and I assume that this conversation is going to take a while. I turn on my good side and face Lydia. "Right, you ready to begin?"

I nod, and Lydia starts to tell me everything about Charles and Jake. I don't interrupt her. I just quietly listen. I am desperately hoping that something she says will jog my memory.

It takes a fair while for Lydia to go through everything. It sounds like some kind of soap opera, but I have to face the fact that it isn't a made-up script. Lydia wouldn't make any of this up, so I need to accept that my life has been a whirlwind over the last few weeks.

When Lydia has finished, I remain silent, processing all that she has told me.

"You and Jake are made for each other, Stace. He's like your knight in shining armour." Her cheesy comparison makes me laugh.

"That sounds so corny."

"It's true," she says, smiling.

"How so?" I would like to see how she can justify her knight in shining armour comment.

"Well... Um... I need to tell you something else, and it's not going to be pleasant for you to hear." She looks nervous.

"Okay. It can't be that bad, surely?"

"It is, Stace. I need you to promise me that if it gets too much for you to hear, then you will tell me to stop."

Shit, she really means what she is saying. Now I'm a little worried.

"Okay. I promise."

"Okay. Here goes..."

CHAPTER SEVEN

STACEY

I sit in silence after listening to what Lydia had to say. It's hard to take it all in.

Lydia is just sat there, staring at me, waiting for me to say something.

"Lyd, would you mind going to get me a cup of coffee, please?"

"Uh, sure." She shifts awkwardly in the chair. "Do you not want to discuss what I just told you?" It's not often that I see Lydia struggling to say the right thing, but this is one of those moments.

"I just need a few minutes to process it all." I smile at her to try and hide my sadness at what has happened to me.

"Okay, babes, I won't be long." Lydia stands up and gives me a hug before picking up her bag and leaving the room.

When the door closes, I let the tears fall. I held them back somehow whilst Lydia was here. There is just so much stuff that I can't remember. Leaving Charles, Donnie assaulting me, and Jake rescuing me. Jake then rejecting me, only to come back to me again, moving in with Lydia, and then Caitlin stalking me and eventually stabbing me. I cannot comprehend it all.

Why can't I remember?

Why has my brain erased all of this?

I lie on the bed, wipe my tears away, close my eyes and pretend that I have fallen asleep as I don't want Lydia to fuss over me. I pull the covers up to my chin and lie still, waiting for Lydia to return, which she does a few moments later. I keep my ears alert as I hear her put a cup down on the table by my bed.

"I'll come back tomorrow, Stace. Keep strong, babes." She kisses my cheek softly, and then I hear her leave the room.

The door clicks closed behind her and I open my eyes, my tears re-emerging.

Tears of sadness and frustration leave me sobbing.

My sobs echo throughout the room and I suddenly feel very much alone.

JAKE

Lydia's name appears on the screen of my phone and I immediately answer the call.

"How is she?" I ask urgently, without even saying hello.

"Not good, Jake. I told her everything, including what happened with Donnie."

"Fuck. Why did you do that?" I feel angry that I wasn't there for that conversation.

"She wanted to know what had been going on. I told her everything about you and about how she left Charles and moved in with me. I had to tell her about Donnie. It's part of what has happened to her." Lydia's voice breaks. "She sent me to get her a cup of coffee, and when I went back to the room, she was pretending to be asleep. She doesn't know that I know that she was pretending. I've only just left. You need to go and see her, Jake."

"I'm already on my way."

STACEY

I have been crying since Lydia left, and there is no sign of me stopping anytime soon.

I am an absolute mess.

I grab a tissue out of the box on the table beside me, blow my nose and try to dry my eyes. I am so glad that the nurse isn't due until this afternoon. It's only eleven-thirty in the morning, so I have plenty of time to pull myself together.

If only there was something to occupy my mind, or to distract me from my thoughts. All I can think about is what Lydia told me. She tried to talk to me about the one-night-stand that I had with Jake, nearly seven months ago. I remember the sex, but the guy doesn't really have a face. It sounds so stupid, but I genuinely can't picture the guy being Jake.

I now have no reason to think that Jake is lying about what has happened between us though. Lydia has confirmed it all.

I am going to drive myself crazy being cooped up in here. There is way too much time to think. My head is whirring, and my emotions are all over the place.

The door to my room opens suddenly, and Jake walks in. My breath catches in my throat as he comes straight over to me and gently wraps his arms around me. I don't try to move away from him, and I sob into his chest, soaking his shirt in the process.

He just holds me and tries his best to comfort me.

I don't know how long it takes me to regain some composure, but he doesn't rush me. He continues to hold me, waiting patiently.

"It's okay, babe. Let it all out," he whispers, his voice soothing.

I pull my head away from him and I look into his caramel-coloured eyes. They really are striking. I bet I look horrific with my red puffy eyes and my snotty nose.

"I'm sorry, Jake. I'm trying to remember, but it's all just blank." I feel so hopeless.

"Hey." He strokes my cheek with his thumb, wiping away some tears in the process. "We will figure it out. We will get through this." He seems so sure, but I am not convinced.

"It's like one big, giant mind fuck." I don't watch my language. I think I can be excused in this instance. "Lydia was telling me all of this stuff, but I just can't imagine it all happening to me. How can I not know any of it? How can my memory just block it all out?"

"I don't know, Stace. I wish that I knew the answers, but I don't. I will help you as much as I can, but you have to let me in. I know it feels like I am a stranger to you at this present time, but maybe, if we spend some time together, it may help to bring your memories back?" What he is saying actually makes sense to me.

Maybe if I do spend time with him, then it will jog something in my mind?

The question is, can I really ask him to put his life on hold, so that I can try and figure all of this out?

I don't know if I can.

Right now, I'm not even sure if I want to remember.

"I can't let you put your life on hold for me. I may never remember."

"You *are* my life, Stacey. I will always be here for you, and if you don't remember, then we can make new memories."

Is this guy serious?

Most men would run a mile if something like this happened.

"Listen, Jake, I don't mean to put even more of a downer on this situation, but what if things don't feel the same for me as they do for you?" If I thought that he had looked devastated before when I didn't know who he was, then that has got nothing on the way that he looks right now. A feeling of guilt starts to settle in my gut.

Maybe I should have kept that question to myself?

"How can you say that?" His voice cracks.

"I'm not saying it to hurt you, Jake. I'm just trying to be realistic." I don't recognise my voice.

This isn't me.

This gorgeous man is saying that he wants to help me, and all I am doing is trying to push him away.

Jake backs away from me and runs his hands through his hair. "Jesus, Stace, I know that you have amnesia, but why wouldn't you feel the same about me? I'm still Jake."

"Yes, but I don't know Jake." I don't want to sound like a bitch, but I'm afraid that is exactly how I sound.

"Well, then get to know me, Stace," Jake raises his voice which makes me jump. "Fuck. I need to get out of here."

I watch as Jake storms out of my room. I actually feel panicked at the thought of him walking away.

What am I doing?

One minute, I don't want him so close to me, and then the next, I want him to come back. I take deep breaths to try and calm myself down. I am disgusted with myself for the way that I just treated Jake. I need to think about how frustrating this situation must be for him.

I let out a cry of rage.

I need to get out of this hospital and start piecing my life back together.

CHAPTER EIGHT

STACEY

I have now been in the hospital for six days, and today I am finally allowed to leave.

My home is at Lydia's, and that is where I will be going. I am so excited to be leaving this hospital. Lydia is picking me up in half an hour and the doctor should be here in the next twenty minutes to discharge me. I am looking forward to, hopefully, getting some normality back in my life.

I still haven't regained any of my "lost" memory. It is still frustrating me, but once I get out of here, I am going to try and do anything that I can to help me remember.

Firstly, I want to visit The Den to see if that conjures up anything. Maybe starting with a bad memory will be more helpful? I don't know if it will be, but I can't think of any other way to approach this. I'm just going to have to go with the flow.

I haven't seen Jake since he stormed out of here. A part of me is pleased. I couldn't stand seeing how much I was hurting him. The other part of me though is a little gutted that he hasn't been back. What I should have said to him was that, I didn't feel like I could focus on a relationship until I had sorted myself out. But no, instead I managed to sound like a first-class bitch by telling him that I may never feel the same way about him again.

I need to engage my brain before I talk sometimes. Me and my big mouth.

I am sat, waiting on the edge of the bed when Doctor Reynolds strolls in five minutes earlier than I expected.

"Wow. Someone is eager to get out of here," he says.

"I can't wait. No offence."

"None taken, Miss Paris."

"I'm just looking forward to getting back to some sort of normality." Well, whatever my normality is going to be from now on anyway.

"That's good, but please, don't go rushing back to work or anything. Your body still has plenty of healing to do. I will need to see you back here in five days to check your wound, and then a nurse will re-dress it for you. If you have any abnormal pain in the meantime, you are to come straight back." He gives me a stern look and I nod to acknowledge that I have heard what he is saying. "I am very pleased with your progress so far, and I will be sending you home with some painkillers to take if needs be. As for your memory, don't force it. I am still hopeful that it will come back in due course."

"But what if it doesn't?" This has been worrying me more over the last couple of days. Doctor Reynolds smiles and places his hand on my arm in a comforting gesture.

"Let's cross that bridge if that happens. Right now, there is no need to worry about it. Now, I just need you to sign these papers and then you can be on your way." Doctor Reynolds hands me the papers and shows me where to sign. As I am signing the last piece of paper, Lydia enters the room.

"She all good to go, doc?" Lydia asks.

"She is indeed," he says, directing his answer at Lydia before turning his attention back to me. "Keep in mind what I said to you, Miss Paris, and I will see you back here on Wednesday. I will get a letter sent out to you to confirm the time of the appointment. Take care of yourself."

"Thanks for everything," I reply. Doctor Reynolds smiles at me, shakes my hand, and then leaves the room.

Lydia picks up my hospital bag, which contains a few items of clothes. "You ready to get out of here?" she asks me.

"You bet I am."

We go to the pharmacy to pick up my painkillers before we leave, then we are on our way out of here, and I follow Lydia to the car park. I said that she could use my car as I wouldn't be using it for a while. She opens the passenger door for me, and I gently lower myself into the seat. Lydia then shuts the door and goes round to the driver's side. I put my seat-belt on carefully and try to make myself as comfortable as possible. My side twinges slightly but I ignore it. I don't want to alarm Lydia by saying anything. Knowing her, she will march me straight back into the hospital, and that is the last thing that I want to happen.

On the drive home, Lydia informs me that she is going to be my personal nurse-maid. She has covered her shifts at The Den for the next week, so I get her company twenty-four seven.

"Lydia, I really don't need you to do that. I don't want to put you out." I don't like the thought of people halting their lives for me. First Jake wanted to, and now Lydia actually is.

"Don't talk stupid. You have just been in hospital for a stab wound and a head injury. Plus, you now have amnesia. I am looking after you. End of discussion."

There is no point in arguing with her. She's the most stubborn person I know, but she means well.

We drive the rest of the way in silence, listening to the radio. When we get to the flat, Lydia parks the car and then comes round to the passenger side to help me get out. She refuses to let me carry anything, so I slowly make my way to the building. Climbing the stairs to the flat is certainly challenging and it seems to take me forever to reach the relevant floor. It's only a couple of flights of stairs, but that is more than enough. At this moment in time, I wish that there was a bloody lift in this building.

By the time we reach the front door, I am exhausted. Lydia instructs me to go and put my feet up whilst she makes us a coffee. I don't need telling twice, so I head straight to the lounge. I gingerly sit down on the sofa and survey my surroundings. I love this flat. It is so cosy and homely.

I prop my feet on the coffee table as Lydia comes in with the drinks. She hands me my cup, and I gratefully take it from her.

"Thanks, Lyd." I take a sip and I appreciate the taste of decent coffee. The coffee that they have at the hospital tastes like cheap stuff.

Lydia takes a seat on the chair, opposite me. "So," she says, "Are you going to tell me why you haven't seen Jake for the last few days?"

Oh God, here we go with the twenty questions.

I groan at her. "There's nothing to say, Lyd. I don't know the guy."

"But you *do*. You guys are perfect for each other."

"Yeah, so perfect that I got stabbed because of him." I roll my eyes and sarcasm drips from my tone.

"Oh, come on now, that's not fair. Jake wasn't to know what that crazy bitch would do."

"Yes, I know." I sigh. "But, I did get stabbed because she was jealous. I mean, if I had never met him, then none of this would have happened." I feel exasperated by it all.

"Stace, you're not being fair. You were head-over-heels for Jake before you lost your memory. I know that you don't remember that, but it's not going to hurt to spend some time with him. It might bring something back to you." She sips her coffee and looks at me expectantly.

"I don't know, Lyd. I was pretty mean to him when I last saw him." I doubt he will ever want to see me again to be honest.

"You were confused and frustrated. It's a lot to get your head around. He will understand that." I really wish Lydia would drop this topic. I don't have the energy to talk about this right now.

"I don't mean to be blunt, but I don't want to talk about Jake any more. I'm just so tired of it all." I finish my cup of coffee, put it down on the coffee table, and slowly stand up. "I'm going to go and lie on the bed."

"Oh, okay. Well, if you need anything then just give me a shout."

"I will." I smile at Lydia as I leave the lounge and walk to the room that is my bedroom. I don't bother to get changed, I just climb straight into the bed and look around at my things in the room.

Even though I didn't want to talk to Lydia about him, my mind shifts to Jake, and it isn't long before I drift off to sleep, thinking about those caramel-coloured eyes.

CHAPTER NINE

STACEY

I don't get up until ten o'clock the following morning. I really needed a decent amount of sleep after being in the hospital, and there is nothing like an uninterrupted night.

It takes me an hour to get up and get dressed. There is really no way that I can rush around, but then I have no need to rush around at the moment. My side is throbbing, so I go to the kitchen to get a glass of water. I take two of my painkillers and fill the kettle to make myself a cup of coffee.

I sit at the kitchen table and look through the pile of trashy celebrity magazines that Lydia buys. She loves to see what the celebs are up to. I have tried to tell her that she shouldn't take any notice of what she reads in them, but she never listens.

The kettle boils, so I make up a pot of coffee instead of just one cup. As I sit back down at the kitchen table, Lydia comes waltzing in.

"Morning, babes. I need coffee, I am caffeine deprived."

"I've just made a fresh pot," I say as I point to the pot on the side. Lydia busies herself getting a cup and making her drink. When she has finished, she sits opposite me at the kitchen table.

"Are you really looking at my magazines?" she asks in disbelief.

"I was just flicking through. There isn't much else to do if you have a stab wound and partial amnesia," I reply sarcastically.

"It's only temporary."

"Hmm." Until I start to regain some memories, I am dubious. "Lyd, you know that you said that you would help me to try and remember?"

"Yeah."

"Well..." I'm not quite sure what reaction I am going to get at my next choice of words, but I need to say them. "I was wondering if... If you would come and see Charles with me?" I squint, unsure of what she will say.

"WHAT?!" she screeches, obviously in shock at my question. She stares at me open-mouthed.

"Hang on a minute, hear me out before you start shouting at me." I sip my coffee as I wait to see if she can remain calm whilst I speak to her.

Lydia closes her mouth and clears her throat. "But he's an asshole, Stace. Why on earth would you want to see him?"

"I don't particularly relish the thought of seeing him, believe me. I just think that, as he is my last memory, it might jog something. He was also a big part of my life for a while. I just need to try something. I need to get my life back, Lyd, and if I sit around here waiting, that could take forever." I hope my explanation has worked, and that she agrees to come with me.

"I don't know, babes. What about Jake?"

"What about him?" I sigh as his name gets mentioned again.

"He's not going to be particularly happy that you are visiting your ex-boyfriend, is he?" She raises an eyebrow at me.

"Lydia, Jake doesn't own me. I can make my own decisions, you know? I don't know Jake. I don't know what it is that Jake and I are supposed to have had together. I need to focus on myself right now, not some guy that I don't bloody know." I feel angry. I understand that he must have been part of my life, but I need to find out for myself what it is that we had.

I just need people to stop trying to force me to be with Jake.

I need to make my mind up on my own.

"I don't like this, Stace, but if it is going to help you with your recovery, then sure, I will go with you." I smile at her, but she doesn't look happy at what I have asked her to do. "But if he starts being a twat towards you, we're leaving. No arguments."

"Deal."

"I know that you probably don't want to hear this, but I think you should tell Jake that you want to go and see Charles."

"What? Why?" *What is her obsession with Jake?*

"Stacey, he loves you. It would be cruel to keep him out of the loop on this." I stare at her, flabbergasted. "And when you do regain your memory, you are going to wish that you had told him." Her stern look tells me that her opinion on this matter isn't going to be swayed.

"Fine. I will tell him, but only after we have been to see Charles."

"Why not tell him now?"

"Because I don't want to tell him now. The only reason I am going to tell him at all is because you feel that I should."

"Stacey—" She sounds unsure as she says my name, but I cut her off before she can continue.

"Look, Lyd, I get that Jake was a part of my life before my memory was wiped, but until I am able to piece things together, can you just support me in my decisions? Please?" I say. I shouldn't have to justify my choices or my actions.

"I will always support you, Stace, you know that." At least she has the decency to look sorry for being pushy about Jake. "When do you want to go and see Charles?" she asks, changing the subject.

"Now."

"Now?" she screeches at me.

"Yes, now. The sooner I get this over with, the better." I know it is my choice to see Charles, but our relationship wasn't exactly a happy one from what I remember.

"Right. Let me just go and get ready and then we can get going." Lydia stands up and leaves the kitchen, heading down the hallway to her bedroom. I get up and go to my bedroom to retrieve my phone, which I left charging overnight. The battery had completely died seeing as I didn't have the charger with me whilst I was in the hospital. I pick it up off of my bedside table, turn it on and it soon beeps to notify me that I have a text message.

> *Hey, baby girl. How are you feeling? Lydia phoned and told me what happened. Are you out of hospital yet? Hit me up, so that I can come and visit my favourite lady.*
> *Martin x*

Martin's text makes me smile. I write back to him whilst I am waiting for Lydia.

> *Hi, Mart. Yes, I am home! Come and visit me, and help me figure out how my life got so crazy. Are you free this evening?*
> *Stace x x*

I hit send and within seconds I have a reply.

> *See you at seven.*
> *Martin x*

I smile at the thought of seeing him. I haven't caught up with him for ages. At least, I don't think that I have. I shake my head at how ridiculous it is that I can't remember if I have seen Martin since my memory loss has taken hold.

I look at my phone screen and decide to take a look at the photos on there. Maybe there will be some photos that will shed some light on my life? I press the relevant button and bring them up. There are plenty of Lydia and I together, and I smile as I look through them.

There are a couple of Martin and I on a night out, and then there is one photo of Jake and I together. I am staring at the camera, and Jake is placing a kiss on my cheek. I look so happy in the photo. Jake's eyes are closed, and his hand is cupping my cheek. He looks handsome, even if it is only his side profile in the photo.

One of my arms is around his shoulders and I am obviously using the other to hold the phone at arm's length so that I can take the photo. Anyone looking at this photo would be able to see that we were a couple. I let out a puff of air at how much the photo has impacted me.

I feel a sudden sadness sweep over me.

How can I not know when this photo was taken?

How can my mind have failed me so badly?

I blink away tears that sting the backs of my eyes.

No, I will not cry.

I need to keep my head in the game.

I need to get my life back on track.

And if I really did feel that strongly about Jake, then I owe it to myself to fight to remember what we had.

CHAPTER TEN

STACEY

Lydia pulls up outside of Charles' offices and switches off the engine. I look at the building that houses Charles' offices and feel nothing. I almost feel empty.

"Are you sure that you want to go in?" Lydia asks me.

I ponder her question for a few moments. The only reason that I am here is to see if anything jogs my memory. I don't particularly want to see Charles at all. Lydia has told me all about why we split. I don't feel the slightest bit jealous that he slept with someone else. Our relationship simply ran its course, I suppose.

"Yeah. Let's go," I say before I have chance to change my mind. I open the passenger door and slowly get out. I am still having slight twinges in my side, but I am getting better with my movements.

I walk around to Lydia's side and I stare at the sign that says, "J & M Accounting." I don't miss the thought of a life with Charles. At the end of our relationship, and for a while before that, I was just like his personal skivvy.

Lydia links her arm through mine and we start to walk forward. We are about to enter the building, when I hear someone shouting my name. I turn around to see who it is and am gobsmacked to see that Jake is walking towards me. He is dressed in a navy-blue suit, with a white shirt and a blue tie. He looks good. Too good actually. He exudes confidence, but not in an arrogant way. His eyes travel up and down my body and I feel a little flutter in my stomach.

Woah, where is this feeling coming from?

The last time I saw Jake, I was horrible to him, and now, I am getting butterflies over him?

Jake comes to a stop in front of Lydia and me.

"Hi," he says in greeting.

"Hi," I say, shyly.

"Hi, Jake," Lydia says.

He turns and smiles at her. "How's it going, Lyd?"

"Oh, you know, this one isn't easy to look after," she says, playfully patting me on the arm. I roll my eyes at her and Jake chuckles, which gives me goose-bumps.

"So, what are you two up to?" Jake asks. He looks to the building behind me and he frowns as he registers where we were going.

"I was going to see Charles," I answer. Jake raises his eyebrows and I quickly continue to speak so that he doesn't get the wrong idea. "I just thought that seeing him might help me to remember something, seeing as my last memory is of him and I going to the Bowden Hall."

"The Bowden Hall?" Jake asks.

"Yeah. We were going to some sort of event for his company. I remember getting out of the car when we got to the Bowden Hall, and then it all goes blank." I shift uncomfortably. I almost feel the need to explain myself which is a contradiction of my earlier feelings about not having to justify to anyone what I am doing.

"Oh, right. Well, if you think it will help then you should see him," Jake says. He might be saying words to encourage me, but I can tell that he doesn't believe them. I can see his jaw ticking. I presume this is something he does when he is pissed off.

"I hope it will help."

"I would say have fun, but seeing Charles Montpellior is probably on the opposite end of the fun scale." Jake is trying to keep things light-hearted, but I can see that the thought of me seeing Charles is hurting him. I don't want to be the one to make him feel like that. "Anyway, I better be going. I have a meeting that I need to get to. Bye, ladies." Jake turns and starts to walk in the direction that he came from.

"Bye, Jake," Lydia calls after him.

The photo on my phone suddenly pops into my brain, and I feel a sudden panic at the thought of him walking off. I don't want him to get the wrong idea about me seeing Charles. I owe it to Jake, as well as to myself, to figure all this out.

Before I know what I am doing, I call out to him.

"Jake," I shout. He turns around and I unlink my arm from Lydia's and start to walk towards him. He stays where he is and puts his hands in his trouser pockets. Lydia doesn't follow me, which I am quite glad about.

When I reach Jake, I stand in front of him and start to speak before I can change my mind. "Jake, I know that this last week has been tough. I know what I said to you in the hospital hurt you, and I am sorry for that. I wasn't being fair to you, and I know it is no excuse, but I was so confused in there. I still am really, but I want to do everything I can to change that." Jake nods but he doesn't go to speak.

I take a deep breath and continue with what I need to say. "I was wondering if you might be free tomorrow night? I thought it might be a good idea for us to talk?"

Jake stares at me as I fidget on the spot, waiting for his answer. I would completely understand if he didn't want to see me again after the way I was with him.

"Just me and you?" he asks.

"Well, yeah. But, if you don't want to then—" I don't get to finish my sentence as Jake interrupts me.

"What time?"

"Um.... What time is good for you?"

"I will be finished with work about five-ish. Do you want me to pick you up when I am done?"

"Okay."

"We can go to my house."

"Your house?"

"Yeah. Is that okay with you?" he asks, seeming somewhat unsure of himself.

"Sure."

"Great. I will text you when I am on the way to yours."

"Okay. I will see you tomorrow then." I give Jake a little smile which he returns, and I turn to walk back to Lydia.

"Bye, Stace," I hear him say as I start to walk off.

I see Lydia is just staring at me, clearly waiting to be told what just happened with Jake. As I get closer to her, she can no longer contain her curiosity.

"Well?" Lydia asks me.

"Well what?" I reply. Lydia rolls her eyes at my casual response.

"Don't act coy with me, missy. What was that between you and Jake just now?"

"If you must know, I am seeing him tomorrow night when he has finished work."

"Really?" She doesn't hide the surprise in her voice. I suppose with the way that I have been acting about the whole Jake situation, it is a bit of a turnaround.

"Yes, really. You can grill me about it later. Right now, I need to go and see Charles."

"Ugh, can't wait," Lydia says, her tone full of sarcasm. I link my arm back through hers and we start to walk to the entrance of Charles' offices. Lydia pushes the door open and we walk inside to be greeted by the most ridiculous looking receptionist that I have ever seen. The girl doesn't look a day over twenty. She has her hair up in a sleek ponytail, she is wearing an obscene amount of make-up, and her blouse shows off her cleavage.

Is this really the look Charles wants when people walk in here?

She doesn't look professional in the slightest. The gum she is clearly chewing doesn't help either. I clear my throat and am about to ask if it is possible to see Charles when I hear him behind me.

"Stacey?" Charles says. I turn around and see him stood there, his mouth dropped open at the sight of me.

"Hi, Charles."

"Charles," Lydia says. I can hear the distaste in the way she says his name. Lydia never did hide her dislike of him.

"Lydia." The feeling is mutual as Charles looks less than thrilled to see her with me.

"Can we talk for a few moments?" I say. I want to get this over with as quickly as possible.

"Uh... Sure. Follow me," he says.

Lydia and I trail behind him as he walks us to his office. I feel the familiarity of knowing where I am going, but it brings me no comfort.

On entering his office, Charles gestures for Lydia and me to sit down. We take the seats that are in front of his desk and after closing the door, he goes and sits in his chair on the opposite side of the desk to us.

I feel awkward being sat here, and I can see that Charles feels the same.

"What brings you here, Stacey?" he asks.

"I don't know really." I'm not quite sure how I saw this conversation going, and now I am here, I haven't a clue where to start.

Lydia remains silent beside me.

"Right. Well, that doesn't give much away. I haven't heard from you in weeks, and then you turn up here and you don't know why?" Charles is clearly irritated that I am here.

"It's complicated. I've... Um... I've been in an accident and I was hoping that by seeing you, I might get some answers."

"An accident?"

"Uh, yeah." Charles just stares at me, and I start to feel that coming to see him was a big mistake. I don't think I am going to get any answers here.

"Are you going to expand on this accident?"

"Well, I was stabbed. And things are a bit hazy, since the stabbing,"

"You were stabbed?" He raises his eyebrows in shock. I nod at him, not knowing what else to say. "And why would coming here give you answers?"

I scoff at his response. I thought that he might have at least asked how I was.

I look to Lydia who is staring daggers at Charles. I shake my head and realise that seeing Charles is probably the worst thing that I could have done. Seeing him isn't going to bring my memory back. All it does is make me realise how wrong we ever were for one another.

"I don't mean to sound rude, but I have a meeting taking place in five minutes. Can we hurry this along?" His tone sounds bored. How foolish I have been to come and see this man. Charles only ever thought about himself, and it looks like things haven't changed in the slightest.

"Are you really not going to be a bit more considerate?" Lydia says, making me jump. "Stacey has been through a traumatic ordeal, and she came here hoping that you might be able to help her, and all you care about is getting her out of here, so you can attend some sodding meeting."

"It's okay, Lyd." I place my hand on her arm to try and get her attention. She looks to me and I can see the fire in her eyes. "This was a waste of time. Come on," I say as I stand up. "Let's go."

Lydia stands up and I lead the way to the door of Charles' office. I place my hand on the door handle and turn back around. "You know what, Charles?"

"What?" he says. He looks completely unfazed by Lydia's outburst.

"I pity you."

"You pity me?"

"Yes, I pity you. It must be very lonely being Charles Montpellior." I don't wait for him to answer me as I open the door to his office and walk out of the building, and out of Charles' life for good.

CHAPTER ELEVEN

STACEY

Lydia and I drive back to the flat and I wearily walk up the stairs to the front door. I unlock it, and Lydia follows behind me. I go straight to the lounge and dump my handbag on the coffee table. Lydia enters the room and I slowly sit down on the sofa.

Today's effort at trying to regain my lost time was a complete disaster.

"Are you okay, babes?" Lydia asks me.

"Not really." I sigh and feel frustration taking hold. "I really thought that seeing Charles would help in some way."

I close my eyes and rub my temples to try and soothe the dull headache that I have acquired since leaving Charles' office.

"You were only doing what you thought was best." Lydia is trying to make me feel better about the whole situation, but it doesn't work.

"Things between us were bad towards the end, but I really thought that some part of him would give a shit about helping me. I feel so stupid."

"You're not stupid. You're just trying to make sense of it all. I can't imagine what you are going through right now." Lydia sits next to me and puts her arm around my shoulders. I rest my head on her shoulder and feel thankful that at least she wants to help me.

"I hope that you never have to. It's so frustrating. But I think the worst part is knowing that this could be permanent."

"It's not permanent."

"It might be, Lyd." My comment halts our conversation.

The reality of the situation is kicking in.

I may never remember what I had with Jake.

I may never remember how I finally came to leave Charles.

I know that Lydia and Jake have told me what happened, but it's almost like I am listening to someone else's story.

"I think I'm going to go and lie on the bed. Martin will be here in a couple of hours and I feel wiped," I say wearily.

"Okay, babes. Maybe getting some rest will make you feel better."

"Yeah, maybe." I stand up, pick up my handbag and walk out of the lounge and to my bedroom. I close the door behind me and sit on the edge of my bed. I take my phone out of my handbag as I feel the urge to look at the photo of me and Jake.

My heart does a little flutter at the sight of him in the photo, and guilt sets in that I chose to see Charles.

What was I thinking?

My fingers tap a few buttons on my phone, and before I realise what I am doing, I find Jake's name in my phonebook and I hit the call button.

JAKE

I am about to leave the office to go and get a late lunch when my phone starts to ring. I look to the screen and see that Stacey is calling me. I don't hesitate to answer the phone.

"Hello."

"Hi, Jake. It's Stacey," she says in greeting. I smile as she announces that she is the one calling me. I decide not to draw attention to the fact that I knew it was her calling before I even answered. I figure that she doesn't need reminding that I already have her number stored in my phone. It's just good to hear her voice, even if I did only see her a couple of hours ago.

"Is everything okay?" I ask her.

"Not really." She doesn't expand on her answer, leaving me in suspense. It looks like I am going to have to help ease her into this conversation.

"Want to talk about it?"

"I guess so," she says with a sigh. "I just..." She struggles to find the words for whatever she is trying to say.

"Stace, what's wrong?" I might as well cut straight to the point. I know that something is bugging her.

"I'm not really sure why I called." My heart drops at her answer. "I just... I found this photo on my phone. It's a photo of you and me, and I just felt like I needed to speak to you." My heart lifts again at the fact that she just wanted to speak to me. "I know that probably sounds silly."

"Not at all."

"I also feel like I should apologise to you."

"Apologise?"

"Yes. I'm sorry that I went to see Charles. It was a mistake to go and see him. Lydia told me not to, but I didn't listen."

"Why would you need to apologise to me for that?"

"Because... Lydia told me that it might upset you." It bugs me that it takes Lydia to tell her that this may have upset me, but I have to think about the fact that she doesn't 'know' me at the moment.

"It's okay. You thought that it would help you and I respect that." *Well done, Waters, keep cool about it.* "Did it help?"

"No." I hear her sigh down the phone. "It was a disaster. Charles is and always will be a selfish prick." I feel relief that she still thinks that Charles is a prick. I must admit that a small part of me thought that she might go back to him, seeing as he is her last memory.

"What happened?" I am intrigued to find out more.

"Well, to cut a short story even shorter, I told Charles that I was stabbed, and he asked me to hurry things along because he had a meeting to get to." I remain quiet as my jaw ticks.

That guy is such a tosser.

As much as I was unhappy about Stacey seeing Charles, I'm even more pissed that he didn't show any interest in helping her.

"Jake?" her voice breaks my thoughts.

"Yeah, I'm still here."

"Are you okay?"

"I'm fine." I need to change the subject. Speaking about Charles makes my blood boil. "So, what are you up to now?"

"Oh, I'm just led on my bed."

Now that is a sight that I can picture vividly. It's also an image that I welcome. It's just a shame that she isn't in my bed, waiting for me. I feel my cock stir at the image and I fidget in my seat.

All in good time, Waters, all in good time.

"Martin is coming to see me later. I presume that you already know that I have a friend named Martin?" Her tone turns playful and I love to hear her sounding more relaxed. I chuckle at her words.

"Yeah, I know that you are friends with Martin." I want to keep the conversation light, even if it is just to keep her on the phone for a bit longer. "I actually met him once."

"Oh, really?"

"Yeah, but from what you have told me about him, he obviously kept his personality very low-key when I met him."

"Of all the things Martin could be described as, I would never have put low-key in the same sentence as his name." She starts to laugh which makes my cock stand to attention. Even her laugh turns me on. "So, anyway, I better let you get back to whatever it is you were doing. Thanks for listening to me, Jake."

"Anytime."

"So, I'll see you tomorrow then?" she asks it as a question rather than a statement. Maybe she thinks that I have changed my mind? Like that is ever going to happen.

"You will. Have a good evening, Stacey."

"You too." The phone goes dead and I pull it slowly away from my ear. I look to the screen and see my background picture before it times out. The image of Stacey and I together makes me yearn for her, more than I am already.

I remember that I was going to get some lunch before she phoned. I stand up, put my phone in my pocket and head out of my office. For the first time in over a week, I feel a sense of hope. Hope that we can put right all that Caitlin's actions have put wrong.

———

STACEY

There is a knock on the door at quarter past seven, and I leave my bedroom to go and answer it. I am so excited to see Martin. His fun-loving nature is just what I need right now. I open the door and see Martin stood there with a bunch of flowers and a big box of chocolates.

"I know that you can't have any alcohol, so I brought chocolates instead," he says as I usher him inside.

"What I wouldn't give for a glass of wine. But chocolate will do for now," I reply. Martin hands me the flowers which are so pretty. Pinks, whites and purples. I couldn't tell you what flowers they actually are though. Green-fingered I am not. "Thanks, Mart. They're beautiful."

"Beautiful flowers for a beautiful lady." He moves towards me and pulls me into a gentle hug. I smile and put my flower-free arm around his waist. "How are you doing, baby girl?" he asks me, sounding more serious.

"Oh, you know, fine." Martin pulls back and looks at my face.

"Well, that was the most unconvincing answer that I have ever heard. Come on," he says as he pulls away from me and takes my hand, leading me into the kitchen. "Get that kettle on and tell Uncle Mart all about it." He points to the kettle and I salute him. I fill the kettle and get two cups out of the cupboard, and Martin takes a seat at the kitchen table.

"So, where's Miss Lydia then?" he asks.

"She's in her bedroom having a lie down. I expect that she will come and join us shortly," I say as I busy myself putting the flowers in a vase.

"So, for the time being, I get you all to myself?"

"You sure do." The kettle finishes boiling, and I make Martin his cup of tea whilst I opt for a green tea.

"Does that mean that I can grill you on that delicious man that you have been getting naked with?" Martin asks as he proceeds to open the box of chocolates.

"Martin!" I exclaim.

"Oh, honey, you know I like to speak my mind."

"Yes, but do you have to be quite so blunt?"

"What's the point in being vague? Now, come on, spill the beans." He sits eagerly awaiting a full report whilst popping a chocolate in his mouth. I carry the cups over to the table and hand Martin his before I sit opposite him and sip my tea, trying to think of where to start.

"There's not much to tell really."

"Oh, please. You could talk about that man's abs all day long and I wouldn't get bored." I burst out laughing. He really has no shame. It takes me a few moments to calm down before I can speak.

"Well, I don't remember what his abs look like, so I can't tell you about those. But I can tell you that I am meeting him tomorrow night to talk." I feel a little thrill shoot through me at the thought of spending some time with Jake. My mixed emotions seem to be changing for the better.

In the hospital, I was scared. Scared of not knowing and scared of being unsure about anything. Now that I am home, and I have had a few days to process some things, I feel more certain. I may still have amnesia, but I am excited to see how things progress with Jake.

The photo of us together was the jolt that I needed.

"Nothing is coming back to you at all?" Martin asks me. I shake my head at him. "Oh, baby girl. Maybe that isn't such a bad thing?"

"How do you mean?" I can think of nothing worse than having part of your life erased.

"Well, this way, you get to forget some of the bad stuff that happened, and you get the thrill of falling in love with Jake all over again." He takes a sip of his tea and smirks at me.

"How do you know that I will fall in love with him?"

"I just know. Trust me, Jake is the one for you."

CHAPTER TWELVE

STACEY

I wake up at ten o'clock the following morning. Martin didn't leave until midnight last night, but it was worth staying up late to spend some time with him. It's going to be so much easier to see him now that I'm no longer with Charles.

I smile as the thought of seeing Jake later pops into my head. Martin helped to put things into context for me. I know that Lydia has been trying to get me to let Jake into my life but hearing it from someone other than her just shows me how much I must have thought of him before I lost my memory.

I get out of bed and go to the bathroom to use the facilities. Once I am finished, I knock on Lydia's bedroom door. There is no answer, but I can hear faint sounds coming from the lounge, so I figure that she must already be up.

I go to the lounge and see that Lydia is sat on the sofa, watching the television.

"Morning, Lyd," I say as I walk in and sit in the chair.

"Morning, babes. You okay?" she asks me.

"Yeah. I feel good actually." It's the first time that I have woken up since the incident and actually felt positive.

"That's great. It was good to see Martin last night." Lydia joined us after Martin had been here for about an hour.

"It was. He helped me to make sense of the whole Jake situation." I instantly regret my words as I don't want to offend Lydia, seeing as she has been trying to help as well.

She frowns at me. "And I haven't helped you at all?"

Oh shit, I need to shut down her overactive mind.

"Yes of course you have. I didn't mean anything by it. It's just that, hearing another person voice their opinion has helped me. I can't explain why. It just has." I shrug and hope that Lydia will be somewhat satisfied with my answer.

"Hmm. It's a good job that I understand what you are trying to say." She smiles at me and I am relieved that she gets it. "So, what are we doing today?" she asks me.

"Well, I was kind of hoping that you would take me to The Den."

"What?" she yells. "No way, Stacey. It's too soon for you to go there. There is no way that you are going there yet."

"Oh, come on, Lyd. I need to see if it will help me remember something. Maybe returning to the scene of the crime will trigger a flashback."

"It's not happening, so you may as well drop the subject now." I knew that she might freak out a little at me asking to go there, but I never expected her to be so set against it.

"Please, Lyd." I pout at her, hoping that she will change her mind.

"Nope."

"But—"

"NO! When you are stronger, I will take you, but not before." She looks at me with her arms folded across her chest, and I know that there is no way that I will change her mind. Lydia can be very stubborn if she feels the need to be, and my hopes plummet.

"You have no idea how frustrating all of this is for me. I want to regain my memory, Lyd." Tears start to fall down my cheeks. Lydia gets up off of the sofa and comes over to the chair. She perches on the arm and puts her arm around my shoulders.

"I will help you, babes. Just not today. I promise that we can go soon though. You are not strong enough right now."

"I am," I protest.

"No you are not. I know you, Stacey, and I know that you are not ready to face the place in which Caitlin stabbed you." I feel crushed at her words. I wipe my tears away and I mentally try to think of ways that I can get there, without the help of Lydia. I can't ask Martin. He would worry too much and end up telling Lydia where we are going, and then she would stop him from helping me.

"I'm going to make myself a drink," I say as I get up from the chair and head out of the lounge. Lydia doesn't follow me, which I am grateful for. I'm a little angry with her right now.

As I make myself a drink, my mind wanders to the one person that I think will help me. I take my drink back to my bedroom and sit on the bed before picking up my phone and scrolling through my contacts. After finding the relevant person, I hit the call button.

JAKE

I sit at my desk, looking at some spreadsheets that have numbers written all over them. I stare at each piece of paper in turn and then I push my chair back from the desk and let out a sigh.

My head isn't in the game right now. Work is the least of my priorities. All I can think about is seeing Stacey later. I keep trying to foresee what might happen, but I really have no idea how it is going to go. I've tried to concentrate on anything else, but it's no use.

My mobile phone starts to ring on the desk, so I scoot forwards on the chair to see who it is.

Stacey's calling me.

My heart leaps into my throat as I fear that she may be calling to cancel seeing me tonight. I toy with the idea of not answering for a few seconds, but I quickly push that thought away. I take a deep breath and I answer the call.

"Hello."

"Hi, Jake."

"Hi. Is everything okay?" I ask. If she is going to cancel tonight, then I would rather get straight to the point.

"I'm sorry to interrupt you. I just... I need..." she trails off and the line goes quiet.

"What's wrong, Stace?" I hear her take a deep breath on the end of the line and I patiently wait for her to start speaking again.

"Okay. Here goes. I need someone to take me to The Den." She says it in a rush, and for a moment, I think that I have misheard her.

"You want to go where?" I ask. I just need to make sure that I heard her correctly.

"The Den."

"Are you sure that's a good idea?" I don't want to sound like I am down on the idea, but she hasn't been out of hospital for that long.

"I think so. I need to do whatever I can to help my memories come back, even if they are bad ones. Seeing Charles clearly didn't help. Maybe I need to return to the place where the attack happened." She sounds so sure of herself. She has obviously given this a great deal of thought. "Lydia won't take me, and you were the only other person that I felt I could ask."

Her honesty floors me. Okay, so I wasn't her first thought, but that's understandable seeing as Lydia is looking after her, but at least I was the next one she felt that she could ask.

Now I am torn between doing something to help her and doing what I think is best for her. I weigh up the options.

"Jake?"

"Yeah, I'm here. I'm just a bit surprised that you want to go back there so soon." I can't help but voice my opinion. I can just picture her rolling her eyes at me. The thought of knowing how she will react makes me smile.

"I need to do this. And I need to go with someone that I can rely on. I expect that sounds crazy to you with the way that I have been acting."

"Not at all." If she feels that she can rely on me, then that's a start. "What time did you want to go?"

"I was thinking that we could go tonight? Before we go to yours, maybe?" I ponder this idea for a few moments, but it doesn't sit right with me. The idea of Stacey walking in there, when The Den is open, doesn't strike me as a good idea. She's still recovering from her ordeal and the last thing that she needs is to deal with drunken assholes whilst she is trying to find herself.

"No."

"No?" She sounds a little panicked.

"I think it would be better to go whilst there is no one else there. Is there any way we can get in without Lydia finding out?" She needs me, and I am going to be there for her. If I know Stacey as well as I think I do, she would just try and go on her own anyway.

"I guess I could try and sneak her set of keys."

"Okay. I'll be there in twenty minutes." I was already struggling to concentrate on work. I might as well leave and put my focus to better use.

"Twenty minutes?" Surprise enters her tone.

"Is that going to be a problem?"

"No, no. It's just... I don't want to disrupt your day."

"You're not disrupting it."

"Well... Okay then. I best go and distract Lydia so that I can get her keys."

"You do that. See you soon." I end the call and I buzz through to my PA, Valerie, and tell her to cancel my meetings for the rest of the day.

Stacey is my top priority right now.

I may finally be on the way to getting my girl back.

CHAPTER THIRTEEN

STACEY

There is a knock on the front door exactly twenty minutes later. If that's Jake, then he is certainly punctual.

Lydia is answering the front door as I walk out of my bedroom.

"Oh, hi, Jake. What are you doing here?" I hear Lydia say as I walk down the hallway. She definitely sounds surprised to see him.

"Hi, Lyd. I'm just here to see if Stacey would like to go and get a cup of coffee," Jake answers.

"Aren't you guys seeing each other later?"

"Yeah, but I fancied a coffee break and decided to drop by to see if I could persuade Stacey to keep me company for a while." Jake doesn't falter in his response and I smile at his quick thinking. If it was me stood at the door, my face would give away that I was lying. I walk up behind Lydia, just as she shouts for me.

"STACE."

"I'm right behind you, Lyd," I say, making her jump.

"Good God, woman, don't do that. You'll give me a heart attack," Lydia exclaims. Jake smiles and I feel my heart melt a little. He really is extremely handsome. His eyes sparkle, and I feel a flutter of butterflies in my stomach.

"Sorry, Lyd. Didn't mean to scare you."

"Uh huh." She smirks signalling that she isn't annoyed with me. "Jake has requested your company for coffee." This puts a massive smile on her face and I can see that, with every fibre of her being, she is willing me to go with him.

My eyes shift from Lydia to Jake, and I feel a little guilty for not being honest with her. I hope that she won't be too mad when I tell her the truth. Jake's eyes bore into mine and I feel a heat start to creep its way up my body.

Where is this reaction coming from?

"So, do you want to go for coffee?" Jake asks me, pulling my attention away from how good he looks in his suit.

"Sure. Let me just go and grab my handbag." I go back to my bedroom and pick up my bag and put my phone inside it, along with my purse, flat keys, and the keys to The Den. I hope to God that Lydia doesn't notice that they are missing.

I walk back to the front door and Lydia and Jake go quiet as I approach. I get the feeling that they were talking about me, but I don't question them. I don't need to lose focus right now.

"Ready?" Jake asks. I nod at him and then I say goodbye to Lydia.

"Don't be too long, missy. You still need to rest," Lydia says as I walk out of the front door.

"Don't worry, Lyd. I will take care of her," Jake answers. I feel a tingle make its way down my spine at his words.

Jake shuts the front door behind me and we walk out of the building and to his car. He has a sporty number which just oozes manliness. I'm a little concerned about how low it is to get into though. Jake opens the passenger door for me and I slowly lower myself down to the seat. I let out a little groan as I feel a twinge in my side. My hand immediately flies to my injury and Jake takes this as a sign to help me sit down.

Once I am inside the car, he puts the seatbelt around me. My entire body is covered in goose-bumps from being in such close proximity of him.

"Thanks, but I can put a seat-belt on, you know?" I say playfully. He smiles, winks and then shuts the door. He goes around to the driver's side and gets himself settled before starting the car.

"I take it you managed to get the keys then?" he asks me. I answer his question by pulling the keys out of my handbag, giving them a little jiggle when they are in the air.

"I feel bad that I have duped Lydia," I say.

"Let's worry about that later. If this feels right for you, then that's all that matters right now." He smiles, and I am grateful for his support. "I am going to ask you one last time though. Are you absolutely certain that you want to do this?"

"Yes."

"Okay. Just had to make sure."

"I'm sure. Now, let's go."

"Yes, ma'am," he replies. Jake pulls out of the parking space and then we are on the way to The Den. It won't take long but trying to walk it would absolutely wipe me out.

"So, how have you been?" I ask him.

"Fine." His answer doesn't seem very convincing, but I don't push him on it.

We travel the rest of the way in silence, but it doesn't feel uncomfortable. We pull up outside The Den five minutes later. I tell Jake to drive around to the parking area at the back of the building. Once he has parked the car, I unbuckle my seat-belt and take a few deep breaths.

"We can go in the back entrance," I tell him.

"Okay."

I go to undo the car door so that I can get out, but Jake puts his hand on my arm which stops me. I turn to face him and search his eyes.

"Wait there," he says before getting out of the car, leaving me to wonder why he told me to wait. I watch as he comes around to my side, opens the door and then he leans in and puts one hand under my legs, and the other around my back.

"Uh, Jake, what are you doing?"

"I'm helping you get out of the car. No arguments." He then lifts me with ease, and I put my hands around his neck as he stands up.

The moment feels charged with emotions.

I can feel a sense of familiarity pull at my gut.

Has he ever done this before?

Am I just getting used to being around him?

I wish that I knew why I was suddenly feeling like this, but of course I don't. Jake smiles and lowers my legs slowly to the floor. I release my arms from around his neck and I stand there feeling like a teenager who is about to go on a date with her crush.

"Thanks," I say a little breathlessly.

"You're welcome. Shall we?" he says, indicating that we need to enter The Den.

"Uh... Yes." My emotions are starting to overwhelm me from being that close to him. I gather myself together and I lead the way to the back door.

As I reach the door, I unlock it, push it open and walk into the familiar building, quickly switching the alarm off as I enter. Jake follows me, and he closes the door behind us.

I walk gingerly through the hallway and then turn right, so that I am entering the main bar area. I stop and look around and feel nothing as I survey the area. I close my eyes and jump when I feel something brush against my hand. I open my eyes and look down to see that Jake is taking my hand in his.

I look into his eyes and he squeezes my hand gently. I smile and feel incredibly touched by the simple gesture. I have said some cruel things to him, but he is standing next to me and supporting me through this. He hasn't gone running off or told me to leave him alone. He just seems like he wants to be there for me, and I am so glad that I asked him to come here with me.

"If anything comes back to you and it becomes too much, then just say and we will leave," Jake says. I smile a little wider at him and squeeze his hand back before I lead us further into the main room. I walk slowly past the dance floor and come to a stop just in front of the bar.

"It all feels normal," I say out loud.

Whether I am saying it for my own assurance, or whether I am letting Jake know that I am okay, I don't know. My eyes roam the bar and then they land on the door to Lydia's office. Lydia has obviously told me that the altercation took place in there, but I suppose I expected it to look a little different somehow. It doesn't. It looks just the same as it always has.

I let go of Jake's hand and start to walk towards the door, feeling Jake close behind me. I reach the door and unlock it using Lydia's keys before I push the handle down and slowly open it. I start to feel a sense of unease as the door opens fully.

As I walk into the room, the hairs on the back of my neck stand to attention. I push forward and come to a halt at Lydia's desk.

I run my fingers along the desk and then look to the floor.

I can see a slight stain on the carpet. I bend down so that I can get a better look at the stain. It's almost like an orangey colour. I study it closely, ignoring the fact that I probably look like I have lost the plot to Jake. I see him out of the corner of my eye, standing in the doorway, watching me.

Come on, Stacey. You can do this. You can remember.

I close my eyes and all I can hear is my heavy breathing and the ticking of the clock.

Fear starts to creep its way into my system, and I know that I am close to remembering something.

I concentrate as hard as I possibly can. I stay like that for a few moments, just waiting for something to come back to me, and when I open my eyes again, I am confronted by the sight of the stain, and then it happens like a bolt of lightning.

I can see myself, led on the floor, blood seeping from my body.

Some woman with blond hair has her hand on a knife that is sticking into my side.

Her face comes into focus.

Her eyes are almost glowing, and her lips are curled upwards into an evil smile.

I can hear screaming that physically hurts my eardrums.

It isn't until I feel Jake's arms around me that I realise that the screaming is coming from me.

CHAPTER FOURTEEN

STACEY

"Shit, shit, shit," I repeat over and over. I am sat back in Jake's car with him. He carried me out of The Den as I couldn't find the strength to walk. The images of me lying on the floor, with Caitlin cackling like a maniac, were too much. I take deep breaths and try to get my breathing back to normal.

"Lydia was right. It was too soon for you to come back here," Jake says. I look to him and his jaw is tense. My hand rests in his and his grip is firm.

"No," I say, making him look at me in shock. "In a way, this is good."

"Good?" Now he looks at me like I actually have gone crazy.

"Yeah. Don't you see?" I say whilst he looks at me perplexed. "I remembered Jake. I actually remembered something. Okay, it wasn't the greatest flashback to have, but it's a start. Granted, the images were terrifying, but at least I know what happened now. And if I have remembered this, then maybe other stuff will start to come back to me?" I feel a sense of hope at the thought of regaining my other memories.

"I guess," Jake answers, but he looks unsure.

"This is a good thing." Elation takes over any other emotions that I am feeling. Elation at having a break through, and it only just occurs to me that I don't know what has happened to Caitlin. "Hey, Jake? What happened to Caitlin?" I can't believe that I haven't thought to ask anyone this question before now.

"She was arrested at the scene." He looks uneasy at having to tell me this information.

"Why do I get the feeling that there is more to that answer?"

"Um..." Jake runs his free hand through his hair and lets out a puff of air.

"Jake, what aren't you telling me?"

"Caitlin was released on bail, pending further enquiries." I feel like I have been punched in the stomach at his words.

Released on bail?

"Why was she released? And why the hell haven't the police been to see me about any of this?" Anger takes hold of me, and I feel myself start to tremble.

"That may be my fault."

"What do you mean?" I feel so confused. *Nothing new there then, Stace.*

"Don't get mad at me. I have only had your best interests in mind."

"Just tell me, Jake." I loosen my hold on his hand as I get the feeling that I am not going to like what he has to say.

"I have been taking the calls from the police for you. I have a friend on the force who is dealing with your case. He is aware that you have suffered a form of memory loss as a result of the attack. They aren't able to convict Caitlin yet. They need your statement to do that."

"Hang on a minute. Why can't they convict her? She was there, I just saw it in my flashback. She had hold of the knife that was sticking in me." My voice raises several notches as I speak. I ignore the fact that he has been taking the calls for me as my real concern is the fact that Caitlin hasn't been convicted yet.

"She's saying that it was self-defence, and without your statement, they were unable to keep her for longer than seventy-two hours." His jaw starts to tick, and I hope that means that he is just as pissed off as I feel right now.

"So, she's still out there? She could come after me at any time to finish whatever she was planning to do?" How can this have been kept from me?

"That's not going to happen."

"How do you know that? She's fucking psychotic, Jake. I am living proof that she has several screws loose." Panic courses through me, and my eyes start to dart everywhere. She could be watching me right now.

"Stacey, calm down."

"Calm down? Fucking calm down? That crazy woman has been allowed to walk free and you're telling me to calm down?" I shouldn't be shouting at Jake, but there is no one else to say this to, so he is just going to have to bear the brunt of my anger.

"She won't get to you, Stacey. Why do you think Lydia booked time off of work?" My eyes look back to him and I can see that he wasn't supposed to tell me that.

"Lydia knew?" I am absolutely raging. *Why didn't she tell me?* "She told me that she wanted to look after me, and now you're telling me that she has just been acting like some kind of bodyguard?"

"No. Lydia wanted to look after you anyway." I can see that he is panicking slightly at dropping Lydia in it.

"Fucking hell, Jake. You have both kept this from me. I should have been told."

"I'm sorry. We just thought that it was best not to stress you out any more than you already were." He looks genuinely sorry, but I can't see past my anger at the moment. "I am just as angry about the situation as you are. They never should have let her go, and I told them so." Jake's hand comes up to my face and cups my cheek. My eyes lock with his and I feel like all of the air has left my body.

"I won't let her hurt you again. Please believe me when I tell you that." I feel tears sting the backs of my eyes. The funny thing is, I do believe him. The familiarity I felt earlier is back, and I know deep down that he isn't just trying to make me feel better. He means every word that is coming out of his mouth.

I fight back the tears and simply nod my head at him. I have no words left. Just when I think that I can't be surprised or confused any more, I am.

I close my eyes and let my head fall against the head-rest. I am tired. Tired of being kept in the dark. Tired of having to try and piece the last few weeks of my life back together. And I'm tired of being in pain, mentally and physically.

Jake removes his hand from mine and I feel the car start to move. I don't ask where we are going because I really don't care. Wherever I go now, I am going to feel trapped. Caitlin still has her freedom, but I don't.

It seems that I am going to be living this nightmare for a while longer yet.

CHAPTER FIFTEEN

STACEY

I keep my eyes closed for the entire car journey. When the car stops, I open them to be greeted by the sight of a stunning looking house. I don't recognise the building.

"Where are we, Jake?" I ask.

"We are at my house. I thought it would be best for you to get some head space before returning to the flat."

"How thoughtful." My tone is sarcastic, and I sound like a bitch. "I'm sorry," I say quickly.

"It's okay. You have had a few shocks today." Jake is being so nice to me that it makes me feel even worse.

"Even so, I shouldn't be taking it out on you." I give him a small smile, which he returns. Even in my stressed-out state, I can appreciate how dazzling his smile is. I bet he has women falling at his feet everywhere he goes.

"Better me than Lydia right now." The mention of Lydia annoys me. She's meant to be my best friend. She should have been the one to tell me that Caitlin is still out there.

"I don't want to talk about Lydia." I sound like a stubborn brat.

"Fair enough. Come on, let me show you around my house, again," Jake says, breaking some of the tension between us. He gets out of the car and I unbuckle my seat-belt. He comes around to my side, and once again he lifts me out of the car. He then picks my handbag up and hands it to me.

"Thanks," I say. I follow him up the steps to the front door and I wait whilst he unlocks it. He pushes the door open and steps aside, gesturing for me to walk in front of him.

"After you," he says. I walk in and am standing in a hallway that is decorated to the highest standard. I hear Jake close the door behind me. "The kitchen is the last room at the end of the hallway. I don't know about you, but I could do with a coffee right now."

"Sounds good." I walk along the hallway and reach the last door, and I walk through it to enter the most beautiful kitchen that I have ever set foot in. The room is huge, and there is a kitchen island in the middle which I place my handbag on. Jake walks over to one of the worktops and starts fiddling about with, what I presume, is the coffee machine.

"Black, no sugar?" he asks me.

"Yes, please." Of course he knows how I like my coffee. It's so unfair that I know nothing about him.

I run my fingers over the worktop of the kitchen island. The surface feels so smooth, and I get the feeling that I have been in this room before. I know that Jake has told me that I've been here, but I actually feel it within me.

I perch on one of the stools that are next to the island and I continue to scan my eyes across the room. Anything could be a trigger.

Jake walks over with the two cups in his hands and places them on the worktop. He then sits down on the bar stool next to me.

"Anything else coming back to you at all?" he asks sounding hopeful that it might be.

"No."

"Oh."

"But..." I see his eyes light up a little at my use of the word 'but.' "I know deep down that I have been here before. It's still hazy, but this place feels familiar. Does that sound weird? I haven't been making much sense lately."

"No, it doesn't sound weird. I'm pleased that you get a familiar feeling with this place." He gives me a heart-stopping grin and I have to stop myself from leaning over to kiss him.

"Why don't you take a walk around. Maybe it will help to explore the whole house?" he suggests.

"Okay. I won't be long."

"Take your time. I'm just going to answer a few emails whilst I drink my coffee."

"Okay." I stand up off of the stool and exit the kitchen. I enter the hallway and go to a door on my left. When I open it, I see that it is a cosy lounge. I scan the room, but nothing is coming back to me. I repeat this in every room that I come to, on this floor and on the first floor. I still have the familiar feeling, but apart from that there is nothing.

I walk up the flight of stairs to reach the second floor. There are only two doors on this floor, one on each side of the hallway. I decide to explore the room on my left first. I get to the door and push it open. It's a bedroom.

Is this Jake's bedroom?

At the thought, a shiver goes down my spine. I walk further into the room and stop at the edge of the bed. I feel that I should have asked Jake permission before I came in this room. It is clearly his bedroom. A man's watch lies on the bedside table and there is a photo frame behind it. I go over and pick up the frame to be greeted by the sight of my smiling face.

When was this photo taken?

I am led on a bed, which I presume is this one, and my face is peeking out from behind the quilt. My body is covered except for my left leg, which is hooked over the quilt as I am led on my side. The smile on my face is natural. I don't know how long I stand there and stare at the photo of myself, and it isn't until I hear Jake walking along the hallway that I am brought back to reality. His masculine frame appears in the door way.

"So, you found my bedroom then?" he teases, playfully.

"Yeah." I sound miserable.

"Hey," he says softly as he walks over to me. He sees that I have the photo frame in my hand and he smiles. "That was taken just before the attack," he informs me.

I look up at him and I see a range of emotions flicker through his eyes. I see hurt, anger, confusion, frustration and love. From what I know about Jake so far, I can see why I must have fallen for him.

I place the frame back on the bedside table and turn so I am completely facing Jake. His hands are in his trouser suit pockets and his hair is slightly ruffled. I don't know whether I am about to do the right thing or not, but I know that I need him in this moment.

I close the gap between us and search his eyes. As our bodies connect, chest to chest, I hear him hitch a breath of air. I erase any thoughts from my mind, apart from the one where I want to kiss him. I reach up my left hand and place it behind his neck, and he closes his eyes at the touch of my fingers on his skin.

Whilst his eyes are closed, I place my lips on his. I apply gentle pressure and the feel of his soft lips on mine makes my sex stir. When he doesn't stop me, I put my other hand behind his neck and deepen the kiss a little. I feel him place his hands on either side of my hips which gives me goose-bumps.

This feels right.

I don't question what I am doing, I just go with it. I open my mouth so that Jake's tongue can explore me further. With our tongues entwined, I feel like I never want this embrace to end. I move my hands into Jake's hair as our kiss becomes more frenzied. Jake lets out a small groan at my actions and I relish in being able to make him do that. I feel my lips shape into a smile against his mouth. This feeling is incredible.

How could I have forgotten how good this sensation feels?

I forget all about my injury as I push my body into his. Jake's hands snake around my waist so that his arms are locked around me. Unfortunately, it is at this moment that I feel a sharp pain in my side. I break our contact and suck in a mouthful of air. Jake loosens his grip on me but he doesn't completely let go. My hand goes to my side to gently hold it whilst I breathe through the pain.

"Stace, what's wrong? Have I hurt you?" Jake asks in a panicked voice.

"No, no. I just need a minute for the shooting pain to pass." Jake manoeuvres me so that I am sat on the edge of his bed. "My painkillers are in my handbag. Could you get them for me?"

"Sure." Jake leaves the bedroom in a hurry to go and get my handbag which I left on the kitchen island. I close my eyes and concentrate on blocking out the pain as much as I can. Jake comes back a few moments later, carrying my handbag and a glass of water. I take my handbag off of him and find my tablets. My hands are shaking which makes getting the tablets out more difficult, and Jake takes them off of me.

"Two?" he asks, referring to how many tablets I am able to take. I nod at him as I continue to breathe through the pain.

"Thank you," I say as I take the tablets from him, putting them in my mouth and taking a few sips of water to swallow them down before placing the glass on the bedside table. I feel exhausted. I think the last few hours have taken their toll.

"Do you need to go to the hospital?" Jake asks me.

"No, no." That is the last place that I want to go. "It's my fault for not taking my tablets on time," I say as I look to the bedside clock and see that I should have taken them about an hour ago.

"Are you sure?"

"Positive." I smile at him to help try and reassure him.

"Why don't you have a lie down? You look tired." I get the feeling that Jake doesn't want me to leave yet.

"Okay," I say. I don't particularly want to leave yet either. We still have a lot to talk about. If I get some rest then we will be able to talk later, like we had planned to. Jake helps settle me in his bed.

"I will leave you so that you can get some rest."

"Thanks, Jake." He smiles at me and I curse my injury for interrupting our embrace a few moments ago.

"If you need anything, just give me a shout," he says before he turns and leaves the room. I pull the quilt up so that only my head is showing. I close my eyes and replay our kiss in my head. I don't know how many times I replay it before I drift off to a state of blissful sleep.

CHAPTER SIXTEEN

STACEY

I wake up and the room is dark. I groggily look around my surroundings, and it comes back to me that I am in Jake's bedroom, but there is no sign of him in here. I look to the clock on the bedside table and see that it is just gone ten past seven.

How long have I been asleep?

I sit up and take a sip from the glass of water on the bedside table. I listen for any noises coming from anywhere in the house, but I can't hear anything. I slowly stand up and walk to the hallway. The lights in the hallway are dim, which I am grateful for. As my eyes adjust to the dim lighting, I make my way down the stairs until I reach the ground floor. The lounge door is shut, so I make my way to the kitchen.

As I enter the room, I see that Jake is sat at the kitchen island, tapping away on his laptop, and I clear my throat to make him aware of my presence. He turns around and flashes his mega-watt smile at me.

"Hey, you're up. You feeling better?" he asks. I wander over to where he is sat, and I stop by the edge of the island.

"Much better. How long was I out for?"

"About four hours."

"Really?" I can't believe that I slept for so long.

"Yeah. You obviously needed the rest, so I decided not to wake you. How's your side feeling now?"

"It's fine. All pain gone." I smile and Jake gestures for me to take a seat next to him.

"Can I get you a drink?" he asks me.

"No, I'm good thanks." I start fidgeting with my hands as the memory of our kiss comes into my mind. I can feel a slight blush graze my cheeks.

"I was about to make some food. Would you like some?" Jake asks me.

"Sure. What are we having?" I like that he is keeping the conversation light.

"I was just going to cook some chicken stir fry. Is that okay with you?"

"Sounds good." Jake gets up and starts to take relevant ingredients out of their various cupboards. He brings everything over to the kitchen island and then he starts to chop up some vegetables.

"Can I help with anything?" I ask. I feel useless just sat here watching him do it all.

"You could finish chopping these things whilst I put the chicken on to cook."

"Okay." I get off of the stool and go around to where Jake is stood. My body hums as our hands briefly touch from him passing the knife to me. Electricity sparks between us and I quickly focus my gaze on the vegetables so that I don't make a fool of myself by saying, or doing, something stupid. I don't want to ruin the calm, comfortable feeling between us.

I pick up a green pepper and start to de-seed it whilst Jake busies himself putting the chicken breasts in a pan to cook.

"Shall I pop some music on?" Jake asks me.

"Sure. Nothing too girlie though," I say teasingly. He laughs and goes over to an iPod dock in the corner of the kitchen. He browses through his music selection before pressing the play button, and I hum along to the song he chooses as it starts to play. Jake casually walks back over to the frying pan to check on the chicken.

As I finish chopping up the vegetables, a different song starts to play, and it sparks familiarity within me, a sense of nostalgia washing over me. I freeze in place and stop humming. I close my eyes and listen to the music intently. The smooth sounds of the music conjures up feelings of happiness for me, and I know that I am close to remembering something.

The chorus of the song kicks in and all of a sudden, there is an image as clear as day in my mind. Jake and I are dancing. As we move our feet in perfect sync of one another, I can appreciate how good we look together. As we move around the dance floor, it is almost like I am transported directly into the moment, and I feel heat rise within my body. My breathing becomes laboured as I revel in the memory of his touch. I watch the scene in my mind as the song plays out. I don't move the entire time.

The song comes to an end, the memory fades, and I open my eyes to see that Jake is sat on one of the bar stools opposite me. I didn't even hear him move from the frying pan. He sits there with his hands linked and his chin resting on them.

"Anything coming back to you?" he asks.

"Yeah," I say, breathlessly. "That song, and us dancing together. How did you know that the song would trigger something?"

"Lucky guess I suppose." He smiles, clearly pleased with himself that I have remembered a part of our time together. I am astounded that he would think to do that. Since spending time with Jake today, I have managed to regain two memories.

One not so great, and another one that kind of makes up for the bad one. "Want to talk about it?"

"Give me a few moments to process it all." Jake nods and stands, taking the vegetables and adding them to the stir fry. He doesn't seem to want to push me, which is good. I feel that I can take my time and gather my thoughts first. Lydia would be wanting to bombard me with questions right about now.

"Hey, Jake?" he turns around to look at me. "Did Lydia try to call whilst I was asleep?"

"She did. She said that she tried ringing your phone a couple of times but there was no answer. She started to worry, so then she called me. I told her that you had fallen asleep and that I would bring you back to the flat later on. She seemed satisfied by my answer."

"I bet she did." Lydia has been rooting for Jake the entire time that I have played emotional tennis with myself. He looks at me and frowns. "Lydia has been fighting your corner this whole time." I may as well tell him.

"Huh. Remind me to buy her a drink sometime to say thank you."

"Okay," I say, laughing. Jake finishes preparing the stir fry and then dishes it into two bowls. He pushes my bowl towards me and fetches some cutlery. He then takes his food and comes and sits next to me.

"This looks great," I say, my stomach rumbling in appreciation.

"Dig in before it gets cold." We sit and eat in silence for a few moments. I don't feel awkward at all, and the food is delicious.

"So, you were at the Bowden Hall that night then? You know, the last memory that I could recollect when I woke up in the hospital."

"I was," Jake confirms.

"And we danced together."

"We did." He grins as he finishes his last mouthful of food.

"Where was Charles whilst I was dancing with you?" I can't imagine that he would have been happy about me dancing with another man.

"He was in the bar area, chatting up the woman that he later slept with behind your back."

"Oh."

"I then gave you a lift home. Well, we actually went for food first, and then I took you back to Charles' house."

"Really? I didn't get that far. I just saw us dancing together." *He gave me a lift home? Why would he have done that?*

"It's a good memory, isn't it?" he asks the question as if awaiting my approval that I think the same as him. I chuckle like a giddy school girl.

"Yeah, it's not a bad one." I put my fork down as I can't eat another bite. I have managed about half of the amount that Jake has put me. He clears away our plates and cutlery. I ask Jake if I can have a cold drink and he goes about pouring me a diet coke. He obviously knows me well enough not to have to ask what I want. I thank him and take a sip.

"I need to ask you, Stace, are you pissed at me that I have been speaking to the police for you?" He leans against the worktop, bracing himself with his hands, and I see his muscles ripple underneath his T-shirt. He must really look after himself to have a physique like that, and that's from me seeing him with clothes on.

"I was pissed when you told me, yes. But in hindsight, there isn't anything I could have done if they had spoken to me. I didn't remember anything until today, so I guess I can forgive you." I see his shoulders slump with relief. "I will need to speak to them though, especially now that I can remember what happened."

"Uh, I wouldn't do anything just yet."

"Why not?" I ask, feeling puzzled.

"Until your memory completely comes back, the defence will say that your recollection is impaired. They are going to do and say anything that they can to get Caitlin off of whatever charges she may be facing."

"Fucking brilliant." Disappointment wades in, dampening my good mood.

"I know it's frustrating, but we are going to see that bitch put behind bars. Don't think that she will get away with it. Today you have made loads of progress. Maybe I am your lucky charm?" he says, raising one eyebrow at me. I laugh and think how true his words might be.

"You just might be, Jake Waters."

JAKE

I took Stacey back to Lydia's just after nine. She looked tired still and I didn't want to keep her up any longer. I would have been more than happy for her to have stayed with me the night, but I didn't want to push my luck. The kiss we shared earlier plays in my mind. She is starting to give into her desire for me, and I am so fucking thankful. The way her body reacted to me makes my cock swell. Her tight body pressed against mine, her lips devouring mine, her hands reaching into my hair.

Jeez, Waters, calm the fuck down.

I am on my way to meet Paul for a drink, so I need to distract my thoughts. I park the car and walk across the road to The Den. Paul is already here, waiting for me, and is sat at a table just to the right of the bar area. I order myself a bottle of beer and then I go and join him.

"Hey, man," Paul says as I take a seat next to him. "How did it go?" Paul knew that I was seeing Stacey tonight.

"It went fucking brilliantly, all being said."

"Yeah?" He knows how much I have missed her. Apart from Eric, he is the one person that I can confide in.

"Yeah. She remembered stuff today."

"I'm guessing that by stuff, you actually mean that she remembered something about you."

"Yes and no. The first thing she remembered was the stabbing. That wasn't so good." I don't go into the finer details. He doesn't need a blow-by-blow account.

"Shit. Bet that was brutal."

"It wasn't great. But then, at my house, she remembered about the night that I saw her again, at the Bowden Hall." I grin like the cat that got the fucking cream. "She stayed for some food and then I took her back to Lydia's. Oh, speaking of which, have you heard from her yet?" I know that Paul has been pining after Lydia since his stupid meltdown over some guy who was trying to hit on her.

"Nope. I don't know what her problem is. She hasn't spoken to me for two weeks." He takes a long swig of his beer before putting the bottle back on the table.

"Give her a break, man. She has been looking after her best friend who was stabbed not long ago." I make an excuse for Lydia, but I do find it strange that she has ceased all contact with him. It was only the other week that they were inseparable.

"I guess. I thought she may have wanted some support herself, but clearly she doesn't."

"Yeah, well, I don't think she would have the same sort of support in mind as you do." I raise one eyebrow at him as he catches onto my drift.

"*Everyone* seeks that type of support from time to time," Paul retorts. He puts on such a front, but I know that he feels differently towards Lydia. I've seen him with plenty of women to know when one affects him more than another. I think he has definitely got his work cut out for him if he decides to pursue her.

"Another beer? And a shot?" I ask him as I drain the last of my drink.

"Now you're talking."

CHAPTER SEVENTEEN

STACEY

The last few days have passed by in a blur. I have experienced more flashbacks and I'm slowly starting to piece my life back together.

Apart from the flashback of Caitlin, all the other things that I have remembered have been good memories. There are some of me and Lydia at The Den, some of me and Martin, but the most dominating ones are the ones of me and Jake. The more that I remember, the more I can feel myself falling for him.

I haven't seen him since the day that I went to his house, but we have kept in contact via text messages and a couple of phone calls. I think that by not seeing him, it has helped me to realise that he is an important part of my life.

He is picking me up later so that we can have dinner together. Before that though, I have a doctor's appointment which Lydia is taking me to. I confessed to her that I had been to The Den and that I had taken her keys. She wasn't very happy with me, which I expected, but I think she is just relieved that things are coming back to me. She seems to be thrilled with the way that things are progressing between me and Jake.

Lydia pops her head around my bedroom door. "You ready to go, gorgeous?" she asks, interrupting my thoughts.

"Be out in a minute." I have decided to wear my boyfriend jeans because they are loose, and a white pullover. I'm only going to the hospital, so there is no need to dress up. I have left my hair in loose waves and I have decided against any make-up. Au naturel is the vibe of the day. I put my phone in my jean pocket and then I am ready to go.

Lydia is waiting by the front door as I put on my shoes. It's not often that Lydia is waiting for me to be ready.

"All set?" she says. I pick up my handbag and nod at her.

She opens the front door and I follow her out, locking it behind me, and we go to my car, which I am still unable to drive. As we set off, I think about how today will be the first time that I will be able to see what type of scarring that I will be left with. Apart from a couple of twinges in the last two days, I have felt much better. I hope that it is all healing as it should be.

"Want to go and get some lunch after your appointment?" Lydia asks me.

"Let's just see how it goes first." I still feel uneasy being out and about with Caitlin still out there somewhere.

"Oh come on, Stace. It might do you some good to be out of the flat for a bit."

"I said I'll see." I'm not going to be forced to go out for lunch if I don't feel like going. Lydia lets out an exasperated sigh.

"I will be with you, Stace. Caitlin won't have a chance to get near you. Plus, in a public place, I highly doubt that she would try anything."

"If you want to go out then that's fine. I can survive in the flat on my own." *With the door locked and bolted*, I think to myself.

"I know that, but I want to go out for lunch with you. Is that so terrible?" Lydia sticks out her bottom lip at me, and I break into a smile at her ridiculous expression. Maybe I do need to relax a little? Lydia is right, in a public place it is highly unlikely that anything is going to happen.

"Okay, fine. But I want Italian food."

"Deal." She smiles, and I know that she is pleased with her persuasion.

I feel my phone vibrate in my pocket as we pull into the hospital car park and I pull it out to see that I have a message from Jake. My heart does a little leap. I have been feeling more and more excited every time he texts me.

Lydia goes to get a car parking ticket, and I read the message.

> *Morning, beautiful. I just wanted to say good*
> *luck at the hospital today. Will be thinking*
> *of you. Still on for later?*
> *Jake x*

He called me beautiful. A ridiculous grin breaks out across my face, and I type back a reply.

> *Yes, definitely. Looking forward to it.*
> *Stace x*

I get out of the car as Lydia returns with the ticket and I put my phone back in my pocket.

"What's putting that great big smile on your face?" Lydia asks me.

"Jake." I don't hesitate to answer, and Lydia does a little squeal of delight. I know that she is pleased that things are getting back to normal. She links her arm through mine as we make our way to the relevant department in the hospital. As soon as I have sat down, I am called in to see Doctor Reynolds. Lydia comes with me and we both enter his office.

"Ah, Miss Paris, please, come in and take a seat." Doctor Reynolds gestures to the chair in front of his desk. I sit in the one directly opposite him, and Lydia takes a seat that is placed just to the left. "So, how have you been feeling?" he asks me.

"Apart from the odd twinge, I've been feeling good."

"Okay. That's promising news that everything is progressing as it should be. The odd twinge is perfectly normal. Any sharp shooting pains at all?"

"Just one, a couple of days ago."

"How long did the pain last?"

"Not long. I took some painkillers and then I went to sleep. When I woke up the pain had gone." I picture myself being led in Jake's bed, but I quickly push it to the back of my mind. I certainly don't need to be getting all hot and bothered at thoughts of Jake whilst I am talking to my doctor.

"Okay. Let's take a look at the wound, shall we?" Doctor Reynolds stands up and walks over to a curtain in the corner of his office. He pulls it back to reveal a hospital bed behind it. "If you come behind this curtain and strip down to the waist, I will then take the dressing off and see how it's doing." I oblige and go behind the curtain. I perch on the edge of the bed and Doctor Reynolds asks if I am ready. I reply that I am, and he draws the curtain back slightly. He closes the curtain again and talks me through everything that he is doing as he undresses the wound.

I notice the curtain twitch as the dressing is pulled away, and Lydia's face pops into view.

"Lydia!" I exclaim, making the poor doctor jump.

"Oh come on, Stace, we have no secrets. I just want a peek to make sure it looks how it should."

"And how would you know what it should look like?" I ask, raising one eyebrow at her.

"I just want to see."

"I'm not some sort of side-show, you know?"

"I know that." Lydia makes no effort to move away. The doctor looks to me as if waiting for approval for Lydia to be seeing this. I nod at him.

"Fine. But you're not taking any photos of it."

"I won't." She smiles. "Scouts honour."

"Scouts honour? Lydia, you never were, or ever would be a scout considering that you are a female."

"I know, but it sounds good though, right?" I burst out laughing as the doctor looks at Lydia with a look of surprise on his face. I would have thought that he had gotten used to her flamboyant nature whilst I was staying in the hospital, but obviously not.

I signal for the doctor to continue with his examination. As I look down to where the dressing has been removed, I see that I have a fairly large scar which looks to be about four inches long. Even Lydia looks a little shocked. Neither of us say anything as the doctor goes about what he needs to do.

So, this is my everlasting reminder of Caitlin. Fan-fucking-tastic. I swear, I will regain all of my memory and make that bitch pay for what she has done.

Doctor Reynolds finishes up and then re-dresses my wound. When that is done, Doctor Reynolds and Lydia leave me to put my clothes back on. After getting dressed, I go and sit opposite Doctor Reynolds, and wait to see what he says.

"Well, it all appears to be healing exactly as it should be. I am very pleased. There has been minimal weeping, which seems to have completely stopped now. Seeing as you have only had a few twinges in the last few days, you can probably start to dwindle down how many painkillers you are taking, if any at all. Obviously, if you get severe or abnormal pain, then I want you to come straight to the hospital." I nod at him to acknowledge what he is telling me.

"You will need to come back in a week's time and a nurse will take a look at the wound again, and if all is well then we should be able to discharge you completely. I will give you some spare dressings to take with you as you will be able to change them yourself every couple of days."

"Thank you," I say. At least I won't have to keep coming to the hospital to have it done.

"Now, I need to ask you how your memory loss has been. Has anything come back to you at all?"

"Yes. I remember what happened on the night of the attack, and how I ended up in here. I also now know that Jake was a part of my life before this happened. Not everything has come back to me yet, but I am hoping that it will do sooner rather than later."

"That's fantastic news. I think that you are showing brilliant progress, it's just a case of being patient and allowing it to come back naturally." The doctor seems extremely pleased with what I have told him, but something is bugging me.

"Doctor Reynolds?"

"Yes?"

"Is there nothing that I can do in order to quicken things up? It's just that, the police need me to regain my full memory before they can actually convict Caitlin." Saying her name makes me shiver.

"I'm sorry, Miss Paris," Doctor Reynolds says with a sympathetic stare. "There really is no quick fix here. I understand how frustrating it must be for you, but your mind will only fix itself when it is ready to."

I can't help but let out a sigh. "Okay. Just thought that I would ask." I try to brush off my disappointment, but I'm pretty sure that I don't hide it well.

I look to Lydia, who looks just as disappointed as I probably do.

"Don't worry, babes, she will get her comeuppance," Lydia says, giving me a sad smile.

I am determined to see Caitlin go down for what she has done.

I will remember everything.

I have to.

CHAPTER EIGHTEEN

STACEY

> *Hey, Jake. I just thought that I would let you know that the doctor is pleased with my progress. I will tell you properly later what he said. Hope your day is going okay.*
> *Stacey xx*

Lydia and I have just got back to the flat after going out for lunch. It was nice to get out and do something normal, even if I was approaching everything with more caution than I would have done previously.

We looked around a couple of shops afterwards, but I soon started to feel tired, so we came back home. I lie on my bed and stare at my phone, waiting to see if Jake will reply. He does so a few minutes later and I feel a jolt of excitement go through me.

> *That's good. My day hasn't been too bad.*
> *I am aiming to finish at about four-ish.*
> *I should be with you by half past four.*
> *Is that okay?*
> *Jake x*

I text back to tell him that that is fine. I have about two hours to kill whilst I wait for Jake. I wish that I felt confident enough to go to Danish by myself and just order a coffee and a croissant. I crave being able to go and sit in my favourite seat, taking my laptop with me so that I can do some writing. Determination starts to course through me at the thought of overcoming my anxiety at Caitlin not being behind bars.

Why the hell should I stay in all the time?
I should be able to go anywhere that I want.
Why should I let what happened affect the rest of my life?
It has already affected enough of it as it is!

With this in mind, I write Lydia a note. She is in the bath, and I know that if I tell her that I am going out, then she will stop me from going. I write in the note where I have gone and that I have my phone with me if she needs to get hold of me. I leave the note on the coffee table in the lounge, and before I can lose my nerve, I pick up my laptop and head for the front door. I grab my handbag on the way to the front door and put my shoes back on.

Fuck Caitlin.
She will not dictate my life anymore.

I open the front door and leave the flat, closing and locking it behind me. My heartbeat races slightly as I get outside and do a quick scan of the area. Satisfied that there is no sign of her, I begin to walk to Danish, but I remain alert the whole way there. If she was to come at me this time, then I sure as hell would be more prepared.

I get to Danish and feel ridiculously pleased with myself that I am out on my own. I walk into the coffee shop and decide to treat myself to a caramel latte and a cream cake, rather than my usual choice of a croissant. I sit near the back, avoiding my preferred seat by the window. Being by the window would make me feel a little too open, even if it is my favourite seat.

I get settled, open my laptop and turn it on. An older lady brings my order over a few minutes later. I thank her and then I start to read the last few chapters of what I have written. I take a bite of my cream cake and I smile to myself.

See? This is good, Stacey. Out, by yourself, being able to do something that you love.

I put the cake down and start to edit some mistakes that I have noticed in the chapter that I am reading. Midway through editing the chapter, I notice that the door to the coffee shop has opened, and Lydia comes storming in. I roll my eyes and prepare myself for the rant that I am about to receive.

It was nice while it lasted, Stace.

"Stacey Marie Paris," Lydia says a little too loudly as she nears my table. A couple of people look over at her and frown. They clearly weren't expecting their quiet coffee break to be interrupted by a fiery red-head. I turn my attention back to Lydia and I can see that she is fuming. "What the bloody hell do you think you are doing?" She stops at my table and takes the seat opposite me. I close my laptop and smile at her.

"Well, Lydia, I am enjoying a delicious cream cake and a latte. What does it look like I am doing?" I can't help but sound sarcastic.

"Don't get smart with me, missy."

"I'm not," I say innocently.

"Do you know how worried I was when I got out of the bath to find that you had buggered off out without me?" she screeches.

"Keep your voice down, Lyd," I reply. "I just wanted to come out, on my own, without being watched for a little bit."

"There is a reason for you being watched, Stace. Jesus Christ, don't you care that Caitlin might appear and do something stupid again?" Her anger is not dissipating.

"Of course I care, but I don't see why I should live my life in fear. She has already taken enough from me, without her having my freedom too." I feel myself getting angry now, and I take a few breaths to keep myself calm. "Lydia, I know that you are just looking out for me and I am grateful for that, but I need to start doing some things by myself. I didn't go far from the flat, did I?"

"That's not the point." Lydia sighs.

"I won't apologise for coming to my local coffee shop and having a drink and a cake."

"I'm not asking you to apologise," Lydia says, her voice becoming calmer. "I just want you to be careful."

"I know, and I was. I survived the walk here and I am fine. I'm great, actually." Lydia just looks at me and I decide to give her a peace offering. "Cream cake?" I say as I pass the plate with my cake on over to her. I see her begin to smile and I know that I have gotten through to her.

"So I don't even get a whole one?"

I grin at her and I get up to go and order her a cake as well. I return to the table, cake in hand, and I place it in front of Lydia. She picks the cake up and takes a huge bite as I return to my seat and sip my latte.

"Good?" I ask as she shovels more cake into her mouth.

"Mmm. Delicious." I laugh at her and it hits me that this is my normal, and I love it. "So, what time is Jake getting you later?"

"He said about half four."

"Are you going to his place?"

"I presume so. He hasn't said otherwise. All I know is that we are having dinner together." Maybe I should have asked him where we were going? To be honest though, I don't really care, I'm just excited at the thought of seeing him. "Hey, I remembered Paul by the way."

"Oh." Lydia sounds downcast as she answers.

"Oh?" From what I have remembered, Lydia and Paul were doing good.

"It hasn't come back to you yet what I did to him, has it?" I shake my head and Lydia groans. "I didn't think so, otherwise you wouldn't be asking me about him."

"What did you do?" I hate to ask, but I really want to know.

"I'll go and order a coffee, and you're going to need another one. We could be here a little while longer."

JAKE

I finally reach Stacey's just before five. Work was a fucking nightmare. Now all I want to do is unwind and spend some time with Stacey.

Things have been going good between us over the last few days. The more she remembers, the more she is opening up to me. I knock on the flat door and wait for either her or Lydia to answer it. A few minutes' pass by and there is no answer, so I knock again. Maybe they didn't hear me the first time?

There is still no answer.

I knock a third time before marching back down to my car to get my phone. I check the message from her earlier, just to double check that she knew what time I would roughly be here. The message confirms I said four thirty-ish. I scan the area, but there is no sign of her.

Where the fuck is she?

What if something has happened?

My mind starts to race with endless possibilities, and none of them are good. I find her name on my phone and hit the call button. It rings a few times, making me more impatient. Finally, as I am about to hang up, she answers.

"Hey, Jake," she says, sounding cheerful.

"Hi. Is everything okay?"

"Yeah. Why?"

"Well, I'm at the flat and there is no answer."

"Oh shit, is it that time already?" She pauses for a second. "I'm sorry, Jake, I just lost track of time."

"That's okay." Relief washes through me. She just lost track of time, that I can live with.

"I'm with Lydia, at Danish. We will be back in ten minutes."

"No, it's okay. I can come there, if that's easier?" I don't want her rushing around and exhausting herself.

"Are you sure?" she asks.

"Yeah. I will be with you in a few minutes."

"Okay. I'll get you a coffee in. Remind me how you take it again?" She says it in a joking manner. She has really started to relax about the memory loss over the last couple of days.

"I'll have a cappuccino, no sugar."

"Got it. See you shortly."

"Can't wait." I hear her giggle as I hang up the phone and it brings a ridiculous big grin to my face.

She's slowly coming back to me.

STACEY

Jake walks into Danish five minutes later looking so good that I could literally eat him. I feel myself swoon as he makes his way to our table.

"Afternoon, ladies," Jake says as he pulls over a chair from another table. He places the chair next to me and I pass his drink to him. "Thanks," he says as he takes a sip.

"Hi, Jake," Lydia says. "How's it going?"

"Better now that I'm not at work."

"Shit day?" Lydia asks him.

"Like you wouldn't believe." I am yet to speak to him, I just drink in how handsome he looks whilst he and Lydia make chit-chat. The more I remember about him, the more it heightens my feelings for him.

"Stacey?" Lydia says, startling me from my thoughts.

"Huh?"

"Where did you go? You zoned out there," Lydia says, giving me a knowing look. I feel myself blush and I clear my throat and try to think of something to say.

"Oh, uh, I was just thinking about…" Nothing comes to me. Jake and Lydia are both staring at me, waiting for an answer. I look to Lydia for help and luckily, she comes to my rescue and changes the subject.

"So, what are you guys up to tonight?" she asks, and I breathe a sigh of relief. Clearly, I couldn't have told them how I was thinking about Jake, in his suit, looking like a God.

"Well, I was thinking that we could go out somewhere for dinner?" Jake says, directing his question at me.

"Sounds good. Where did you have in mind?" I ask, my brain finally able to piece together a sentence.

"I was thinking about Claringtons."

"Claringtons? Seriously?"

"Oh my God," Lydia chips in. "That place is so swanky. The food is to die for. Oh, you have to go there, Stace." She seems more excited than me about the idea of Jake taking me there.

"Have you never been?" Jake asks me.

"No," I answer, feeling a little nervous at the prospect of going somewhere so posh. It is an exclusive restaurant and some people book months in advance to go there. "Won't it be fully-booked?" I ask.

"No, it's fine. The owner uses my firm for his accounts, and I use them for business meetings, so it's fairly easy for me to book a table."

"Oh," I say. *Oh God, does that mean that I have to get all dressed up?*

"We don't have to go there. We can go somewhere more low-key, if you like?" Jake says, clearly noticing my hesitance.

"What?" Lydia screeches. "Don't be silly, she would love to go there." I raise my eyebrows at Lydia, but she ignores my questioning look. Jake is looking at me for an answer, ignoring Lydia's over the top reaction.

"No, it's okay. We can go to Claringtons." I don't want to sound like a buzz kill by suggesting the local pizza place.

"Great. I will give them a call to book a table. Is seven o'clock okay?"

"That's fine," I answer. Jake gets up from his chair and goes outside to make the phone call. As soon as he is out of ear shot, I stare daggers at Lydia.

"What?" she says, innocently.

"Lydia, I can't go to Claringtons."

"Why not?"

"Because I don't have anything appropriate to wear." It's the first excuse I can think of.

"Yes, you do," Lydia says dismissing my excuse.

"But—"

"Stacey, let him take you out and treat you how you should be treated. Let him have this." I think about her words and I allow them to sink in. I look out of the window at Jake and I think about what he has been put through in the last couple of weeks. Lydia is right. Jake deserves a break from the rollercoaster that has been my life since the stabbing.

"Okay," I say. Lydia squeals with excitement.

"Yay!" Lydia claps her hands together and I laugh at her reaction. She stands up and gestures for me to do the same. "Come on then, we need to get you ready for your date."

CHAPTER NINETEEN

STACEY

By half past six, I am dressed and ready to go. Lydia has had me holed up in her bedroom since we returned from the coffee shop. Jake drove us back from Danish and was then ordered to go and wait in the lounge, and as far as I am aware, he has complied.

Lydia has done my hair and make-up, which I am yet to see. She has also made me wear my little black dress, which shows off my long legs. The dress is one of my favourites, but I am a little worried that it may be a little too much. I voice as much to Lydia, to which she replies that I am talking nonsense. She then informs me that Paul took her there before she decided to avoid him like the plague, so she clearly knows what the people there wear. I suppose I just have to trust her on this one, seeing as I have never been and have no clue what I would be expected to wear.

She finally lets me look in the mirror, and I have to say, she has done an amazing job. My hair is hanging in loose waves around my face, the make-up she has used has accentuated my cheekbones and highlighted the colour of my eyes, making them stand out more. I run my eyes over the dress and I feel like a completely different person.

I am not Stacey who was attacked nearly two weeks ago.

I am just Stacey, going on a date with an incredibly hot guy.

The dress comes to just above my knee, which is acceptable. I wouldn't have wanted to wear anything that was shorter. The long sleeves of the dress mean that I won't need to cover myself over with a cardigan. Lydia retrieves my pair of black shoe boots from my bedroom, and I put them on. She then hands me her black clutch-bag and I transfer my phone, purse and keys into there.

"Wow, Lyd, you really missed your calling to be a stylist or a make-up artist." I am in awe of what she can make me look like when the need calls for it.

"You do look good, girl." She smiles and admires her handiwork. "It helps though that you're naturally gorgeous anyway." I roll my eyes at her and do a twirl. "Jake isn't going to know what's hit him when he sees you." She says his name, and the butterflies start to flutter madly in my stomach.

"Oh God, Lyd. What if I act like a prat when I'm at the posh restaurant?" I ask her nervously.

"Well, then it will be no different to normal." She laughs, and I swat her on the arm. "You will be fine. Just go, have fun and relax. God knows the two of you deserve it."

"You're right," I say, psyching myself up.

"I know. Now, enough chit-chat, you need to be going." She opens her bedroom door and gestures for me to walk out. I take a deep breath, hold my clutch-bag tightly, and I walk down the hallway to the lounge.

I appear in the lounge doorway and Jake is sat in the chair. As I come into view, his eyes look up from his mobile phone and over to where I am stood. His gaze travels slowly from my feet and all the way up my body until his eyes meets mine.

"Wow," he says on a breath. I'm not sure if he was meant to voice that out loud, but it certainly does wonders for my self-esteem.

"You ready to go?" I ask him, deciding to take the lead as he seems to have lost the ability to speak. Jake clears his throat and I hold back a chuckle.

"Yeah." He stands up and I turn and walk to the front door. Lydia is in her bedroom doorway and she gives me a thumbs up as I pass. I give her a quick smile and then open the front door. Jake follows behind me as I walk down the stairs and out into the fresh air. At this point, I turn to him and smile. He still looks slightly wide-eyed, which I am hoping is a good thing. He directs me to his car and opens the passenger door.

"Thanks," I say, as I lower myself into the seat. Once I am in, he shuts the door and goes around to the driver's side, getting in and starting the car. I put my seatbelt on and wait for Jake to start driving. When a few seconds' pass by and the car still hasn't moved, I turn to look at him. His eyes search mine as he holds my gaze.

"You look incredible," he says. I blush and feel my heartbeat accelerate. The moment is charged with the sexual tension radiating between us.

"Thank you." I don't know what else to say.

Jake leans closer to me and I feel like I am going to pass out from the suspense of the moment.

Is he going to kiss me?

Oh God, please let him kiss me.

We haven't kissed since I was last at his house, and that moment was abruptly cut short. His face comes closer to mine and I hold my breath with anticipation. He stops just before he connects our lips.

"May I?" he whispers.

"Yes," I whisper back, and I close my eyes at the feel of his lips on mine.

I bring my hand up so that I am cupping his cheek, and I can feel his stubble lightly graze the palm of my hand. Our tongues entwine, getting themselves reacquainted with each other. My sex awakens and all I want to do is give myself to him. I desperately want his hands to explore my body.

I have had a few flashbacks of Jake in the bedroom, and even those leave me wet with need. His hand rests on my knee, causing goose-bumps to race up and down my body. We stay connected like that for a few moments before the kiss draws to an end. I open my eyes as our lips break apart and I catch my breath before I remove my hand from his cheek and place it in my lap. Jake smiles and I mirror him.

"You ready to go?" he asks. I nod my head and then he diverts his attention to driving.

I feel like I am floating on cloud nine.

I can't believe that I ever forgot this guy. I may not have fully recovered my memory yet, but from what I do know and remember, I feel lucky to have met him.

We drive to the restaurant, listening to the radio in the background and we arrive at Claringtons just before seven o'clock. Jake, ever the gentleman, opens the car door for me and helps me out.

"Are you sure that I look okay?" I ask, my eyes darting to a couple walking in. The woman is wearing a long dress and I start to doubt Lydia's choice of outfit for me.

"You look more than okay," Jake says taking my hand in his. He hands his car keys to a valet, who will go and park the car us before he leads me into the restaurant, and I am immediately bawled over by how upmarket it is.

The hardwood floors are varnished, the décor is all in cream and gold, and the lighting is intimate. Jake and I wait at the hostess table for a waitress, or waiter, to return and I survey the bar area to my left. The bar looks like it is made of solid gold. Even the bar stools ooze class.

The diners all look relaxed and each table is lit by candles. The tables aren't crammed in together either, so there is plenty of space to give a feeling of privacy. Large leather sofas are situated all of the way down the right-hand side of the building, allowing for a relaxing lounge area. The place looks amazing. I hope that the food is just as good.

A waiter comes over to the hostess table and greets both of us. Jake states that he has a reservation and the waiter checks a seating chart on a stand to the left of him. He then asks us to follow him. As we pass through the restaurant, I notice some of the women looking at Jake with a lust filled expression.

Do they really think that by looking at him like that, that he is going to go over and speak to them?

They seem to take no notice of the fact that he is holding my hand, clearly indicating that he is here with someone. The waiter leads us to the back of the restaurant to a table in the corner of the room. Jake pulls out my chair for me and I sit down, thanking him as I do. Jake then sits opposite me and the waiter asks us what we would like to drink. I ask for a diet coke and Jake orders the same.

"I will be back in a moment with your drinks," the waiter says, his eyes lingering a little bit too long on me. Jake notices and I can see his jaw twitch.

When the waiter has gone, I look around me. I feel a little out of place here and I see one woman looking at me. She must be in her fifties, and she sticks her nose up in the air at me. I divert my gaze from her and look back to Jake.

"This place is beautiful," I say. I don't hide how impressed I am at the grandeur of it all.

"It is. Wait until you taste the food." The waiter returns at this point with our drinks. He places mine on the table first and then Jake's. He then starts to tell us what the speciality dish of the night is. The dish is roasted leg of minted lamb with fondant potatoes and seasonal vegetables, with a minted gravy. My mouth waters at the sound of it and I order that without even looking at the menu. Jake orders the same and then dismisses the waiter.

I am about to ask Jake about his day when the waiter returns with two glasses of champagne on a tray.

"I'm sorry to interrupt, but these have been sent to you both as a gift." The waiter places my glass on the table and is about to give Jake his when Jake stops him.

"Hold on a minute. Who sent these?" Jake asks. The waiter looks slightly miffed at being asked this question.

"They didn't give a name, sir."

"Well, if they didn't give you a name, then what did they look like?"

"Um, it was a woman. Blond hair, average height..." his voice trails off as I stand up abruptly and scan my eyes across the room. My eyes dart from left to right.

It has to be Caitlin. No one else with blond hair would buy us both a drink.

In my peripheral vision, I see the waiter pushed aside by Jake, and then he is standing next to me. Jake puts his arm around my shoulders, but I don't feel any less threatened.

"We're leaving. Tell Dean that I will settle the bill when I see him," Jake says to the waiter, even though all we have been brought so far is two soft drinks.

"But, sir, I can't just—" The waiter is trying to stop us from leaving. I want to slap him.

"You can't what?" Jake bellows. "Just tell Dean that Jake Waters had to leave unexpectedly." With that, Jake guides me to the exit as fast as possible.

No one else tries to stop us from leaving. I'm still looking for any signs that Caitlin may be near. She can't have gone far, seeing as we only received the drinks moments ago. Jake instructs the valet to retrieve his car keys. The valet clearly senses the urgency and returns seconds later with the car keys. We walk to Jake's car and he basically lifts me into the passenger seat. I feel like I am in some sort of daze, and my body starts to shake. I am unsure if it's from fear or anger, or both. Jake gets into the driver's side and he drives us away from the restaurant quicker than he probably should.

Why can't this nightmare be over already?

CHAPTER TWENTY

STACEY

I wake up the next morning to Lydia knocking on my bedroom door. I groggily sit up and tell her to come in. She pushes the door open and sits at the end of my bed.

"Morning, babes. How are you feeling?" she asks me. My mind takes me back to last night and I groan. Jake brought me back from the restaurant and filled Lydia in on what had happened. He wanted to take me to his place, but I just wanted to be at the flat. Lydia promised that she would take care of me, but Jake was taking no chances and he ended up sleeping on the sofa.

"I'm just so fucked off with it all, Lyd. Why won't she leave us alone?"

"I don't know the answer to that. I just know that we need to make sure that she doesn't come near you again."

"She's ruining my life, Lyd. What the hell did I ever do to her?" I feel myself start to get so angry over the whole situation.

"Nothing. You have done nothing wrong in any of this. The crazy bitch should be locked up." Lydia is just as mad about the whole thing. I sigh and throw the covers off of me.

"Has Jake gone?" I ask as I put my dressing gown on.

"Yeah. He had to go into the office, but he said that he would call you later."

"Okay." I feel a little disappointed that I didn't get to say goodbye to him before he left. Things were going so well between us last night before the champagne incident. "I'm going to go and make a coffee. Want one?" I ask Lydia.

"Yes please." She follows me into the kitchen and sits at the table. I busy myself making the coffee, but I can feel Lydia's eyes on me the whole time.

"Why are you staring at me?" I ask her. My tone comes across more irritated than I would like it to.

"I'm just worried about you, Stace. I don't like seeing you this angry."

"Well, I'm sorry to upset *you,* Lydia. Forgive me for being a bit pissed off at life right now." I shouldn't be snapping at Lydia, I know that. It's just getting so difficult to keep a lid on my emotions. "I don't deserve any of this. I know that I'm far from perfect, but how did I fuck up so badly that I now have some deranged ex of Jake's, basically, stalking me? It's clearly not enough for her that she has already injured me and given me some sort of memory loss in the process. I just want it to stop, Lyd. I want it to stop."

I start sobbing in the kitchen and I no longer have the strength to continue with any of this. I slide down the cupboard until I am sat on the kitchen floor. I pull my knees up to my chest and hug them with my arms. I bury my face in my knees and I let out all of the anger and frustration that I am feeling.

Lydia's arm goes around my shoulders as she sits beside me, and just holds me. I don't know how long we sit there for, and to be honest, I don't really care.

I need all of this to stop once and for all.

JAKE

I bang my desk with my fist after speaking to the police. Stacey and I called them last night to update them on what had happened at the restaurant. I thought that it might help with bringing Caitlin back into custody. Turns out that I was fucking wrong. Apparently, Caitlin has an alibi for last night. I know that her alibi is bullshit. She was at Claringtons, and she was the one who sent over those drinks. She's fucking with us.

I wish that Stacey's memory would return completely, then she could give a solid statement, and all of this could be over a damn sight quicker.

I feel like I am losing my mind.

I need to think of a way to help her out of this situation.

If only there was some way that Caitlin would confess...

STACEY

It's been a couple of hours since my epic meltdown. I apologised to Lydia for my behaviour, and she was completely understanding which made me feel even more guilty for the way that I spoke to her. I need to keep my emotions under control. I can't go taking it out on the people closest to me.

As I lie on my bed, staring at the ceiling, my phone vibrates on the bedside table. I pick it up and see that I have a message from Jake.

Hi, Stace. Sorry I had to dash off before you woke this morning. I was going to come and see you when I had finished work, but I have an urgent meeting to attend. I will call you tomorrow.
Jake xx

I sigh and chuck the phone on the bed. I'm disappointed that I won't get to see him today, especially after last night. I hear a knock on the front door and I lie still.

I see Lydia walk past my room and I call out to her. "Lydia."

"Yeah?" she says, back tracking so that she is stood in my doorway.

"Don't answer that. It could be Caitlin." Even a simple knock on the door has me questioning whether it should be answered. This is no way to live life.

"It's fine, babes. I know who it is." With that she disappears from sight and I hold my breath as I hear her answer the front door. I hear a lot of shushing, but I can't make out who it is. I sit up, waiting to see who has called round. I don't have to wait long, and when I see who it is, it brings a massive smile to my face.

"Martin!" I squeal as I get up off the bed and walk over to give him a hug.

"Baby girl," he greets me, giving me a gentle squeeze.

"Why didn't you tell me that you were coming over?" I ask him.

"Lydia and I thought that it would be a nice surprise. I'm guessing that it is?"

"Of course it is." I release him, and I see that he is holding a bottle of wine in his hand.

"Lydia also tells me that you are no longer on any painkillers." He waggles the wine in front of my face and I can think of nothing better than sharing a bottle of wine with my two closest friends.

"Lydia would be correct."

"Well, come on then, let's get this baby poured." Martin turns, and I follow him into the lounge. Lydia has already gotten three wine glasses out and placed them on the coffee table. I take a seat on the chair, leaving Lydia and Martin to share the sofa. Martin opens the bottle of wine and pours each of us a glass. We all pick up a glass and Lydia announces that she wants to make a toast.

"To Stacey. I know that the last couple of weeks have been tough, but you have handled the situation better than either of us would have. You are the strongest person that I know. I'm proud of you, babes." I smile at her and am touched by her words.

"And can I just add," Martin says. "Thank you for letting the gorgeous Jake Waters back into your life. I may have only met him once, but fuck me, he is a sight to behold." Lydia and I burst out laughing and we clink our glasses together.

I take a sip of my wine and close my eyes at how delicious it tastes. This is the first drop of alcohol that has graced my lips since the attack. I am not a big drinker, but it is nice to be able to share a drink with my friends.

"So," Martin says, interrupting my silent appreciation of the wine. "When am I going to be properly introduced to Mr Waters then?"

I roll my eyes at him. "You're incorrigible," I reply.

"Just want to get to know the guy in your life, baby girl," he replies.

"I promise that you can meet him again, soon."

"I'll hold you to that promise," he says with a wink.

"How is Clayton anyway?" I ask, changing the subject. "I haven't seen him for ages. Didn't he want to come over tonight?"

"Oh, he's passed out on the sofa. His job is just so demanding, you know?" If Martin wasn't a close friend of mine, then I wouldn't bat an eyelid at his answer. Unfortunately for him, I notice the way in which he avoids my gaze as he answers. I know Martin and I know that something isn't right with the two of them. I don't pry as he obviously isn't ready to tell me yet. Either that, or he doesn't want to say anything in front of Lydia.

"Maybe he can come to lunch with us next week?" I say.

"Yeah. Maybe." Martin doesn't expand on his answer and the flat goes silent for a few moments. Lydia breaks the silence by suggesting putting some music on. She goes over to the stereo and pops on a CD. As music plays quietly, Martin finishes his first glass of wine and pours himself another one. "So, Lydia, how is your love life going?"

"Not great," she answers miserably. I give her a sympathetic look as I know that she is missing Paul.

"Oh no. Want to talk about it?" Martin asks. I expect Lydia to say no, but she doesn't. She surprises me by starting to tell Martin about how she made the mistake of sleeping with someone else.

As she tells the story, I start to get another flashback. It is of the moment that Lydia is talking about. I listen intently, and I let the memories back in.

I can picture everything that she is saying. The images are of her telling me that she slept with someone else. I sip my wine quietly and wait to see if the memory is going to stop, but it doesn't. It carries on.

I usually only remember snippets of things, but this is different.

As I finish my glass of wine and let Lydia and Martin carry on their conversation, I am overcome with what I am experiencing. I close my eyes for a moment and images flash through my mind at quick speed.

From the moment that I saw Jake at the Bowden Hall looking so handsome in his suit, to the way in which he made my heart flutter as we danced together.

From Jake taking me home in his limo, to me leaving Charles after he confessed to sleeping with someone else.

From moving in with Lydia which leads to the awful moment when Donnie assaulted me. Jake was the one to come to my rescue, he was the one who cared for me in the aftermath of the assault.

From the night that Caitlin slashed Jake's arm with a broken vase, to my altercation with her in Jake's kitchen the next morning.

From Jake and I kissing at his place, to him rejecting me, leading to me returning to Lydia's flat.

From me re-starting to work at The Den, making up with Jake, and dress shopping for an event at Waters Industries which led to Jake and I giving into our feelings and spending the night together.

From Caitlin becoming more and more erratic in her behaviour, to the attack that has left me with an everlasting reminder in the form of a stab wound. I can picture myself led on the floor, eyes closed, ears alert as I hear Jake and Eric enter the office, then I see Jake cradling me in his arms, speaking three words that left me feeling some sort of peace despite the dire situation I was in.

"I love you."

Three words that cause my heart to beat rapidly and my adrenaline to accelerate as I remember. It's all just come back to me, as if the memories hadn't disappeared in the first place. No warning and no signs. It's all just there, like something has clicked into place again.

My eyes fly open and I take a few breaths. Lydia and Martin haven't noticed that I zoned out for a short time as they are still deep in conversation. I want to burst with excitement at the fact that I have remembered.

I can't keep quiet. I have to tell them.

"Holy shit," I say, making them both jump and look at me with wide eyes at my outburst. "I've remembered, guys. I've remembered everything."

They both stare at me for a moment like I have lost my marbles. I stand up and put my wine glass down with shaking hands.

"Everything?" Martin asks, and I nod my head at him frantically.

"That's awesome," Lydia says as she also stands up.

"It's all just slotted into place. You were telling Martin about Paul, and the next thing I know, everything that I had forgotten is rushing back to me." My lips pull into a smile at the amazing thing that has just happened. "I can't believe it."

There was a part of me that genuinely thought that I wouldn't regain my full memory. I start to laugh and cry at the same time as relief washes over me. Lydia and Martin both come over and envelope me in a hug, one stood either side of me.

"Baby girl, that's fantastic news," Martin says.

"It was like watching a film, but it's actually my life." I regain some composure and excuse myself to go and use the bathroom where I splash some water on my face and stare at myself in the mirror.

I'm back. I'm completely back.

I feel a little shaky as I dry my face and return to the lounge. Lydia and Martin are looking at me expectantly and I see that my glass has been refilled.

"You okay?" Martin asks.

"Yeah. I'm great." *If a little overwhelmed by my emotions.*

"Stace, when you say you have remembered everything, do you remember what happened with Donnie?" Lydia asks.

"Yes." Not the most pleasant thought, but at least I know now exactly what happened.

"And you're okay with that?" she says.

"Of course I'm not okay with it, but the fact that I have remembered everything far outweighs what he did to me. I know now that I have already dealt with that part of my past. Jake was there. He helped me."

Jake.

Jake is always helping me.

He has done nothing but be there for me, even when I forgot him.

I suddenly have the urge to see him. I know that he said that he had a meeting, but he might be back home now. I go to my bedroom and grab my phone, but I don't have any messages from him.

Maybe he is still busy?

I walk back to the lounge and an idea strikes me.

"Hey, guys," I say getting Lydia and Martin's attention. "How do you feel about accompanying me on a little trip?"

CHAPTER TWENTY-ONE

STACEY

Lydia, Martin and I are on our way to Jake's house, in a taxi. Seeing as we have all been drinking, no one would have been able to drive. I know Jake said that he had a meeting, but it's late evening, so I can't imagine that he will still be at work.

Lydia and Martin were thrilled with my idea of turning up on Jake's doorstep to surprise him. As we get nearer to Jake's place, I feel myself getting more excited. I really hope that he is there.

"This is so exciting," Martin says. He is bouncing up and down in his seat.

"We're nearly there, guys," I say as we turn into Jake's road. I can see his house in the distance and I see that the lights are on.

Oh, please God, let that mean that he is home.

The taxi pulls over outside his house and I look to the other two for reassurance that I am doing the right thing by turning up here.

"What are you waiting for?" Lydia asks me.

"Maybe I should have called first?" I reply.

"Nonsense. Now, get your butt out of the car and go and see him," she says.

"Yeah," Martin chimes in. "Go and see your man, baby girl." I give them both a nod and open the car door.

"Could you guys wait here until you see him open the door? He might not actually be here. He may have just left some lights on."

"Yes we will wait," Lydia replies.

"Hell, I'm going to be peeking the whole time. I want to see what happens," Martin says. I roll my eyes at him and close the car door as I look to Jake's house. I can't see any movement, but that doesn't mean that he isn't home.

I walk towards the driveway and the gravel crunches under my boots as I make my way to the front door. I walk up the steps and before I can change my mind, I knock on the front door. I fidget on the spot as I wait to see if he is home. My heart is pounding, and I start to get the familiar feeling of butterflies in my stomach.

It feels like I am waiting forever, and I am about to give up, when I see a figure through the frosted glass of the front door. The figure is making their way to the front door and I hold my breath when the door starts to open.

And there he is, stood before me, looking more handsome than when I last saw him.

Jake's eyes go wide as he sees me stood there, and I drink in every bit of him that I can. His jeans, his black shirt which is untucked, his unruly hair and his caramel eyes which bore into mine.

"Stacey," he says, breaking the silence. "What are you doing here?" He looks puzzled by my appearance, and his greeting certainly isn't what I was expecting. I thought he may have been pleased to see me.

"Um, I just..." My voice trails off as I see someone appear at the end of the hallway, behind Jake, and my gaze travels to the figure behind him.

Recognition of who it is slowly sweeps over me.

No way.

It can't be.

Jake wouldn't do this to me, would he?

The figure slowly starts to move forwards and my blood runs ice-cold through my body. I freeze and take in the scene before me.

Caitlin is in Jake's house.

Why the fuck is she in his house? I don't understand.

Her beady eyes zone in on me and she starts to smirk. My mouth drops open and tears sting the backs of my eyes.

Don't cry, Stacey. Don't give her the satisfaction, or him for that matter.

I blink furiously, and my gaze travels back to Jake. Any words that I may have wanted to say to him have left me, leaving me speechless.

I can feel the blood pounding in my ears and my whole body begins to tremble.

I frantically try to think of some sort of explanation for what I am seeing, but there isn't one.

"Trust me," Jake whispers, breaking my frantic thoughts.

I scoff at him in response. *Trust him? That's all he has to say to me? Is he for real right now? He's got the bitch that stabbed me in his house, and I'm supposed to trust him?*

I start to slowly back down the steps until my feet hit the gravel of the driveway.

"You bastard," I whisper back to him. They are the only words that I can say to him before I turn and run. I run as fast as I can, ignoring the pulling of my side as I pick up my pace.

The taxi that brought me here has gone. Lydia and Martin must have seen Jake answer the door and then decided that I wasn't going to be coming back with them. I can't blame them, I thought the same myself, to be honest.

I manage to run to the end of the road before I need to stop. I clutch my side as it aches, and I try to catch my breath. My mind races.

Why is Caitlin at his house?
It doesn't make any sense.
I thought that Jake hated her as much as I do?
Are they back together?

That last thought alone makes tears cascade down my face. I start walking as I realise that she could leave his house at any moment and come after me.

I have my phone on me, so I try to call Lydia, but it goes to answerphone.

"Fuck," I say out loud as I try Martin's number instead. Martin's phone rings but he doesn't pick up, so I start walking in the direction of the flat as fast as I can manage.

Multiple questions enter my head on the way back to the flat, and none of them can be answered.

It takes me nearly half an hour to reach the flat and I am exhausted by the time that I get there. I climb the steps and reach the front door, banging on it loudly, hoping that Lydia and Martin didn't stop at a bar or anything on their way home. I didn't bring my keys with me which was a bloody stupid thing to do. I continue to bang the door, each knock louder than the last.

"Alright, I'm coming," I hear Lydia shout from the other side. Thank God for that, she is home. She unlocks the door and I can see she is about to bollock the life out of the person banging on the door, until she sees that it is me.

"Stacey? Why aren't you with Jake?" she asks as her eyes go wide.

"He's a fucking bastard. That's why I'm not with Jake." I march into the flat, past Lydia, and go into the lounge. There is still a bit of wine left in the bottle that we had opened earlier, so I pick it up and take a swig. Lydia comes rushing in the room after me.

"What are you talking about? What's he done?" She searches my face for an answer, but she would never guess what has happened in a million years.

"He's got Caitlin there," I say, taking another mouthful of wine.

"You what?" she says, frowning at my words.

"Caitlin is in Jake's house. I saw it with my own eyes." My whole body is trembling with shock and anger.

"Caitlin? In Jake's house?" Lydia seems just as confused by my words as I was when I saw Caitlin in Jake's hallway.

"Yes, Lydia. Jake opened the door, and then Caitlin was stood behind him, in the hallway." I sigh and flop down on the chair, throwing my phone onto the coffee table as I do.

"But... But... That doesn't make any sense." Lydia takes a seat on the sofa and stares at me, aghast. Before either of us can say anything else, my phone starts to ring on the coffee table. We both lean forward to see who it is, but a part of me already knows that it will be Jake before I see his name on the screen. A part of me wants to hear what his explanation would be, but the other part of me is so mad that I wouldn't trust myself to not completely lose it with him.

"Are you going to answer?" Lydia asks me.

"No. I may want to hear his excuses, but that's all that it would be. Excuses. There isn't any way that he can get out of this one, Lyd." My heart plummets as the adrenaline coursing through my body starts to wear off, and the phone stops ringing. "How could he do that to me, Lyd? How could he have that woman in his house after what she has done?"

"I don't know, Stace." Lydia shrugs her shoulders and I can see that she is disappointed by this turn of events. She was so pleased that Jake and I were getting back on track, and now this has happened.

My phone beeps to signal that I have a text message, and I wearily lean forwards to pick up my phone. Of course the message is from Jake.

Trust me.

I scoff and put the phone back on the table. It's the exact same words that he said to me when I was stood on his doorstep. My mind is all over the place and my heart is shattering into millions of tiny pieces.

"What is it?" Lydia asks.

"It's a message from Jake. It just says, 'trust me.'"

"Trust me?"

"Yeah. I mean, really, how the bloody hell can he ask me to trust him after what I have just seen? I've been so stupid, Lyd."

"Oh no. There is no way that you are blaming yourself for this," she scolds me. She knows me well and knows how my mind works.

"I thought that things were good between us, even with everything that has happened. I had fallen for him again, Lyd. I've fallen for him so hard, and it fucking hurts." I choke on the last word as I let the tears spill down my cheeks.

Lydia comes over and nudges me so that I move over, allowing her to sit in the chair with me. She hugs me, but I take no comfort from it.

Jake has destroyed me. A part of me now wishes that I hadn't remembered just how strongly I felt for him before the attack.

I may not be certain of a lot of things right now, but there is one thing that I am certain of, and that is the fact that it is going to take me a hell of a long time to get over Jake Waters.

CHAPTER TWENTY-TWO

STACEY

At some point last night, Lydia and I fell asleep on her bed. I don't recall what time it was, I was too distraught over what I had seen earlier that evening.

My head is pounding as I groggily sit up and check the time. It is only eight-thirty in the morning. I feel awful. I am about to get up to go and get a glass of water for my dry mouth, when someone starts banging on the door. The bang on the door jolts Lydia awake and she jumps to a sitting position beside me. I look at her and wait for her to come around somewhat. The door bangs again and we both look at each other puzzled.

"Who the hell is that at this time of the morning?" Lydia asks out loud.

"No idea," I answer. "But if it's Jake, then he can just bloody well stay out there." Lydia starts to get out of bed, putting her dressing gown around her as she goes.

"I'll go and see." With that, she plods out of her bedroom and walks down the hallway to the front door. She disappears from sight and I strain to listen to who it is. I half expect Jake to come barrelling in here. I sit with my knees clutched to my chest, waiting to see what happens, and then Lydia's voice breaks through the silence that surrounds me.

"Stacey, there is someone here to see you," she shouts.

It better not be Jake. I told her I didn't want to see him.

Reluctantly, I get out of bed. I don't have to worry about wearing a dressing gown as I am wearing a pair of leggings and a baggy jumper. I tentatively walk down the hallway, psyching myself up as I go. I round the corner and see that there is a man stood in the doorway. It's not Jake. It's a guy that I have never seen before. I give Lydia a questioning look when the guy starts to speak.

"Miss Paris?" he asks me.

"Uh, yeah, that's me." I feel slightly nervous as I answer him.

"I'm D.C. Sykes," he says as he flashes his police badge at me. "I'm here to speak with you regarding the incident with Caitlin Carter a couple of weeks ago. May I come in?" I nod, and Lydia moves to one side, allowing room for the officer to pass through.

My eyes go wide as he passes, and my gaze meets Lydia's. She just shrugs at me and closes the front door.

"The door on your left is the lounge, we can sit in there," I say, managing to find my voice. D.C. Sykes nods and leads the way to the lounge. Lydia and I follow him, and he opts to sit on the chair. I slowly take a seat on the sofa and wait to see what is about to happen whilst Lydia stands awkwardly in the doorway.

"Come and sit down, Lyd," I say to her, and her eyes shift to D.C. Sykes as if she is looking to him for an answer. I quickly cotton on to her thinking and I ask the officer a question. "Is it okay if Lydia stays with me for this conversation?"

"Of course," he answers. I turn to Lydia and pat the sofa beside me. She quickly sits down, remaining quiet, and I clasp my hands together to stop myself from fidgeting. "I won't keep you long, Miss Paris, and I apologise for the early call, but there has been a development that you need to be made aware of."

"Okay," I answer. *A development?* I am intrigued, and I want to hear more.

"Miss Caitlin Carter has made a full confession about her involvement in the attack on you. We will still need a statement from you, but with her confession, she will be prosecuted anyway." As he stops talking, I feel like all of the air has left my lungs. I'm not sure that I heard him right. *Maybe I am dreaming?*

"I'm sorry, did you just say that she confessed?" I ask.

"Yes. Last night. She also admitted to stalking you."

"That's great news," Lydia pipes up.

I stare at the officer as I process his words.

Prosecuted.

Stalking me.

Full confession.

"I'm sure that this is a lot for you to take in, Miss Paris, especially as this is the first time that I am meeting you to discuss it."

"Uh, yes, it is a lot to process. I was actually going to the doctors today to tell them that I have regained my full memory about everything."

"Well, that's good," D.C. Sykes answers. "It must be a relief for you."

"It is," I say as I sit there in shock at what I am being told.

"Would anyone like a drink?" Lydia asks.

"A coffee would be great. Black, two sugars, please," D.C. Sykes answers.

"No problem. Stace?" Lydia gives me a nudge to get my attention.

"Uh, yeah. Thanks." Lydia gets up and leaves the room. "Um, D.C. Sykes, I'm struggling to understand why Caitlin would come to you and confess. Didn't she say that she stabbed me in self-defence? Why would she have a sudden change of heart? It doesn't make any sense."

"Well, you would need to thank Mr Jake Waters for her confession." Now that was not the answer that I was expecting.

"How do you mean?" My eyebrows knit together at his words.

"Mr Waters invited Miss Carter around to his house last night with the excuse that he wanted to talk to her. What Miss Carter didn't know was that Mr Waters was wearing a wire. An officer and myself were parked close by and we were listening to the entire conversation. Miss Carter made her full confession as well as admitting to threatening you on a previous occasion, and she admitted that she has been following your movements for the last few weeks.

"Once we had acquired all of the information that we needed, we arrested her. Miss Carter is now in custody and she will remain there until she is sentenced." Lydia returns to the room at this moment and places our drinks on the coffee table. She is unaware of what I have just been told as she sits back on the sofa, next to me.

D.C. Sykes takes a sip of his coffee as I digest what he has just said.

Jake did all of this?

He did all of this for me?

He invited that woman into his home just so that he could get a confession out of her. This is why he told me to trust him.

How could I have gotten it so wrong?

"Um, D.C. Sykes, where is Jake now?" I ask.

"He said that he would be at work if we needed to contact him further as he gave a full statement last night. I do have to say that we were a little worried when you showed up at his house. Luckily, it didn't impact on any evidence that we obtained."

"Oh my God."

"What? What did I miss?" Lydia asks, clearly wondering why the hell I am asking where Jake is. I don't answer her. I am in a daze.

Jake was setting her up. My assumptions have been way off the mark on this one.

I stand up and wordlessly, I leave the room, going to the hallway to put my trainers on. I do a quick check of my face in the mirror. I don't look too bad, all things considered. I go to my bedroom and run a hairbrush through my hair before returning to the lounge to get my phone off of the coffee table.

I turn to D.C. Sykes. "Thanks for coming to let me know about Caitlin. I will come to the station later to give my statement, if that's okay?"

"Sure. I will be there until five o'clock, so if you can make it before then, that would be great."

"Will do." I then turn to walk from the living room, but Lydia's voice draws my attention.

"Where are you going?" she asks me.

"I just need to be somewhere."

"Say hi to Jake for me," D.C. Sykes says, clearly being able to read my intentions. "And tell that son of a bitch that he owes me, big time." A massive grin spreads across his face as I nod my head. I then leave the flat, grabbing my bunch of keys on the way out. I still can't drive my car, so I walk along the street as fast as I can. I could have asked Lydia to take me, but I need to be on my own for this. Also, with Caitlin in custody, I have no need to worry about her coming after me.

I am on autopilot as I walk to the other side of town, and I reach the Waters Industries building twenty minutes later. I walk into the foyer and march straight towards the lifts, and I get thrown a few funny looks due to what I am wearing. I guess they don't see many girls come in here dressed in leggings and a baggy jumper, but I don't care.

All I care about is seeing Jake.

I press the button for the lifts and one opens immediately, so I get in and press the number for Jake's floor. Before the doors have a chance to shut, six more people get into the lift. Each one of them presses a different button and I curse the fact that they couldn't all be going to the same bloody floor. I tap my foot impatiently as the lift keeps stopping and starting.

Once the other six have vacated the lift, I take a look at my reflection in the lift doors. My cheeks are flushed, and my hair has gone a bit fly-away from the walk here. Unfortunately, Jake is just going to have to excuse my scruffy manner today. My appearance is irrelevant right now. The urge to see him far outweighed my desire to put on make-up and nicer clothing.

The lift stops, and the doors open on Jake's floor. I walk out and march in the direction of his office doors. I walk past his PA, who is sat at her desk, talking on the telephone. She abruptly ends her phone call and shouts out to me as my hand goes to the handle of Jake's office door.

"Oh, Miss, I'm afraid that Mr Waters is with clients. You can't go in there." She looks flabbergasted, and I make a mental note to apologise to her later.

"Oh yes I can," I say, and I open his office door before she can stop me.

I walk in and see that he is sat at a large table to my left, with four other men. Jake is sat with his back to me, so he has no idea that it is me who has just barged in here. The four other men who are sat on the opposite side of the table to Jake, all look at me with wide eyes.

I just stand on the spot like an idiot, waiting for Jake to turn around.

He seems to take forever to do so, but when he does, he stands up and fixes his gaze on me. His eyebrows are slightly raised, suggesting that he is shocked to see me here. He steps around his chair and stands there, putting his hands in his trouser pockets.

He's waiting to see what my next move is going to be.

I don't keep him waiting long.

I start to cross the room, keeping my eyes fixed on his caramel pools. I don't give a shit that there are other people in here. I take a few deep breaths to steady my nerves at how Jake will react. Adrenaline is spiking through my body, and I pray that he won't tell me to leave.

The closer I get to Jake, the more I am convinced that he can hear my heart pounding.

As I reach him and align my body with his, I can feel the heat emanating from his body. He hasn't told me to leave so far, so I take that as a good sign. I reach up both of my hands and I put one on each side of his face. I can feel the slight stubble and the softness of his skin beneath my fingertips. I push up on my feet, so that I am stood on tiptoes, and I close the space left between us.

My face tilts up and I press my lips to his. I kiss him gently to start with, unsure of whether he will tell me to stop or not, but when he doesn't pull away from me, I move my hands to the back of his neck.

I feel his arms wrap around my waist and I open my mouth to him, letting our tongues become entwined. He pulls my body tighter to his as our kiss deepens, and I let my fingers snake their way into his hair.

I am completely lost in this moment.

No one and nothing else matters.

I pour all of the passion that I am feeling into our kiss. I need Jake to know how I feel about him, and how I feel about everything that he has done for me.

My body hums.

My lips tingle.

It's like we are the only two people in the world.

It isn't until I hear someone clear their throat behind Jake, that I am brought back to reality. I pull my face back slightly, but I keep my focus on Jake.

"Thank you," I whisper to him. I don't need to explain why I am saying this to him. He knows what I am thanking him for.

"You're welcome."

"I'm sorry about interrupting your meeting."

"Don't be. It's the best interruption that I have ever had." I giggle at his comment and I feel relieved about the fact that he doesn't seem to care that we have had an audience watching us.

"I thought that I should let you know that my memory's back. I can remember everything."

"Everything?" he asks as if needing me to confirm what I just said.

"*Everything.*" I lick my lips as I answer, and I can see the heat in Jake's eyes.

One of the men sat at the table coughs, making me peer around Jake's head. Each one of the men sat there are all staring at us with open mouths.

"Maybe we should continue this later, in private?" I say.

"Sounds good. I'll call you when I am finished here."

"I'll be waiting."

"I look forward to it." Jake smiles, releasing his grip on me, and I step out of his arms. I turn and start to walk from the room and see that Jake's PA is stood by the doors, smiling. I look at her sheepishly as I feel a blush creep up my neck and graze my cheeks.

As I reach her, I apologise for not listening to her when she tried to stop me from coming in here. She waves her hands at me in a manner that suggests she isn't bothered by my ignorance to her earlier request.

"Hey, Stace?" Jake says, stopping me in my tracks. I turn around and our eyes lock onto one another.

"Welcome back, baby," he says, grinning like the cat that got the cream. Butterflies are going crazy in my stomach as I smile and turn to walk out of Jake's office.

I leave with a bounce in my step and feeling more positive than I have in weeks.

It's all going to be okay, I just know it.

CHAPTER TWENTY-THREE

STACEY

I return to the flat at half past three. After leaving Jake's office, I went straight to the police station to give them my statement. It is a relief to finally get it over and done with.

D.C. Sykes was the one who dealt with me and he made me feel completely at ease. He said that he will let me know as soon as a court date has been set for Caitlin's trial. I won't need to attend if I don't want to. It's nice to have the choice as with the way I feel about her right now, I never want to have to see her again.

The flat is quiet when I open the front door and there is no sign of Lydia. There is however a note scribbled on the kitchen table from her. She has had to go to The Den to sort out some paperwork. I bet it is killing her not knowing how things went with Jake. I know that as soon as I see her, she will want all the details.

I decide to have a shower and freshen myself up whilst I wait for Jake to finish work.

Once showered, I dry myself and put my black, silk dressing gown on. Jake said that he would call me when he had finished work, so I have plenty of time to get ready. I tidy the bathroom after I use it and then I go to my bedroom and dry my hair. Once dried, I style my locks into soft curls. I want to look better than I did earlier for when Jake comes over.

I make my way to the kitchen and flick the kettle on. I take a quick look at my phone, which I left on the kitchen table, but there have been no missed calls. I hum quietly to myself as I wait for the kettle to boil, but a knock on the front door breaks my peaceful moment. I bet it's someone trying to sell something.

I walk down the hallway and open the front door, expecting to dismiss whoever it is very quickly, only to be confronted with the sight of Jake standing there.

"Oh," I say, surprised to see him here already. His eyes roam up and down my body and I become very aware of the fact that I am completely naked beneath my dressing gown. "Um, I thought you were going to call when you left work?" I am thrown by his sudden arrival.

"I thought that I would surprise you. Can I come in?" he asks in his smooth tones.

"Oh, uh, yeah, sure." I sound like a bumbling idiot.

I step back to allow him to enter the flat. "I was just about to make a coffee. Would you like one?" I ask as I shut the door after he has walked past me. As I close the door, I feel Jake's lips by my ear and I almost orgasm on the spot.

"I didn't come for coffee," he purrs in my ear. His breath heats my cheek and he pulls my hair back over my shoulder. I am still facing the door as his hands go either side of me and his palms go flat against the door, his body encasing mine.

I close my eyes and inhale his scent. He smells spectacular. I can't believe that I ever doubted him.

I try to keep my breathing as normal as possible, but it's hard to do with him this close to me. My whole body becomes covered in goose-bumps and my sex starts to awaken. He must be able to sense how turned on by him I am.

Jake's breath travels from my cheek to my neck, and then his lips make contact with my skin. He places light kisses on the side of my neck and I lean into his body so that my back is resting against his chest. I give a moan of approval and I feel his lips curve into a smile against my skin.

I keep my eyes closed and relish in the feel of him. I feel his hand cup my cheek before he gently turns my head to the side. I can feel his lips centimetres from mine.

"Open your eyes," he says in the sexiest voice that I have ever heard. I do as he says, and I am penetrated by his caramel pools. So many emotions pass between us. "God I've missed you." I am unable to reply as his lips crash onto mine.

We devour each other hungrily and Jake turns me, so that we are chest to chest. He then pushes my back against the door and I love the way his macho side makes an appearance.

He is all man, and he is all mine.

His hands travel downwards, and he starts to caress my ass. I moan into his mouth and I grip his biceps. My body responds to him in a way that it never has with anyone else.

Jake's hands move to the backs of my thighs and he lifts me up. I wrap my legs around his waist and link my arms around the back of his neck. Our lips break apart and we both pant as we try to catch our breath, and I feel the overwhelming need to tell Jake that I am sorry.

"Jake, I'm sorry for everything that I have put you through these last few weeks. I can't thank you enough for what you have done for me." I feel tears sting the backs of my eyes, but I need to say more. "I never should have doubted you, and I am sorry for that."

I feel a single tear start to roll down my cheek. Jake's hand comes up and he wipes the tear away with his thumb. The gesture is so tender that it almost makes me cry more.

"It's okay. You don't have to explain," Jake says. He has been so understanding about everything.

"Yes, I do," I whisper. I tighten my grip on Jake's waist with my legs. I never want anything to break us apart again. "My life has been like a rollercoaster since I woke up in the hospital, and you have been there every step of the way. I'm sorry for pushing you away at the beginning, and I'm sorry for some of the uncaring things that I have said to you. But out of everything, there is one thing that I am most sorry for..." My voice trails off as my throat clogs with unshed tears. Jake is looking at me expectantly, waiting for me to finish what I need to say. I am grateful for his patience whilst I start to fall apart in his arms. "Most of all, I'm sorry that I forgot *you*."

I see his eyes glaze over, and I know that my words have touched him. I know that my words have meant something to him.

"I'm just glad to have you back," Jake says, placing a light kiss on my lips.

"What did I ever do to deserve you, Jake Waters?" I will never know the answer to that question.

"You're just lucky, I guess," he says, teasingly.

I laugh at his answer. "I guess I am."

"How does your side feel now?" he asks, changing the subject.

"It's fine. No pain."

"Is that so?" He cocks one eyebrow at me and I hope that I am thinking the same thing that he is. "In that case, what do you say about removing some of these layers between us?"

I can think of nothing better.

"There isn't much to remove on my part. I'm only wearing this dressing gown."

"Oh really?" Jake starts to walk with me still straddled around him, to my bedroom. He closes the door behind us as we enter, and he gently lowers me to my feet. "Well then, I guess I better even things out a bit."

I stare at him as he takes off his suit jacket and starts to unbutton his shirt. At the first sight of his chest, I inhale a sharp intake of breath. His body is perfect. Ripped abs and smooth, tanned skin.

He drops his shirt to the floor and then his hands find the belt of my dressing gown. He undoes the belt and the dressing gown splits down the middle. He pushes the material to the sides and then slowly pushes it down my arms. My skin prickles and I feel the cool air touch my naked skin.

I stand there, immobilised by his actions. I can now remember how good the sex was between us, so I am already anticipating what he may do to me.

Jake undoes his trousers and lets them fall to the ground. I watch as he then pushes his boxers down his legs and I lick my lips at the sight of him in all his naked glory. Beautiful.

He steps out of the clothes and kicks them to one side before gently pushing his body against mine and lowering me onto the bed. He treats me like I am going to break, and I know that he is worried about hurting my side even though I have told him that it isn't painful anymore. I still have the dressing covering it, but it should be able to come off completely in the next couple of days. I push the thought out of my mind and focus on Jake's eyes. I can't believe that we have lost weeks of intimacy, of the connection that we share.

Jake covers my body with his and I move my legs to either side of him, so that he can slide in-between them. I feel the head of his long, hard cock nudge at my entrance, and I am already wet with my need for him to enter me.

He looks to me for reassurance that I am okay, and I nod my head slightly at him. He pushes slowly into me and I groan as I feel him fill me. He moves so that he is all the way in and I tremble.

"Okay?" he asks me.

"Yes." He lowers his face to me and I put my arms around his shoulders. His lips cover mine and he slowly starts to move in and out of me.

This isn't going to be rushed.

This is us rediscovering each other's bodies.

This is us celebrating our reunion.

This is us erasing all the bad of the last few weeks.

This is us, making some perfect memories.

CHAPTER TWENTY-FOUR

STACEY

I lie there after making love to Jake, and I revel in the feel of his arms wrapped around me. I am led so that I have my head resting on his chest and one leg straddled over his. He holds me tight against his body, and I savour every bit of this moment, this pure state of bliss that I have been missing for the last few weeks. The way Jake made love to me just now has left me speechless. I wouldn't have had it any other way. It was perfect.

"That was incredible," Jake says, mirroring what I was thinking. I smile at the fact that he found it just as amazing as I did. He was gentle with me, almost as if he thought that I would break, but it made it more intimate somehow. The way he seems to know what my body needs is mind-blowing.

I run my fingers across his abs, loving how they ripple. His physique is outstanding. It makes me think that I should tone myself up a bit more. I am about to voice this to Jake, when there is an almighty banging on the front door. I jump from the loud noise.

"What the hell was that?" I say out loud. I feel myself start to become irritated that, whatever it was, it has interrupted our blissful moment.

"I have no—" Before Jake can finish his sentence, there is another bang.

I disentangle myself from Jake's arms and I jump out of the bed. I find my dressing gown on the floor and I quickly put it on. Jake follows me out of the bed and there is another bang. I open my bedroom door before Jake has got his boxers on and go to the front door. I can hear a lot of giggling from the other side and then I hear my name being called.

"Stacey, open the fucking door." It's Lydia. She must have forgotten her keys.

I breathe a sigh of relief that it is her. I unlock the door and open it, only to be knocked backwards as Lydia comes flying through the door. I land on my ass with a thud as Lydia lands beside me, and some guy lands on top of her. She is laughing like a maniac.

Good grief, how much has she had to drink?

I feel a twinge in my side which makes me suck in a sharp breath of air as Jake appears to my left, fully dressed, taking in the scene before him.

"What the fuck happened?" he says as he comes over and helps me to my feet.

"Nothing, I just fell over. It's fine," I say. I really don't want him to fuss over me.

"No, it's not. What about your side, Stace?" he says, angrily. I wave a dismissive hand at him.

"I landed on my ass. I'm sure that my side will be fine." Jake wraps one arm around my waist to keep me steady as I look down at Lydia. I have never seen her this wasted before. "Lyd, are you okay?" I ask as I lean over her. Her eyes are glazed over, and she seems to be having great difficulty in focussing on me.

"Hey, babes," she slurs. "Have you met..." Her voice trails off and she waves her hand in the direction of the guy, who has now rolled onto his back on the floor, next to her. The guy's eyes are half closed, and I bet he hasn't got a clue where he is.

"Do you want a coffee or something?" I ask, not quite knowing how to deal with Lydia and this strange man.

"No thanks. We're just gonna go and, you know..." She doesn't manage to finish her sentence as her eyes close and her head turns to the side. I look from Lydia to Jake and then back to Lydia. I stare open-mouthed at the state of her. Her hair is a mess, she has mascara smudged underneath her eyes, and her clothes look like they need a damn good ironing.

"Lydia," I say loudly, trying to get her attention. There is no response, so I crouch down beside her, ignoring the pain in my side as I do. I nudge her gently to start with, and then a little bit harder as she doesn't respond.

"Lydia," I say a little more urgently. She gives a small moan and I nudge her harder. "Lydia, wake up." She groggily moves her head and slightly opens her eyes. She mumbles something, but I have no idea what. "Lyd, get up." She needs to get to bed and sleep off the ridiculous amount of alcohol that she has consumed.

I look up to Jake helplessly and he runs his hands through his hair.

"She is completely out of it," he says, stating the obvious. "Who's the guy with her?" he asks me.

"I have absolutely no idea. Maybe I should try and lift her to her room?" I say, more to myself than to Jake.

"Oh no you're not." Jake's tone is adamant.

"But I can't just leave her led in the hallway all night."

"I'll lift her to her room." With that, Jake signals for me to move out of the way so that he can carry Lydia to her bedroom. I slowly stand up and go and open her bedroom door. I put her bedside lamp on so that Jake can see where to go. He carries her in with no problems and then places her on the bed. I manage to take Lydia's shoes off of her feet and then I cover her over with her quilt.

"What about the guy she brought back?" I say to Jake.

"Well, I'm not lifting him into bed," Jake says, making me laugh. The look on his face is priceless.

"Do you think that we can wake him up?" I ask once my laughter has subsided.

"I know," Jake says, walking out of Lydia's room. I follow him, curious to see what he is going to do. He disappears into the kitchen and I come to a stop by the guy who is currently sleeping in the hallway.

A few seconds later, Jake emerges from the kitchen with a glass of water in his hand. Before I can ask what he is going to do, he pours the water over the guys face, making him splutter and open his eyes. I put my hand to my mouth to stifle the laughter that is threatening to burst out of me.

"Hey, bud," Jake says, leaning over the guy to get his attention. "Time for you to leave." Jake then helps the guy to his feet and directs him out of the front door. I don't think the guy knows what planet he has woken up on, as his eyes are wide with shock as Jake shuts the front door on him. Jake then turns to me, with an innocent look on his face.

"What?" he asks, putting his arms out either side of him.

"I can't believe that you just did that," I say, no longer able to contain my laughter.

"It got him out of here, didn't it?" he says whilst smiling.

"It sure did." I chuckle as I make my way over to him. "Thank you for lifting Lydia into her bedroom," I say as I come into contact with him.

"No problem," he says, moving his hands so that they are holding my hips.

"I wonder how I can show you my appreciation," I tease. I lay my hands on Jake's chest and his hands move around so that they are cupping my ass.

"I'm sure that you can think of something." Jake leans down and kisses me. I move my hands up his chest and am about to move them to his shoulders when I feel a sharp pain in my side.

"Ouch," I say, interrupting the moment. I bring my hands back down and curse myself for not masking the pain.

"Babe, what's wrong?" Jake looks concerned as he steps back from me and gives me a quick look over to see if he can see what the problem is.

"It's nothing. I just had a little shooting pain in my side. It won't be anything to worry about."

"Let me see."

"Jake, don't fuss. I will just take some painkillers and it will be fine." I try to reassure him, but I should have known that wouldn't work.

"Stacey, let me see," his tone is commanding, and I know that he isn't going to back down on this one. I sigh and take his hand, leading him into my bedroom. I pop the light on and close the door. Jake sits on the bed and I stand in front of him. I undo my dressing gown and Jake moves the material to one side.

I watch Jake as his eyes go wide before I follow his gaze and notice a tiny patch of red on the dressing. It isn't much, but it is enough to cause alarm bells to go off in my head.

"Fuck. I'm taking you to the hospital." Jake stands up off of the bed and goes to walk out of the room.

"Wait," I say, stopping him from going further. He turns to look at me. "I need to get dressed first, I can't go in just my dressing gown."

"Why not?" Jake asks.

"Because I won't feel comfortable being naked beneath just a dressing gown." I am not going to budge on this one, blood or no blood.

"Fine." Jake sighs. "But we need to be quick. You need to see a doctor."

"Yes, I am fully aware of that," I say as I grab my jogging bottoms to put on. Unfortunately, I have a bit of trouble bending to put them on.

"Stop," Jake says as he takes the jogging bottoms off of me and kneels to the floor to help me put them on. "You are going to be the death of me, woman." I smile as he pulls the jogging bottoms up and then helps me slip on a T-shirt. He then puts my socks and shoes on for me.

He kisses me on the nose and takes my hand in his. "Can we go now?" he asks.

"Yes."

Jake takes his car keys out of his pocket and guides me out of the flat.

CHAPTER TWENTY-FIVE

STACEY

After spending a couple of hours at the hospital, I am given the all clear to go home. I had managed to tear a couple of stitches that hadn't yet knitted my skin back together. The on-call doctor did a thorough examination and then cleaned and re-stitched the part that had torn.

After thanking the doctor, Jake takes my hand and we walk out of the hospital and back to his car. He helps me get in before getting into the driver's seat. As he starts the engine, I notice that his jaw is clenched, so I move my hand and place it on his knee. He turns to look at me, his eyes softening a little.

"Are you okay?" I ask him. I know damn well that he is pissed off, but I would like to ease the tension radiating from his body.

"Yeah, I'm fine," he answers, very unconvincingly.

"Jake, it was just an accident." I don't want him to think badly of Lydia.

"That may be, but I'm taking you home with me." I roll my eyes at him, but inside I am secretly thrilled that he wants to take me to his place. "Don't roll your eyes at me. You heard the doctor in there, you need to take it easy, and you can't do that with Lydia coming home all shades of fucked up."

"That's not fair, Jake. Lydia has been good to me since the attack. She didn't mean to do it."

"I don't care. I'm going to look after you now, and that's final." He starts to pull the car out of the hospital car park and we turn onto the main road. "We can go to the flat and you can pack some things. That way, we can check on Lydia at the same time, if that makes you feel better."

"Okay." I don't elaborate on my answer. I may be pleased that Jake wants to look after me, but I don't want him thinking that I am completely useless.

We drive in silence back to the flat and when Jake has parked the car, he helps me out and up the stairs to the front door. I unlock the door and go straight to Lydia's room to check on her. She is led exactly as we left her, and I close her bedroom door after being satisfied that she is okay.

I walk to my bedroom and find Jake sat on my bed. He still looks pissed off, so I go and stand in front of him. I nudge his legs so that he opens them slightly, allowing me to walk into the gap he has just created.

He looks up to me and I place my hands on his shoulders. "Relax. I'm fine."

"I just don't like to think of what would have happened if I hadn't been here." His eyes bore into mine. "I nearly lost you once, Stace, I can't even contemplate what I would do if it happened a second time." I am touched by his honesty, but I need to de-dramatise this situation.

"I only tore a couple of stitches, Jake. It's nothing to worry about. You were here to help me and that's all that matters." I bend down slowly and kiss him on the lips. It's a tender kiss that leaves me feeling weak at the knees.

When I come up for air, I can see that some of the tension from his body has dissipated. I quickly change the subject to get Jake's mind off of what happened. "Right then, there is a pink holdall in the bottom of the wardrobe, could you get it for me, please?" I step away from him and start picking out some underwear to pack as he gets the holdall for me. He places it on the bed and unzips it. I pack my underwear and then I start looking for some comfortable clothes to take with me.

"You know, I think that the underwear is enough clothing," Jake says with a twinkle in his eye. I laugh at him as I grab some leggings and jogging bottoms, popping them in the holdall along with some tops and a couple of jumpers. I ask Jake to unplug my laptop and pack that for me, with the charger. I also pack my phone charger, and then I go and collect my toiletries from the bathroom. I pack some make-up and my hairbrush, and I quickly scan the room to see if I have forgotten anything that I might need. I spot my dressing gown on the floor and ask Jake to pick it up for me. He does, and I place it on top of all the other items that I am taking.

"I think that will be enough. I'll be coming back in a few days' time, so I shouldn't need anything else."

"Hmm. We'll see about that," Jake mutters as he zips up the holdall and exits my bedroom. I ignore his comment and follow him into the hallway. I go into the kitchen and write a quick note for Lydia, so that she knows where I am, and I leave the note on the kitchen table before walking back to Jake. I pick my handbag up off of the side which already has my phone, purse and keys in it, and then I take Jake's waiting hand.

I lock the door as we leave, and we make our way back to Jake's car. Jake pops my holdall into the boot and then, as seems to be normality at the moment, he helps me into the passenger seat. Once Jake is in the car, I buckle up and then we are on our way to his place.

"So, do you have to put up with Lydia behaving like that often?" he asks me. Lydia clearly hasn't made a very good impression of herself tonight.

"No," I say on a sigh. "I don't know why she got so wasted." I do know, but I am not about to tell Jake why. I know that Lydia is still struggling with the whole Paul situation. I am worried about her, but I also need to get myself back to full health.

"Well, whatever the reason, she needs to get her shit sorted," Jake says, his tone harsh.

"Give her a break." I really can't go into any details.

"Give her a break? Stacey, her behaviour tonight resulted in you having to go to hospital." He's not going to let this issue go easily.

"Jake, if you are going to keep going on about it then you can turn the car back around and drive me home," I say in a firm tone. "I will not listen to you going on about it all night. It was an accident, end of story." I hear Jake chuckle beside me and I whip my head around to look at him. "What's so funny?" One minute he's annoyed, and the next he is laughing.

"Nothing."

"No, go on, I want to know." Now it is me that is sounding annoyed. I impatiently sit there and wait for him to answer.

"You know, you're sexy when you're being feisty." Jake grins and I feel a smile tug at my lips. I wasn't expecting that answer.

He glances at me and I quickly divert my eyes so that I am looking out of the window.

"I wasn't going for sexy, Jake," I answer, but my tone has definitely lost its firm edge.

"I know. That makes it even sexier."

I laugh at his answer and just like that, all the tension from his beautiful face, and body, has vanished.

JAKE

Fuck me. This woman really knows how to get under my skin.

I take in her perfect profile as I glance at her in the passenger seat, and my cock stirs in appreciation of her. Her creamy skin, her twinkling blue eyes, and her full lips makes me want to do all sorts of things to her. Of course, we won't be doing anything for a while as she needs to get better, but when she is fully recovered, I am going to catapult her into another world.

My mind wanders back to our tryst, earlier this evening. Her petite but curvy body led on the bed. Her pussy wet with her need for me. Her moans as I rode her slowly like music to my ears. Her breasts pushing against my chest as our tongues were entwined makes my cock start to harden.

Damn, Waters, get a hold of yourself.

I fidget slightly in my seat to ease the pressure on my groin.

I make a promise to myself right here, right now.

She is my life.

I am going to do everything I can to keep her safe. I've finally got her back. There is no way I am going to lose her again.

I'm going to look after her so good that she is never going to want to leave my place.

CHAPTER TWENTY-SIX

STACEY

We arrive back at Jake's and he unlocks the front door. He lets me enter first and then follows behind me, carrying my holdall with him. I stop awkwardly in the hallway and wait to see which room Jake is going to go into. He places my holdall by the stairs and then offers to make us both a drink. I follow him into the kitchen and I take a seat on one of the bar stools, placing my handbag in front of me on the worktop.

"Hot chocolate?" he asks me.

"Yes, please." It's far too late for coffee, and if I drink one now, then I will be up all night. Jake busies himself getting the cups and making the drinks as I scan the room. I think this is one of my most favourite rooms in this house. It's got a homely feel to it.

"Can I get you anything to eat?" Jake asks as he brings over the hot chocolates.

"No thanks. The hot chocolate will be fine." Jake takes a seat next to me and we sit in comfortable silence for a few moments. It doesn't take me long to finish my drink, and my body warms from the inside at the chocolatey goodness. I stifle a yawn and my eyes flick up to see what the time is. It's gone eleven, and from the events of the day, it's no wonder I'm tired. Jake sees me trying to stop myself from yawning.

"Come on you," he says as he places his now empty mug on the worktop. "Let's go to bed." Jake stands, and I follow suit, and he leads the way up the stairs, picking up my holdall on the way. I wearily reach the top of the second flight of stairs and Jake puts his arm around my waist to help me along. He can clearly see that my body is losing its strength as tiredness takes over.

"Thanks," I say as we walk to his bedroom. Jake guides me to the bed and I sit down on the edge, groaning in pleasure as my ass meets the soft mattress. Jake places my holdall to the side of the room and then helps me out of my clothes. I stand up and let Jake take my jogging bottoms off. I don't have any underwear on as we were in a rush to get to the hospital earlier.

As I lift my arms up for him to take my T-shirt off, I wince slightly. My side is sore after being messed about with. Jake gently moves my T-shirt up my arms, and his hands graze the sides of my breasts, making my nipples instantly harden. Even though I am in pain, my body craves his touch.

Jake throws my T-shirt on the floor and eyes me approvingly before walking to his wardrobe. He disappears for a few seconds and then emerges, carrying one of his shirts.

"Wear this," he says as he holds the shirt open for me to put my arms into. "It will be less painful to take this on and off than one of your tops." I slide my arms into the fabric and inhale deeply as the scent of him encases me. I button up the shirt and Jake goes to my holdall, bringing a pair of my lacy knickers with him. I step into them and he pulls them up as I raise an eyebrow at him quizzically. I thought that he would like the thought of me being commando. "It's hard enough to keep my hands off of you, without the added enticement of you wearing nothing under that shirt."

"Yeah but think about how good it will be when I'm all better," I tease him.

"Oh trust me, I am. And it won't just be good. When the time comes, Stacey Paris, I am going to make you delirious with pleasure." The heat emanating from his eyes makes me feel weak with need for him. I step up on tip toes and place a light kiss on his lips.

"I look forward to it," I whisper to him. He smiles, and it makes my heart flutter. His smile really is gorgeous.

"In the meantime, you need to get some rest." Jake twirls me around so that I am facing the bed and he pulls the quilt cover back. I get into the bed and he covers me with the quilt. He then starts to undress himself and I can feel myself salivating at the sight of his naked flesh. He strips down to his boxers and then disappears into the ensuite, emerging a few minutes later and climbing into the bed behind me.

I can't lie so that I am facing him as I need to stay led on my good side.

I feel his chest against my back and his hand rests on my leg. He can't put his arms around me, because if he does, his arm will be resting on my wound. He nuzzles his face against my neck and I giggle as it tickles. I feel feather-light kisses start to inch their way around to my lips. I turn my head to look at him and his lips cover mine.

He kisses me softly and I love the feel of our tongues merging together. We take our time exploring one another's mouths. His hand leaves my leg and comes up to caress my cheek. I so badly want to take things further, but I know that Jake would stop it. He wouldn't want me to end up hurting myself again, so I know that there is no point in even trying.

"Hey, Jake?" I say as our kiss comes to an end.

"Yeah?" His face is inches from mine and I love the intense look in his eyes.

"I know that I apologised to you earlier, but there was something else that I didn't get the chance to say." I turn so that I am led on my back, enabling me to look at him properly.

"Okay." He looks wary of what I might be about to say, but I am hoping that when he hears it, it will make him happy. I hold his gaze as I feel my eyes start to well up. I have never felt this strongly about anyone else. I may not have known Jake for long in reality, but I feel like I have known him my whole life. And, I know that I have only just got my memory back, but it has only made how I feel about him even stronger, if that is at all possible.

As I study every aspect of his handsome face, I bring my hand up and trace his lips. He plants a kiss on my fingers and then takes hold of my hand, lowering it to the bed.

"What is it, Stace?" He searches my eyes for an answer.

"I heard you, when I was lying on the office floor. I heard what you said to me."

"You did?"

"Yes, and I just wanted to tell you that, I love you too." I have never said those words to him before, so it is kind of a big deal for me. I have also never meant them as much as I do now. His face breaks into a massive smile and he kisses me again.

"You have no idea how long I have been waiting to hear those words," he says as his hand entwines with mine.

"I think I do." I have been waiting forever for someone to mean it when they say they love me. I know that Charles never did, not in the way that he should have, but Jake does.

He places his hand back on my leg and I get as comfortable as possible. With Jake curled around me, I close my eyes, feeling like I am on cloud nine despite what transpired earlier this evening.

"You were made for me, Stacey Paris," Jake says, his voice soft and low. I smile, and with those words in mind, it's not long before I fall into a deep, blissful sleep.

CHAPTER TWENTY-SEVEN

STACEY

I wake up to find that I am alone in bed. There is no sign of Jake in the room. I sit up groggily, and a smile begins to form on my face from the memory of last night. Happiness consumes me as I get out of bed and go to the ensuite. I use the facilities and then take a look at myself in the giant mirror. I look flushed and my hair is a mess, but even I can see that my eyes are sparkling.

I go and get my hairbrush from my holdall and take my toothbrush with me at the same time. After tying my hair into a ponytail and freshening up my breath, I leave Jake's bedroom to go and find where he has disappeared to.

I get to the first floor and I can hear him talking in one of the rooms, so I walk along the hallway and come to a stop at his office door. When he sees me, he looks up and smiles. He hasn't put a T-shirt on and I appreciate his manly form as he sits at his desk. He gestures for me to walk over to him and as I approach him, he moves his chair back and pats his lap for me to sit down. I sit on his lap and start to plant light kisses on his neck. He is still on the phone and I have to stop myself from laughing at the fact that he has all of a sudden become a little tongue tied.

"I'm sorry, Valerie, I'm going to have to call you back later. I have something that I need to attend to." He leans over and puts the phone down and lets out a low growl as I kiss my way to his lips. After I am finished, I pull my face away from his slightly.

"Good morning, handsome."

"Good morning to you too." He doesn't seem remotely bothered that I interrupted his phone call.

"Shouldn't you have left for work by now?" I ask, noting that it is half past ten in the morning.

"I'm not going into work today."

"Why not?"

"Because."

"Oh, Jake, I don't want you to put your life on hold for me any more than you already have." I don't want to be seen as a burden in his life.

"I'm not. I want to spend the day with you. Is that a problem?"

"Well, no, but—"

"No buts," he says, cutting me off before I can finish. "I have employees and if they can't manage without me, then they shouldn't be working for me." Well, I wasn't expecting that answer.

"Want some breakfast?" he asks, changing the subject.

"Sure," I say as I realise just how hungry I actually am. I stand up and lead the way downstairs to the kitchen.

"What would madam like? Bacon? Eggs? Toast?"

"Whatever you're having is fine by me."

"Bacon and eggs it is." He starts to get the relevant ingredients out and busies himself turning the grill on. I sit at the kitchen island and draw in a breath as the coldness of the seat touches my legs. I push past it and then see that my handbag is still on the worktop. I unzip it and take my phone out, hoping that Lydia may have called me.

As I look at the screen, I see that I only have one message, and it's not from Lydia. However, the message still brings a smile to my face.

Hey, baby girl. How's things going with that delicious man candy of yours? Want to come out for some drinks at the weekend? I am in desperate need of a wild night, and it wouldn't be the same without my girl there. Hit me up.

Mart x

His message makes me laugh, causing Jake to turn around and look to see what I am laughing at.

"What's so funny?" he asks.

"I just got a text from Martin, that's all. He makes me laugh. He's invited me out for drinks this weekend."

"Uh, I don't think so," Jake answers. I raise my eyes from my phone to his face and I can see his features are stern.

"Why not?" I ask as the smile disappears from my face. *Who does he think he is? I can make up my own mind.*

"Stacey, the doctor said that you have to take it easy and going out for drinks isn't taking it easy."

"It's not like I would be break-dancing on the tables. It's just drinks with a friend."

"No."

"No?" I can feel myself starting to get angry. I know that Jake is only saying it for my benefit, but it annoys me that he is telling me what to do. "You listen to me, Jake Waters, if I want to go out for drinks then I will, whether you say so or not."

"When you're better you can go for all the drinks you like, but until then, you're not going. Plus, you're back on your painkillers, so you can't drink anyway." He seems to think that the discussion is over as he turns his attention back to the bacon and eggs that he is cooking. I stare at him, my mouth open in shock. I feel like a child who has just been told "No" to going to the school disco. I scowl at Jake's back and type out a reply to Martin.

*Sounds good, Mart. Man candy being
annoying. Will call you later to discuss.
Stace xx*

I put my phone back in my handbag, only for it to start ringing. I pull it back out as Jake serves up the bacon and eggs and see that it's Susie's name across the screen.

"Hey, Susie."

"Thank God you answered your phone," Susie says, sounding flustered.

"What's wrong?"

"Listen, I'm sorry to bother you when you're currently signed off work, but do you know where Lydia is? She's meant to be here right now, but she's not answering her phone."

"Oh, um, I'm not at home right now and I haven't seen her since yesterday." I can't tell Susie that Lydia was wasted beyond belief last night. It wouldn't look good seeing as Lydia is her superior.

"Oh. Okay. Just thought that I would ask."

"If it's a shift that you need covering then maybe you should phone the agency staff for the time being?" I suggest.

"Do you think that Lydia would mind?"

"Not at all. And if she does, then just tell her that I gave you the go ahead."

"Thanks, Stace. You're a star. And sorry again for bothering you." Susie sounds a little bit calmer now that she can call someone else in.

"It's no problem. If you need anything else, then just give me a call."

"Thanks, hun. Take care."

"Bye." I hang up the phone and try to call Lydia. Her phone just keeps ringing until it eventually goes to voicemail. I try another three times, all with the same result.

"Problem?" Jake asks as he puts a piece of bacon into his mouth.

"Nope." My answer is short as I am still pissed with him. I pick up some bacon and take a bite, although I'm not really very hungry anymore. My mind is now on Lydia and how she is doing.

"Are you really not going to tell me?" he asks, and I can see the amusement in his eyes.

"Why do you look like you are enjoying the fact that I am pissed off?"

"I'm not enjoying it. You just look cute when you're moody." I scoff at his answer. He really does know how to push my buttons.

"Stop trying to butter me up, Jake." I sigh in frustration.

"I'm sorry. Go on, tell me what's bothering you." He pushes away his empty plate and waits for me to answer.

"I may be your girlfriend, Jake, but you don't own me. I don't like being told what I can and cannot do. I have had that done to me before, and I sure as hell won't let it happen again."

"Whoa, whoa, whoa." Jake looks genuinely shocked by my outburst. "Stacey, I'm not trying to tell you what to do, and if it came across like that, then I apologise. I would never tell you that you couldn't go somewhere. I just think that whilst your body is recovering, going out for drinks isn't a great idea." I soften slightly at his words and at the genuine look on his face. "Do you really think that I would try and control you like that?"

Oh shit, I have really taken his words out of context. He looks distraught at the thought.

"No, of course I don't," I say with a sigh. "I'm sorry. I shouldn't have jumped to conclusions." I take his hand in mine and link my fingers through his. "I know that you're not like that. I guess I'm just frustrated that I can't do things for myself at the moment and I took it out on you. I apologise." Jake kisses the end of my nose and I know that he has forgiven my over-reaction. "I'm also worried about Lydia. She's not answering her phone, and after the state of her last night, I'm just hoping that she will be okay."

"Do you want to go to the flat and check on her?" Jake asks me.

"You mean, I can go out?" I say playfully.

"Ha ha," Jake answers sarcastically.

"You really don't mind if we go and see her?" I don't want to put him out but checking on Lydia will put my mind at rest.

"As long as it makes you happy, then I don't mind."

I stand up off of the bar stool and, carefully, wrap my arms around Jake's neck. "I really do love you, Mr Waters."

"You better." He puts his arms around me and places his hands on my ass, causing a tingle to work its way up my body. "Have you taken your painkillers yet?" he asks.

"No. I'll take them now and then we can go and get dressed and go to the flat." I disentangle myself from Jake and walk over to where he left my painkillers last night. I grab a glass from the cupboard and fill it with water then put the pills in my mouth, swilling them down with the cold liquid.

"Are you not going to eat any more of your breakfast?" Jake asks as he looks at the minimal amount that I have consumed. I put the glass of water down, grab a piece of bacon off of my plate and take a bite.

"Come on," I say to him as I walk out of the kitchen. "We need to get dressed and get going."

"Already?" he moans as he follows me up the stairs.

"The sooner we go, the sooner we can come back." I reach the second floor and enter Jake's bedroom and ask Jake to lift my holdall onto the bed, which he does. I sift through the few clothes that I packed and decide to wear my black leggings. I keep Jake's shirt on as it doesn't involve having to struggle into a T-shirt. I am only going to the flat so it's not like I need to get dressed up.

Jake helps me into my leggings and then he puts some socks on for me. It's nice that he wants to do these things for me, but I can't wait until I don't have to rely on somebody else for help. Jake keeps the jogging bottoms on that he is already wearing and pulls a T-shirt over his head. He looks gorgeous with his hair all ruffled up. I lick my lips at the sight of him and he catches me staring as my tongue darts back into my mouth.

"See something that you like?" he asks, one eyebrow raised. I feel a blush creep its way across my cheeks and I suddenly become a little flustered.

Jake stalks towards me and all I want to do is rip his clothes back off of him. He takes my head in his hands and kisses me passionately, leaving me breathless when I finally come up for air.

"Mmm," he murmurs. "I could get used to having you here, you know?" he says as he lets go of my face and walks to the ensuite. I stare after him and wonder if he meant anything by that comment.

I could get used to it too. I won't be telling him that though. We are only just getting back on track after the whole Caitlin fiasco.

I walk to the ensuite doorway to see that Jake is just finishing brushing his teeth. He spits the toothpaste out and wipes his mouth on a towel before swilling his toothbrush off and putting it back into the holder. He leans his hands on the sink and looks at my reflection in the mirror. I must look ridiculous in his shirt and I suddenly feel a little self-conscious of the fact that I haven't made much of an effort with my appearance. I break my gaze away from him and look down to the floor.

"Everything okay over there?" he asks me.

"I just think that I look a little bit silly going out dressed like this, that's all." I keep my eyes down and I see Jake's feet appear beside mine. His hand comes to my chin and he tilts my face so that I am looking at him.

"You look beautiful." I scoff at his compliment as I know that I really don't look good right now. I divert my eyes from his and feel a little bit silly for telling him.

"Look at me," he says. My eyes are drawn back to him and his caramel pools burn into me. "You do not look silly. If anything, wearing my shirt makes you look even more sexy than you normally do. Stop putting yourself down."

"You are just saying that because you're my boyfriend."

"No I'm not. I would be saying it even if we weren't together because it's the truth." I know that Jake wouldn't lie to me, so I guess I am just feeling a bit self-conscious about myself right now. I'm hardly the catch of the century, what with the gash on my side and the fact that I can't spruce myself up as I normally would.

Jake places a kiss on the end of my nose, which seems to have become a new thing that he likes to do. "Now, let's get going." He takes my hand and leads me back down the stairs. Helping me into my shoes, he then goes to the kitchen to retrieve my handbag for me. I thank him and follow him out of the front door and to his car.

I can't help but feel a little nervous about what state I might find Lydia in when we get there. I just hope that she is okay.

CHAPTER TWENTY-EIGHT

STACEY

Jake and I arrive at the flat and I take a deep breath as I unlock the front door. I push the door open and the first thing to hit me is the smell inside. I instantly cover my nose to stop the rancid aroma from infiltrating my nostrils any further.

"What the hell is that smell?" Jake says behind me. I turn to look at him and see that he has his nose screwed up in disgust.

"I guess there is only one way we're going to find out." I walk into the flat with Jake following close behind me. I walk to the lounge and stop in the doorway at the sight that I find. I stare open-mouthed at the mess that greets me.

There are beer cans strewn everywhere and cigarettes spilling out of a cup on the coffee table. My eyes scan the room and they land on a suspicious looking wet patch on the sofa. I make my way to the window so that I can open the curtains and get a good look at what the wet patch is. As I allow light to enter the room, I see that the wet patch is a pile of sick.

Oh lovely.

"Fucking hell," Jake says, voicing the words that I felt like saying.

"I don't understand why the place is in such a mess?" I say. You would think that I had been gone for weeks rather than just the one night.

I open the windows wide to let some of the stench out. At least we can see why it smells so bad now. Alcohol, cigarettes and sick are not a good scent combination.

I make my way out of the lounge and go into the kitchen. This room isn't in much better shape. There are some wine bottles on the kitchen worktop and it looks like a plate has been smashed over the floor.

What the fuck has gone on here? The place looks horrendous.

I stalk out of the kitchen and go straight to Lydia's bedroom. Jake follows me, and I'm glad that he does because God knows what I will find in there. I can hear the faint sound of her television on from behind the closed door. I don't bother to knock, I just barge my way into the room, ready to confront Lydia about the mess. However, on opening the door, I am greeted by the sight of Lydia hunched over on the bed, asleep, along with some guy led next to her. Recognition dawns on me that it is the same guy that Jake kicked out of here last night before we left for the hospital.

As if seeing the flat in such a state wasn't shocking enough, I then spot the white powder that is strewn across Lydia's bedside table.

Fucking hell. What has Lydia gotten herself into?

I rush over to Lydia's side of the bed and try to wake her up.

"Lydia, wake up," I say as I start to nudge her. There is no response, so I push her gently onto her side and place my hands on her shoulders. I give her a little shake, but there is still no response.

"Lydia," I say, more loudly this time. I shake her a little harder. Still nothing. "Jake, she's not waking up," I shout as tears gather at the backs of my eyes. Jake strides over to me and removes my hands from Lydia. He then lifts her arm and checks her pulse. After a few tense seconds, Jake lays her arm back down and turns to me.

"It's okay, she's just sleeping." I feel the air whoosh from my lungs and tears start to fall down my cheeks. Jake envelopes me in his arms and I hug him fiercely. He holds me like that until I have calmed myself down a bit.

"Sorry," I say as I wipe my face with the sleeve of Jake's shirt that I am wearing.

"It's okay. She just needs to sleep off whatever she has taken." His eyes look at the white powder and he shakes his head slightly. He then looks to the guy sleeping next to Lydia and sighs. "I guess I better wake him up with the old water trick again."

I smile at him and he disappears from the room, so I busy myself by opening the curtains and windows. Jake returns with a glass of water in hand and goes to the side of the bed where the guy is sleeping.

"Here goes," he says as I watch him tip the water over the guy's face. The guy instantly springs up, spluttering. His eyes look wild, as if he has pulled an all-nighter, which I presume he pretty much has.

"What the fuck are you doing, man?" he says as his eyes focus on Jake. "Are you fucking crazy?"

"Time for you to leave. Get your shit and get out." Jake's tone is powerful, and his stance is intimidating. Even in this crazy scenario, I am attracted to Jake's control of the situation.

The guy clearly senses that Jake isn't messing around. He holds his hands up and stands off of the bed. He is fully-clothed, so at least we don't have to wait for him to get dressed. The guy even has his shoes on for goodness sake.

As the guy walks past Jake, his head turns in my direction. He obviously didn't realise that I was in here until just now. I see his eyes rake over me and I outwardly cringe at his unwelcome perusal of me.

"Wow. Lydia said her friends were pretty, but you are off the charts. Wanna hook up later?" Oh shit, that was just about the worst thing that the guy could have said to me. Before I know what is happening, Jake is dragging the guy out of Lydia's bedroom and down the hallway. The next thing I hear is the front door opening, and then slamming shut.

Jake stalks back into the room a few seconds later and I can feel the irritation coming off of him in waves.

"Fucking low-life," Jake mutters. He looks to me and I give him a smile which he returns, and I know that I am going to thank him in more ways than one, when my body has healed.

I return my attention to Lydia, who is still out of it, oblivious to anything that has just happened.

"I never should have left her on her own." I should have been here. It's clear that she needed a friend, and I wasn't around for her.

"*You* needed to go to the hospital, and *I* insisted that you came back to my place. No one was to know that this was going to happen." I know deep down that he's right, but the guilt that I am feeling right now is awful. "Let's leave her to sleep whilst we tidy this place up."

"You don't have to tidy up, Jake. You have done enough."

"I'm helping and that's final. I'll go and make a start in the kitchen." I walk over to him and place a light kiss on his lips.

"You're going to get sick of helping me and my friends one of these days," I say to him, fearing that it may become true if much more happens.

"That will never happen, babe. You're stuck with me."

My heart starts to beat a little faster. I could certainly think of worse things to be stuck with, that's for sure.

"I'll make it up to you later," I answer as I lick my lips. He lets out a low growl and squeezes my ass with both of his hands.

"I look forward to it, Miss Paris," he says as he lets go of me, turns and walks down the hallway.

JAKE

I stalk into the kitchen and survey the mess that I have offered to clean up.

Fucking brilliant.

This is not how I thought that I would be spending the day.

My original plans were to keep Stacey holed up in my bedroom all day long. I know that we can't have sex right now, but I imagined us spending our time cuddled in bed, watching shitty movies, and making out like a couple of teenagers. Instead, I am clearing up a flat that looks like an absolute shit tip.

I go through the cupboards until I find some black bags, and I start to throw the rubbish in there. Lydia really needs to sort out whatever fucked up shit is going on with her. Stacey needs to get herself better, but instead she has to put up with her best friend bringing home random men and getting as high as a kite on whatever substance is sitting on the bedside table.

I sigh and continue to throw empty beer cans into the rubbish bag. Once all of the rubbish has been cleared, I find a brush and sweep up the mess of the broken crockery on the floor.

Fucking animals.

I open the kitchen window and inhale the fresh air. If I hadn't seen the mess caused from just one night, then I never would have believed that it was this bad.

After clearing the floor, I spray the shit out of the sides with bleach and wipe them all down. I tie the bag of rubbish and put it by the front door, ready to take out to the rubbish bins later.

I go back to Lydia's bedroom to see how Stacey is getting on. The musty smell has started to subside from the room and the bedside table has been cleared of whatever drug was on offer last night. Lydia still lies in a heap on the bed. I look at her in disgust.

What a state to get into.

There is no sign of Stacey in here, so I go to the bathroom, but she isn't in there either.

Where did she go? She's not in the lounge as I would have seen her walk in there.

It isn't until I am passing by her bedroom door, that I see it is slightly ajar. I peer in the crack of the door and I see Stacey sat on her bed, her head in her hands. I push the door open and walk in.

"Stace?" She looks up and I see that she has been crying. I go to her and kneel in front of her. "Don't cry, babe. Lydia is going to be fine."

"It's not about that," she chokes out in-between sobs. I stare at her puzzled. *If it's not about Lydia, then what else could it be?*

Stacey looks at me and her eyes look pained. Her hand goes to the side of her and picks up a small black box that I hadn't noticed before. I look at the box which is open, but there is nothing in there. "My parents wedding rings have been taken. It's all I had left of them."

"What?" I say, a little louder than intended. That scumbag that was in here. It must have been him. I feel anger rise within me and it takes all of my control not to go and find the fucker. Stacey sniffles and then throws the box back on the bed.

"What kind of person does that?" She looks at me hopelessly and I feel my heart pang for her.

"A low-life asshole, that's who. I'm so sorry, babe."

"It's not your fault." She shrugs, and I pull her into my arms. She hugs me tight, so I just hold her and make a promise to myself that I will find those rings and get them back for her. We stay like this until we hear the sound of Lydia throwing up in her bedroom. Stacey releases her grip on me and I move so that she can stand up. She rushes out of the room and I follow her. Lydia is on her side and she is being sick all over the bed and herself. The smell hits me and my stomach churns in protest. Stacey is beside Lydia, moving her hair back so that it doesn't get tangled up in the sick.

"She needs a doctor, Jake. We have to get her to hospital."

"I'm on it," I say as I pull my phone out of my pocket and make a call.

STACEY

Lydia continues to throw up as I hopelessly try and keep her hair out of the way. Seeing her like this is awful. Jake has disappeared, and I hope that he is phoning for an ambulance.

After a few long, painful minutes, Lydia's heaves start to subside. She is gasping for breath as she recovers from her vomiting episode. I talk to her quietly, so she knows that I am here. Her eyes are streaming, and my heart goes out to her.

"Stace?" she croaks, her throat sounding harsh.

"Yeah, I'm here, Lyd. You're going to be okay."

"I need water."

"Okay, I'll be right back." I leave her and go to the kitchen to get a glass of water for her. Jake must have gone into the corridor outside as the front door is slightly ajar. I don't have time to see what he is doing, I have to look after Lydia.

I go back to her bedroom and help her to sip the water. The smell of vomit is making me want to be sick myself. I try not to breath in too deeply, but the putrid scent still wafts up my nostrils. Lydia gulps the water hungrily until she has finished the whole glass.

"Thanks," she says, and I place the glass on her bedside table.

"Lyd, you need to move so that you can get cleaned up."

"I can't," she groans. "I feel awful."

"No shit, Sherlock!" I can't help the slight sarcasm in my tone. "You can't lie in this bed, in your own vomit." I watch as Lydia flops to the other side of the bed. "Uh, that isn't really what I had in mind, Lyd." I wait for her to answer, but her eyes are closed again. I sigh and start to strip the pillows that Lydia has just rolled off of. I chuck them in a pile on the floor, but the actual pillow is saturated as well. I throw that onto the pile deciding that the whole lot will need to be chucked out.

I pull the quilt off of the bed and add that to the pile as well. I will just have to go and buy Lydia a new set of bedding. The sheet is my next problem as Lydia is still led on one half of it. I pull the sheet down as best as I can, and I go around to the other side of the bed. I am about to try and lift the top half of Lydia's body, so I can shimmy the sheet down beneath her, when Jake comes storming into the room.

"Don't even fucking think about it." I look at him in shock. "You are not jeopardising your own recovery by lifting her. I'll do it." He moves me out of the way and I watch him as he lifts Lydia with ease, sliding the sheet beneath her. "There.

All done." Jake looks to me, seeming pleased with himself as I stand there with my arms folded. "What?"

"I'm not an invalid, Jake. I can still do stuff."

"Not lifting you can't. Don't argue with me on this one, Stacey. You won't win." I blow out a puff of air as I bundle the soiled sheet up and I add it to the pile of bedding to be chucked out. "The doctor will be here shortly," he says.

"As in, here? In the flat?"

"Yeah. It's my private doctor. I figured that trying to get Lydia to hospital would be too much for her."

"Oh." He really does think of everything. I walk over to him and place a kiss on his cheek. "Thank you."

He just keeps continuing to surprise me with what he is able to do.

"No problem. I'll go and wait out the front for him to arrive."

CHAPTER TWENTY-NINE

STACEY

I start to tackle the mess in the lounge as I wait for the doctor to arrive. I have cleared all of the empty beer cans and I am emptying the make shift ash tray when I hear the front door opening. I go to the lounge doorway as Jake is leading the doctor towards Lydia's room. I decide to leave them to it for the moment and I carry on with the cleaning.

Jake comes into the room as I am disinfecting the coffee table. He inspects the chair and then flops down into it. He gestures for me to sit on his lap and I happily oblige.

"I'm sorry for all of this, Jake." I feel guilty that he has spent most of the day helping me tidy up and look after Lydia.

"It's fine."

"No, it's not, but I do appreciate everything that you have done." If it wasn't for him, I don't quite know how I would have handled this situation. I lean on his chest and his arms come around me. I close my eyes and just enjoy a few minutes' peace with him. He makes me feel as if I can get through anything when he is with me. I can't imagine my life without him.

"Shall I go and make us a drink?" I ask him.

"Sure. I could do with a strong coffee." I get up off of his lap and go to the kitchen, putting the kettle on to boil and rewashing the cups in the cupboard, just to be certain that they are clean. Jake comes in as I am washing the last cup and he takes a seat at the kitchen table.

"What do you say we get a take-away when we leave here and spend the rest of the day in bed?" Jake says.

"I would love nothing more than to do that, but I can't go back to yours, Jake. I need to stay here and look after Lydia." I dry up two cups to keep myself distracted from his gaze that I can feel burning into my back.

"There is no way that you are staying here."

"I have to. I can't leave her."

"Then she can come to mine as well." I whirl around and look at him. His jaw is clenched, and I know that he isn't joking around.

"I can't put you out like that, Jake. You have done enough to help as it is."

"It's not putting me out. I want you with me, and you want to look after Lydia. It's a perfect solution to a shitty situation."

"But—" I am cut off by the doctor walking into the kitchen. "How is she?" I ask before he can speak.

"Lydia is going to be fine. I've done a thorough check of her and whatever she has taken seems to be wearing off." I breathe a sigh of relief at his words. "She's lucky though. Whatever it was that she took, in my opinion, was impure. She needs to rest, but she should be feeling better within the next forty-eight hours."

"Thank you, doctor," I say.

"It's no problem." He smiles at me before turning to Jake. "Good to see you, Jake. Although, let's hope that I don't have to do another home visit like this one again."

"I appreciate it, Harley." Jake stands up and shakes his hand before walking him out of the flat whilst I go to see Lydia, who is still asleep. I haven't been able to go out and get new covers for her bed yet, so I go and get the quilt off of my bed so that I can cover her over. Once I have done that, I sit by the side of her on the bed.

"I'm going to help you, Lyd. Whatever the problem is, I will help you figure it out." I know that she is asleep, but a part of me hopes that she can hear what I am saying.

Jake comes into the bedroom and perches next to me, on the end of the bed.

"Please come and stay at mine, Stace. You will be safe at my place. That guy Lydia had in here could come back at any time, and he could bring God knows who with him."

Shit, I never even thought of that.

I take hold of his hand and I give it a gentle squeeze.

"Okay." Jake smiles at my answer and I can see some of the tension leave his body. "Let's go and have that cup of coffee and then I will pack some of Lydia's things." Jake follows me to the kitchen and he sits back at the table. I make the drinks and take them over, sitting opposite him, sipping my coffee.

"Listen, Stace, I need to tell you something." Jake shifts and looks uncomfortable.

"Oh God, what now?" I ask as a feeling of dread settles in my stomach.

Surely nothing else could possibly go wrong?

"Well, when I was waiting outside for the doctor, I got a phone call. It was D.C. Sykes calling to say that they have set a date for Caitlin's sentencing. He said that he has left a message on your phone with the details." I suck in a deep breath and gesture for him to continue. "It's two weeks Monday at nine in the morning."

"Right... Well... That's a good thing." I haven't let myself think too much about it to be honest. It's a part of my life that I would rather not think about. I'm just glad that I don't have to endure the process of it going to trial to determine who is telling the truth. Her confession has made the whole situation less complicated.

"Do you want to be there when she's sentenced?" Jake asks. I ponder his question for a few moments.

Do I?

Do I really want to see her face again?

Would it bring me any satisfaction by going?

I take a deep breath and let it out slowly.

"You know what? I don't think that I do." Jake looks a little shocked at my answer and I feel that I should explain myself. "That woman ruined a part of my life. She took away a part of me for a short while. I know that I am okay now, but I think that seeing her again will bring back too many painful memories."

"I understand."

"Are you going to go?" I ask him.

"I'm not sure yet. Half of me wants to go and see her get her comeuppance, but the other half of me doesn't want to be in the same room as her. She hurt you, Stace, and nothing is more important to me than you are."

"In that case, don't you think that it is best to stay away? I mean, she will probably be expecting to see us there. I think it may shock her more if neither of us go." Jake sips his coffee and appears to be lost in thought.

"I don't think that I will be able to make my mind up until the day." I just nod at his answer and we sit in comfortable silence for a few minutes. Life really has been crazy lately. "Are you hungry at all?"

"Not really."

"You need to eat." Jake gives me a stern look and I know he thinks that I should be focussing on myself more than I am.

"I will later. I still need to finish cleaning the lounge."

"Well, come on then," Jake says as he finishes his cup of coffee. "Let's do that, get Lydia's things packed, and then we can go and pick up some food and go back home."

"Home?" I say, not missing the meaning behind it. He just grins at me and walks out of the kitchen and into the lounge. I smile and shake my head.

He really is too good to be true.

CHAPTER THIRTY

STACEY

Jake and I made quick work of cleaning the rest of the lounge, and then I packed some of Lydia's things ready to go to Jake's house. Jake and I are sat on the chair in the lounge, watching some television, when Lydia appears in the doorway. It's only been a couple hours since the doctor left, and I'm surprised to see her up and about.

"Hey, Lyd," I say, keeping my voice low. "How are you feeling?"

"Like shit," she replies as she collapses onto the sofa. Good job I took the cover off there and put it in the wash, otherwise she would be sat in a patch of sick right now. She looks horrendous. Her face is pale, her eyes have lost their usual sparkle and have bags under them, and her hair is lank and greasy. She hasn't gotten changed out of her clothes and the faint smell of sick reappears. "Why do I feel so bad?"

"Um... To cut a long story short, you got totally wasted, spent most of the day sleeping, threw up everywhere and now you have the hangover from hell." It's the only way that I can think to explain it to her. "I'm guessing that you don't remember much?"

"Not really." Her hands go to her head and she rubs her temples.

"Listen, Lyd," I start as I go over to her and sit next to her on the sofa. "Jake has offered for us to both go and stay at his place for a few days. I've already packed you some stuff, so we can leave whenever you're ready." Her eyes focus on me and she looks confused at what I am saying.

"Why the hell would I go and stay at Jake's?"

"I just don't think that it's safe for us to stay here right now."

"Why not?"

"Do you have any idea what's been going on here? Do you even remember what state this place was left in? Do you even remember who the guy was that you brought back here last night?" I can feel rage boiling up inside me, but I need to keep a lid on it.

"Of course I remember the guy," she answers, looking a little uncertain of her answer. "Stop being so bloody dramatic."

I scoff at her words. "*Dramatic? You think that this is dramatic?* This flat was a complete fucking mess, Lydia. Beer cans, wine bottles, broken plates, and sick on the sofa are not a welcoming sight. Jake and I have spent all day cleaning the place up."

"Oh, well, thanks so much." Lydia's tone is full of sarcasm which does nothing to help calm me down. She sits there, picking at her fingernails, clearly not giving a shit about what I am saying. I need to get through to her.

"I had to go to the hospital last night, Lydia. When I opened the front door to you and your *guest*, you knocked me over, resulting in my some of my stitches tearing." I am hoping that this information will jolt her out of her self-absorbed state. She looks up to me momentarily, before turning her attention back to her fingernails. I look to Jake. He is sat there, watching me, his jaw clenched tight. I know that he wants to remove me from this situation.

I turn back to Lydia and sigh in exasperation. "Lydia, the guy you had in here last night went into my bedroom. My parents wedding rings are missing." I feel the sadness grip me. The invasion of my privacy makes me feel too open.

"You probably just misplaced them somewhere."

"You know as well as I do that I would never have just misplaced those rings." I give her a stern look and she at least has the decency to look a little bit worried.

"What is it that you want from me? An apology?"

"No, I'm not asking you for an apology, but I would like a little bit of gratitude."

"Gratitude? Since when did you become all high and mighty?" Lydia has clearly got over the tiny bit of worry that I spied in her moments ago.

"What the hell is wrong with you?" I am flabbergasted at her reaction. This isn't my best friend sat before me. I don't know who this person is.

"You're the one sat there, having a go at me. Maybe if you loosened up and had some fun once in a while, then you wouldn't be acting like this. When did you become so fucking boring, Stacey?" My mouth drops open and I stare at her, aghast.

How dare she treat me this way.

I am incensed at her words, and I can no longer contain my fury.

"Fun?" I screech at her. "You call the state that you got yourself into fun?"

"Yeah. You should try it some time."

"Are you still high or something? I have been worried about you, I have cleaned up after you, and this is how you choose to treat me?"

"Oh, that's right, Stacey, play the role of the fucking martyr. Let's make everything about you, shall we? Being assaulted, being stabbed, and losing your memory hasn't been enough for you, so now you have to make another drama." Lydia's tone is evil, and I don't like it.

My whole body starts to tremble as I take in her words.

"That's enough, Lydia," Jake's voice cuts in. His tone is firm, and his eyes are narrowed on her.

"I wondered how long it would take for you to chip in," she says, turning her attention to him. "You have only been around for five minutes, so why don't you just back off, buddy." Oh God, I want the ground to swallow me up. She is making such a fool of herself.

"Lydia," I say in shock. "Why are you being like this?"

"I'm not being like anything. It's you two that seem to have some sort of problem, not me."

"Us? We are the ones with the problem?" I scoff. "Look at the state of you, Lyd." My voice is getting louder and louder with each word I speak. "We are not the enemy here. We're trying to help you."

"I'm not a fucking charity case. I don't need any help," Lydia screams at me. She stands up off of the sofa and storms out of the room.

I stare after her, my mouth hanging open in shock.

"She's not in her right frame of mind. She doesn't mean any of what she just said," Jake says, grabbing my attention.

"Oh yes I fucking do!" Lydia shouts, coming back into the lounge. "I don't need you two here, bringing me down. I'm fine on my own. Why don't you both run along and play house together."

"Lydia," I say as I stand up. "Please, just listen to me." She turns and leaves the lounge, and I follow her into the kitchen. She goes to the fridge and pulls out a bottle of wine, grabbing a glass from the cupboard and pouring herself a large amount.

Shit, I should have gotten rid of all the alcohol when we were clearing up.

"Don't you think that you have had enough of that over the last few days?" I say, indicating to the wine bottle.

"No, actually, I don't. If I want a glass of wine, then I will fucking well have one." She drains the entire glass and pours herself another.

"Lydia, please come to Jake's with me," I plead with her. I can't stand to see her do this to herself. She slams the glass down on the worktop, making me jump, and she stares daggers at me.

"Fuck off, Stacey." She mouths each word slowly, enunciating each word. "Just leave me alone." A tear rolls down my cheek as I feel the hurt from her words. "That's right, turn on the water works."

"You really want me to leave?" I whisper, not able to make my voice any louder.

"Yes." There is no hesitation in her answer. I look at her and I see the determination in her eyes. I feel defeated.

"Fine," I say as I turn and see Jake standing behind me. "Let's go, Jake. It seems that we're not welcome here."

CHAPTER THIRTY-ONE

STACEY

Jake and I arrive at his place, and I go straight to his bedroom and curl up under the duvet. Jake climbs in behind me and wraps his arms around me. I let my tears flow freely. I never thought that Lydia could be so hurtful. She is like a sister to me.

"How could she be like that, Jake?"

"She's clearly not in a good place. Try not to take what she said to heart. She doesn't mean it."

"How can I not?" I say, turning so that I am led on my back, allowing me to look at him. "How am I meant to feel? She won't let me help her." I feel totally useless.

"I don't know, babe. Has she got any family that you could call?"

"I don't really relish the thought of phoning her mum. They aren't close, and Lydia certainly wouldn't thank me for contacting her."

"Well, even though they aren't close, it might be the push that Lydia needs to see sense," Jake suggests. I think about it for a moment, and I realise that Jake may have a point. Something, or someone, needs to shock Lydia, seeing as I am having no effect on her.

"I could phone her brother, Nick." I bite my lip as I consider this option. Nick and Lydia aren't close either, but it would be a better option than her mum. I am also hesitant of phoning Nick seeing as we used to hook up, before I was with Charles.

"There you go. Give him a call," Jake urges. I battle with my inner thoughts before deciding that I need to ignore whatever happened between Nick and me.

This is about Lydia. I shouldn't let any awkwardness stand in the way of helping her.

I dry my eyes on the quilt, get out of bed and ask Jake where my handbag is. He informs me that it is on the stairs, so I go down to retrieve it. I return to the bedroom and pull my phone out of my bag. I have no messages or calls from Lydia, but then, I didn't expect to see any. I scroll through my phone and find Nick's number. Sitting on the edge of the bed, I take a deep breath, and hit the call button. The phone rings three times before it is answered.

"Hey there, gorgeous. Long-time no speak. How's it going?" Nick's use of the word gorgeous has me cringing slightly.

"Uh, hi, Nick." I stumble on my words and Nick picks up on this instantly.

"Whoa, why do you sound so nervous? Are you calling to hook up again?" Oh Christ, I really hope that Jake can't hear what he is saying to me.

"Uh, no. I'm calling about Lydia." I try to keep my voice even as I speak to him. Lydia and Nick have a lot of history that they need to try and resolve one day, and I am hoping that I am not about to make their relationship worse.

"Okay. What's up?" He sounds so calm and relaxed and I hate that I am about to burst his bubble.

"Is there any chance that we could meet up and talk?" I decide that I don't want to try and explain the situation over the phone to him.

"Sure. How about one evening next week?"

"No, Nick, it can't wait until then. Are you free tonight?" Nick goes quiet on the line, and I presume that he is processing my urgency to see him tonight.

"Well, I did have plans." I roll my eyes as Nick's plans probably include hooking up with some girl that he has on the go.

"Can you cancel them? This is important." I stress my urgency in my tone.

"Uh, I suppose so," he answers warily.

"Good. Can you meet me at Lydia's in twenty minutes?"

"Yeah, okay." He sighs down the phone. "But this better be worth it. I had a hot date planned for tonight." Bingo. I knew that he would just be trying to get his end away.

"It is worth it." I don't know why Lydia and Nick can't put aside their differences and just appreciate that they are family. "See you soon."

I end the call, put my phone back into my handbag and turn to look at Jake, who has a serious expression on his face.

"We're going back to Lydia's?" he asks, raising one eyebrow at me in question. Relief shoots through me that he didn't hear what Nick said on the phone.

"I figured that it's better to explain in person rather than over the phone. Plus, this way, he will be able to see the state of her for himself."

A knot forms in my stomach and I feel a wave of nausea sweep over me.

"Okay, babe. Let's go."

JAKE

We drive back to Lydia's flat and my mind processes what Nick said to Stacey on the phone. I realise that the issue here is to get Lydia well, but it grates on me that he thought she was calling him for a hook up.

The thought of another man touching her makes me want to punch the steering wheel.

I get that Stacey has a past, as do I, but it still fucking narks me. Stacey clearly doesn't think that I heard what he said, and I get why she wouldn't want to tell me, but I'm still going to speak to her about it later. I now have to spend time in the company of some guy who has fucked my girl. Bloody fantastic.

I pull into the car park for the flats, and I switch the engine off. I can feel the tension coming off of Stacey in waves. I am unsure if the tension is just being caused by Lydia, or if she is stressed about seeing Nick. Her leg is fidgeting up and down and I place my hand on her knee, hoping that it will calm her down. She looks at me and smiles, making me want to rip her clothes off and fuck her on the back seat.

"When all of this shit is sorted, we're going away somewhere," I blurt out. I can think of nothing better than whisking her away from here and shutting us off from the world.

"Sounds good." Huh. I wasn't expecting her to agree so easily.

"Oh, it will be. Sun, sand, sea, and just us." I lean towards her and she hums in appreciation. My mouth covers hers and I take my time in caressing her tongue with mine. She groans into my mouth, sending a direct signal to my cock. As I end the kiss and look into her eyes, I can see that they are burning with desire for me.

I swear that when her body is healed, I am going to fulfil that desire.

I'm going to make her scream my name over and over.

"I can't wait, but right now, I have to go and speak to Nick." She looks to the side of me and I turn my head to see this Nick guy getting out of his car. I reluctantly move away from her and exit the car.

Keep yourself in check, Waters. She's yours now.

Stacey is already out of the car before I can walk around to help her. I see the guy staring at her, looking her up and down, and I want to punch him. His eyes look hungry as he assesses her. I have to remind myself that Stacey is only here to help Lydia.

The guy's eyes move to me as I feel Stacey take my hand in hers. He is sizing me up, and I can't help but smirk.

She's mine, asshole.

I feel Stacey tug at my hand and we start to walk over to him.

Here we go.

STACEY

Nick stands by his car with his arms crossed. He looks the same as he did when I last saw him, and that was a while ago. With his shaved head, strong jaw, sparkling green eyes, and stocky frame, he is every bit as good-looking as he was when I first met him. Of course, he doesn't compare to Jake, but I can appreciate a handsome man when I see one. No one compares to Jake, so if our relationship ever does crumble, I'm going to be screwed for meeting anyone else.

"Hey, girl," Nick says as he uncrosses his arms and envelopes me in a hug. I reluctantly return his hug as Jake still has hold of my hand. I quickly move back from Nick and give Jake's hand a little squeeze. I can feel the tension radiating off of Jake's body.

"Hi, Nick. Let me introduce you to Jake, my boyfriend." I gesture to Jake, who puts his hand out for Nick to shake. I can practically feel the macho hormones radiating around us. Nick shakes Jake's hand, but neither of them smile in greeting.

"You're a lucky man, Jake. This girl is special," Nick says smiling at me.

Oh Christ, why did he have to say that?

I fidget awkwardly at his compliment. Nick always wanted to take things to the next level with us, but I always resisted. At that time in my life, all I wanted was a bit of fun.

Jake's jaw starts to tick, and I decide that now would be a good time to tell Nick about Lydia to divert attention away from me.

"Nick, Lydia is in a bad way. I know that things have been strained between you both, but you know that I wouldn't call you without good reason." Nick nods and his eyebrows furrow questioningly. I hear the sound of loud music start to play and I know that it is coming from Lydia's flat. "Maybe I should just show you. Come on."

I let go of Jake's hand and enter the flat block, Jake and Nick following behind me. The music gets louder as we approach the front door. I unlock the door and walk in. The music is so loud that I can barely think.

I walk to the lounge and stop in the doorway. I am astounded to see that the guy from this morning is sat on the chair.

There are a further three strange looking guys sat on the sofa.

The coffee table is littered with little packets of white powder.

Lydia is kneeling at the end of the coffee table with a rolled-up note to her nose, snorting some of the powder.

I step to the side and usher Nick to go in front of me. The guy in the chair looks at us and alerts the other three to our presence before turning the music down slightly. Lydia remains oblivious. She is clearly too busy taking drugs to notice anything else going on. The look of shock on Nick's face says it all.

"What the fuck is going on here?" Nick roars.

Even though the music is painstakingly loud, Lydia's head snaps up at the sound of her brother's voice. The colour drains from her face and she drops the rolled-up note onto the floor. Nick has gone a deep shade of red and I know it is because he is angry. I wouldn't be surprised to see steam coming out of his ears at any moment now.

The guy in the chair switches the music off and my ear drums breathe a sigh of relief. My heart is pounding so hard that I am sure they can all hear it.

No one says a word until Lydia averts her gaze from her brother and rests her eyes on me.

"You fucking bitch," she screeches at me. "You of all people. You called my fucking brother?"

"Damn right she did, and with good fucking reason, Lydia. What the hell do you think that you are doing?" Nick shouts, defending me and releasing a bit of his anger at the same time. Nick then turns his attention to the four strange guys. "You four, get the fuck out. NOW!"

The three guys on the sofa quickly stand up, grab as many bags of the white shit that they can, and then they all stumble past us to the front door. They can't seem to get out of here quick enough.

The guy from this morning however, remains seated.

"Did you not hear me?" Nick says, moving closer to him. "I said, get out."

"I'm not going anywhere, pal," the guy answers. I feel Jake grab my hand and pull me into the kitchen doorway.

"Stay here, Stacey," Jake commands. I don't argue. I stand there, my whole body shaking as I realise that this situation could turn very nasty, very quickly.

Oh God, I don't want anyone to get hurt.

I just want Lydia to be safe.

"It's okay, Callum," I hear Lydia say. "You go, and I'll phone you when they have gone."

Yes, Callum, get out of here.

I hear some shuffling and then Callum exits the lounge, coming to a stop in the hallway. He turns his head and looks at me stood in the kitchen doorway. His pupils are dilated, and he smirks cockily.

"Well, well, if it isn't the little stunner from this morning. Thought anymore about my offer of fun yet?" I inwardly cringe at his words.

"Back the fuck off," Jake snarls. He is beside Callum in a nanosecond, and his gaze is menacing. This is the second time today that this Callum guy has tried to hit on me. I swear that he has a death wish. Callum winks at me and that's all it takes for Jake to grab him by the throat and physically march him to the front door.

"Don't come back here again," Jake says before pushing him into the corridor and slamming the door in his face. I breathe a sigh of relief that Jake didn't punch the guy. I saw what he did to Donnie, and it wasn't pretty.

Jake stalks back over to me and the cold look in his eyes instantly warms as he locks his gaze with mine. He pulls me into his arms and I wrap my arms tight around his waist.

"You okay, babe?" he asks me.

"Yeah, I'm fine. I'm just glad that you didn't do anything stupid."

"Oh, believe me, I could have quite easily."

"I know." I lean back and see emotion flicker through his eyes, but I can't quite place what emotion it is. I am abruptly pulled out of my embrace with Jake by the sound of Lydia sobbing. I side-step Jake and poke my head around the lounge doorway.

The scene before me breaks my heart.

Nick is sat on the floor, cradling a sobbing Lydia in his arms, and he looks up at me, giving me a sad smile. I suddenly feel like I am intruding on a very private moment. I gesture for Nick to call me later and he simply nods his head at me.

"Come on, Jake," I say as I take his hand. "Let's leave them on their own. They have a lot of talking to do."

CHAPTER THIRTY-TWO

STACEY

I am exhausted by the time we return to Jake's. It's been a hell of a day, and I drag my weary body upstairs to his bedroom. I enter the ensuite and as I look in the mirror, I see that I look drained. I rub my hands over my face. All I could do with right now is a long, hot bath, but I can't even do that with the bloody dressing still covering my wound. The hospital issued me with a few special dressings so that I could take a quick shower though, so I start to undress, put one of the special dressings over the existing dressing, and am just stood in my bra and knickers when Jake comes into the room. His eyes hungrily survey me, and I feel sparks shoot straight to my sex.

"Now that is a very welcome sight at the end of a very hectic day," he says as he stalks towards me. I feel a delicious shiver go through me as he pulls his T-shirt over his head and throws it on the floor.

"Want to join me in the shower?" I ask him, drinking in the sight of his abs. He smirks and stops in front of me, unbuttoning his jeans and pulling his boxers down with them. He steps out of his clothes and then gestures for me to finish undressing. I undo my bra and drop it to the floor. I then, slowly, take off my knickers and kick them to one side.

"After you," he says, motioning for me to get in the shower. I reluctantly turn away from him, switch the shower on, and step in, being instantly warmed by the hot water. I feel Jake step in behind me and his hands rest on my hips. Goosebumps cover my entire body as he pushes his chest into my back, his cock resting at the bottom of my spine. Desire ripples through me and I lean back into him as his hands snake their way to my stomach, moving slowly upwards until he is kneading my breasts. I moan at his touch.

"Jake?"

"Hmm."

"I want you inside me." It seems like forever since we last had sex. He nibbles on my ear lobe and I arch my back so that my breasts push harder into his hands. He growls and turns me around, pushing me against the shower wall. I gasp as the cold wall makes contact with my skin. His mouth covers mine and I move my hands to his shoulders, my fingers digging into his skin.

"Stop," Jake says abruptly. I whimper at his words and at the loss of his lips on mine. His face is only inches away, but it feels too far. "We can't. I don't want to hurt you." I see the worry in his eyes at the thought that he might do something to cause me any pain.

"You won't hurt me. I need to feel you," I plead. I wrap my arms around his neck and I see him struggling with what he thinks is best for me, and with what I need from him. I place kisses along his jawline, enjoying the feel of his light stubble against my lips.

"Oh Jesus," he says as my tongue licks along his bottom lip.

"Please, Jake." He looks into my eyes, and just when I think that he isn't going to give in, he moves his hands underneath my ass and lifts me, so that I slide up the wall. I give a squeal of delight as I feel his erection pressing against my opening.

"If you get any pain in your side at all, then promise that you'll tell me."

"I promise," I answer, desperate for him to push inside of me. I cup his face in my hands and kiss him softly.

As I feel Jake's length enter me, I cry out in pleasure.

"Fuck," Jake says as he eases slowly back out of me, and then pushes back in even slower. I bite my bottom lip and close my eyes. Jake's mouth closes over my nipple and I let my head fall back against the wall. As he sucks gently, I tighten my grip on him.

"Oh God," I say as I can already feel my orgasm building. Jake proceeds to give my other nipple the same treatment as the first. He continues to ease in and out of me at a torturously slow pace. As my orgasm gathers speed, my body starts to tremble. "Jake, I'm close." I don't know how much longer I can hold on for.

"Look at me," he says in that commanding tone of his, making the moment more intense than it was before. I open my eyes and stare deep into his caramel pools. I can see from the look in his eyes just how much he loves me. This thought, along with the sensations that I am experiencing are quickly bringing me to climax.

"Jake," I say breathlessly as my core tightens. I can sense that he is getting close too as I desperately try to hold onto my release.

"You know that you're mine, right?"

"Yes." I don't hesitate to answer him.

A silent understanding passes between us.

I am his, and he is mine.

"I love you, Stacey Paris." Those words are my undoing. I cry out as my orgasm hits, my sex tightening around Jake's length, and he follows me seconds later. As we both pant and try to catch our breath, I place my lips by Jake's ear.

"I love you too," I whisper, needing to tell him. He moves back slightly, and I lower my shaky legs to the ground. He cups my face in his hands and places a light kiss on the end of my nose.

"Good, because I'm never letting you go." I smile at him and thank my lucky stars that he came into my life. Jake has opened my eyes to emotions that I never thought I would feel.

He is my soul mate, my love, my perfect stranger.

―――

JAKE

I love her.

With every fibre of my being, I love her.

It's that simple.

I don't need to ask her about any other guys that she may have been with. I know that those guys don't mean anything to her.

I know that she loves me, and as long as we are together, then nothing else matters.

CHAPTER THIRTY-THREE

STACEY

A few days have passed since the Lydia fiasco. I've received a couple of text messages from Nick about how she is doing, but I haven't heard from Lydia herself. Nick has informed me that Lydia is staying at his place for the time being. I'm so glad that her brother has stepped up and is helping her, but a part of me wishes that she had let me in. I also told Nick that I would see that The Den was okay whilst Lydia concentrates on getting better. I might not be able to actually return to the physical side of work yet, but I have been in contact with Susie each day to discuss the staffing issues. Unfortunately, agency staff are the only way to go at the moment. It's already costing a fortune to hire them, but there is no other way. Understandably, Susie has asked questions about Lydia's absence. I have just told her that Lydia has a flu-type bug. I don't know if Susie believes me or not, but that is the least of my worries.

Jake has been absolutely amazing through all of this. He took a few more days off of work, just so that he could spend some more time with me. I will forever be grateful for all of his support. Today is his first day back at the Waters Industries offices, and I am led alone, in his bed, thinking about how much I miss him already. He's only been gone for an hour and I am already pining for him.

Oh God, I'm like one of those sappy women you read about in a bad romance novel.

With that thought in mind, I make myself get out of bed to go and have a shower. I look at the small bundle of clothes that I brought here with me nearly a week ago, and I sigh. I have none of my, what I would call, "nice" clothes here. All I brought with me was comfy attire as I thought that I would be back at the flat with Lydia by now. I could go and pick some clothes up, but I don't feel like I can go to the flat just yet. It just wouldn't feel right without Lydia being there.

I pick out my "boring" clothes and am about to go into the ensuite when my phone starts to ring. I walk over to the bedside table and see that it is Martin calling me.

Oh shit. I completely forgot to call him back the other day. Bollocks.

I pick up my phone and brace myself for the ear bashing that I know I am going to get.

After a deep breath, I answer the call. "Hi, Martin."

"Don't you 'hi Martin' me. Where the hell have you been? And why haven't you called me?" Martin is pissed off, and I can hardly blame him. With everything going on lately, I haven't exactly been the most attentive friend.

"I'm sorry, Mart. Things have just been so crazy. I meant to call you back, but then something happened with Lydia. I know that's no excuse though, I should have called you." I don't want Martin to think that I am fobbing him off with some excuse.

"Yes, you should have."

"I know, and I'm sorry." I let the line go quiet, hoping that Martin will forgive my shitty behaviour towards him. "I don't suppose that you're free for a coffee today at all?"

"Well, I am, actually."

"Great. Want to meet at Danish in the next hour?"

"Well... I suppose so." I smile at his acceptance of my coffee invitation. "It doesn't mean that you're forgiven though. I'm still pissed at you, baby girl." I smile at his "baby girl" reference to me, which means that he is already on his way to forgiving me.

"I know." I am still smiling as I hang up the phone and place it back on the bedside table. I dash into the ensuite and get undressed to have a shower. As I place my clothes in the wash basket by the door to the ensuite, I hear my phone ringing again. I curse under my breath and stalk back into the bedroom. I am annoyed at being interrupted, but that annoyance soon melts away once I see that it is Jake calling me.

"Hi, handsome," I say as I answer the phone and sit on the edge of the bed.

"Morning, beautiful," he replies. I literally swoon. *Will I ever tire of hearing his voice?*

"Everything going okay?" I ask.

I hear him sigh down the phone and I can imagine him running his hand through his hair. "It's not too bad."

"You're a shitty liar at times, Jake." He can't fool me.

"Okay, it's been fucking awful so far. All that's getting me through is the thought of being with you later." I hear the shift in his tone of voice and it's like my whole body become alert. "I miss you," he says, and I smile at his words.

"You've only been gone an hour." I feel pleased though that he has been feeling the same way as I have.

"It feels like longer than an hour, and from the looks of things here, I'm going to be late finishing tonight." He sounds just as disappointed as I suddenly feel.

"Oh. Well, maybe I can cook us something nice for when you get back?" I ask, suddenly perking up as an idea forms in my head.

"Sounds good. I will let you know roughly what time I will be home."

"Great."

"So, what are you up to?"

"Well, Mr Waters, right now, I am sat on the bed... Naked." I hear the slight intake of his breath on the other end of the phone and I take delight in the way that I can make him react. "You called as I was about to get in the shower."

"I knew I should have stayed at home." I laugh at his answer.

"Well, just think about the fun we can have once you get back here." I can't help but tease him. He growls down the phone and I feel butterflies flutter in my stomach.

"Oh, I will, but with the thought of you naked, it's going to be pretty hard to concentrate for the rest of the day."

"I'm sure you'll find a way to get through it. In the meantime, I need to be getting ready. I'm going to meet Martin for coffee." I don't want to end our conversation, but if I don't hurry up, then I will only be late to meet Martin, and I have already been a crap friend to him lately without adding anything else to the mix.

"Okay, babe. Make sure that you call Eric to come and pick you up."

"I don't need to call Eric, I am perfectly capable of walking." I hear him sigh at my answer and I know that it frustrates him that I don't ask Eric unless I absolutely have to.

"Please, just call him." I decide not to make his day any shittier, so I refrain from arguing about it.

"Okay. If it will make you happy then I will call him."

"Good. I'll see you later."

"You will indeed."

"Bye, beautiful."

"Bye." I hang up the phone and shake off the shiver going through me. Jake can literally make my body respond to him in any way he wants it to. I place the phone back on the bedside table and go to take a quick shower. I wash and dry myself, and then I put on my unflattering clothes. I call Eric and he says that he will be here in the next ten minutes. I have a funny feeling that Jake had probably alerted him to the fact that I would be needing a lift.

I quickly dry my hair and put it up into a ponytail before applying minimal make-up and putting everything I need into my handbag. I walk down the stairs and put my shoes on and then pick up my set of keys to Jake's house. I walk outside and lock the front door to see that Eric is standing beside the limo, waiting to open the door for me. As I approach he smiles.

"Miss Stacey," he says, his usual greeting for me.

"Morning, Eric. How are you?"

"I'm okay, thank you." He opens the door and I ask him to take me to Danish before I thank him and get in the car. I nearly have a heart attack as he shuts the limo door and I see that Jake is sat opposite me.

"Oh my God, Jake. You scared me," I say as my hand clutches my chest from the shock of seeing him sat there. "What are you doing here?"

"I thought that I would come along for a ride. Is that a problem?" he says as he moves off of the seat and kneels between my legs. Arousal instantly flows through me. Before I can answer, he moves forwards and places his lips over mine. I close my eyes and moan as his tongue meets mine. My hands find their way into his hair and I tug gently.

Jake pushes his body against mine, his cock brushing against my sex through our clothes, and I move my hands so that they find the zip on his trousers. I slowly pull the zip down, undo the button on his trousers and push them below his ass, along with his boxers. Jake moans into my mouth, which turns me on even more.

My hand grips around his cock firmly, and I find that he is already hard for me. I smile against his lips and he pulls his head back, breaking our contact. I gently push him away, indicating that he should sit back on the seat behind him. He does and the fire in his eyes makes me want to straddle him right here, right now. Unfortunately, we don't have time for that, so I lower my head and wrap my lips around his length.

"Holy shit," Jake cries as I start to move up and down, sucking gently. I keep a firm grip around the bottom and move my hand at the same pace as I move my mouth. I hear Jake's breathing shift and I apply more pressure with my hand, whilst sucking him a little bit harder.

I intend to give him a blow job that he will think about for the rest of the day.

I move my other hand and cup his balls, massaging gently.

"Stacey," he says my name, his voice sounding hoarse and I know that he is close. I swirl my tongue around the tip before plunging him back into my mouth. I take him all the way in and as I feel his length hit the back of my throat, he groans in pleasure and his juices start to fill my mouth. I suck harder, until there is nothing left for him to give me.

As I slow down my movements, I hear Jake trying to catch his breath. I give his balls a gentle squeeze as I release his cock from my mouth and look up to him. His eyes are sparkling, and a gorgeous grin graces his face.

"Better?" I ask him, raising one eyebrow in question.

"Fuck, yeah," he answers as he grabs me by my arms and lifts me onto his lap. His hand comes around to the back of my head and he presses his lips against mine. It's a hungry kiss, like he wants to devour me, and it isn't until I feel the car pull to a stop that I pull my head back from him.

"Enjoy the rest of your day at work," I say, and before he can stop me, I pick up my handbag and quickly open the car door and get out. I hear him call my name as I shut the car door behind me. I know that I can't see him, but he can see me, so I blow a kiss and walk towards Danish, smirking at how I left him. The limo stays parked there as I enter the coffee shop.

I scan the room for Martin and see that he is sat in the far corner. I wave to him as I walk over, chuckling away to myself. I sit down and see that he has already got me a coffee waiting.

"Why do you look so pleased with yourself?" he asks, eyeing me suspiciously.

"Let's just say that Jake won't be thinking about much else but me at work for the rest of the day." I pick up my coffee and take a sip.

"Oooo, do tell." Martin sits forward on his seat and I know that he is no longer pissed off with me.

I am about to tell him, when I see his gaze shift to look behind me and his jaw drops open. I look around, curious to see what has gripped his attention. As I do, I see that Jake is coming in the front door. My heart starts to accelerate as he sees me and stalks over, looking all kinds of dominant in his posture. I gulp and feel a blush rise on my cheeks. His hair is slightly scruffy where my hands were tangled in it not so long ago.

My God, he is just perfection.

I stand up on shaky legs and as he reaches me, he grabs me and pulls me against his body. I don't have time to do anything other than meet his ferocious kiss, which renders me speechless.

When he has finished devouring me in front of everyone in the coffee shop, he puts his lips by my ear and whispers. "That's just a taster of what I'm going to do to you later."

I gasp and then Jake is retreating from the coffee shop. He doesn't turn back around as he leaves Danish and gets into the limo, but I know that he is smiling away to himself at his little display. I stare through the window until I see the limo drive away.

"Holy shit, baby girl. That was hot," Martin says, breaking my dazed state.

I do a quick look around the room and see that everyone is staring at me. I smile shyly and then sit back down.

"That man is just..." Martin trails off, clearly going into a little daydream of his own.

"Perfect." I finish the sentence for him. No other words come to mind.

CHAPTER THIRTY-FOUR

STACEY

It has now been a week since I last spoke to Lydia. I sent her a text yesterday, but I haven't had a reply yet. I know that she is doing okay as Nick is still updating me, but it's not the same as being able to ask her myself. She still isn't back at the flat yet, and I have been at Jake's since the night that I had to go back to the hospital.

As much as I miss living with Lydia, in my heart, I feel like Jake's place is my home. I love it here. I love being here when he gets home from work, I love going to sleep with him, and I love waking up to see his gorgeous face. We have become even closer, if that is possible, and I can't imagine not staying here with him. He hasn't mentioned me going back to the flat, and I haven't brought the subject up either.

We have been through so much in such a short amount of time, and I think that we are both just enjoying how uncomplicated our lives are at the moment.

To make life even simpler, I have just had my last hospital appointment. I didn't tell Jake about it as he has rearranged his life for me far too much in the last few weeks already. I know that he will be pissed off that I haven't told him, but I am hoping that the plan that I have forming in my mind will be enough to make up for not telling him.

I have finally been given the all clear, meaning that I can return to work. I am so pleased, and I don't want to have to see the inside of a hospital again for a long time.

I am currently stood outside Martin's office block, waiting for him to start his lunch break. As I wait for Martin, I see Charles walking towards the entrance of the offices.

Bollocks. I was hoping not to have to see his smug face.

His gaze zeros in on me and he roams his eyes up and down my body. I cringe and suddenly feel self-conscious that I am flashing too much flesh. I am wearing my denim shorts, black vest top, black cardigan and black converse. The weather is warm, but all of a sudden, I feel a chill wash over me. Charles' eyes linger on my legs and I feel icky.

Whatever did I see in him? He's wearing a tweed suit for fuck's sake.

"Well, well, well," Charles says as he gets closer to me. "Look who it is. Good to see you, Stace." *God, even his voice repulses me.* "Come to your senses, have you?"

"What?" I say abruptly, having no idea what he means.

"Well, waiting outside my offices, you must have ditched that idiot and come to beg me to take you back." He comes to a stop in front of me. He is standing far too close and I inch myself back a few paces.

"If by "idiot" you mean Jake, then no, I haven't ditched him. We are still very much together. And as for begging you, in your dreams is the only place that that will ever happen."

"Shame. You will come to your senses in time, I'm sure." His cocky expression makes me want to slap him. At that moment, Martin comes out of the building and stands beside me. He looks from me to Charles and a worried expression crosses his face.

"Martin," Charles greets him sternly. There is no friendliness to his tone.

"Mr Montpellior," Martin replies, clearly in employee mode around his dickhead boss.

"Don't be late back from lunch," Charles states. *What an asshole.* As far as I am aware, Martin has never been anything other than an exceptional employee, and he has certainly never been late to work.

"I won't be, sir," Martin responds.

I know that Charles is Martin's boss, but it makes me so angry that Charles speaks to him like that. I bite my tongue as I don't want to give Charles any reason to harbour any animosity towards Martin by me saying anything.

Charles goes to walk into the building but turns back around before he disappears. "When you change your mind, Stacey, you know where to find me." He smirks and my face screws up in disgust. He walks off laughing to himself.

"Do I even want to know?" Martin asks me.

"No. It's just Charles being his usual arrogant self."

"Ah. Say no more then." Martin hold his arm out and I link my arm through his. "So, to what do I owe the pleasure of your company for lunch?"

"Well, firstly I wanted to see you seeing as we haven't caught up since last week, and I still need to make it up to you for being a shitty friend." Martin laughs, and I smile at him. "Secondly, I do actually need your help with something."

"And what could you possibly need my help with?"

"Let's go and get some lunch and then I will tell you. My treat."

We walk to a cute little deli at the end of the road and as we enter, we choose a table for two that is situated by the window, but private enough for us not to be overheard. A waitress comes over, takes our order, and returns in record time with our drinks. I moan as I take a sip of the full fat Frappuccino that I have sat in front of me.

"Jeez, baby girl. People are going to start staring if you keep making those noises." I swat at his arm and move the Frappuccino to one side. "So, come on then, don't keep me in suspense any longer. What's going on in that gorgeous mind of yours?"

"Well, I want to do something nice for Jake. I figure that he deserves a surprise after the shit he has had to put up with over the last few weeks."

"Okay, but what exactly is it that I can help you with?"

"How likely is it that you can get me exclusive access to the Great Ballroom at the Bowden Hall?"

"That's easy. I could probably arrange something for you for as early as next week."

"Um, that's not quite what I had in mind." Martin raises his eyebrow at me. "I was kind of hoping that you would be able to get it for me tonight."

"Tonight?" Martin screeches as he splutters his mouthful of milkshake at me. The waitress chooses this moment to bring our sandwiches over and I politely thank her whilst wiping remnants of milkshake off of me.

"Sorry," Martin says, looking apologetic and a little amused at the same time. I try to give him a stern look, but I fail miserably as we both burst out laughing. I pick up one of my sandwiches and take a bite.

"I know that it's a lot to ask."

"A lot to ask? Baby girl, the ballroom is usually booked up months in advance. I would only have been able to get it for you as early as next week because I have contacts." I pout at him and give him my best puppy-dog-eyes look. "Don't look at me like that. You know that I'm a sucker for those beautiful blues of yours."

"I don't know anyone else who would be able to swing this for me. Please, Mart, I really just want to show Jake how much he means to me."

"Why don't you tell me exactly what you have got planned, and then I will see what I can do." I break into a grin, stand up, walk to Martin and throw my arms around him. "Steady on," Martin says whilst laughing. "I haven't done anything yet."

"If anyone can pull this off then it's you," I say.

Martin's ego is clearly boosted by my comment. He waves me off of him and I take my seat back at the table and take another bite of my sandwich. I excitedly fill Martin in on what I want to do as we finish our lunch. He thinks that my idea is fantastic, and he is soon on the phone to one of his contacts at the Bowden Hall.

With the first part of my plan in action, I decide to tackle the second part. I pull my phone out of my handbag and dial Eric's number.

"Miss Stacey. Do you need to be picked up?" Eric asks.

"Not just yet, Eric. I actually need to ask you a favour."

"Okay. What might that be?"

"Before I ask you, I need to promise that you won't tell Jake anything I am about to say to you." There is a moment's silence before Eric speaks.

"Well, that depends on what it is that you need to ask me. I don't like keeping things from Jake."

"I know that, but I wouldn't ask you to keep quiet if it wasn't important. Jake has been so good to me over the last few weeks and I want to surprise him, and I need you to help me do that. I promise that he will love what I have planned." I don't want to give Eric all the sordid details. He is like a father-figure to Jake and I just feel it would be a bit weird for me to tell him exactly what I had planned. There is silence as Eric processes my words.

"Please, Eric? Jake deserves a night where he can relax and not have to plan every detail himself." I hold my breath and cross my fingers as I wait for him to answer.

"You make a good case, Miss Stacey. What is it that you need me to do?" I punch the air in triumph as I reel off instructions to him. "Okay," he says when I finish telling him what I need him to do. "I will have him there after work."

"Thanks, Eric. I owe you one." I hear Eric laugh on the other end of the line before I hang up.

Martin signals that we need to leave the deli and I go to the counter to pay the bill. He is still deep in conversation on the phone, and I just hope that means that he is having progress.

We leave the deli and I walk back to Martin's work with him. He finishes up his phone call as we reach the entrance.

"You owe me big time, baby girl. The ballroom is yours for the night." I let out a squeal of delight and pull Martin into a hug as I thank him over and over again. "Okay, Stace, calm down."

"You really are a legend, you know?"

"Oh, I know," Martin replies, as modest as ever. "I better get going. Charles will no doubt be watching for my return like a hawk."

"It's a shame that you work for a bastard like him. You're much too good for his company."

"I know, but what can I do? It pays well, and I love my job. Now, enough about that, I want details about how it goes tonight as soon as, baby girl."

"Drinks tomorrow night?" I ask.

"Sounds good. Oh, and if you want to bring that hunk of a man that you are lucky enough to be fucking with you, then please, feel free." I roll my eyes and tell Martin that I will text him tomorrow to arrange a time to meet. I wave to him as he disappears into the building. If only he could work for someone who would appreciate his talent and good nature.

I turn and walk in the direction of the high street. I need to do some retail therapy for tonight. My thoughts however keep straying back to Martin and how I wish that I could help him find another place to work...

CHAPTER THIRTY-FIVE

JAKE

"What a shit day," I say as I collapse into the back of the limo.

"That bad, huh?" Eric says as he pulls away from the curb and starts to drive.

"You would think that with all of the money that I pay out for employees, that they would be able to sort out the little problems, but it appears not."

I close my eyes and rub my temples as I feel the start of a dull headache approaching. I try to shut my mind off of work and instantly I am flooded by images of Stacey. I can't wait to get home and bury myself in her. Just the thought of her being at home, waiting for me, has gotten me through the day.

I picture her petite body with curves in all the right places. Her skin soft and her beautiful face make my cock twitch. I was so lost before she came into my life. It's nice to have someone to look after and love, rather than just having a life that revolves around work and meaningless sex with women that I would never want to see again.

I decide to ask Eric to stop at the florists on the way home, so that I can get Stacey some flowers. I open my eyes and am about to ask him, when I notice that we are not going in the direction of my house.

"Eric, where the fuck are we going?" I ask in an abrupt manner. Eric doesn't answer me, acting like he hasn't heard me. I repeat my question, but I still get no response. "Eric, will you tell me what the hell is going on?" Still silence.

Why the fuck isn't he answering me?

I quietly start to seethe with anger at the fact that I am being ignored, and at the fact that I have no idea where he is taking me. I just want to go home and relax.

With every mile that we drive, I feel myself becoming more agitated. I try a couple more times to ask Eric where it is we are going, but he continues to ignore me, and I keep my eyes firmly fixed on the road ahead.

I sit forward as Eric takes the turning for the Bowden Hall.

What the hell are we doing here?

"Eric, mate, either you tell me what we are doing here, or you're fired." I don't mean it, but I am hoping that it will make him talk. It doesn't. He still remains silent, his eyes fixed on the road ahead, and I throw my hands up in exasperation.

We continue down the long driveway and eventually stop in front of the building. I jump out of the limo and wait for Eric to get out of the driver's seat. He doesn't. Instead, to my amazement, he starts to drive off.

What the fuck?

I am beyond pissed off now. I am going to be having some serious words with him when I next see him. I watch the limo disappear down the driveway and I whirl around to see a young man standing at the entrance to the building. I march up to him and he looks petrified.

"Young man," I say, making my tone as demanding as possible. "I need a taxi, and I need it now." I am aware that I sound like a complete ass, but I don't care. I'm too mad to care. I just wanted to go home, but instead I have been stranded here, for reasons I cannot fathom.

"Mr Waters?" the young man stammers in a shaky voice. I frown at him. *How does he know who I am?*

"Yes?"

"Um, could you please make your way to the Great Ballroom?" he asks me. I am sure that he was supposed to sound more confident than he actually does.

"Why would I do that?" I am beyond confused.

Why would I go to the ballroom? Have I forgotten about a meeting? Impossible. I would remember having to come here.

"There is someone waiting for you, sir."

What? This has to be some kind of mistake. Either that or Valerie has fucked up and not told me that I am expected here.

I let out a puff of air, run my hands through my hair, and I stomp through the entrance and up to the doors of the Great Ballroom. I can barely contain my anger at being here.

I reach the doors to the ballroom and I push them open with more force than I meant to.

As the doors swing open, I walk into the room and come to a stop at the sight before me. My mouth drops open as I see that Stacey is here.

She is here, and she looks fucking edible.

She is stood by a table that has been set for two, with a smile on her face. My eyes roam up and down her body. She is wearing a red, lace dress that is similar to the one she wore when we were last here. The dress hugs her tight little body and I feel jealous that it gets to do that.

For fuck's sake, Waters, it's a dress. Get a bloody grip.

She's wearing come-fuck-me black stilettos and her hair hangs down in loose waves, framing her beautiful face. She looks exquisite.

"Good evening, Mr Waters," she purrs at me, making my already alert cock stand to attention. "Would you like to join me for dinner?"

Would I? Fuck, yeah, I would.

I make my way towards her, taking long strides, but as I try to reach out to her, she backs away and wags a finger at me.

"Uh uh," she says as she shakes her head. "Sit." She points to one of the chairs at the table. I consider my options. I can ignore her request, grab her, and make her body melt against mine, or I can play along and see where she is going with this. I opt for the latter and I sit down. My anger has completely evaporated. It's amazing how much this woman can control my emotions without even realising it.

Stacey sits down opposite me and sips some wine from her glass. I notice that my glass is also full, so I take a few mouthfuls. In front of each of us is a plate that is covered. She gestures for me to uncover my plate and as I do, I start to laugh.

There on the plate is a meal consisting of a burger and fries. I look to Stacey and she is grinning at me.

Fuck me, she is stunning.

Her eyes sparkle as our gazes connect, and desire fizzles through my body. I have to fight the urge to stand up, walk around to her, and kiss her. My cock is twitching and straining against my trousers.

All in good time, Waters. All in good time.

"How did you manage to arrange all of this?" I ask her. I'm intrigued to see how she pulled this off. I know that the Bowden Hall is not an easy place to book something unless you have it reserved months in advance. She takes a bite of her food and gives me the most arousing look that I have ever seen.

"I have my ways, Waters." She winks at me and then she stands up. I watch her ass sway from side to side as she walks over to a portable CD player that has been put on the front of the stage. She presses a button and the music that played on the night that we danced in here all those weeks ago starts to filter out of the speakers.

"Would you like to dance?" she asks me. I smile at her and stand up, forgetting about the fact that I haven't even taken a bite of my food yet.

Food is the last thing on my mind right now.

I walk over to her and take her in my arms.

She feels so good.

Her body moulds against mine.

A perfect fit.

Her hands rest on my biceps and she places her head on my chest. We dance in silence and I am transported back to the very first time that I danced with her to this song. I smile at the image of her battling to keep her desire in check. She looked just as stunning that night as she does now, and I tighten my arms around her.

Stacey moves her head off of my chest, stands on tip toes, and puts her lips by my ear. "I have a room booked for the night, and today the doctor gave me the all clear. Feel free to be as rough as you like."

Her words send a signal straight to my cock, and my sharp intake of breath makes it obvious that her words have affected me.

I pull my head back so that I can look at her. "You had a doctor's appointment today? Why didn't you tell me?"

"You had work to do, and you have done enough for me already." I am about to respond when she puts her finger over my lips to silence me. "Question time is over, Waters. Now, how about we go and make use of that room that I have booked?" She raises one eyebrow at me in question.

She doesn't have to ask me twice.

STACEY

I tell Jake which room we are staying in and he leads me to the correct one. I unlock the door using a key card that I obtained earlier, and we walk into the magnificent suite. It's just as breath-taking to me now as it was when I first saw it earlier today. The gold and cream décor makes it feel elegant and plush. The four-poster bed is huge, and the furnishings are exquisite. The lighting is dim, setting the tone for what is about to happen.

"I just need to use the bathroom. Make yourself comfortable," I say to Jake as I make my way to the ensuite. I shut the door behind me, wanting what I am wearing for Jake to be a complete surprise. I put the lingerie in here earlier so that I wouldn't have to keep either of us waiting for too long.

I carefully take off the lace dress and hang it on the back of the bathroom door. I then put on the expensive lingerie that I purchased earlier today. I smile as I assess my appearance in the mirror. Barely-there red lace covers my breasts and the thong is so small that it should come with a health warning. I know that Jake will appreciate it though.

I arrange my hair so that it falls around my shoulders, and I decide to leave the stilettos on, just until we get down to business anyway. I exit the ensuite to see that Jake is already naked, led on the bed, waiting for me.

My God, he is perfection personified. I could look at him all day long.

His eyes widen, and his mouth falls open as he takes in my appearance. He intakes a sharp breath as I reach the bed.

"Fuck me," he says on an exhale.

"That's what I was hoping for," I tease. I bend over, giving Jake a good look at my cleavage as I take off my shoes. I stand back up slowly and relish in the desire radiating from Jake's eyes. He comes to the edge of the bed, so that he is kneeling in front of me. His hands grip my waist and I can already feel how drenched I am.

"You are so beautiful," Jake whispers as I lean my head down to him and brush his lips with mine. He groans, and it takes all of my willpower to pull back from him.

I push him back on the bed and straddle him, loving the feel of his muscly physique between my legs. I undo my bra and slowly pull the straps down my arms before I throw it onto the floor. Before I know what is happening, Jake flips our positions so that I am led beneath him. His mouth finds my breast and he starts to lick my nipple, causing sparks to shoot straight to my core. I arch my back in order to gain more friction. My sex is throbbing, and I desperately need him to relieve the dull ache that has settled there.

"Jake, please," I beg him.

So much for me being in control.

I hear Jake chuckle and it does glorious things to my insides. He removes his mouth from my breast and moves, so that we are eye level.

"Please what?" His hand dips below the front of my thong and his fingers brush against my clit. I cry out in pleasure from the gentle touch. "Jesus Christ, you're soaked."

He brings his hand to his mouth and licks my juices off of his fingers. I don't know how, but that one action is so erotic that I almost orgasm.

"I want to feel you inside me," I say to him, breathlessly. "I want you to fuck me, Jake."

I feel Jake rip the thong from my body at my words. *Well, that didn't stay intact for long.*

"You ready to scream, baby?"

"Hell yes," I manage to answer as I feel Jake's cock pushing against my entrance.

"Get ready. It's going to be a long night," Jake says in that seductive voice of his.

I'm not going to argue.

A long night of Jake is just what I was hoping for.

CHAPTER THIRTY-SIX

STACEY

I wake to the feel of soft kisses being trailed up and down my spine. I stay led on my front, not moving as I enjoy the sensation.

Jake slowly makes his way up to my neck, and then he kisses a trail from there to my lips. I give up the pretence that I am asleep, and I press my lips to his mouth hungrily. A deep chuckle sounds in Jake's throat which makes my heart skip a beat.

"Morning, babe," Jake says between kisses.

"Good morning, handsome." I turn onto my side so that I have a full view of my man.

"I hate to say this, but we need to leave in an hour." I groan in protest and shove the pillow over my head. I don't want to leave yet. Last night was amazing. I know that sex with Jake has always been fantastic, but last night was out of this world. We had it rough, then slow, then rough, then slow. I lost count of the amount of times that I orgasmed.

Jake starts to tickle me which makes me chuck the pillow away and start to try to wriggle from his grasp. It doesn't take long for me to hold my hands up in surrender and admit defeat.

"Okay. Okay," I say whilst trying to catch my breath. "I'll get up. Just stop tickling me." Jake stops, and I take that as my opportunity to pounce on him. I may think that I have him pinned to the bed, but I know that he could easily move me off of him if he really wanted to.

"Surely we have time for one more round before we go?" I purr in his ear.

He smacks my ass and stands up off of the bed, with me wrapped around him.

"Why do you think I woke you?" he says with a cheeky glint in his eye. "Shower?" he asks.

"Perfect." My insides turn to jelly as Jake walks us to the ensuite, and his mouth breaks into a grin that makes me wet before we even reach the bathroom. "I love you, Mr Waters."

"I love you too."

JAKE

Christ, this woman is going to be the death of me.

I watch Stacey as she gets out of the limo, her sweet ass inviting me to touch it. I thought that my sex drive was high, but she certainly gives me competition in that department. The woman is insatiable. Not that I'm complaining. What she did for me last night is something that I will never forget.

I follow her out of the limo and carry our few items into the house. I tell Eric that I will call him later as I walk through the front door. I obviously didn't say anything to him about his part in Stacey's plan. I should probably be thanking him, actually. I certainly had one of the best nights of my life, that's for sure.

I close the front door as Stacey heads to the kitchen. She goes to the coffee machine and sets it all up. She really is a bit of a caffeine addict. Still, better caffeine than anything else.

"Would you like one?" she asks me as she goes to the cupboard where the cups live.

"Yes, please. Only a small one though, I have to leave for the office soon." I sit down on one of the bar stools and I watch her as she comfortably moves around my kitchen.

It hits me that I don't ever want to not see her in my kitchen.

When she is here, it makes the place so much more homely. I find myself racing to get back from work as I know that she will be here.

I know that she is staying with me for now, but there will be a point when she returns to Lydia's. That is a point that I don't ever want to come.

Stacey brings the coffee's over and sits beside me at the kitchen island.

"So, I take it that you enjoyed your surprise?" she asks, her eyes looking all innocent as she peers over the coffee cup that she is sipping from.

"Best surprise ever." I think that it is amazing that she thought to try and re-create our meeting at the Bowden Hall. No one has ever gone to so much trouble for me. I'm going to have to figure out a way of topping that one. Although, I really don't know if I ever will.

"So listen, Jake, I need to talk to you, about me returning to work." She looks worried about broaching this subject, but little does she know that I already have an idea up my sleeve. I need to put on my best acting skills if I am to pull this off without her suspecting anything.

I stay silent and drink my coffee, waiting for her to continue. "Um, seeing as the doctor has now given me the all clear, I really need to get back to work and earn some money."

"Okay."

"Okay," she repeats after me, sounding relieved. I decide to drop the bombshell now, so that she has time to stew whilst I return to the office.

"You're not returning to work at The Den," I say, mustering all of my acting skills to keep a straight face.

"What?" she says loudly, looking a little fazed by what I just said. "Why not?"

"Are you being serious?" She looks at me, her eyebrows raised in question. "It's not safe for you there." I keep my voice even, giving nothing away.

"Oh for goodness sake. Don't be so ridiculous. Donnie is no longer around, and Caitlin is in prison. The two culprits that have caused me harm are no longer here. It's more than safe for me to return to The Den."

"No."

"No?" she screeches. "Since when do you decide where I can and cannot work?" She is angry with me, but I need to keep her in the dark for now.

"I'm not deciding for you." I sigh. "I just think that The Den is unsafe." She sits there with her arms folded, glaring at me.

God, she looks sexy when she's angry.

"Jake Waters, I will work wherever I bloody well choose to, and if that means that I choose to work at The Den, then you are just going to have to deal with that." She gets up off the bar stool and marches out of the kitchen. I follow her into the hallway and put my hand on her arm, turning her to face me.

"Stacey, I don't want to argue with you. Why are you being so stubborn about this?"

"Me? Stubborn?" She scoffs. "You're the one being unreasonable. Ass." She shrugs me off and bolts upstairs. I chase her and grab her around the waist as she enters my bedroom. She squeals as I lift her to the bed and pin her down so that she is facing me. "Jake, get off of me."

"Not until you calm down and listen to my reasoning." I fight back the urge to chuckle. She may think that I am being an ass, but she will thank me when I surprise her later. She is still glaring at me, and my cock can't help but twitch. "Do you know how turned on I am by you right now?"

"Ass," she whispers but I see her eyes sparkle. That does it for me. I crash my lips against hers and devour her mouth. I release her arms and she links them around my neck. She may be pissed off with me, but she can't deny the sexual attraction between us. Even during a disagreement our sexual chemistry can't be stopped.

I fumble about, undoing my trousers before lifting her skirt and ripping her thong from her, throwing it behind me onto the floor. "Hey! That's the second pair of panties that you have ruined in the last twenty-four hours."

"I'll buy you more." I plunge my cock into her which has her immediately gasping for breath. "Now, here's the deal. We're going to talk about this later because I have a proposition for you." She moans as I pull my cock back and thrust into her. Her eyes glaze over, and I know that she isn't thinking about anything other than me being inside her. "As for right now, I'm going to fuck you before I have to leave for work."

I plunge into her again and she screams out my name in pleasure.

"Deal?" I ask her as I pull my cock back out slowly and wait for her reply.

"Deal, baby."

CHAPTER THIRTY-SEVEN

STACEY

I lie on the bed, in my post orgasmic state, after Jake has left me feeling more than satisfied.

The man is an animal.

I don't know how long I lie there for, but the sound of my phone ringing breaks my blissful state. I throw on one of Jake's shirts and a pair of knickers, and I fly down the stairs to get my phone. It stops ringing just before I reach the bottom of the stairs, where it is in my handbag which I left on the floor when we arrived back here earlier. I pick up my bag and dig out my phone to see that it was Lydia who tried to call me. I quickly dial her number back, needing to see if she is okay. It's been far too long since I last spoke to her, and I wouldn't want her to think that I am ignoring her.

The phone rings twice before she answers.

"Hi, Stace," she says shyly.

"Hey, Lyd. It's so good to hear from you." The phone stays silent as I think that maybe I should have said something different. "How are you?" I ask, wanting the awkward silence to disappear.

"I'm good thanks. Much better than I was anyway."

"That's great." The conversation stalls again and I rack my brains for what to say next, something that I have never had to do before when talking to Lydia. "So, are you back at the flat yet?"

"No, I'm still staying with Nick. It's been so good to be able to lean on him through everything." I am pleased that she is getting better, but I can't help but feel a slight pang in my chest at the realisation that she wouldn't let me help her at all. "Listen, I just wanted to call and say that I'm sorry for everything. I didn't mean those awful things that I said to you. You are my best friend, and I hope that I haven't ruined that."

"Of course you haven't," I say, wanting to put her mind at rest.

"Don't give me an easy-out, Stace, I acted like a bitch towards you. I took my frustrations out on you, and I shouldn't have done that."

"I'm not giving you an easy-out, Lyd. I just want to forget it all and put it behind us." There is no need to rehash the past in this case.

"I don't suppose that there is any chance that you might be free for coffee this afternoon is there?" she asks. The nerves in her voice are evident.

"Sure. What time were you thinking?"

"Um, shall we meet at Danish in an hour?"

"Sounds good."

"Great. I'll see you there." We wrap up the call and I quickly run around getting myself ready. I go back up the stairs to Jake's bedroom and put on my skinny jeans with silver sandals, and my grey sleeveless shirt. The shirt is a little see through, but not in a slutty way, so I make sure that I put a black bra on. I put my hair up into a high ponytail, check my make-up and I retouch my mascara and eyeliner.

Once satisfied, I grab my grey clutch-bag and leave Jake's house. It is another glorious day outside meaning the walk to the coffee shop is enjoyable. The sun is beaming down on my skin and it feels heavenly. I am in my own little world when my phone beeps to signal that I have received a message. I pull the phone out of my pocket and see that it is Martin.

Hey, baby girl. I need drinks, TONIGHT!
You still up for it?
Mart x x

The urgency in the word "tonight" screams that something is wrong.

Sure. Meet you at The Den at 7pm?
Stace x

Martin replies seconds later saying that he will be there. Oh, and he also says that he wants updating on the dirty details of what happened with Jake last night. I smile at the memory, but my concern for Martin outweighs my delight. I know that things with Clayton haven't been good, he hasn't needed to tell me about it, I just know. I hope that, whatever it is that they are going through, they can work it out.

I decide to send Jake a quick text to let him know that I will be going out tonight. Even though he acted like an idiot over the work issue, I don't want him to worry about where I have gone.

Hi, Jake. Just a text to let you know that I
am going out for drinks tonight.
Stace x x
P.S. you're still an ass!

I can't resist putting that last bit on.

I put my phone away as I reach the coffee shop, and as I enter, I scan the tables for Lydia. She is sat by the window with a coffee in front of her, and another one waiting for me. She looks over as I approach, and before I can sit down, she stands up and flings her arms around me. I return her hug and feel tears start to well in my eyes.

I have missed this lady being a part of my life.

She pulls away and smiles at me before sitting back down. I take my seat and can see that she looks like she is getting back to her old self. Her hair is full of its usual bounce, her skin is clearer, and her eyes look brighter.

"You look good, Lyd." I can't help but remark on her appearance. Hardly surprising though seeing as she wasn't looking her finest when I last saw her.

"Thanks. I feel good." I smile at her and take a sip of my coffee. "So, what have you been up to? You look amazing by the way. I'm presuming that your time with Mr Jake Waters has something to do with the healthy glow currently radiating off of you?" And just like that, I know that Lydia is returning to her old self.

I waste no time in telling her some of the things that have been going on between Jake and me. She seems engrossed in my words, but then I suppose she hasn't had much to gossip about with Nick. "Wow. You and Jake sound like you are definitely on the right track after everything that has happened."

"I hope so, Lyd, I can't imagine my life without him in it." I hate to sound so soppy, but it's the truth. "Anyway, enough about me. Tell me, how have things really been between you and Nick?"

"It's been really good, actually. I think that we needed something to get us to put aside our differences. I'm just sorry that it took me getting into such a state for us to start talking properly again." She looks down in shame.

"Hey," I say, reaching over and putting my hand on her arm. "The main thing is that you're getting back to your old self. That's all that matters, Lyd. Just, promise me that you won't go down that self-destructive route again?"

"Oh, don't worry, I won't. Taking drugs messed my head up. I barely remember what I was doing whilst I was on the stuff. I don't know why I felt the need to take it. I think I just felt like life was getting on top of me, and I didn't know how to deal with the emotions that I was feeling. Taking the drugs and drinking alcohol seemed to blot it out. Well, for a while it did anyway."

"You know that you can always talk to me, Lyd. You shouldn't keep things bottled up."

"I know." She smiles at me. "But you had your own shit to deal with. You didn't need me bringing you down with my trivial problems."

"It doesn't matter how trivial things may seem, I always have your back, you know that."

"I do know that." Her eyes start to glisten as she speaks. "Wow, look at me getting all sentimental." She tries to make a joke of it to lighten the mood.

"It's understandable. You have been through a lot." I sip my coffee and decide that a change in topic may help. "Anyway, I haven't told you about Charles trying to crack onto me the other day."

Lydia's mouth drops open and her eyes go wide with shock. "Shut the fuck up. Does Jake know?"

"Hell no, he would go ballistic. No point in getting him worked up over that bellend." Lydia and I burst out laughing at the same time at my choice of words.

"Well, come on then, tell me more. Where and how did this happen?" I smile at her and take comfort in the fact that I have my best friend back.

"I love ya, Lyd."

"I love you too, girl. Now, spill."

CHAPTER THIRTY-EIGHT

JAKE

I don't get to leave the office until just after seven o'clock. If it's not the accounting department fucking up, then it's the event planners. I seriously need to consider hiring some new staff to help with the workload. Business is booming, which is great, but I have so much to deal with that I need to employ people who can make decisions without my need for approval.

Eric is waiting outside Waters Industries when I exit, and I practically run to the limo, gratefully sinking into the back seat. I instruct Eric to take me straight home as I check my phone messages. There are twenty of the damn things, but the only one that I am interested in reading is from Stacey.

I open the text message and start to read it, and when I finish reading, I feel myself getting annoyed that I wasn't able to read it earlier. Fuck. I wanted to speak to her about her job tonight. I try to call her, but it goes straight to voicemail. Bollocks.

Where the bloody hell would she be?

I sigh and try to think of where she might have gone. It doesn't take me long to figure it out, especially after our conversation earlier today.

"Change of plans, Eric. Take me to The Den."

STACEY

"Dang, baby girl, your booty is looking mighty fine in that itty-bitty dress," Martin says as I walk up to him. I place a kiss on his cheek and we enter The Den. My choice of a black bodycon dress appears to be a good one. "Your man is not going to be happy when he sees you wearing that."

"Pfft. Tough."

"Oooo, fighting talk, I like it. Don't ever lose that sass of yours, babe."

We reach the bar and order some drinks. There are still agency staff working here, but I'm hoping that I can rectify all of that as soon as possible.

We choose to sit at the corner of the bar counter, and I perch myself carefully on a bar stool.

Maybe this dress is a bit too short? One wrong move and I will be giving the patrons an eyeful.

"So, where is Clayton tonight?" I ask, wanting to get to the bottom of what is going on. I sip my cocktail and enjoy the cool sensation working its way down my throat.

"Oh, uh, you know, busy working," Martin stammers.

"I'm not buying it, Mart."

"What do you mean?" he says, avoiding eye contact with me.

"I know that something is going on between you guys. Are you having problems?"

"If you must know, Clayton and I are taking a break. He moved out a couple of days ago," Martin says with a sigh. My eyes go wide with shock. I knew that something was amiss, but I never imagined that Clayton would have moved out.

"Why didn't you say anything?"

"You don't need to hear about my failing love life, baby girl. Not when yours is so freakin' hot right now."

"That's a shitty excuse, Martin. You are my friend, and you should have told me. I feel awful that you have been going through all of that on your own." First Lydia keeps things from me, and now Martin. Am I sending some sort of signal out for my friends to keep quiet about anything that is troubling them?

"I haven't told anybody, Stace. I was hoping that he would be back after one night away. I think that it's over, for good." Martin looks so sad.

"Oh, honey, I'm so sorry."

"It's okay," he says with a shrug of his shoulders. "If it's meant to be then we will find a way back to one another."

"I hope you do." I give him a smile but inside I feel sadness for my friend. Martin seems to be consumed by his own thoughts for a moment and I sip my drink as I wait for him to gather his thoughts.

"Anyway," he says suddenly, making me jump. "Enough about Clayton. Are we here to party or not?" He drains his cocktail and attracts the bar tender. He orders two more drinks and a couple of tequila shots.

Shit, this is going to be a messy one.

JAKE

I spot Stacey from across the room. She looks fucking hot in a figure-hugging black dress. Too fucking hot, actually. I almost barrel over there and carry her back to mine like some macho caveman. However, I manage to restrain myself.

It doesn't escape my notice that there are several men drooling whilst watching her dance.

Fucking letches.

I can see that she is with Martin. I have only seen him a couple of times, but I can tell that his dress sense was toned down on those occasions. He's wearing a lime-green shirt and electric-blue trousers. It's enough to give you a headache from looking at him.

I watch Stacey as she laughs and shakes her ass in time to the music. I stalk her with my eyes, like prey as she walks to the bar and leaves her companion to tear up the dance floor, and I smile to myself.

I think now may be the time to surprise her.

STACEY

I wait at the bar to be served, when some guy stands beside me and decides to try and chat me up.

"Did you fall from heaven?" he shouts in my ear. I roll my eyes and try to catch the bartender's attention. The guy continues to try his luck. "You are bloody gorgeous. Can I buy you a drink?"

"No, thank you. I can buy my own."

"Ah, come on. One little drink won't hurt."

"I said no."

"Just one drink. No strings." Fair play, this guy isn't going to give up easily.

"Look, mate," I say as I turn my body to face him with one hand resting on my hip. "I'm not interested. I don't need you to buy me a drink because I'm not going to dance with you, I'm not going to kiss you, and I'm not going to sleep with you. You are wasting your time. Why don't you run along and try your *charms* on someone else?" I turn back to face the bar, hoping that he will go away now that I have made it clear to him that I have no desire to do anything with him.

"Oh, so you play hard to get, do you? I like that in a woman."

Ugh, is this guy for real? What is it with men who think that they can hassle women on a night out? I'm going to have to be even more blunt with this moron.

"You have a couple of options here, so listen carefully." The guy looks like it's Christmas morning as he leans in closer. "Option number one, you can continue to harass me, and I will have your ass kicked out of here. Option number two, I can knee you in the crotch which would be highly embarrassing for you. And then there is option number three—"

"What's that then?" he interrupts, not looking quite as jolly as he did a few minutes ago.

"Option three is that you turn around and walk back over to your group of buddies over there, and we can forget that this conversation ever happened." I smile sweetly as he looks at me and then looks to his friends who are unsubtly trying to egg him on.

"I think I'll just leave you to it," he answers, clearly sensing that I am being completely serious.

"Good idea," I say. I wave him away and he walks back to his friends, his shoulders slumped slightly. I shake my head and return my attention to the bartender, who is now on the opposite side of the bar serving a group of ladies who are clearly half pissed already.

I sigh and close my eyes, taking in a few deep breaths. I feel someone brush against my arm and I swallow down my annoyance.

I swear, if that's another asshole who is going to try his luck, I am going to punch them.

I open my eyes and look to the side of me.

My heart starts to pound, and my breath catches in my throat.

"Good evening, Miss?" His voice is like liquid gold. Smooth and silky. His chiselled features are beautiful, and the slight stubble on his chin makes him look sexy as hell. He holds his hand out for me to shake.

"Paris." I answer, trying to stop my hand from trembling. I place my hand in his and immediately I feel the electricity zip between us. I gulp as his eyes settle on my lips.

"What a beautiful name. I saw you shoot that other guy down, but may I buy you a drink?"

Hell yeah you can buy me a drink. I obviously don't say this out loud thank goodness.

"No, I'm okay, thank you. My friends always told me not to accept drinks from strange men."

"Is that so?" he says, seeming slightly amused. "Your friends must be very wise people." He grins at me and my knees almost give way. I slowly pull my hand out of his grasp and grip the edge of the bar for support. "So, you're not looking for any male attention this evening then?"

"Uh, no," I reply quickly. "My boyfriend wouldn't appreciate me interacting with other men." My voice has become raspy, my throat dry.

"I can't say that I blame him. Whoever he is, he is a very lucky man." I can feel the blush creeping up from my neck and to my cheeks. The bartender chooses this moment to come over, allowing me to divert my attention. I order two shots of tequila as one isn't going to be enough. I wait for the bartender to bring me my shots, and I can feel the guy's eyes on me the whole time.

The bartender brings my drinks over and I down them both before he has even brought my change back. I need to see if the alcohol will calm my nerves.

"Wow. Thirsty?" the guy asks me.

"Yeah. It's all the dancing," I reply feeling a little foolish at giving such a crappy answer.

"Hmm. I did see you up there earlier," he says, indicating to the dance floor. "I must say, you do know how to, uh, move, shall we say?"

Christ, he was watching me?

How long for?

The mere thought turns me on more than it should.

"Uh, anyway, I better be getting back to my friend," I say, needing to get away from him.

"Sure. Nice to meet you, Miss Paris. I hope to run into you again some time." I nervously smile and return to the dance floor, on shaky legs.

Luckily, Martin remains unaware of my altercation at the bar. I can still feel the guy's eyes on me as I start to dance. Ciara's, "Dance like we're Making Love," starts to play and I become very aware of my dance moves.

I bump and grind as my skin heats. I turn to face the guy at the bar, and our eyes lock. The sizzle between us is so immense that I almost orgasm there and then.

What the fuck are you doing?

You shouldn't be acting this way in front of all of these people.

I can't help it though. I am drawn to this man like a magnet. I thought that I had felt attraction before, but this is a whole new feeling entirely.

I shake my head and avert my gaze. I need to stop behaving this way. I turn back to dance with Martin, and to forget about the beautiful man that is sat at the bar.

"Baby girl, you are on fire," Martin shouts at me. I just smile at him and let my body go with the beat of the music.

As I continue to dance, I feel someone tap me on my shoulder from behind. I stop dancing and whirl around to see that the bartender is stood there. I look at him and I can feel my face pull into a frown.

"Are you Stacey?" he asks me.

"Yes. Is there a problem?"

"I'm afraid so. The owner would like to see you in his office." *What? The owner?*

"Why would the owner want to see me?" I ask.

"I don't know, but he said that it was urgent. If you could please follow me, I'll take you to his office." I turn to Martin and tell him that I will be back shortly, and he waves me off as he dances with a couple of lads.

I follow the bartender and rack my brains as to why the owner would want to see me. Even in the time that I have worked at The Den, I have never met him. I wouldn't even know what he looks like, actually.

I expect to be taken to Lydia's office, but the bartender leads me down the corridor that goes past the toilets. We keep going until we reach a door right at the back of the building. The bartender stops outside the door, turns to me, and tells me to go on in before he heads back out to the main room.

I feel slightly nervous as I stare at the door. I consider bolting, but my curiosity gets the better of me. I take a deep breath, open the door, and walk in.

The room is dimly lit and straight away I can see that it is an office, but a much plusher one than Lydia's.

How come I have never been in here before?

There is a massive black, leather corner sofa dominating the right-hand side of the room, with a sleek coffee table in front of it. Opposite the sofa is the most beautiful carved oak desk that I have ever seen. I walk over and run my hands along the cool wood. There is a large television screen on the wall to my left, and then there is a door to the right of it.

I wonder where that door leads?

I am tempted to take a look, but I don't know where the owner is, and I wouldn't want him to catch me snooping. I am about to walk over and take a seat on the sofa whilst I wait, when the door I have just been wondering about opens, and out steps the handsome guy I was talking to at the bar. He closes the door behind him and smiles.

"Take a seat, Miss Paris," his voice booms over to me. "Would you like a drink now?" He makes his way to a small cabinet in the corner of the room and waits for me to answer.

"Yes, please," I manage to squeak out. I feel my legs go weak as my eyes focus on his ass. He is wearing suit trousers that are just snug enough to give me a glimpse of how firm it is.

Somehow, I make myself walk to the sofa and take a seat. The guy brings over two glasses containing a light brown liquid. Exactly what it is doesn't really bother me at this point in time. My hairs stand on end as he decides to come around the table and sit on it, so that he is inches from me. If I were to shuffle forward slightly, then our legs would be touching.

"Here," he says, handing me one of the glasses. I take it from him, drain the contents and put the glass by the side of him, on the coffee table. The liquid burns as it slides down the back of my throat.

"You are quite a little tease, aren't you, Miss Paris?" My eyes go wide at his comment. "Oh, I'm not complaining. I do believe that your dancing out there was for my benefit?" he asks, his mouth pulling into a slight smile. I can't answer him. My mouth has lost its main function, so I just nod. "I thought so."

He takes a sip of his drink and leans in close to me. So close that I can feel his breath on my skin. I feel like I could almost faint from the proximity of this ridiculously hot guy. This man is making me experience a level of desire that I haven't experienced before. His hand comes to my chin and tilts my face up so that I am eye level with him.

"Well, Miss Paris, shall we relieve some of your sexual tension?" I whimper at his words. He seems to take that as a yes and his lips lock with mine.

Our kiss starts out soft, but it soon becomes frenzied. My hands move of their own accord up to his hair and I run my fingers through his silky locks. His hands find their way to my thighs, and he begins a slow caress until he reaches the hem of my dress. He lifts me up slightly and shimmies my dress up, exposing my lace thong.

He breaks away from my lips and pulls my dress up further, essentially unwrapping me in one fluid motion. His gaze roams over my lingerie clad body, and I bite my bottom lip as I await his next move.

"Such a beautiful body," he whispers as he kisses my neck.

I feel like I have died and gone to heaven.

I unbutton his shirt and push it off of his shoulders. His hands caress my breasts, and I moan into his mouth, causing him to growl in response.

"Please," I whisper. "I need to feel you."

He unclasps my bra and lets it fall to the floor. His finger brushes over my thong, touching my clit through the fabric, and I cry out in pleasure. He stands up, pulling me with him, and I undo his trousers. I pull them down to just below his ass, freeing his erection. I pant as I admire his manhood and then move down his body until I am able to lick his length with my tongue, making him gasp.

"You are a bad girl, Miss Paris." I take his full length into my mouth and begin to move back and forth. I become like a woman possessed as I devour him. He groans in pleasure as I roll my tongue over the tip of his cock. I grip his firm ass as I move him all the way to the back of my throat.

"Jesus," he cries out. He then abruptly manoeuvres himself so that he is no longer in my mouth. I look up at him in question.

"Stand up," he commands. I do as he asks, and he hooks his fingers into my thong, pulling it down my legs and then motioning for me to step out of them. I stand before him, in nothing but my shoes and I don't feel the least bit shy.

He steps back towards me, closing any gap between us. His hands rest just under my ass and then he lifts me up. I lock my legs around his waist and his cock touches my sex, making me quiver.

He moves so that my back is against the wall and gives me no warning as he plunges into me, making my sex convulse around him. I grip his arms with my fingers, and I scream at the sheer force as he starts a punishing rhythm.

Fuck, this is good.

I can feel my insides clench as my orgasm approaches fast. I try to hold back from my release, but this feels so good that I can't control it.

"I'm close," I whisper.

"Hold on," he says in that smooth voice of his. I whimper at his words, trying desperately not to give in and let go.

"I can't," I say breathlessly.

"You can. Just wait for me."

The pleasure is building inside of me, and I know that I am going to shatter into a million pieces. Just when I think that I can't hold on any longer, he speaks.

"Come for me," he says, locking his eyes with mine.

I allow myself to relinquish the tiny bit of control that I had left, and I scream out in pleasure, feeling his hot liquid shooting into me seconds later.

My body turns to jelly in the aftermath and I cling onto him limply as he carries me back to the sofa. We are both panting, and that has got to be one of the most intense encounters that I have ever had.

He lies me down and then covers me with his body. I start to shake from the sheer violence of my orgasm. He looks into my eyes and I feel like he is penetrating my soul with his stare. We have such a strong connection, on every level.

"That was incredible," he says, mirroring my thoughts exactly.

"Mmm," is all I can muster the energy to say. He places a gentle kiss on my lips.

"You are quite the game player, baby."

"You're not so bad yourself, Mr Waters."

CHAPTER THIRTY-NINE

STACEY

After sorting ourselves out, so that we look presentable, Jake and I leave the office and go to the bar to get a drink.

As I enter the main room, I see that Martin is still on the dance floor, completely unaware that I have just been thoroughly fucked senseless in the back room. Jake orders us some drinks and I perch on one of the bar stools. He moves so that he is stood behind me, his arms going around either side of me, his hands resting on the bar. I can't help but turn and give him a kiss on the cheek, inhaling his scent as I do.

I really cannot get enough of him.

Our little role play just now was so exciting.

The bartender brings our drinks over and I take a sip, turning my body on the stool, so that I am facing Jake, our faces inches apart.

"So, tell me, how did you manage to get access to that back room?" I ask him.

"Did the bartender not tell you that I am the owner?"

"Oh, ha ha, very funny. We're not in role play mode now, Mister."

"Who said anything about role play?" he says looking deadly serious. I frown as I try to process what he is telling me.

"Jake... Are you saying what I think you are saying?" I ask, astonished at how this conversation is going.

He leans in closer so that his mouth brushes against my ear. "Well, if what you are thinking is, 'I have bought The Den,' then you would be correct." He pulls back, and my mouth drops open.

"What? Why on earth would you want to buy this place?" My voice is high-pitched and squeaky. He just looks at me, and it suddenly dawns on me why he bought this place. "Oh, Jake. Please tell me that you didn't just buy this place because I wanted to come back to work here?"

"Look, you want to return to work, and I want to keep you safe. If I own the place, then I have more chance of doing that. This way, I can put extra security measures in place. It seemed like the logical answer." He shrugs and takes a sip of his drink.

"Logical?" The disbelief in my tone is evident. I shake my head at him. "You are crazy, you know that?"

"Crazy about you." He rubs his nose against mine, and just like that he has managed to win me round to his way of thinking.

"So, this morning, when you were being an ass about me returning to work here, that was just you putting on an act?"

"Guilty," he says with a cheeky smirk on his face. Unbelievable.

"You really had me fooled, you know?"

"I am well aware of that." That cheeky smirk of his is not disappearing.

"You're still an ass," I reply which results in Jake bursting into laughter.

"Oh, and there is one more thing," he says, once he has managed to stop laughing at me. I groan and roll my eyes at him.

What more could there possibly be?

"What is the one more thing?" I ask.

"Well, I want you to be in complete control of running the place." At his words, I come to the conclusion that Jake has lost his mind. I am about to answer him when Martin comes strolling over and drapes his arm around my shoulder.

"There you are, baby girl. Where did you disappear to?" he slurs in my ear. His eyes move from me to Jake and he literally swoons on the spot. "Fuck me, aren't you a delightful sight." I burst out laughing as Jake's eyes go wide with shock. "I could melt on the spot."

"Martin," I swat at him playfully, trying to get my laughter under control. Jake looks like a cat caught in the headlights. "I know that you guys have met before, so I don't need to do any introductions."

"We certainly have," Martin replies. "And may I say, I am very pleased to meet you again, Jakey boy." Martin holds his hand out and Jake shakes it warily. "You certainly are the hottest man candy in here tonight. Tell me, do you have any homosexual brothers?" Martin asks a flustered looking Jake.

Jake looks so uncomfortable at Martin's forwardness, but I think that this is one of the funniest things that I have ever seen. Jake struggles to form any words, so I decide to help him out.

"Martin, stop," I say, still chuckling.

"What?" Martin says, looking at me all innocent, but grinning at the same time. I roll my eyes at him.

"Leave my man candy alone."

"I tell you what, Stace, how you ever leave the bedroom is beyond me. I could ruin a man who looks like that." This is definitely the first time that I have seen

Jake go red in the face. I am never going to let him forget this moment. It will forever be ingrained on my memory.

"Listen, honey," I say to Martin. "I'm beat, are you ready to take off?"

"Hell no, I see a beautiful blond man over there just begging for me to take him home and teach him a thing or two." I look to where Martin is pointing and there is indeed a blond man giving him the eye. "You go ahead, baby girl. Go and enjoy your man candy." He points to Jake and my laughter returns in full force.

"I'll call you tomorrow," Martin says.

"Make sure that you do," I say as I kiss his cheek. Martin looks to Jake and moves closer towards him.

"Such a shame I can't tempt you to sample a bit of the Martlove."

"Uh..." Jake is literally speechless.

"Don't look so worried, I'm only messing about. You'll get used to me. Nice to see you again," Martin says as he turns to walk away. He only takes a few steps before he turns back around again. "Look after her. She's one in a million." He then winks at me and heads towards the blond guy that he has set his sights on.

I see Jake smile at his parting words, and a warmth fills me.

"Can we go now?" Jake asks.

"Sure, babe." I hop off of the bar stool, take a few more sips of my drink and then I grab Jake's hand and lead him outside. I see the limo waiting across the road, and Eric gets out of the driver's seat as he sees us approach. He opens the back door for us and smiles.

"Good evening, Miss Stacey."

"Hey, Eric," I say.

I get into the limo as I hear Jake mumble something to Eric. I relax into the seat and Jake gets in, sitting next to me. I link my hand with his and rest my head on his shoulder. Suddenly, I sit upright as I have a brainwave and Jake looks to me in question.

"I will run The Den for you, on one condition," I say firmly.

"And what would that condition be?"

"You offer Martin a job at Waters Industries, in the event planning department."

"Are you serious?" Jake splutters. I turn so that my body is facing him.

"Yeah. He's amazing at his job. One of the best. I hate the thought of him being treated like shit working for Charles. He deserves better."

"You want me to hire him after the comments he made tonight?"

"Yes. He was only having a laugh." I will not back down on this negotiation. "Honestly, Jake, he's a good guy. I wouldn't be friends with him if he wasn't."

"And if I hire him, then you will run The Den?" Jake asks, needing this confirmed again.

"Yes." He takes a few moments to mull over what I have said.

"Well," he starts as he strokes my hand with his thumb. "It looks like I will be offering Martin a job then."

I smile and throw my arms around him. He pulls me tight to his body and I pull my head back to look at him.

"I love you," I say as I place a kiss on his lips.

"I love you too. More than you will ever know."

JAKE

We get back to my place, and Stacey has fallen asleep. I manoeuvre her, so that I can exit the limo whilst being able to carry her.

"Goodnight, Eric. Thanks for bringing us back home, I'll see you in the morning."

"Night, Jake. Take care of her. She's good for you."

"I know." I sometimes think that she is too good for me.

I walk up the drive and take the steps leading to the front door. I unlock it and close it behind me before I carry Stacey up to my bedroom and gently lie her on the bed. She gives a little moan as she shuffles onto her side, curling up into a ball.

I take her shoes off and pull the duvet over her before sitting on the edge of the bed, just so I can look at her.

This woman has made my life worth living.

She has made me whole.

I can't imagine my life without her in it.

One day, she will become Mrs Waters, I am sure of that.

First things first though, after Caitlin's sentencing on Monday, I am going to ask her to move in with me, properly.

I kiss Stacey on her forehead before going to the bathroom to get undressed. I return to the bed and get in, curling around her, enjoying the feel of her warmth. Shame she's wearing her dress still though. I breath in the scent of her shampoo and count myself as one of the lucky ones.

I have found my soul mate.

CHAPTER FORTY

STACEY

Monday morning has come around far too quickly, and this Monday happens to be a bit different to all of the others.

Today is the day of Caitlin's sentencing.

I am on my way to Lydia's flat, so that I can try to take my mind off of it.

Oh, who am I kidding? I can't think about anything else. I just want it to all be over.

I get to Lydia's at just gone half past eight, bringing with me coffee and fresh doughnuts. Lydia answers the door and she looks radiant. Her hair and skin are glowing, and her eyes have fully regained their mischievous sparkle.

"Morning, babes," she says, her eyes falling to the bag in my hand. "You brought breakfast. Fab. I'm starving."

"You're in an awfully good mood this morning," I say as I make my way inside and head through to the kitchen.

"I am indeed. I feel great," she says as she trails behind me.

"I wish I could say the same," I reply, my stomach churning at what today's outcome might be. I put the bag of doughnuts and the coffees on the table and take a seat. Lydia sits opposite me, peering into the bag.

"Oh, yum, doughnuts," she says as she pulls one out and takes a bite. I'm not feeling hungry at all. My stomach is in knots. I just sip my coffee, but even that is leaving a bitter taste in my mouth.

"Are you not having one?" Lydia asks, thrusting the bag towards me.

"I can't eat yet. Not until the sentencing is over." Lydia's hand reaches for mine, her grip firm.

"She's going to get her comeuppance, babes. I hope that they lock her up and throw away the damn key." I nod in agreement with her, but inside I'm not so sure.

I don't want to get my hopes up, only for them to be dashed. I try to change the subject.

"So, how's things going since we last spoke?" I ask.

"Awesome." Lydia smiles and I know that there is more to her happiness than meets the eye. "Having my brother back is great, we have become close in such a small amount of time. I didn't realise how much I missed him until now." I am so pleased that I called Nick on that awful day. If I hadn't, things could have been very different.

"I also have something else to tell you," Lydia says, breaking my thoughts. Her eyes sparkle, and she fidgets excitedly.

"Okay, what is it?" I feel my own mood lifting at watching her become so animated.

"I'm back in contact with Paul."

"Really?"

"Yeah. We're going out for dinner later in the week. I really like him, Stace, and I think that he could be good for me, if I let him in."

"I agree." I feel a surge of happiness for her. All I want is for Lydia to be happy and content with her life.

My eyes flit to the clock on the wall. It is just before nine. It's getting close.

Jake decided to go to the sentencing in the end. He wants to be there in person to hear the verdict for himself. I take a few deep breaths and try to calm my nerves.

"Stace, stop it. You're getting yourself all worked up."

"I'm sorry, I can't help it. It's just, this is the last day of that chapter in my life. The aftermath of what she did, it still pains me that she managed to take so much away from me for a short time. I just want it all over with so that I can fully move on."

"I know," Lydia says, giving me a soft smile. "Why don't you tell me what you got up to over the weekend?" She's trying to divert my attention. I tell her all about going out with Martin and how Jake and I had the most glorious sexual encounter together.

"Wow, he's a keeper, babes," she says when I am finished.

"I know. I just hope that I have what it takes to keep him."

"Of course you have." Lydia scoffs. "Anyone can see how much he loves you, Stace. Just enjoy the feeling and go with it."

"I've never felt this way about anyone before, Lyd. Sometimes, it scares me how powerful my feelings are for him."

"I don't think that you are alone in that thought, Stace. The feeling is clearly mutual—"

My phone rings, interrupting Lydia. I look down to the screen, petrified as I see that Jake is calling me. I pick up my phone with trembling fingers, and answer.

"Hey," I greet him, quietly.

"Hey, babe. You okay?" he asks me. His voice invades my mind and eases the knot formed there a little.

"Not really," I reply honestly. "You?"

"I'm fine. I'm just worried about you." There is a brief silence as I painfully await the news of the verdict. I look to the clock and see that it is only just gone half past nine. It didn't take them long to come to a decision.

Maybe they are running late?

Maybe she got off scot free?

I shut down the questions and decide to get to the point.

"Has she been sentenced yet?" I ask Jake.

"Yes," Jake states. I feel nervous at his answer, and I take a couple of breaths before responding.

"And?" I prompt him when I am ready to hear the answer.

"Eight years, baby. She got eight years with no chance of early release." I let out a puff of air and tears start to roll down my cheeks. I feel overwhelmed with emotion.

Lydia comes around the table and puts her arm around my shoulders, and Jake stays silent on the phone, letting me cry it out.

"I'm sorry," I say a few moments later. "It's all just a bit over-whelming."

"Don't apologise," he says. "Did you go to Lydia's in the end?"

"Yes, I couldn't be by myself."

"I'm coming to get you. I'll be there in twenty minutes." There is no room for argument, but to be honest, I want him to come and get me.

"Okay," I whisper as I end the call.

Lydia is waiting expectantly to see what the outcome was.

"Well?" she asks.

"She got eight years, Lyd. Eight long-ass-years."

"That's great," she says as she gives me a hug. "I told you that she would get what she deserved, didn't I? The psycho bitch that she is."

"Yeah. That's the kind of crazy that no one needs in their life." I breath in and out as I feel like a weight has been lifted off of my shoulders.

With that part of my life all wrapped up, I can now look forward to my future with the man that I love.

CHAPTER FORTY-ONE

STACEY

Jake picks me up from Lydia's and we go back to his place. I didn't get a chance to tell Lydia about Jake buying The Den, but there is plenty of time for me to do that. I don't even know the finer details myself yet. I just hope that she doesn't mind me running the place.

Jake and I walk through the front door and go to the kitchen. I sit on one of the bar stools and Jake wraps his arms around me, enveloping me in a hug. I wrap my arms around his waist and take comfort in our embrace. I could stay like this forever.

I nuzzle into his chest as he gently strokes my back.

"It's over, babe. It's all over," he says. I take notice of his words and pull my head back to look into his gorgeous caramel eyes.

"No, it's not," I reply. He frowns at me, waiting for me to continue. "It's only just beginning." He smiles at me and places a light kiss on my lips.

He moves his head back, so that it is only a breath away from mine. His eyes mesmerise me and emotions pass between us.

"Move in with me," he says, breaking the hypnotic spell that his eyes had put me under. I feel a slight smile tug at the corner of my mouth at his words.

I don't keep him waiting for an answer. "I'd love to."

The grin that appears on his face is heart-stopping and makes me feel giddy. He lifts me up and I wrap my legs around him. His lips crash onto mine and I link my arms around his shoulders.

He pulls back a few seconds later and I don't think that I have ever seen him look so happy.

I'm sure that the same look is mirrored on my face. "Here's to making more perfect memories, baby."

PERFECT DISASTER

CHAPTER ONE

STACEY

I stand with my arms folded across my chest, and I survey my surroundings. I watch as people all around me are enjoying themselves, drinking and dancing to the music. Most of them are unwinding after a long week at work. I smile as Susie catches my eye. She is busy behind the bar, serving drinks to a rowdy hen party.

As I look around, I can see that all of my hard work has paid off. My eyes wander to the dance floor and I see Lydia and Martin bopping away to the nineties dance music.

Tonight, I stand here as the new manager of The Den. I have had complete control of the refurbishment that I have been working hard on, all week long. Now that this place is under new management, I thought that it would be good to put my own stamp on the place.

I had various workers in here early in the mornings, who then worked late into the night, so that the place was ready for tonight, the opening night. Being able to manage this place has brought out a drive in me that I didn't expect at all. I have actually quite enjoyed myself, even if it has been a little stressful at times.

The Den's makeover has given the place more of a modern feel. The walls are now black and white monochrome, and the sleek new furnishings have helped to give a sexy but hip vibe. The black enamelled tables and chairs look great in contrast to the grey flooring.

The dance floor has been made up of black and white squares, which has added a retro aspect. Lydia and Martin thought that the place looked fantastic. The energy filling this room tonight is infectious, but I can't fully absorb it as there is something missing.

Actually, what I should say is, there is someone missing.

Jake.

He had to go away on a business trip a week ago, meaning that he hasn't been able to make the opening tonight. He actually went the day after I moved in with him.

Talk about shitty timing.

What makes it even worse is that I have only spoken to him a couple of times since he has been gone as we keep missing each other's calls. Either he has been in meetings or I have been busy getting this place ready. I have no idea when he is due back either.

Apparently, the deal that he is trying to negotiate is taking much longer than expected. I miss him like crazy. It doesn't feel right for him to not be here.

I sigh, blowing a lock of my hair out of my eye and see Martin making his way towards me, so I force a smile.

"Baby girl, this place is banging. You have done a fabulous job."

"Thanks, Mart," I say, mustering up as much cheeriness as I can.

"Why the sad eyes? I thought that you would be pleased with the number of people that have turned out tonight to see the place?"

"I am pleased," I reply. "I just miss Jake, that's all." I sigh.

"Ahhhh, look at you. I never thought that I would see the day when you became a love-sick puppy," Martin teases.

"Fuck off," I retort.

"Oooo, bitchy." It's a good job that Martin and I understand each other's sense of humour. He knows that I am only playing with him.

"Want some more champagne?" I ask as I make my way behind the bar before Martin can answer. He is bound to say yes, so I don't know why I bothered to ask in the first place.

I take a bottle of the finest champagne from the fridge and return to Martin, who is now sat on one of the bar stools. I grab two glasses from behind the bar and place them in front of us.

"Is it on the house?" Martin asks me.

"Yes, Mart, it's on the house." I pop the cork and pour us each a glass.

"I knew that there was a reason why I became friends with you," he says, winking at me. I poke my tongue out at him and he starts to laugh. We clink our glasses together and I take my first sip. This is the first drink that I have allowed myself so far tonight. I didn't want to drink alcohol too early on as I know that I am here until closing time, and I moan quietly in appreciation as the bubbles slide down my throat.

I spot Paul weaving his way through the crowd, heading towards Martin and me. I grab another champagne glass and by the time he has reached us, I have poured his drink and am holding the glass out to him.

"Thanks, Stace," he says as he takes the glass, sits down on a bar stool next to Martin, and takes a big gulp of his drink. "That's some good shit," he comments, taking a sip this time.

"Ah, a man who appreciates the finer things in life," Martin says as he turns to

Paul. Martin is always flirting with Paul, but Paul doesn't seem to mind. In fact, the two of them are forming quite a bromance.

"Hey, Paul?" I cut in before they start a full-blown conversation about whatever random topic they decide to debate today. "Have you heard from Jake today at all?"

"Nah. He's busting his balls to close whatever deal it is that he has gone to negotiate. I guess he's too busy to bother with us little people right now." Paul laughs, clearly cracking a joke, but I flinch a little at his words. He quickly sees that I am not amused and abruptly halts his laughter. "Oh God, I was only joking, Stace," he says, looking panicked.

"I know, I guess I'm just a little sensitive at the moment," I reply, trying to brush off my reaction to his comment.

"Have *you* not heard from him then?" he asks, looking a little shocked at having to ask me this question.

"I had a text from him this morning to wish me good luck for tonight. Apart from that though, I haven't heard a thing from him."

"Oh, Stace, you know that he wouldn't miss tonight if this deal wasn't really important." I know that what Paul is saying is the truth, but I still feel disappointed that he isn't here.

"I know, I know," I say, dismissively. I really did think that he would have been back by now though. It better be a great fucking deal that he is negotiating. "It just doesn't feel right with him not being here. I miss him."

"Oh, baby girl," Martin chimes in. "He's the one who is missing out tonight. I mean, look at you. Talk about rocking the sexy-boss-lady vibe. You got it going on."

I frown as I look down to my clothes. I have no idea what Martin is talking about. I picked the simplest outfit for tonight, consisting of black leather trousers, a black sleeveless shirt that is tucked into the front of my trousers with the back hanging down loose and dark grey shoe boots. I raise my eyebrows at Martin. He must be more pissed than I thought.

"You're clearly more pissed than I realised," I say to Martin as I voice my opinion out loud.

"Seriously, you are one hell of a hot boss and you don't even realise it. That makes the vibe that you are giving off even more sexy."

"He's got a point," Paul says, making me feel a little awkward that he is in agreement with Martin.

"You guys are both being ridiculous." I walk away before they can comment on my appearance any more.

I walk out of the main room and go to my office, which just happens to be the room that Jake fucked me senseless in not so long ago. I unlock and open my office door, closing it behind me once I have walked in. I can still picture Jake and I, against the back wall, passion controlling our encounter. A shiver of delight goes through me at the thought. I smile and make my way over to my desk to check my phone. I unlock the screen and see that I have no new missed calls or texts. The smile quickly disappears from my face and turns into a scowl.

I fire off a quick text to Jake.

> *Hey, babe. I miss you like crazy. Tonight is going well, but it's not the same without you. I know that you have to work, but hurry up and come home! I love you.*
> *Stace xxx.*

I put my phone back on the desk and leave my office, closing and locking the door behind me. I walk back down the corridor and stand at the entrance to the main room, scanning my eyes around the place to make sure everything is still running smoothly.

The dance floor is packed, and the crowd go wild as the DJ starts to play Another Level, "Freak Me." I smile and tap my foot in time to the beat.

I watch as Lydia and Paul start to bump and grind together. They seem to be getting things back on track between them which is brilliant. My eyes find Martin next, and I break out in laughter as I see that he is basically humping a bar stool. His dance moves leave a lot to be desired.

The staff are still busy at the bar, and it will be interesting to see how much money we have taken tonight. I am about to go and give them a hand behind the bar, when I feel two hands grip my waist from behind.

I freeze, and my heartbeat starts to accelerate.

I go to turn my head, but a hand comes up and grips me by my nape, meaning I have to stay facing forward.

I am gently pulled backwards so that my back comes into contact with a firm, hard chest.

I keep my head facing forward as the hand that was holding my nape trails down the side of my neck, sweeping my hair to one side.

Heated breath warms my skin and teeth start to nibble at my ear lobe.

The hand returns to my waist and two arms lock around my midriff.

I moan as light kisses are placed along my neck and back to my ear.

"Hey, baby. Did you miss me?" Jake's voice purrs in my ear.

I reach one hand up and place it behind his neck, turning my face to look at him. I smile as I drown in his caramel depths.

He's here! I can't believe that he's here!

Butterflies are going crazy in my stomach and I feel a little light-headed. I pull his head down and angle myself, so that I can feel his lips on mine.

Our lips connect and nothing else in the room exists.

I open my mouth to him and let our tongues dance together. His hands loosen around my waist and I take that as my cue to turn my body to face him. Lips still connected, I turn in his arms and he clamps me to his body.

I love the feel of him against me, and I love that I know that he is just as turned on as I am right now.

His effect on me is powerful.

I feel him smile against my lips and I pull my head back from him.

"I'll take that as a yes," he says, his eyes sparkling.

I bury my face in his chest and enjoy just being held by him. I can't begin to describe my joy at him being here. He brings one hand to my chin and moves my head, so that I am looking up at him.

"I missed you so much," I say to him.

"I can tell." He grins, and I melt. The effect he has on me is still as strong as the day that I first met him.

"How come you didn't tell me that you were coming back tonight?" I ask.

"You know that I like to surprise you," he says with a wink.

"Oh, Mr Waters, you are going to get so lucky when we get out of here."

"I was counting on it."

CHAPTER TWO

STACEY

Jake and I are the last ones to leave The Den at just gone half three in the morning. It has been such a fantastic night, made all the better by Jake's surprise return. Everyone that I care about came to celebrate with me, and I couldn't be happier right now.

Eric is waiting by the limo as usual, when we approach.

"Good evening, Miss Stacey," Eric says, his normal greeting for me.

"More like good morning. I hope that he is paying you well, Eric, dragging you out at this time," I say playfully. This earns me a smack on my ass from Jake, and I hear Eric laughing as I climb into the limo.

Jake follows me and as soon as he is sat down, I straddle him. Luckily, the partition is up, meaning that Eric can't see my desperation for the man who is currently trapped between my legs.

"Someone's keen," Jake says with a cheeky smirk.

"And you're not?" I retaliate.

"Oh, babe, it's been a week, I'm gonna blow your mind." My lips part at his suggestion and my whole body becomes aroused. Jake presses the button for the intercom and starts to speak to Eric. "Eric, would you mind driving around for a while?"

"No problem," Eric replies, his voice booming back through the speaker in the door.

"Why aren't we going straight home?" I question, frustration apparent in my tone.

"I can't wait until then. I need you, *now*."

Oh my, Jake is certainly the sexiest predator that I have ever had the fortune to meet.

"In here?" My eyebrows raise as I contemplate the thought of sex in the limo.

"That's right. Unless you don't want to?" Jake nibbles at my earlobe and I know that there is no way that I can resist him.

His hands fondle my breasts over my shirt, and I arch my back. Jake traces his tongue down my neck and comes to a stop when he reaches my breast bone. He looks up at me with a wicked glint in his eyes and I melt.

Fuck, I really do love this man.

He smiles, which makes me quiver, and I can't wait any longer, I start to unbutton his shirt, needing to feel his bare chest. When his chest is exposed, I lean down and gently lick and suck his nipples in turn. I can hear a low rumble in his throat which turns me on even more.

I move my hands to his trousers and unbuckle them as I slide my body down, so that I am kneeling on the limo floor. I gaze up at him and see that he is trying to calm his breathing. I smile and snake my hand into his boxers, freeing his erection before wrapping my hand around the base and beginning to move up and down in gentle strokes.

"Fuck, yeah," Jake mutters. He closes his eyes and his head rolls back.

I lower my head whilst he isn't looking and take him in my mouth. He groans in pleasure as I circle his tip with my tongue and then plunge his full length deeper into my mouth, taking him all the way.

"Ah, Jesus, that's good." His words do things to my insides.

I don't think that I will ever get my fill of this man.

I increase my speed and his breathing quickens, and I moan around his cock as I get ready to taste him. Just when I think that Jake is about to reach his climax, he pulls me off of him and gently shoves me onto the seat opposite. I whimper at the loss of him in my mouth, but before I can ask why he stopped me, his mouth crashes onto mine, rendering me speechless.

Our embrace becomes frantic as we both crave the feel of each other after a week apart. Our tongues entwine, and our hands roam each other's bodies. He finally undoes my trousers and shimmies them down my legs, taking my knickers with them. I don't have any time to prepare myself as he plunges his length into me, hitting my core and making me cry out from the feel of him inside me.

My body is on fire as he pounds into me. With his powerful body on top of me, and his punishing rhythm hitting me just where I need it to, my climax gathers force. My hands fly into Jake's hair and my fingers tangle with his silky locks.

I close my eyes as sensations tingle through me. Jake's heated breath is on my face and his lips find mine, kissing me as if our lives depend on it.

"Eyes, baby. Let me see your eyes," Jake says, inches from my face. As hard as it is to open my eyes, I do, and I am penetrated by his heated stare. His jaw is tense, and I know that he is close to his release.

My hands move up to his face, cupping his cheeks, his light stubble grazing against my palms. I tilt my head and place a soft kiss on his lips.

The moment is so tender, despite our erratic love making.

Jake groans as I pull my lips away.

"I love you," I whisper, emotion pulsing through me.

"Oh God," he says, holding my gaze as I feel his release pump inside of me. This triggers my own climax, and together, we ride out the height of our pleasure. Jake buries his face in my neck as we both lie there, panting, trying to catch our breath.

That was awesome.

As I lie there, in my post orgasmic state, I run my fingernails up and down Jake's back, enjoying the feel of goose-bumps rising on his skin.

"I can't believe we just did that," I say, suddenly embarrassed at my actions. Jake pulls his head up and places a kiss on the end of my nose.

"Well believe it, babe. I'm going away more often if I get a welcome home like that every time." I swat Jake's arm with my hand and I hear a rumble of laughter deep in his throat.

"It's not funny, Jake. What if Eric heard us?"

"So what if he did?" Jake seems completely unfazed.

"I'll never be able to look him in the eye again. I blame you for this."

"You blame me?" Jake raises his eyebrows in question.

"Yes. It's your fault for being so bloody handsome," I say, knowing that he will love that answer. He gives me the most gorgeous smile, and if we hadn't already had sex, then that smile would most definitely make me do naughty things to him, despite my embarrassment at the possibility of us being heard.

I feel his cock twitch within me and my eyes widen in surprise.

He can't possibly be ready to go again?

"Maybe we should get back home now," Jake says, pulling out of me. He sits back on the opposite seat to me as I sit myself up and start to make myself look presentable.

"I think that is a good idea," I reply.

Jake speaks to Eric through the intercom and asks him to take us back to the house, he then switches the intercom off and looks at me, heat blazing in his eyes. "When we get home, I'm going to take my time with you. I want to taste every inch of you."

I gasp and my sex, which hasn't calmed down from round one yet, tingles in anticipation. Jake gestures for me to sit on his lap, and I happily comply.

I place my arms around his neck and Jake cups my face in his hands. "I'm going to make love to you, worship you, and make you scream."

I bite my lip to stop myself from moaning out loud. Jake's eyes are hungry, and I am sure that the same feeling is reflected in mine. He runs his tongue across my bottom lip and I shiver with delight, imagining what he is going to do to me when we get home.

"I can't wait," I whisper.

CHAPTER THREE

STACEY

I am up, showered and dressed before Jake is awake. I have only had a few hours' sleep, and as much as I want to spend longer in bed with Jake, I have to go to The Den. My limbs ache, but in a good way. Jake wasn't exaggerating when he said he was going to worship me and make me scream last night. I lost count of how many times he brought me to orgasm.

We made love in the hallway, in the shower, and in our bed. Jake took his time with me, almost torturing me with desire. Our love making last night was deeper and more meaningful than it has been before. I'm not quite sure how, it just was. Jake and I have always had an amazing sex life, but last night surpassed every other time.

I smile as I write a note for Jake, telling him that I have had to leave and that I didn't want to disturb him. I leave the note on the front of the coffee machine as that will be the first place Jake goes when he wakes up. I make myself a coffee, put it in my travel mug, pick up my handbag and keys, and leave our house.

I get into my car with a bounce in my step. I put my seatbelt on, start the car, and turn the music on. The smooth sounds of Usher fills the sound system. I wind down my window as it is already hot, even though it is only ten o'clock. I put my sunglasses on and pull off of the drive way, singing along to the music as I drive. I feel great. All of the sexual release last night has done wonders for my mood.

The drive doesn't take long, and I am soon pulling into the car park for The Den. Now that I am the manager, I have my own designated parking space. There are definitely some perks to running this place.

I get out of my car, grab my handbag and travel mug, and head for the back door of the building. I enter, disable the alarm, and lock the door behind me before going to my office and finding the relevant key to unlock it. I keep the office locked at all times when I am not here. I don't want any of the staff, or God forbid customers to be able to walk in and do whatever they like.

I unlock the door and enter, going straight to my desk and putting my handbag down. I then go to the main room to check that the place is clean and tidy for opening time later. The cleaners come in early every morning, escorted by a security guard. The security guard has keys, but the cleaners don't. I didn't want to start dishing keys out to just anybody. It may seem a little bit silly, and I know that Caitlin is no longer around, but you can never be too careful about who you trust. The security guard is a guy that used to work for Jake at Waters Industries, and if Jake trusts him, then that is good enough for me.

I look around the main room and admire the way the place looks. I really did work hard to bring this place up to scratch. The bar stools are almost gleaming and the black glass table tops shine. Satisfied with the upkeep, I take a sip of my coffee and return to my office. I leave the office door open and go to my desk. I sit down, loving how comfortable my chair is, and I fire up my laptop. I take a look at the rota for the coming week and feel deflated as I look at it. I am working every evening until next Monday, something that I haven't yet told Jake. I hope that he understands, what with him being a businessman, that I need to be here for the time being.

I want this place to be successful. I feel like I need to prove to myself that I can do this.

I have Lydia and Susie working tonight, along with two new temps called Stephanie and Darren. I am going to be here to supervise and help train the temps to see if they are suitable for bar work. Stephanie has no experience, but she seemed likeable, so I thought that I would give her a chance. She is only twenty-two, and although a little shy, she assured me that she could hold her own. Only time will tell I guess.

Darren was a completely different kettle of fish. He's thirty-two, and he has done bar work since leaving college. I decided to give him a shot due to his experience, and the fact that he's a little easy on the eye. Not my type, but I think that the ladies will like him. It may seem a bit shallow of me, but I need to think about what is best for business.

Stephanie and Darren are the only temps that I have hired so far, and I really need to pencil in some time to hire a couple more staff members. I just haven't had time to interview anyone else, what with the re-modelling of the place.

I get my diary out of my desk draw and look to see when I am free to conduct interviews. I literally have no time this week, so I resign myself to the fact that I am going to have to keep using agency staff to fill the void for the time being, but I make a note in my diary to advertise for some more temps as soon as possible.

I am about to take a look at the profit for last night, when my phone starts ringing. I take it out of my handbag and answer, without checking who it is calling me.

"Hello, Stacey Paris," I say, in an official tone, just in case it is work-related.

"Babes, why the fuck are you being formal?" Lydia's voice says. Never one to sugar coat her words.

"Oh, hey, Lyd. Sorry, I answered without checking who was calling. What's up?" I ask her.

"I need to talk to you. It's urgent." A feeling of dread creeps up my spine at her words. Please don't say that she has had a setback. She has been doing so well since her episode with drugs that I find myself hoping that she hasn't taken anything.

"Okay. Where are you now?"

"Stacey Marie Paris, you took far too long to answer me. I know what you are thinking, and no, I haven't taken anything." She knows me far too well.

"I wasn't—"

"Don't try and bullshit me, lady, I have known you far too long," Lydia says, cutting me off before I can try and defend myself. I almost feel like a naughty school girl who has just been caught smoking behind the sports block.

"Sorry, I shouldn't have thought that you would do that." There is no point in trying to excuse what I was thinking. It would only piss Lydia off if I was to lie to her.

"It's okay, I would have thought the same if it had been the other way around. Anyway, where are you?" she says, changing the subject.

"I'm at The Den, but I can leave and be with you in ten minutes?"

"No, no, I'll come to you. Nick's at the flat, and I need to talk to you without anyone else around. I have my keys on me and I will be as quick as I can."

"Okay, Lyd. See you soon."

"Bye, babes," she says and hangs up the phone.

I wonder what could be so urgent that she needs to see me right now? If it's not the drugs thing, then I can only guess that it is Paul-related. God, I hope that things haven't gone wrong between them. They have been getting on so well recently. They make a cute couple and he actually treats her with respect.

I turn my attention back to the computer screen and bring up the profit count for last night. The amount made is far more than I had predicted. I feel a sense of achievement, but I know that I have to work hard to keep the profit up. I understand that, being opening night last night, the profit would probably be more than it would be on a normal night, but I still need to aim high.

My phone starts to ring, interrupting me again. This time I look at the screen and see that Jake is calling me. I feel a tingle go through me as I answer the call.

"Good morning, Mr Waters," I purr into the phone.

"Don't you good morning me, Miss Paris." Oh dear, he doesn't sound very happy.

"What's wrong with you?" I ask, wondering what could have possibly put him in a bad mood.

"Why the bloody hell didn't you wake me up this morning?"

"Because you were sleeping, duh." I can't help but sound sarcastic.

"Not in the mood, Stace."

"Oh cheer up, stroppy. What's bit you in the ass?"

"Well, let's see, I was hoping to be woken up by my sexy, beautiful girlfriend this morning, but instead I get left a crappy note. I envisioned us spending the day together, preferably naked, but obviously not." He really is in a sulk.

At the mention of us naked in bed together, my sex stirs. I squeeze my legs together and try to shut down the ache, deep within me.

"Listen here, Waters, your girlfriend is very busy running one of *your* businesses. *If* you had told me that you were coming back last night, then I could have gotten today covered, but you didn't. I'd say that's bad planning on your part, baby." I know that I am fuelling his annoyance, but I love to tease him.

I can hear him breathing down the phone and it makes my body shiver.

"You just wait until I get my hands on you, Miss Paris."

"I will look forward to it," I whisper into the phone before I cut the call. I smirk at the fact that he is going to be wound up all day now. Excellent. He will be like an animal by the time I get home tonight. My sex quivers with excitement at what will await me.

I shake my head and pull myself from my fantasy before returning my attention to my computer screen and printing out some paperwork for Stephanie and Darren to look through before they start their shift tonight.

Sipping my coffee, I sit back, and my eyes go to the picture of Jake and I on my desk. He is standing behind me, with his arms wrapped around me. Our heads are angled, so that we are staring into each other's eyes, and we both look so happy.

I smile and think about how lucky I am, when I hear the back door open and slam shut. I jolt out of my thoughts and sit up straight. My heart starts to pound a little. I listen carefully and that's when I hear Lydia curse before she strides into my office. I flop back in my chair with relief. I don't know who I was expecting to see other than her. The only people with keys are myself, Jake, Lydia and one of the security guards. I need to stop being so jittery.

Caitlin is gone, behind bars. She isn't coming back here for you.

I take in Lydia's frazzled state as she flops down on the sofa opposite me. She is breathing heavy and looks a little wind swept.

"Jeez, did you sprint here or something?" I ask her.

"Pretty much," she says as she tries to catch her breath.

"Really?" Lydia never runs, so I know that whatever she needs to tell me must be serious. She nods at me and I see that her eyes are puffy. She has been crying, and she also looks a little pale.

"Lyd, what's wrong?" She looks at me, and her eyes mist with tears.

Oh shit.

I put my coffee down and walk over to her, taking a seat by her on the sofa and putting my arm around her shoulders. "Oh God, what is it, Lyd?"

Tears start to fall down her cheeks and she looks at me like she is in pain. I wait for what feels like an eternity for her to speak, but when she does, her words shock the hell out of me.

"I'm pregnant."

CHAPTER FOUR

STACEY

After getting over my initial shock at Lydia's news, I manage to find my voice.

"Are you sure?" I ask her.

"I did six separate tests, Stace. They can't all be wrong."

Well, no-one can accuse her of not being thorough.

"No, I guess not. Have you made a doctor's appointment yet?" It seems like the next logical question to ask.

"Yeah. I go this afternoon at three."

"I'm coming with you." She smiles, and I know that she is grateful for my support.

"What the hell am I going to do, Stace? I'm just getting my life back on track, and now this." She looks to me for an answer, but I don't have one. I just stare at her blankly. "Oh God," she says and hangs her head in her hands.

"What made you think that you were pregnant in the first place?"

"I've been feeling sick the last few mornings, and this morning I threw up. I only had a couple of glasses of champagne last night, so I couldn't understand why I felt so bad, and then it hit me. With my head down the toilet, it hit me. My period is also a few days late, but I just put that down to stress from recent events." She takes a deep, shaky breath and looks at me. "I rushed out this morning and bought some pregnancy tests, and hey presto, the little window of truth confirmed it."

"Shit." My response isn't great, but I don't know what else to say.

"I know. Talk about terrible fucking timing." Lydia lets out a sigh.

"Oh my God, is Paul the dad?" I ask her. She doesn't answer me, but the look on her face tells me all that I need to know. "You don't know, do you?" She shakes her head and fresh tears fall down her cheeks.

"Oh, Lyd," I say as I pull her into a hug. My mobile phone starts to ring, but I ignore it. Whoever it is can wait. My phone stops ringing, and then my office phone starts to ring.

"Don't you want to get that?" Lydia asks me.

"No." I move off of the sofa and go to my private toilet to get Lydia some tissues. I return to her and hand her a bunch of them.

"Thanks," she says as she wipes at her eyes.

"Do you want a drink?" I ask her.

"Sure."

I leave my office and go to the main room, making my way behind the bar. I grab two bottles of water from the fridge and then I place them on the side. I rest my hands against the bar and try to process my thoughts. Poor Lydia. She has just gotten herself to a good place in her life, and now she has this bombshell to deal with. I hope, for her sake, that Paul is the father. I dread to think what will happen if it is that Callum guy, or even worse, Donnie. The thought makes me shudder and I quickly push it away, reasoning that Donnie has been gone for a while now, so it couldn't be his baby.

My thoughts are interrupted, and I jump in shock as the front door to The Den bursts open. I squeal in surprise and stand there looking dumbfounded as Jake comes marching in. He sweeps his eyes across the room before they land on me behind the bar.

"Why the fuck aren't you answering the phone?" His face is like thunder.

His day clearly isn't getting any better yet.

"Because it's in my office and I am out here," I reply, annoyed that he has come bursting in here and scared me half to death.

"For Christ's sake, woman, I was worried that something had happened to you." Jake reaches the bar and walks behind. He comes towards me and pulls me to him, enveloping me in his arms. I relax against his body, loving the feel of him.

In Jake's arms, I always feel safe.

I breath in his scent and then lean my head back to look at him.

"Sorry, I didn't mean to worry you." I move back, so that I am resting against the bar. Jake's hands move to either side of me, resting on the bar, effectively encasing me. "Why didn't you just check the cameras? You have access to them. Would that not have been easier than storming in here like a raging bull?"

Jake had high-tech cameras installed during the re-modelling, allowing him to monitor them from his computer.

"I wasn't in the office or at home, so I have no access to either computers to check the damn cameras."

"Oh." I'm flattered that he was worried about me, but his reaction is a little dramatic. His stare is penetrating me as I look up at him from under my lashes.

God, I could get lost in those eyes all day long.

My body reacts to him without me even telling it to. My nipples harden, and I feel a warmth spread through me. I push off of the bar and place a light kiss on his lips. He moves closer and leans into me, his crotch pressing against my stomach.

I sigh at the feel of him and it takes all of my willpower not to rip his clothes off. I clench my jaw and see that Jake is doing the same thing, his eyes blazing with desire. I clear my throat and find my voice again, needing to diffuse this sexually charged moment, seeing as Lydia is in my office and could walk out at any minute.

"So, now that you have checked on me, don't you have a company to run?"

"Mmm." He steps back slightly and grabs one of the water bottles off of the bar, opening it and taking a few gulps. His eyes are drawn back to the second bottle and he stops drinking.

"Is someone here with you?" he asks.

"Yeah, it's my lover." I can't resist the urge to tease him. His face quickly turns into a scowl and I stifle a giggle that has worked its way up my throat.

"Not funny, Stace."

"What?" I feign innocence.

"You know what," he replies, his voice sounding dangerous, causing my skin to tingle.

"Okay, okay." I decide to back down now. I think I may have wound him up enough already today. "Lydia is in my office."

"Oh, right. Is everything okay?"

"Yeah. We're just going over the rota for the coming week." I feel awful not telling him about Lydia being pregnant, but I don't know if she wants others to know about it yet.

"Well, in that case, I will leave you guys to it. How about I cook for us tonight and we can have a quiet evening?" His question is loaded with expectation, and I know that I am about to piss him off with my answer.

"I would love to, but—"

"Oh no, please don't tell me that you're working?" he says, cutting me off.

"Unfortunately, I am." He sighs in frustration and runs his hand through his hair. "I'm sorry, but I need to help train the new temps tonight."

"Fuck's sake."

I step forwards and press my body up against him whilst linking my arms around his neck. I tilt my head, so that my lips are angled to touch his. I lightly brush my lips across his and then I let my tongue dart out, licking his bottom lip.

"I will make it up to you when I get home." I make my tone as enticing as possible and that is all it takes for Jake to wrap his arms around me and lift me up his body. I instinctively wrap my legs around his waist and crash my lips down on his. I savour the taste of him, knowing that I won't see him until late tonight.

When we finally come up for air, I run my hands through his locks.

"I promise that it will be worth the wait," I whisper, enjoying the feel of his hands cupping my ass.

"Oh, I have no doubt about that. I just don't like that I have to wait so long." I laugh at him as he pouts at me.

"I know." He releases me, and my legs slide down his body until I am standing on my feet again.

"The things you do to me, woman." I smile, and he starts to walk out from behind the bar. "I love you," he says as he walks towards the front doors.

"I love you too." He turns around, smiles and then opens the front door, disappearing out of it. I sigh and grab the bottles of water. That man can turn me to putty in his hands, most of the time.

I tingle with delight as I walk back to my office.

I know that tonight will be a night worth waiting for.

CHAPTER FIVE

STACEY

The doctor's waiting room clock says that it is five to three, meaning its nearly time for Lydia's appointment. I know that she is nervous as her leg is twitching up and down like crazy.

"Calm down, Lyd, everything is going to be okay," I try to reassure her. She doesn't acknowledge me, but she does stop the leg twitching.

Lydia's name is called out a few seconds later and she stands up.

"Will you come in with me?" she asks, looking pale.

"Of course." As if she even had to ask me.

I follow her to the correct room and Lydia knocks on the door.

"Come in," a male voice says on the other side. Lydia takes a deep breath and pushes the door open, me following behind her. I close the door when I have entered the room, and I follow Lydia to the seats in front of the doctor's desk. I sit in the left-hand seat and my eyes lock with the doctor's.

Wow, he's handsome.

He smiles warmly at me, which I return. His looks are striking. He has short, black, cropped hair, and a strong jaw line. There is no stubble on his chin, giving him the appearance of baby soft, smooth skin. His skin is lightly tanned, but it is his eyes that give him his stunning quality. They are brown, but they appear to have gold flecks in them.

I feel a little bit guilty assessing another man, but no one can hold up against Jake.

"Good afternoon, ladies," the doctor says. "I'm Doctor Bradley. Which one of you is Lydia?"

"I am," Lydia answers in a small, quiet voice. "This is my friend Stacey." Lydia points at me as if it wasn't already obvious.

"Hi," I say, not wanting to appear ignorant.

"Nice to meet you, Stacey," Doctor Bradley replies before he turns his attention back to Lydia. "So, Lydia, what can I do for you today?"

"Well, I'm, um..." She stops speaking and closes her eyes, taking a deep breath. "I'm pregnant," she says, only opening her eyes after she has spoken those words.

"Okay. I'm guessing that by the look on your face, that this isn't a planned pregnancy?" he asks.

"No," Lydia replies.

"Right. Well, Lydia, I need you to do a urine sample for me. It's so that I can confirm your pregnancy for our records." Doctor Bradley pulls open one of the draws on his desk and produces a urine sample container. He holds it out to Lydia and she stares at him, looking shocked.

"You want me to do it now?" she asks.

"If you feel that you are able to, then yes, please." I hear Lydia gulp as she reaches for the pot. She looks at me nervously, and I smile and nod my head, trying to encourage her. She rises from her chair, and I watch her leave the room, the door clicking shut behind her.

I turn back to face the doctor and he is looking at me. I sit there feeling slightly awkward and avert my gaze. I don't really know what to say, so I pull my phone out of my bag and I pretend to type out a text message for something to do.

Doctor Bradley doesn't speak, but I can feel his gaze on me. If that was Jake sat there, looking at me, I would be on cloud nine, but although this doctor is handsome, it is just making me feel uncomfortable.

After what feels like forever, Lydia returns, and I put my phone away, feeling grateful that she has come back into the room. She hands the sample pot to the doctor.

"Thank you, Lydia," he says, taking the pot off of her. She sits back down in her seat and looks at me. I put my hand on hers and give it a squeeze as Doctor Bradley walks over to a sideboard and pulls out a little strip of paper.

I watch as he pops on a pair of latex gloves, opens the pot, and dips the strip of paper into the urine for a few seconds. He then pulls the paper out, looks at his watch and waits. I watch the clock on the wall and three minutes later Doctor Bradley throws the strip of paper away and disposes of the pot and its contents. He pulls the gloves off, throwing those away too, and washes his hands before coming to sit back down.

"Well, you were right, Lydia. Congratulations, you are indeed pregnant." Lydia doesn't move a muscle, but her eyes start to mist over. The doctor notices and starts to speak again. "Lydia, if this isn't something that you want, then you do have other options." He speaks in a soft and gentle voice, obviously realising the sensitivity of the situation.

I hold my breath at his words.

The doctor clearly hasn't looked back at Lydia's medical history. If he had, then he would see that this is a topic that would affect Lydia, badly.

Lydia had an abortion when she was sixteen, and she has told me that it was the hardest decision that she has ever had to make. I can't begin to imagine what she must have gone through.

Lydia lets a few tears fall down her cheeks and the doctor starts to pull some pamphlets out of another draw at his desk. He places them on the top of the desk and I quickly whip them away, shoving them into my hand bag. Doctor Bradley furrows his brows at me, obviously wondering why I have been the one to snatch the pamphlets away.

"Uh, thanks," I say, not knowing how else to respond. I smile awkwardly, and I know that he is assessing my behaviour. I couldn't really give a shit what he thinks, I just know that I need to get Lydia out of here as soon as possible.

Doctor Bradley clears his throat and then starts to ask Lydia a series of questions. Lydia answers every question, and I know that she is as desperate to leave here as I am.

"I will need to book you an appointment with the midwife. Is there any particular time that is good for you, Lydia?" he asks whilst looking at his computer screen.

She looks to me and I answer for her.

"Anytime is fine," I reply, and the doctor looks up at me once again, looking confused. "I'm her boss," I say with a shrug of my shoulders as a way of an explanation. He nods at me and looks back at the computer before he writes down an appointment time on a card and hands it to Lydia.

"Thanks," she says as she stands up. I follow suit, and so does Doctor Bradley. He holds his hand out to Lydia and she shakes it quickly before turning and heading for the door. I am about to follow her, when Doctor Bradley thrusts his hand in my direction. I hesitate for a moment before taking his hand. He's looking at me, and I feel a bit silly for feeling awkward, so I try to shake off my weird feeling. His grip is firm as he shakes my hand and his thumb brushes my wrist. I pull my hand away as quick as I can and mutter a goodbye as I go to leave the room. Lydia has already gone, and as I go to close the door, Doctor Bradley speaks.

"See you soon, Stacey," he says. I don't know why he has said it. Shouldn't he have said that to Lydia? She is his patient after all.

I don't know how to respond, so I give a nod of my head and close the door, breathing a sigh of relief as I get outside and inhale the fresh air.

Why the hell did I just feel so awkward in there?

I look for Lydia and see that she is stood by my car, waiting for me to join her. I unlock the doors and we both silently get in. I look across to Lydia, and she just looks deflated.

"Hey," I say softly. "How are you feeling?"

"Like crap." She runs her fingers through her wild hair and sighs. "Thank you for cutting the abortion talk short. I know that I was only young when I first got pregnant, and I know that it was the right thing to do, but it is still painful to think about it."

"I know." I start the car and put my seatbelt on. "Listen, I'm going to cover our shifts at the bar tonight—"

"No, Stace, you don't have to do that," Lydia says, cutting me off.

"Yes, I do. You are coming to my house and staying the night. No arguments." I start to drive out of the car park and turn in the direction of my place.

"Stace, you have the temps coming in tonight. You have to be there."

"No, I don't. Susie can show them what to do." I sound more confident than I feel. I really should be there, but Lydia needs me more right now.

"But, won't Jake mind?"

"Of course he won't." *Yes, he will.*

Lydia goes silent for a few moments, and I think that she is going to try and talk me out of covering our shifts, but she surprises me.

"Thanks, Stace, I couldn't face going back to the flat right now." I look over at her and see some relief across her face. I smile at her and turn my attention back to the road. I'm pretty sure that Jake is going to be really pissed off, but I can't worry about that.

"Stace?" Lydia says, interrupting my thoughts.

"Hmm?"

"Please don't tell Jake that I'm pregnant. I don't want anyone else to know yet." I hesitate to answer her. I don't want to have to lie to Jake. Lydia must sense my discomfort. "Please, Stace. I need to work it out in my head first. I also don't want to run the risk of Paul finding out before I have had the chance to speak to him." I can hear the desperation in her voice and my heart goes out to her.

"Okay," I say. "I won't tell Jake." I look across to her and she smiles.

"Thank you."

I turn my attention back to the road.

How the hell am I going to keep this from Jake?

I'm going to have to pull off some major acting skills, so that he doesn't see that I am hiding something from him.

CHAPTER SIX

STACEY

Lydia and I are sitting at the kitchen island, drinking hot chocolate. I have just gotten off of the phone to Susie who is more than happy to show the temps the ropes tonight. I have also contacted some agency staff to come in tonight to cover Lydia and myself.

The last call I need to make is to Jake. I scroll through the names on my phone until I find him, and I am about to press the button to call him, when I hear the front door open. I hear Jake talking, followed by another male voice. I look at Lydia and she has paled considerably.

"Oh shit," she says as realisation dawns on me that the other male voice is Paul. "Paul can't see me, Stace. I can't speak to him right now." The desperation in her voice makes me jump into action.

"It's okay, I'll get rid of him." I hop off of the stool and practically sprint to the kitchen door. I need a really good reason for not wanting Paul here.

Think, Stacey, think.

Jake and Paul have their backs to me as I enter the hallway. I close the kitchen door behind me and they both turn around.

"Hi, guys," I say, a little too high-pitched.

"Hi, Stace," Paul says. I give a little wave as I continue to rack my brains for a good excuse.

"Stace? I thought you were working tonight?" Jake asks.

"Oh, um, I was, but, uh..." *Oh Christ, he's going to know that something is wrong if I don't form a sentence quick.*

It is at that moment that the excuse I need enters my head. And that excuse consists of making Jake think that I came home to spend some *alone* time with him.

"Is everything okay?" Jake asks, looking a little perplexed.

"Oh, yeah. Everything's fine. I just... I covered my shift so that we could, you know, spend some time together." Jake raises one eyebrow at me and puts his hands in the pockets of his trousers.

"Is that right?" he says, his mouth twitching as he clearly tries to hold back a smile.

"Um, yes. I just thought that we could have made the most of tonight as I'm working every other night this week, but it doesn't matter. I guess I should have called you earlier, but, um, sorting out cover for my shift took longer than I thought." I try to sound as convincing as possible. Paul starts to fidget on the spot and I feel a little bit guilty about lying to both of them. "So, what do you guys have planned then?"

Hopefully it isn't too important, and Jake will ask Paul to leave.

"Not much. Just thought that we would have a few beers and watch some sports," Jake replies.

"Oh," I answer. "Okay." *Just sports. Nothing too dramatic.* "Well, I will just go and have a long soak in the bath and let you guys enjoy your evening."

At the mention of having a bath, Jake's eyes light up and I sense that I might be getting somewhere. I make my way to the stairs, giving Jake a quick kiss on the lips as I pass. I make it to the top of the first flight of stairs when I hear mumbled voices coming from below. I can't make out what they are saying, but I pray that my feeble plan has worked. If it hasn't and they both walk into the kitchen and see Lydia sat there, they are going to know that something is going on.

I continue to make my way to the second floor and head for mine and Jake's bedroom. I make my way to the bed and am about to sit down and wait to see what happens, when I feel two hands grab me from behind, pulling me backwards. I connect with Jake's hard chest as he wraps his arms around me, nuzzling his face in my neck. I giggle as his stubble tickles and I squirm in his arms. He loosens his grip, so that I can turn to face him before pinning me on the bed, arms above my head. His eyes sparkle with mischief.

"So, you said something about a long soak in the bath?"

"I did, but shouldn't you be entertaining your guest?" I say as Jake rubs his nose against mine.

"Paul kindly left." I feel a pang of guilt. Jake lowers his lips to mine and kisses me tenderly. I moan against his mouth, enjoying the sensation of his lips on mine. He lets go of my hands and I bring them to his chest.

I push against his chest slightly, causing him to pull his head away from me.

"Jake, I need to tell you something," I say, feeling nervous.

"Okay." He looks at me with those intoxicating eyes of his and I pray that he isn't going to be too pissed off with me.

"Um, I may have told a little white lie, just now, downstairs."

"What do you mean?" Jake asks. He moves off of me and sits on the edge of the bed, and I sit up, so that I am beside him.

"Well, I wasn't completely honest about the real reason that I covered my shift tonight."

Jake doesn't say anything, clearly waiting for me to expand on my answer.

Oh boy, here goes. "I couldn't tell you the real reason before because Paul was there." He frowns at me, clearly wondering why Paul being here would be a problem. "Lydia is currently sat in our kitchen and she didn't want to see Paul, but obviously I couldn't tell you guys that just now. I was about to call you as you walked in the front door. She's staying here tonight." I am well aware that I am rambling right now.

"Hold on a sec. Why doesn't she want to see Paul? I thought that those two were doing good now?"

"They are, she just, um..." I rack my brains for why the hell she wouldn't want to see him. I don't want to have to lie to Jake about why, but I've promised Lydia that I will keep her pregnancy a secret. I decide to be as honest as I can, considering I lied to him a few minutes ago. "I can't tell you."

"Why the hell not?"

"I just can't. I'm sorry, but I promised Lydia."

"But it's me, Stace. You can tell me anything." Oh God, does he have to make me feel guiltier than I already do?

"Yes, I know that I can. It's not that I don't trust you, I just can't break my promise to Lydia."

"For fuck's sake," Jake mutters as he stands up and runs his fingers through his hair. He walks into the ensuite and takes his jacket off, throwing it into the washing basket.

Oh yeah, he's pissed.

I watch him as he turns the shower on and starts to undress himself. He doesn't look at me, and then he disappears out of my view as he enters the shower.

Bugger. I knew he would be annoyed, but I thought that he would understand why I had to lie and why I can't tell him anything.

I run down the stairs to the kitchen to check on Lydia.

I open the kitchen door and see that she is still sat at the kitchen island. She turns around at the sound of someone entering and looks relieved that it is me.

"Oh, thank God it's you," she says.

"Don't worry, Paul's gone." She smiles at me and I try to return it, but my mind is on Jake right now. "Do you mind just chilling in the lounge for a bit whilst I speak to Jake?"

"Sure, babes. Is Jake okay?" She gets off of the stool and walks over to me.

"He will be."

"Oh no, I don't want to cause problems for you. I'll just go back to the flat, Stace—"

"No you won't," I say, cutting her off. "Jake will be fine." I walk to the lounge,

Lydia following me. I pick up the television remote and hand it to her. "You make yourself at home, I won't be long."

"But—"

"No buts, Lydia. Now, I'm just going to go and soothe a man's ego and then I will cook us some food, and after we can watch a film." I wink at her as I leave to the sound of her chuckling.

I race back up the stairs and see that Jake is still in the shower. *Good.*

I close our bedroom door and strip my clothes off. I enter the ensuite and see that Jake has his back to me. I quietly climb into the shower, standing behind him, and admire his naked form.

God, he really does have an ass to die for.

I carefully make my way over to him. As I reach him, I place my hands on his shoulders and start to trace light kisses across his back. Jake stops washing himself and I feel his body respond to me. I kiss my way down to his ass, my hands going around to the front of his thighs before I move my body around his legs, so that I am kneeling in front of him, the water pounding on top of me.

I close my eyes to shield them from the water, and I take his length in my mouth. I place my hands on his ass and caress his gloriously smooth skin. His hands run through my now sodden hair, and I lick and suck him, making him groan in pleasure.

I hear his breathing quicken and I increase the pressure, knowing that he is close to climax.

"Stace," he says on a whisper as he explodes into my mouth. I suck him gently, swallowing all of his juices. When I have wrung him dry, I release his length and kiss my way up his torso, running my hands up the sides of his body.

I kiss his neck and along his jaw line, finding my way to his lips. He pulls me close to his body and our tongues entwine. Our kiss is gentle and loving. I gently bite his bottom lip before pulling away and wiping the water from my eyes, so that I can look at him.

"I love you," I whisper, overcome with the intensity of his eyes on mine.

"I love you too."

I rest my head against his chest. "I'm sorry that I lied, and I'm sorry that I can't tell you what's going on with Lydia."

"Shhh." He places a hand under my chin and moves my head, so that I am looking at him. "Don't apologise, it's fine. I didn't mean to act like a prick earlier. I just miss having you to myself."

"I miss that too." I smile at him and see that any annoyance that he may have had about the situation has dissipated. He lowers his head to mine and kisses me, taking my breath away.

I feel his cock harden against my stomach and I break away from his lips, raising my eyebrows in question. "Really?"

He just smiles at me, confirming all I needed to know, and I lose myself in his embrace.

Right now, in this moment, this is the only place that I want to be.

CHAPTER SEVEN

STACEY

Jake, Lydia and I are all sat at the dining table, ready to eat the lasagne that I have just finished cooking.

Jake has been more relaxed since our escapade in the shower. He has been laughing and joking with Lydia and me, and I think that Lydia's mood has lifted somewhat.

"This looks great, Stace," Lydia says as she licks her lips at the sight of the food on the table.

"It's just lasagne and garlic bread, Lyd," I reply. "Go ahead and help yourself."

Lydia wastes no time in filling her whole plate with lasagne, as well as taking a couple of slices of garlic bread. I watch in amazement as she starts to shovel the food into her mouth. It's like she hasn't eaten for days.

Jake was putting food on his plate, but his hand has frozen in mid-air at the sight of Lydia. I nudge him under the table with my foot. He looks to me and I indicate for him to stop staring. Luckily, Lydia hasn't noticed anything. She seems far too interested in the food to take any notice of us.

Jake finishes spooning lasagne onto his plate, handing the serving spoon to me. I take a spoonful and then a slice of garlic bread. Lydia has already demolished half of her plateful before I have even taken my first bite. She's going to give away her secret if she keeps eating like that.

"So, what film do you fancy watching later, Lyd?" I ask her, trying to take the attention away from her hoovering up her food.

"I don't mind," she replies, taking another slice of garlic bread.

Huh. Well, that cut that conversation short.

I look to Jake and his eyes have returned to watching Lydia. I roll my own eyes and start to eat my own food. We all remain silent whilst we eat which makes me feel a little awkward. I don't like how uncomfortable the atmosphere is right now. I also don't understand it. I just want to finish this meal and get the hell away from the table.

"Fair play, Stace," Lydia says as she eats her last mouthful. "That was tasty. Does anyone mind if I have some more?" She looks to both of us and I hear Jake scoff in surprise. I nudge him again with my foot, and he scowls at me. I smile sweetly, not wanting Lydia to feel embarrassed.

"No, you go ahead, Lyd," I answer. Lydia dishes out the remaining lasagne, and literally inhales it. I put my fork down, having lost my appetite, and take a gulp of my wine. I patiently wait for Jake and Lydia to finish, and then I busy myself by clearing the table.

"That's better. I was starving," Lydia declares.

"Glad you enjoyed it," Jake manages to respond, and I can hear him stifling his laughter. He glugs back his beer and goes to the fridge to get another one.

"Why don't you go through to the lounge, Lyd? I'm just going to finish cleaning up in here and then I'll come and join you."

"If you insist." Lydia gets up and leaves the room, rubbing her belly as she does. Jake looks at me and mouths the words, "Oh my God." I roll my eyes at him and start to load the plates into the dishwasher. Jake waits patiently for me to finish and then pulls me through the patio doors and out into the garden.

"What the hell was that about?" he asks me, surprise and amusement evident in his tone.

"What was what about?" I feign ignorance.

"You know what. She just inhaled her food in there, barely stopping for breath." He looks astonished, and it takes all of my skills to keep my face neutral.

"Don't be silly. She was just hungry." I really hope that he doesn't say too much more on the subject. I hate not being able to tell him.

"Hungry? Jesus, I thought that she was going to eat the tablecloth at one point." I bite my lip to stop myself from laughing.

"Jake, don't be so mean," I say, the chuckle escaping into the back of my throat.

"I'm not, but come on, babe, that was something else." He bursts out laughing and I crumble. I'm not making fun of Lydia, I'm just laughing at the whole situation. The look on Jake's face throughout that meal was a picture. I hold my stomach as the laughter starts to hurt.

"Stop it," I say as I try to catch my breath. "It's not funny."

"Oh, it is."

"Seriously." I wipe my eyes and the laughter starts to subside. One day, when Lydia has made her secret public knowledge, she will laugh about this with us. I know she will.

"Anyway, I'm going to my office to send some emails. If you two are watching a chick flick, then I would rather opt out."

"Okay. As long as you don't mind."

"Of course I mind," Jake says as he steps closer to me, invading my personal space. An invasion that I most certainly welcome. His arms go around my waist and I place my hands on his shoulders. "I wanted you all to myself, but seeing as we have company, I will just have to leave you with this…"

His lips crash down on mine as his voice fades off. I mould myself against him; my nipples harden, my sex stirs, and my senses come alive. One of his hands travels around my waist and heads south, skimming the hem of my skirt and trailing its way up the inside of my thigh. His fingers graze over my sex, rubbing, teasing, and sparks fly through my body.

His gentle touch makes me want to rip his clothes off here and now. As I am losing my mind from his actions, Jake abruptly pulls away from me and steps back. I stand there, gasping, a little uncertain of how I was in his arms one minute and the next he is backing away from me. He smirks, doesn't say a word, and just walks back into the house.

What the hell?
Why would he do that?
Why would he just…
The realisation hits me like a lightning bolt.
Ah, I get it. Mr Waters wants to play games.

He is clearly showing me a taste of what I will be missing seeing as we won't be on our own tonight. Getting over my initial shock at his abrupt departure, I start to smile.

If Mr Waters wants to play, that's fine by me.
Bring it on.

I walk back into the house and go through to the lounge. Lydia is sprawled out on the sofa, watching, The Notebook, which is one of my favourite films. I flop down beside her, suddenly feeling tired from the day's events.

"I take it that Jake is okay with me staying here?" Lydia asks me.

"Of course he is. I told you earlier that he would be fine."

"I feel guilty that I am making you keep my pregnancy a secret from him."

"Don't worry." I sigh. "You just need to figure it out for yourself first." I smile at her and she nods her head.

"Thanks, Stace. You're a good friend."

"Just a good one?" I say playfully.

"The best."

"That's better." We both laugh and then turn our attention to the film. It's about three quarters of the way through, and we watch the rest in silence. The end of the film always chokes me. The love that they have for each other makes me hope that love like theirs isn't just in films or written in books. It's the kind of love that I hope that Jake and I will always have. Unconditional.

"Want to watch another one?" Lydia asks, disrupting my thoughts.

"Sure." I don't really, but I don't want to be rude. She starts to flick through the movie channels and stumbles across our all-time favourite.

"Dirty Dancing. Oh, yes," she says as she snuggles further into the sofa.

"I'm just going to go and check on Jake quickly," I say. It may be my all-time favourite film, but my all-time favourite man is upstairs, and I want to get him back for his panty-dropping antics earlier.

"Uh huh," Lydia mumbles, already engrossed by the sight of Patrick Swayze on the screen.

I leave the lounge and make my way to Jake's office. As I stand in the doorway, I see that he is on the phone. I study him for a few moments, revelling in the fact that he's mine. He could have his pick of women, but he chose me.

Me.

I smile and tap lightly on the door. His eyes shoot up and lock with mine, his face breaking into a grin, and he motions for me to come in. I walk over to his desk, his eyes never leaving mine, and I perch on the edge, so that I am facing him. He's still on the phone, and I decide that I will use this moment to push his buttons.

I lower myself, so that I am kneeling in front of him before I move my hands to the zip on his trousers and I slowly pull it down. I undo the button and then snake my hand into his boxers, enjoying the feel of how hard he is when I haven't even done anything yet.

I make him feel like this, and that is beyond thrilling.

He is trying to speak to whoever is on the other end of the phone, managing to keep his voice even, until the moment that I pull his cock out of his boxers and place my lips over the tip. I hear the intake of his breath, and his words become staggered. I look up at him from underneath my lashes, and his expression is one that makes my knickers wet with desire.

I start my movements slow and tantalising. He is desperately trying to keep control, but he is failing. I chuckle around his length and then increase the pressure, sucking harder. Jake lets out a gasp.

"I have to go. I'll call you back," he says, his tone dominating. He chucks the phone on the desk and then places his hands on either side of my head. I work him until he is reaching his peak. The shallowness and the speed of his breathing, and the low groan all signal that he is close. His hands have moved to grip the arms of his chair, and just when I know that he is about to explode with pleasure, I pull away, freeing him from my mouth.

His eyes are still closed as I stand up and quickly make my way to the other side of the desk. When his eyes open, he looks dazed, dumbfounded. I smirk and stand there with my arms folded, waiting to see what his next move will be.

"Uh, why are you all the way over there?" he asks, his expression one of complete confusion.

"It's not nice being left all hot and bothered, is it?" I raise one eyebrow at him, turn on my heel, and exit the room. I giggle to myself at the look on his face.

Maybe he will think twice before he tries to leave me high and dry again.

CHAPTER EIGHT

STACEY

I wake up to the sound of Lydia snoring. I groggily open my eyes and see that she is sprawled out on the sofa. We must have both fallen asleep whilst watching the television last night.

I stretch my arms above my head and yawn. I need a cup of coffee.

I move off of the part of the sofa that Lydia hasn't occupied, and I quietly start to make my way to the kitchen. I don't want to wake Lydia as she needs her rest, especially after the events that transpired yesterday.

I shut the lounge door behind me and walk through to the kitchen. The sight of Jake's back greets me, his shirt slightly stretched across his broad shoulders. I shiver in delight. I make my way over to him, put my arms around him from behind, and place my lips by his ear.

"Good morning, handsome," I purr. He puts down the cup of coffee that he is holding and turns his head to look at me.

"Good morning." His reply is a little abrupt and I get the feeling that he is pissed off with me about last night. I place a light kiss on his lips and then I go to make myself a coffee.

I smile to myself as I hum along to the radio that Jake has playing in the background. He doesn't say another word, but I can feel his gaze boring into my back. I decide to take my coffee upstairs with me whilst I get ready for the day ahead. I am hoping that it will just be a straight forward day, but my life of late is anything but straight forward, so I don't get my hopes up too much.

I smile at Jake as I make my way out of the kitchen and upstairs to our bedroom. I put my coffee down on the bedside table and go to the ensuite. I take a quick shower, reasoning that my coffee will be cool enough to drink by the time that I have finished. I wash quickly, get out and wrap myself in a towel.

I am picking out my clothes to wear for the day, when Jake walks in. As I pick out a pair of tailored grey trousers and a black, fitted shirt to wear, I watch him out of the corner of my eye. He stands there, with his hands in his trouser pockets, looking like a God. I fight the urge to go to him as I select my underwear to put on. I choose a red lace bra and matching thong, knowing that Jake loves to see me in the colour red.

I saunter past him, faking ignorance of him as I return to the ensuite. I close the door behind me, smirking and start to dry myself off with the towel. The smirk is soon wiped from my face though as Jake bursts through the door, making me drop the towel in shock.

Damn him for not having a lock on this door.

"Do you mind?" I say as I watch his eyes rake over my naked body. "I am trying to get dressed." My nipples harden from his penetrating stare. In a flash, he comes towards me and has me pinned against the wall.

The heat in Jake's eyes is enough to make me weak at the knees, but I somehow manage to contain my excitement from his body being pressed up against mine.

I know that he is looking for a bit of payback after I failed to finish him off last night.

I maintain eye contact with him, all the while fighting the urge to kiss his full, inviting lips. His head swoops down and he trails kisses from my neck, up to my cheek. I resist the urge to close my eyes from desire. With my arms pinned above my head, and Jake's body pressing against mine, I am unable to move. Not that I really want to move. I can think of nothing better than having Jake pressed up against me.

His lips trail from my cheek and down to my breasts, where he flicks each nipple in turn with his tongue. I let out an involuntary moan as he continues his delicious assault of my nipples. He shuffles my hands slightly, so that he is pinning them to the wall using just one of his hands rather than both. His free hand comes down and trails across my stomach. He licks his way back up to my neck and his hand fondles one of my breasts. My breathing becomes staggered as my senses heighten. The combination of his mouth on me, and his tweaking of my nipple causes me to cry out in pleasure.

I feel his lips pull into a smile against my skin. His hand traces its way down to my sex, which is already wet and ready for him. He strokes me and my body shudders.

"Your body betrays you, my love," he whispers in my ear, causing my skin to heat from his breath. I look at him and see the cheeky smile spread across his face.

He knows that I can't deny him.

He knows that I lose all sense of reason when he touches me.

I know that he is about to leave me wanting more, just like I did to him last night. Suddenly, my idea for payback doesn't seem like it was a very good one.

"Ass," I whisper, making him chuckle deep in his throat.

"Yours will be mine later," he says as he cocks an eyebrow, releases me, and walks out of the ensuite. That is the second time in less than twenty-four hours that he has gotten me all hot and bothered and then just left me hanging. Bastard.

It takes me a few moments to regain any sort of composure.

Once I do, I get myself dressed and then head into the bedroom. I style my hair, so that it is poker-straight.

I need to think of a way to get Jake back for his little performance just now.

There is no way that he is getting away with it again.

I grab my phone off of the bedside table and dial Martin's number.

"Hey, baby girl. What's shaking?" he says as he answers after only two rings.

"I need your assistance with a sexual revenge plan." I get straight to the point.

"Lunch break at one o'clock."

"Great. I'll come to your office and I will bring lunch."

"Excellent. Oh, how I do love a good bit of sexual revenge," Martin says, chuckling down the phone. I smile as an idea starts to form in my head already.

Mr Jake Waters is going to wish that he had never started this game with me.

CHAPTER NINE

Stacey

I arrive at Waters Industries just after half past twelve, after dropping Lydia back at her flat. I spent all morning trying to keep her mind occupied, but it was no good. She is still worried about what to do. I told her that I would phone her later, but she just seemed to be consumed by her own thoughts.

I enter the lobby and walk straight to the lifts. I'm too early to meet Martin for his lunch break, but that's okay as I need to see Jake first. I enter the lift when it opens, and I push the button for the floor that houses Jake's office. I'm alone in the lift, so I admire my appearance in the mirrored walls.

I decided against wearing the grey trousers and black shirt and opted for something sexier. I'm wearing my fishnet tights, tight black pencil dress and my red stilettos. I left my hair down, seeing as I straightened it earlier, and I have teamed my ensemble with a sleek, black briefcase. The professional but sexy vibe has never been more appropriate.

My make-up is more striking than usual. I have gone for the smokey-eye-effect and a dark shade of red lipstick that will have Jake eating out of the palm of my hand. The lift opens, and I exit, making a beeline for his office.

I stop in front of Valerie's desk and she looks up at me and smiles.

"Oh, hello, dear," she greets me. She really is a lovely woman and always has a welcoming smile on her face. "Mr Waters is just finishing up a meeting. Shall I inform him that you are here?"

"Yes, please, Valerie," I reply sweetly. I take a seat outside his office and wait.

I listen to Valerie buzz through to Jake, and within a minute a couple of men walk out of his office. I have my legs crossed in front of me and the men eye me appreciatively. I smile back at them, so as not to appear rude, when I see Jake stood in his office doorway, scowling at me. I know that he isn't happy that the men were looking at me in a hungry manner.

I keep the smile plastered on my face as I approach him, swaying my hips as I move. I squeeze past him and enter his office, making my way to his desk.

"No interruptions," I hear Jake say to Valerie. I put my briefcase on his desk and then I turn around and lean against the edge of the desk. Jake clicks the office door shut and puts his hands in his trouser pockets. I love it when he does that, it makes him look so powerful and dominant.

He stalks towards me and I start to get a flutter in my stomach.

Good grief, he is so hot. Will I ever tire of looking at him?

He stops a couple of feet in front of me and raises his eyebrows in question.

"Hi, baby," I purr at him. I know that he will be wondering why I am not in a bad mood from him leaving me in the ensuite this morning.

"Hi." His reply is short as his eyes roam my body from top to toe. His eyes twinkle as he drinks in my appearance, signalling that this was definitely the right choice of clothing to wear. I clear my throat to get his attention. His gaze snaps back to mine, and I would like nothing more than to make love to him on this desk, but I have a plan to stick to.

"I can't stay long as I'm meeting Martin for lunch." I need to stay focussed and keep my head in the game for this to work.

"You mean, you haven't come to have lunch with me?"

"No, afraid not." He looks disappointed, but I brush it off. I push myself off of the desk and saunter to him, placing my hands on his firm, toned chest. "I just wanted to say that, I'm sorry for leaving you high and dry last night. I feel bad and I was hoping that we could make up for it tonight?"

"Hmm, and what exactly did you have in mind?" he asks.

I run my hands up his chest and link them around his neck, bringing his lips down to mine. I kiss him slowly, and I move one of my hands down to his crotch.

"I think that you can guess but let me spell it out for you. I want this," I squeeze his crotch gently to indicate what I am talking about, "Inside me. I want these," I take my other hand and brush my thumb over his lips, "All over me. I want every inch of my body to be worshipped by you."

I plant another kiss on his lips and he groans deep in the back of his throat. "And I want this," I grab one of his hands and place it on my ass, "To be broken in by you."

That does it, I am pushed back onto the desk and laid down, Jake's body covering mine. His lips crash down onto mine, and my hands grab Jake's hair, pulling gently.

My plan is working.

He is putty in my hands.

I mentally give myself a high-five. The buzzer on Jake's desk rings and Valerie's voice informs us that Jake's one o'clock meeting has arrived early, even though he told her not to interrupt us. I'm guessing that the meeting is important though for

Valerie to go against Jake's orders. Jake breaks our kiss and grunts in frustration. He stands up, pulling me with him.

"Fucking meetings," he curses as he straightens out his jacket. "You're a bad girl, Miss Paris."

"I prefer the term dirty, but I suppose bad is okay," I tease.

"How am I meant to concentrate on my meeting now?"

"I'm sure you'll manage," I whisper in his ear. I stand tall and pick my briefcase up off of the desk. "See you at home, handsome." I side-step him and walk to his office door.

I turn my head before I open the door, and I find Jake transfixed on me, just as I knew he would be.

"I'm going to ruin you, Miss Paris."

"That's what I'm counting on." Inside I am doing a little victory dance at how well this part of my plan has gone.

"Before you go, could you try and do me a favour?" Jake asks.

"Sure, what is it?"

"Can you try not to give any of my business associates a heart attack on the way out. That outfit is far too sexy for you to be wearing out in public." I smile at him, give him a wink and I open the door. I walk out of his office feeling more than satisfied with myself.

I wave goodbye to Valerie and ignore the guy that is currently waiting to see Jake. I return to the lifts and wait for one to become available. When one does, I press the button for Martin's floor and I make my way to his office.

I get to Martin's office and I knock on the door. I don't want to barge in if he is busy.

"Come in," I hear him shout. I open the door and I get a wolf-whistle off of him as I walk in. "Hey, baby girl."

"Hi, Mart," I reply, taking a seat on the chair opposite him.

"I take it by the way you are dressed, that the sexual revenge plan is in full swing?" he asks, one eyebrow raised.

"It is indeed."

"You don't waste any time, do you?"

"Nope."

"Did you bring lunch?" I roll my eyes at him and place my briefcase on my lap, clicking it open. I pull out two large trays of sushi and place them in front of Martin. "OMG. I fucking love you. You do know how to spoil me," Martin says. He doesn't waste any time in opening up one of the trays and shoving some salmon into his mouth. "Mmm, mmm, mmm. Delish."

"Okay, calm down there. It's just sushi." I laugh as I take a piece of salmon for myself.

I know that sushi is Martin's favourite food, but I didn't expect him to almost orgasm over eating it. I pull two bottles of iced tea out of my briefcase, and hand one to Martin.

"Ah, I love you even more." Martin opens his bottle and takes a few swigs. "Mmm. Heaven."

"Can we stop climaxing over the food and drink choices now, please?" I say playfully.

"Sorry." He doesn't look sorry.

"So, how has your first week here been?" I ask after finishing my mouthful of food.

"It's fabulous, darling. I have so many events to plan, and I love the atmosphere in this place. I owe you one, baby girl. If it weren't for you, I would still be working for that douche-bag Charles."

"No problem. I'm glad that you like it here." I'm so pleased that Jake hired Martin. I think he is really going to appreciate having Martin on his payroll.

"Now, stop stalling, and tell me about this plan of yours that you have already put into action." I chuckle to myself and take a sip of my drink. Martin places his hands under his chin, resting his head on his palms, waiting for me to fill him in. I quickly tell him about what happened last night, and this morning, and then I finish off with what I just did in Jake's office.

Martin gasps. "Stacey Paris, I never had you down as such a hussy. I love it!" I laugh at his reaction.

"What I really need now though is a pair of handcuffs." Martin splutters, and bits of sushi fly across his desk. "Ewww," I squeal as I push my chair back slightly.

"Sorry," he says, once he has swallowed the remainder of his food. I sit there and patiently wait for him to regain his composure. "It takes a lot to shock me, and I certainly never had you down as a handcuff kind of girl."

I shrug my shoulders at him. "What can I say? Jake brings out my naughty side."

Martin laughs and opens one of his desk drawers. He pulls out a pair of handcuffs, still in their packaging, and places them on the desk. My mouth drops open.

"Martin," I say slowly. "Do I even want to know why you have a pair of handcuffs in your desk drawer, at work?"

"You never know when an opportunity may present itself," he answers with no shame. "You need to be prepared, darling." He is completely unfazed by my shock. "As you can see, I am yet to use them." I scoff and he pushes the handcuffs towards me. I pick them up and put them in my briefcase.

"Uh, thanks," I say, still shocked that he produced the very item that I needed.

"No worries. My gift to you." He bursts out laughing and I join in with him.

Tonight is certainly going to be a night that Jake will remember forever.

CHAPTER TEN

STACEY

I leave Martin's office once his lunch break has ended, and I head to the lifts. The doors ping open and I falter as I enter. Jake is stood there, by himself, looking devilishly handsome.

How any of the women working here get any work done is beyond me. I would be rendered useless every time that Jake was in sight.

I stand beside him and face the lift doors. I see that Jake is travelling to the ground floor, so there is no need for me to push the button. My heart rate speeds up as the lift doors close.

We stand there, staring at each other in the mirrored walls.

"A pleasure to see you again, Miss Paris." I love the way he says my name, and I smile at him.

"You too, Mr Waters."

"If only there weren't any camera's in here." I raise my eyebrow in question. "If there weren't, then you would be up against the wall right now, gasping for breath," he says, calmly. I intake a sharp breath and keep my eyes fixed on him. I can feel the heat rushing up my body.

The lift stops, and the doors open on the ground floor. We both stride out and into the lobby, Jake placing his hand at the bottom of my spine. I see a few envious looks from some of the female staff, but I ignore them.

We exit the building and I see Eric is waiting outside with the limo.

"Hi, Eric," I say, giving him a wave.

"Miss Stacey," Eric replies with a nod of his head.

I turn to Jake and put my hand on his chest to stop him from walking any further.

"You know," I whisper in his ear. "It would have been *you* gasping for breath in that lift." Jake raises his eyebrows. "I'll see you later, handsome." I place a quick kiss on his cheek as I walk in the direction of the car park.

"Stacey," I hear Jake call my name. I stop and turn my head to look at him. He stands there with a sexy as hell glint in his eye. "I'll be home at five. You better be ready for me."

"Oh, I will be, don't you worry about that." He grins, and I turn back around and carry on walking. He really won't be expecting what I have in store for him.

I reach the car park, get in my car and drive to the mall as I need to purchase some attire for this evening's plan. I really should be at The Den catching up on paperwork, but my sex revenge plan trumps the idea of work.

I fire off a quick text to Susie telling her that I will be unavailable tonight after all. I hope she doesn't get too pissed off. I reason with myself that she enjoys filling in for me when I am not there. I will definitely need to spend the day there tomorrow though.

When I reach the mall, I park the car and head straight to the designer lingerie shop. I walk in and there are hundreds of beautiful pieces to choose from. However, I am not just looking for something beautiful. I am looking for something that stands out and screams sexy but classy and stunning at the same time.

I make my way through the shop, perusing every item that I can see, but it isn't until I reach the back of the shop that I find what I am looking for. On the back wall is the most gorgeous white lace bodysuit that I have ever seen. The intricate detail of the lace gives me a shiver down my spine as I picture Jake's face at seeing me in this garment. I look through the rack and locate my size. The bodysuit has a plunging neck-line and pretty, small and delicate rhinestones running down the sides.

I don't bother to try it on. I know that this is the perfect choice.

I hurry to the counter to pay for it, and I nearly faint at the price when the sales assistant scans the barcode. I hand over my card, trying to conceal my shock at the amount. As I put my pin in the card machine, I realise how ridiculous it is that I am spending such an obscene amount of money on one item. I argue with myself that I am making good money now, and there is no better way to spend it. If I can't buy something that is definitely going to bring Jake to his knees begging, then it's a poor job.

After purchasing the bodysuit, I go to the shoe shop and buy some white stilettos to complete the look that I will be going for. I have everything else that I need at home, so I return to my car and pump up the music as I drive back.

I get back to the house at half past three, leaving me an hour and a half to get ready before Jake arrives home. I run up the stairs, shower, shave and moisturise every part of my body. I decide to put my hair up into a high ponytail, so that it doesn't cover up the top part of the bodysuit. I slip the white lace bodysuit on and assess my appearance in the mirror. I admire how the bodysuit hugs my curves and how it accentuates my breasts. I put the white stilettos on and I apply some nude make-up to finish the look.

I can't wait to see the look on Jake's face when he sees me.

I check the time and see that I have ten minutes left until he arrives home. I race downstairs and carry one of the chairs from the dining table up to the bedroom. I position the chair to the side of the bed, and I take the handcuffs out of my briefcase. I rip the packaging off of them and hide them under my pillow on the bed before I race to the hallway window.

The limo is pulling onto the driveway and my heart starts to beat wildly. Jake gets out of the limo and my whole body shivers with excitement. He is so perfect that sometimes I feel the need to pinch myself, just so I know that I am not dreaming.

I watch him walking up the steps to the front door, and I race back to the bedroom. I take a few deep breaths as I take my white silk dressing gown off of the back of the bedroom door. I put it on and tie it around myself.

"Stacey?" I hear Jake shout out from downstairs. I check myself over in the mirror once more, and I walk to the top of the stairs.

"Up here," I call down to him. I wait as I hear him approaching.

When he finally comes into view, my heart does a little flutter. His eyes peruse my attire, and he raises one eyebrow in question. I try to stop my body from shaking. I need to remain in control.

"Good afternoon at work?" I ask him, innocently.

"Not too bad." He slowly starts to walk up the stairs towards me, like a predator about to strike for its prey. "And what have you been up to?" he asks as he reaches the top of the stairs. I take a few steps backwards, needing to leave some space between us.

If he touches me, then my plan will go to hell.

"Oh, nothing much."

"May I ask why you are standing there looking insanely fuckable in those heels?" I smile at his comment.

"Wait and see, baby. Want to follow me into the bedroom?"

"Hell yeah." I turn and walk to the bedroom, Jake following behind me. I stop when I reach the bed and whirl around, so that I am facing him. He stops and looks at the chair, eyeing me suspiciously.

"What's the chair for?" he asks.

"You'll find out soon enough. Now, strip." Jake's eyes go wide at my commanding tone. I keep a straight face and hope to God that he does as I ask.

After a few moments, Jake starts to remove his clothes, keeping his eyes on me the whole time. I feel my face flush as more and more of his naked body is revealed. I struggle to regulate my breathing as he removes his boxers and stands there in all his naked glory. His body really is spectacular.

I clear my throat and find my voice. "Get on the bed and lie facing upwards."

"Feeling dominant, are we?" he teases, but I can tell that he is getting turned on by my tone.

"Get on the bed, Waters." I keep my voice firm, ignoring his question. He lets out a low growl and does as I ask. I keep the dressing gown on, and I sit by him on the bed.

He goes to touch me, but I waggle my finger at him and shake my head. He reluctantly puts his hands back by his sides and waits to see what I am going to do next.

"Arms above your head," I instruct. He complies immediately.

I lean over him, placing a soft kiss on his lips as I pull out the handcuffs and shake them in front of his face. I smirk at him and place one of the cuffs on his wrist. He watches as I hook the handcuffs around one of the wooden rails on the headboard, and I then put the other cuff around his other wrist, locking it in place.

Well, that was easier than I expected. I thought that he would make a fuss.

"Um, babe, I can't touch you if I'm handcuffed like this."

"Exactly." I smile, stand up off of the bed and face him. He watches me intently as I untie the belt on my dressing gown and take it off, letting it pool at my feet.

"Fuck me," he exclaims as he admires my choice of lingerie. "You look like an angel." I smile at him and climb back onto the bed, so that I am straddling him.

Bringing my face down to his, I allow our lips to touch and sparks fly immediately, as they always do. He groans as I massage his tongue with mine. I can feel his cock standing to attention, and it takes all of my effort to break our kiss and pull away from him.

He looks at me with a dazed expression on his face. I move off of him and stand by the side of the bed. He frowns at me, clearly annoyed that I have halted proceedings.

"Uh, what are you doing?" he asks, looking puzzled.

This is the part of the plan that I have been looking forward to the most.

"Well, baby, this is called payback."

"Payback?"

"Yes. Payback." I smile and wait for it to dawn on him.

"Payback for what?" Clearly, he isn't quite there yet.

"For this morning." I see that realisation hits him, and he doesn't look amused.

"Okay, I get it. Very funny. You have made your point. Now, can you please let me out of these handcuffs?"

"No."

"Why not?" He is not happy with how this little scenario is panning out.

"Because, Mr Waters," I answer, sweetly. "I'm not finished with you yet."

He stares at me as I start to remove my bodysuit. I make sure that I take my time as heat builds in his eyes. I slide the bodysuit down my torso and I place it to one side.

I take a seat on the chair and I smile.

"Now what?" he asks me.

"Now you get to watch me whilst I pleasure myself."

"Oh, fuck no. Stace, you can't do that to me. Come on, just let me out of these handcuffs."

"No way, Waters. I'm just finishing what you didn't." I bring my hand up to my neck and I slowly trail my fingers down my body until I get to my stomach.

I pause my hand, and I spread my legs wide, giving him a perfect eyeful.

He looks like he is going to pass out, but in a good way.

I start to move my hand down lower, and when I let my finger brush against my clit, I let out a low moan.

"Babe, please," he pleads with me. "I need to touch you." I ignore him and continue to stimulate myself. My hand moves in a circular motion, allowing me to slowly build up my climax. My breathing quickens, and my eyelids grow heavy. I won't break eye contact with Jake though. The desire burning in his caramel pools is making me wet.

"Stacey, please. I'm sorry about this morning. Just let me out of these fucking handcuffs." Jake's voice is urgent, but I refuse to answer him. I teeter closer to the edge of release.

"Oh God," I say breathlessly.

Jake grits his teeth and I see his jaw flexing. He tries pulling his hands away from the headboard, but there is no way that he will be able to free himself.

I increase the speed of my finger and use my other hand to tweak my nipple. Jake watches me open-mouthed as I reach my climax.

My body convulses as I ride out my orgasm, and Jake watches on as I work myself down from my release.

When I am finished, he opens his mouth to speak, but stops as he watches me put my finger in my mouth. I lick my own juices from my finger and moan in approval.

"Ah, you are fucking kidding me," Jake says, his voice still sounding urgent. "Please let me out of the cuffs now, Stace."

I sit there, in my post orgasmic state, relishing the feel of this moment. I have never done anything like this before, and I have to say, I loved every minute of it. I can tell that as much as he is annoyed that he can't touch me, Jake has enjoyed my little show.

I don't think that he will be leaving me hanging again anytime soon.

I stand up, pick my dressing gown up off of the floor and put it on. Jake is still staring at me, and I give him a smile.

"I'm just going to go and get a drink whilst you calm down," I tell him. I can see his jaw ticking.

"Are you not going to let me out of these cuffs first?" he asks in disbelief.

"Nope." I turn on my heel and walk from the bedroom as he shouts out my name.

I make my way to the kitchen and get myself a cup of coffee. Sitting at the kitchen island, I laugh to myself at how easy my plan was to pull off. I drink my coffee quickly. I might have wanted to teach him a lesson, but I actually don't want to leave him too long. He's frustrated enough as it is.

I finish my drink and head back upstairs. Jake is lying there with his eyes closed. I walk over to the bed and open my bedside drawer. Jake opens his eyes as I produce the keys that will free him.

"Have you calmed down yet?" I ask.

"Yes."

"Are you sure?"

"Yes." He sighs. "Can you just unlock the cuffs?"

I move to his left wrist and unlock the first cuff. I have barely unlocked the other one before Jake's hands are grabbing me by my waist, and then I am pinned underneath him on the bed.

"You're a bad girl. Do you know how horny and frustrating your little performance was to watch? To not be able to touch you?"

"I have a rough idea."

"The things you do to me."

"Well, maybe next time you will think twice about keeping me waiting." I keep an innocent look plastered on my face, but let's face it, I am far from innocent here. He chuckles, and I know that he has forgiven me for handcuffing him.

"Noted." He brings his lips to mine and kisses me, his movements slow and sensual.

It doesn't take long for us to forget about our game-playing as we get lost in each other, setting a precedent for what the remainder of our night together will entail.

JAKE

I watch Stacey as she sleeps beside me.

This woman mesmerises me.

She excites me, pleases me, thrills me, but most of all she challenges me.

The little performance that she put on earlier was mind-blowing.

I have never experienced anything like it.

I don't know what, or who, brought this woman into my life, but I thank my lucky stars that she is in it. The women I used to date, or just sleep with, just used to fall at my feet. They were boring and un-exciting. They just used to hang on my every word and hope to God that they were going to be the one to make me settle down.

Stacey is nothing like that.

I love how unpredictable she is, and I hope that we never lose the chemistry that we share.

Stacey turns and faces the other way, giving a little moan as she does.

God, even her back is sexy.

I get out of bed and go to use the ensuite. Even after our marathon lovemaking, I can't sleep. I don't want to disturb Stacey, so I decide to go to my office and check some emails. Maybe doing that will help tire me out?

I switch the office lamp on, turn on my laptop and take a seat on my leather swivel chair. I wait for the computer to load and then I pull up my emails. Most of the ones that I check are just to confirm business meetings, a couple of them are junk mail, and then there is one that stands out.

I inwardly groan as I see my brother's name on the sender column.

He only ever contacts me when he needs something, and that is usually money.

I open the email, figuring that the quicker I read it, the quicker I find out what the hell he wants.

Hey, bro,

I know that we haven't spoken for a while, but I thought that I would let you know that I am back in the area. Things didn't work out in America. I've been back a few weeks and was hoping that we could catch up?

You are my big brother after all.

Hit me up via email and we can arrange a day and time.

Laters,

Brad.

Oh, fuck.

He's back? Why is he back?

I drop my head in my hands as I feel the beginning of a headache coming on. I'm not exactly close to my brother. His top priority in life is chasing after some skirt, normally resulting in him getting himself into stupid situations.

Of course, I usually have to bail him out of whatever situation he has gotten himself into. I find his behaviour embarrassing. I just wish he would grow up and act his age. He's thirty-one, so there isn't a big age gap between us.

We used to be close when we were younger, but as we got older, we drifted apart.

I became a serious businessman and I think he resented me. I could never understand why though, seeing as he has a decent career himself. He is a general practitioner, and for all I know, he may have retrained to become a surgeon or something.

Brad moving to America was a blessing. It meant that I wouldn't have to worry about what he got up to next. It's a bit like the saying, out of sight, out of mind. I haven't heard anything from him for two years. The day he left for America was the day that I thought that he was out of my life for good.

Fuck, this means that I am going to have to tell Stacey more about him.

That is a thought that I do not welcome. She knows limited information about Brad, and I wanted to keep it that way.

Brad is a massive flirt and he won't care about the fact that Stacy is my girlfriend, if he ever meets her. I should know, he has form. Brad doesn't care who gets hurt, as long as he gets what he wants. He used to try and steal any girl off of me when we were younger.

As we drifted apart, he seemed to want to have anything that was remotely linked to me. He succeeded in stealing a couple of girls from me. Luckily, they never meant anything to me.

What irritated me was the way Brad treated me. I am his brother, and he should have just been happy for me. But no, he was incapable of doing that.

There is absolutely no fucking way that I will let him take Stacey away from me.

She is mine.

I close down the email and decide to deal with it at a later date. I rub my temples, trying to soothe away the impending headache.

"Babe?" My thoughts are interrupted by my gorgeous girlfriend standing in the doorway, naked. "What are you doing?"

"I couldn't sleep, so I was just checking some emails."

"Oh. You okay?" She rubs her sleepy eyes and stifles a yawn.

"Yeah, I'm fine." I smile at her to reassure her that there is nothing wrong. I don't want to talk about Brad now.

"Well, in that case, are you coming back to bed? I could do with a reminder of our earlier encounter." She cocks one eyebrow at me.

Fucking hell, she is outrageous.

"Already?" I ask in disbelief, not that I will ever complain about her wanting to fuck me. She nods her head at me, and that is all the persuading that I need.

I turn off the computer and the light and walk towards her. When I get to her, I grab her around the waist and lift her up. She wraps her legs around me and I can feel her wetness against my bare stomach. I place a kiss on her nose and carry her back to our bedroom.

Oh yes, Waters, this girl is definitely a keeper.

CHAPTER ELEVEN

STACEY

Jake has left by the time that I wake up. I stretch across the bed and my arm brushes against his pillow. I turn my head as I feel something on there, and I see that he has left a note for me. I pick it up eagerly.

> *I left you to sleep after all the exertion last night.*
> *Rematch later? Call me when you wake up.*
> *I love you.*
> *Jake x x x*

I smile at his note. His personality is just perfect. He's loving and sweet, as well as being powerful. I grab my phone from the bedside table and call him, but it goes straight to answerphone.

Damn, he must be in a meeting.

I scroll through the contacts on my phone and call Lydia instead.

"Hi, babes," she says as she answers the phone.

"Morning, Lyd. I just wanted to see how you were feeling this morning?"

"I'm good. Actually, I'm great. I'm seeing Paul after work tonight, and I'm going to tell him everything."

"Really?" I can't hide the shock in my voice. I wanted her to tell Paul, but I thought that it may have taken longer than a couple of days for her to conclude that telling him was the only option that she actually had.

"I'm guessing that you didn't expect me to be saying that," she says as she chuckles down the phone. At least she isn't annoyed by my obvious shock. "I figured that, if I want to build a future with him, then I have to be honest with him. Well, that's if there even will be a future with him after tonight."

"I'm sure it will be fine. Paul's a good guy, Lyd."

"I know." As she answers her voice is quiet and I know that she deeply regrets ever meeting that Callum guy.

"If you need me at any point, promise that you will call me."

"Of course I will. And, Stace?" She pauses, and I can hear her voice crack a little as she says my name.

"Yeah?" I prompt her.

"Thanks for not telling Jake. I know that you don't like keeping stuff from him. And thank you for being there for me after everything." I know what she is referring to. I know that she still feels bad about the things that she said to me during her bad patch. As far as I am concerned though, it is in the past, and that is where it is staying. I hold no malice against her.

"That's what friends are for, Lyd." I have nothing but love for this girl.

"I know, but you have done more for me than anyone else ever has. Even if I don't always realise that." I smile at her words. "Oh, and I bumped into Martin yesterday. He told me to ask you about a pair of handcuffs." I can hear the mischief in her voice.

"Uh..." I'm lost for words, and Lydia starts to laugh.

"I want details when I next see you, missy. There is no way that I am letting you keep that secret to yourself. Anyway, I best go, Nick is waiting to take me out for breakfast. Talk to you later, babes."

"Bye, Lyd." I hang up feeling relieved that I didn't have to tell her all about my sexual revenge plan over the phone. I will be having words with Martin when I next speak to him. He's got such a big mouth sometimes.

I get out of bed and get showered and dressed. I really need to get to The Den and do some bloody work.

JAKE

Fucking hell, how is it only just half past ten?

My day has already gone to shit, and I have hours left yet.

The accounting department are really trying my patience. I dropped the idea of buying Charles Montpellior's business when most of his clients left him and came to my company anyway. The only problem is, my accounting staff are snowed under and clients are being kept waiting. I pride myself on dealing with issues quickly and efficiently, so I need to figure out a plan of action on how to handle all of the extra work.

The ideal solution is to employ more staff. I could leave it to the accounting manager to deal with, but I like to make the final decisions on who I hire and fire. Trouble is, I don't have a free day in my diary for weeks. I know that I need to relinquish some control, but after successfully building up my business alone, it's hard to let others take over.

I grab my phone out of my desk drawer and switch it on. I need a distraction, but there is only one distraction that will be sufficient, and that is Stacey. The screen lights up and I am notified that I have a missed call from her. I call her back, hoping that she can lighten my shitty mood. The phone rings and rings and then goes to answerphone. I sigh and hang up.

The buzzer on my desk goes, signalling that Valerie needs to speak to me.

"What is it, Valerie?" My tone is harsher than intended.

"I'm sorry, sir, I know that you are very busy, but there is a gentleman here that says he needs to see you urgently."

"You need to be a little bit more specific, Valerie. There are plenty of people who want to see me. What's his name?" I ask, irritation evident in my tone.

"He won't say, sir. I have tried to tell him that you have no free time, but he says that he will wait all day if he has to." She sounds a little nervous answering me.

"Okay. Go ahead and send whoever it is in." I sigh and keep my eyes fixed on my office door. I want to see who the hell needs to interrupt my time so badly.

As the door opens and the guy in question comes into view, I immediately wish that I hadn't told her to send him on in. I have a feeling that my morning is about to get a whole lot worse.

"Hey, my man," says Brad as he confidently strides into the room. He takes a seat in the chair on the other side of my desk and sits back, looking relaxed and comfortable. "It's been a long time, brother." His familiarity immediately pisses me off.

"Yes, it has. So, what trouble have you gotten yourself into now?" I decide to get straight to the point of why he is here. Brad makes a big show of pretending to be offended by my comment.

"Now what makes you think that I would be in trouble?" His hand goes over his heart as if he is wounded. I roll my eyes at how dramatic he can be. He definitely missed his calling to be an actor.

"Brad, the only reason that you ever come to see me is if you are in trouble. I haven't seen or heard from you in two years, and here you are, casually waltzing in here as if we spoke just yesterday. Forgive me for side-stepping all of your usual bullshit and getting straight to the point."

"I came here to catch up with my bro. That's all. No ulterior motive, I swear." He holds his hands up in surrender and I raise my eyebrows at him.

I don't believe him for one second.

"Uh huh." I can't be bothered to play along with his stupid games, so I decide to be blunt. "Look, Brad, I'm busy. If this is just a social call, then it's going to have to be done some other time."

"Wow, things really don't change, do they? Still the boring, hard-nosed boss man that you always were."

"A little ambition never hurt anyone." I refuse to rise to his taunts.

"I agree, but you are obsessed by it. Why don't you just relax and take a chill pill once in a while? There's more to life than work, Jake." We have pretty much the same conversation every time that we see each other. I smirk at the fact that he doesn't know how much fun I actually do have in my private life.

"You're not still pissed with me over Tara Benson, are you?" he asks, and I laugh at his ridiculous question.

"Grow up, Brad. I couldn't give a shit about you and Tara." Tara is the girl that he took to America with him. The girl that I slept with once before she realised that I wasn't going to settle down with her. Brad swooped in and charmed her, and she fell for whatever crap he fed her. If he thinks that I am pissed off by it, then he is sadly mistaken.

"Just checking."

"Still as cocky as ever."

"The ladies love it," Brad replies, grinning. "Listen, bro, why don't we catch up over a few beers? Say, tonight? I can't imagine that you have anything exciting planned."

"I'm busy tonight." My mobile phone chooses this moment to start ringing. I look to the screen and see Stacey's face lit up, telling me that she is the one calling me. I smile and am about to answer the phone, when I stop myself. I don't want Brad eavesdropping on my conversation with her. I will phone her back when he has fucked off and left me alone.

I hear him wolf-whistle as he hovers over my desk. His eyes are on my phone.

"Wow. Nice work, bro. She is hot." I feel my blood boil at his comment.

"Why are you still here, Brad?" I can't hide the anger in my voice.

"Whoa, calm down. What's your problem?" he asks me.

"I have already told you that I don't have the fucking time for a social call. Either you tell me what you really want, or you get the fuck out of my office." I know that I am being a little unreasonable, but I can't help it. The thought of him being attracted to Stacey riles me. She is my whole fucking life. He is not going to charm her and steal her away from me.

Brad stands up, giving me a wary look.

"Look, bro, I didn't come here with an agenda. I simply came because I figured that we could try and forge some sort of relationship again. I know that I have been an asshole in the past, but I have changed. I'm a different person now, Jake." I scoff which interrupts his little speech. He shakes his head and turns, walking towards the door.

He places his hand on the door handle and then turns back around to face me. "If you want to talk like adults at some point, then feel free to call me. I sent you an email earlier with my number on." With that, he opens the door and leaves, slamming it behind him.

"Fuck it," I say out loud to myself. I rub my temples and will the impending migraine to piss off.

Maybe he's right?

Maybe I do need to chill out a bit more?

However, deep down, I know that it is just his presence that has me feeling like this. He really is a pain in my ass.

I pick my phone up to call Stacey back. I need to speak to her. She will be able to calm me down. It rings and goes to answerphone again.

Bollocks.

I chuck my phone onto the desk and sit back in my chair.

I need to get out of here and clear my head.

CHAPTER TWELVE

STACEY

I arrive home just after five o'clock.

It has been a long day.

I have been sorting out paperwork all day at The Den, and now I have to get changed, ready to go back in an hour and start the evening shift. All I really want to do is relax with Jake, but I can't ask Susie to cover for me again. It wouldn't be fair to her. Plus, I need to show that I am an active member of the team, even if I am the boss.

I run upstairs and go straight to my mobile phone which I left on the bedside table when I left home this morning. I put my bag on the bed and sit on the edge. Looking at my phone, I see that I have a couple of texts from Jake, and a shit load of missed calls.

I sigh and decide to read the messages before I call him back.

Hey, baby, we seem to keep missing each other today. I have no more meetings now, so call when you can. Love you.
Jake x x x

This is ridiculous, I miss your voice. Call me asap.
Jake x x x

I smile at his eagerness to speak to me. It's exactly the same for me when I haven't spoken to him for a while.

I hope that this feeling never fades.

I open the last message from him, and my smile soon disappears as I read the words.

> *How the fuck could you do this to me?*
> *Don't look for me.*
> *I don't want to see you right now.*

Huh? Is this message meant for me?

I call Jake's phone, but it goes straight to voicemail. I call his office next, but there is no answer. I even try to call Eric, but his phone goes to voicemail too.

What the hell?

I start to panic at the fact that I can't get hold of him. I take off my shoes and rack my brains for a reasonable explanation for his message. I change out of my skirt and shirt combo, and I put on my skinny jeans and a fitted white T-shirt. I put on my black shoe boots and pick my bag up off of the bed. With my phone in hand, I try to ring Jake again, but it still goes to voicemail. I make my way downstairs, still feeling confused by Jake's last message.

As I enter the kitchen though, I freeze.

My eyes widen as I stare at the leaflets that litter the kitchen island.

"Oh no," I say out loud. I walk slowly over to the island, and my heart starts to beat faster. My eyes scan the leaflets and it dawns on me what Jake's message was about. Panic starts to course through me at the sight of the abortion leaflets that Jake has clearly seen, and my breathing starts to speed up as I realise how stupid I have been.

I should have thrown the leaflets away.

The bag that I had put them in is on the floor, with all the contents spilled out. I can only assume that Jake knocked it over and the leaflets fell out.

Fuck.

I can also only assume that Jake thinks that these leaflets belong to me.

Of course he thinks that they belong to you, Stacey. They were in your fucking bag.

I let out a sound of rage.

I need to find him.

God knows what is going on in his head right now.

I pick up the leaflets, tear them into pieces and throw them in the bin. Nausea overwhelms me, and I grab the edge of the counter to steady myself.

Where would he have gone? His office? Paul's house?

I rack my brains, but ultimately, he could be anywhere. I am about to try and phone him again, praying that his phone has miraculously switched on, when the screen lights up, making me jump. Lydia's name is across the screen and I hurriedly answer, needing to speak to someone.

"Lyd, thank God you called—"

"Babes, you need to get your ass to The Den. *Now*," she says, cutting me off mid-sentence. I don't fail to notice the urgency in her voice.

"What's going on?" I ask, suddenly getting a bad feeling settling deep in the pit of my stomach.

"Jake's here, and he's not alone." My heart fills with dread at her words, and I slowly sit on the stool as my knees go weak.

"What do you mean he's not alone?" I whisper. I speak so quietly that I am surprised that she can hear me.

"Just get down here. I'll be waiting at the back door for you."

"Okay." I hang up the phone and take in what she has said. She obviously doesn't want to tell me over the phone, and that just makes me more nervous about what I might see when I get there.

A few minutes go past before I feel like I can stand. When I do, I take my phone and handbag, and walk into the hallway. As I reach the front door, I pick up my keys and leave the house, locking the door behind me. I feel like I am in a daze as I get in my car and start to drive to The Den.

It's like I'm on autopilot as I pull into The Den car park. Lydia is waiting by the back door, and when she sees me, she comes walking over. I park the car and get out. The look on her face is grim and I know that I am not going to like what I am about to see.

My whole body starts to shake as Lydia stops in front of my car.

"Where is he?" I say in a firm tone. I sound a lot more confident than I feel right now.

"He's sat at one of the tables at the back of the dance floor, in the corner. Stace..." I don't hear anything else she says as I march through the back door and head straight for the main room.

As I enter the main room, my eyes scan the tables at the back. My gaze zones in on Jake straight away. He is sat there with some young woman draped all over him. She is sat on his lap and she's whispering something in his ear.

I feel my blood boil and my hands curl into fists at my sides.

I know that there is no way that I am going to remain calm for the scene that will unfold in the next few moments.

I feel Lydia put her hand on my arm, but I shrug her off. I am in a state of shock at the sight of Jake with another woman. Before I can think about my how I am going to approach this scenario, I am walking over to him. As I get nearer to the table, Jake's eyes lock with mine. I can see hurt and anger clouding his vision, but I am sure that mine reflect the same feelings.

I reach the table and stand there with my hands on my hips. I don't think that I have ever been so mad with someone in my entire life. I am physically shaking with anger.

"What the fuck are you doing?" I shout at him. I don't give a shit if other people hear me. Right now, all that exists is my idiot boyfriend, and the tart that is currently sat on his lap.

The woman's head whips round so fast that I am surprised that she doesn't give herself whiplash. The smile quickly disappears from her face and her eyes widen with surprise.

Jake's arm is around her waist, and it takes all of my willpower not to rip his arm off of her and physically drag her from his lap. He takes a sip of his drink, never removing his gaze from mine. It feels like I have been stood here forever waiting for him to answer me, but in reality, it must only be a few seconds.

"Stacey, this is Gemma," he says as he points to the woman on his lap. I don't fail to notice that his eyes are glazed over, indicating that he has had more than a few drinks.

My eyes narrow on him before I divert my attention to this Gemma woman. When my eyes connect with hers, she looks like she is going to have a panic attack.

"Um... Hi," she mumbles, her voice irritating me instantly. I am not really sure what point Jake is trying to make here. I just need to get that woman off of him.

"Hi, Gemma," I say a little bit too sweetly. I smile at her, which she returns warily before I go in for the kill. "Let me give you a piece of advice."

I lean forward, so that my hands are resting on the table, allowing me to be eye level with her. She arches herself back a little, clearly uncomfortable. "The image of you sat on my boyfriend's lap is pissing me off, which I am sure you can understand. So, here is what I think you should do."

Her eyes widen some more, and she quickly looks to Jake before looking back at me. His gaze hasn't left me the entire time. "Get up and walk away before I really lose my cool, and before I give you the ass-kicking of a lifetime." I sound evil. I almost don't recognise my own voice. I know that Jake has been the one to create this situation, but my focus is just on getting her to leave. I see her gulp and look back to Jake.

"You have a girlfriend?" she asks him.

"I did have." His answer stings me. He doesn't look at her when he answers, his eyes remain on me. His deep caramel pools that have always captured me are now devoid of any warmth.

"Oh my God," she says as she scrambles off of his lap. "I am so sorry," she says to me. "I didn't know."

"Forget it. Now, run along." She scurries away as fast as she can.

Out of the corner of my eye, I can see that Lydia is standing off to the side, clearly wary of how this situation will play out. I return my eyes to Jake, and his body radiates anger.

"Now that your little plaything has gone, are you going to tell me what the fuck you think you are playing at?" I snarl at him and he scoffs.

"Me? What am I playing at? You're the one with the fucking abortion leaflets, Stace, so why don't you tell me what the fuck *you* are playing at?" His tone is harsh, and I hear Lydia gasp.

"They're not mine, Jake."

"Oh please, don't give me that bullshit. They were in your bag, Stacey. Why the fuck would you have them if they weren't yours?" He downs the rest of his drink and slams the glass on the table. "Do you know how it feels to find something like that? Fucking heart wrenching, that's how."

"They are not mine," I say again, this time through gritted teeth.

"Liar," Jake spits at me.

"Jake, they're not Stacey's," I hear Lydia say. I push myself off of the table and turn to face her. Paul has emerged from somewhere and is now standing by her.

"Don't, Lyd," I warn her. I try to plead with her using my eyes, but she just looks at me and places her hand on my arm. She nods at me and I see that she has unshed tears in her eyes.

"No, Lydia, don't try to cover for her," Jake snarls. "It's better that I find out now what a heartless bitch she is, rather than find out further down the line."

It takes all of my control not to turn around and slap him across his face.

Lydia steps around me and starts to speak.

"Those leaflets are mine, Jake." Jake blinks a few times and I turn to see that Paul is frowning at Lydia. I could throttle Jake for this. "Stacey came with me to a doctor's appointment the other day to confirm that I am pregnant. I was a bit of a mess in the doctor's, so Stacey took the leaflets for me. I forgot that she had them to be honest. That's why I stayed at your place the other night. I didn't want to go back to the flat and Stacey said that I was welcome to come and stay at yours. I asked Stacey not to tell you anything until I had figured out what I was going to do." I see Lydia's body start to shake slightly, and I know that it is taking all of her courage to admit to this, especially with Paul listening.

Jake's expression changes to shock whilst Paul looks completely blown away by Lydia's announcement.

"You didn't have to do that, Lyd," I say to her.

"Yes, I did." She smiles at me and then turns to Paul. "We need to talk," she says to him. He appears to be in a daze as he just nods his head at her.

"Use my office if you need to," I say to her.

"Thanks, babes. Call me later." I smile at her as she leads Paul across the main room and out towards my office.

I turn back to Jake and my smile vanishes. His eyes eventually look to mine, and I can see the shame on his face.

"Stacey, I'm so—"

"Sorry?" I cut him off before he can finish. "Save it, Jake. I'm not interested in listening to some pathetic apology." I turn on my heel, needing to get as far away from him as possible. I don't get far as he grabs my arm and turns me around to face him.

"Get your fucking hands off of me," I shout in his face as I yank my arm from his grasp.

"Please—"

"No, Jake. I suggest that you leave me the hell alone." I turn and run through the main room and make my way to the back door. I can hear Jake shouting my name, but all I want to do is get in my car and drive away.

I make it out of the back door and am just opening my car door, when Jake comes behind me and slams the car door shut. I turn, so that I am facing him, and he puts his arms either side of me, resting his palms on the car. He has effectively trapped me.

"Get away from me," I say in a low voice.

"No. I'm not going anywhere. We need to talk."

"No, we don't. You're drunk, and I am way too pissed off to have a rational conversation with you right now." I try to push his body away from me, but he doesn't budge. I desperately try to fight the tears that are threatening to emerge. I look past him, not wanting to have any eye contact with him right now.

"Please, Stace," he says, the overpowering smell of whisky on his breath is wafting over my face. "I'm sorry that I thought the worst. I just saw those leaflets and—"

"And you jumped to fucking conclusions," I finish for him.

"What was I meant to think?" he says, exasperated. I close my eyes to avoid seeing the devastation on his face. "I accidentally knocked your bag onto the floor, and the leaflets fell out. I saw them, and I just…" His voice trails off as he tries to find the words to justify his actions. "I just lost it."

I open my eyes and look at him. His eyes are swimming with the pain that he is feeling right now. My heart aches for him, but I quickly shut it down. The image of that girl on his lap, his arm around her waist, makes my hands curl into fists at my sides. I grit my teeth to stop myself from saying something that I will regret. "I'm so fucking sorry, babe."

I swallow past the lump that has formed in my throat.

I need to get away from him.

I need to get some head space.

"Your words don't mean anything right now." My voice sounds cold, devoid of all emotion. "I need some time to think." It's almost like I am in a daze.

"No, Stace, we need to sort this out. I can't lose you." His arms have moved and are gripping the tops of mine in desperation. I can see that he is sorry, but it may not be enough. The pain that sliced through my heart at the sight of him with another woman is a pain that is not going to heal quickly.

"Please," he pleads with me. "I love you. I made a massive fucking mistake. I should have spoken to you when I found those leaflets, I just couldn't see past the anger and the hurt that you might have been considering aborting a baby of ours." His words cause the rage that I am feeling to boil over.

"How could you ever think that I would do something like that?" I shout back at him. "How could it even entertain your thoughts that I would get rid of something that was part of both of us?" My whole body is shaking. "Do you not know me at all?"

"Of course I do."

"I beg to fucking differ, Jake. How low must your opinion be of me to not only think that I would kill our baby, but also for you to let some other woman sit on your lap and touch you. Your hands were around her, Jake, her lips were by your ear, whispering God knows what. What would you do if some other guy had his hands on me?" My words have an effect immediately as Jake lets out a low growl and his face contorts with fury at the thought of another man touching me.

"Tell me, Jake, what the fuck would you be feeling if you were me right now?" He moves his hands and runs them through his hair as he lets out a cry of rage. He turns away from me momentarily, and I take that as my chance to get the hell out of here.

I quickly open the car door and get in, locking the door from the inside, so that Jake can't open it. He turns around at the sound of the door shutting and tries the handle. When he realises that I have locked it, he starts to bang on the window. I ignore him and start the car.

"Stace," he bellows through the window.

All I can think about is getting away from him.

Getting away from a man that I love, a man that I put my complete trust in, only for him to throw it back in my face.

I reverse, Jake still by the window.

"Please don't go, Stace," he shouts, and I can see his eyes start to glaze over. "We can work this out."

As I stare into his handsome face, I realise that I may never be able to come back from this. I may never be able to forgive his actions.

"It's too late," I mouth through the window, and I know that he has made out the words that I have spoken. He backs away from the window and I pull out of the parking space and start to drive away.

The tears that I have managed to hold back are now streaming down my face.

As my eyes drift to the rear-view mirror, I see Jake on his knees, his head hanging in shame at what he has done.

―――

JAKE

I've lost her.

I have acted like a complete fucking asshole, and it has come back to bite me in the ass. She couldn't even bear to look at me.

I hang my head in shame, unable to look at her car driving away.

What the fuck have I done?

CHAPTER THIRTEEN

STACEY

I get back to the house and find myself standing in mine and Jake's bedroom, feeling lost and alone. The tears won't stop flowing, and it feels as though my heart is shattering into a million pieces.

How could he do that to me?

The image of that woman sat on his lap will be forever ingrained on my memory. He should have just asked me about the goddamn leaflets.

I thought that he knew me.

I thought that I knew him.

I guess I was wrong.

I go to the wardrobe on autopilot and pull out my pink holdall. I can't stay here. I need to get away. Everything here is just a painful reminder of the life that Jake and I have together. Or maybe I should say the life that we *had* together.

I throw some essentials into my holdall and leave the house. I don't leave a note. Jake can't be stupid enough to think that I would stay here now.

As I make my way to the front door, I realise that I have no idea where the hell I am going to go. Lydia is busy trying to sort things out with Paul after Jake's monumental fuck up. Martin has his own relationship problems to deal with, he doesn't need me bothering him with my issues.

I make my way out of the house, holdall in hand, and I sit back in my car. I try to slow my racing mind, hoping that some inspiration will hit me about what to do. My phone starts to ring which breaks my thoughts. My stomach churns, thinking that it might be Jake calling me. I brace myself and look at the screen of my phone. I almost breathe a sigh of relief when I see that it is Lydia.

"Hello," I answer, glumly.

"Babes!" She sounds relieved to hear me. "Where are you?"

"I'm just at home, sat in my car." I sound so distant. "I'm just trying to decide where to go. I can't stay here."

"Come to mine," Lydia says instantly.

"No, I can't, Lyd. You have stuff to figure out with Paul. You don't need me intruding on your life."

"Don't be so fucking stupid. Get your ass round to mine, now. Paul and I are fine. We have talked, and we're going to work through things." I smile at the fact that Paul is prepared to see it through with Lydia. I knew that he was a good guy. She deserves that. "You, however, are not fine."

"No, I'm not," I say quietly.

"Stacey, listen to me. Paul is with Jake as we speak. Paul is trying to convince Jake to give you some space, but it's like he has lost all sense of reasoning. He's on his way to yours right now. If you don't want to see him, then you need to leave, pronto."

"Shit," I say, starting the car up.

"Come to mine and you can try to figure out what to do." I have no time to think of any other plan right now, so I take Lydia up on her offer.

"Okay, I'll be there soon."

"Okay, babes." I hang up the phone and pull off of the driveway.

As I pull onto the main road, I see Jake and Paul on the opposite side. Jake clocks my car straight away and I start to panic. I put my foot down as I see Jake start to run towards my car. I race past him, going faster than I normally would. I can hear him shouting my name, and the pain in his voice almost makes me stop the car. I don't though. I need to sort myself out before I can even entertain the idea of speaking to Jake.

I pass the turning for Lydia's and carry on along the main road. He will expect me to go to Lydia's. I knew that all along. I never should have agreed to go to hers.

My mind is a cluster-fuck of emotions as I continue to drive.

My phone is ringing like crazy on the passenger seat, but I ignore it.

I drive for about half an hour, when I spot a bed and breakfast on the side of the main road, and I pull into the car park, which is just to the right of the building. I park the car and take a look at my phone. Lydia has tried phoning me a couple of times, and the rest of the missed calls are from Jake. I will call Lydia back later. Right now, I need to see if I can get a room at this bed and breakfast for the night.

I wipe my eyes, put my phone in my pocket, and pick up my handbag. The bed and breakfast is very pretty from the outside. It is a quaint cottage that looks like it has been extended at some point. Flowers adorn the window boxes in an array of colours. I exit the car and wearily walk to the front door. I ring the doorbell and wait patiently for it to be answered. It takes a few moments, but the door is eventually opened by an older lady who has a friendly smile plastered across her face.

She's very petite and must be in her late fifties. She has her grey hair pulled back into a neat bun and her blue eyes sparkle, instantly making me warm towards her.

"Good evening, dear, my name is Melody. How can I help you?" Her voice is quiet, so I have to strain to hear her properly.

"Oh, hello. I was wondering if you might have any vacant rooms available for the night?" I ask, praying that she has.

"I do have one room left. It is a double room with an ensuite. Would you like to take a look?" Melody asks me.

"Yes, please," I answer, feeling relief that my snap decision to stop here is going to pay off. Melody ushers me in and shuts the door behind me. I walk into a large foyer which has yellow pastel coloured walls and hardwood floors. There is an oak staircase directly in front of me, and there is a cabinet to the left which appears to have a guest book on the top.

Melody walks over to the cabinet and unlocks it. She takes a key off of one of the hooks and then locks the cabinet back up again.

"Follow me, dear," she says as she starts walking to the staircase. I follow her, taking in the surroundings as I do. There are pictures hung on the wall all the way to the top. Each one is of beautiful countryside.

As we reach the top of the stairs, Melody turns to the left and then stops outside a room which has the number five on the front. She unlocks the door and ushers me in. When I enter the room, I see that it is decorated in much the same way as the foyer. Yellow walls and gold furnishings. There is a double bed against the back wall, a table and chairs by a window to the left, a television hangs on the wall opposite the bed and there is a wardrobe and dressing table to the right. A cabinet, just along from the dressing table, houses a kettle and any necessary accompaniments to make tea or coffee.

Melody walks over to a door, which is to the left of the bed.

"This is the ensuite," Melody says as she switches on a light and I peer around the door. The bath tub is larger than I thought it would be, and the whole room sparkles where it has been cleaned.

"This is perfect," I say as I proceed to tell Melody that I will take the room for the night.

"Wonderful, dear. It's sixty pounds for the night, and breakfast is served in the dining room between eight and ten. There is also a communal room, if you feel that you would like to relax in the company of others." She smiles at me and I find it no effort to smile back, her kind nature making me momentarily forget my troubles. "If you could just follow me back downstairs, then we can get you signed in."

"Great." I follow Melody back to the foyer, and she asks me to sign the guest book.

"Will it just be the one night that you will be staying, dear?" she asks me.

"Oh, um, I'm not really sure yet." I can barely think about what I am going to do in the next hour, let alone think about how long I want to stay here for.

"Not to worry," Melody says. "Are you here on a business trip?"

"Uh, not exactly." I don't really know how to answer the question. I can hardly say that my boyfriend mistook abortion leaflets to be mine, so he went and pulled some tart to make me jealous. "I just need a bit of a time out."

"Ah, career girl, huh?" I just smile at her and she seems to take my smile as a yes. "Well, I don't have anyone booked into this room for a few days, so you are welcome to stay until then."

"Thank you," I say, grateful that she doesn't ask any more questions about why I am here.

Melody hands me the key to my room and then shows me around the dining area and the communal room. The dining room has six oak tables, with matching oak chairs and the yellow theme continues in here. White tablecloths are edged in pretty lace, and deep red curtains hang at the windows.

The communal room blows me away. In the middle of the back wall is the most intricate fireplace that I have ever seen. It is beautiful and is definitely the main feature of the room. There are comfortable armchairs situated around the fireplace, and then over by the window are two tables and beautifully upholstered chairs. There isn't anyone in here at present, but I imagine that the guests are attracted to the warmth and comfort of this room. I can just picture myself curling up in one of the chairs, fire roaring, reading a good book and sipping a glass of wine.

"Well, that's the tour over," Melody says, diverting my attention back to her.

"This really is a beautiful place, Melody."

"Thank you, dear. I hope that you enjoy your stay here, however long that may be." She smiles at me and I thank her again before going to retrieve my holdall from the car.

When I return, Melody is in the foyer and I open my handbag, pulling out my purse. Luckily, I have some cash on me, so I pull out sixty pounds for tonight and hand it over to her.

"You know that you don't need to pay until you have finished your stay," she says, clearly taken aback at me having the money ready to give her.

"Oh," I say, not at all accustomed with the way Melody does things. Usually, in a hotel, you pay up front before they allow you to set foot in the room. I feel a little bit silly that I practically thrust the money in her face.

"It's okay, dear, I know that other places require money upfront, but I have never had any problems in asking guests to settle their bill." She really does seem like such a lovely, trusting lady.

I pull my hand back from her and shove the money back into my purse. I smile shyly and make my way up the stairs, holdall in hand. I reach my room and unlock the door, closing and locking it behind me. I leave my holdall by the door and walk over to the bed. I sit on the edge and pull my phone out of my pocket. I find Lydia's name and give her a call. She answers on the first ring.

"Stacey," Lydia practically shouts down the phone. "Where the bloody hell are you? I thought that you were coming to mine?" I can hear the panic in her voice, and I feel bad that I didn't call her back earlier.

"Sorry, Lyd, I didn't mean to worry you. I just... I couldn't come to yours."

"Why not?"

"Because your flat is the first place that Jake would think to look for me." Lydia stays silent and I know that Jake has already been round there, but I ask the question anyway. "He came round, didn't he?"

"Yes." Lydia's voice is quiet.

"See, I knew that he would."

"I know that you don't want to hear this right now, but he was a mess, Stace." She sounds like she feels sorry for him.

"He's drunk," I reply bluntly.

"No, babes, he wasn't drunk. I think that maybe the shock of everything has sobered him up somewhat. Paul is still with him. He has gone back to yours with Jake, so that he can keep an eye on him."

Although I am mad with Jake, my heart aches at the thought of him hurting. His actions may be beyond repair, but it doesn't mean that I can turn my love for him off. I can't just stop caring about him. I wish that I could.

"Lyd, I need to ask you to do me a favour."

"Okay. What is it?"

"I know that this is terrible timing, but could you run The Den for me? I can't face being there right now. I know that it is a lot to ask, but I can't risk seeing Jake until I am ready. If he knows that I am at The Den, then he will show up."

"Consider it done," Lydia replies, no hesitation in her answer.

"Thanks, Lyd."

"So, are you going to tell me where you are?" she asks.

"I'm just at some bed and breakfast. I saw it as I was driving, and I just stopped and asked if they had any rooms." I shrug my shoulders, even though I know that Lydia can't see me.

"How long will you be there for?"

"I don't know. I just need some time to process everything." I sigh in frustration at how things have dramatically changed in the last couple of hours. "So, are you going to tell me properly how things went with Paul now?" I ask, changing the subject.

"He was great, Stace. I told him everything, including how I took drugs. He said that he likes me too much to walk away." She sounds giddy with happiness.

"That's awesome, Lyd. I'm so happy for you." Even if my own love life is in tatters, at least Lydia's is improving.

"Thanks, babes."

"Listen, Lyd, I think I'm going to try and get some rest now. I feel exhausted all of a sudden."

"Okay. Call me tomorrow, yeah?"

"Sure. Love ya."

"Love you too, babes."

"Bye." I hang up the phone and it immediately starts to ring. Jake's name flashes across the screen and I chuck the phone on the bed as if it has burned me. I can't speak to him yet.

I lie down and curl up into a ball. The tears start to fall again and the pain slicing through my heart is horrendous.

After everything Jake and I have been through, why the hell did it have to come to this?

CHAPTER FOURTEEN

STACEY

I must have fallen asleep, because when I open my eyes the room is pitch-black. I sit up, feeling disorientated, and I feel my way across the bed to the bedside lamp. I switch it on and rub my eyes, which are sore from crying.

I make my way over to the window and close the curtains before going into the ensuite. I use the facilities and then stare at my reflection in the mirror. My eyes are puffy and red-rimmed. My face is pale, and my blue pools convey all of the misery that I am feeling.

I splash my face with water and then dry myself on the plush yellow towel that is hanging on the heated rail. I return to the bed and climb under the duvet, failing to take off my clothes. I don't have the energy to get undressed.

I pick up my phone which is still on the bed from earlier. I have five more missed calls, one text message and a voicemail, all from Jake. My stomach churns as I contemplate deleting the text and the voicemail without reading or listening to them. It takes me a few minutes to decide that I can't delete them. As much as I know that it would be best to ignore them, I have to look.

Curiosity gets the better of me and I open the text message.

Stace, please speak to me. I'm such an idiot. Not being able to speak to you is killing me. I'm so sorry for what I did. Please, just think about calling me back. I love you more than you will ever know.

Jake x x x

My breath catches as I re-read the message a few times.
Why did he not just ask me about the damn leaflets?
Why did he have to go and chat up some other woman?
I could be at home with him right now if he hadn't jumped to conclusions.

I take a deep breath, and before I can chicken out, I listen to my voicemail. I put it on loud speaker and wait for the message to begin.

> *"Baby, I am so sorry. I know that I have said that already,*
> *but I need you to believe how sorry I am. I wasn't thinking*
> *straight after finding those abortion leaflets. I just... I*
> *thought the worst, and I shouldn't have done that. I know that*
> *you would never do that to me."*

I hear his voice break at this point, and it makes my heart constrict with pain.

> *"I don't want to lose you, Stace. We have come through so*
> *much. I don't want us to be over. I didn't mean to hurt you.*
> *I love you so much. I don't know how to be without you.*
> *You are my whole fucking world. I wish I could take it back.*
> *Please talk to me. Please..."*

The message ends with the sound of Jake breaking down and then cuts off. I delete it straight away. I can't listen to that again.

The pain in his words and the anguish in his voice makes me want to get in my car and go to him. It would be so easy, but I know that I would regret it. I need to give myself time to decide what I want to do.

I turn my phone off and place it on the bedside table. I lie there, staring at the ceiling for God knows how long before I decide to turn the television on. I just need some sort of background noise to try to distract me.

I need to stop hurting, just for a little while.

I flick through the channels but seeing as it is just after three in the morning, there is nothing decent on. I mindlessly stare at the screen whilst some woman gives the weather report. I don't take in anything she is saying. I just stare and will myself to feel numb.

My head whirrs with what I should do, and I keep replaying the events that transpired with Jake.

Can I really be with a man who would use another woman to try and piss me off?
How many more hurdles am I going to have to face by staying with him?
Can I really give him up?
Can I throw away everything we have worked for over a misunderstanding?

My thoughts consume me until I am so tired that I finally drift off to sleep again.

CHAPTER FIFTEEN

STACEY

I don't wake up in time for breakfast, which is just as well seeing as I have no appetite. It is just after eleven in the morning when I wake up. At least I managed another few hours of sleep. I still feel exhausted though.

I get out of the bed, use the ensuite, and decide that running a nice, hot bath might help to relieve some of the tension in my body. I start running the water and then I go to the bedside table and turn my phone on. Before I can do anything, my phone starts to ring.

It's Jake again.

I toy with the idea of answering, my finger hovering over the answer button, when the ringing cuts out. I place the phone down on the bedside table and return to the ensuite. I wait for the bath to fill up, shutting the door. I take my clothes off, feeling icky that I slept in them all night. I finish running the bath and get in, enjoying how the hot water makes my skin tingle.

I stay in the bath until the water becomes lukewarm. As I drag my weary body out, I dry myself and I hear my phone buzzing in the next room. I ignore it for the time being, taking my time to get dry. I then go to my holdall and take out a pair of leggings and my off the shoulder jumper. Or my comfy jumper as I call it. I grab some clean underwear and then go back to the ensuite to get dressed.

I dry my hair with the towel and tidy up the ensuite, ensuring that I have dried any water on the floor. My phone starts to buzz again, and I sigh as I roll my eyes and walk over to it. Jake's name appears across the screen again and I wait for the call to end. I desperately want to speak to him, but I still need time, so I decide to call Lydia.

"Hi, babes," she says as she answers the phone. "How are you feeling today?"

"I'm okay," I reply sullenly.

"Really?"

"No."

"Look, Stace, I know that this is a shitty situation, but maybe it would help to talk to Jake?" I know that she means well, but with her saying that I should speak to him, it is slowly chipping away at any resolve I have to ignore his calls.

"No," I reply bluntly as determination courses through me to stand my ground. I hear Lydia sigh and I know that she is frustrated with my stubbornness.

"Jake has been round here again this morning." I groan out loud at her words. He can't hound my best friend. No wonder she wants me to speak to him.

"Was he hoping that I would be there this time?"

"I think so. I had to tell him that you have gone away for a few days. He looked devastated, Stace. Paul said that Jake was pacing the house all night long, trying to figure out where you could have gone."

"I'm sorry that he is bothering you, Lyd."

"Don't you apologise. This is all my fault anyway."

"Oh no, don't you dare—" I don't get to finish my sentence as Lydia cuts me off.

"Stacey Marie Paris, I know what you are going to say, and I also know that this whole situation *is* my fault. I don't need you trying to tell me that it isn't. If you hadn't taken those abortion leaflets for me, then none of this would have happened. You know that as well as I do." She pauses, and I hear her take in a deep breath. "Babes, I know that you are hurting, but can't you just give him a call? I know that what he did was out of order, and I'm not sticking up for him, but you guys are made for each other."

"I will speak to him when I am ready, and that's not yet."

"Okay," Lydia replies, exasperated. "I just don't want you to regret not talking to him."

I need to get off of the phone.

"I need to go, Lyd, but I will call you tomorrow."

"Oh, okay." She sounds a little shocked that I am ending the call, but I don't need to hear her fighting Jake's corner any longer.

"Speak to you soon."

"Bye, Stace." I hang up the phone and let out a groan of frustration. I think about what Lydia said, and I scroll through the phone and find Jake's name.

I stare at his name and am so close to pressing the dial button, but I can't make myself do it. I throw the phone down on the bed and decide that I need to get out of this room. I need to go for a walk.

I put my shoes on, grab my handbag and exit my room, leaving my phone on the bed. I don't want to take it with me.

I leave the bed and breakfast and there is no sign of any other guests. I walk through the car park and head left, along the main road. I don't worry about being seen by Jake as he has no idea where to look for me. I walk about ten minutes along the road and I come across a newsagent, so I decide to take a look inside and maybe pick up a newspaper.

I enter the shop which is actually bigger than it appears from the outside, take a look around, and grab a daily newspaper to read, just for something to do. As I look around the store, I notice a stationary section near the back. I peruse the notepads and pens and decide that a spot of writing may take my mind off of my personal life.

I pick up a couple of notepads and a pack of pens and take them to the counter to pay. After paying and leaving the shop, I head back to the bed and breakfast. Walking along, I am scared to death when a car starts beeping its horn at me. I jump in shock and freeze on the spot, my thoughts immediately thinking that it is Jake.

As I look up though, I see that it is Martin's car. He pulls over, puts his hazard lights on, and jumps out of the driver's seat.

"Baby girl," he screeches at me as he comes running around the car. "What are you doing here?" he asks as he envelopes me in a hug. I take comfort in his arms holding me as I feel fresh tears spring to my eyes.

No, Stacey, don't fucking cry now.

When I don't answer, Martin steps back and takes a proper look at me. "Baby girl, what's wrong?" he asks, concern replacing his happy demeanour from a few seconds ago.

Instead of answering him, I let the tears fall. I can't hold them back any longer.

Martin puts his arm around my shoulders and guides me towards his car. He opens the passenger door and manoeuvres me into the passenger seat. The sobs rack my body as he puts my seatbelt on and then hurries around to the driver's side. Martin starts to drive, and I don't ask where we are going. I don't care where we are going either. I let all the emotions flow through me as I continue to let the pain take over. Anger, hurt, betrayal, disappointment, and sadness consume me.

I felt like my heart was shattering into a million pieces last night, but right now, in this moment, I know that I am heartbroken, and I worry that it may never be repaired.

CHAPTER SIXTEEN

STACEY

I return to the bed and breakfast just after six, after spending the remainder of the afternoon with Martin at his house. I promised that I would call him tomorrow before I waved him off, assuring him that I would be okay. He offered for me to stay at his, but I didn't think that it was fair of me to put him out like that. I also didn't want to annoy Melody by not letting her know if I was staying again or not.

I enter the foyer and Melody comes waltzing out of the communal room.

"Hello there, dear," she says, smiling at me.

"Hi, Melody. I just wanted to make sure that it was okay for me to stay again tonight?"

"Of course it is. You look a little pale, dear, are you feeling okay?" she asks me, her brows furrowing with concern.

"It's just been a long day." I don't care to divulge my personal problems to her. I spent the afternoon doing that with Martin and I feel drained. "If you're not too busy, could I possibly have a large glass of white wine?" I ask her, feeling that I need something to drink after an emotional day.

"Coming right up. You go on through to the communal room and I will bring it in to you."

"Thank you," I say as she rushes off into the dining area.

I enter the communal room and choose to sit in one of the chairs by the window. I place my handbag and my bag of shopping that I got from the newsagent earlier, on the table. I am the only person in here and it feels peaceful. I stare out of the window and enjoy the view of the gorgeous sunset.

Melody comes in a few moments later with my glass of wine and places it on the table in front of me.

"There we are, dear. I will add it to the tab for your room."

"That's great," I say, hoping that I won't have to force myself to make polite conversation.

"I'm so glad that you have decided to stay another night. It's nice to have someone young here. Don't get me wrong, I love anyone coming here, but most of the people who walk through that door are old fuddy-duddies." She chuckles, and I laugh along with her. It's the first time I have laughed in two days, and it feels good. "Anyway, I must dash, lots of work left to do before tomorrow." She gives me a wink and then leaves the room.

I shake my head and smile. She really is a character, and her easy nature has made me feel so comfortable here. I pick up my glass of wine and take a sip, closing my eyes as the cool liquid slides down my throat. I take another sip and let my mind drift to the conversation that Martin and I were having earlier.

Martin was wonderful. He let me vent, cry, and then vent some more. He listened to my fears and worries. He didn't try to convince me to speak to Jake. He was just there for me, and that is just what I needed.

I take another sip of wine and nearly drop the glass when someone clears their throat right behind me. I turn around to see who it is and am gobsmacked by the person standing there.

"I'm sorry, I didn't mean to make you jump." *Holy shit, it's Doctor Bradley.* He smiles at me and my mouth drops open in surprise. He indicates to the chair on the other side of the table. "Do you mind if I join you?"

"Uh, no, not at all." *Why would he want to sit with me?*

"It's Stacey, right?" he asks as his eyes linger intently on my face.

"Yeah." I don't know what else to say. I sit awkwardly, racking my brains for something to say. He has a glass of scotch in his hand, and he takes a sip.

"So, how are you?" he asks, placing the scotch glass on the table.

"Uh, I'm okay, thanks. You?"

"I'm great. How's your friend? Lydia, isn't it?" *Should Lydia's doctor be asking me this?*

"Oh, she's fine." I feel my face frown. "Excuse me for being blunt, but can I ask why you wanted to sit with me?" I decide that I don't have the energy or the inclination to pussy-foot around someone right now.

"Oh, well, I just moved back to the area and I don't really know anyone. I saw you sitting here and recognised you from the other day. I can leave though, if you like?" He looks a little wary and I instantly feel like a bitch for being so blunt.

"No, it's fine. I'm sorry, I'm just not very good company at the moment. I didn't mean to come across as rude." The guy is only looking for some friendly chit-chat. I bet he wishes that he hadn't bothered coming over now.

"No worries. So, you don't mind if I sit with you then?" His striking eyes look to me for confirmation.

"No, of course not." I smile at him. "So, how long have you been staying here?" I ask, feeling that I now need to make a little bit of effort to show that I am not just some rude bitch.

"A couple of weeks now. I just moved back from America."

"Wow. Why would you do that? I would love to live out there." It has always been a dream of mine to go to America. One day I hope that I will make that dream come true.

Doctor Bradley chuckles at my reaction. "I guess you could say that I felt homesick. I missed certain aspects of living here. I also have a brother who I am hoping that I can reconnect with. I left on bad terms with him, and I am hoping to gain back his trust." He looks sad as he speaks, and I can't help but feel sorry for him.

"Oh." Well, that conversation turned a little more serious than I thought that it would. I'm a little surprised that he has just divulged personal information to me, seeing as I am a virtual stranger to him. "I'm sorry to hear that." There really is nothing else that I can say at this point.

"It's my own fault. I acted like a complete ass when I was younger." He stares out of the window as he speaks. "I am hoping to change my brother's opinion of me, and I'm hoping that he will be able to see that I am not the same person that I once was." His head turns, and his eyes lock with mine.

"I'm sure that it will all work out."

"Fingers crossed." He smiles and clears his throat. "So, what brings you to this bed and breakfast?"

"Um, let's just say that I needed a time out from life." I give him the same reason that I gave Melody.

"Huh. I'm guessing that there could be a man involved in that statement." I let a sad smile form on my lips, not bothering to hide the fact that he has hit the nail on the head.

"I would rather not talk about it." I'm not about to place my trust in this guy. He may be a doctor, but that doesn't mean that I have to tell him my secrets. I take a few gulps of my wine and Doctor Bradley nods towards my glass.

"Another?" he asks, picking his scotch glass up off of the table.

"No thanks. I really should be getting back to my room." I stand up and the doctor does the same, holding his hand out for me to shake. I place my hand in his and I don't fail to notice how he tightens his grip on me.

"It was nice talking to you, Stacey. We should do it again soon." He flashes me a killer smile and I quickly pull my hand away, feeling like I am betraying Jake by being near this guy. I can appreciate that he is handsome, but that's as far as it goes. I don't get butterflies from looking at him. I don't feel a blush creeping over my cheeks. I don't feel my sex stir with need at the thought of his skin on mine.

Jake has officially ruined me for any other man.

I doubt that anyone will ever make me feel the way that Jake does.

I smile at Doctor Bradley before picking up my bags off of the table. I turn and exit the communal room, making my way up the stairs to my room. I unlock the door and enter my room, putting my bags on the floor and locking the door behind me.

I feel my body sag against the closed door and I close my eyes, hoping to God that I can find a way out of the hell that I am feeling sometime soon.

CHAPTER SEVENTEEN

STACEY

It's six in the evening, and I have spent the whole day locked in my room, writing. I woke up this morning and took out the notepads and pens that I bought from the newsagents yesterday, and I sat by the window, pouring my heart out onto the pages in front of me. It feels therapeutic to write about the way that I am feeling. It also lets me maintain a sense of privacy that I have put all of my emotions into characters that I have made up.

I have been running on caffeine all day long. I didn't make it to breakfast again this morning, but I still have no appetite. I know that I should really eat, but I have been so consumed with getting my thoughts down on paper that I haven't thought about anything else. My phone has been off all day, and it's been quite nice to shut myself off from the outside world. I know that I need to switch it on and check in with Lydia and Martin, but I am enjoying my last few moments of peace before I do that.

I sip the last of my coffee and walk over to the bedside table. Picking up my phone, I turn it on and wait to see what messages await me today. I have two, one from Lydia and one from Martin. They are both just asking how I am doing. I have nothing from Jake.

I feel a pang of disappointment within me. I know that I asked for space, and I know that I am the one who has been ignoring his calls, but I would hate to think that he has given up on me. My mind is still all over the place as I realise how ridiculous that sounds. I want him to leave me alone, but then I'm disheartened that he hasn't called.

I need to get my shit together.

I decide to give Martin a call to distract my confused thoughts.

"Baby girl," Martin exclaims as he answers the phone. "How are you doing?" His voice softens as he asks me the question.

"I'm okay, Mart. How are you?"

"Oh, I'm just peachy." I sense a hint of sarcasm in his answer.

"What's wrong?" I ask, feeling concern for my friend.

"I don't know if I should tell you."

"Why not?"

"Because it's work-related." I instantly know that his problem is with Jake and I sigh into the phone. I don't want him to feel like he can't talk to me just because Jake is his boss.

"You can tell me, you know? I'm not going to fall apart at the mention of his name." I would have done two days ago, but I feel like I can't cry over Jake any more than I already have.

"Well, to put it bluntly, Jake has been a fucking nightmare. He was in work today, and all he did was shout and ball at anyone who spoke to him. Honestly, it was horrendous. He's clearly not handling this situation very well."

"I'm sorry, Mart."

"What the hell are you sorry for? You haven't done anything wrong." He sounds genuinely perplexed by my apology.

"Well, the reason he is in a foul mood is because of me. I'm just sorry that he is taking it out on everyone else."

"Don't. Don't you dare apologise for his behaviour. He only has himself to blame, baby girl." I know that Martin is trying to make me feel better, but I don't like the thought of him getting shit at work. "Listen, I know that you need your space and I totally understand that, but can I just say something that has been on my mind since yesterday?"

"Sure." I know that I am not going to want to hear this by the tone of his voice, but I feel that I should listen to him. He has been good to me, and I don't want to make him feel like his advice or opinion doesn't matter to me.

"I know that what he did to you was totally out of order. I understand that you are hurt and feel betrayed by his actions. I would be mega pissed if my partner did that to me, so please don't think that I am sticking up for him." Martin stops talking and I can practically hear his thoughts through the phone.

"I keep running over what happened between you guys in my head, and I just can't believe that Jake would have done anything with that woman. He isn't the type to cheat, Stace. He shouldn't have jumped to conclusions about those leaflets, but I just keep thinking what I would have done in his shoes. I mean, if it had been me that had found those leaflets, I think I would have jumped to the same conclusion as he did. I know that might make me a shitty person for saying that but hurt and anger can make you do stupid things." I let out the breath that I have been holding at hearing Martin's opinion. The line stays silent as I process his words.

Have I blown this out of proportion?

Should I give Jake the benefit of the doubt?

"Stace?" Martins voice interrupts the questions swirling around my head.

"Yeah."

"I thought that you had put the phone down for a minute." Martin sounds a little wary.

"No, I'm still here."

"I'm sorry, baby girl, I know that you probably didn't want to hear what I just said, but I just thought that maybe it might help you decide what to do."

"It's certainly given me something to think about." I'm not pissed off with Martin for voicing his opinion. He's just trying to help, but I know that whatever I decide to do, he will support me. As will Lydia.

"Do you feel like you might return to the real world soon?"

"Maybe. I don't know. Listen, Mart, I'm going to go and grab a drink and then have an early night."

"Okay, baby girl. Make sure that you don't stay away too long."

"I won't." I smile as we say our goodbyes and hang up the phone.

I scroll to the pictures on my phone, looking at the ones of Jake and I together. We look so happy in each and every one.

Am I really prepared to throw away what we have?

Can I get past the hurt that he has caused me?

Can I repair my broken heart?

I sit there and replay my conversation with Martin over and over in my head, willing myself to look at it from Jake's point of view. I can sort of see what Martin was saying. I understand that as a human being, we can sometimes overreact and judge things without knowing the facts. I get that. I think what I am struggling with is that fact that Jake allowed another woman to touch him. I don't know if I can get over that.

A message pings on my phone and I see that it is from Jake. I take a deep breath and open the message to see that it is a link to a song. I click on it and let the music start to play.

The words are clearly relevant to how Jake feels. When the words are sung, it penetrates straight to my heart, and by the time the song finishes, I am a mess. The tears that I thought I had cried enough of have re-emerged. I make my way over to the bed and torture myself by listening to the song on repeat, the thought of getting a drink disappearing from my head. It's like I need to punish myself in some way by listening to the lyrics.

I am the reason that Jake is struggling, and I hate the thought of it.

I eventually drift off to sleep, the music playing in my subconscious, making my dreams just as painful as my reality.

CHAPTER EIGHTEEN

STACEY

I am up and dressed in time for breakfast this morning. I figured that after two days of eating nothing, I really could do with some food inside me. I make my way down to the dining room just before nine o'clock to be greeted by Melody as soon as I enter the dining room.

"Morning, dear," she says to me in her usual cheerful manner. "Come and take a seat." She guides me to a small table by the window and I thank her as I sit down. "You're the first person to show up for breakfast this morning."

"Really?"

"Uh huh. They must all be having a lie-in. Well, what can I get for you, dear? Full English? You could do with some meat on those bones of yours." I take no offence to her comment. I don't think it is in her nature to be malicious in any way what so ever.

"A full English sounds great. Thanks, Melody."

"Excellent." Melody potters through a door to the back of the dining room, which I presume is the kitchen. I spot a table with drinks on it near the back of the room. I walk over to it and pour myself a glass of orange juice as well as a cup of coffee. I take the drinks back to my table and sit down, enjoying the aroma of the coffee beans.

As I take my first sip, I see Doctor Bradley walk into the dining room. He looks very smart in black suit trousers and a crisp, white, long sleeved shirt.

"Good morning," he says as he acknowledges me.

"Morning." He gives me a megawatt smile and then makes his way over to the table with the drinks on. Melody returns to the room, carrying my breakfast.

"There we are, dear. Enjoy," she says as she puts the plate in front of me. My eyes boggle at the amount of food on the plate. The breakfast is huge. I quickly mask my shock at all of the food and proceed to thank Melody. She gives me a smile and then turns to Doctor Bradley. "Good morning, Doctor. What can I get for you this morning?" she asks him.

"Whatever she's having," he says as he nods to my plate.

"Fabulous. Take a seat and I'll be back in a jiff." She once again leaves through the door at the back of the room. Doctor Bradley chooses to sit at the table opposite me.

I pick up a piece of toast and take a bite. My stomach growls in response. I can feel Doctor Bradley's eyes on me as I chew my piece of toast. I look up at him and he quickly looks away, obviously trying to hide the fact that he was watching me. I decide that I don't particularly want him gawping at me eating my breakfast, so I make a snap decision.

"Would you like to join me?" I ask, gesturing to the vacant chair opposite me. If he sits with me, then maybe he will feel the need to stop staring.

"And there was me thinking that you would never ask." He gets up, chuckling to himself, and brings his drink with him. Melody returns to the dining room with his breakfast and places it on the table as he sits down.

"This is just what I need to start the day," he says, eyeing the food appreciatively. Melody chuckles and I can see her eyes darting from Doctor Bradley and over to me. I squirm slightly in my seat. I can practically see the excitement in her eyes that we are sitting together.

"You two would make a cute couple," she says before she notices another guest walk into the dining room. She chuckles again as she walks away, and I decide to ignore her comment. I have no interest in Doctor Bradley in that way.

"So," I start to say, not wanting Doctor Bradley to think too much about Melody's comment. "Busy day at the surgery, doc?" I ask him as I place a piece of bacon in my mouth.

"Actually, I'm only in the surgery this morning. I have the afternoon off, and I intend to visit my brother and try to talk to him."

"Oh. Well, good luck. Not that you will need it. I am sure that he will be able to see that you have changed, whoever he may be," I say, trying to be positive.

"Thanks. I think that I might need more than luck though." I can see on his face that he is worried about how this meeting with his brother might go.

"Hey, you will be fine. Family is important. I'm sure that the two of you will work out your differences." I give him a reassuring smile and he returns it, his face relaxing.

"I hope so." He takes a bite of his sausage and swallows before speaking again. "Have you got any plans today?"

"I thought that I would do some writing."

"Writing?" Doctor Bradley asks. It is at this point that I realise that he won't have a clue that I love to write. I wasn't exactly very forthcoming with information the other night.

"It's my dream to become a published author. So, whilst I am here having a time out, it seems like a perfect opportunity to get some writing done."

"Wow. That's awesome. What kind of stuff do you write?" he asks, seeming genuinely interested.

"Well, my first novel is a crime novel, but I didn't bring my laptop with me, so I can't do anymore to that at the moment. I did start working on a new novel yesterday, which is about romance and heartbreak." I don't tell him that it is due to my current love life that I have decided to put pen to paper. I wouldn't want anyone to read it and compare it to the life that Jake and I shared up until a couple of days ago.

"Well that's informative," Brad says sarcastically but playfully.

"Hey," I say as I smack his arm gently. "If I tell you anymore details then you won't buy the book when I'm rich and famous," I tease back. It feels good to have some friendly banter.

"Well, I would expect a free copy, of course." He laughs, and I laugh along with him. I put my knife and fork down and finish drinking my coffee. I feel bad that I have left half a plateful of food, but I couldn't eat another bite. I am absolutely stuffed.

Doctor Bradley mops his plate up with his last piece of toast and then sits back, his eyes moving to my plate.

"Weak effort, Stacey," he says, shaking his head at me. "What's wrong with this bacon?" he asks as he points to a couple of rashers left on my plate.

"I'm too full to eat anymore." Doctor Bradley takes this as a cue to take a rasher off of my plate and eat it. My mouth falls open. "Did you really just take food off of my plate?" I ask, astonished.

"I did."

"But you're a doctor."

"So?"

"And you hardly know me. How do you know that I haven't got some sort of illness or something?" Surely as a doctor, he must be a little more cautious about germs.

"I'm not worried about eating anything that you have touched. Besides, I would like to think that we have some sort of friendship going on here, and friends eat each other's bacon." His eyes twinkle as his gaze moves to my lips. I feel a little awkward at him looking at me in this way. I fidget in my seat and put my coffee cup down on the table, just for something to do.

"Anyway, I best be going. Patients to see and brothers to visit," he says as he stands up, thankfully leaving me no room to comment on his words about us forming a friendship.

"I hope it goes well for you."

"Me too. Fancy grabbing a drink later? It will either be in celebration, or I will be trying to drown my sorrows."

"Sure." I smile at him as he leaves the dining room, wondering if I have made the right decision to join him for a drink later.

JAKE

"Is this really the best that you can come up with?" I shout at Martin. He sits on the other side of my desk looking petrified.

"I'm... I'm sorry, sir, but I think that it is a great idea for the Waters Industries summer ball." His voice is timid, which is hardly surprising seeing as I am acting like a complete and utter asshole towards him. I know that he doesn't deserve to face my wrath, having done nothing wrong, but I can't help it. I am fucking miserable and I am making that known to everyone around me.

"No. It's not good enough. Go away and think of something else." I wave him away with a flick of my hand. Martin doesn't need telling twice, and he quickly gathers up the paperwork that he brought in with him and leaves my office. I hang my head and feel ashamed of myself. I am not the type of person to belittle my employees like that. I hate what I have turned into in the last few days, but I can't seem to control the emotions flowing through my body.

I shouldn't even be at work.

My head is not here.

My head, and my heart, are with Stacey.

I hate myself for what I have done to her. I hate that I have hurt her. And I hate that I didn't have enough faith in her to just ask her about the fucking leaflets in the first place.

I sigh and pick up my mobile phone. I haven't tried to contact her since yesterday.

I wonder if she read my message?

I wonder if she listened to the song that conveys how my heart feels right now?

I'm trying to give her the space that she needs, but it is so fucking hard. I just wish that she would speak to me.

I scroll to her name in my phonebook and am about to try and call her, when my office door flies open. I look up, in the hope that it might be her, only to be disappointed that it is Brad.

"Oh for fuck's sake," I say out loud. "Can this day get any worse?"

"Oh, thanks, bro. That's quite a welcome that you have going on there." Brad strides in, shutting the office door behind him. He makes his way to the chair that Martin vacated minutes ago.

"What's bit you in the ass today?" he asks, looking far too fucking happy for my liking.

"I've just had a shit day so far." I keep my answer short and sweet. I don't want him to know anything about how I have lost the one person that means more to me than anything else.

"More like a shit week," Brad remarks. I eye him suspiciously. *How the fuck would he know?*

"What is that supposed to mean?" I ask cautiously.

"Well, I have some info for you, but you have to promise to listen to me before you react." I think about this for a few minutes. He has to be bluffing. There is no way that he could know what has been going on with my life. I decide to entertain him by playing along with whatever he thinks he might know.

"Go on, what is it?" I tap my fingers on my desk as I wait for him to speak.

"When I was here the other day, you got a phone call from some woman. Her name's Stacey, yes?" I instantly feel my hackles rise at his words, and I grit my teeth together to refrain from reacting to him. I need to see where he is going with this.

I nod to confirm that the woman phoning me was indeed Stacey. For all I know, he just saw her name on my phone when she tried to call me. "I had the pleasure of meeting her the other day when she came to the surgery with her friend. Anyway, last night, I saw her again. I recognised her and asked her if I could join her for a drink."

"What?" I shout at him, my brain picturing all kinds of scenarios and each one fills me with rage. His words are like a punch to my gut.

"Calm down, I haven't finished talking yet."

"I swear, if you have touched her, I won't be able to control my actions." My voice is filled with hate. I am hanging onto any rational thoughts by a mere thread.

"Jake, for fuck's sake, man, chill out." He sighs in exasperation. "Just to be clear, I haven't done anything but talk to her, so there really isn't any need for you to go all caveman on my ass." He holds my gaze, and I get the feeling that he is telling me the truth.

"Continue." It's the only word that I can form right now.

"As I was saying, I asked to join her for a drink because she looked like she needed cheering up. She is staying at the same place as me. I asked her why she was there, and all she said was that she needed a time out. I then saw her at breakfast this morning—"

"At breakfast?"

"Yes, Jake, at breakfast. She was eating her breakfast in the dining room, and when I walked in, she asked if I would like to join her." I feel as if each one of his words is like a stab to my heart.

He gets to have breakfast with her? It should be me, not him.

"Excuse me for interrupting, but where exactly are you going with this? I mean, if you are just here to wind me up, then you are doing a fucking cracking job of it."

"I'm not here to wind you up, Jake. I'm here to fucking help you. God knows, I owe you a favour or two." *Help me? He wants to fucking help me?* I snort in response. "She has no idea that I am your brother."

"Well, I figured that much. If she knew that you were, then I am positive that she wouldn't have spoken to you at all. Not after what I have done..." I let my voice fade off, already knowing that I have told him too much.

"I'm sure that whatever you have done, it isn't as bad as some of the shit that I have done." He chuckles at his words, obviously thinking that now is the perfect time to try and crack a joke. I give him a stern look and his laughter quickly dies.

"Look, I kind of appreciate what you are trying to do here, but I don't think that she will ever be able to forgive what I did." I don't look at him as I speak. Shame consumes me once again.

"Shit, what the hell did you do?" Brad asks, his eyebrows shooting up in question.

"I would rather not talk about it."

"Okay, fair enough. I just want you to know though that I am here if you ever need to talk." I can see that he is trying to make an effort, but I don't know if Brad and I can ever salvage our relationship. It has been hanging by a thread for years.

"Listen, I am meeting her later for a drink. Do you want me to call you after I have seen her?" he asks. I hate the thought of him having a drink with her. I hate the thought of him talking to her. I hate the thought of him being anywhere near her, but what other choice do I have? If I tell him to fuck off, then I will remain as clueless as I have for the last couple of days.

"Yeah." Brad smiles but I don't return it. "Where is it you said that you were staying?"

"Oh no, I'm not telling you that."

"Why the fuck not?" I bite back.

"Because you would go straight there and try to speak to her. I can see that she means a lot to you, but for the time being, I think that you need to give her the space that she needs. I may not understand what is going on, but I know that doing the opposite of what any woman asks is just going to piss them off." I clench my jaw, knowing that he is right.

Just how much more space is she going to need though?

It may have only been a couple of days, but it feels like a lifetime.

"Fine." The buzzer goes on the intercom, interrupting our conversation.

"I better get going anyway," Brad says as he stands up. I stand up and reach across the desk, grabbing his arm to get his attention. He looks at me questioningly.

"I meant it when I said don't touch her." My tone is laced with warning.

"I'm not going to, bro. Jeez, I have learnt from my past mistakes. You're just going to have to trust me on this one." He shrugs out of my grasp and walks to my office door.

"I'll call you later," he says as he opens the door, and then he is gone.

To say I am shocked by the conversation that we just had is an understatement. Half of me is pleased that I am finally able to find out how Stacey is, but the other part of me is extremely wary of Brad's motives. I just have to hope that he is being true to his word.

Trusting Brad is like swimming in a sea of sharks with no cage.

CHAPTER NINETEEN

STACEY

I have spent the whole day writing again, and it feels so liberating. At least I have managed to do something productive in the last two days, instead of just wallowing in misery.

I click the kettle on to make myself a drink and my phone starts to ring. I check who is calling before answering and see that it is Martin.

"Hey, Mart, how's tricks?"

"Oh, baby girl, I have had the most awful day," he says sounding glum.

"Oh no, what's happened?"

"Ugh, what hasn't happened. First of all, work was totally shite, and then Clayton phoned me to say that he wasn't coming back. He doesn't see a future for us."

"Oh, honey, I'm so sorry." I feel awful for him. I know that he loves Clayton, and I was rooting for them to work out their differences. "Did Clayton say why he didn't see a future for the two of you?" I ask, ignoring the work problem for now.

"He just said that he feels like we have grown apart, and that he loves me, but he isn't in love with me anymore. I had a feeling that this was coming, but actually hearing him say it hurts like hell." My heart goes out to him. I know how he is feeling right now. I know that we are both going through different circumstances, but heartbreak is gut-wrenching, no matter what shape or form it comes in.

"Oh God. Do you need me to come and give you a hug?" I feel like such a shit friend for shutting myself away in this bed and breakfast. I should be there for him.

"I appreciate the offer, baby girl, but I think that I just need to be by myself for tonight. It's a lot to take in. At the moment I just feel sad, but I know that anger will kick in shortly, and I don't want anyone to witness me screaming the place down like a baby." I hear him take a deep breath on the other end of the phone. "I really thought that he was for keeps, Stace." His voice breaks, and I know that this break up has deeply affected him.

"Oh, Martin." The line goes silent for a few minutes as I listen to my friend weep for his broken relationship. "Please let me come and see you," I say, wanting to be there for him.

"No, I can't face seeing anyone. I feel like someone has come along and ripped my heart from my chest." I have never heard Martin talk like this before, and it scares me. Martin has always been fun, bubbly and flamboyant. Yes, he has had down moments before, but he has always tried to make a joke out of things. He isn't known for taking life too seriously. I could kick Clayton's ass for doing this to him. "I just... I feel hollow."

"I know the feeling well." Too well, actually.

"It's not quite the same though, is it?" Martin says, causing me to question what he means.

"How so?"

"Well, I know that you are hurting, but at least Jake still wants you. He loves you and would do anything to get you back. Clayton doesn't want me. He isn't going to try and fight for me." Martin's words cause my heart to thump in my chest. He doesn't say it maliciously, he's just voicing his view of both situations.

He's right. Jake has done nothing but try to get me to speak to him.

All of a sudden, I feel ridiculous that I have let this situation drag on for the last few days. Here's Martin, on the end of the phone, in bits. He has lost the guy that he loves more than anything.

My guy is still waiting for me.

My guy hasn't ended things with me.

"I'm sorry," I whisper into the phone.

"Don't be sorry, Stace, just make sure that you are staying away from Jake for the right reasons. If you still love him and want to be with him, then make it work. I don't want you to lose him and feel like I do right now." I don't know what to say in response. I let a tear fall down my cheek, and I hear Martin blow his nose into a tissue. Maybe a change of topic will help?

"How about you tell me what happened at work today?"

"Ugh, where do I start?" he says, sighing in exasperation. "Basically, I came up with this fabulous idea for the Waters Industries summer ball. I have been working on it all week long, but today, when I showed Jake my ideas, he completely shot me down. It was humiliating. He's still not handling things well." Although the change of topic gives Martin something else to focus on for a few minutes, hearing that Jake is still struggling causes a pain to travel straight to my heart.

"He shouldn't be treating you badly, Martin."

"He can't help it. He's hurting. I get it." His short answer halts our conversation, and I decide to change the topic again.

"Listen, why don't we hit the town on Saturday night? I feel like we could both do with a good night out."

"Okay." I expected a little more enthusiasm, but then I remember how numb I felt when I left Jake in The Den car park the other day.

"Great." I inject some cheer into my voice.

"Listen, I'm going to go and take a long, hot bath. Thanks for listening to me, baby girl. And keep in mind what I said. I don't want you to lose your happy ending." I smile, even though I know that Martin can't see me. I know that he is just looking out for me.

"I'll call you tomorrow. If you need me before then though, just let me know and I will be straight there."

"Will do. Love you, baby girl."

"Love you too, Mart." We end the call and I feel the need for a glass of wine.

Martin's words have really hit home.

I leave my phone in my room and make my way down to the communal room. When I enter, I see that Doctor Bradley is sat in the same chair that he was sat in last night when we were talking. He has a bottle of beer in his hand, and I see that there is a full wine glass on the table. He looks up at me and smiles, gesturing me over to sit with him.

"There you are," he says as I take a seat opposite him. "I was beginning to think that you had stood me up." He laughs at his joke and I take a sip of my wine.

"Mmm, I need this." I say, taking a few more sips.

"Bad day?" he asks me.

"It was okay until a few moments ago. I just finished up a call with a close friend. He's having some trouble and I feel awful that there isn't anything that I can do for him."

"That sucks, but you seem like you have your own problems that you need to sort out before you start to worry about anyone else's."

"I may have my own problems, but my friends are important to me," I say defensively.

"Whoa, I didn't mean anything by it." He holds his hands up in surrender and I instantly feel guilty for snapping at him.

"Sorry."

"It's okay. You know, I am here if you need to offload about anything." I know that he is dying to know why I am here, but I still don't want to tell him too much. It's actually been nice having a bit of company here, but I don't expect to see him after I leave.

I shake my head at him, smiling. He doesn't give up easily.

I place my wine glass back on the table and let my gaze wander to the window. It's raining heavily, the sound of the rain on the glass putting me at ease. I always love it when it is raining, and I am sat indoors just listening to it patter on the window. The sound relaxes me.

"Stacey?" Doctor Bradley says after a few moments, making me pull my gaze away from the window to look at his face.

"Yeah?"

"There is something that I need to tell you."

"Okay." I feel my eyebrows knit together, wandering what on earth he could have to tell me that has caused him to have such a serious look on his face. He puts his beer down and leans forward, his arms resting on his knees as he looks at me. His look is intense, and it is starting to make me feel slightly uncomfortable.

"I don't quite know how to tell you this, but I feel that you have a right to know." He takes a deep breath, and his words leave me feeling more confused than ever.

Oh God, please don't let him tell me that he is some kind of deranged stalker or something? I have already had to deal with one of those, and that was enough to last me a lifetime.

"Stacey, I am Jake's brother." And just like that, I feel like the wind has been knocked out of me. I can't have heard him correctly. This must be some kind of joke.

"Excuse me?" I say, finding my voice, even if it is quiet.

"I'm Jake's brother. I know that this must be a shock, but you had a right to know." He pauses and picks his beer back up, taking a long gulp.

"What the hell are you talking about? I don't understand. Your surname is Bradley. Jake's surname is Waters."

"My surname is Waters too. Bradley is my first name. I have called myself Doctor Bradley for years. It sounds less pompous than Doctor Waters."

Is this guy for real?

"No, no. This is a wind up, right?" I say, my hands starting to shake.

"Afraid not." He's being deadly serious.

"Oh my God." I close my eyes and feel stupid for not spotting the connection earlier.

Jake's brother moved to America.

Jake's brother is a doctor.

Jake's brother is called Brad.

How the hell did I not put two and two together in the first place?

"I saw Jake today. He knows that I have met you. I only realised who you were when I saw you calling him the other day when I was at his office—"

"Whoa, whoa, whoa. This is too much." I am way out of my depth here. It feels like the room is closing in on me.

I abruptly stand up and bolt from the room. I run up the stairs to my room, and can hear Doctor Bradley, or just Bradley as I now know him, calling my name. I unlock the door to my room quickly and slam it shut behind me. My breathing is laboured, and I feel shaky. I lean against the door and process the limited information that Bradley just told me.

Bradley is Jake's brother.

Did Jake send him here to keep an eye on me?

What the hell is going on with my life?

Will this madness never end?

I make my way over to the bed on shaky legs, and I sit on the edge.

How did my life become so complicated? It's like a fucking soap opera.

I almost laugh at how eventful my life has become over the last couple of months, but I am broken from my thoughts by a knock on the door to my room.

"Stacey, please open the door." It's Bradley.

Fuck.

What the hell do I do?

"I just want a chance to explain things to you."

Do I trust what he is saying to me?

I know that Jake doesn't have a very high opinion of him. They haven't been close for years.

Would Jake really want me speaking to him?

My legs seem to make the decision for me. They take me to the door and I unlock it before my brain has caught up with what I am doing. I open the door and Bradley is stood there with fresh drinks in his hands.

"I thought that you may need a refill after hearing what I just told you." He holds the wine glass out to me and I take it. "Please can I come in?" he asks.

"I don't think that is a good idea."

"Please, just five minutes. If after that you want me to leave, then I will."

In this moment, he seems so genuine that I decide to hear him out, so I step to one side, allowing him to enter my room. I close the door behind him and walk over to the table and chairs by the window. I sit down and gesture for Bradley to sit in the chair opposite me. He takes a seat and I wait to see what he has to say.

"I'm sorry if I went about telling you that Jake is my brother all wrong, but it didn't feel right to keep it from you any longer." He puts his beer down on the table and runs one of his hands through his hair. The action makes me picture Jake, seeing as it is something that he also does.

I study Brad's face, and now that I know they are brothers, I can see similarities. They both have the same strong jaw line, the same shaped nose, and similar striking eyes. "When I went to see Jake today, I told him that you were staying at the same place as me."

"Oh God, does that mean that Jake knows where I am?" I ask, panic engulfing me.

"No. I refused to tell him where we were staying." I breathe a sigh of relief at his words. "I have done some awful things to Jake in the past. I have fucked up in so many ways, but he has always helped me out of the shitty situations that I found myself in. I don't know how much you know of mine and Jake's past."

"Not much. He doesn't really talk about you."

"I figured as much. If you knew half of the stuff that I had done, then you probably wouldn't even give me the time of day. When we were younger, we were close, but as we got older, I became jealous of Jake. He was always the together one. He always knew that he wanted to be a successful businessman, and he made that happen.

"I resented his success, so I tried to piss him off in other ways. Before I left for America, Jake was seeing this girl. I was always a bit of a jack-the-lad, and anything

Jake had, I wanted. Jake wasn't serious about the girl, but I didn't know that at the time. I slept with her behind Jake's back, and then I took her to America with me." I gasp at his admission.

"It's safe to say that Jake lost all trust in me at that point. I think that it hurt him that, as his brother, I could do something like that to him. You can imagine how he first reacted when I told him that I had met you." He pauses and stares at the floor, clearly ashamed of his actions.

"I haven't been in Jake's life since the day that I left, but I still know how he works. He's always been the same, but I have never seen him like this. He's a mess. He's suffering, and I think that you are suffering too. I know that I don't really know you, but I feel like we have a connection. I just want to help the both of you in any way that I can. I don't know the ins and outs of what has happened between you and Jake, but I know that he regrets whatever it is that he has done.

"He's a good guy, Stace. Don't tell him that I said this, but he's one of the best. Don't let a mistake he made ruin what you two have together." He takes a swig of his beer and I am left reeling from his confession. He looks at his watch and sighs. "I guess my five minutes is up."

He stands and starts to walk over to the door. He places his hand on the door handle and turns to look at me. "If you need to talk, I'm in room number twelve. Thanks for listening to me." With that, he opens the door and leaves my room whilst I sit in complete shock.

I grab my wine glass and drain the whole thing in one go, slamming the glass back down on the table when I have finished.

Well, fuck me.

JAKE

My phone rings and I see Brad's name across the screen. I answer immediately.

"Is Stacey okay?"

"And hello to you too."

"Cut the shit, Brad." I'm not in the mood for idle chit-chat right now.

"Jeez, you really need to loosen up, bro." I clench my jaw in frustration.

"Just tell me how she is." It took every ounce of willpower that I possess not to follow him to wherever he is staying earlier and see how Stacey is for myself.

"Honestly, I don't know. I told her that I am your brother."

"Fuck." *Why the hell did he do that? I don't want Stacey to think that I have been keeping tabs on her by using him.*

"Yeah. To say that she was shocked is an understatement, but I guess that is hardly surprising. She ran off when I first told her and locked herself in her room, but I managed to get her to let me in to speak to her."

"Wait a fucking minute. You were in her room?" *He shouldn't be anywhere near her room.*

"Yes, Jake, but I was only in there for five minutes. She listened to what I had to say, and then I left." He sounds exasperated saying this, but I don't like the thought of them being alone together, especially in the privacy of her room. I know that Stacey wouldn't do anything with him. I trust her implicitly. I just don't fucking like it. "I think that she is going to need some time to process everything that I told her. You need to leave her to think things through."

"That's easier said than done."

"I know, but you need to do this, for her sake. Keep your cool, and if anything else happens, I will phone you."

"Fine." There isn't really anything else that I can say. "I suppose I should thank you for helping me."

"Never thought I would hear you saying that to me," he chuckles.

"Me either."

"Listen, do you want to grab a beer on Saturday night? I won't pull any crazy shit, I promise."

"We'll see." I hang up the phone and chuck it beside me, on the sofa. I hope to God that Brad hasn't fucked things up further for me. I want to believe that he has changed. I want to believe that he is helping me out of the kindness of his heart, but I'm still not convinced. I guess that I will just have to wait and see what the outcome is.

The trouble is, I hate fucking waiting.

CHAPTER TWENTY

STACEY

I am stood on the driveway of mine and Jake's home before nine o'clock in the morning. I woke up early at the bed and breakfast, paid Melody the money that I owed for the room and any expenses, said my goodbyes, and then I left. Melody made me promise that I would pop by sometime to see her.

Part of the reason that I left early was so that I wouldn't bump into Brad. After last night's revelations, I feel that is only right that I see Jake before I see or speak to anyone else.

I thought long and hard about what Brad told me. It played on a loop in my mind for most of the night. I then factored in Martin's words to me over his break up with Clayton. Between the two of them, they helped me reach an answer to the soul-searching that I have been doing over the last few days.

I look up to the house, and I realise how much I have missed this place. It may not have been my home for long, but I feel like I belong here.

There is no sign of Jake's car, so I presume that he has already left for work.

I open the boot of my car and take out my holdall and handbag, then lock the car and make my way to the front door.

―――――

JAKE

I feel like shit.

After drinking half a bottle of scotch last night, after talking to Brad, I am left with a pounding headache.

I make my way down the stairs and to the kitchen, where I proceed to make myself a coffee, drink a pint of water, and take a couple of tablets to curb the pain in my head.

I sit at the kitchen island, close my eyes and sip my coffee. After finishing the first cup, I immediately make another one. Sitting back on one of the stools, I place my head on the counter top and allow my coffee to cool.

I think back to what Brad told me last night, but my thoughts are interrupted by the sound of the front door opening. I sit up and strain my ears to make sure that I'm not hearing things.

When I hear the front door close a few seconds later, I quietly stand up and make my way to the kitchen doorway. If this is some fucker trying to break in, then I don't fancy their chances of getting away unscathed.

As I peer around the kitchen door, I am blown away by the sight before me. I move into the hallway and just stand there, looking at the vision before me.

Stacey.

Her back is to me as she places her pink holdall on the floor and takes off her shoes. I watch her, drinking in the sight of her, almost afraid to blink in case it turns out that my mind is playing tricks on me.

Her long hair is in a high ponytail, her petite frame is masked by a jumper that is slightly too big for her. She places her keys on a hook by the front door and then I hear her take in a deep breath.

She's here.

She's really fucking here.

She starts to turn around and my heart feels like it is going to jump out of my chest. Her head is down as she turns in my direction, and she takes a few steps forward before she freezes on the spot.

Her head whips up in surprise, and her wide eyes lock with mine.

It takes every ounce of control for me to stay where I am.

All I want to do is go to her, hold her, and never let her go.

STACEY

When my eyes lock with Jake's, I freeze.

He stands at the end of the hallway, his hands by his sides, his jogging bottoms hung low on his hips, and his chest bare.

My heart does a flutter at the sight of him.

This man takes my breath away.

He may have hurt me, but that doesn't take away the chemistry that is between us.

My body hums in response to him being so near.

He doesn't speak.

He doesn't move.

He just watches me.

Waiting.

It's now or never, Stacey.

I came here to speak to him. I came here to repair our relationship. I came here to put the bad behind us, but as I stand here and look at him, I realise that I don't need explanations.

I don't need to rehash what happened at The Den.

I don't need him to apologise over and over again.

I don't need him to promise me that he won't ever hurt me again.

I don't need any of those things, because deep down, I know that he loves me, and I know that he would do anything for me.

I know that he would never have done anything with that woman.

I know that he was just looking for a reaction that day because he was hurting.

I know that he regrets his actions, and I suppose that I regret mine too.

We are both to blame here.

If I had just been honest with him about Lydia, then none of this would have happened. I thought that I was doing the right thing by Lydia by keeping quiet, but in the end, all I did was hurt myself and Jake.

I make a promise to myself that I will never again keep anything from him, no matter who asks me to.

Adrenaline pumps through my body as I start to move forwards. I take slow, steady steps towards Jake, and I can see his chest rising and falling with each breath he takes.

I keep my eyes locked with his as I come to a stop in front of him. I don't leave much room between us as I tilt my head to keep his eyes on mine.

"Stace—" Jake starts to speak, but I move my hand up to his lips and place my fingers over them to stop him from saying anything.

I don't need him to speak.

I can see everything that he wants to say just by looking into his eyes.

I let my other hand come upwards and I place it on his bare chest. The heat coming from him and the feel of his skin on mine makes my body sizzle.

He is the only man that has ever lit me on fire.

I move my hand from his lips, and I move it to the back of his neck. His body vibrates with the need to touch me, but he is still holding back. I apply pressure to my hand behind his neck, and I bring his face down to mine. He closes his eyes as his face comes closer, and I stand on tip toes and brush my lips over his.

He omits a low growl in his throat and it makes my insides turn to jelly. I close my eyes and I let my lips connect fully with his. As I move my other hand up his chest, I let it travel to my other hand and I link my hands behind his neck. I push my body into his and that is all it takes for Jake to lose control.

His hands find my ass and he lifts me up. I move my legs and wrap them around his waist, still not feeling as if I am close enough to him. I open my mouth to him and our tongues entwine, our kiss deepening by the second. The desire coursing through me becomes overpowering and I moan into his mouth.

His hands kneed my ass and it makes my sex stir with desire. I run my hands through his hair, loving the feel of his silky locks between my fingers. I cup his face in my hands and relish in the feel of his stubble on my palms.

Jake turns me and pushes me up against the wall, allowing his hands to move freely. He brings one hand up to the nape of my neck, his grip holding me firm. His other hand has snaked around my back and is holding me against him.

I don't think that I will ever be able to get my fill of Jake.

I whimper as he pulls his lips away from me and lets his forehead rest against mine. We're both panting, trying to catch our breath, and I let my hands rest against his back, the smooth feel of his skin sending signals straight to my core.

"You came back," Jake whispers, emotion rife in his voice.

"I did." He moves his head back slightly, so that he can look into my eyes.

"I fucking love you, Stacey Paris." His voice cracks slightly and it makes tears sting the backs of my eyes. I don't want to cry though. I don't want to shed anymore tears. I blink a few times and gulp down the lump that has formed in my throat.

"I know," I say breathlessly.

"I'm so sorry that I hurt you."

"I know that too." I smile at him and he opens his mouth to speak again, but I cut him off. "Take me to bed, Jake."

CHAPTER TWENTY-ONE

STACEY

I lie in bed with Jake's arms wrapped tightly around me, my back pressed firmly to his chest and his legs entwined with mine. I lightly stroke his arm, enjoying the feel of goose-bumps rising on his skin from my movements. His lips are placing soft kisses on my shoulder and the side of my neck, bringing a smile to my face. The feel of his lips on my skin makes me want to make love to him all over again.

When Jake brought me upstairs, he stripped me of my clothes slowly, savouring every moment of our reconciliation. Once I was completely naked, he took his jogging bottoms off and stood before me with his arousal on display. He gently lowered me onto the bed and began to devour every inch of my body.

He reigned kisses on every inch of my skin, taking his time, allowing me to become more aroused with every second that passed by. What transpired between us just now was nothing short of magical. There was nothing hurried or rushed, we simply just took our time with one another, and I loved every single moment.

With my body spent, Jake pulled me into his arms and he hasn't let me go since. His strong, muscular arms make me feel secure, safe and loved.

Our time apart has made me realise that I never want to be without him.

He owns my mind, body and soul.

He may not believe it, but my heart belongs to him. No one will ever be able to take that away from him.

His teeth nip at my earlobe, sending sparks shooting down to my core. I turn my face to look at him and his lips capture mine in a slow and sensual kiss. I am still being held firmly in his arms, almost as if he is frightened to let me go.

When he pulls his lips away from mine, I pout slightly, making him chuckle.

His eyes hold mine, and I know that I made the right choice by coming back. I know that I would have been miserable without Jake.

"What's running through that beautiful mind of yours?" he asks me, placing a kiss on the end of my nose.

"I just... I missed you," I whisper to him.

"Oh God, I missed you too. I really thought that I had lost you." He rests his forehead against mine and closes his eyes. His words pull at my heart.

"Hey," I say softly, nudging his head with mine, so that he looks at me. His eyes open and I can see that it is taking everything for him to keep control of his emotions right now. "You never lost me, Jake. I will always belong to you." I pour every bit of emotion into my words. He needs to hear this. "We both made mistakes, and we are both to blame for what happened."

"No," he says abruptly, his head whipping up so fast that I am surprised that he doesn't pull a muscle. "You did nothing wrong. You were just being a good friend to Lydia. I was the one who jumped to conclusions. I was the one who got it wrong. I should have known that you would never take the life of something that was mine and yours. I know you, but when I saw those leaflets, I lost myself for a few moments, and those few moments was all it took for me to turn into a complete asshole. I will regret that day for the rest of my life." His voice fades into a whisper and I let a single tear slide down my cheek.

Jake notices and kisses the tear away. His grip on me has loosened slightly, allowing me to free my hand, so that I can bring it to his face. I cup his cheek in my palm, and as I look at him, I see the pain and the guilt that he is still carrying from that day. I don't want him to feel guilty. I don't want him to carry that on his shoulders. I need him to understand that we have to move past it and learn from it.

"Jake, you need to stop. I don't want you to let what happened eat away at you. If I had told you about Lydia in the first place, then none of this would have happened. I forgive what you did. I forgive all the hurt, and you need to do the same." He frowns at me as if he doesn't understand what I am saying to him. "I need you to forgive me for not telling you the truth in the first place."

I can see that he wants to argue with me about how he doesn't think any of it is my fault. I give him a death stare, as if daring him to argue with me, to which he starts to smile. I feel myself relax as his gorgeous smile lights up his face.

"I love it when you look at me like that," he growls in response. Jake has always told me that there is a certain look that I do that makes him hard. And true to form, I can feel his length pressing against my leg.

He moves so that he is nestled between my legs, his body covering mine and my legs parting so that he can get comfortable. He kisses the tops of my breasts and my hands run through his hair. I sigh as his kisses start to travel downwards. My eyes close and I press my head into the pillow as he reaches my sex. He parts my legs more, so that I am exposed to him. He lightly blows over my clit and excitement races through my core. I can feel his lips hovering above me, making me wait.

"Eyes, baby," he says, making me lift my head to look at him. "I want you to watch as I make you come." His words and the glint in his eyes make me wet with want.

I watch as his tongue darts out to lick my sensitive bud. He looks up to me every so often to make sure that I am watching. It takes all of my strength not to throw my head back and cry out in pleasure.

As I feel my orgasm approaching, I part my legs wider, giving him more access. His fingers make their way to my opening and he inserts two, all the while keeping his lips attached to my clit.

His eyes fix on mine as I start to tighten around his fingers. My hips move, so that I can rub against his mouth, and I start to pant as my climax gathers speed.

Jake increases the pressure slightly with his tongue, and that is all it takes to tip me over the edge. I cry out his name over and over again. My eyes are still connected with his, making my orgasm more powerful.

He intently watches me as he slowly works me down from my orgasm. When I feel that I can give no more, I let my body relax onto the bed and Jake quickly climbs up my body and inserts his cock at my opening. His lips cover mine and I can taste my arousal on him.

He plunges himself into me, making me scream into his mouth. I wrap my legs around his waist and push his ass with my feet, making sure that he has buried himself in me as much as possible.

My hands fly up to his shoulders and I grip on for dear life as Jake starts a punishing rhythm. Straight off of the back of my first orgasm, I feel another one building. With Jake's hard thrusts and his lips on mine, it doesn't take long for my climax to ignite.

I break my lips away from his as I moan and writhe beneath his strong body. My sex pulses around his cock, and a few seconds later, Jake roars from the impact of his orgasm.

As I wrap my arms around his neck, I pull his body as close to me as possible. I squeeze my muscles and bite Jake's ear lobe as he calls out my name. He collapses on top of me when he is finished, and I let my hands move up and down his back. My legs are still wrapped around him, and he is still inside me.

"Fucking hell," he says quietly into my ear. I smile and place a kiss on his cheek. He places his arms by the sides of my head and lifts himself up slightly, allowing him to look at me. "That was—"

"Amazing," I finish his sentence for him.

"I'm never letting you go again." I take comfort in his words, and I know that he means them.

Jake doesn't open himself up to people often, but when he does, it's pretty special.

I count myself as lucky to be one of the special ones.

He rolls over, taking me with him. He lies on his back, me on top of him, and I know that there is nowhere else in the world that I would rather be right now.

We have been through a lot in the short time that we have known each other, but whatever we face, we always seem to come through it stronger.

Every hurdle we jump brings us closer.

Every obstacle that stands in our way, we manage to find a way through it.

I close my eyes and place my head on Jake's chest, so that I can hear his heart beating.

His heart beats for me, and mine beats for him.

I will fight for this man every step of the way.

Our relationship is worth every single moment of pain that we have endured.

I close my eyes with a smile on my face and with the simple knowledge that I am home.

CHAPTER TWENTY-TWO

JAKE

I am the luckiest son of a bitch in the world.

I watch Stacey as she shakes her fine ass on the dance floor. She is wearing the sexiest come-fuck-me heels ever, and her long legs are on display due to her wearing a pair of black, tailored shorts. The silk and lace camisole top that she wears shows off her womanly curves, and her long hair is straightened, flowing down her back, begging for me to grab hold of it and tug gently as I fuck her from behind.

I have noticed several men looking at her this evening, but I stand here with a smug smile on my face, because they will never get their hands on her.

She is mine.

They can look all they like, but I'm the one who gets to take her home and touch every inch of her body.

I am the one who makes her scream in pleasure.

I am the one that she chose.

Even after what I did to her, she still loves me.

She still wants me, and I am going to do everything in my power not to fuck up again.

When she left me for those few days, my life went to shit. I can't function without her. I never thought that I would ever be one of those men who needs a woman in their life. I never thought that I would ever give my heart over to another person, but here I am, letting her have it.

As she dances with Martin, I smile at the friendship that the two of them share. I have grown fond of Martin in the short time that I have known him, and I feel awful for the way that I have treated him at work recently. I have apologised to him for my behaviour, and he was understanding, just brushing it off. Stacey told me that Martin and his partner have called time on their relationship and that she wants to support Martin as much as she can. She hasn't told me what Martin said about us during our time apart, but I have a feeling that he was rooting for Stacey and me to work it out, and for that I will always be grateful to him.

Lydia is working at The Den tonight, and I made it my mission as soon as we arrived to apologise to her. She, like Martin, brushed the whole thing off like I had done nothing major to affect her life.

Paul however is a different matter. I haven't seen or heard from him since that fateful day. I know that he stayed with me initially, to make sure that I didn't do anything stupid, but that was the last time that I saw him. I have tried to call him, but he has been ignoring my attempts to contact him.

Paul is my best friend, and one of the only people that I have trusted through my adult life, and I feel like a complete wanker for the way the news about Lydia's pregnancy was broken to him. Lydia has assured me that Paul is just busy with work, but I think that she is trying to spare my feelings. Why she would bother, I really don't know. I deserve to have them raging at me. I know that when I do eventually see Paul, that he is going to want to have his say on the matter. I expect that, and a part of me welcomes it. I almost feel that I have gotten away with my actions far too lightly.

When Stacey walked back through the front door yesterday, she didn't want to talk about it. She didn't want to go over what happened. All she wanted to do was immerse herself in me, and I wasn't about to stop her. We spent the whole day in bed together, switching between making love and fucking like animals. It has to be one of the best days of my life. My cock stirs at the memory of her body against mine, her lips against my skin, her legs straddling me as she rode me to release. I lost count of the amount of times I made her come.

"Hey, bro." I turn to look at Brad, almost scowling at him for interrupting my thoughts. His voice next to my ear acting like a cold bucket of water being poured over my cock.

"Hey," I say as I swig my beer. "You made it then?" I had invited Brad along tonight, seeing as he wanted us to go out for a beer anyway.

"'Course I did." He sips his drink and his attention turns to the dance floor. I follow his gaze, and I find his eyes watching Stacey and Martin, just like I was only seconds ago. "So, you guys all good now?" he asks, nodding his head towards Stacey.

I am wary of answering his questions. I still don't trust Brad, but he did help me when Stacey was gone, so I suppose I should cut him a little slack.

"Yeah." That's about as much slack as I am willing to give him, but it's more than he would have got out of me a few days ago.

My attention moves to Stacey as she saunters towards me, her eyes glittering.

Jesus Christ, she is fucking stunning.

Her gaze drifts to Brad and she smiles at him to acknowledge that he is standing there. She doesn't let her gaze linger on him for long though, returning her blue eyes to lock with mine.

As she reaches me, she places her hands on my chest and lets them slide up to the back of my neck. She brings my head down and places her lips by my ear, licking my ear lobe before speaking.

"I hope that you haven't had too much to drink, Mr Waters. I was hoping that we could pick up where we left off this morning." Her voice purrs in my ear and sends signals straight to my cock, who has decided to wake up again since she walked over here and pushed her tight little body up against mine. She pulls her head back and brushes her lips against mine, before pushing away from my body and turning towards Brad.

"Hi, Brad," she says before I can respond to the words that she whispered in my ear.

"Hey, Stace," he replies, completely at ease around her. I feel a pang of jealousy that he got to know her a little whilst I was out of the picture. I push the feeling down and clench my jaw.

Relax, Waters. They have barely said two words to one another. Stacey has no interest in Brad, in that way.

I try to reason with myself, but I don't fail to notice the look in Brad's eyes as he looks at her appreciatively. His gaze flicks to me and I give him a cold stare, silently challenging him to look at her like that again. He shrugs his shoulders at me and turns away as Martin comes over.

"Hi, dolls," Martin says as he bumps his hip into Stacey's making her giggle. "Where are those drinks, baby girl? I am fucking parched."

"I'm just about to go and get them." She turns back around to look at me and Brad. "Do either of you guys want another?" I shake my head and Brad says that he would love another beer, proceeding to down the contents of the one that he is currently holding. It is at this moment that Martin seems to realise that we have an addition to our group. He looks at Brad and I stop myself from laughing at what I imagine it about to happen. If my first proper meeting with Martin is anything to go by, then this is going to be a fucking treat.

I slide my hand around Stacey's waist and bring her to my side. She looks up at me and smiles, knowing as I do that Martin is about to unleash his personality on Brad.

"And who do we have here?" Martin asks as he runs his eyes up and down Brad.

"Martin, this is Brad, Jake's brother," Stacey says. "Brad, this is Martin." She leaves it at that and goes silent to watch the show that Martin is about to put on.

"Hi, Martin," Brad says as he holds his hand out for Martin to shake.

"Well, well, well, aren't you a treat," Martin says as he takes Brad's hand and shakes it. Brad's face changes to one of shock and I bite on my lip to stop myself from laughing.

"Let me ask you something, Brad," Martin says as he moves towards Brad and leans in to whisper in his ear. I can't hear what Martin has said, but from the look on Brad's face, it has clearly rendered him speechless.

Brad stands there and splutters as he tries to form words, and I can no longer hold back my laughter. My body starts to shake, and I can feel Stacey's doing the same.

"Uh..."

"Oh relax," Martin says, letting Brad's hand go. "God, he's just as prudish as you, Jake."

"Hey, I am no prude," I say through my laughter.

"I beg to differ. There was a time when you had the same look on your face as he does right now," Martin says smirking.

"Yeah, okay." I concede defeat as he is absolutely right. I was shocked as shit when he first offered me the 'Martlove.'

"Come on, baby girl," he says, taking Stacey's hand in his. "Let's go and get the drinks. Brad looks like he could do with a beer to cool down." He winks at Brad and then him and Stacey walk off, heading to the bar.

"What the fuck was that about?" Brad says, still looking shocked.

"That was the whirlwind that is Martin." I take a swig of beer, chuckling away to myself.

"Fucking hell, I don't think I have ever met someone who is so forward."

"Really?" I find that very hard to believe, knowing what some of the women were like that he used to bring home.

"Seriously, bro. No woman has ever said what Martin just said to me." He sees the look on my face and then bursts out laughing himself.

We stand there, roaring with laughter, and it feels good. I know that I am still wary of Brad, and I don't completely trust his intentions, but right now, for the moment at least, it feels good to be laughing with my brother.

STACEY

I carry mine and Brad's drink back over to where Jake and Brad stand. Martin follows behind me, carrying his cocktail. Lydia informed me that Darren has been a godsend over the last few days. It seems that my choice to hire him was a good one. She doesn't mention Stephanie, but from what I can see, she seems to be holding her own.

I assure Lydia that I will return to work on Monday, which I think that she is grateful for. She has been a rock for me, running this place, but I can tell that she is tired. I feel bad that I am here having fun whilst she is working, but when I said as much to her, she just waved off my concerns and told me to enjoy myself.

As I reach Brad, I hand him his drink which he thanks me for. I place my drink on the table by Jake and am about to speak to him, when I hear "Starboy" by The Weeknd start to pump through the speakers. Martin's squeals behind me, grabs my hand, and drags me onto the dance floor. Ever since the song came out, Martin has said that it is his jam. I laugh as we both shake our hips to the music, people around us making room for Martin and his flailing arms. I enjoy the beat of the music as it pumps through the system, making the dance floor vibrate.

My back is to Jake, but I can feel his eyes watching me. As the song winds down and the DJ remixes in the next one, I feel my inhibitions leave me. Nine Inch Nails, "Closer," starts to play, making me very aware of Jake and his eyes roaming over my body. I turn to face him, his eyes filled with heat as I move to the beat. I feel Martin come up behind me, and I swear, he is the only guy that Jake would ever let me bump and grind with.

Martin's hands hold onto my hips and I move my ass in time with his, all the while keeping my eyes on Jake. He looks like he wants to pounce on me and rip my clothes off. I turn in Martin's arms, allowing Jake a view of my ass writhing to the beat. Martin grabs my ass, making me squeal from his actions.

"Martin!" I shout at him over the music.

"Oh relax, baby girl. Jake won't mind. In fact, I would say that our little dance is turning him on, if the bulge in his trousers is anything to go by." I gasp at his words.

"You shouldn't be looking at his bulge," I say playfully.

"It's kind of hard to miss." I laugh at him and we continue to dance to the song. I feel another pair of hands on my hips from behind and Martin lets go of me, giving me a wink before he turns and starts to grind up on some unsuspecting male.

I keep my body moving to the song, and I feel my hair being moved away from my neck. Lips graze my earlobe, and Jake's masculine scent swirls around me. Jake speaks the lyrics of the song, his voice low and filled with heat. My hand flies up to his neck, and I bring his lips down so they connect with my skin.

As he begins a delicious assault of kisses on my neck, everything around us disappears. In my mind, it is just Jake, me and the music. His hands grip my waist tighter as I grind my ass against his crotch. I don't fail to notice the low groan that he emits.

I close my eyes and enjoy the feel of him against me. As the song continues to play out, I can no longer hold onto my need for him.

I move my lips to his ear so that he can hear me when I speak. "I need you, Jake, *now*."

He moves quickly, jolting me back to reality in the process. He grabs my hand, pulls me off of the dance floor and in the direction of my office. He opens the door, and slams it shut behind us, pushing me up against the door and devouring my mouth as if he hasn't tasted me for days. I groan and claw at him, my hands roaming everywhere, and it still doesn't feel like it is enough.

I bite his bottom lip and our actions become frenzied. We pull at each other's clothes, our hands clumsy with our desperation for one another. I free Jake's cock and run my hand up and down it, feeling that his tip is already wet.

He pushes my shorts down, sliding my thong to the side and I lift my leg and hook it around his waist. I place his cock at my opening and take in a sharp breath as Jake slams into me. I cry out, grabbing his ass, needing more friction from him.

He begins a punishing rhythm as he grunts into my mouth. My back is slamming against the office door, but I don't care. All I care about right now is what this man is doing to me. Over and over again he plunges into me, and my grip on his ass tightens as I barrel towards my release.

"I'm coming, Jake, I'm coming," I say breathlessly. As I feel myself free-falling through my orgasm, Jake tightens his grip on my thighs and I feel him burst inside me.

"Fuck," he shouts as I tighten my muscles around him, determined to ride both of our releases to their full potential.

I place my hand over Jake's heart and I bring his hand up, so that it is placed over my heart too. I want him to feel how hard it is pounding. His is pounding just as much and he stares at me, questioningly. I lick my lips and take a few deep breaths before speaking.

"It's all for you, Jake," I say as I answer his silent question. "My heart beats for you, and only you." He rests his forehead against mine and, if it's possible, his heart beats even harder.

"I love you so much, Stace," he whispers. "I never thought that I would be lucky enough to find the great love of my life that people talk about."

He pulls his head back, and my eyes search his as he puts his feelings into words. "The very first time that I laid eyes on you, I knew that I had to have you. All those months ago, I watched you from across the dance floor. I was mesmerised by you back then, and I still am today. I used to laugh at those blokes who gushed over their partners, but that was because I didn't understand what they had."

He takes a few deep breaths before continuing. "Now, I understand. You are the reason that I understand." I let my hands come up to his face, placing my palms on his cheeks. "When you agreed to go home with me that night, all those months ago, I knew that it wouldn't be the end of us. I had no idea when I was going to see you again, but I knew that it would happen.

"When I saw you at the Bowden Hall six months later, my heart beat so fast that I was sure that you were going to be able to hear it. You looked incredible in your red dress." He closes his eyes, obviously picturing me in the red dress, and I am captivated by his words. "I can picture everything about that night as if it happened yesterday. That was the night that you stole my heart. I had no idea that I was going to fall for you so hard and so fast."

Tears well up in my eyes as I swallow down the lump that has formed in my throat. Jake opens his eyes and they are glistening, just as mine are. "I promise that I will love you, cherish you and worship you until the day that I die." A tear rolls down his cheek and it breaks me. I let a sob escape my throat as this man declares his love for me. I never realised that his feelings ran just as deep as mine do for him.

I press my lips to his, our tears mingling together, our breathing shallow, and our bodies heaving against one another. As our lips break apart, I wipe my thumbs across his cheeks, taking away the wetness that our tears have left. "You are my life, Stacey. All I want is for you to be happy."

"I am," I say, no hesitation in my reply. He smiles, and it makes my insides melt. I will never take our love for granted, and I know that we will always do everything that we can to make our relationship work.

Jake places a light kiss on my nose and pulls himself out of me. I pout at the loss of him inside me, and he chuckles. Guiding me to my private bathroom, we both clean ourselves up and then make ourselves presentable to return to the main room.

I go to open the office door, but Jake stops me.

"You know, if you had danced with any other man the way that you were dancing with Martin earlier, there would have been some serious punishments in store for you, lady." I raise one of my eyebrows in challenge to his words.

"Is that so?" He nods his head at me, making me want to behave badly just to see what punishments he might have in store. "Well, you could always give me a taster when we get home of what those punishments might be."

"You're a bad girl, Miss Paris."

"And you love it," I say as I open the door and start to lead Jake from my office.

"More than you know." His words bring a smile to my face as we enter the main room and proceed to spend the rest of the night dancing, drinking, laughing, and having fun.

CHAPTER TWENTY-THREE

STACEY

Monday has been a bitch of a day, and I still have another five hours before I can finish up and go home. I have been at The Den since nine o'clock this morning, catching up on everything that I have missed over the last week.

Lydia came in at ten o'clock to bring me up to speed with what she had done in my absence. It is now six o'clock, and The Den has just opened, students filtering in already after the start of their week at college or uni.

Darren and Susie are working the bar at the moment, but I am on hand for when it starts to get busy. Lydia sits at the end of the bar, waiting for me as I pour us both a drink. Non-alcoholic of course.

As I finish pouring our diet coke's, I walk around the bar to Lydia and sit down beside her.

"Listen, Stace, I had a thought," Lydia says, grabbing my attention. "Why don't you and Jake come round to mine for dinner on Thursday night? I think it's about time that we got Paul and Jake in the same room together and let them sort their shit out."

"I don't know, Lyd." I'm wary of her idea as I know that Jake has tried to contact Paul, resulting in Paul ignoring him.

"I feel like we need to do something. I know that Paul misses Jake, he's just too stubborn to admit it."

"Is Paul really still that mad with him?" I ask.

"I don't know." Lydia shrugs her shoulders as she speaks. "I have tried to get him to talk about it, but he just shuts down. I think that he is just pissed at how the whole situation turned out."

"I know that it was bad, but if you and I can get past it, then why can't Paul?" I don't really understand why he seems to have a bigger issue with it than the rest of us.

"I think it's more to do with how Jake handled it all. Jake went from being angry, to trying to hurt you, and then he took it out on everyone around him. In all the years that Paul has known him, he said that he had never seen Jake act that way before. Paul was mad on my behalf because I was mad at how Jake had treated you." I process what Lydia is saying, but it still confuses me that Paul is having difficulty with it all.

"Let me speak to Jake first. I don't really want to walk into anything that he doesn't feel comfortable with." There is no way that I am springing this on him by just showing up at Lydia's place. We are just getting back on track and I am not doing anything to fuck up our progress.

Lydia is about to reply to me when some guy goes crashing into the back of her, shoving her forward on her seat. I see her hands shoot out in front of her to stop her from smacking into the bar counter. I jump up off of my stool and whirl around to look at the guy who just knocked into her.

"HEY, ASSHOLE," I shout at him, as I move myself to stand in front of Lydia. The guy struggles to stand up straight and I see a couple of his mates laughing behind him.

"Sorry, love. I tripped," he slurs.

"You tripped?" I screech at him. "Did it ever occur to you to drink less and be more fucking careful?"

"It was an accident," he says with a shrug of his shoulder.

"It may have been an accident, but your accident has resulted in you smacking into a pregnant woman." His face pales at my comment, but I am not finished with him yet. "You need to leave, now." I am filled with rage as I feel Lydia's body shaking behind me.

The guy takes a step forward, obviously hoping that he is going to intimidate me.

"Who the fuck do you think you are?" he spits at me. "What's a pregnant woman doing in here anyway?" My eyes shift to look at his two pals, who are no longer laughing. They are slowly backing away instead of trying to take their repulsive friend with them.

I remain where I am, hands on my hips, unwilling to let this piece of shit make me feel threatened by him.

"Get out," I say the words loud but slow, just so he understands.

"I'm going nowhere, sweetheart." I am about to retaliate when a voice from behind him shouts out.

"I think that you are," the voice says as the guy is pulled away from me. He stumbles backwards and falls to the floor. My eyes fly up from the sprawling mess on the floor and I see that Brad is stood there, his hands balling into fists as he leans down and says something into the guys ear.

My eyes are wide as the guy scrambles to his feet and the bouncers come over to escort the guy off of the premises. I turn my attention to Lydia and put my arms around her.

"Are you okay, Lyd?" I ask her, worry threatening to overpower me.

"Yeah, I'm fine. Just a bit shaken." Her voice breaks, and a tear slides down her cheek.

"You need to get to the hospital and get checked over," I tell her.

"No, Stace, I'm fine. I don't want to go to hospital."

"Tough."

"Stace, please, I don't want any fuss. I'm just a bit shocked, that's all." She tries to plead with me, but I am taking no chances. I grab Lydia's phone out of her hand, find Paul's number, and hit the dial button. He answers immediately.

"Hi, beautiful," he says as he answers the phone.

"Uh, Paul, it's Stacey."

"Oh shit, sorry. Is everything okay?" he asks in a panic, clearly wondering why the hell I am phoning him from Lydia's phone.

"Not really. Lydia needs to get to a hospital. Some guy knocked into her, so she needs to go and get checked over."

"Fuck. I will be there in five minutes." The line goes dead and I place Lydia's phone in front of her, on the bar counter.

"You didn't have to do that," Lydia says to me as she sits back down on the stool.

"Yes, I did. You're pregnant, Lydia, and you need to make sure that everything is okay." I would never forgive myself if I just let her sit here and not get checked over.

My gaze wanders to Brad, who is stood behind Lydia, and I rub Lydia's back as she takes a sip of her drink.

"Thanks for that, Brad. That guy was a real asshole," I say to him, giving him an appreciative smile for his help.

"No problem. Although, I have to say, you are definitely one feisty chick," he says, chuckling.

"Just looking out for my friend."

"Remind me never to piss you or your friends off." He smiles at me and then turns his attention to Lydia. "Does it hurt anywhere?" he asks, and it is at this moment that I remember that he is a fucking doctor.

"Not really," she replies. We don't get to continue the conversation as Paul comes striding over, his eyes wide with worry. He clearly broke several speed limits to get here as it has only been about two minutes since I spoke to him. He envelopes Lydia in his arms and helps her up off of the stool. He promises to let me know what the hospital says, and then he whisks her away, leaving me feeling helpless as I stare after my friend. I hope that everything is okay.

I bite my lip and realise that I need to do everything I can to make Lydia's job safe whilst she is with child. Brad sits down on the stool that Lydia has just vacated and goes to order a beer, but I stop him. I make my way around the bar and pull a bottle of beer out of the fridge, opening it and placing it in front of him.

"On the house," I say, feeling like I need to thank him.

"Thanks," he says as he takes a swig of the drink. "So, anything else need doing around here, seeing as you seem keen to hand out free beers?" I laugh at his comment and shake my head.

"Not right now. You just relax and revel in the fact that you are the hero of the moment." My attention is diverted away from him by my phone ringing. "Excuse me," I say as I pull my phone from my pocket and answer the call.

"Hey, babe," I say as I see that Jake is the one calling me.

"Hi, gorgeous. How's things going at The Den?" he asks me. I spoke to him briefly earlier and told him that my head was fried from all of the paperwork that I had to catch up on.

"It's okay, well, it was until five minutes ago. Lydia has just been taken to hospital."

"Why?"

"Some drunken idiot shoved into her. I called Paul and he came to get her. They left a few moments ago. I figured it was better for her to get checked out than leave it and then something happens later on."

"Shit. I hope she's okay."

"Me too. Paul said that he would let me know."

"Maybe I should give him a call or something?" Jake says.

"I think that might be a good idea," I reply, knowing how much I need my friends in times of turmoil. It may be just what Jake needs to do to get Paul to speak to him again. "Anyway, it turns out that your brother is a bit of a hero right now."

"Brad?"

"Yeah. The guy that knocked into Lydia was getting in my face, Brad showed up and put the guy on his ass." The line goes silent and I wonder if the call has been disconnected. "Jake?"

"Yeah, I'm still here." I hear him let out a sigh and I know that it is because Brad is here. I know how Jake's mind works. We may have all had fun the other night, but Jake still doesn't trust Brad. He especially doesn't trust Brad's intentions around me. "I'm coming to see you."

"Don't be silly, Jake. You have had a long day."

"I don't care. I want to come and see you." I know that there is no point in arguing with him. He will come here now whether I tell him to or not.

"Okay. See you soon." I hang up the phone and place it back in my pocket.

Jake and I had a long talk about Brad yesterday. Brad was a bit of a bastard towards Jake for years, so it is hardly surprising that he is wary of him.

"Everything okay?" Brad asks me, downing the rest of his beer.

"Yeah. All good. Jake's on his way here now."

"He's pissed that I'm here and he's not, isn't he?" Brad asks me. I sigh and decide not to sugar coat my answer.

"Can you really blame him?" I say, raising my eyebrows at him.

"I guess not." He looks sad as he answers, and I feel a little bad that I am having this conversation with him, but my loyalty lies with Jake.

"You did some shitty things to him when you guys were younger. You just need to give him some time to get used to you being here again. If you want to be part of his life, then you need to show him that you have changed. You need to gain his trust back, and that is going to take more than a few days to achieve." Brad looks surprised by my words.

"You don't beat around the bush, do you?" he says, and I shrug my shoulders at him.

"What's the point in pussy-footing around?" Brad smirks at me and I see his shoulders relax a little.

"See, feisty," he says as he nods in my direction.

"I fight tooth and nail for the people that I love, and Jake is one of those people." My hands are braced on the bar counter and Brad moves his hand so that it covers mine. I still at his movement.

"Jake is lucky to have met you." His voice is so quiet that I almost don't hear him. I pull my hand away, feeling a little uncomfortable. Unsure of what to say, I let my eyes drift past Brad and I see that Jake is walking over to us. I smile and busy myself pouring him a scotch. I figure that he needs something a little stronger than a beer to put him at ease.

Jake reaches the bar counter and leans towards me, placing a kiss on my lips. As he takes a seat next to Brad on one of the bar stools, I place his drink in front of him.

"Thanks," he says as he picks up his drink and takes a sip.

"I like to look after my favourite customers," I say with a wink before I go to help Susie serve drinks to a group of students.

———

JAKE

As I sit and sip the glass of scotch that Stacey had waiting for me when I arrived, I watch her behind the bar as she busies herself with serving customers. She is wearing her skinny jeans which hug her ass, allowing me to see her curves, a white figure-hugging T-shirt, and her come-fuck-me black work boots.

I watch as she commands the bar, running it efficiently and smoothly whilst keeping the customers happy. Out of the corner of my eye, I notice that Brad is watching her also and I feel my jaw clench.

I rip my gaze from Stacey and turn my head to look at him. He must notice my movements as he fidgets on his seat and turns to face me.

"What are you doing here, Brad?" I ask him, wanting to know his reasons for being here.

"Enjoying a drink, bro. Why else would I be here?" he answers cockily. I finish the rest of my scotch and place the glass back on the bar.

"I don't know," I answer honestly. I have a fair idea of why he might have come here, but I am trying to be reasonable and put my thoughts to one side.

"Listen, bro, I have no hidden agenda here. I finished work and fancied a beer. I didn't want to go back to my room at the bed and breakfast, so I thought that I would come here." At this point, Stacey comes over, replacing my empty scotch glass with a full one. She winks at me and then returns to the other end of the bar.

"She's a good one," Brad says, nodding in Stacey's direction.

"Yes, she is."

"So, tell me, how did you two meet?" he asks. I don't particularly want to tell him the ins and outs, so I keep my answer short and simple.

"We met here, actually."

"Wow, don't go overboard with the details," Brad says sarcastically.

"I don't really see what business it is of yours," I answer, to which I hear Brad sigh loudly.

"I was just asking. Seeing as we have been getting on okay recently, I thought that I might get the chance to know more about your life. You know, for most families, this would be a normal conversation."

"Most families don't fuck the other ones over." I can't help the bite to my words as I speak.

"Jesus Christ, Jake, you gotta let that shit go, man." Brad runs a hand through his hair and I stare at him. "I know that I have fucked up in the past. I don't know how many times I can say sorry for that."

He takes a swig of his beer before continuing. "I know that you have bailed me out of plenty of situations in the past. I know that I have tried to fuck up every relationship that you have ever had. I know that you don't trust me, but I am telling you that I have changed. Believe me when I say that, moving to America showed me just how fucking lonely my life was."

He looks down at the bar, a sad look crossing his face. If I hadn't been burned by Brad before, then this would be the point where I would feel sorry for him. "Just give me a chance, bro."

I look to Stacey who gives me a smile as she walks to the till. I know that she wants me to give Brad a chance. She lost most of her family when she was a child. I know that she doesn't want me to throw away the chance to mend fences with Brad. I think about how emotional she got when she first told me about losing her parents, and then, in later years, her nan. I know that if I give Brad a chance to prove himself, then Stacey will be there for me every step of the way.

There will always be a part of me that is expecting him to fuck up again, but maybe it is time to let go of some of the resentment? I know that even if he wanted to, he would never be able to take Stacey from me. There is nothing he could do, or say, that would make her turn her back on me.

If there is some master plan behind his insistence to mend our broken relationship, then more fool him. As long as I have Stacey, I can get through anything.

"Okay," I say.

"Okay?" Brad says, looking a little confused by my answer.

"One more chance, Brad."

"Seriously?" he says, shock evident in his voice and on his face.

"Seriously." I give a nod of my head and then pick up my fresh glass of scotch. I sip the contents and see Brad down the remainder of his beer.

As his eyes settle back on Stacey, I make a promise to myself. I promise that if he ever does anything to show his true colours, then I will be ready for him.

Nothing mattered in my life when he screwed me over before, but now that I have something worth fighting for, he better be prepared to go to war.

STACEY

I am exhausted by the time that Jake and I get back home. He stayed until I had closed up and had Eric pick us up and bring us home. Brad stayed until the end too and then made his own way back to the bed and breakfast.

As I wearily get undressed and then make my way to bed, Jake is already waiting for me. I pull the cover back and he envelopes me in his arms.

We lie there, and I relish in the feel of his warm body curled around mine. We talked in the limo about his conversation with Brad, and I am glad that he is going to give him a chance to make things right between them. I know that Jake is still wary, but he is willing to try, and that is all that matters. I would give anything to have some family left around me, and I think that might have played a part in Jake's decision. I just hope that Brad is true to his word, and that he really does want to put the past behind them.

As I snuggle myself against Jake's body, I close my eyes and feel peace wash over me. My worries about Lydia were put to rest tonight when she text me to say that the doctor had checked her over and had said that she was fine. I told her that I would give her a call tomorrow and see how she is doing. I need to come up with a plan for her to be kept out of harm's way during her pregnancy whilst she is at work.

I feel Jake place a kiss on my shoulder as sleep starts to claim me. With the rollercoaster that we have been on for the last couple of months, I figure that this is our time for everything to run smoothly.

Jake and I deserve happiness, and I will do everything in my power to make sure that we don't let the actions of others ruin that.

CHAPTER TWENTY-FOUR

STACEY

Jake has already left for work by the time that I wake up. I have the day at home before I go to The Den tonight for the evening shift.

After catching up on all of the paperwork yesterday, I decide that today I will blitz the house and give it a clean. I get dressed in a pair of leggings and a long sleeved top and put my hair up. I make my way downstairs, my mobile phone in hand, and make myself a coffee. I sit at the kitchen island, and as I wait for my coffee to cool, I give Lydia a call.

"Morning, babes," she says as she answers the phone.

"Morning, Lyd. How are you feeling today?" I ask her.

"Oh, I'm fine, and so is the little jellybean."

"Jellybean?"

"Yeah, jellybean." She chuckles, and I laugh along with her.

"Well, I'm glad that the jellybean and you are okay."

"Me too, and despite my insistence that I am okay, Paul has taken the day off. He's currently making me some breakfast whilst I lie in bed. Honestly, he's more dramatic than me."

"Uh, I doubt that, Lyd," I say, laughing.

"Shush you. Anyway, how did the rest of your shift go?" she asks me.

"No problems. Brad stuck around until closing, and Jake showed up when I told him that Brad was there."

"Oh dear. Do I sense trouble?" Lydia knows bits about Brad and Jake's history, but she doesn't know all of it. Hell, I still don't think that I know the half of it. My knowledge of the situation stretches to knowing that Brad has always needed Jake to help him out, mostly with money, and of course the fact that Brad went off with the woman Jake was seeing before he went to America.

"Well, Jake says that he is willing to give Brad a chance, and I support him in that decision."

"I guess that only time will tell, huh?"

"I guess so."

"So, now that Jake and Paul are on speaking terms again, can we discuss you guys coming round on Thursday night?" Lydia asks me.

"Well, I guess it couldn't hurt." I haven't actually spoke to Jake yet about how things went down with Paul when he phoned him last night to check on Lydia.

"Fantastic! Come round for seven and I will cook." I can hear how excited she is, and I hope that this turns out to be a good idea.

"We can talk about your new role at work then too."

"New role?" she asks.

"Yes, but I'm not discussing it now. I will speak to you about it on Thursday. In the meantime, you are off work with full pay." I don't want her to worry about her finances at a time like this. The last thing that she needs is to be stressing about money.

"But—"

"No buts, Lydia. As your boss, I order you to take time off and relax."

"Uh, if you're sure?" she sounds a little hesitant, but I think that it is best for her to have some time off.

"Of course I'm sure." I can hear Paul speaking in the background and I presume that he is bringing her her breakfast. "Now, you enjoy your breakfast and get some rest."

"Thanks, Stace. I'll give you a text later."

"Love ya, Lyd."

"Love you too, babes." The phone goes dead and I place it on the kitchen island and pick up my now cooled down coffee. I finish my drink quickly and decide to get cracking on the housework, so that I can get it done and out of the way.

I go to the hallway and open the cleaning cupboard, taking the hoover out and through to the lounge. I pop a CD into the stereo, turning the volume up full when "Formation" by Beyoncé starts playing. I plug the hoover in and begin to clean, singing and dancing to the music at the same time.

The time passes quickly, and before I know it, I have cleaned the whole lounge. With the hoovering, polishing, and the fluffing of cushions done, I move into the kitchen. I start cleaning the worktops and "Try Me" by Jason Derulo starts playing. I flick the coffee machine on and make myself another cup whilst I dance to the beat of the music. Of course, when Jennifer Lopez starts to sing on the track, I think that I have morphed into her. I sing and dance around the kitchen as if my life depends on it, shimmying the cloth along the worktops, lost in my own little world.

When the song winds down and I stop shaking my hips, the sound of someone clapping behind me makes me scream. As I am screaming, I whirl around and see that Brad is stood in the kitchen doorway. He's grinning at me, but I am too shocked at seeing him standing there to register any words that he might be saying. My heart literally jumped into my throat when I heard him clapping behind me. I try to calm my erratic breathing, feeling irritation build up within me, and I feel my face form into a scowl as my mind wonders what the hell he is doing here.

"Brad," I say breathlessly, once I have managed to get my mouth to form words. "What the hell is wrong with you? You almost gave me a heart attack."

"Sorry, I didn't mean to scare you." He doesn't look too apologetic though if the smirk on his face is anything to go by.

"How did you get in here?" I ask.

"Through the front door, funnily enough," he responds sarcastically.

I didn't unlock the front door. How in the hell did he open it? Maybe Jake left it unlocked?

"Haven't you heard of knocking?" I say loudly as another song starts to play, making it impossible to talk at a normal level.

"I did knock, but clearly you couldn't hear me. Do you even have eardrums, Stace?" he shouts, chuckling at the same time. I huff and walk past him, going to the lounge to turn the music off. I walk back to the kitchen and see that Brad has made himself comfy on one of the stools at the kitchen island.

"What are you doing here anyway?" I ask, my tone a little bit harsher than intended.

"Well, I just wanted to see if you fancied grabbing some breakfast." He says it so innocently, as if we do this kind of thing on a regular basis. Thoughts of how he got in here fly from my head at his suggestion.

"Me?"

"Yes, Stace, you."

"But, why?" I am more than a little confused as to why he would want to get breakfast with me.

"I just thought that, with Jake deciding to give me a chance to make things up to him, that it would be a good idea to get to know you better. You are the most important person in his life after all."

"Um..." I have no idea what to say. I don't want to offend him, but I know that Jake wouldn't be comfortable knowing that I was out with Brad. I feel awkward, something that Brad obviously picks up on.

"Don't worry, Stace. I get it," he says, looking a little downcast as he speaks. "I guess Jake wouldn't be happy with me taking you out. I'm sorry, it was stupid of me to ask you."

I rack my brains for something to say, but there is nothing. If Brad had been in Jake's life when I first met him, then I am sure that this wouldn't even be an issue. But Brad wasn't here back then.

"Hey," I say quietly to get Brad's attention. He looks up at me from under his lashes. "It's a nice thought and all, but I think that you need to give Jake more time to get used to you being around before you suggest anything like this. You just need to be patient. It won't be easy, but it will be worth it in the end." I smile and hope that my words have softened the blow of me not taking him up on his offer. "Maybe we could all go out for drinks this weekend?" *In a neutral setting with plenty of other people around,* I add silently in my head.

"Will Martin be there?" He looks a little scared at the thought, and I laugh out loud. Martin really did put his personality on full display for Brad. It was hilarious to witness.

"I'm sure that he will be if he knows that you're going to be there. He has taken a shine to you," I say with a wink. He seems to relax at my comment and he starts to smile.

"Yes, he told me as much."

"I'm sure he did," I say, barely containing my laughter.

"Listen, Stace," he says, his tone turning serious. "I just wanted to say thank you to you."

"What for?" I ask, truly perplexed as to why he would be thanking me.

"For trying to help me. I know that you are the reason that Jake is tolerating having me around." I have no answer for him. I just nod my head and smile at him. "Anyway, I guess I should be going. I don't want Jake to have any reason to cut me out, and I guess by being here, that is a possibility."

I think he is hoping that I won't tell Jake that he showed up here unannounced, but I can't promise him that. I have no intention of hiding this from Jake.

"Jake will be fine," I tell him, not believing my words for one minute. "I will get him to call you about drinks at the weekend," I say as I walk him to the front door.

"Thanks, Stace. Take care," he says as he leaves, and I shut the front door behind him.

I let out a long breath of air and lock the front door before I go upstairs to get washed and changed, needing to go and see Jake straight away. I take a quick shower and pick out some clothes to wear. I put on my black, bootcut trousers, a purple fitted top and my shoe boots. I redo my hair and put it back into a ponytail, and I apply a light touch of make-up.

I am not looking forward to telling Jake about Brad, but I know that it has to be done, and there is no way that I want to tell him what just happened over the phone.

With adrenaline pumping through me, I make my way out of the house and to my car to drive to Jake's office.

———

JAKE

"Mr Waters, Miss Paris is here to see you," Valerie tells me through the intercom on my desk.

"Send her through, Valerie." I sit back in my office chair and watch the doors to my office. Stacey walks in a few seconds later, looking as delicious as ever. My cock starts to twitch, something it does every time I lay my eyes on this woman.

She walks around my desk and I turn my chair around, so that she can sit on my lap.

"Hi, handsome," she purrs before giving me a quick kiss on the lips. Even the sound of her voice gets my juices flowing.

I put my arms around her and hold her against my body. I pull her head down to me, the first kiss not being long enough. She opens her mouth, allowing my tongue to massage with hers. I hold the nape of her neck in place, and only when I feel that I have had my fill of her, do I loosen my grip.

She pulls back slightly and smiles. "I hope that you don't greet all of your visitors in that way, Waters," she says in a teasing tone.

"Of course not. I only reserve this type of treatment for special guests." She chuckles, and I love that we can have a bit of banter without her becoming needy or offended by my comments. "To what do I owe the pleasure of this unexpected visit?" An unexpected visit that I most definitely welcome.

"Well, I, uh... I have something to tell you," she says looking downwards, instantly putting me on edge. I know this woman's body language better than she does, and I know that she doesn't feel comfortable with whatever it is that she needs to tell me.

"What's wrong, Stace?"

"Why would there be anything wrong?"

"I know you, and I know that something is bothering you." I can see the worry in her eyes as she places her hands on my chest and takes a deep breath.

"You have to promise me that you won't get mad at what I am about to tell you."

"That's not exactly a great way to start the conversation, babe."

"Well, I'm not telling you until you promise," she says stubbornly. I study her face and I know that she is not willing to budge on this condition. If I want to know what is bothering her, then I need to keep my cool.

"I promise," I tell her. "Now what is it?"

"Brad came to the house just now." My body tenses at her words, but I remain silent, so that she can continue to speak. "He came by to ask me to go out to breakfast with him." My jaw clenches with each word that she speaks.

What the fuck is he playing at?

"I told him no, obviously," she says hurriedly. "He figured that by taking me out, he could thank me."

"Thank you for what?" I interrupt.

"He seems to think that the only reason that you are giving him a chance is because of me. He really does seem like he wants to build bridges with you, Jake."

"There's building bridges though, Stace, and then there is just going one step too fucking far." I can't help but be pissed off that he even suggested the idea of taking her out.

"That's why I said no. Obviously, I think that it would be good for you two to be on good terms again, but I would never jeopardise us by doing something that I know would upset you."

God, this woman is incredible.

She gets me.

She understands what makes me tick.

I lean forward and place a gentle, tender kiss on her lips.

"What was that for?" she asks, her eyes sparkling, the tension visibly leaving her body.

"Just because." I really didn't think that I could love her any more than I already do, but I guess that I can. "Thank you for telling me."

"You're welcome. I must say though, you are a lot calmer about this than I was expecting."

"I promised you that I wouldn't get mad, so I'm not." *Not on the outside anyway.*

"I said to him that we could go for drinks at the weekend, if you wanted to. He then looked a little scared about the fact that Martin could possibly be invited along." She laughs at the last bit and a smile crosses my lips.

"I think that Martin should definitely be invited."

"I thought that you might say that. Is Martin in today?" she asks me.

"Yeah. He was out this morning scouting out a possible location for the summer ball, but he should be back by now."

"Great. I'll stop by his office before I leave." She places a quick kiss on my cheek and then jumps off of my lap. "Don't forget that I am working tonight, so I will be home late again."

"I know," I say, giving her a playful pout in response. She rolls her eyes at me and starts to make her way to the office door. She stops before opening it and turns back to me. "Hey, Jake?"

"Mmm?"

"Did you lock the front door this morning when you left for work?"

"Of course I did. Why?"

"Oh, no reason. I'll see you tonight, if you're awake."

"Oh, I will be awake, don't you worry about that." She gives me her radiant smile and then closes the office door behind her.

Questions run through my head about what the hell Brad thinks he is playing at by going to my house and asking Stacey to go out with him.

But there is one question that is burning at the front of mind more than any others.

Why in the world would she ask me about locking the front door?

CHAPTER TWENTY-FIVE

STACEY

I manage to sneak out of work early as it is pretty quiet tonight. I leave Darren, Susie and Stephanie to it and drive myself back home. I haven't told Jake that I am coming home as I want to surprise him.

I pull onto the driveway to see that the house is in darkness and there is no sign of Jake's car. I exit the car and go to the front door, unlocking it. As I enter, I put the hallway light on and lock the door behind me, straining my ears for any indication that Jake may have decided to get Eric to drive him home.

The house is completely silent, so I shrug my shoulders, take my shoes off and make my way to the kitchen. I proceed to pour myself a glass of white wine which I then take upstairs with me. I enter our bedroom and take my wine through to the ensuite. A nice relaxing bath sounds like heaven right now, seeing as Jake isn't here to occupy my time.

I begin to run the bath and put the wine on the side so that I can undress. I put in an obscene amount of bubbles and inhale the lavender scent as the water continues to fill the bath tub. I leave the ensuite door slightly ajar, so that I can hear when Jake gets home. I strip off my clothes, leaving them in a pile on the floor and I finish running the bath.

As I get into the tub, goose-bumps rise on my skin from the welcoming heat. I sit back and take a sip of my wine as I try to relax, but it has been bugging me all day about how Brad got in here this morning. I believe Jake when he says that he locked the door, but that doesn't explain how Brad got in here.

With a weary sigh, I slide further down the bath tub, so that the bubbles are touching my chin. I could mention my concerns to Jake, but I don't want to give him even more doubts over Brad than he already has. Then again, I don't want to piss him off by not telling him seeing as I promised myself that I would never keep anything from him again after the abortion leaflets misunderstanding.

I close my eyes and will my brain to switch off for a while.

I need to stop obsessing over something so trivial.

JAKE

By the time I return to my house, it is just gone half past nine. I decided that it was time that I just went round to Paul's and spoke to him, face to face. We have been friends for a long time, and I think of him as more of a brother than I do Brad. I caught him just before he was about to leave to go and see Lydia. I may have spoken to him on the phone when Lydia had to go to hospital but speaking on a phone is different to speaking in person.

To start with, I thought he was going to tell me to fuck off, but he didn't. He invited me inside and offered me a beer, which I declined due to driving. I didn't want to keep him from Lydia, so I got straight to the point.

Once I asked him what was wrong, he let me have it. He shouted at me about how I handled the whole abortion situation, and I let him rant and rave at me. He was pissed that I had made Lydia feel as though she had to speak up and tell him the truth in front of others. He was pissed at how I had treated Stacey, knowing that it had made Lydia worry about her. I apologised to him, told him that he could hit me if that made him feel better, but he decided against that.

Once he was done shouting at me, he seemed to relax more. I think that he needed to tell me what an asshole I had been, and I completely agreed with him. He needed to rant at me, face to face, in order to feel better. He then told me that Lydia had invited Stacey and I over to her place on Thursday night for dinner, and that he hoped that we would both be there.

We shook hands before I left, and now I presume that it will all go back to normal again.

As I pull onto the drive, I see Stacey's car parked there and the lights on in the house.

Huh? She must have been able to get off of work early.

I waste no time in getting out of the car and making my way inside the house. I make sure the front door is locked behind me, Stacey's question from earlier about locking the front door bugging me, and I race upstairs to see where she is.

As I enter our bedroom, I see that the ensuite door has been left ajar. I quietly walk over and peek inside to see that Stacey is led in the bath, her head facing away from me. I push the door open some more and quietly step into the room.

I watch her as she lies there peacefully. I can't see any of her body, other than her head, as she has a ridiculous amount of bubbles filling the bathtub. I tip toe across the room, so that I am just behind her, and am about to lean down and place a kiss on her lips, when she startles me by speaking.

"I know that you're there, Waters," she says as she opens her eyes and stares up at me with those captivating blue pools of hers. "Why are you creeping about the place?" she says with a cheeky smile.

"I wasn't creeping," I reply.

"You so were."

"Would you prefer it if I were to creep somewhere else?" I ask, enjoying the easy flow of banter between the two of us.

"No. I would prefer it if you could undress yourself quickly and creep into this bath tub with me." She raises one eyebrow and her tongue runs along her bottom lip.

I don't need to be asked twice.

I strip my clothes off, leaving them on top of hers on the floor, and I jump into the bath tub, making some of the water and bubbles splash onto the floor.

"Jake!" she shrieks as water splashes her face and bubbles fly into the air. I laugh and pull her against me, angling her face and moving her closer, so that I can feel her lips on mine. She straddles me as her legs go either side of my hips, her sex hovering just above my, now hard, cock. My hands roam up and down her back, sliding against her smooth skin. I can feel her nipples harden against my chest, and I love how I have the power to turn her on so much.

I do that to her.

Me.

Her hands move to the tops of my thighs and my cock gives a twitch at her hands being so close. She glides her palm across my thigh and wraps her fingers around the bottom of my cock. I break my lips from hers and I take in her glazed eyes and flushed cheeks.

"Are you sure that you don't want me to creep away?" I whisper to her, teasingly.

"No way, Waters," she says against my lips, running her tongue along my bottom lip, making my body tingle. I watch her as she lowers herself onto my cock, taking me all the way. She slowly begins to rise and fall, making each plunge inside of her deliciously torturous.

I take her nipple into my mouth and suck, causing her to groan loudly. Her hands fly to my head, holding me against her breast. I flick her nipple with my tongue and then move to the other breast to repeat my actions.

I feel Stacey tighten around me, and it makes me want to take charge, but I don't. It's always hard for me to hold back and let her control our movements.

I will never get enough of her.

She speeds up slightly as her body shudders, and I know that she is close to her release. I place my thumb over her clit and move it in small circles. Her eyes connect with mine and she whispers my name. I hold the nape of her neck to stop her from looking away from me. I love watching her come. It's the most erotic thing that I have ever seen.

My release is building slowly, and I remove my hand from her clit, so that we can reach our heights at the same time. With her hips grinding and her breathing becoming laboured, her movements become quicker. Just when I think that she is about to come, she lifts herself up and slams down on me, causing my release to rush to the surface. I call out her name as she slams down on me again and then I am unfolding inside of her.

She cries out on the third slam and I feel her convulse around me, making my climax more intense. She moves one last time, and then her body collapses on top of mine.

I hold her shaking body close and bury my face in her neck as I catch my breath. Stacey lets her hands run up and down my arms, sighing with satisfaction.

"Now that is much better," she says against my ear.

"So, I take it that I am free to creep about the place in future then?"

"If it results in pleasure like that every time, then feel free to creep about all you like, Mr Waters."

CHAPTER TWENTY-SIX

STACEY

Jake and I are sat at the dining table, enjoying a cooked breakfast that I made for us before we both have to go to work. As I finish my food, I pick up mine and Jake's cups and make us another coffee. When I return, Jake has finished eating and is looking at his phone.

"Thanks," he says as I place his cup of coffee in front of him. I resume my place on the other side of the table and sit back in the chair.

"Everything okay over there?" I ask him, seeing that his brows are furrowed.

"Yeah," he replies, placing his phone on the table. I raise one eyebrow at him to question his answer and he sighs. "I tried to phone Brad yesterday and got no reply about going for drinks Saturday night. I also sent him a message about it, but he hasn't gotten back to me yet."

"Okay," I say slowly, wondering why Jake is worrying over Brad not texting him back. "Maybe he's just busy with work or something?"

"Hmm."

"Oh, I forgot to tell you that Lydia has invited us over for dinner on Thursday night," I say, diverting the conversation away from any mention of Brad.

"I know, Paul told me. I went to see him last night, before you had your wicked way with me in the bath tub." He winks at me and I smile at him, understanding why he never mentioned speaking to Paul before now. As soon as we got out of the bath and got dried, we went to bed and as soon as my head hit the pillow, I fell asleep.

"How was it when you saw him?"

"It was fine. He told me what had pissed him off and that's it." He shrugs his shoulders and sips his coffee. It always amazes me that blokes can move on from things quickly. If only it was that easy for us women.

"So, you're okay with going round there on Thursday?"

"Yeah."

"Okay then." My phone beeps to alert me to a text and I see that Martin has replied to the message that I left him yesterday. I stopped by his office after seeing Jake yesterday, but he wasn't there, so I sent him a text asking if he was free to come out on Saturday night.

Hell yeah, I'm free! What's the plan?
Martin x x

I send a text back informing him that I will pick him up and he can come to my house for drinks beforehand. Martin is yet to see where I live, so I figure it's about time that I show him around the place. I get a reply from him seconds later, and it seems that he can barely contain his excitement at coming to see the house. I laugh at his reply and Jake looks at me, clearly wondering what has made me chuckle.

"Martin is coming out on Saturday with us. It seems he is a little bit excited about me inviting him here first."

"Oh lord, he's going to inspect the place with a fine-tooth comb, isn't he?"

"Probably," I say, smiling.

"Listen, I have been thinking," Jake says, changing the subject. "I know that we talked about going away a while ago, but we haven't sorted out any dates yet."

"Well, I guess we could do something in a couple of months' time?" I say, not really wanting to up and leave when I haven't long gone back to work.

"A couple of months? I was hoping we could go before that."

"It's a nice thought, Jake, but I can't take time off from work again. I've only been back there a few days as it is, and I need to start interviewing people, to employ someone to take Lydia's place. There is no way that she can work the bar after what happened to her the other day." Jake sighs in frustration. I reach across the table and place my hand on his. "I would love nothing more than for us to get away for a break, but right now, it just isn't feasible." I give his hand a little squeeze and he gives me a slight smile.

I know that he is disappointed with my answer, but he can't expect me to drop everything, just like I wouldn't have thought that he would be able to with his business. I stand up, picking my plate and cup up at the same time, so that I can load them into the dishwasher.

When I return to the table to get Jake's plate, he grabs my hand and turns, so that he is facing me. I look down at him and am instantly captivated by his caramel pools.

"You are such a stubborn woman," he says in a low voice.

"I prefer the term assertive to stubborn," I reply with a shrug of my shoulders.

He laughs, and I smile at the sound that it makes. He stands up and his tall frame means that I have to tilt my head slightly to look at him.

"You know, when we do go away, it's going to be the best fucking holiday ever. Just the two of us. Work always used to come first in my life, but all that has changed. You come first now, and I can't wait to spend some time away from reality with you." *How does he always know just the right things to say?*

"You know it's my birthday in a couple of months' time?"

"Yes, Stace, I know when your birthday is." He furrows his brow, clearly not seeing why I am bringing this up.

"Well, why don't we go away then?"

"Really?"

"Yes. Really." I smile at him and a warmth spreads through me at the grin that spreads across his face.

"Done. I will book it today. Anywhere in particular you want to go?" he asks me, looking ridiculously excited.

"Surprise me," I whisper. He cups my face in his hands and brings his lips to mine. My phone ringing interrupts our embrace and we both groan in unison at having to pull apart. I walk to the kitchen island and see that Lydia is calling me.

"Good morning, Lyd. How's things?" I say as I answer the phone.

"Uh, are you free for a chat this morning?" She sounds a little nervous.

"What's wrong?"

"Nothing. I just need to speak to you. Can you come round to mine?"

"Okay, I can be with you in ten minutes."

"Great. I will have the coffee waiting." She clicks the phone off and I wonder why she sounds so cagey.

"I have to go," I say to Jake. "Lydia needs to see me."

"Is she okay?"

"I don't know as she didn't say much. I hope that nothing is wrong with the baby." I grab my handbag and give Jake a quick kiss. "What time will you be home?" I ask him.

"Not sure. I have a meeting at three this afternoon which could go on for a while."

"Okay, well, I will see you later then." I am not down to work tonight, so at least we will be able to spend some time together. I start to walk from the room, only to be stopped by Jake calling my name. I stop walking and turn to look at him.

"Let me know how Lydia is when you have spoken to her."

"Will do."

"I love you."

"Love you too," I say as I blow him a kiss. I rush out of the front door to my car and hope to God that Lydia is okay.

CHAPTER TWENTY-SEVEN

STACEY

I get to Lydia's and she ushers me into her flat, and through to her lounge. I take a seat on the sofa and see that she has coffee and biscuits laid out on the table. Lydia sits on the chair opposite me and I stare at her, waiting for her to speak.

"Thanks for coming round," she says.

"No problem. Now, what's the matter?" I don't beat around the bush.

"Paul has asked me to move in with him," she says quietly.

It takes me a few moments to answer her. I thought that she was going to tell me some bad news, but from what I can see, this is a good thing.

"Okay," I say slowly. "And that is a bad thing because?" She's going to have to help me out here as I am a little lost as to why she looks so downcast.

"Oh my gosh, I don't even know where to start." She sounds exasperated as she speaks. "Do you not think that it is too soon? What if I move in with him and everything goes to shit? My track record with men isn't great. What if I do something to mess our relationship up? What if I live with him and he decides that he doesn't want me anymore?" Lydia is rambling so fast that I almost can't keep up with her.

"Lyd, slow down. One question at a time."

"Sorry. I guess I'm just freaking out a little."

"A little? I would say that you are freaking out a lot," I point out to her.

She puts her head in her hands and sighs. "I just... I don't want to screw this up. I love Paul, and I don't want to do something to make him hate me."

"Why on earth would you ever make him hate you?"

"This is me, Stace," she says, her voice rising a little. "Nothing ever runs smoothly with me. I just keep thinking that, one day, Paul is going to wake up and wonder what the hell he ever saw in me." She has tears in her eyes when she looks at me, and my heart goes out to her.

"Stop that right now," I say firmly. "Stop putting yourself down, Lydia. Paul loves you, and he just wants to be with you. You guys are having a baby together for goodness sake."

"Exactly. What if he is just asking me because of the baby?" *Oh jeez.*

"Lydia, you need to calm down and take a breath." She actually does take a deep breath as she looks to me for answers. "Paul wouldn't ask you to move in if he didn't want you with him. You need to have more faith in yourself. Yes, you have had the misfortune of being with men who are assholes, but is there anyone who hasn't?" She doesn't answer me, but I can see that she is thinking about what I am saying. "Plus, you're going to be a little family in the near future. Do you really want to live in separate places when the baby is here?"

"I guess not," Lydia says.

"And who is to say that it is too soon? What happened to the hopeless romantic that is my best friend?"

"She got wise."

"Well, maybe she needs to remain wise but let that romantic spark back in. You deserve to be happy."

"Do you think?" She still sounds uncertain, but she doesn't look as downcast as she did when I first arrived here.

"Yes. Don't let your past experiences affect what you have now."

"Hmm."

"Do you not think that maybe, there is the slight possibility that your hormones are all over the place right now?"

"No. Why would my hormones have anything to do with this?" Lydia says, jumping on the defence rather quickly.

"Well, you are pregnant, as if that isn't stating the obvious, so you could just be overthinking things due to being hormonal."

"Well, I'm not," Lydia replies matter of factly. "You sound just like Paul. He said the same thing to me last night when I got annoyed that he hadn't picked a towel up off of the floor. I mean honestly, talk about an overreaction on his part." Lydia rolls her eyes and picks up a biscuit. I stifle a laugh as I hide my face behind my coffee cup. Yes, hormones are definitely playing a factor in all of this, but I am not going to be the one to argue that with her. If there is one thing that you should never do, it's piss a pregnant woman off.

"Listen, Lyd, whilst I'm here, I might as well tell you about the plan for work."

"The plan?"

"Yes. I thought that it would be a good idea for you to be paperwork based for the time being." I can see that she isn't overjoyed by this idea, but she needs to understand that she needs to be more careful now.

"Paperwork? But it's so boring."

"Believe me, I know, but it wouldn't be forever." Lydia goes quiet and it is at this moment that I hear her front door opening and closing. I turn my head to look at the hallway and see Nick appear a few seconds later. He leans against the door frame, hands in his pockets and a big grin on his face.

"Morning, ladies," he says, looking smug.

"Morning, Nick," I reply.

"Morning," Lydia says. "And I presume that the dopey look on your face is due to some piece of skirt that you spent the night with?" she asks him, not hiding the disgust in her voice.

"Oh, come on, sis, lighten up, will you?" Nick says, and I take that as my cue to leave.

"Lyd, I need to get to The Den. Think about what I said, and I will speak to you later." I stand up and walk over to give her a hug before turning to leave the lounge. Nick is still leaning against the door frame and I have to squeeze past him as he clearly doesn't want to move.

"See ya later, Stace," he says to my back as I walk towards the door. I wave without turning around and can hear Lydia shouting at him as I close the front door. With her moods all over the place, I don't envy Nick for the bollocking that I am sure she is giving him right now.

I walk out of the building and head to my car, only for my attention to be grabbed by a white piece of paper under my wind screen wiper. I frown as I approach the car and take the piece of paper out. It is folded in half, so I unfold it to see what it says.

Just to let you know that I am missing you already.
xxxxxxx

My first thoughts immediately go to Jake. He would be the only one to leave me a note like this. I smile at his thoughtfulness, even though it would have been easier for him to just text or ring me.

He must have been passing by this way for a meeting or something.

I fold the note back up and place it on the passenger seat of the car as I sit in the driver's seat. I push all thoughts of nice notes and naughty thankyou's out of my head as I drive to work. I have a busy day ahead and I can't let myself be distracted.

I am making today my mission to advertise for new bar staff.

CHAPTER TWENTY-EIGHT

STACEY

I have no idea where the last few days have gone. It has been nothing but a whirlwind, what with setting things up ready to interview potential new staff members as well as doing my bar shifts at The Den. I have also been showing Lydia all of the paperwork side of the business which has added to my workload.

I have barely seen Jake for the last few days. He has been busy trying to acquire another new deal, and by the time that I have arrived home from work, I am so tired that I have fallen asleep as soon as my head has touched the pillow. I am looking forward to tonight though. Jake and I are going to Lydia's flat for the evening and I can't wait to just unwind and spend some quality time with the people closest to me.

As I sit at my desk, I let out a loud groan. Lydia looks at me, raises one of her eyebrows and allows a smirk to grace her face. She is sat next to me, at my desk, and has been helping me conduct interviews for the past two hours.

The way that I am feeling right now, I would rather employ a couple of trained chimps than anyone that has walked through my office door.

"It's no good you smirking, Lydia."

"Oh, come on, Stace, even you have to admit that the last guy we interviewed was funny." I think that Lydia may have taken leave of her senses for a moment, but then she bursts out laughing and I can't help but laugh along with her.

The last guy we interviewed had said that he had previously worked at a hotel bar and had plenty of customer service skills. What he actually meant was that he had worked in a strip club some years ago, and by customer service skills, what he actually meant was that he knew how to spout cheesy chat-up lines and that is about it.

"Okay, the situation was kind of funny, but the guy himself, not so much."

"You mean you didn't like his opening line of, "Baby, did you fall from heaven, or am I dead?"" Lydia says in a badly put on male voice before she erupts into more laughter, wiping away the tears streaming down her face.

"Ugh. I think it's fair to say that he fluffed the interview before he even sat down on that seat," I say, pointing to the chair on the other side of my desk.

"I'm so glad that you asked me to do the interviews with you. I needed a good laugh," Lydia says, finally calming down a little.

"Glad to be of service." I smile at her and am pleased to see that she seems more relaxed than she has been in a while. Lydia picks the list of names up off of the desk and starts to study it.

"So, what's the name of the next potential candidate?" I ask her, leaning back in my chair and stifling a yawn. Lydia doesn't get a chance to answer as my office door opens, and Susie walks in with the next interviewee trailing behind her. Recognition washes over me as Susie steps to one side and Bonnie makes her way to the vacant chair on the other side of my desk.

"Bonnie?" I screech, sitting bolt upright.

"Hey, Stace. It's good to see you," she says cheerfully.

"Oh my God, it's been way too long since I last saw you," I say as I stand up and walk around the desk to give her a hug.

"It has. What happened to you? You always used to come to Danish for coffee, but then you just stopped?" Bonnie asks me as I gesture for her to sit down.

I take my seat back behind my desk and give her an apologetic look.

"I'm sorry. Things have just been a little hectic lately. I have been meaning to come and see you, but with running this place, I haven't had much spare time." It sounds like a lame excuse, but it is the truth. Things have been up and down for the last few months, but I don't have time to go into detail about it all now.

"Well, it would be nice to catch up with you when things aren't so crazy," Bonnie says, smiling.

"That would be good," I say as Bonnie and Lydia exchange hello's and how are you's. At the sight of Bonnie sat here, I suddenly feel hopeful. I know that Bonnie is a fantastic worker. She would be perfect for this place.

"So, shall we get on with the interview?" Lydia asks, placing the piece of paper in her hands down on the desk.

"Sure," I reply and direct my attention back to Bonnie. "So, what happened with your job at Danish?"

"New owners happened. They weren't very accommodating with the shift patterns, so I had to leave. I have been looking for something a little different. I saw the advert for bar staff a couple of days ago and, hey presto, here I am."

"Well, do you know how to pour drinks, open bottles, and mix cocktails?" I ask her.

"Um, yes, I can open bottles. I have poured pints at a previous bar job, but the only cocktails I have ever made have been the ones that I have prepared at home before a night out." She chews her lip nervously.

I look to Lydia who is sat there with a big grin on her face. She knows that I always got on well with Bonnie, and she knows what a hard worker Bonnie is from all of our times of going to Danish. I think Lydia already knows what I am about to do.

"That sounds good enough to me. Cocktails are easy to learn. You're hired," I tell her. Bonnie's eyes go wide, and Lydia starts nodding in agreement with me.

"Really? But don't you want to ask me anything else?" Bonnie says, clearly surprised by my offer of employment.

"Trust us, honey," Lydia says, "You are like a breath of fresh air in here today."

"It's true. Before you walked in, I had lost all hope," I say.

"I... I don't know what to say," Bonnie says.

"Just say that you accept the job," I tell her.

"Yes. Yes, I accept."

"Fab. Your training will start on Saturday night. Be here for six o'clock, and bring your relevant information, so that I can get you on the payroll as soon as possible," I say, putting a great big tick next to her name on the list.

"Yes, of course. Thank you so much, girls. I'm so grateful."

"No problem. The dress code is pretty casual. Just smart jeans or trousers, and a black or white top will be fine, and a pair of black shoes or boots," I inform her.

"Okay," Bonnie says, still looking shocked.

"Great," I say standing up. Bonnie follows suit and I walk around the desk, so that I can walk her to the office door. "We'll see you Saturday then."

"You sure will. Thank you," Bonnie says as she hugs me and then walks out to the main room where Susie will show her out.

I close the office door behind her and breathe a sigh of relief.

"Thank God she walked in," Lydia says, mimicking my thoughts.

"I know. She has certainly brightened up the day. Who have we got next?" I ask as I make my way back to my seat.

"Larry Darlington," Lydia answers.

The office door opens, and Susie escorts a young man into the room. Susie makes a swift exit as the man takes a seat, and Lydia's mouth drops open at the sight of Larry sitting before us. He has long pink dreadlocks, his T-shirt and jeans have rips everywhere, his face is covered in multiple piercings, and I can't see a scrap of skin that doesn't have a tattoo on it.

I turn to look at Lydia and she catches my eye. I bite my lip to stop myself from laughing.

I think it is safe to say that our afternoon may just be more interesting than our morning.

JAKE

I told Stacey that I would meet her at Lydia's due to my meeting finishing late. It's just gone seven by the time that I get to Lydia's flat, and I feel bad that I am so late for dinner. I know that Stacey has been looking forward to tonight, but a part of me wishes I could just have her to myself. The last few nights she has been exhausted when she has come home from work, and we have barely had any time to ourselves. I understand that she wants to prove that she can run The Den, but I really hope that the interviews she conducted today were a success. I miss my girl.

As I knock on Lydia's front door, I can hear laughter inside. I smile as I hear Stacey laughing. The door is swiftly opened by Paul.

"Hey, man," he says. "Come save me from the women. They have been talking in code ever since they got back from work. Whoever they interviewed today has sure given them some comedy value."

"I can hear them laughing from out here," I say as I enter the flat and take off my jacket. I hang it up by the door and follow Paul into the lounge. Lydia and Stacey are sat on the sofa, Stacey with her back to me, and Lydia is wiping tears from her face.

"Hi, Jake," Lydia says, prompting Stacey to turn around and look at me. I nod to Lydia, but my eyes are fixed on Stacey.

"Hi, babe," she says. She stands up off of the sofa and comes over to give me a hug. I wrap my arms around her waist and pull her against me, inhaling her scent as I bury my nose in her hair. I place a kiss on the end of her nose and she smiles at me.

"Hi, yourself," I reply as she steps out of my embrace and resumes her seat next to Lydia. She pats the sofa on the other side of her and I take that as my cue to sit down.

"Beer?" Paul asks me, and I nod my head in response. He disappears into the kitchen and I turn my attention to the ladies, who are still chuckling away.

"How did the interviews go today?" I ask and am greeted with another round of laughter from them. Paul comes back into the room with my beer and he takes a seat in the chair.

"See what I mean? I can't get any sense out of them," Paul says, sitting back in the chair and sipping his own beer.

"Oh, shush you," Lydia says. "If you had seen what we have today, then you would be laughing just as much as us."

"It's true," Stacey interrupts.

"Please tell me that you were able to hire someone?" I ask, needing her to tell me that she is going to lighten her workload.

"Actually, I hired two people."

"Seriously?" I ask her.

"Yeah. I'm not quite sure how I managed to get two though as it was slim pickings all day long." Stacey reaches forward and picks up her glass of wine and takes a sip. I watch as the liquid wets her lips and I have to clench my teeth together, so that my cock doesn't start to twitch at the mere sight.

A beeping starts going off in the kitchen, prompting Paul and Lydia to jump up at the same time.

"That's dinner ready. Give me a few minutes to dish up," Lydia says as she goes to exit the lounge. Paul follows her, ever the doting boyfriend. I can hear Lydia telling him that she is quite capable of dishing up the food by herself, but he doesn't come back to the lounge, so I presume that he is choosing to ignore her.

"So, if you hired two more people to work behind the bar, and Lydia is taking over the paperwork side of things, does this mean that I get you to myself a bit more?" I ask Stacey, pulling her closer to me. She slides onto my lap and links her hands behind my neck.

"Maybe," she teases as she lowers her lips to mine and kisses me. Her lips taste of the wine that she has been drinking, and she keeps the pressure minimal. She runs her tongue along my bottom lip and I have to remind myself that we are about to eat dinner with our friends.

"I can't wait to bury myself in you tonight, Miss Paris." She bites her bottom lip which makes me want to bite it for her. It is at this moment that Lydia calls out to us that we can go through to the kitchen. Stacey chuckles and jumps off of my lap, holding her hand out to me. I take her hand and stand up, groaning a little that we have been interrupted so quickly.

"All in good time, Waters. All in good time."

CHAPTER TWENTY-NINE

JAKE

I am led on the bed, flicking through the television channels, when Stacey walks out of the ensuite looking like a million fucking dollars. I have to physically stop myself from pouncing off the bed and ripping every piece of clothing from her body.

"See something that you like?" she asks me like the fucking minx that she is.

"Always," I reply honestly.

My eyes roam over her, from head to toe, and I honestly think that this woman, somehow, manages to become more beautiful by the day. Before I can say anything else, the doorbell rings. Stacey squeals and makes a hasty exit from the bedroom. I make myself get off of the bed and go to the ensuite to get myself ready. I know that this is going to be Martin arriving, and as much as I like Martin, I know that he is going to be so dramatic about every detail of the house that I feel the need to hide for a little longer.

STACEY

I run down the stairs and reach the ground floor, flinging the front door open to be greeted by the sight of Martin in the most outrageous outfit that I think I have ever seen him wear. A purple satin shirt, complete with billowing cuffs, red skinny jeans and a pair of blue dress shoes adorn his body.

"Baby girl," he says as he throws his arms around me and pulls me into a bear hug. When he steps back a few moments later, he looks me up and down and nods in approval. "Oh yes, I like it. Sexy black playsuit, check. Fuck me silver heels, check. Sexy, sleek hair, check. Dramatic make-up, check." I laugh at him and usher him inside.

I give Eric a wave and beckon him over, but he politely declines and gets back into the driver's seat of the limo. Jake organised Eric picking Martin up tonight in the limo, and I tried to object, but once Jake mentioned it to Martin there was no way that I was going to win that argument.

As I close the front door, Martin has already started walking down the hallway, so that he can start his inspection of the place.

"Oh my God. This house is like a mini mansion," he exclaims as he enters the lounge.

"Don't exaggerate, Martin." I roll my eyes at him.

"I'm not. Seriously, why the hell haven't I been invited here before now?" he asks as he collapses onto the sofa and sinks into the seat. "Wow. This sofa is like butter on your butt cheeks." He closes his eyes and lets out a loud sigh. I laugh in response and go to pull him off of the sofa, so that we can go to the kitchen and get a drink.

As I take hold of his hand, he playfully swats at me. "Oh no, just two more minutes. This is bliss."

"Come on, Martin. There will be plenty of other times for you to pamper your butt cheeks, but now isn't one of them." I pull on his hand and he reluctantly stands up.

"I seriously want to come for a sleepover."

"Fine. We will sort something out. Now, can we please go and get a drink?"

"Sure." Martin is still gawping around the room as I drag him behind me. Jake comes down the stairs at the same time as we enter the hallway. He looks divine in his dark denim jeans, ice blue shirt and black dress shoes. I swear, the man doesn't have to do anything to make himself look this good. I let my eyes rake over him and he grins at my obvious perusal of his body.

"Fucking unbelievable," Martin exclaims behind me, making me jump. "A limo, a gorgeous house, and you also have the perfect man in your life. Ugh. It's so not fair," he says as he flounces into the kitchen. Jake raises one eyebrow at me.

"Do I dare ask?" he says.

"Probably best not to," I advise him. "You look good, Waters."

"Just good?" he says as he stalks towards me, and I feel my heart beat speed up a notch.

"Okay, not just good. You look fucking hot." There is no point playing down how hot I think he looks. He can probably tell just by my body language alone anyway.

He smirks as he backs me up against the wall.

"Just so you know," he whispers in my ear, his heated breath causing goose-bumps to rise on my skin. "All I have wanted to do since you came out of the bathroom wearing that get up, is rip it off of you." His hands skim my sides and I shiver at his touch.

I am about to retaliate when a squeal from the kitchen brings me back to reality. I gently shove Jake away from me and rush into the kitchen to see if Martin is okay.

"What's wrong?" I ask Martin as I go and stand beside him, my eyes scanning everywhere to see why he squealed.

"Please tell me that you do not have a fucking hot tub in that garden?" he says comically, pointing to where the hot tub is situated.

"Um, okay. We don't have a hot tub in the garden," I say, sarcastically with a shrug of my shoulders.

"Don't play games with me, baby girl. A hot tub to add to your list is just even more unfair. Ugh. I am staying here for a whole weekend. I don't just want one night, I want two." I laugh at his dramatics.

"Whatever you say, Mart. Now, let me pour some drinks and then we can be on our way." I pull on his arm and drag him away from the sight of the hot tub. He sits on one of the stools at the kitchen island, and watches as I pour us each a gin, lemonade and lime. I pop a straw into Martin's glass and hand it to him.

"Thanks, baby girl." Jake walks into the kitchen just as I am finishing pouring him a scotch. I hand it to him and he places a kiss on the top of my head as he says thank you.

"Hey, Jake," Martin says.

"Yeah?"

"This house is the bomb." I stifle a laugh at Martin's description.

"Uh, thanks," Jake replies, taking a healthy swig of his scotch. Martin asks if he can go and use the toilet, so I direct him to the one on the first floor. I know that he will be snooping for a good ten minutes before he returns, giving me enough time to finish my drink before we leave.

"Did Brad ever get back to you about tonight?" I ask Jake.

"Nope. I guess he must have found a new 'hobby.'" I don't fail to notice the sarcasm in Jake's tone. I guess by 'hobby' he means woman.

"Oh, well, his loss," I say flippantly. I hear another squeal come from upstairs and I roll my eyes. "I better go and see what is making Martin squeal this time."

As I go to exit the kitchen, Jake stops me.

"Can I just ask, did I hear Martin say something about him staying here at some point?" he asks me, making me grin from ear to ear. "Oh God."

I laugh as I walk off and go in search of Martin and his screeching.

CHAPTER THIRTY

STACEY

We arrive at The Den just before six o'clock. Eric drops us off in the car park at the back as the place isn't open for customers yet. I let us in through the back door and I can already hear activity in the main room. Jake and Martin follow behind me as I head for the bar area, where Darren is currently trying to impress Bonnie by attempting to juggle with some lemons. Susie sees me and just rolls her eyes, and then goes back to getting things ready for opening time.

As I reach the bar counter, I clear my throat loudly, making Darren drop the three lemons that he was using for his entertainment. He whirls around and has wide eyes as he sees me stood there. I'm not sure why he looks so petrified though, it's not like I am the strictest boss in the world.

"Sorry, boss," Darren says as he scurries around on the floor to retrieve the lemons.

"Uh huh," I mumble as I look to Bonnie and see her trying to stifle a giggle. She has certainly dressed accordingly, which I knew that she would. She looks cute in black jeggings, black kitten heels and a white wrap around top. Her hair is pulled back into a high ponytail, and her minimal make-up allows her natural features to shine through.

"Is Tom not here yet?" I ask, to no one in particular.

"Who's Tom?" Susie says.

"He's the other new bar staff member."

"There's two new people?" Darren asks, still looking red-faced from his lemon juggling disaster.

"Yes. Is that a problem?" I ask him.

"No. No problem."

"Don't worry, Darren, I'm not replacing any of you guys." I see him physically breathe a sigh of relief at my words. Out of the corner of my eye, I see that Jake and Martin have taken a seat at the bar. Susie goes over to them and asks them what they want to drink. I don't even have to ask her to go over to them, she knows the drill.

Darren goes to the back of the bar and finishes setting up the cocktail station. He doesn't ask who Jake and Martin are, but I do notice that he keeps glancing at them. No doubt he will be asking Susie about them when I am out of ear shot.

"Bonnie," I say, startling her. "We can't wait any longer for Tom. It's nearly opening time and I need to show you a couple of things before then."

"Okay," she says coming to stand beside me.

"We'll go through to my office and then I will show you where you can put your stuff," I say, indicating to her handbag and coat.

"Cool."

"First though, there is someone that I would like you to meet." I smile at her and lead her over to Martin and Jake. "Obviously, you know Martin from our trips to Danish, so I don't need to introduce you to him."

"Hi, Bon," Martin pitches in.

"And this is Jake Waters. He owns this place," I tell her. Her eyes go wide, and she shifts on the spot. I guess she didn't expect to meet the owner on her first shift.

"Pleased to meet you," Jake says, ever the gentleman. He holds his hand out for her to shake, which she does.

"You too," Bonnie stammers.

"She forgot to mention that I am also her boyfriend," Jake says, nodding in my direction.

"I was just getting to that part," I say as I place my hands on my hips. "You'll have to excuse him, Bonnie, he can be a little needy at times." Jake chuckles and I know that he has taken my comment at its comedy value. Bonnie smiles as she watches the easy banter between us.

"Oh, please," Martin says as he sips his drink. "These two are just as bad as each other," he says, pointing at both me and Jake.

"Shush you," I say, smacking him playfully on the arm. I cut the conversation short because I don't have time to carry it on. I tell Jake and Martin that I need to show Bonnie a few things before we open and then I lead Bonnie to my office.

We go through some forms and Bonnie gives me her relevant information for the payroll. After that, I show her the staff room, which is Lydia's old office, and then I give her a quick rundown of the protocols expected.

I show her the weekly rota, which is up on a noticeboard in the staff room. I have already added her name to it for the coming week. I take her back to the bar area and see that customers are already starting to filter in. There is still no sign of Tom, so I busy myself showing Bonnie the ropes.

Darren is already busy making up cocktails and Susie is serving a couple of guys that have taken up residence at the bar. I see Jake's glass is empty, so I ask Bonnie to pour him a scotch and take it over to him. I decide that I should go and phone Tom to see where he is. I tell Bonnie that I will be back in a minute and go to my office and close the door behind me.

I walk to my desk and freeze on the spot when I see that there is a huge bouquet of flowers sitting in a vase on my desk. The flowers are beautiful, and I can see a card poking out of the top. I take the card and open it.

Nowhere near as beautiful as you.
Hope you like them.
xxxxx

I smile as I read the note and I instantly forget to ring Tom as I rush back out to the bar to thank Jake for the flowers. I come up behind him and place my hands on his shoulders, leaning down, so that my lips are by his ear.

"Thank you," I say as move my body to the side of him, so I can look at his handsome face.

"Thank you for what?" he asks me, looking genuinely confused. I know that Jake can put on an act when he wants to, so I take no notice of his confusion.

"For the flowers. They're stunning." I place a light kiss on his lips.

"What flowers?" I roll my eyes at him.

"The ones that are sat in my office. The ones that you had delivered here with this note," I say, handing him the piece of card with writing on. He takes the card and reads it, but he doesn't smile. In fact, he looks pissed off.

Before I can say anything else, Jake grabs my hand and leads me out of the main room and back to my office. He closes the door behind us and looks over at my desk.

He inspects the flowers as if they are omitting a nasty stench.

"I didn't send you these, Stacey." His mouth sets into a line and I can see that he is clenching his jaw.

"You must have," I reply, but I don't sound so sure. "Who else would send me flowers?"

"Fuck knows, but it wasn't me." He walks over to the offending flowers and studies them like he is going to get answers from them. I wrap my arms around myself and start to feel uneasy.

If it wasn't Jake, then who was it?
Someone has obviously been in my office and I don't know who the hell it is.

A sense of unease creeps through me.

The last person to creep about this place was Caitlin. I know that it isn't her this time, but some of the same feelings resurface.

"The camera's," I say to Jake as I have a lightbulb moment. He turns to look at me, clearly understanding where I am going with this. He takes a seat at my desk and switches my laptop on. Thank God Jake had extra cameras installed after the Caitlin fiasco. Looking at the footage will hopefully show us who has been in here.

Jake brings up the relevant programme and brings up the camera footage.

"So, these weren't in here when you came in with Bonnie?" Jake asks me.

"No."

"So, it has happened in last thirty minutes or so?"

"I guess so."

"Right. I'll go back and find you and Bonnie in here, and then we will just have to watch to see who came in here and left the flowers."

"Okay." I peer over Jake's shoulder as he finds the correct place on the footage and hits the play button. I can feel the tension pulsate around us as we watch avidly to see who is going to appear on the camera.

After ten minutes, Jake pulls me onto his lap and wraps his arms around me. I take comfort from him and hope to God that we don't have another Caitlin-type-scenario on our hands. I know that I am probably overreacting, but being stabbed has made me warier, as it probably would most people.

Another five minutes go by of watching nothing, but then the office door opens, and I sit forward to get closer to the computer. Jake does the same and we watch in silence as someone in a black hoody walks into the room with the flowers. The person keeps their head down the whole time. It definitely looks like a man from the build of the person and from the baggy jeans and trainers.

"Who is that?" I whisper as the person places the flowers on the desk and then they leave the room just as quickly as they entered it.

"I don't know, but I intend to find out," Jake says. He gently lifts me off of his lap, so that I am standing, and then he gets to work looking at all of the other cameras in the building.

"I'll go and get us a drink," I say, knowing that Jake will be reluctant to leave my office until he has found answers.

I return to the main room and go behind the bar to pour Jake and I a drink. I also make another drink for Martin, but there is no sign of him. I leave it behind the bar and tell Susie to let Martin know that I am in my office when he returns. I quickly check in with Bonnie, but she waves me away and says that she is doing fine. The Den is busy but the three of them can handle it for now.

I return to the office, drinks in hand, and give Jake his as he keeps his gaze fixed on the computer screen.

"Any luck?" I ask him.

"I've traced the person through the whole building, but I am yet to be able to see their face clearly. Whoever this is, knows where each and every camera is. They don't want to be caught."

"Great," I say sarcastically. I can't believe that yet another person is trying to mess with us. I feel anger build inside of me.

Why can't we just be left alone?

"I will find out who this is," Jake says, taking my hand in his and squeezing gently.

"Even if you do, when will this end?" I say, exasperated by it all. Jake frowns at me and I quickly explain my outburst. "Why are there so many people willing to interfere in our lives, Jake? I'm so fed up of fighting. I don't want to fight anymore."

Jake stands up and pulls me into his arms, holding me close to his chest. I wrap my arms around his waist and close my eyes. I may not want to fight, but I will. I would fight with everything that I have for our relationship.

It is at this moment that I remember the note that was left on my car.

"Oh my God, the note," I say out loud, causing Jake to loosen his grip on me a little.

"What note?" he asks.

"There was a note left on my car the other day. I presumed it was you that had left it."

"When was this?"

"When I went to Lydia's the other morning. I came out of her flat and the note was on the windshield. It just said, 'missing you already,' so I thought that maybe you had driven past and put it there. I forgot to mention anything as it has been so busy around here."

"Where is the note now?"

"Still in my car." I see Jake's jaw begin to tick.

My office door bursts open, startling me, and Martin walks in.

"There you two are. God, a man goes for one little dance and the two of you bugger off like he never existed," Martin says, waltzing in and taking a seat on the sofa.

"Sorry, Mart," I say, breaking away from Jake and going over to Martin and sitting beside him.

"It's okay. I actually found a rather nice young man to talk to."

"Oh yeah?" I say, and Martin starts giggling like a love-struck teenager. "Well, why don't we get out there and show him how to party?"

"Yes!" Martin says, jumping up from the sofa. I look to Jake as I stand up and he gives a slight nod of his head towards the computer, signalling that he will be staying in here, and probably keeping an eye on me in the process.

"Come on, baby girl. Let's go and booty shake," Martin screeches as he grabs my hand and pulls me out of my office. We hit the dance floor and start to move in rhythm to the music.

Tonight should have just been about having fun, but instead, I now need to find out who has been leaving stuff for me, and why.

I thought I was done with being followed, but obviously not.

Martin and I dance through a couple more songs and then I leave him to go and get us some more drinks. I need to try and distract my racing mind and not give Martin any cause to worry that I am acting differently. So far, I seem to be doing a good job of that.

As I approach the bar, I see that Bonnie is serving a guy who has his back to me, and she looks all dopey-eyed. I stand beside the guy and when I look to see his face, I see that it is Brad. He hasn't noticed me yet as he is too busy gazing at Bonnie. I smile and lean closer, so that he will be able to hear me speak.

"You're not distracting my new staff member are you, Brad?" I ask him, making him jump. He turns to face me and smiles.

"Not at all. I'm just checking that this young lady isn't being hassled by any men," he replies.

I raise an eyebrow at him. "Right, you mean besides being hassled by you of course?"

"Hey, I am a gentleman. I don't hassle, I just charm."

"Uh huh." I notice that Bonnie is looking from me to Brad and I inform her that Brad is Jake's brother.

"Wow. Good looks really do run in the family, huh?" Bonnie says. I'm guessing that she didn't mean to say that out loud, seeing as her hand is now clamped over her mouth.

"I guess so," I say, grinning at her faux pas. She quickly scurries away, her face red with embarrassment.

"Ah, Stace, I was making good headway until you came along." He says it in a joking manner and then pouts at me, making me laugh.

"Don't blame me if your techniques aren't having the desired effect. Maybe you should up your game?"

"Hmm. Maybe I already have." The way he speaks and stares at me, makes me feel like he is talking about something else. I don't know what, but his answer definitely has a double meaning. Luckily for me, Martin comes bounding over and puts his arm round my shoulders.

"Where are those drinks, baby girl," he asks impatiently. His eyes wander to Brad, and he starts to grin. "Oh, well, if this is why you are taking so long then, please, take all the time in the world." I roll my eyes at him and Brad's smile suddenly drops from his face.

"I'll just go behind the bar and get our drinks myself. Brad, do you want another?" I ask him.

"Yes, please," he says, gulping back the rest of his beer. I chuckle as I make my way behind the bar and busy myself getting the drinks ready. I only have a diet coke as I need to keep a clear head, just in case I need to serve on the bar at some point. If that Tom guy had bothered to show up, then I wouldn't have had to worry at all. I decide here and now, that Tom is a lost cause. If he hasn't showed up for his first shift on time, then he clearly doesn't want the job that much.

I sigh as I take Brad and Martin their drinks. I will probably end up having to select one of the other not-so-great candidates that I interviewed the other day. I groan at the thought.

I pick up my drink and tell the guys that I am going to my office to check on Jake. Brad decides to follow me, but Martin returns to the dance floor. I open my office door and Brad follows me inside. Jake looks up from the computer screen and I see his face harden slightly when he sees Brad emerge from behind me.

"Hey, bro," Brad says, taking the seat opposite Jake, on the other side of my desk.

"You showed up then," Jake says, his jaw ticking with annoyance.

"Of course I showed up. Didn't you think that I would?" Brad asks, a smirk crossing his face. I walk around to stand by Jake and to take a quick look at the computer screen to see if he has found any clearer images. Jake doesn't answer Brad and instead turns his attention back to the computer. "What are you guys doing anyway?"

"Oh, we're just—"

"Checking some accounts," Jake says, interrupting me. I give him a quizzical look and the look in his eyes tells me that he doesn't want Brad to know what we are looking for. I close my mouth and take the silent hint that he is giving me.

"Seriously? On a Saturday night?"

"Yes, Brad. It's part of running your own business," Jake replies.

"Jeez, it's the weekend, man, leave work alone for one night." Brad rolls his eyes and I start to feel a little bit awkward at the uneasy words between the two brothers. "Nice flowers," Brad remarks, his eyes settling on the large bouquet that sits on the floor, beside my desk.

I tense at his words and place my hand on Jake's arm to steady myself.

"Uh huh," is all I can think to say.

"What's he done this time to buy you a bouquet like that?" Brad says, nodding his head towards Jake but keeping his eyes fixed on me for an answer. I immediately try to rack my brains for a suitable answer to cover up the fact that they have been left by some creep.

"They're not from me," Jake says, startling me.

"Wow, you got some competition then, bro," Brad says, chuckling away at his own comment.

"They're from a supplier who won't take no for an answer," I say, pleased with myself that I have thought of something to say.

"You wanna keep an eye on that supplier, Jake," Brad says with a wink.

"He doesn't need to worry," I say, putting my arms around Jake. I lean down and put my cheek next to his. "I'm not going anywhere."

I place a kiss on Jake's cheek and I feel some of the tension leave his body from my touch and my words.

"Uh, I think I'm gonna head back to the bar and get another drink. Are you two coming?" Brad asks as he stands up.

"Be there in a minute," Jake says as he fixes his eyes on mine. I hear Brad sigh and then turn to leave my office.

When I hear the door click closed, I move my head forward and lock my lips with Jake's.

"Do you know how much I love you?" Jake says when we break apart.

"Hmm, you may have mentioned it once or twice." I love that he has no hang-ups about telling me what I mean to him.

"Come on," I say, grabbing his hand. "Let's go and have some fun. We can worry about the flowers tomorrow." I expect him to argue with me, but he doesn't. I just want to have a good time, enjoy myself and forget about whoever it was in my office.

The problem will still be there tomorrow, and I have no doubt that Jake will be doing everything that he can to find out who the culprit is.

CHAPTER THIRTY-ONE

STACEY

It's been a couple of days since the offending flowers were delivered to my office. Jake has been scouring the camera footage morning, noon and night. I finally took the laptop off of him last night and hid it from him. He's driving himself crazy trying to figure out who it was that sent them, and also the note that was left on my car. He has upped the security at The Den, and I swear that he is watching the cameras each and every time that I am here.

I am currently sat in my office and I know that he will be sat at his desk, watching me. It doesn't creep me out that he does this as I know that he is just worried about my safety. I know that after what happened with Caitlin, it frightens him that there is some other loon out to get me. I have tried to reassure him that the security guys wouldn't let anything happen to me, but if watching the cameras gives him peace of mind, then I'm not going to argue with him.

I am typing up the rota for next week when there is a knock on my office door.

"Come in," I shout out, looking up from the computer screen. Bonnie appears from behind the door and walks over to my desk. "Everything okay, Bonnie?"

"I guess so," she says as she takes a seat and lets out a loud sigh.

"Uh huh. Out with it." I know that something is bugging her. She's usually so upbeat, so I am not used to seeing her looking so fed up.

"I feel a bit silly saying this out loud, but... I can't get him out of my head, Stace."

"Who?"

"Brad." She sighs again, but this time she has a dreamy look on her face. "He's got the most mesmerising eyes that I have ever seen." I smile at her. I can definitely agree with her that the Water's family gene for eye colour is strong. Jake's striking eyes were what first attracted me to him.

"Continue," I prompt her, knowing that there is probably more that she wants to say.

"I just can't stop thinking about him. I feel like I am going crazy. Maybe I am crazy? No guy has ever made me think about them like this before. He just... He oozes sex appeal and masculinity. You know what I mean?" she finishes, looking at me for answers.

"Well, I can understand the way that you are feeling. What you are experiencing right now is similar to what I felt about Jake. Hell, I still feel that way about Jake." Now I am probably the one looking all dreamy-eyed. I shake my head to snap myself out of my daze. "Maybe you could ask Brad out for a drink?"

"I can't ask him out!" Bonnie exclaims.

"Why not?" I laugh.

"Because he is way out of my league, Stace."

"Don't be ridiculous," I scold her. "What is it with my friends and putting themselves down?" I don't expect her to answer that, I am just venting out loud. "Listen, I can have a word with him, if you like?" Bonnie's eyes widen at my suggestion and I quickly try to put her mind at ease. "I would be subtle, I promise."

Before she can answer me however, there is another knock on my office door, and the man in question comes breezing into my office.

"Shit," Bonnie whispers as her head whips round and clocks Brad walking towards my desk.

"Well, well, if it isn't the beautiful Bonnie," Brad says, working his charm. Bonnie blushes and giggles like a school girl.

"That will be all, Bonnie. You can go back to the main room now," I say, dismissing her. She nods her head and scrambles to her feet. I watch her as she casually tries to saunter out of the room, but the slight shake in her knees is a dead giveaway that she is putting on a front.

"Good to see you again," Brad says, sitting in the chair that Bonnie has just vacated.

"You too," Bonnie replies. I roll my eyes and cringe slightly at the way her voice sounds all breathless.

Bloody hell, is that what I sound like when I am around Jake? I'd like to think that I have a little bit more sass than that.

Bonnie eventually leaves the office, shutting the door behind her, and I turn my attention to Brad as I wonder why on earth he is sitting in my office.

"So, what brings you here?" I ask, knowing that Jake won't be too pleased if he is watching the cameras.

"I just thought that I would come and see my favourite sis-in-law."

Sis-in-law? What is he talking about?

He obviously notices the shock on my face from his comment and he smirks. "Calm down, only joking. Although, you practically are. Jake has never been serious about anyone else."

"Why are you really here, Brad?" He seems to be side-stepping whatever it is that he came to say. I may sound blunt, but I just want him to get to the point.

"What, no offer of a drink first?" he asks, putting his arms out either side of him in astonishment.

"You have just walked by the bar. You could have gotten yourself a drink then." Brad starts to laugh, although I don't really see why.

"I can see why my brother loves you, Stacey. You are one special lady. I just hope that he realises how lucky he is to have you." His words leave me shocked.

"Uh, thanks," I say, awkwardly.

"Relax, I don't mean anything by it. I'm just pleased for Jake, that's all." I know that Brad is speaking, but I fail to see any sincerity in his face. It's almost like the words have been rehearsed, and I start to feel uneasy.

"So, you came down here, just to tell me how lucky you think Jake is?"

"No." Brad clears his throat and shifts in the chair. He brings his left leg up and crosses it over his right leg. This may be a perfectly normal action, but it makes my blood run cold. The reason being that, his shoes look just like the ones that the flower guy had on. I should know, Jake blew the images up and has looked at them countless times. "I came to see what you really thought of the flowers now that Jake isn't here."

My eyes fly up to his face, and my mouth drops open.

"What?" I say in a small voice.

"I asked you what you really thought of the flowers that I left for you."

"That was you?"

"Yes. Although, I did have some help." I stare at him, flabbergasted. He decides to take my shocked state as a sign to continue talking. "I know that this place is fitted with cameras, so I needed someone to scope the place out for me properly. Did you not wonder why Tom never showed up?"

"You and Tom?"

"Yes, Stacey. Me and Tom. You see, I needed to get an idea of where all of the cameras were, so that I could hide my face. I also know that it is only a matter of time before Jake finds out that it was me who sent you the flowers, and of course the note that I left on your car. I knew that he would want to know who sent them, but I didn't expect him to go all FBI on my ass."

"But... Why?"

"I like you. Simple." He says it without a care in the world. I don't know what planet that he thinks he is living on, but once Jake finds out, I am certain that he is going to brought back down to earth with a bump.

"But you don't have to buy flowers or leave notes for someone just because you like them." I am trying to think of an appropriate reason for him doing this, but nothing is coming to me.

"When they have a connection, like we do, then people send flowers." He speaks with such confidence that I almost want to laugh at him.

He can't be serious right now.

"What connection?" At this point, he stands and comes around the desk. I shift back in my seat, feeling more than a little uncomfortable. He perches on the edge of my desk, facing me, and smiles.

"You must feel it, Stace. Don't deny it. Since the first day I met you, there has been something. In my doctor's office, you wanted me. I know that you did." My heart rate accelerates, but not in a good way. I have been trapped in an office before, and right now, I feel on edge. I don't like it, and I need to diffuse whatever the hell is going on.

My brain spins as I process the amount of people who have tried to screw Jake and I over. My eyes stare at the floor, and Brad takes this as his opportunity to take hold of my hand. I try to pull it out of his grasp, but his grip is firm.

"Brad, I have no idea what you are talking about. What I do know though is that you need to let go of my hand," I say as I try to free myself from his grasp. He doesn't listen. He holds on tighter, and I pray that Jake isn't witnessing this. If he is, then he is going to be going mental.

My office phone starts to ring, and I peek around Brad at it. I desperately want to answer it. I go to move, but Brad blocks my way.

"You can't dismiss me, Stacey." He places my hand over his heart and it is beating wildly.

"Please let go of my hand."

"No. I need you to admit what you feel for me. I need to hear you say that you want me."

"But I don't want you. I love Jake!" I screech at him, my patience running thin.

"I'm not saying that you don't, but you can want me at the same time." His eyes plead with me to give him the answer that he wants, but I can't.

"I'm sorry, Brad," I say with a shake of my head. "I just don't feel that way about you."

"Yes, you do."

"No, I don't!" I close my eyes in frustration and Brad finally lets go of my hand. My eyes snap open and I hold my hands to my chest, so that he can't grab one of them again. "You need to stop this, Brad. If Jake finds out about this, then he is never going to speak to you again."

"I don't care," he replies with a shrug of his shoulders.

"You don't care? You don't care?" I shout, my anger rising to the surface. "If you don't care then why the fuck did you come back?" I am on my feet now. Rage courses through me.

"To screw with him. I came back to screw with Jake." My next move shocks Brad and myself as my hand flies out and slaps him hard across the face. His head turns from the force of my slap, and it is at this moment that I see that Jake has entered my office.

CHAPTER THIRTY-TWO

JAKE

Two seconds ago, I had a smile on my face.

Two seconds ago, all I wanted to do was have a quiet drink whilst I surprised my girlfriend with a visit to her office.

Two seconds ago, all I wanted to do was relax.

That is clearly not going to be the case as I have just walked into Stacey's office to the sight of her smacking Brad around the face.

Shock doesn't even come close to what I am feeling right now.

"What's going on?" I say, finding my voice. I close the office door and step closer to Stacey's desk. Her eyes are wide, and I keep my gaze fixed on her, ignoring Brad, who is rubbing his cheek.

"She's fucking crazy," Brad says, his answer instantly pissing me off. I clench my fists at my sides and turn to look at him.

"Don't talk about her like that."

"Fucking hell, she really has done a number on you, hasn't she?" Brad's cocky nature shines through. He moves around her desk and away from her.

"You bastard," Stacey says, her words directed at Brad.

"Me? You're the one who just tried to hit on me," Brad says. My pulse quickens, and I have no doubt in my mind that he is lying. "You clearly don't know her very well, bro. You wanna get rid of her before she fucks you over."

With that, Stacey rounds her desk and is walking towards Brad, but I catch hold of her arm, halting her in her tracks.

She looks at me, her eyes pleading. "He's lying, Jake."

"I know," I whisper to her, not doubting her for a second. I say the words quietly, so that Brad can't hear me answer her. I can feel her body trembling with rage, and all I want to do is take her in my arms and make her feel better, but I can't do that right now. I need to deal with Brad first.

I move her, so that she is stood behind me, effectively making my body a shield between the two of them. I face Brad and stare at him intently.

"It would be a really good idea for you to tell the truth right now." I fold my arms across my chest and I try to push down the anger that I am feeling. I need to hear his explanation and see if he is going to spout a load of bullshit at me.

"I came in here to see if she wanted a drink, and that is when she made a pass at me."

"What?" Stacey screeches behind me. I move my hand back and take her hand in mine, squeezing gently to let her know that I am not buying his story.

"She grabbed hold of my hand and started going on about how we had a special connection. When I turned her down, she slapped me and that is when you walked in." He shrugs his shoulders as if this is a normal, everyday occurrence for him. For all I know, it is, but I will be damned if he is going to try and wreck what Stacey and I have together. I can feel the tension pouring off of Stacey behind me. Her breathing is loud, and I know that it must be taking all of her willpower to keep quiet. "You have to believe me, bro."

I actually want to laugh at him at this point, but I don't. I turn my body, so that I am looking at Stacey.

"Would you like to tell me what really happened now?" I say to her. Stacey starts to speak, and each time Brad tries to interrupt, I tell him to shut up. I heard his pathetic version, now I want to hear the truth.

When she has finished, I simply place a kiss on her hand and then I turn back to Brad.

"You're not going to believe the crap that just came out of her mouth, are you?" he asks, and I can see that he is starting to look worried.

He knows that I believe her.

He knows that I know that he is lying.

I am quite proud of myself for not flying across the room and punching him in the face.

I let the tension simmer for a few minutes as I watch Brad start to squirm. If I'm not mistaken, I can see beads of sweat forming on his brow.

Good. Let the fucker panic. I should never have agreed to let him back in my life. I know what he is, and I now know that he will never change.

He came back here to fuck with me.

"Let me give you a piece of advice, Brad." I say the words slowly so that they sink in. He stares at me, waiting. "Run."

"Run?" He almost looks like he doesn't understand what I am saying.

"Yes. Run. Get the fuck out of here before I really lose my shit."

"Oh my God, you are actually going to take her word over mine?" he says as he points at Stacey. "Clearly a good fuck is more important than family."

Before I know what I am doing, I am across the room and have Brad pinned against the wall. Not losing my shit didn't last long.

"Jake, bro, calm down."

"Calm down? Fucking calm down?" I shout in his face. "You expect me to be calm when you talk about Stacey like that?"

"She's just some woman." I tighten my hold on him, making it clear that his words were the wrong ones.

"Jake," Stacey's voice says softly from behind me. "Jake, let him go. He's not worth it." Stacey knows what I am capable of when it comes to her. She saw me beat the shit out of Donnie when he attacked her. She will know that I have no qualms about doing the same thing to my brother if he continues to be disrespectful about her.

"Please, Jake." Her pleading voice is the only thing that makes me let go of him. If it was anyone else trying to talk me down, then it wouldn't make a difference.

Brad sags against the wall as I step back from him slightly.

"Get out," I say, my voice low and menacing.

"So, that's it? You want me gone?" Brad says, his arms held out either side of him.

"Yeah, I want you gone." I have never said these words to him before. I have been pissed off with Brad many times in my life, but I have never actually told him to go.

"You're gonna regret this. She won't be around for you forever. I was just trying to show you what a tart she really is." I feel Stacey's hands clamp around my arm to stop me from doing anything.

I clench my jaw and try to take a few deep breaths to calm myself down a little.

"This has nothing to do with Stacey. This is about you wanting to screw me over as much as possible."

"Damn straight I want to screw you over," Brad shouts, his true colours shining through. "Why did you get to be the one with the great fucking business? Why did you always get the girls running after you? What makes you so fucking special? I always got glanced over. I was always the one on the side-lines, watching everyone fall over their feet to speak to you. What was wrong with me? Why did you get all the glory?"

Brad's 'nice guy' act has well and truly left the building. "I never thought the day would come where Jake fucking Waters would have someone that he cherished more than his own life. When I came back here, I already knew that you had fallen hard for Stacey. It's amazing what you can find out if you know the right people to contact. I must thank Caitlin for all of the information that she gave me about the two of you." I hear Stacey gasp, and even I am a little shocked by his admission of speaking to Caitlin.

"You spoke to Caitlin?" Stacey says from behind me.

"Oh yeah. She was more than willing to help me try and split you two up. It was her idea to leave the note on your car and the flowers in your office. She thought it would be a nice touch, seeing as she stalked you for weeks before she stabbed you."

"You sick, twisted—"

"Yeah, yeah. Call me what you like, but you can't deny that it was a good fucking plan," Brad says, cutting Stacey off mid-sentence. "It's just a shame that it hasn't ended in the way that Caitlin and I had hoped."

"And what was the end game?" I ask, almost wishing that I hadn't voiced my curiosity.

"To gain your trust and leave you heartbroken, bro. To make you feel worthless, like I have done all of these years." I scoff at his and Caitlin's ridiculous plan.

Is this the best that they could come up with?

They clearly underestimated mine and Stacey's commitment to one another.

"Brad?" Stacey says from behind me, making me turn around to look at her. Her eyes are wide, and she has gone pale.

"Yes, Stacey?" Brad replies.

"That morning that you came to the house to invite me to breakfast, how did you get in?" I turn away from Stacey to look at Brad as it finally clicks into place for me that she didn't actually let him in the house on the morning in question.

"I was wondering when you were going to ask about that," Brad replies, a smirk crossing his face. "During my time of plotting with Caitlin, she divulged the information that she had hidden a key to the house."

I hear Stacey gasp again and my hands ball into fists at his answer. "You see, when Jake and Caitlin were fucking one another, she had the sense to borrow Jake's key and make a copy." I clench my jaw as the anger within me starts to boil over. "Jake never knew about the key that she had copied, obviously. She hid the key in a safe place, just in case she ever needed to use it."

"Oh my God," Stacey says in a whisper.

"Thanks to Jake's carelessness before you came along," Brad says directing his comment to Stacey, "He gave Caitlin the opportunity to have access to his house keys."

"I feel sick," Stacey says.

"You need to leave, Brad," I say, needing him to get as far away from me as possible before I wrench my arm out of Stacey's grasp and launch myself at him.

"And what are you going to do about it if I don't?" he says, cockiness taking over.

He is going to regret asking me that question.

"If you stay around here, then I will ruin you. I will have you discredited as a doctor, and I will make sure that you never work anywhere near here, ever again."

"You don't have the power to do that."

"Don't be so sure, Bradley." I only ever use his full name when I mean business. He knows that. He looks at me warily, clearly assessing his options since his plan has backfired. "I have money, and you and I both know that money talks. I have connections due to my business, and I have ways of making your life hell."

"You wouldn't do that."

"If you believe that I wouldn't, then you're more stupid than I thought. The line that you have crossed this time can never be repaired. As far as I am concerned, I have no brother." I can see that my words have stung him, but I couldn't give a fuck. He has never been a brother to me, so it's not really any loss.

"You know, it was fun while it lasted. I would like to say that I regret my actions, but all I regret is the fact that I wasn't able to play this out a bit longer. I reckon another month or two and she would have been putty in my hands," Brad says, pointing at Stacey.

I feel Stacey's grip on my arm tighten, so that I don't go over to him and unleash my full fury. I grind my teeth together so hard that I am surprised that I don't chip a tooth.

As I look at Brad, with what I am sure is a death stare, he finally shakes his head and turns away from me. He walks to the office door, opening it.

"Brad?" I say, getting his attention before he walks out of my life for good. He looks at me, and I can see the hate filling his eyes. "Don't ever come back."

CHAPTER THIRTY-THREE

JAKE

Stacey flops down onto the sofa in her office after getting us both a drink from the bar. I have watched the footage of what happened before I got here, and I am furious. Watching it has done me no favours whatsoever. Stacey told me not to torture myself by looking at it, but it turns out that I am a glutton for punishment.

When his hand grabbed hers, I wanted to hurl the computer across the room. I don't understand how he thought that he was going to get away with lying. The cameras prove what really happened, and he knew that cameras were in here. I don't think that I will ever understand how he thought his plan would work.

"How are you doing?" she asks me, her hand covering mine.

"I've been better," I admit. I'm annoyed at myself more than anything. I'm annoyed that another person came into our lives and tried to destroy what we have.

"I'm sorry about Brad," she says.

"Don't be," I say, pulling her close to me, my arm around her shoulders. She snuggles her head against me and I inhale her scent.

"I really thought that he wanted to be part of your life. I never would have tried to convince you to let him back in if I had known what he was really like. I should have listened to you."

"Hey," I say softly as I use my free hand to lift her chin up, so she is looking at me. Her eyes look sad and I want to take away that look more than anything. "Don't you dare go blaming any of this on yourself."

I know how her mind works, and I am not prepared to let her think that she had any influence on Brad's intentions.

"But—"

"No buts. He's out of our lives for good. All that matters is that we have each other." I sound like a soppy sod, but I don't care. I need her to know that she is all that I care about. She sighs and takes a sip of her drink.

"We need to get the locks changed at the house," Stacey says.

"Already on it. There will be someone out first thing tomorrow morning."

"Phew. That's one less thing to worry about, I suppose."

"I'm also having some security cameras installed outside, just for the time being." I say. I need to make sure that Stacey is safe.

"Do we really need to do that?" Stacey asks. "I mean, Caitlin is in prison, and if Brad has any sense, then he will be gone."

"I'm not taking any chances. They're both screwed in the head." I'm not one hundred percent convinced that Brad will go, so it is better to be safe than sorry.

Stacey lets out a loud sigh. "Are things ever going to run smoothly for us, Jake?" she asks me.

"Sure they will. Whatever we face only makes us stronger. No one is going to break us."

"Promise?"

"Promise," I say as I lean down and place a kiss on the end of her nose. She smiles and rests her head on my shoulder.

As I sit here, her body close to mine, I feel thankful that she is willing to stick around and put up with all of the shit that comes from being with me. This woman has been stabbed, stalked, and hit on by my brother, because of me. If she were any lesser woman, she would have run a mile ages ago.

I know that she isn't going anywhere.

I know that I will do everything in my power to make her happy.

I also know that one day soon, I am going to ask this woman to be my wife.

PERFECT BEGINNINGS

CHAPTER ONE

STACEY

I sit in one of the plush chairs on the balcony of my hotel room, thinking about the last six months of my life.

Where the last six months have gone, I have no idea. My life has been like one big whirlwind that shows no signs of slowing down.

At times, it has been incredibly difficult, but I wouldn't be where I am today without the obstacles that I have previously faced.

As I look out at the sunrise, I smile and feel thankful for everything and everyone present in my life. I have great friends, my dream job, and a wonderful boyfriend. Lydia is due to give birth any day now, Martin is just as crazy as ever, and Jake is still the man of my dreams. To be fair though, Jake is probably the man of most women's dreams, it just so happens that I was lucky enough to hold his interest. My close circle is only small, but I value each one of them.

I sip my coffee and close my eyes, revelling in the taste of the exquisite coffee beans. I am staying at one of the most luxurious hotels that I have ever stepped foot in. My room spans across the entire top floor of the hotel.

Oh yes, nothing but the best for me.

Jake wouldn't hear about me staying in one of the perfectly adequate hotel rooms on the lower floors. He had to make sure that I had the penthouse suite, even though I am staying here all by myself.

My book tour has been going on for two weeks now, and whilst I am incredibly grateful to be given the chance to publish my novel, I do miss being at home.

Two weeks ago was the last time that I saw Jake.

I miss him like mad.

I miss everything about him.

I dread to think what I am going to be like when I have to take my book tour overseas.

I think about how much Jake and I have overcome in such a short space of time. What with Donnie, Caitlin, and Brad, you would think that the universe was trying to tell us to give up on one another. Most couples probably would have, but we haven't.

In fact, we are stronger now than we ever have been.

Neither of us have heard from Brad since he tried to come between us all those months ago, and I hope that it stays that way. Jake sneakily hired a private detective to find out as much about Brad as he could. I wasn't on board with this idea to start with, but when Jake explained that he wanted to find out how much contact Brad and Caitlin had had, I quickly got on board. The thought of that woman infiltrating our lives again made me want to know everything possible.

It turns out that Caitlin had somehow contacted Brad and told him everything. She is the reason that he came back from America. She is the reason that his hatred for Jake was so bad. I'm just glad that she is safely locked away behind bars.

The private detective also managed to find out that Brad had made a complete mess of his life in America. He had gotten himself into serious debt and had several loan sharks looking for him. I have no idea where he is now, and I don't particularly care. It seems that he has gone into hiding somewhere, and for his sake, I hope that he stays there. Jake being Jake, paid off all of Brad's debt, even after what he had tried to do to us. I couldn't be mad at him for that though. It's just the way Jake is. Brad probably doesn't even know that Jake has paid it all off for him either. Jake told me that it was to be the last act of kindness that he would ever do for his brother.

Jake is such a good, kind-hearted person, and it pains me that Brad wanted to hurt him. It still angers me to this day that Brad thought that I would choose him over Jake. I know that Jake will never forgive him, and I would never try and convince him otherwise.

I have been there for Jake as much as possible, because he is my life. But when my book took off so quickly, and unexpectedly, it took me away from him more than I thought that it would.

Hell, it is still keeping me away from him.

Jake has been so supportive, but I can't help but feel a little bit selfish. I mean, this is my dream career, but I never really thought about book launches and book signings. My debut novel has been so popular that I have been commissioned to write a follow up. I haven't started the second book yet, but I plan to once this book tour is over and done with.

It turns out that, in a time when I thought that my heart was breaking, I managed to write a number one best seller. When I was holed up in the bed and breakfast after Jake had misunderstood the abortion leaflets, I poured my heart out in the form of fictional characters. Readers seem to love a romance gone wrong, only for it to go right again.

My phone rings breaking my thoughts. I look to the screen and see that Lydia is calling.

"Good morning, Lyd," I greet her as I answer the phone. "What are you doing up so early?" I double check the time and it is only just gone quarter past six.

"Stace, the baby's coming."

"What?" I screech as I sit forwards on the edge of my seat.

"The baby. It's coming." Lydia sounds panicked, and I wish more than anything that I could be there with her.

"It's okay, Lyd. Take deep breaths and calm down."

"Calm down? Calm down?" Oh shit, Lydia is about to blow her lid. "I can't fucking calm down. A baby is going to be shooting out of my nether regions at some point very soon, and you're telling me to calm down?" Lydia's voice has gone so high-pitched that I have to move the phone away from my ear slightly. "Oh shit, here comes another one."

I wait and listen to Lydia screaming down the phone. I'm guessing by another one that she means that she is having a contraction. My heart goes out to my best friend. Hearing her in pain is not pleasant.

"Stacey, I really do think that this baby is trying to kill me." I can't help but smile at Lydia's reference. And here was me thinking that Martin was always the more dramatic one.

"Now you listen to me, Lydia. The baby is going to make the pain all worthwhile once it has arrived. You are a strong woman and you have Paul by your side. You can do this, Lyd."

I can hear Paul in the background, trying to help Lydia.

"Oh for fuck's sake, Paul, get away from me. Jeez, and here was me thinking that he would be helpful when it came to the giving birth part." I know that Lydia doesn't mean what she is saying, and I hope that Paul doesn't take her words too seriously either. "Stace, I wish that you were here with me. I can't do this without you."

I want to cry at her words.

"I wish that I could be there too, Lyd. How far apart are your contractions?" I ask, trying to take the heat off of myself for not being there. Lydia starts to scream again, so I am guessing that the contractions aren't very far apart.

I patiently wait for Lydia to work through the pain.

"They're coming quicker, Stace."

"You need to go to the hospital. And when you have given birth to my beautiful god-daughter, I want you to call me."

"Yes. Hospital. Right." Lydia seems to be in another world entirely. Unfortunately, I can't relate as I have never given birth.

"I love ya, Lyd."

"You too, babes. Paul," I hear Lydia shout. "Get the car ready. We need to get to the fucking hospital." Lydia then hangs up the phone and I stare at the screen, tears forming in my eyes.

I can't believe that I am missing this.

I was supposed to be with Lydia at the birth. I know that she has Paul there, but she needs all of the support that she can get. Paul probably does too to be honest.

Without thinking about what I am doing, I go back inside my hotel room and start putting my clothes on. I pull on my grey pencil skirt, a black vest top and a black roll-neck jumper. I put on some socks and my black, knee-high, boots and pull my hair into a ponytail.

I call my car service, all part of being a famous author, and tell them to pick me up as soon as possible. I then call my agent, Chloe, and tell her that due to an emergency, I need to leave and go back home. Of course, Chloe tries to persuade me otherwise, but I don't listen to her. By the time that I get off of the phone to her, she is beyond pissed with me.

I have a book signing in four hours, but I don't care. Lydia needs me, and I am going to try my hardest to be there, preferably before the baby arrives.

I put the things that I need in my handbag, grab my grey swing coat, and race out of my hotel room. I run to the lifts and press the call button, the lift seeming to take forever to arrive. The doors ping open a few painstaking minutes later and I silently curse Jake for getting me the penthouse suite. If I had been in one of the other rooms then I would have been closer to the ground floor. I realise that this is a ridiculous thing to think about, but I need something else to concentrate on other than my worry for Lydia.

When the lift eventually reaches the ground floor, the car service phone me to let me know that they are outside. I run out of the hotel lobby and practically barrel into the back seat. I instruct the driver to go to the hospital that Lydia has chosen for the birth. I know that I am a couple of hours away, but I am hoping that I will make it in time.

I try to call Jake as we set off, but there is no answer. He must still be sleeping.

I relax back into the seat of the car and gaze out of the window as I watch the scenery rush by. Half an hour into the journey, my phone begins to ring.

"Hello," I answer, without checking the name on the screen.

"Hi, Stace, it's Paul."

"Hi, Paul. How's Lydia? Is everything going okay?" I ask, desperate for information.

"Yeah everything is fine. Well, as fine as it can be with Lydia threatening to kill me every thirty seconds." I can't help but let out a little chuckle.

"She's just in pain, Paul. She doesn't mean it."

"Oh, believe me, if I thought that she meant it, then I would be in hiding somewhere." He laughs, and I laugh along with him. "Listen, I was actually calling to ask you a favour."

"Sure. What is it?"

"Well, I know that you are busy with your book tour and everything, but is there any way that you can get back here? I mean, I know that I am here, but I'm not sure that I am helping much. I know that Lydia really wanted you here, and—"

"I'm already on my way," I cut him off, stopping his rambling. "When I got off of the phone to Lydia, I called my car service and got them to come and get me. I'm just over an hour away."

"Oh, that's great." The relief in Paul's voice is obvious. "I won't say anything to Lydia just yet. It will be a nice surprise for her when you turn up. It might even cheer her up a little. Just try and get here before the baby does." His voice is pleading.

"I'm doing my best," I reply. "I've instructed the driver to take me to the hospital as I am guessing that is where you are now?"

"Yes, we are on floor five, and its room number thirteen."

"Thirteen, huh?" I doubt very much that Lydia will be pleased with that number.

"Uh, yeah, Lydia has already remarked about it. Her and her bloody superstition." I laugh and say goodbye to Paul, telling him to give me an update if the baby makes an appearance before I arrive.

I try to call Jake again, but there is still no answer.

Damn it.

I guess that I will just have to surprise him with a visit, once Lydia has had the baby.

CHAPTER TWO

STACEY

I get to the hospital just after eight o'clock. I thank the driver and tell him that I may be some time before I dash into the hospital. I find the nearest set of stairs and run up them until I reach floor five. Thank goodness that I started using the gym a few months ago as if I hadn't, that would have taken me longer and I would have been a sweaty mess by the time that I reached Lydia.

I race to find room number thirteen, my eyes scanning both sides of the corridor. When I spot the room number, the sounds of Lydia screaming halt me in my tracks. I presume that she is having a contraction, so I decide to wait outside the door until it has passed before I announce my surprise appearance.

Whilst I wait, I send a quick text to Jake, telling him that I am at the hospital with Lydia, and then I turn my phone off. Once I hear the screaming stop, I open the door and am greeted by the sight of Lydia led on her back, sweating profusely. Paul looks petrified as he stands by her bed, holding her hand, patting her forehead with a wet cloth, with a midwife writing notes on a chart at the end of the bed.

It takes a few moments for Lydia to register that I have entered the room. She looks at me dazed, and before I can speak, Paul comes walking over to me and embraces me in a bear hug.

"Thank you," he whispers as he hugs me tight.

"Uh, no problem," I answer him, shocked by his greeting for me.

"For fuck's sake, Paul, let her in, will you?" Lydia snaps at him. My face pulls into a grimace at Lydia's tone and Paul releases me, stepping back.

"See?" he says with an exasperated look on his face. I smile at him and then turn back to look at Lydia.

"How are you feeling, Lyd?" I ask her, instantly wishing that I had asked something else instead. Lydia looks at me like I am an alien.

"How am I feeling? Well, I'll bloody well tell you, shall I?"

"Oh boy," Paul says from behind me.

"Apart from the fact that my vagina is going to be ripped apart at any moment, my back is killing me, and this gas and air is fucking shit." Lydia then proceeds to take a deep gulp of the 'shit' gas and air whilst keeping her eyes fixed firmly on me.

"Well, okay then," I answer, not really knowing how to respond to her outburst.

Lydia continues to suck the life out of the gas and air, and Paul excuses himself to go and get a drink. I ask him to grab me a coffee on his travels and he seems more than happy to grab a few minutes' peace from Lydia's wrath. Can't say that I blame him. I have only been here about a minute and I feel that I am going to face more of Lydia's acid tongue.

I put my bag on the chair in the corner of the room, and then I go to stand by the side of Lydia's bed. The midwife is still looking at Lydia's charts and I don't interrupt her to introduce myself. She doesn't exactly exude a very friendly vibe. Her grey hair is pulled back into a tight bun and she is short and dumpy. The buttons on her nurse's uniform look like they are about to pop off. She must be close to retirement age. Her name badge says that her name is Cynthia. I turn my attention back to Lydia, who has gone extremely red in the face. She screws up her face in discomfort and I decide to take over what Paul was doing when I walked in, and I start to mop her brow to help keep her cool.

"Right, Lydia," Cynthia says, her voice booming into the silence. "I am going to go and check on another one of my patients. If you need to get hold of me, just press your buzzer." With that, Cynthia leaves the room.

"Wow. She seems like a bundle of joy," I say to Lydia, hoping to raise a smile from her with my sarcasm.

"Pfft. Miserable old battle-axe. I mean, honestly, they could have given me a cheerful midwife. Anyone would think that she is the one being put through this immense bloody pain."

"Where is your midwife from the doctor's surgery?" I ask her.

"She broke her ankle last week," Lydia answers, not sounding impressed in the slightest.

"Oh, right. Well, I suppose that she can't help breaking her ankle," I reply.

Lydia scoffs at my answer. "She could have waited until I had had my baby before she decided to go on a bloody skiing holiday."

Lydia really does sound hard done by. I quickly agree with her to avoid a Lydia-style-rant. Another contraction takes hold and I do my best to help her through it. Lydia manoeuvres herself, so that she is led on her side, and I rub her back for her.

The door to her room opens and in walks Paul with a cup of coffee in each hand.

"Thanks, Paul," I say as he deposits my coffee on a table, which sits under the window behind me. He smiles and then goes round to the other side of the bed to face Lydia.

"Hey, baby," he says to her. He crouches down, so that he is eye level with her. I step back, wanting to give them a moment together. I turn to look out of the window and it hits me just how much I wish that Jake was here.

Jake is going to be the baby's god-father. We were both thrilled when they asked us to be the baby's god-parents.

I wonder if he has seen my message yet?

"Stace?" Lydia says, breaking through my thoughts. I turn away from the window and go back to her bedside.

"Yeah?"

"Can you give us a minute, please?" she says, gesturing to Paul.

"Sure," I reply. I pick my coffee up off of the table, and I leave Lydia's room, closing the door behind me. I decide to walk along the corridor instead of waiting outside like some kind of eavesdropper. I imagine that at this moment, Lydia is either apologising for her behaviour so far or she is scratching Paul's eyes out. I'm hoping that it's not the latter.

I walk to the end of the corridor, hearing various women in stages of labour as I do so. It almost sounds like a bloody horror film with all the moaning, screaming and swearing. It's enough to put anyone off of childbirth for life.

I reach the end and turn around to make my way back to Lydia's room, and as I do, I feel my body tingle. I look up and see that Jake is walking down the corridor towards me.

My heart does a flutter and butterflies flap wildly in my stomach.

It amazes me that I still get these feelings even though we have now been together for eight months. For some people, the butterflies disappear long before now.

Jake looks incredible as he stalks towards me. His hair is messy, just how I like it, and his eyes are burning into mine. After two weeks of not seeing him in the flesh, he manages to somehow look even sexier than he did before I went away.

He's wearing his office attire and he radiates masculinity. I start to quicken my pace, needing to feel him against me.

When I reach him, he wraps his arms around me and pulls me to his body. I have my coffee in one hand and I try not to spill it all over the corridor floor. I wrap my free arm around his neck and nuzzle my face into him. He feels so good. His grip on me is reassuring and comforting. I breathe in his scent and let the aroma of his aftershave fill my nostrils.

One of his hands goes to the nape of my neck and he gently pulls my head back. His caramel coloured eyes are like a magnet for me. I love how they convey so much emotion, and I love that they only convey that emotion to me.

He looks over my face, almost like he is mesmerising every single detail.

"Hi, babe," I whisper. He smiles at me and then his lips are on mine, his gentle pressure leaving me wanting more.

If only we weren't standing in a hospital corridor right now.

Oh, the things that he would do to me.

I smile against his lips at the thought. I am well aware of what Jake can do to my body.

He pulls back slightly and gives me a questioning look.

"What's the cheeky smile for?" he asks me, his deep voice making my insides tremble.

"I was just thinking about what we could be doing right now, if we weren't here." I immediately see the desire burning in his eyes. It's been two weeks since we made love. Two fucking weeks. I know that Jake must be just as frustrated as I am. I mean, sure, we have had phone sex whilst I have been away, but nothing compares to the real thing.

"I swear, when I get you home, you are not going to be able to walk after I'm finished with you." Jake's voice is low, and his words take my breath away. I know that he is capable of achieving this, and I can't wait until he makes his statement come true.

We are broken from our moment by Paul shouting down the corridor.

"STACE! GET IN HERE!" Paul's voice is urgent and panicky. I pull away from Jake and run back to Lydia's room, not giving a shit that I am now spilling coffee everywhere. I can hear Jake running behind me.

As I enter her room, I see that Lydia is crying, but my eyes are drawn to something else. Blood. All over her bed.

Oh fuck.

I place my coffee cup on the table and go to Lydia, taking her hand in mine.

"It's okay, Lyd. You're going to be okay," I say to her, keeping my voice as even as possible.

"Why am I bleeding? What's happening?" Lydia looks scared shitless, and to be honest, I can't really blame her for looking like that. The fear going through me is bad enough, so God knows what Lydia is experiencing.

"Where's the doctor, Paul?" I ask him.

"I don't know. I pressed the buzzer, but no one is coming," Paul replies. I look at him in disbelief. He is seriously just waiting for someone to turn up? I feel anger flood my body. This must be the one and only time that I have witnessed Paul being a useless lump.

"Go and find a fucking doctor, Paul. NOW!" I shout at him. Paul's eyes go wide, and he nods before racing from the room. Jake is standing in the doorway. "Jake, make sure that he finds a doctor, and quick." Jake nods at me and then leaves.

I turn my attention back to Lydia. She is sobbing and battling contractions at the same time as worrying about all the blood that covers her bed.

"You're doing good, Lyd. Keep going," I say, trying to support her through the pain. I keep hold of her hand and put my other arm around her shoulders. The blood looks terrifying, but I am hoping and praying that it looks worse than it actually is.

Eventually, after what feels like a lifetime, Paul returns with a doctor in tow, and Jake follows after them. The doctor comes over to Lydia and does a quick assessment of the situation. He then presses a blue button behind Lydia's bed, and informs us all that Lydia could be haemorrhaging and that the baby needs to be delivered pronto.

I gasp and see the colour completely drain from Paul's face. Cynthia and another nurse come in and are instructed by the doctor about what to do next. Soon they are wheeling Lydia's bed into the corridor with Paul, Jake and I following behind them. The doctor asks who is to be in the delivery room and Paul immediately answers. Jake and I stop following them as they are about to wheel Lydia through the operating theatre doors. I feel tears sting the backs of my eyes and my whole body begins to shake.

Oh God, please let Lydia and the baby be okay. Please, please, please...

"STACEY!" Lydia shouts at me before the operating theatre doors close. "I need you with me." My heart literally leaps into my throat and I run through the doors after them.

As I follow them, I look to Paul and see that he still looks like he has seen a ghost.

As we walk along, I reach for his hand and gently squeeze it. He looks at me and all I see in his eyes is fear. A fear that I am sure is mirrored in mine. I give him a small smile and then we are entering a delivery suite. The nurses position Lydia's bed and then Cynthia hands Paul and I some very unflattering green gowns to put over our clothes. We also have to wear a plastic cap that looks like a giant blue condom.

As we are getting all geared up, I take this moment to speak to Paul.

"Are you sure that you want me in here, Paul?" I ask. He needs to be okay with me being in here too.

"Yeah. Lydia wants you here, and whatever makes her happy is all that matters to me."

"Okay," I say softly.

When we have finished putting on our awful gowns and condom cap, we go to a sink basin and wash our hands thoroughly before putting a special gel on them. The nurses have been prepping Lydia and there is now a curtain covering the lower half of her body. I have seen this on various television programmes, but never in real life. I know that the curtain is there so that Lydia doesn't see anything going on behind it.

Paul is by Lydia's side, holding her hand and placing gentle kisses on her forehead.

I feel out of place.

I shouldn't be in here.

I almost feel like an intruder.

This moment should just be for Paul and Lydia.

"Stacey Marie Paris, get your butt over here," Lydia says. I walk to the bed and stand on the opposite side to Paul, taking her other hand in mine and blinking back the tears that are threatening to emerge. "God, you two look like you are about to pass out."

I know that Lydia is trying to make light of the situation, but I can see the worry in her eyes. I give her a smile and try to rack my brains for something to talk about that will take her mind off of the worry somewhat.

"Hey, Lyd?"

"Yeah?"

I frantically continue to think of something to say when the doctor interrupts us, so that he can talk Lydia through the procedure that he is about to perform. I don't take any of his words in as I am still in too much shock at what is happening.

Once he has finished speaking, he disappears back behind the curtain. Lydia looks to Paul and then back to me.

"You were saying?" she prompts me to speak.

"Right. You remember that holiday that we took to Spain a few years ago?" I say. Lydia gives me a nod. "Well, remember how we said that we would always go back for your thirtieth?"

"Actually, I think that we said that turning thirty would bring about some sort of breakdown, so we should go back there and party like we were still in our twenties."

"Oh, yes, that's right. Well, how about we make it even more memorable and go to America?"

"America? Seriously?" Lydia asks in disbelief.

"Seriously."

"That sounds awesome."

"I was thinking that we could lounge on the beach in Mexico, and the guys can do all of the babysitting."

"Hey," Paul cuts in. Lydia and I both turn to him with a questioning look on our faces. "Do Jake and I get a say in this at all?"

"No," Lydia and I both answer in unison, making us both laugh.

"Oh, well, as long as I know," Paul replies, but I know that he is just trying to help me keep Lydia's mind off of what is happening. "Will Jake agree to this little holiday that you two are planning?"

"Oh, please," Lydia says. "Jake is so in love with Stacey that she could tell him to run in front of a bus and he probably would."

"Fair point," Paul agrees.

"Um, I am still here you know," I say, giving them a little wave just to make sure that they see me.

"We know," they both answer at the same time, and we all laugh at the little comedy sketch that we are most definitely giving the hospital staff. The easy banter between us just shows how close we have all become in recent months. Before I can answer them, the next thing we hear is the sound of a baby, crying.

We all stare at each other with wide eyes at the noise. Such a beautiful sound.

"Oh my God," I say as Lydia looks to Paul, tears shining in her eyes. The doctor appears from around the curtain, carrying their beautiful baby.

"Congratulations, Mum and Dad," the doctor says. "You have a little girl."

Lydia starts to cry, and I squeeze her hand and let a tear run down my cheek at this beautiful moment that I am witnessing. The doctor asks Paul if he would like to hold her whilst they stitch Lydia back up. He nods, and their baby girl is placed in his arms.

I feel that now is the time for me to leave the room.

I let go of Lydia's hand and slowly start to move towards the door. The sight of the three of them together leaves me speechless. I smile and exit through the door, taking off the gown and cap as I get back into the corridor.

I walk along the corridor in a daze at the amazing experience that I just had. Seeing my best friend giving birth to my god-daughter is nothing short of a miracle.

I reach the operating theatre doors and push them open. My eyes fly to Jake, who stands up off of the chair that he was sitting on. I let the happy tears flow down my cheeks as I walk over to him, smiling. He embraces me in his arms and I bury my face in his chest.

"It's a girl, Jake. Lydia and Paul have a beautiful baby girl."

CHAPTER THREE

STACEY

Jake and I wait back at Lydia's room for her and Paul to return. Paul comes back first and tells us that Lydia needs to rest under the doctor's orders. We congratulate Paul on the safe arrival of their little girl and we leave the hospital. I tell Paul that I will be back later on to see how they are all doing. Sod the bloody book tour.

Jake drove himself to the hospital, so we head to the car park and climb into his sexy black Porsche. The car is so sleek, and it is so very Jake.

As Jake drives us out of the car park, I turn my phone on and am immediately greeted by a string of voicemails from my agent, Chloe. I groan as I start to listen to them one by one. There are six altogether, and each one sounds more urgent than the next. I grimace at the last one as Chloe sounds like a banshee. In fact, she is so loud that Jake can hear the message, and I haven't even got it on speaker phone.

"Jeez, she sounds pissed," Jake comments.

I sigh and let my head fall back against the head rest. "I know. I guess I'm going to have to call her back and have her bollock me for the next hour or so."

I really don't enjoy the thought of being told off like a child.

I look at my phone and scroll through my contacts until I find Chloe's name. I am about to press the call button, when Jake stops me by placing his hand on my arm.

"Don't call her yet, babe. I haven't seen you in person for two weeks. Can't we just get back to the house and spend a bit of time together before you are taken away from me again?" Jake sneaks a look at me, making me melt with his gorgeous eyes. I cannot resist him. I smirk and turn my phone off, putting it back into my bag. The grin that spreads across Jake's face is just breath-taking. "That's my girl."

He winks at me and then turns his attention back to the road. I notice that he puts his foot down a little bit more than usual. I guess that's what happens when you are sex deprived and in need of an imminent release.

We pull onto our driveway and I have never seen Jake exit a car so quickly before. He is round my side of the car before I have even taken my seatbelt off. I unbuckle myself and laugh as he lifts me out of the seat.

"I can walk, you know?" I say, chuckling at his macho display of affection.

Jake smirks at me. "I know. I'm just in a rush to get you in the house and get you naked, seeing as we are on a schedule." His tone is so arousing that I am already wet for him.

Jake unlocks the front door, I throw my handbag on the hallway floor and I squeal as he literally runs up the stairs with me. We enter our bedroom and Jake throws me on the bed.

Oh yes, I'm getting animal Jake. Fabulous.

Jake strips off as if his life depends on it, and then he starts to undress me. I don't try to help him with my clothing. It excites me to see how much he wants me. Once I am completely naked, Jake covers me with his body and then roughly claims my mouth with his.

I moan with my desire for him, which spurs him on even more. He trails kisses all the way down my body before reaching my sex and devouring me, hungrily. I am bucking and trembling within a minute. Jake knows exactly how to work me into a frenzy and I absolutely love it. Our bodies are so in tune with one another.

My impending orgasm starts to mount, and I moan his name out loud. Jake reaches up with his hands and starts to fondle my breasts at the same time as his tongue is swirling around my clit. I try to hold off my climax for as long as possible, but it's no use. I can't control it any longer. I let myself go as Jake takes me through my high and then slowly works me down. He trails kisses back up my body until his eyes are level with mine.

"Did you enjoy that?" he asks me in a breathy voice.

"Oh yeah," I pant. "But I'm going to enjoy the feel of your cock inside me even more." Jake claims my lips again and plunges his length into me quickly. I try to gasp, but Jake's mouth on mine stops me from doing so.

Jake begins a punishing rhythm that has me feeling like I am on another planet. I am delirious with my love for this man. Our lips are still connected as Jake pounds into me harder with each stroke, and I start to build up to my second orgasm.

Jake is the master of multiple orgasms. I have only ever experienced these with him.

I break away from his lips as I bury my face in his neck and scream out his name in pleasure.

"Fuck," Jake moans as we both come together.

Once finished, Jake collapses on top of me and I clamp my legs around his waist. I literally cannot be close enough to him. I scratch his back lightly, moving my hands up and down slowly.

"Mmm," Jake mumbles in my ear, indicating that he is enjoying my hands roaming over his back. The sound he omits makes goose-bumps appear all over my body. The effect that he has on me is so strong. Jake shifts, so that his body is lying beside mine and I turn on my side, so that I am facing him.

He lightly trails his fingers down the side of my body and I shiver with delight.

"I've missed this," Jake says, his tone soft.

"Me too," I reply, giving him a gentle peck on the lips.

"Stace, I want to talk to you about something," Jake says, looking serious, instantly putting me on alert.

"Sure. What's up?"

"I've been thinking about this for the last few months but being at the hospital today made me realise something." Jake takes a deep breath before continuing. "I want us to try for a baby."

His words blow me away.

I frown as he just looks at me, waiting for my reaction.

"You want a baby?" I say in a quiet voice.

"Yeah, I want *our* baby."

Well, fuck me, I wasn't expecting that.

"Jake," I say his name softly. "I don't really think that now is the right time for us to be trying for a baby." The look of disappointment on his face doesn't escape my attention. "Don't get me wrong, one day the idea of us becoming a little family is wonderful, but..." My voice fades off as I see the hope in his eyes die.

I don't want to crush his dreams, but I am just not ready to be a mother at this point in my life.

Jake moves so that he is sitting on the edge of the bed, and I suddenly feel very cold. Our reunion is about to go pear-shaped unless I can get this situation under control.

"It's just not the right time." There really isn't any more I can say other than this.

Jake pushes himself up off of the bed and starts to put his clothes back on. Feeling very uncomfortable with this turn of events, I pull the quilt over me, so that I don't feel quite so exposed.

"Are you just going to ignore me?" I ask him. Jake finishes buttoning up his shirt and turns to face me.

"I thought that we both felt the same way, Stace." His statement shocks me. He knows how I feel about him. Or at least, I thought that he knew.

"I love you more than anything or anyone else, Jake. I couldn't bear the thought of you not being in my life. I just don't feel ready to be a mother yet. I've got my book tour to finish here and God knows what it is going to be like when I have to go and promote it in other countries." I am being realistic, but I don't think that Jake is on the same page as me.

"I don't see why that should stop us?" Jake answers.

Is he for real right now?

"Seriously?" I say, eyebrows raised. "You don't see how me being in another country or travelling on the road would be a problem?"

"No. If it is something that we both want, then why should some stupid book tour stop us from doing that?" Jake clearly didn't think about his wording before he spoke out loud. My eyes narrow on him, and I feel anger rise within me at his flippant comment of my book tour being 'stupid.'

"Stupid book tour?"

"I didn't mean it like that."

"Oh, really?" I throw the quilt off of me, get off of the bed, and start to get dressed. "I thought that you supported my career, Jake? I thought that you were proud of me? And I thought that you understood how much this means to me?"

"I do, babe. I really didn't mean it to come out that way. I just meant that, even with you doing your book tour, we could still try for a baby. Why does it matter where you are for us to do that?"

"I don't want to be in another country when I am pregnant, Jake. I want to be here, with you, but as for the foreseeable future, that isn't going to happen. I need to concentrate on my career." My voice is getting louder with each word I speak.

"Are you saying that your career is more important than our life together?"

Oh, I can't believe that he has just said that.

"You know that nothing is more important to me than us." I walk closer to him and am stood inches from his face, anger seeping through me. "How dare you try to make out that I don't value what we have together. After everything that we have been through, Jake, I thought that you knew better. My career is just something that I need to pursue right now."

"Oh, I get it. I'm just supposed to wait here until you decide that the time is right for us to have a family?" Jake's tone is firm, and I don't see either of us backing down from this.

"Don't be so ridiculous," I say, throwing my hands up in exasperation. "Now you are just trying to make me sound like a bad person. Starting a family is something that we both need to agree on, Jake. It's okay for you, your career has been booming since you were twenty-five years old. Mine is only just beginning. Don't make this into something that it isn't. I don't want to argue with you, but sometimes you can be so damn difficult." My hands are on my hips as I continue to hold my own.

I will not back down on this.

"I'm difficult? I think that you will find that you are the one being difficult on this matter. You haven't even given the idea a chance." Jake isn't going to budge. But then, neither am I.

I sigh in exasperation. "We are clearly going to have to agree to disagree for the time being. We can discuss this another time. I have some phone calls that I need to make." I walk around Jake and out of the bedroom.

God, he really knows how to ruin a beautiful moment.

Ten minutes ago we were having amazing sex, and now we are arguing.

I stomp down the stairs and retrieve my phone from my handbag. I turn it on and go to the kitchen to get a cup of coffee. As my phone turns on, I see that Chloe has left another two messages. I take some tablets out of the cupboard as I feel a headache looming.

I make my cup of coffee and swallow down two tablets, rubbing my temples as I try to calm my rage. I lean against the work top and close my eyes.

Why did Jake have to do that?

Why did he have to bring up the subject of a baby?

I open my eyes and see that Jake has appeared in the kitchen doorway. I suck in a breath at the sight of him. He looks pissed off.

"I'm going to the office," he says before he turns and leaves the house. I hear the front door close and I let out a cry of frustration.

He really wants to leave things between us like this?

My phone starts to ring in my hand, breaking through my thoughts. I look to the screen and see that it is Chloe calling, again. I groan out loud. I don't want to answer this, but I know that I have to.

I take a deep breath and answer the call.

"Hi, Chloe," I say tentatively.

"Where the hell are you, Stacey? I have been trying to get hold of you all morning," she screeches down the phone at me, making me grimace.

"I told you that I had an emergency. I'm coming back tonight. Re-schedule the book signing for another time." I keep my voice even as I try to hold on to calm thoughts. Not an easy task when Chloe is screaming at me and Jake is being a stubborn ass.

"Do you really think that it is that simple?" Chloe says. "Oh, just re-schedule for another time. Why didn't I think of that?"

"I apologise for the inconvenience, Chloe, but there really was nothing that I could do. I had to leave and that's that." I am not in the mood to be lectured.

"I just don't think that you understand the full implications of missing your book signing today, Stacey. I just—"

"I get it, Chloe," I say, cutting her off. "I have apologised for leaving, but it was urgent. I do have a life outside of this book tour, you know? Now, if you could cut your rant short and leave it there, then I would appreciate it. I will be back at the hotel by seven tonight." My tone leaves no room for any more discussion on the matter.

Chloe goes quiet and I take that as my cue to end the call. "I will see you in the morning, Chloe."

I hang up the phone without saying goodbye. I have more important things to deal with than some pissed off agent. I'm the one making her money for fuck's sake.

I alert the car service to pick me up from the hospital at five this afternoon. There is no way that I am leaving here until I have seen Lydia and my gorgeous god-daughter again.

First things first though, if Jake thinks that I am going away and leaving things like this between us, then he has got another thing coming.

With determination, I get ready and call a taxi to come and pick me up.

Jake storming out of here like a child is the quickest way to get me to react, and boy, is he going to wish that he had stayed at home for this conversation.

CHAPTER FOUR

STACEY

I arrive at the Waters Industries building just after quarter past two. I pay the taxi fare and march my way through the front doors, going straight to the lifts and waiting for the doors to open. They do so a few moments later, and Martin comes walking out.

"Baby girl," he says as he gives me a quick hug.

"Hey, Mart."

"What are you doing here? Shouldn't you be on your tour right now?" Martin asks me.

"I should be, but Lydia had the baby early this morning, so I came back." Martin starts to clap with excitement at this news, making me smile.

"Oh, I must go and see her. How are they both doing?" I give Martin a quick rundown of what happened. When I have finished, he frowns at me. "Why are you so tense, baby girl?"

"Jake."

"Oh. You two had a tiff?"

"Something like that."

"Ah, so that is why the God-like-creature came storming in here not so long ago then."

"The God-like-creature?" I raise one eyebrow at Martin's reference to Jake.

"What?" he says innocently. "I like it. It has a nice ring to it, don't you think?"

"If you say so," I reply, smiling. "Listen, I need to go and see him before I have to head back to the hotel, but I'm back next week. Fancy a night out then?"

"Absolutely."

"Fab, I'll call you when I wrap up the tour."

"You sure that you're not too busy for us little people now that you're a hot-shot author?" Martin teases.

"Don't be silly. I do however have a God-like-creature's ego to attend to though." The determination in my face must be evident.

"Oh shit, look out Jakey boy." Martin chuckles and gives me a kiss on the cheek. "Hit me up when you're back."

"I will." We say our goodbyes and I enter another waiting lift. I missed the first one due to my conversation with Martin. There are a few other people in the lift, meaning that it takes me longer to reach Jake's floor than I would like.

When the lift pings open on the relevant floor, I march out and go over to Valerie's desk.

"Hi, Valerie," I say, startling her. She looks up from her computer screen and smiles. "Is Jake in there?" I ask her, pointing to his office.

"He is, dear. Go on through."

"Thank you," I reply.

I walk to his office doors and throw them open. Jake is sat behind his desk, talking on the phone. I enter his office, closing the doors behind me, and his eyes penetrate me. I don't know who he is speaking to, and to be quite honest, I couldn't give a fuck either.

I stalk over to his desk and fold my arms across my chest. Jake is muttering something about acquisitions, showing no sign of ending his conversation, and he raises one eyebrow at me.

I wait a few seconds to be courteous, but my patience is rapidly wearing thin.

I wait precisely ten more seconds before I blow.

"Are you going to get off of the phone? I don't have all day to wait around for you, Waters." I say loudly, wanting the person on the other end of the phone to hear me.

Jake looks at me with shock at my outburst. When he makes no move to end the call, I place my hand over the phone with my finger hovering on the button to cut the call. He looks to my hand and then back at me, almost giving me a challenging look. I stare back at him, never averting my gaze.

"I will do it," I say, smiling sweetly. Jake seems to process my words for a few seconds, and then quickly comes to the decision that I am being serious. He clears his throat, ends the call and then slams the receiver down. He stands up and braces his hands on the desk.

"What the hell do you think you are doing? I was in the middle of an important phone call," he says, his anger apparent.

"You could be talking to the Prime Minister for all I care. How dare you just leave the house without talking to me rationally. How bloody old are you?" My voice is high-pitched, making my rational comment seem a little hypocritical.

"And storming in here, interrupting my phone call isn't childish?" Jake asks me. His eyes blaze into mine and I raise my chin defiantly.

There is no way that he is turning this around on me.

"Well if you had just spoken to me at home, instead of going off in a strop, then

I wouldn't have had to come down here and interrupt your phone call," I answer him, sweetly.

"What is there to talk about? You don't want kids. End of discussion."

"I don't want kids *right now*. You are making this a bigger deal than it needs to be, Jake."

"Oh, I'm so sorry," Jake says sarcastically. "I just thought that having a baby with the woman that I love would have been perfect. Excuse me for getting it so wrong."

"Aaargh," I let out a cry of frustration. "Will you just stop." I hold my hands up in front of me, palms facing Jake. "I do want kids with you one day, I really do." My tone softens slightly. "Just not right now. It doesn't mean that I don't love you. It just means that I want to finish my book tour and then have some time for just me and you."

I start to walk slowly around his desk until I am standing before him. I place my hands on his chest and tilt my head to look into his eyes. "I love the fact that you want us to start a family. But you need to understand that at this point in my life, I need to follow my career. And I want us to share some more memories together before we embark on parenthood." I can feel some of the tension leaving Jake's body at my words.

"We haven't even been together a year yet, Jake. There is no need for us to rush anything. We have the rest of our lives together. I don't want to leave here with us mad at each other."

I look into his caramel pools and see the anger subsiding. I reach my hands up and entwine them around his neck, pushing my body against his.

"Can't we just enjoy what we have right now?" I say as I stand on tip toes and place my lips on his. Jake's hands come to rest on my hips as he returns my kiss. All too soon, the kiss turns more passionate and I am clawing at his clothes to get them away from his body.

We become a frenzied mess as I push Jake's trousers and boxers down and he lifts my skirt up. He picks me up and places me on the edge of his desk, pulling my knickers to one side and before plunging his hard length into my opening. I lean back on a groan and close my eyes.

I feel Jake's lips connect with my skin as he trails kisses up my neck. His rhythm is steady as he thrusts into me. I put my arms behind me, hands face down on the desk, so that I can meet his thrusts.

I open my eyes to see his blazing with emotion, and it almost takes my breath away.

"I'm close," I whisper in-between pants.

"Wait for me," Jake says, placing his thumb on my clit which he moves in small circles.

As I moan with desire, Jake's breathing starts to quicken. I bite his bottom lip and he growls like a predator. A few thrusts later and I know that he is about to let go.

"Come for me, Stacey," he says, his voice hoarse.

I let my climax take hold and we both ride out or releases together, holding each other close.

As my body goes limp, Jake pulls me into his arms, his grip on me tight.

As my breathing starts to slow to a normal pace, I look up at him.

My beautiful man.

"I love you," I say to him as all the anger I was feeling earlier disappears.

"I love you too." His smile melts my insides.

He pulls out of me and we both sort ourselves out, so that we look presentable to the outside world. I look to the clock on his office wall and see that I need to leave to get to the hospital. If I don't go now, then I won't see Lydia and the baby before I have to return to the hotel.

"I have to go," I say as Jake groans at my words.

I give him a lingering kiss to cushion the blow of my absence.

"I'm sorry," Jake says, his eyes conveying his sincerity for his earlier actions. "I am so proud of you, but I will be glad when this book tour is over, and I get to have you back home with me."

"Me too."

CHAPTER FIVE

STACEY

Jake insists that Eric drives me to the hospital, and I don't argue. I say my good-byes to Jake and go and wait outside the building for Eric. He pulls up to the curb a few minutes later and gets out to open the car door for me.

"Hi, Eric."

"Miss Stacey," he says with a simple nod of his head.

I get into the back of the limo and relax into the plush seat. The partition is up, and as much as I don't want to be rude, I am not really in the mood to make chit-chat right now. I just watch the scenery go by as Eric drives me to the hospital.

When we arrive, Eric opens the car door for me and I thank him for the lift and tell him that I will see him soon. After bidding Eric farewell, I make my way into the hospital and up to Lydia's room.

The door is closed when I get there, so I gently knock and wait to be invited in.

"Come in," Lydia shouts. I open the door and am greeted by the sight of Lydia propped up on the bed, with her little girl cradled in her arms.

Lydia breaks out into a big smile when she sees me. "Hey, babes."

"Hi, Lyd. I hope that you don't mind me coming back, but I couldn't leave to go to the hotel without seeing you guys again." I walk over to the side of Lydia's bed and my heart melts at the sight of her little girl's face. She is gorgeous. Her eyes are closed, and she looks so peaceful.

"Oh, Lydia, she is so beautiful," I exclaim. I reach out and brush the baby's cheek with my finger. "Ah, her skin is so soft."

"I know, right?" Lydia answers. "I can't believe that she is here." Lydia's eyes are full of love as she gazes at her little girl. "She is just so perfect. Do you want a cuddle?"

"Oh my God, yes." I feel excited and nervous as Lydia hands me her baby. I gently cradle her in my arms and take a seat on the chair, next to the bed. "She's so tiny and precious."

I coo over the baby for the next few minutes as Lydia looks on proudly.

"Where's Paul?" I ask.

"He went home to get a change of clothes for me, as well as a few other bits I asked him to bring in. He's been great, Stace, even with me threatening to emasculate him during the labour."

I laugh at her. "Yeah, Paul did mention something about you wanting to kill him."

"Oh well," Lydia says as she shrugs her shoulders. "Blame it on the hormones." She smiles but then winces slightly.

"You okay?" I ask, concerned by her expression.

"I'm okay, just a bit sore. I need to take it easy for the next few days."

"I should think so."

"Paul's got the next couple of weeks off of work, so that we can get settled at home, and hopefully, by the time that he goes back to work, I will be healed and in a routine."

"I'm so proud of you, Lyd. You did amazing."

"Thanks, babes."

We sit in silence for a few moments, both looking at the little bundle of joy in my arms. "Have you thought of a name yet?" I ask her.

"Actually, we have." Lydia doesn't expand on her answer as she looks at me.

"And?" I ask her, the suspense nearly killing me.

"We're going to name her Amber."

"Oh, Lyd, that is such a beautiful name. Hello, Amber," I say, talking to the baby. "I'm your Auntie Stacey." I know that the baby is sleeping, but I just feel the need to talk to her. "And when your mummy is being unreasonable, just give me a call and I will sort her out."

"Hey," Lydia pipes up. "I am going to be a cool mum. There will be no sorting out needed," she says whilst smiling.

"Uh huh. If you say so. I will remind you of this moment in years to come though."

We both laugh in unison. I know that Lydia is going to be so protective of Amber.

"Do you want to know her middle name?"

"Yeah."

"Stacey."

"What?" I reply, wondering why the hell she is saying my name out loud when we are already having a conversation.

"Her middle name is Stacey. Amber Stacey Connors." I feel tears sting the backs of my eyes at Lydia's words.

"You're naming her after me?" I ask in a hushed voice. The emotion of this moment is threatening to get the better of me.

"Yeah. Who better to name her after than my best friend who has always been there for me?" Lydia's eyes also fill with tears and when Paul enters the room, we are both crying.

"Oh my God, what's wrong?" Paul asks, looking at both of us with worry etched all over his face.

"Oh, nothing," Lydia says with a wave of her hand. I can't speak right now. Lydia wipes some of her tears away. "I've just told Stacey the baby's name and, you know how us women are, emotional and all that nonsense."

"Ah," is all that Paul says, instantly understanding the tears. He puts down the bags that he brought in with him and then he goes to give Lydia a kiss on the cheek. He is looking at her like she is the only woman in the world. I love that he looks at her in that way. Lydia deserves this happiness, and I am so glad that Paul has been the one to give it to her.

I smile and attempt to wipe away my tears with one hand.

I stand up and give Amber back to Lydia.

"I really wish that I didn't have to go, but I need to get back to the book tour," I say, feeling regret at being pulled away from my closest friends so soon.

"Okay, babes. When are you back?" Lydia asks me.

"In a few days hopefully, but I want daily pictures of this little beauty sent to me." I point to Amber and Lydia nods her head. Somehow, I think that I am going to be inundated with photos.

I say goodbye to all three of them, giving Amber a kiss on her forehead before I leave the hospital, despite feeling an overwhelming urge to cancel going back to the hotel. It's a nice thought in hindsight, but in reality, I know that I can't cancel.

I need to see this book tour through, and then hopefully everything will be a bit more normal.

CHAPTER SIX

STACEY

The last few days have dragged by.

I have travelled to four different counties and all I want to do now is go back home. I have one more book signing tomorrow, and I can't wait for it to be over. I am so grateful for all of the fans that have turned up to my signings, but my face is literally aching from the constant smile that I have to keep plastered to my face.

It is only just after eight at night, but I am already in my pyjamas and led in bed.

Who would have thought that becoming an author could be so tiring?

I am waiting for room service to arrive with my evening meal of a chicken salad. I am too tired to go to the restaurant this evening.

I am about to watch a film on the television which is situated at the end of my bed, when there is a knock at the door. I get out of bed and plod over to the door, taking my purse with me, so that I can give the room service a tip.

However, I open the door to find that Chloe is stood there, holding my food in her hands.

"Uh, hi," I say, stunned to see her here. "Thinking of a change in career?" I ask her, not able to keep the playfulness out of my tone.

"Absolutely not," she says, screwing her face up in disgust. *God, she really is stuck up at times.* "I happened to see that the bellboy was going to knock on your door when I stopped him and said that I would deliver this to you."

"And why would you do that?" I ask. I am not in the mood for her this evening.

"I need to talk to you. Are you going to let me in?" she asks. I sigh and take a step back from the door, allowing her to enter my room.

Chloe walks in and sets the food down on the coffee table, which is positioned between two armchairs by the window. She sits down and perches on the edge of the seat with her back perfectly straight and her legs crossed in front of her. I roll my eyes, shut the door, and make my way over to the vacant armchair.

I sit down and curl my legs underneath me. I have no issues with making myself comfortable. If Chloe wants to sit there like her shit doesn't stink, then she can carry on.

She fidgets and clasps her hands together, and I wait to see if she is going to speak, but when she doesn't, I start to get impatient.

"Chloe, I don't mean to be rude, but I'm hungry and tired, so if you could get to the point of why you are here, then I would be grateful."

"Oh, yes, of course," she says, looking a little put out from my words. "Well, I know that your last book signing is tomorrow, but I have some news for you."

"And what news might that be?" If she says that they have added more dates to my tour, then I am going to be pissed off. I need a break.

"This is so exciting, Stacey," she says, looking the most animated that I have ever seen her. "After Christmas, we are taking your book tour to America." Chloe's voice has gone high-pitched and I can see that it is taking all of her willpower not to start bouncing up and down on the seat. The shock on my face must be apparent.

America?

Seriously?

"America?" I say with disbelief.

"Yes. America. Your first book signing over there is looking likely to be at the end of January. The book is going to be promoted within the next week."

"Wow, I wasn't expecting you to say that when I opened the door to you." I am flabbergasted.

America really want me?

I knew that we would be going overseas at some point, but I never dreamed that it would be to America. This is a massive breakthrough for a debut novelist. I know exactly what this could do for my career.

"I am still ironing out all of the details, but I will inform you of everything as soon as possible. This is a huge deal for you, Stacey."

Yeah, and no doubt the commission that you are going to be earning is a huge deal too, I think but I don't voice this out loud. Chloe will be making a pretty packet from this type of exposure.

"Anyway, that is all that I came to say. I just couldn't wait until tomorrow morning to share the news with you." Chloe stands up as I stare at her, still in shock. "I'll see myself out. I will be waiting outside for you tomorrow morning at nine o'clock, sharp." With that, Chloe heads to the door and exits my room.

I process her words for the next few moments as I slowly come to terms with what she has just said. If I thought that the success over here was overwhelming, then America is going to be a whole other feeling entirely.

I have lost my appetite as nerves and excitement course through me. I numbly rise from the chair and crawl back into the bed.

I grab my phone from the bedside table and call Jake.

"Hey, gorgeous," Jake answers. "Are you missing me?"

"Always." I hear him chuckle at my words and it warms me on the inside.

"To what do I owe the pleasure?" he asks me, his voice husky.

"Um, well, I have some news." Some news that he will be pleased about, but at the same time he won't be thrilled with me going away again.

"Okay," he answers warily.

"I'll get straight to the point. Chloe came over just now and told me that..." I struggle to form the words that I need to.

"Please tell me that you are still coming home tomorrow?" Jake asks, taking my silence as bad news.

"Yeah, I'm still coming home."

"Thank God for that," he says, relief laced in his tone. I suddenly get the overwhelming urge to scream. I want to scream from the rooftops that I am going to America to promote my book. I must be getting over the initial shock, and I feel a huge grin start to form on my face.

"My book tour is going to America, baby." I can hear the excitement in my voice, and I hope that Jake will mirror my emotions.

"That's great news," he says, sounding genuinely pleased.

"I know. I can't quite get my head around it. Me, in America, promoting my debut novel. This is what I have dreamed about, Jake. I never ever thought that this would happen to me." My words all come out in a rush as I experience a range of emotions.

"Babe, you are a fantastic writer. I never doubted your success for a second."

"Thank you." I am touched by his words. He really is one of a kind.

I guess I was wrong about him being annoyed about me going away again.

"I'm so proud of you." Jake's words cause my smile to get even bigger, if that is at all possible.

"I love you."

"I love you too."

"So, um, now that I have told you my news, how about we spice this phone call up a little?" I tease.

"Feeling frisky, are we?" Jake asks.

"Oh yeah."

"Well then, lie back and spread your legs, baby. I'm going to make you so wet that you are going to be rushing to get back to me tomorrow." I whimper at his words and his deep voice.

"I'm already wet for you," I say breathlessly.

"You're a bad girl, Miss Paris."

"Only for you, Waters."

CHAPTER SEVEN

STACEY

My final book signing goes well, and I am back at the hotel, packing my stuff away. It's just gone ten past three and my car service will be here at half past three.

When all of my belongings are packed, I take one last walk around the suite to make sure that I haven't missed anything. Once satisfied, I make my way out of the hotel suite and along the corridor to the lift, pulling my suitcase along behind me.

I decide to wait out the front of the building for the car service, so that I can jump straight in and get home as soon as possible. The car pulls up just before half past three, and the driver gets out to open the door for me.

"Thank you," I say as the driver starts to put my suitcase into the boot of the car.

I sit back and relax, ready for the two-hour car journey home.

We set off and my mind starts to wander. I may have only been gone for a few days since Lydia had Amber, but I feel like I have missed so much more than that. Lydia has sent me countless photos of Amber, and I can see changes in her already. I know that sounds ridiculous seeing as she is only a few days old, but it's true. I am looking forward to spending some time with both of them over the next few weeks.

I haven't even had a chance to speak to Martin properly, but I am hoping that we are still having a night out when I am back. I will arrange it with him tomorrow at some point.

I have heard nothing from Susie at The Den, so I am guessing that all is running smoothly. I appointed Susie as the acting manager when my book took off. My first choice would have been Lydia obviously, but she has decided to devote her time to Amber. Susie is more than capable, and I know that she would have contacted me if there was anything that she may have needed help with.

I kind of miss working at The Den. It was my first managerial role, and I loved it.

Unfortunately, a book tour doesn't allow you to keep a steady job. Not that I need to work in The Den anymore. I mean, I have made more than enough money from my book, but it doesn't stop me missing the daily routine of working there.

Maybe I could do a couple of shifts when I am back? It would just help to keep me in the loop.

It is Jake's business after all, so I would hate to see it fail in any way.

My mind then wanders to Jake. I am so looking forward to going home and just being with him. I smile at the image of him in my head. Tall, handsome, well-defined muscles, and those gorgeous caramel coloured eyes that always leave me weak at the knees.

The things that he has done for me during our time together, have been mind-blowing.

I have never felt so loved and cared for.

I have never felt so cherished and like I am someone else's everything.

Jake has made me feel those things.

Jake has made me believe in love again.

I think back to my birthday a few months ago. Jake surprised me with a weekend away to Rome. It was truly romantic. Nothing else in the world mattered to either of us during that weekend. We turned our phones off and just enjoyed being with one another. He wined and dined me, and then fucked me like only Jake can. My body shivers at the recollection of our sex sessions.

Maybe we could recreate some of those over the next few nights?

My phone beeps, breaking my thoughts. I look to the screen and see that it is a text message from Jake.

Speak of the devil, or think of the devil I should say.

I open the message and begin to read.

> *Stace, there is a problem at The Den.*
> *Is there any chance that you can come straight here when you get back? I'm sorry, but it is an emergency.*
> *I love you.*
> *Jake x x x*

Oh, fucking marvellous. I sigh with frustration.

Why hasn't Susie called me about The Den?

It must be bad if Jake has gotten himself involved.

I quickly text him back.

*Is it really so important that it needs
to be dealt with today?
Stace x x*

I await Jake's reply. He doesn't keep me waiting long.

*Afraid so babe.
Jake x x x*

I let out a groan and reluctantly type out a text saying that I will be there within the next hour. I am so tired from the book tour, and I was really looking forward to just going home after living out of a suitcase for the last few weeks.

I close my eyes and hope that whatever the problem is, I can help get it fixed quickly.

―――

JAKE

Nervous doesn't even come close to what I am feeling right now.

I have always been a fairly confident person, but today, I am a fucking wreck…

CHAPTER EIGHT

STACEY

I get to The Den just after six o'clock. We hit a little traffic during the journey back, so it took longer for me to get here than expected. The driver of the car service opens my door for me, and then retrieves my suitcase from the boot of the car. I thank him and wearily make my way to the front doors of The Den.

I find it strange that there are no security guys waiting out the front. Normally, when the place is open, there are two security guys waiting at the front doors at all times.

Maybe they are inside trying to help Jake with whatever the emergency is?

As I get to the front doors however, I find that they are locked.

What the hell?

Why are the doors locked?

I grunt and haul my suitcase around to the back entrance.

I don't understand why the place would be closed?

Whatever has happened must be pretty bad for it to be shut.

Dread settles in the pit of my stomach. The few bad memories I have of this place always come back to haunt me when shit goes wrong.

As I feel anxiety building within me, I try the handle for the back door.

It's open.

I wait at the entrance after opening the door and listen for any sounds. There's nothing.

I look around the car park and see that Jake's car is parked in one of the spaces towards the back. I shake my head, feeling a little silly that I am feeling so anxious. Jake is clearly here, and nothing bad is going to happen to me with Jake around.

I lug my suitcase inside and take a deep breath.

As I walk into the building, I let go of my suitcase and close the door behind me. I slowly make my way along the corridor and keep my ears pricked for any sounds.

All of a sudden, music starts to play softly.

I freeze as the opening lines of Miguel, "Adorn", filters through the sound system.

What is going on?

I feel my face pull into a frown as I continue to move forward. I pass my office and peak inside, but there is no one there.

Huh.

I move around the corner of the corridor, making my way past the toilets, and I can see dim lighting in the main room. I keep walking and come to a halt when I see that the main room has been decked out in fairy lights. My mouth falls open and my eyes come to rest on a table in the middle of the dance floor. The table has been set for two, and there is a bottle of wine chilling in a cooler to the side of the table.

I slowly spin in a circle, taking in the breath-taking sight. It all looks so pretty.

When I turn back to face the table, Jake is stood beside it, looking devilishly handsome.

He is wearing his grey suit, which happens to be my favourite, and a black shirt with the top few buttons left undone. His hair is a little messy, like he has been running his hands through it.

I lick my lips hungrily as I assess him.

His eyes are fixed on mine and he starts to walk towards me. I move too, meeting him at the end of the dance floor. The sexual tension between us is evident, making my body sizzle with desire.

My body hums, something that it always does when I am around Jake.

He stops a few inches in front of me, with his hands in his trouser pockets.

"Hey," he says softly as the song starts to play again from the beginning.

"Hi," I say breathlessly.

All I want to do is touch him.

All I want to do is feel him, but I need to wait and see what all of this set-up is about.

"Jake? What is all of this?" I say as I gesture around the room. His eyes remain fixed on mine, burning into me.

"I missed you and I wanted to do something special." Jake removes his hands from his pockets and takes both of my hands in his. My heartbeat accelerates from the contact. "Babe, I need to say some things to you."

He stops talking and I gulp so loud that I am sure that Jake can hear it. A soft smile grazes his lips, making me feel more at ease. It can't be anything too bad otherwise he wouldn't be smiling.

"There is no emergency, as you can see. I just wanted to get you here, without you suspecting anything," Jake says, making me feel more puzzled than before.

Suspecting anything?

I cannot take my eyes off of him. He is like a magnet. I am mesmerised by him. Jake slowly starts to sink to the floor, keeping hold of my hands, and my eyes widen.

Is this what I think it is?

My whole body feels like jelly, but somehow, I manage to stay standing.

Jake closes his eyes and takes a deep breath before opening them again. It is in this moment that I register that Jake is nervous. This is something that I am not used to seeing from Jake. He always exudes confidence, so I know that what is about to happen is a big deal to him, and his caramel centre's burn into mine.

"Stacey, the day that you walked into my life, I knew that I would never recover. The moment that your lips touched mine, I knew that I was addicted. My feelings for you grow more powerful by the day. I know that at times things have been hard, but we have overcome the obstacles that we have faced. I know that we are stronger together than we are apart.

"We have made some amazing memories together, and I hope that we will make many more in years to come. You were always the missing piece of my life. You make me feel complete.

"I love you, Stacey Paris, and I always want you to be able to picture this moment, right here, right now. I always want you to remember that this is the moment that I asked you to be my wife." I let out a gasp and tears are falling down my cheeks.

Jake reaches one hand into his pocket and produces a little blue, velvet box. I watch him open the box, using both of his slightly shaking hands, and the most gorgeous diamond ring is revealed. It is just one simple square-cut diamond, and the band is made of white gold. I feel my eyes go wide, and Jake takes one of my hands with his. My eyes travel back to him.

"This may not be the ideal place to propose to you, but this is where I first met you, and in that moment, my whole life changed. You changed me, Stace. You are my perfect everything. Stacey Marie Paris, will you marry me?" Jake's voice breaks, and I feel like I am going into meltdown.

He looks at me with anticipation, waiting for my answer.

I can't speak.

My throat feels like it is about to close up.

I swallow and blink a few times, taking in everything from this moment. Jake's expression starts to look worried and I mentally curse myself for making him wait. I realise how he must be feeling, and I quickly want to put any doubts about my answer out of his mind.

I move down, so that I am on my knees in front of him. I cup his face in both of my hands and feel a smile spread across my face. Tears are still falling from my eyes, but they are tears of happiness.

"Yes," I say quietly. In fact, I say it so quietly that, for a moment, I am not sure that Jake has heard me. I repeat my answer but make my voice louder. "Yes, I will marry you, Jake."

Jake lets out the breath that he has been holding and then he grabs me. He places a kiss on my lips and I wrap my arms around his neck. I feel him grin against my lips and I pull my head back to look at him. He looks deliriously happy, and I know that I am mirroring his look.

He moves his hands and body away from me slightly, and he takes the ring out of its box. I stare at his movements, hardly daring to blink in case I miss anything.

He takes hold of my left hand and then slowly places the ring on my third finger. He kisses the back of my hand when the ring is in place and then he looks back to me. I feel like my heart is about to burst with all of the emotion that I am feeling.

"I love you," Jake says, his eyes brimming with tears.

"I love you too," I manage to choke out.

This moment is definitely going down as the most perfect moment of my life.

―――――

JAKE

She said yes.

She said fucking yes.

I don't think that I have ever felt so relieved at someone's answer before.

I can't wait to make her Mrs Jake Waters.

CHAPTER NINE

STACEY

I wake up to the feel of Jake's arms wrapped around me. I smile and snuggle closer to him as the events of yesterday come rushing back to me.

The way that Jake proposed was special.

Special to me, and special to us.

He couldn't have made it anymore perfect.

I look at the ring on my finger and I have to stop myself from shouting out with excitement.

I am engaged.

Me.

Engaged.

Engaged to the most handsome man that I have ever had the fortune of laying my eyes on. The ring is perfect for me, and he is perfect for me. I feel so lucky to have found him.

There is absolutely nothing that can bring down my mood today, and God help anyone that attempts to.

"What are you thinking?" Jake asks, startling me.

"I thought that you were still sleeping?"

"I was until a moment ago." Jake wriggles down so that he is eye level with me. "Good morning, Mrs Waters-to-be."

Oh my God! Mrs Waters! Mrs Stacey Waters! I love the way that sounds.

"Morning to you too, handsome."

"So, come on, tell me what thoughts were running through that beautiful mind of yours." Jake starts to kiss my neck and I struggle to concentrate on the question that he has asked me. I let out a small groan and I feel Jake's lips curve into a smile against my skin. "I'm sorry, am I distracting you?"

"Yes."

"My apologies. I'll stop," Jake says, pulling his lips away. I frown at him in frustration, but all this does is make him laugh.

"No fair," I say, pouting like a stroppy teenager.

"All in good time, babe." He smiles at me and I can't help but soften towards him. He knows me far too well. "Come on. Thoughts." I am a little surprised that he so desperately wants to know what I was thinking about.

Maybe he thinks that you are having second thoughts and he just needs a little reassurance?

If that is why he wants to know, then I need to shut down that line of thinking.

"I was just thinking about how perfect last night was." My hands reach into Jake's hair and I give a gentle tug. The growl in the back of his throat hits me straight at my core, making me wet with desire for him. His tongue traces my bottom lip and then he places a light kiss on the end of my nose.

"I'm glad that you liked it," Jake says, grinning at me.

"I didn't just like it, Jake. I loved it. It was the best moment of my life." I am fully aware that I sound like a soppy romantic, but I don't care. Sometimes being a soppy romantic is called for.

"I am going to go and make some breakfast," Jake announces before leaping from the bed.

"Why?" I whine.

"Uh, because it is morning, Stace. Generally, people have breakfast in the morning."

"Ha ha, very funny wise-ass," I reply sarcastically. "What I mean is, why are you doing that now when we could be working up more of an appetite?" I wiggle my eyebrows at him and he laughs.

"Oh, don't worry, you will be more than hungry by the time I have finished with you, but that's after breakfast," Jake says, raising his eyebrows at me in a suggestive manner.

"Well, then who am I to argue," I reply, conceding defeat.

Jake gets out of bed and pulls on his jogging bottoms. He goes to leave the bedroom, but not before giving me a cheeky wink. I laugh and throw a pillow at him. I hear him chuckling down the hallway, the sound making me wish that I had grabbed him and pulled him back into bed just now.

I sigh with contentment and go to the ensuite to use the toilet and assess my appearance in the mirror. My face is flushed, my lips are swollen, and my hair is going to be a nightmare to try and get a brush through. I attempt to tidy it up as best as I can and then I brush my teeth. I splash some cold water over my face and look down at my ring finger. The ring really is stunning. I couldn't have chosen better myself.

Jake gets me, and he knows exactly what I like.

I can't believe that I have found my soulmate, in every aspect of the word.

What I had with Charles seems foolish compared to what Jake and I have together.

I walk back into the bedroom with a smile on my face as Jake enters with a tray consisting of coffee and toast.

"I know that it's not exactly the ideal breakfast for a newly engaged woman, but there isn't much shopping in," Jake says, looking and sounding apologetic.

"Things really have gone downhill since I have been away," I tease.

He places the tray on the bed and comes over to me. He pulls me into his arms and I nuzzle into him. His chin rests on the top of my head and I close my eyes, feeling more content than I ever have before.

"I can't wait for you to be my wife," he whispers.

"Me either."

"Well, in that case, let's set a date."

"Seriously?" I ask, my eyes springing open as I pull my head back to look at him.

"Yeah. Why should we wait? I want to call you Mrs Waters sooner rather than later," Jake says, astounding me.

"But doesn't it take months to plan a wedding?" I ask, my eyebrows raised.

"You do know me, don't you, babe?" he says with a mischievous look in his eye.

I laugh. "I do, yes, but a wedding usually takes a while to plan, Jake. I don't want us to rush it."

"It won't be rushed. There are plenty of people that I can hire to make it the wedding of your dreams. What do you say?" Jake looks so excited and I can feel my heart flutter at his urgency to marry me.

"You're a hard man to deny, Waters," I say, making him grin. "When were you thinking of?"

"Next week."

"Next week?" I screech at him. He can't be serious. "Jake, there is no way that we can arrange everything for next week."

"Want a bet?" he asks me. I am unsure whether he is joking or not, but my gut feeling tells me that Jake is being deadly serious.

"Impossible," I say in a challenging tone. "There's the venue, the dress, the guests to invite, the reception. Do I need to go on?"

"You forgot cars, music and flowers," he says making me widen my eyes with shock. He starts to laugh at my reaction. "Stace, I am fully aware of what goes into a wedding. I have thought about nothing else since I decided to ask you to marry me."

Jake literally blows me away.

Just when I think that he can't shock or surprise me anymore, he does.

"Really? I think that maybe, on this occasion, you are being just a tad optimistic about getting everything done."

"Leave it with me." With that, Jake lets go of me and leaves the bedroom. I stand, frozen to the spot for a few moments as I try to gather my thoughts.

A wedding next week?

He really is insane.

JAKE

Stacey really does underestimate me at times.

I have been in my home office for an hour and I have already secured a venue and arranged cars for our wedding. It's amazing what you can achieve when your name is Jake Waters. I don't like to use my name to get what I want, but on this occasion, I am making an exception.

I am about to phone Martin and ask him to plan the reception when Stacey enters my office. She looks incredible, even if she is only wearing leggings and a loose-fitting jumper. She walks over to my desk and perches on the edge, facing me.

"What are you doing?" she asks.

"Planning our wedding," I answer. "I have booked the venue and the cars so far." Her face really is a picture at this point. Her mouth has fallen open and her eyes look like they are about to pop out of their sockets.

"I need you to choose what flowers you want, and you need to book a day to go wedding dress shopping. Oh, and I was about to call Martin as I thought that he could arrange the reception for us—"

"Whoa, whoa, whoa," Stacey says, holding both of her hands up in front of her. "Jake, I think that you may have actually lost the plot." She looks flabbergasted and it is taking all of my willpower not to burst out laughing at her. "I don't suppose that you would mind telling me what day we are getting married on?" I can hear a touch of sarcasm in her tone, but I choose to ignore it.

"Next Friday."

"Uh huh. And where is it that our nuptials are taking place, exactly?"

"At the Bowden Hall."

"You're not even joking, are you?"

"Nope." I reach my arms out and pull her off of the desk and onto my lap. "I told you that I want you as my wife, Stacey. You are mine, and I want the whole world to know it." I may sound possessive, but I don't care. She is mine, and she always will be.

She puts one of her hands on my cheeks and lightly rubs her fingers up and down.

"You amaze me, Waters." I can see tears glistening in her eyes and it makes my insides flip. She has been the only woman to ever make me feel like this, and I will never let go of that.

"Why thank you." I place a quick kiss on her lips. "Now, we have a lot left to organise, so we need to get a move on. No interruptions."

"Not even just a five-minute interruption?" she teases.

"You know as well as I do that it won't just be five minutes." I raise one eyebrow at her and she pouts at me. God, her pout is so sexy that it sends signals straight to my cock.

Fuck, I'm going to be a goner if I don't distract myself from her.

"But as your wife to be, shouldn't you cater to my every need?"

Oh, she's good.

She's real good.

She looks innocent enough, but I know what game she is playing. And by the looks of it, it is a game that she is going to win. I stand up, lifting her with me, and she lets out a squeal of delight as I race like a lunatic back to the bedroom.

"This will be quick," I tell her, not believing a word of it.

"That's fine by me. You can make up for it again later."

CHAPTER TEN

STACEY

Okay, so our 'five-minute interruption' ended up being a lot longer than five minutes. I knew that it wouldn't be quick. It was ridiculous for Jake to think otherwise.

I look over at him on the phone, and I admire the way in which he commands every situation. We just had mind-blowing sex, and now he is in business mode.

He is extremely hot in business mode.

I am meant to be looking at flowers on the internet, but I am too transfixed by him to concentrate. He finishes his phone call and looks over at me, sat on the sofa, in his office. I avert my eyes too late as he catches me staring at him. He smirks, and I know that he loves the fact that I can't get enough of him.

"Aren't you meant to be looking at flowers?" he asks me.

"I am."

"Liar." I can't argue with him, because on this occasion I am lying. I sigh as I return my eyes to the computer screen. I am not a massive fan of flowers. I mean, they can be very pretty, but I don't know the first thing about what types of flowers people have at weddings.

I scan down the page and see nothing that interests me. All of the different flower names is also playing havoc with my concentration. I wouldn't know the difference between any of them. I search through a couple more pages, but nothing catches my eye.

I am about to give up and let Jake take over the choosing of the flowers, when I click on the fifth page and am astounded by a flower bouquet on there. It is stunning, as well as managing to stay simple and elegant. According to the description, this particular bouquet consists of pure white roses, orchids, and freesias. The arrangement of the flowers has been done beautifully, and I excitedly take the laptop over to Jake and point the bouquet out to him.

"I want those," I tell him. He studies the flowers and makes a "Hmm" sound as he does.

"Okay. Done."

"Done?"

"Yes, I will order them in a minute. Now you need to decide when you are going to go dress shopping, and where." God, he really has got this all figured out. I feel like I should be the one bossing him about.

"Um, I'll need to talk to Lydia first to see if she can come with me."

"Give her a call now."

"I can't tell her over the phone, Jake."

"Why not?"

"Because I just can't. I want to tell her in person."

"Well, get your ass round there now and tell her then," Jake says, keeping his tone light but dominant at the same time. I'm not quite sure how he manages to maintain a cool-yet-commanding vibe.

I stand to attention and salute him playfully. "Yes, sir."

"Don't take the piss, Stace." He pulls on my arm and I lean down to give him a kiss. "Hurry back. We have lots more to organise." I smile at him and go to walk out of his office.

Just as I am about to step into the hallway, I turn back around and face him. "Don't tell Martin. I want to be the one to tell him."

"Okay, fine." Jake is already phoning someone else as I flounce from the room.

I start to feel really excited as I return to the bedroom and throw on more acceptable clothing. I grab a pair of jeans and a fitted V-neck pink jumper. I run a brush through my hair and leave my face make-up free. When satisfied, I go downstairs, put my boots and coat on and shout bye to Jake. I pick up my car keys and head out of the front door. It is bitterly cold outside, and we have been forecast some snow, but I can't remember the last time that we had snow in December, so I don't hold out much hope.

I get in my car and turn the heater up full blast. Once the car has de-misted, I pull off of the driveway and begin the short journey to Lydia and Paul's house. I wonder if Lydia will be as excited as I am feeling right now when I tell her that I am getting married in a week's time.

The idea of it is crazy, but Jake and I have never been known to follow any protocols when it comes to our relationship.

I let my thoughts consume me as I pull onto Lydia's driveway. It still feels weird not driving to her flat. Lydia and Paul moved in together six months ago, and they have a four bedroom detached property with an annexe built onto the side. It's not quite as big as mine and Jake's house, but it is so pretty.

I get out of the car and walk to the front door. As I knock on the door, I can hear the faint sound of Amber crying. The front door whizzes open a few seconds later and I am greeted by a frantic looking Lydia. As soon as she registers that it is me, she engulfs me in a bear hug.

"Babes, thank fuck you are here," she says as she pulls me into the house. "I don't know what to do. Paul has nipped to the shop, and Amber has been crying the whole time. I have tried everything I can think of to soothe her, but she just won't stop crying." Lydia is rambling. She stops as we enter the lounge, and I see that Amber is led in her moses basket. I turn to Lydia, feeling that she needs my attention just a little bit more than Amber does at this point.

"You go and make us a drink, and I will try to calm Amber down." Lydia looks so tired and I feel like she is going to burst into tears at any moment. She doesn't argue with me. She gives a slight nod of her head and then turns and leaves the lounge.

I walk over to Amber, placing my car keys on the sofa, and I pick her up. She is screaming as if her life depends on it. I am pretty sure that I am going to leave here deaf. I turn Amber, so that her head is resting on my shoulder and I start to gently rub her back, hoping that it will create a settling feeling for her. She continues to cry, and then all of a sudden, she lets out a massive burp. I giggle and continue to rub her back, just in case she needs to burp again. Amber immediately stops crying and when I look at her, her eyes are closed.

She is such a gorgeous little girl. Her little tuft of hair adds to her cuteness factor. I daren't put Amber back in the moses basket for fear of waking her, and for fear of my ear drums becoming permanently damaged. Instead, I sit on the sofa and settle back with Amber still resting her head on my shoulder.

Lydia comes in just as I get myself comfortable. She is carrying the drinks and looks astounded that I have managed to make the crying stop.

"How the hell have you managed to get her to stop crying?" she asks me in disbelief.

"She had wind. I presume that was the issue and she must have exhausted herself from crying, so she fell asleep." I smile at Lydia, but she looks outraged.

"Honestly, Stace, I tried to wind her, but do you think that the stubborn little madam would bring it up for me? She certainly doesn't take after me."

"I think that we both know that isn't the case," I say, making Lydia narrow her eyes at me. "You can be quite stubborn yourself when you put your mind to it."

I am quite glad that I am holding Amber, she acts as a shield from Lydia who looks like she wants to scratch my eyes out.

"Whatever," Lydia says, conceding defeat and flopping down on the sofa opposite me.

"So, how are you doing? Apart from having your ear drums deafened that is," I say, keeping my tone light.

"Oh, I'm just peachy. Tired, frazzled and bedraggled looking. It's such a wonderful feeling," Lydia says sounding miserable.

"Oh dear. Do I detect a hint of the baby blues?" I ask, hoping that this comment won't set her hormones raging.

"That's what Paul keeps saying. Maybe I should speak to my midwife about it when she comes here tomorrow to do the final checks?"

"Final checks?" I ask, not having a clue what she means. I always thought that the midwife buggered off from your life once the baby was born.

"Vaginal checks. You know, make sure everything is still as it should be." Lydia looks unfazed by her answer. She just comes out with it so bluntly.

"Oh." I have no idea what to say to this, so I opt to change the subject. I'm also hoping that my news may cheer Lydia up a little bit. "Well, I have something to tell you."

"Unless it is the fact that you are getting married or having a baby, then I don't wish to know."

Christ, Lydia really is grouchy today.

I wait for her to engage with me before answering. Her eyes look at me a minute later as she registers my silence, and I see a tiny flicker of hope spark to life within her with her next words.

"Oh my God, *are* you pregnant?" she asks, excitement at the thought clearly visible on her face.

"Uh, no." Lydia's shoulders slump. "But I am getting married." I hold my hand out to her, so that she can see my engagement ring. Her eyes go wide, and she jumps up with a shriek.

"Ahhh!" she shouts, making Amber stir.

"Shhh," I say to her. "You'll wake the baby." Lydia instantly looks terrified and stops jumping up and down. She sits back on the sofa and looks at me with a massive grin on her face.

"Oh God, babes, this is so exciting."

"Wait, there's more."

"More?"

"Yeah. I'm getting married next week, and I would like you to be my maid of honour." I wait with baited breath for Lydia's reaction. I think that she is about to start screeching again, but she manages to exert some self-control.

"Holy shit. Next week?"

"I know that it sounds crazy, and I know that there is a lot to do, but it feels right, Lyd. I want this. Jake has already booked the venue and the cars, and by now he has probably booked the flowers as well."

"Wow. You guys don't hang around, do you?"

"Apparently not. So, what do you say? Will you be my maid of honour?"

"Of course I will, babes. I'd be honoured."

"Fabulous. Now, we need to pick a day to go dress shopping." Lydia looks like she could burst at any moment. Maybe this is just what she needed to take her mind off of the baby blues?

CHAPTER ELEVEN

STACEY

I return to the house a couple of hours later. It was so nice to spend time with Lydia and Amber.

I head straight to the kitchen and make myself a cup of coffee, which I take upstairs to Jake's office. As I approach the doorway, I see that Jake is still sat behind his desk, staring at his computer screen.

"Hey, babe," he says, keeping his eyes fixed on the computer.

"Hey, handsome. Everything okay?"

"Yes," he answers, still keeping his eyes glued to the computer screen.

"Are there naked chicks on that screen?" I ask as I walk over to see what has captured Jake's attention. He quickly shuts the lid of his laptop down.

"Uh, Jake?" I say his name questioningly, wondering what he would need to hide from me.

"You can't look."

"Well, I gathered that. Why the hell not?"

"Because... It's a surprise."

"A surprise?" I ask, my interest piqued even more than it already was.

"Yes." I am itching to ask more questions, but from the look of determination on Jake's face, I'm guessing that my efforts would be wasted.

"So, not only do you surprise me with a quickie wedding, but now there is something else to look forward to?"

"Our wedding is not going to be a quickie wedding, Stace. A quickie wedding implies that we are eloping, which we are not. Ours is just being planned faster than usual, that's all."

"If you say so," I reply in a teasing manner. "So, you're not even going to give me a clue about this new surprise?" I ask, just giving it one try to see if he will give me any hints.

"Nope. Not a chance."

"You're no fun, Waters."

"I think we both know that that's not true," Jake says. "And you may be cute when you pout, but I'm still not telling you." Jake starts to smirk, and I poke my tongue out at him. His smirk turns into a full-on laughing fit.

I take a sip of my coffee cup and walk out of his office and am climbing the stairs when Jake grabs me from behind, resulting in my coffee spilling everywhere.

"Jake," I shriek at him. "Now look what you have done." When he finally lets go of me, I point to the spilled coffee all over the plush carpet. "That's going to leave a stain."

"So? I'll just have it cleaned," Jake says with a shrug of his shoulders. He's not concerned about a coffee spillage in the slightest. I playfully smack him on the arm. "Can we go out to dinner tonight? I can tell you about all of the other arrangements that I made whilst you were at Lydia's. How did that go by the way?"

"Good. Well, when I got there Lydia seemed to be having some sort of nervous breakdown, but I soon cheered her up. She is thrilled to be my maid of honour."

"Excellent. Although, I didn't ever think that there was any doubt that she would say yes. That reminds me, I need to give Paul a ring and ask him to be my best man." Jake starts to walk back to his office.

"And you need to call Martin before I do," he shouts at me, not even bothering to turn around. I watch him disappear from sight, admiring his physique as he goes before I go up to our bedroom, put my half empty coffee cup on the bedside table and pick up my phone, which I left here in my haste to go and see Lydia.

I look at the screen and see that I have a picture message from Lydia waiting to be opened. I open the message quickly as I know that it is going to be a picture of my beautiful god-daughter. I am greeted by the sight of Amber sleeping. Lydia has put a little caption by it that says, "she is still sleeping! You are a life saver!" This is followed by the image of a thumbs up sign. I smile and am so pleased that I was able to help, even if the peace will only last for a little while. I save the picture to my photos and then pull up my contacts list, selecting Martin's name when I get to it. It only rings twice before he answers the call.

"Hey, baby girl. What's shaking?"

"Hey, I need to speak to you about something."

"Oooo, intriguing. Is this another sex revenge plan? Oh, please tell me that it is. They are so much fun." Martin sounds very excited by the prospect of another one of these plans.

"Afraid not, but I am sure that there will be another one of those in the pipeline at some point." I hear Martin tut and sigh, clearly disappointed by my answer.

"Okay, so what's up?" he asks me.

"Well, uh, something happened last night that I need to tell you about. Are you sat down?"

"No. Do I need to be?"

"Depends on how shocked you are going to be, I suppose," I say, wishing that I was having this conversation with him face to face.

"Oh God, nothing bad has happened, has it?"

"No, no. It's good news," I say reassuringly.

"Well, come on then, woman, don't keep me in suspense," Martin says a little impatiently. I take a deep breath and get ready for what I know will be his fabulous over the top reaction.

"I'm getting married—" I am cut off by the sound of Martin screaming down the phone. It appears that I was wrong when I thought that Amber would be the one to deafen me today. It turns out that it will be Martin instead.

I pull the phone away from my ear until I hear him quieten down. "That's not the best bit."

"How is that not the best bit?" Martin says, excitement evident in his voice.

"Will you let me finish?" I pause for a second to make sure that he is going to remain quiet. When I am satisfied that he isn't going to speak, I clear my throat and carry on. "I am getting married next Friday, and I would like you to plan the reception." I hear Martin gasp.

"Oh my gosh, baby girl. Are you serious right now?"

"Deadly."

"Of course I'll bloody do it. O.M.G. I am going to make it oh-so-fabulous."

"I know. But nothing too over the top." I know exactly what will happen if Martin is left to his own devices without a bit of guidance. I'll end up with pink flamingos in a fucking fake pond if Martin were to have his own way. "It needs to be simple and tasteful."

"Of course it will be. What do you take me for?"

"Do you really want me to answer that?" I ask him playfully.

"Probably not."

"Whilst we are on a roll, there is one more thing that I need to ask you."

"There's more?"

"Uh huh." I hope to God that he says yes to my next question.

"Okay. What else could there possibly be?"

"Well, I would rather have asked you this question in person but seeing as it is going to be manic around here for the next week, I need to ask you sooner rather than later." I pause and take a deep breath, feeling a little bit nervous all of a sudden.

"I would love it if you would walk me down the aisle and give me away." Another gasp on the end of the phone ensues and I wait with baited breath. When Martin doesn't answer after a few minutes, I start to panic that he doesn't want to do it. "Listen, if you don't want to then that's okay."

"No, I..." Martin's voice breaks, and I hear him sniffle.

"Are you crying?" I ask.

"Of course I'm fucking crying. You have just asked me to do the most precious thing, so I apologise if I have come over all emotional," he says, a hint of sarcasm lacing his tone.

"Okay, I'm sorry," I say. "So, is that a yes then?"

"Of course it's a yes. Oh, baby girl, I am so privileged." The smile beams from my face. I couldn't think of anyone else I would want to give me away.

"Yay! Oh my gosh, we need to go out and celebrate. Are you free tomorrow night?" I ask him.

"You bet I am."

"Great. Meet you at The Den at eight?"

"It's a date. You know though that this means that I get to boss you about, being your substitute father and all."

I laugh at his response. "Don't let it go to your head. I'll see you tomorrow."

"You sure will, baby girl. Oh, I am so excited."

"Me too. Bye, Mart."

"Byesy bye." I hang up and sigh with relief.

Well, that's two more things crossed off of the list.

I best get showered and dressed to go out to dinner with my husband-to-be.

CHAPTER TWELVE

STACEY

Jake takes me to the upscale restaurant that is Claringtons. Thank goodness I opted to wear a dress, as he didn't tell me beforehand that we would be coming here. I have on a long grey dress that hugs my body. The fabric feels like silk against my skin. There is a slit in the side which goes to just above my knee. It has spaghetti straps, and down the sides runs a line of little diamanté gems. I teamed it with my old faithful black stilettos and I decided to leave my hair down after taking an age to straighten it.

Jake looks very handsome in his black suit, grey shirt and black tie. In fact, he looks so good that I would rather eat him than anything from the actual menu, but I will restrain myself.

Eric drove us here in the limo, so that Jake can enjoy a few drinks with his meal. We enter the restaurant and the hostess immediately recognises Jake. She is tall with her red hair swept to one side, and she is wearing a little too much make-up in my opinion. Her black dress hugs her frame and shows plenty of cleavage. She thrusts her breasts forward as we approach her. I roll my eyes at how obvious she is being, but Jake doesn't seem to notice.

"Good evening, Mr Waters," she says in a low voice. I presume that she is going for a husky tone, but she actually just sounds like she has a sore throat. "If you could follow me, I have your table all ready for you."

Jake just nods at her whilst I narrow my eyes at her. She puts her nose in the air, doesn't greet me at all, and then sashays her way to our table. We follow her, and Jake lets me go in front of him, placing his hand on my lower back. As we walk through the restaurant, I see several of the female diners' glance in our direction. They are all hungrily assessing Jake with their eyes and it starts to piss me off.

Am I invisible to these women?

The hostess stops at a table for two, at the back of the restaurant. It is in a secluded corner which means that we will have some privacy from all the wandering eyes. At least I won't have to watch all these women ogling my man.

Jake pulls out my chair for me and I graciously thank him as I sit down. He then goes around to the other side of the table and takes his seat before ordering a bottle of wine without looking at the menu.

"Excellent choice, Mr Waters. I will have it brought over to you right away," the hostess says.

"Thank you," Jake replies, ever the gentleman. He keeps his eyes fixed on me and I continue to quietly rage at the hostess' ignorance of me. She walks away, and I see Jake begin to smirk.

"What are you smirking for?" I ask him.

"I must say, Miss Paris, it's a major turn on for me seeing you jealous." His voice is low and laced with desire.

"Pfft. I'm not jealous. I am simply irritated by her snotty attitude," I reply with a casual wave of my hand.

"Uh huh," Jake mumbles as he picks up the menu and peruses the various courses on offer.

The last time that we came here, it ended in us having to leave before actually eating any food, so I am hoping this time it will be a much more enjoyable experience. I open the menu in front of me and my eyes go wide at the prices.

Eighty-five pounds for a friggin' steak! That is just ridiculous.

"Don't look at the price," Jake says. He knows me far too well. "Just enjoy being spoilt for the evening."

"But, Jake, these prices are extortionate. How am I meant to enjoy myself and relax when I know that the food costs more than what my shoes did?" I know that Jake has money, and I know that we won't ever struggle, but I can't help my reaction.

"Stacey," Jake says as he leans across the table and places his hand on mine. "We don't go to fancy places like this often, so just enjoy it. I want to treat you tonight without you freaking out over the cost. You are going to have to get used to having money, Stace. I know that you're not comfortable with over the top expense, but you are going to be Mrs Jake Waters in a week's time. That means that you are going to have access to my money, and you need to get used to it."

"But—"

"No buts. You will enjoy tonight, or so help me, I will have to punish you." The fire in his eyes leaves no room for misunderstanding.

"But I like your punishments," I say, batting my eyes at him.

"Hmm. Point taken. Just enjoy it, babe, that's all that I ask."

"Okay." I don't want to argue about the price of the food. If he wants to spend a ridiculous amount on a meal, then who am I to stand in his way? I will be having words with him about having access to his money though. I have no interest in his millions. I earn my own money, so I don't need him to give me access to any more.

The hostess returns with our wine and places the bottle on the table.

"Would you like me to pour your drinks, Mr Waters?" she asks, her tone laced with sex. How she does that I really don't know.

"No, thank you. We can manage."

"Oh, okay." She looks put out by his answer and I mentally jump up and down. *Ha, take that you snotty bitch.*

"Are you ready to order?" At no point has she addressed me at all.

"Actually, we need a few more minutes," I say to her before Jake can reply. She turns her head to me and scowls. I feel anger rise within me, but I need to remember that I am in a classy restaurant and to cause a scene in here would just be tasteless. She nods at me and then walks away.

"The fucking nerve of her," I say to Jake.

"Just ignore her. Tonight is about me and you."

"You're right," I say, not wanting to let her wind me up any more than she already has. I smile and return to looking at the menu. "So, what would you recommend on the menu tonight, sir?"

"Well, the lobster is excellent."

"I'll have that then."

"Me too." Jake picks up the wine bottle and proceeds to pour us both a glass of the crimson liquid. I take a sip and moan at the taste.

"Wow, that's lovely."

"Only the best for you," Jake replies.

"I dread to think of how much the bottle cost." I immediately cringe at myself for voicing my opinion out loud about the price.

"Well, it's a good job that you're not going to find out," Jake says as the snotty hostess comes back over to take our order. I swear that she has popped her cleavage out a bit more since she last came over here. Jake orders our lobsters and then dismisses her. I try not to laugh at how put out she looks.

"So," Jake says. "Did you decide when it is that you are going dress shopping?"

"Yes, Lydia and I will be going on Monday."

"Okay, Eric will take you and pick you up when you are ready."

"There's really no need."

"Yes, there is." I roll my eyes at him. "I will be busy at the office for most of next week, so I will be driving myself, therefore freeing Eric up from his usual routine." I decide to just go along with him. If it makes him happy for Eric to chauffeur me around, then who am I to argue?

"Fair enough. Hey, I forgot to tell you earlier that I asked Martin to give me away. As you can probably imagine, his reaction was beyond dramatic," I say with a smile.

"I wouldn't have expected anything else."

"Actually, he was really sweet. He started to cry on the phone. Oh, and I am meeting him at The Den tomorrow night at eight for drinks."

"Is it invite only, or can anyone come along?" Jake asks me.

"Hmm, well, seeing as you are going to be my husband by this time next week,

I suppose that I can allow you to tag along," I say playfully. I love the banter that we have.

"Tag along? Oh, that's charming." Jake pouts, making me laugh out loud at him.

"Ah, poor baby. Did I hurt your feelings?" I say in a babyish voice, ribbing him. He does a crap job of scowling at me, which makes me laugh even harder.

A waiter arrives at our table with our food, interrupting our conversation. I see that the hostess opted against bringing our food over. Maybe she got the hint? The waiter introduces himself at Claude and places our food in front of us. We both thank him, and he leaves us to enjoy our meal as I stare at my plate in awe. The food is placed intricately on the plate and looks so pretty that I almost feel bad about the fact that I will be eating it.

I pick up my knife and fork and try to attack the lobster with as much finesse as I possibly can. I fail miserably as one of the lobster claws goes flying off of the plate and off of the table. I feel my face colour instantly as it hits another lady who is sat on the table across from us, on her foot. I can see out of the corner of my eye that Jake is trying not to laugh. The woman looks round at me and I literally wish that the ground would swallow me up.

"I'm so sorry," I say to her. She just snorts at me and then turns back around, kicking the lobster claw away from her as she does. I look to Jake and his eyes are watering from trying to hold in the laughter.

"It's not funny," I whisper to him.

"Oh, I beg to differ."

"See? This is what happens when you bring me to fancy places. I end up making myself look like a complete twit." My comment seems to be Jake's undoing as he can no longer suppress his laughter. His laughing fit lasts for a couple of minutes and all I can do is stare at him incredulously.

"Jake, stop it. She keeps looking round at me." The woman looks at me again and gives me the evil eye. "Christ, the way she keeps looking at me, you would think that I had thrown the lobster at her on purpose."

"Just ignore her," Jake says now he seems to have composed himself. "This kind of thing must happen all the time." Jake is trying to reassure me, but I know that it is complete and utter bullshit.

"Next time can we just order in a pizza? At least at home I only have you to watch me make a prat of myself."

"Sure," Jake says grinning. "Now, eat up. We need to get to dessert. And I don't mean the ones on the menu."

CHAPTER THIRTEEN

STACEY

The music is loud, the beat is throbbing through my body, and I let myself go to the music.

The Den is packed, as it usually is on a Saturday night. Martin comes bobbing his way through the crowd to join me on the dance floor.

"Shake it, baby, shake it," he shouts at me. I laugh and put a bit more oomph into shaking my booty at him. "Work it, girl."

Martin starts to get his groove on and it isn't long before he is dancing with some guy. Martin has been single since him and Clayton split. I know that he still isn't over the hurt that Clayton caused him. Martin thought that Clayton was the one for him. I haven't heard from Clayton since he left, even though we were friends, and I don't wish to either. My loyalties lie with Martin and I just hope that he finds happiness soon. He's got a lot of love to give.

The Weeknd, "I Feel It Coming," comes on over the speakers and the crowd starts to cheer. I am having such a good night. Susie has been doing a great job of running The Den, but I have to admit to myself that I am a little jealous. This was my project not so long ago. Don't get me wrong, I'm pleased that Susie has taken over the role, but I do miss it.

I spot Jake snaking his way towards me, and as usual my heartbeat accelerates. He is looking mighty fine in his dark denim jeans and black shirt. I lick my lips as he makes his way closer and I can feel him devouring my body with his eyes. He reaches me, grabbing me around the waist, and his body moves in sync with mine to the beat of the music.

Not only is Jake seemingly perfect in every other way, but he can actually dance as well. He really doesn't make it fair for other men. I know that I am probably the envy of most women here tonight, but all this thought does is bring a smug smile to my face.

In just a few short days, I am going to be Mrs Jake Waters. I never thought that we would get to this point, what with everything we have been through. Just shows how much I underestimated our strength as a couple.

"Penny for your thoughts?" Jake whispers in my ear.

"Just thinking about our wedding."

"Oh, really? And?" Jake prompts me for more detail as he grinds his hips against mine.

"I just... I can't believe that we made it. After everything, we are still together."

"We're soulmates. We are meant to be, and the more that life throws at us, the more we put two fingers up and work through it together."

He is so right.

My life would be incomplete without him now.

"Come with me," I say as I grab his hand and lead him to, what was, my office. I open the door and pull Jake through.

I turn to make sure that the door is shut when Jake pushes me against it, lifting my hands above my head. His lips are on mine before I can speak, and our kiss is hot and fevered. I moan into his mouth as he continues to hold my hands above my head with one of his hands, whilst the other snakes its way down my body. His hand finds my sex and his fingers begin to work their magic. I push my body against his to increase the pressure, and my legs begin to quiver as he plunges two fingers into me, making me cry out with pleasure.

"Jake," I say breathlessly against his lips.

"Shhh," he says, his lips still pressed against mine. My whole body begins to tremble as my orgasm builds. I am desperate for him to be inside me, but at the same time, I don't want him to stop what he is doing.

With no prior warning, Jake pulls his lips from mine and drops to his knees. Within seconds his tongue is swirling against my clit as his fingers continue to plunge in and out of me. It takes every ounce of self-control for me to remain standing as Jake brings me to climax.

I hook my leg around his shoulder for extra support as he rides my orgasm out as much as he possibly can.

"Is that what you were after when you pulled me in here?" Jake asks as he licks his lips which are covered with my juices. I keep my eyes locked with his as he slowly stands back up, pushing his body against mine.

"Something like that," I say as I try to regulate my breathing. Jake places a light kiss on the end of my nose before lifting me and carrying me over to the sofa. He deposits me on the cushions and then takes a seat beside me.

"You wait until our honeymoon. I am going to make you orgasm so much that you will be begging me to stop."

"I highly doubt that I would ever tell you to stop," I scoff. The very idea of Jake pleasuring me non-stop is divine.

Hang on a minute, did he just say honeymoon?

"Honeymoon?" I ask him.

"Well, yeah. You don't think that I'm going to marry you and then not whisk you away somewhere so that I can have you all to myself for a while, do you?"

"I just didn't think that there would be enough time for a honeymoon. I mean, my book tour starts again in a few weeks, and I have things to prepare for before it starts. And what about your work?" I am aware that I am rambling, but I have a hundred different questions and thoughts going through my mind all at once.

"Stacey," Jake starts, "I am not waiting for us to have a honeymoon. You're going to be away again soon, and I just want to enjoy some time together before that happens. My company can manage without me for two weeks. I have excellent staff who can oversee everything."

"Two weeks?" I say, interrupting him. I can't go away for two weeks. Chloe will have a fit.

"Yes, babe, two weeks. Two weeks of alone time. Two weeks with no one bothering us." Jake looks so pleased at the thought, and normally I would be ecstatic by this news, but I have Chloe's nagging voice working its way into my thoughts.

"I can't go for two weeks, Jake."

"Why not?" His tone changes from happy and light to one of confusion.

"I don't want to sound ungrateful, but I have things to do before I go to America. Chloe will expect me to be in meetings leading up to the day we leave." I hate to be the one to put a downer on his honeymoon plans, but I have to be realistic. "I would love to go for two weeks, but it's just not going to be possible."

"I'll speak to Chloe," Jake says, his jaw set firm.

"Uh, no you won't."

"If you don't speak to her about this, Stace, then I will. She can sort everything out without you." Sometimes I really wish that Jake could understand the process of being a book author.

"No, she can't. How about a compromise?" I pause and wait to see Jake's reaction. He doesn't speak but he nods his head for me to continue. "We can go for one week now and then we can have another break once my book tour is finished."

I feel that I am being fair.

With this idea, we still go away after the wedding, but I can also be back home and have enough time to finalise everything for when I go to America.

"Are you taking the piss?" Jake says, clearly not loving my idea of a compromise. "We are getting married, Stacey. A honeymoon is a celebration of that. I don't want just a week with you. God knows when I am going to be able to see you whilst you are in America, and now you are telling me that I need to limit our honeymoon time?"

Jake stands up and starts pacing up and down in front of me.

"I thought that you were okay with me going to America?" I ask, needing him to be honest with me.

"Of course I'm not okay about it." Jake stops pacing and kneels down in front of me, taking my hands in his. "I am so happy for you, I really am, but I am going to miss you so much. And I don't even know how long it is that you are going for because you don't even know yet."

I grimace at Jake's comment.

I do know, I just haven't broken the news to him.

He sees my reaction before I can mask it and he starts to frown.

"You do know how long you are going for, don't you?" he asks me, accusingly.

I remain silent as I know that he is going to hate how long we are going to apart for. "Stacey, how long are you going for?" His voice is quiet, and his eyes are fixed on mine.

I take a deep breath and mentally prepare myself for the reaction I am going to get from him.

"Six months," I whisper as my eyes fixate on some imaginary piece of fluff on my knee.

"Pardon? I don't think that I heard you correctly."

"Six months," I say again, only a tiny bit louder than before. I chance a quick look at Jake and the look on his face is one of horror.

"Six fucking months?" he exclaims. I just nod at him. He stands up and runs his hands through his hair. "Bloody hell, Stace. Six months is half of the fucking year. Why haven't you told me this before now?"

"I haven't long found out myself. I was going to tell you last night, but we had such a lovely meal and I didn't want to spoil it." I stand up and walk over to him, placing my hands on his chest. "I know that it's not ideal, but I have to do this."

I start to move my hands up his body and I place them on his broad shoulders. "Besides, there is a thing called a phone, and we can face time, and maybe there will be a break in my schedule allowing me to come back home for a few days. Or you could come and see me whilst I'm over there. It's not the end of the world, Jake."

"Well, it fucking feels like it." Jake sounds like a stroppy teenager.

I smile and stand on tip toes to place a kiss at the edge of his mouth.

"Stop sulking. I have already told Chloe that once I have finished the tour around America, I want a couple of months off. That means you will get me all to yourself. Well, apart from Martin and Lydia of course. They need some Stacey time too." I can see that Jake is trying to fight the smile that is tugging at his lips.

"You do realise that they won't be getting any Stacey time until we have had our second honeymoon, don't you?" Jake says, and I know that he is coming around to my compromise idea.

"I'm sure they will be able to live with that." I link my hands around his neck and pull his face to mine. I stick out my tongue and run it over his bottom lip. "Now, have you quite finished stropping, Mr Waters? Because if you have, then your wife-to-be would very much like to be ravished, right here, right now." Jake chuckles and it warms my heart.

"Well, when you put it like that, what kind of a man would I be to deny you such a request?"

"Exactly. Pants off, Waters."

CHAPTER FOURTEEN

STACEY

I stand and stare at all of the beautiful dresses around me.

The designer wedding gowns are exquisite.

The shop assistant brings me a glass of champagne and I take it from her, grateful for the silky bubbles that are sliding down my throat. The shop assistant is called Holly, and she must only be about twenty-five. I feel ancient compared to her, even though I am only three years older. She is dressed in a chic pant-suit and her blond hair is pulled back into a neat bun. She seems pleasant and has been very welcoming, but I can't help but feel out of place.

I am not used to this lifestyle.

Even though I have been with Jake for nine months now, we have always just been so comfortable and casual with one another. I have never seen his money as a reason to be with him. I have never been interested in his wealth. But he wants me to have the dress of my dreams, so here I am, in the most expensive wedding dress shop in the whole of London. Lydia is absolutely giddy with excitement. She revels in the glamour and designer names. Each dress in here is one of a kind, so I know that there isn't a chance in hell that anyone else would ever be seen wearing the same dress as me.

"Have you had a chance to peruse some of our selection?" Holly asks me, distracting me from my thoughts.

"Oh my gosh," I hear Lydia say as she stands with her back to me. "Stace, this dress is perfect for you." She moves to the side and I get a look at the dress that she is referring to. It is gorgeous. The ivory bodice is covered in lace and is strapless. The dress is floor length, with a very small train on the back.

"Sorry, Holly," I say. "You will have to excuse my friend's excitement." Lydia has gasped at every dress that she has laid eyes on so far. This is now the sixth dress that is apparently perfect for me.

"No problem." Holly smiles at me. She must get over-excited people in here all of the time. "Although, I have to agree, that dress would look beautiful on you." I am not so sure that I could pull off wearing the design, but what the hell, I may as well try it on. "Would you like me to put it in the dressing room for you to try on?"

"Sure," I reply.

"Size ten?" Holly asks me.

"Yes." I guess that working in a high-end wedding shop, you become accustomed to guessing the correct size for the brides-to-be.

"Fabulous." I guess this means that the dress in question is my size. "Would you like me to bring anymore dresses that may suit your figure."

"That would be great," I say. Holly nods and walks away, leaving Lydia and I alone. Lydia is scouring some more dresses.

"There are too many to choose from," Lydia says, more to herself than to me. I stay routed to the spot and try to pinpoint where to start looking. It is a little daunting that this is happening so fast.

"Stacey," I hear Lydia say, pulling me from my inner thoughts. I turn to look at her and she has a puzzled look on her face. "What's wrong, babes?"

"I just... I don't feel comfortable here, Lyd. I don't fit into this world. This is all too fancy for me," I say with a sigh.

"Hey, now cut that out," Lydia says, her tone sharp. "You deserve to have a beautiful wedding dress, Stace. Now, will you please start enjoying yourself, otherwise I may be forced to slap you."

"Sorry, ma'am," I say sarcastically.

"So you should be. This is something that you have probably been dreaming about since you were a little girl. Not every bride-to-be gets the chance to look at dresses like these. Just enjoy being pampered and go with it." I understand what Lydia is saying, but it is hard to change my opinion. I have always been a simple person. I would be happy buying a wedding dress from a high-street store seeing as I am only going to wear it once.

Holly returns and ushers me towards the changing room at the back of the shop, and I see that she has already hung some dresses in there for me.

"If you need any help at all then just push the button by the mirror," Holly says pointing to the button.

"Thank you, Holly." She smiles and pulls the curtain shut.

I sigh as I look at myself in the mirror. I look tired. I still haven't caught up on sleep from Saturday night. I thought that yesterday was going to be a relaxing day, but Jake had other ideas. He had me up at nine in the morning to help him make more decisions for the wedding. Don't get me wrong, it's great that he has so much interest in our big day, but I always thought that the woman was meant to turn into a bridezilla, not the man.

I sigh again and put on the first dress. I don't need any help with this one as the zip does up at the side. This dress is not one that I would have chosen myself, but I don't want to appear rude by not trying it on. The top half of the dress is just plain white and strapless, but the bottom half could not be more different. The meringue on it is ridiculous. I feel like one of those ladies that people have in their toilets to cover their loo rolls. Just to add to its ridiculousness, it looks like someone has emptied the entire contents of a glitter bottle all over it.

I pull back the changing room curtain and see that whilst Holly is smiling, Lydia is grimacing.

"You look wonderful," Holly says. She must have been trained well as her smile never falters, even though I actually look hideous. I just stare at her with one eyebrow raised.

"Um, I don't think that this is the right dress for me," I say. I don't ask Lydia her opinion, it's bloody obvious from her lack of excitement and gritted teeth.

I pull the curtain back across the changing room and start to take the dress off. Once I am out of the monstrosity, I put the dress back on the hanger and hang it on the other side of the changing room. The next two dresses I try on are not much better than the first.

As beautiful as they may look on the hanger, they just don't suit my figure at all. I start to doubt Holly's ability to help me find the perfect dress.

With another sigh, I look to the next dress to try on. This one happens to be beautiful, but simple. The top half has long sleeves which are made of lace, leading to a flattering neck line cut which dips slightly to give some cleavage but not too much. The bottom half of the dress is ivory silk which looks exquisite and feels so soft. I admire it on the hanger for a few moments before attempting to put it on.

This dress has no signs of glitter, or big frills. It is floor length and it has no long train hanging from the back of it either. I take the dress off of the hanger and undo the side zip. I slip into the dress and do the zip up before looking in the mirror at my reflection. The feel of the material is wonderful, and I take a tentative look in the mirror and gasp.

The dress hugs my figure in all of the right places and it accentuates my breasts. It is flattering, and I really hope that Holly and Lydia have the same reaction as me. I pull back the curtain and look up to see that Lydia has her mouth covered whilst Holly is smiling. My eyes stay on Lydia. Holly has smiled at every dress so far, so I should probably disregard her opinion.

I stand there and hold my breath as I wait for Lydia to speak, and I see tears begin to fill her eyes.

"Oh, Stace, you look absolutely gorgeous. That is *definitely* the dress for you," she says as a dopey smile starts to cross her face.

"Really?" I ask as I release the breath that I have been holding.

"Yeah, Jake is going to have a hard time keeping his hands off of you when he sees you wearing it."

Thank God for that. That is exactly the reaction that I was looking for.

"Oh, yes, you really do look lovely," Holly chips in.

"Well then, that's settled. This is the dress that I shall be getting married in." I beam as Lydia lets out a little squeak and we all continue to admire the dress.

"Fabulous choice," Holly says coming over to me and smoothing down the material, even though it doesn't need to be smoothed down. "I must say that you have chosen your dress quicker than any other bride-to-be that I have had in here."

"I guess I'm just lucky that you picked this dress out for me to start with," I say. I probably wouldn't have noticed this one, so I can forgive Holly her horrendous choices before I tried this one on.

"Indeed. Would you like to take a look at our range of shoes to see which ones will complement the dress?"

"Yes!" Lydia says as she stands up and answers for me. Lydia has a bit of an obsession with shoes, so I know that she has been looking forward to this part. I laugh and nod to Holly who leads us to the left of the store and through a small corridor which then opens out into a much bigger room.

My jaw drops open as the shoes come into view. There are hundreds of pairs, again each one of them is, like the dresses, one of a kind.

"I think that I have died and gone to heaven," Lydia says as she starts to peruse the rows of shoes.

I am not a massive fan of shoe shopping, so I let Lydia do her thing and she starts to pick out shoes that will match the dress. I sit and try on each pair that she hands me. Choosing the shoes is taking far longer than choosing the dress.

Holly refills my champagne glass, which I am grateful for. I lose count of how many shoes I try on. My feet are aching slightly, so it is with relief that, after two hours, we find the perfect pair. I opt against wearing a veil, something Holly clearly disagrees with. She tries to persuade me to wear one, but she isn't successful in her attempt.

"Now we need to choose your dress, Lyd," I say to both women. I need to get the attention off of me for a while. Lydia starts to clap her hands and gives a little jump of joy. I smile, and Holly leads us to the bridesmaid section.

I sit on one of the plush chairs and make myself comfortable. I told Lydia that all she has to abide by is the colour, which is to be a dark purple. Holly starts trying to pick out dresses for Lydia, but Lydia just bats her away.

I stifle a smile as Holly soon realises that Lydia is going to be worse than any bride-to-be that she has ever had in here.

CHAPTER FIFTEEN

STACEY

I arrive back at the house just after six in the evening and I feel exhausted. As I knew it would, Lydia's dress took ages to choose, but we finally settled on one that is perfect for her. She's a little self-conscious about her figure since having Amber. She has no reason to be, but seeing as I have never had a baby, I wouldn't have a clue how it impacts on the mind of what you look like after.

I exit the limo, say goodbye to Eric, and I make my way to the front door. I don't have any bags to hide from Jake as Lydia has taken everything to her place.

As I walk through the front door, I am greeted by the enticing scent of roast beef, and my stomach grumbles in appreciation.

"Hey, babe," Jake says, startling me, seeing as I was taking off my shoes and didn't notice him enter the hallway.

"Hey."

"How was your shopping trip?" he asks as he comes over and envelopes me in his arms. I wrap my arms around his waist and enjoy the feel of his embrace. I still can't quite believe that this man is going to be my husband in a just a few short days.

"It was good. We got everything, so that's another thing to cross off of the list."

"Do I get a sneaky preview?" Jake asks.

I pull back from him slightly to look at him. "No way, Waters."

"Why not? You've seen my suit."

"And that's my prerogative. You on the other hand don't get such privileges, so you will just have to wait and see." He does a playful pout at me, making me laugh. I gently push him away and place my handbag on the stairs. "Anyway, I'm absolutely starving, and the smell of roast beef is making my mouth water."

"Well, far be it for me to keep you from the roast beef. Come on," Jake says taking my hand in his and leading me to the kitchen. I see that the table has been set for the two of us, complete with a couple of candles. I take a seat and lick my lips at all of the food laid out in front of me. Beef wellington and a variety of roasted vegetables. I wait for Jake to sit down before I delve into the food. He sits opposite me and raises his beer bottle.

"Not long to go now until you are officially my wife. Here's to us," he says. I pick up my wine glass which he has already filled, and I clink it against his beer bottle before taking a sip. Jake places his bottle down and gestures for me to help myself to the food. I happily tuck in. My eyes close at the gorgeous taste of the beef wellington. It literally melts on my tongue.

"Oh my God, Jake. This is delicious. You actually cooked this?" I ask him, amazed that he is keeping this kind of cookery skill from me.

"Not exactly."

"Huh?" I mumble through another mouthful of food, giving him a puzzled look.

"This food was cooked by the caterers for our wedding. I booked them this morning. I know that I should have waited for you to decide, but there is only four days left and they need the menu plan tomorrow."

Thank God Jake is on the ball with this planning as I hadn't even thought of the food arrangements. Hardly surprising seeing as I have had so many other decisions to make so far.

"Well, this food is fantastic. If this is what the food will taste like on our wedding day, then you made a good choice."

"Thank Christ for that," Jake says, looking relieved. He takes a mouthful of his food and groans. "They are the best caterers for miles."

"It certainly tastes like it." I appreciate the food and we eat in silence for the next few moments.

I am half way through my meal when I decide that now is the time to broach the subject of the hen and stag nights.

"So, what are you doing for your stag do?" I ask him.

"I'm not having one," Jake answers.

Huh? Why the hell wouldn't he want a stag do?

"Why not?"

"I just don't feel the need to have one."

"But it's tradition." I cannot believe that he doesn't want to celebrate his send off into married life.

"Stuff tradition." Jake puts his knife and fork down and looks at me intently. "Stacey, the only celebration that I am interested in is the one where we are wed, and of course the night of our wedding." His lips curve into a wicked smile. I feel myself blush and butterflies start going crazy in my stomach.

"Already made plans for that, have we?" I ask him a little breathlessly.

"Hell yeah. You have no idea." Just his mere words have me wet for him already.

"Um..." I struggle to form words and Jake chuckles.

"Let's just say that it's going to be a long, and very pleasurable night," Jake says slowly, giving me a wink.

"Oh yeah? Want to give me a few clues?"

"Nope."

"Spoil sport," I say as I stick my tongue out at him.

"I could give you a clue, but then that would mean that you would have to give me a sneak preview of your dress."

Oh, touché, Mr Waters.

"You sneaky sod. I am not showing you a thing. I would have a hard job anyway, seeing as the dress is in hiding somewhere else." I waggle my eyebrows at him, making him laugh. "Anyway, back to the stag and hen night conversation. You do know that Lydia is taking me out tomorrow night, don't you?"

"No, I didn't know that, but I do now."

"So, that means that you and Paul can do something."

"Stace—" Jake says, but I cut him off before he can continue.

"Listen, Jake. A stag do doesn't mean that you have to get blind drunk. You guys can just hang out here if you don't want to go out. Don't be such an old fart."

"Old fart?" Jake's eyebrows raise, and I burst out laughing. His expression grows serious and his eyes begin to darken. I cease laughing at the look of desire in his eyes. "Why don't I show you that I am anything but an old fart, as you so kindly put it."

He stands up and stalks around the table. He is looking at me like I am his prey, and I love it.

Unfortunately, this prey is going to make him work for his reward.

I quickly push my chair back and run around the table and out of the kitchen door.

"You'll have to catch me first," I shout as I run up the stairs. I can hear him following me and just as I reach our bedroom, his hand comes around my waist. I let out a squeal and am lifted off of my feet before Jake throws me onto the bed. I laugh as I try to regulate my breathing.

"This old fart is raring to go. You ready?" he asks as he leans over me and lets his lips hover over mine.

"I was born ready," I whisper. Jake's mouth touches mine and sparks fly. He makes me crazy. Crazy for his mind, crazy for his body, and crazy for his touch.

I can't wait to see what he has in store for our wedding night.

CHAPTER SIXTEEN

STACEY

My hen night consists of Lydia, Martin, Bonnie, Susie, Chloe and myself. I am more than happy with it just being a small group of us. We arrived at The Den at seven o'clock, and we have been here for an hour already. The drinks are flowing, we have a VIP table, and I have been made to wear a bride-to-be sash. I also have on a tiara and a couple of 'L' plate signs are attached to my back and front. It may seem tacky, but I love the cheesiness of it.

I didn't want too much fuss, but I have to say that I am enjoying the fact that my closest friends want to celebrate with me. Well, I wouldn't call Chloe one of closest friends, but she is my agent, so I felt that she needed to be invited. Maybe being in a social setting will help her to loosen up a little bit? She seems like she needs to let her hair down more.

My evening started off with Lydia and Martin surprising me at home with my outfit for the night, which consists of white tailored shorts, a sparkly white vest top and white stiletto's. Lydia referred to it as the virgin bride look. Luckily, I quite like the outfit, so I didn't argue with her. My hair has been styled into a mass of curls, but I fully expect it to look frazzled by the end of the night.

Jake wasn't allowed to see me before I left, and Lydia roped in Paul to keep him away from me. I was a little disappointed that I didn't get to say goodbye to him earlier. I didn't even have time to grab my phone or anything, so I can't even text him.

I take a sip of my cocktail and give my head a little shake.

For goodness sake, Stacey, you're going to be seeing Jake later when you go home. Just enjoy yourself.

I smile as I look to Lydia who is dancing with Martin. She is wearing the most gorgeous green baby-doll dress. She also dons a sash with hers saying 'Maid of Honour.' Martin was most displeased that he didn't get a sash of his own. He is wearing a hot pink suit with a black shirt, and black shoes. Where he got the outfit from, I have no idea, but at least the colours don't clash on this occasion. It certainly is a classic Martin look.

Susie and Bonnie are deep in conversation on the other side of the table from me, and Chloe looks like she is completely out of place. She is wearing one of her business suits for goodness sake. She sits just along from me, her back straight, and her head poised high with her nose in the air. I roll my eyes and decide that I should make some effort to speak to her on a friend level rather than an agent level. I move to sit on the stool next to her.

"You okay there, Chlo?" I say, shortening her name. She jumps slightly and turns to look at me. I can't quite read the expression on her face. It seems to be a cross between a grimace and a look of pure confusion.

"Oh, yes, I'm fine, thank you," she says sounding as bored as she possibly can. I grit my teeth as I try to think of some way to get her to let her guard down.

"Want a shot?" I ask her.

"A what?"

Oh good grief.

"A shot, Chloe, would you like a shot?"

"What is a shot?"

She can't be serious?

How can she be in her mid-twenties and have never heard of a shot before?

"You know what, I'll just go and get some so that you can see for yourself." With that, I leave her sat at the table and make my way to the bar. I get served quickly, seeing as the workers know exactly who I am, and I hardly fade into the background with my outfit. I order two shots of tequila for each of us, along with lemon and salt.

Whilst I wait for the drinks to be poured, I take a look around. I still feel a sense of sadness that I no longer work here. I wouldn't give up the success my book has had for anything, but I miss the daily routine of this place.

Darren is the one serving me, and he finishes pouring the shots and tells me that he will carry them over to our table. I try to tell him that I can manage, but he refuses to listen as he picks up the tray of drinks and makes his way out from behind the bar. I follow him to the table and resume my seat next to Chloe. She looks at the tray of drinks and her eyes widen a little.

"Don't worry, they're not just for us two," I say, wanting to put her mind at ease.

"Here you go," I say, handing her one of the shot glasses. She takes the glass off of me and gives me a questioning look. "Okay, Chloe, this is called a shot. It's a shot of tequila..." Before I can finish speaking, Chloe has downed the shot and is sat there with her face screwed up from the taste. My mouth hangs open as I stare at her. She grabs the remainder of her cocktail and takes a few sips.

"God that is gross," she says, turning to look at me.

"Well, you're meant to do the shot with salt and lemon, but you didn't give me a chance to tell you that part."

"Oh."

"Don't worry, I ordered two each, so there's another one for you," I reply with a wink. I then show her the correct way to drink a shot of tequila, and she does her second shot with less fuss than the first one. Lydia and Martin come back over to the table and both drink their shots in quick succession.

"You having a good night so far, baby girl?" Martin shouts to me over the table. I nod at him and am about to suggest that we all go dance together when the music stops, and the DJ starts to speak.

"Stacey Paris," the DJ says into the microphone. I freeze on the spot and my eyes fixate on Lydia, who is grinning like a Cheshire cat. The whole place is silent as every other person in the building looks to see who Stacey Paris is.

"Come on, girl, you're needed on the stage," the DJ continues. I immediately let my gaze narrow on Lydia and I can see that she is struggling not to laugh at my reaction. I told her that I didn't want a big fuss.

"Go on, babes, don't keep everyone waiting," she says, the grin still firmly in place. I scowl at her and allow my legs to walk me around the table. I see eyes start to turn in my direction and I feel so uncomfortable.

I gulp as I move forward, wanting to reach the stage as soon as possible and get whatever is planned for me over and done with. I reach the stairs and on shaking legs I climb each one until I am stood beside the DJ booth.

"Everyone give Stacey a hand," the DJ says, leading the whole room into a clapping frenzy. I force a smile, but I am trying so hard not to cringe that I imagine that I probably look a little bit deranged.

My table of hens and Martin are all hollering and whooping. Except for Chloe of course. She is just sat there taking everything in.

"Now, we were told earlier this evening that Stacey is getting married in two days' time." Some of the crowd cheer at this point, but I hear one voice shout out that I "Must be mad." A few people laugh at this and I allow a genuine smile to grace my lips. "Congratulations by the way," the DJ continues, aiming that comment solely at me. "Your friends thought that they would send you off into married life in style..."

The music starts up again and "Peaches and Cream" by 112 plays through the sound system. I stand routed to the spot, not knowing what the hell is coming next. I can see that Martin is jumping up and down, clearly unable to contain his excitement of what is coming up.

I look around and the crowd start cheering loudly. It isn't until I feel two hands land on my shoulders from behind me, that I realise why the crowd is cheering so much.

Well, the women are at least.

I turn around and come face to face with some guy that I have never seen before. The guy, dressed in a grey suit and wearing dark sunglasses to give him a suave look, leads me over to a chair that has been placed in the middle of the stage. He doesn't speak to me, he just smiles as he turns back to face the crowd. He leads the crowd into a frenzy and then from out of nowhere, two other guys join him on the stage and then they start to dance to a choreographed routine.

I watch as women scream, and men start to back away from the front of the stage. It is at this point that it finally dawns on me that my friends have got me a stripper. No, they haven't just got me one stripper, they have got me three!

I cover my face and start to laugh as the three guys turn around to face me and they start to take their suit jackets off. They then make their way closer to me as their shirts come off, and then their trousers.

I let myself scream along with the other women as I get swept up in the atmosphere of the moment. The music continues with a sexy beat as Usher, "Love In This Club" starts to play. The strippers are dancing around me in just their thongs at this point.

I let my eyes roam the room for a moment to find that Lydia and Martin have made it to the front of the stage and they are cheering away. I smile at them and am thankful that I have great friends who want to make sure that I have fun going off into married life. I blow them both a kiss as the strippers continue to gyrate around me.

I don't worry about Jake being annoyed that my friends have gotten me strippers for my hen night. He will just see it as a bit of fun.

In fact, it has given me an idea for what I can do when I get home…

JAKE

It's just gone two in the morning when I hear the front door open, quickly followed by the laughter of two drunken women. Paul and I are sat in the dining room just finishing off a game of poker. Eric joined us for a couple of games earlier, but he left just before midnight to go home. Stacey refused to have Eric pick her up tonight as she wasn't sure what the plans were going to be.

Paul looks to me as we hear the girls coming down the hallway.

"They sound like they have had a good night," Paul says as he takes a sip of his beer. I just smile at him. Drunk Stacey is certainly entertaining to see. I sit back and am about to continue to play my hand when the girls come bursting through the kitchen door.

"Shhh, Lyd," I hear Stacey say as she struggles to control her laughter.

"I am shushing," Lydia replies as she tries to walk in a straight line. Lydia notices Paul and I sat at the dining table before Stacey does and she starts to walk over. I say walk, but it is more like watching a toddler attempting to walk for the first time.

"Babe," she shrieks as she barrels her way towards Paul and flings her arms around his neck. Paul has to be quick with stopping his chair from toppling backwards. I stifle laughter as Paul struggles to gain control of a drunken Lydia lounging on top of him. Paul's eyes are wide, but his mouth is curved into a smile, so I know that he finds this whole scenario just as funny as I do.

I turn my attention to Stacey who is stood, leaning against the kitchen island, her eyes trained solely on me. I stand up from the chair and walk over to her, seeing that her eyes are a little glazed over as I do so. When I reach her, I place a light kiss on the end of her nose.

"Good night?" I ask her.

"Yeah. We had so much fun. What about you guys, what did you get up to?" she asks, her words sounding slightly slurred.

"Oh, we just played some poker and had a couple of beers. Would you like some water?" I ask her, figuring that she could probably do with some before she goes to bed.

"Yes please." I grab her a glass of water and she drains it all in one go. "That's better," she says as she puts the glass down on the island. She then wobbles her way over to sit at the dining table. She flops down in my chair and lays her head on the table.

"Um, Stace?" I say, making my way over to her. She mumbles something and closes her eyes. I smile and look to Paul who still has Lydia led on top of him. "Do you guys just want to stay in one of the guest bedrooms tonight?" I offer as I think he may struggle to get Lydia into a taxi.

"That might be the best idea," he says as manages to stand up whilst keeping hold of Lydia. "We need to leave at about ten in the morning to go and pick Amber up from my mum's."

"That's okay, I can drive you to yours to get your car."

"Cheers, mate."

"No problem."

Paul proceeds to leave the room and make his way to the first floor. He knows where the guest bedrooms are, so I have no need to show him where to go. I pick Stacey up and lift her up the stairs to our bedroom, kicking the door closed behind me when I get there. I lie her on the bed and make my way to the ensuite to use the toilet. I wash up and get undressed, so that I am only wearing my boxers. I decide that I should try and get Stacey out her hen night attire. She can hardly sleep with a bloody tiara on her head.

I exit the ensuite but am surprised to see that Stacey is no longer led on the bed. My eyes scan the room but there is no sign of her. I frown as I wonder where the hell she has gone. I am about to make my way out of the bedroom, and my hand is on the door handle when I hear faint music coming from the walk-in wardrobe.

Puzzled, I pull my hand away from the door and I wait to see what is about to happen.

STACEY

I did a pretty good job of pretending to be so drunk that I fell asleep on the dining table. I smile as I watch Jake through the crack in the wardrobe doors. His hand is resting on the door handle and I take that as my cue to start playing the music that I have chosen for this exact moment, Ariana Grande, "Everyday." I turn it up slightly as Jake pauses and removes his hand from the door handle.

As the beat of the music kicks in, I appear from behind the wardrobe doors. I strike a sexy pose and lean against the side of the door, with one hand on my hip.

"Stace? What's going on?" Jake asks me.

"Well, I thought that, seeing as I had three strippers for my hen do, it would only be fair for you to have at least one."

"You had three strippers?" he asks, his eyebrows raised. I nod at him slowly and I start to saunter towards him. His lips start to twitch as I make my way closer to him.

"I thought that I would surprise you," I say as I throw the tiara off of my head and onto the floor. He looks to where the tiara has landed, and he has a wicked glint in his eye. "I thought that I would pretend to be drunk, and then I could give you your pre-wedding treat without you suspecting anything."

I reach him, and I place my hands on his chest, letting them slowly trail down his body until I reach his hands resting at either side of him. I take his hands in mine and I pull him over to the bed, indicating for him to sit down on the edge, which he does willingly.

I start to do a provocative dance to the music, slowly taking my clothing off as I go along. First, I take my top off before bending over and facing away from him, so that he has a perfect view of my ass. I let my shorts and knickers fall to the floor and I continue to gyrate in front of him. His arousal is evident, and I decide to give him a bit of a lap dance for good measure.

I straddle him and rub my body against his as I reach behind and unclasp my bra. I pull my bra off of my arms and then throw it behind me as I grind my hips into his. His hands come to my waist and as much as I want to continue this little role play for him, I can't wait any longer for my lips to touch his. I lower my head and push myself against him as our lips connect.

Jake lies back on the bed, with me on top of him. I kiss him slowly as I want to take my time. I move my hand down and snake my fingers into his boxers, wrapping them around his full length. He gives a groan at my touch. I break my lips from his and just hold his gaze as I begin to pleasure him.

The music ends, and another track starts up. Rita Ora, "Body on Me," starts to play and it makes the moment so much more heated than it was a second ago. Before I know it, Jake has flipped me so that I am on my back and he makes quick work of undressing, so that we are both fully naked. He pushes against my opening and I jerk my hips up for him to enter me. He kisses me as he does so and then he begins to slowly pull out and push back in.

I wrap my arms around his neck as we make love to the music. Our bodies are so in tune with one another. We hold each other's gaze the entire time. I have never been shy about making eye contact with Jake. I think it makes our love making more intense.

Our breaths mingle together and we both try to hold onto our release for as long as possible.

I never want to be without this man. Ever.

He owns me, and I am going to do everything in my power to make sure that I am the best wife to him that I can possibly be.

CHAPTER SEVENTEEN

JAKE

I am standing here, in my wedding suit, and I am waiting for my wife-to-be to walk down the aisle. It feels like I have been waiting for hours, but in reality, it is probably only a few minutes. I know that it is the bride's prerogative to be a few minutes late, but it's making me nervous.

I kept the wedding small as I didn't see why we should share our actual nuptials with business associates or mere acquaintances. Of course I invited most of them to the evening reception, but the wedding day itself I wanted to be more personal. Stacey agreed with me as she only cares about her nearest and dearest being here.

The only ones joining us for this part of the day are obviously Lydia, Paul, Amber and Martin, as well as Eric and his partner Grace, Bonnie, Susie, and Valerie. I suppose it may seem extravagant for me to have booked the Bowden Hall for such a small amount of people, but this place means something to Stacey and me, and I couldn't picture anywhere else that either of us would want to get married.

The Great Ballroom has been transformed for the ceremony. The flowers that Stacey chose decorate the ends of the seating and run all the way up to where I am stood. There is a violinist playing by the doors, and each one of our guests keeps looking from me, to the doors, and back again.

I fidget on the spot, willing Stacey to get her ass in here so that I can marry her.

STACEY

I notice that I am now five minutes late for my own wedding. Lydia is faffing with last minute checks, but all I want to do is go and marry Jake.

Martin takes hold of my hand and gives it a squeeze as I take in a deep breath to keep my cool.

"Lydia, I think we need to be going now," Martin says, clearly sensing my stress levels rising.

"I know, but we have to make sure that we are all looking nothing short of perfect."

"Lyd," Martin says, going over to her and placing a hand on her arm. "We all look great, but we are already late for the ceremony." He speaks to her in a soft voice, but I see him out of the corner of my eye giving a slight nod towards me, so that Lydia takes notice.

"Oh God, I'm so sorry, Stace," Lydia says as she comes over and gives me a gentle hug. "Here's me fucking about and all you want to do is go and get married." She smiles at me and I see her eyes fill with tears. "You really do look beautiful, Stace. Jake is going to be pinching himself when he sees you walk down that aisle."

I smile at her words and blink a couple of times so that I don't ruin my make-up by letting any tears fall just yet.

"She looks so good that she almost turned me when I first saw her in that dress," Martin chimes in, making Lydia and I burst into laughter.

"Thanks, guys," I say once I have stopped giggling. "You both look great too."

Lydia looks stunning in her bridesmaid dress, with her hair pinned up and the odd ringlet hanging down. Martin looks very handsome in his grey suit and white shirt combo. I opted against the men wearing black suits. My favourite suit of Jake's is grey, so I thought that it would be fitting to use the colour that I most like him in.

Martin picks up mine and Lydia's bouquet of flowers and turns to us.

"Come on, ladies, let's get out there and get Stacey married to that beautiful man, who is probably waiting and thinking she's run out on him," Martin says with a wink.

I give him a smile, take my bouquet and link my arm through his as he leads me to the double doors of the Great Ballroom.

Lydia follows behind, her bouquet in hand.

I take a couple of deep breaths as I hear the music begin to play, ready for me to walk down the aisle.

"Here we go, baby girl," Martin says. "You ready?"

"Oh God, yes," I say as the doors begin to open...

JAKE

Just when I think that I am going to lose my shit if I have to wait any longer, the music starts to play for Stacey to walk down the aisle to. The few guests stand, and Paul and I turn to face the doors.

I can't wait to see her in her wedding dress.

The doors begin to open, and I keep my eyes fixated, not wanting to miss a second.

As Stacey comes into view, her arm linked through Martin's, I let the biggest grin grace my face. Her eyes find mine straight away, and they are sparkling. I let my eyes take in her dress as Martin starts to walk her forwards. The dress is perfect for her. She looks mind-blowing.

She isn't wearing a veil which I am secretly pleased about. I didn't want her to cover her face, but I never told her this as I wanted her to wear what she wanted, not what my preference was.

She sashays her way towards me and I let my eyes lock back with hers. Her hair has been pinned back from her face but left down, so it cascades in soft waves down her back.

It seems to take forever for her to walk down the aisle.

When she eventually reaches me, Martin gives her a kiss on the cheek and her smile for him is infectious. They have such a close bond and I know that Stacey classes her friends as her family.

As Martin unlinks her arm from his, I hear him whisper something to her and then I see Stacey's eyes fill with unshed tears, and she frantically tries blinking them away. Martin gives her hand a kiss and then he goes to sit behind us, on one of the chairs. Lydia is behind Stacey and she walks around to take her place by Stacey's side.

I hold my hand out for Stacey to take, and she does so without hesitation.

"Hi, handsome," she whispers, her shoulder brushing my arm as she stands next to me.

All I want to do is grab her and devour her in that dress, but I restrain myself.

Before I can answer her, the registrar starts to speak and we both turn to face him. As the registrar speaks, I can feel myself getting more nervous about having to say my vows. We decided to write our own, and I hope that mine convey everything that I feel for the woman standing next to me.

I look out of the corner of my eye and see that Stacey is biting her bottom lip. She must be feeling nervous too. I give her hand a little squeeze as the registrar asks us to face one another and then gives me the go ahead to say my vows.

I take a deep breath and begin to speak.

STACEY

As I face Jake, I find myself holding my breath as he begins to recite his vows.

"Stacey," he begins after clearing this throat. "I wrote my vows out a hundred times trying to get them word perfect, but now, standing here before you, I am just going to speak from my heart."

At this point, he takes a piece of paper out of the inside pocket of his jacket and tears it up into little pieces before letting the pieces flutter to the floor. I watch the pieces of paper fall to the floor, and Jake's hand comes under my chin, tilting my head back, so that I am looking at him. He then takes my hands in his and gives me a small smile.

"I never thought that I would be lucky enough to find the woman that would capture my heart. I never thought that I would find the one that I was meant to be with for the rest of my life." Jake pauses and takes a deep breath before continuing.

"But one fateful night, just over a year ago, I had the fortune of meeting you. You captivated me from the moment that I laid my eyes on you. You're smart, funny, beautiful, and you challenge me in every way possible. We have faced our ups and downs, but each one has made us stronger.

"I promise that I will spend the rest of my life making you happy. The day that you walked into my life, you made me complete. I love you, Stacey Marie Paris, and nothing and no one will ever change that.

"I thought that the day that you agreed to be my wife was the best day of my life, but I was wrong. *Today* is the best day of my life, because today you actually *become* my wife." Jake moves closer to me and places a light kiss on the end of my nose.

"I love you," he whispers before standing back and giving me his heart-stopping grin. I feel a few tears fall down my cheeks, but I don't try to stop them. Jake's vows were beautiful.

I hear a couple of sniffles coming from behind me and I know that Jake's words have touched my heart as well as our guests. The registrar then speaks, indicating that it is my turn to say my vows. I take a few deep breaths as I try to regain my composure, so that I can speak.

"Jake," I start, hearing a slight wobble in my voice. "The day that you came into my life, I knew that I was a goner." Jake chuckles quietly at this. "I tried to fight my feelings for you, but it was hopeless. And I am so glad that it was hopeless.

"Meeting you has proved to me that dreams really do come true. I couldn't imagine my life without you, and I don't ever want to." I feel my lip start to tremble as I struggle to control my emotions. Jake gives my hand another squeeze and I see that his eyes have glazed over.

"I have never been interested in your money, or your businesses. The only thing that held my interest was you. Just you. Your personality and your kind heart. Of course it also helps that you are insanely good-looking." This comment causes everyone to laugh, which is what I was hoping for.

"I love you, Waters, and that will never change. I look forward to sharing my life with you, and I will try to make you as happy as you make me. Here's to making more perfect memories," I say, finishing my vows off with a cheeky wink at Jake. His laugh rumbles deep in his chest, making me want to do all sorts of naughty things to him. I don't have time to do anything yet though as the registrar starts to speak again and then we come to exchanging rings. Neither of us saw the other one's ring choices.

Paul steps up and hands Jake the ring, which he places on my finger. It is gorgeous. It's simple, elegant and very similar to the design that I chose for his ring. It just shows how in tune we are with one another. I also had Jake's inscribed on the inside to simply say, 'Hi, handsome.' Not very imaginative I know, but I know that Jake will love it.

When I take Jake's ring off of Lydia and show him the inscription, he grins and then takes my ring back off of my finger. I frown as I wonder what the hell he is doing, but then he shows me that he has also had mine inscribed. I read the words and feel myself laughing at his choice. It says, 'Perfect Stranger,' which would only mean something to him and me.

It takes me back to the moment that we were dancing together, and I accidentally called him my perfect stranger. At that moment in my life, I wanted the ground to swallow me up, but I don't feel any embarrassment now. I smile as Jake puts the ring back on my finger. I proceed to put his ring on his wedding band finger, and then we face the registrar for the last time.

"I am now pleased to announce that you are husband and wife. Congratulations, Mr and Mrs Waters. You may now kiss the bride." The registrar is smiling, and I turn back to face Jake. He looks so happy and content.

He pulls me towards him until there is no space left between our bodies. He lowers his head and lets his lips hover over mine for a few seconds. I link my arms around his neck and await the anticipation of his lips touching mine.

"I love you, Mrs Waters," he whispers, making me giddy with excitement.

"I love you too, handsome." Jake's lips then lightly brush against mine before he picks me up and makes our kiss more urgent. I hear our guests cheering and clapping in the background and I know that nothing will ever top this moment.

This is our new beginning.

This is us confirming to everyone our love for one another.

This is us kissing goodbye to the bad and embracing only the good, and I can't wait to see where this chapter of our lives takes us.

CHAPTER EIGHTEEN

STACEY

As I stand by Jake's side and greet our guests, I am overwhelmed with the amount of people that have shown up. The wedding was such short notice that I imagined only a handful of people would be able to accept our wedding invitation. How wrong was I? It just shows that if you are Jake Waters, then you are very much in demand. I know that a lot of these people are just business acquaintances, but it still shows how powerful Jake actually is.

Jake's arm is around my waist and it brings me comfort. I love that he wants to tell the whole world that I am his wife.

Wife!

I am a wife!

I manage to stop myself jumping up and down with complete and utter joy. As I look around the Great Ballroom, I see people laughing and enjoying themselves. Lydia and Paul are cooing over Amber and Martin is making sure that the evening reception is running smoothly.

As I hear the band doing their last-minute checks, I know that it won't be long until Jake and I have our first dance as man and wife. I chose the music for our first dance. Jake doesn't know what it is for definite, but I am sure that he has a pretty good idea. There is only one song that I would want to have our wedding dance with him to.

"Would you like a drink?" Jake asks me after we greet the final guest.

"Yes, please," I say as Jake leads me to the bar that has been set up at the back of the ballroom. He orders us both a glass of champagne, and the bar staff don't keep us waiting long, seeing as we are the guests of honour today.

Jake hands me my glass and I clink it against his.

"To us," I say as Jake moves his body closer to mine.

"To us, baby." We both take a sip of our drinks and then I hear the lead singer of the band begin to speak.

"Good evening," he says into the microphone. Everyone stops what they are doing and turns to face the stage. "It is a pleasure to be here with you all tonight to celebrate the union of Jake and Stacey."

The whole room begins to clap as everyone turns to look at us. "I would like to invite the bride and groom onto the dance floor for their first dance as man and wife." There are a few cheers as Jake takes my hand and leads me to the dance floor that has been set up in front of the stage.

The opening lines of the song starts to play, and Jake takes me in his arms, holding me close to his body. I chose the song that we danced to all of those months ago, when Jake came back into my life. It's significant to us, and I couldn't have imagined any other song for us to dance to as man and wife.

"Great song choice," he says into my ear.

"I thought that you might like it." I rest my arms on his shoulders and we begin to dance.

I close my eyes and block everything else out, except for Jake. We dance in silence for the first half of the song, just soaking up the memories.

When I open my eyes, I see that a couple of others have joined us on the dance floor. I smile at the happy faces around us and I pull my head back, so that I can look at my husband. He places his forehead against mine and I feel his breath feathering over my face.

"So, considering we only had a week to plan everything, do you think we did good?" Jake asks me.

"Yes, I wouldn't have had it any other way."

"Me either." I place a light kiss on his lips and feel my sex begin to stir. "And just so you know, I am very much looking forward to our first night together as a married couple." I waggle my eyebrows at him, making him laugh.

"Oh, babe, you have no idea how much I have been fighting the urge to carry you out of here like some kind of caveman." Jake's eyes burn with desire.

"How long do you think we need to stay before we can be by ourselves?" I ask, eager to see what he has planned for me. Before Jake can answer me, Martin appears at my side.

"Sorry to interrupt, guys, but may I have the pleasure of dancing with the bride for this next song?" Martin asks.

As the band begin to play the next song, I start to laugh. Martin has clearly asked for this song to be played. The opening lines of Will Smith, "Gettin' Jiggy With It" starts to play and I burst out laughing.

"Come on, baby girl," Martin says, taking my hands in his. "Time to show these lot how we really do it."

I watch Jake back away as Martin leads me to the front of the dance floor, clearly wanting everyone to see our moves. We dance away in tune with one another, not caring what we might look like. There's us dressed up, me in my wedding dress and Martin in his smart suit, and we're jumping up and down like a couple of excited teenagers.

I look for Jake and see him laughing along with Paul and Lydia at mine and Martin's display of madness. Martin and I sing the words of the song to one another, and then I beckon for others to join us. Some guests look positively astounded to see us letting go and having fun, and others clearly can't wait to join in.

Lydia is beside me moments later and she soon gets into the swing of things. As the song comes to an end, Martin pulls me into a bear hug. I hug him tightly around his waist and then I feel Lydia throw her arms around the pair of us.

"I love you guys," she says as we stay in our little bubble for a few moments longer.

I am so glad that these two played such important roles in my wedding. They have been there for me through thick and thin. We may have had our disagreements in the past, but nothing can break the bond that we all share.

JAKE

We have now been at the reception for a couple of hours, and I am more than ready to get out of here and have Stacey all to myself. I have watched her dance animatedly with her friends, I have watched her politely talk to guests that are complete strangers to her, and I have watched her beam from ear to ear all night long.

I make my way over to her as she talks to Eric. When I reach her side, she puts one finger up to stop me from interrupting them. I raise one eyebrow at her in question, but she continues to speak to Eric. I place my hands in my trouser pockets and wait as patiently as I can for her to finish.

A few moments later, she pulls Eric into a hug and then places a kiss on his cheek. Eric smiles and then turns to me to shake my hand.

"Congratulations again, Jake. Today was lovely, and I thank you for inviting Grace and I to be a part of it."

"My pleasure," I reply.

"I wish you both all the happiness in the world. And I know that I don't need to say this but look after her. She is the best thing that has ever happened to you," Eric says, nodding towards Stacey.

"I know." Eric then excuses himself to go and find Grace.

Stacey steps to me and places her hands on my shoulders.

"You ready to get out of here, Waters?" she says, her voice seductive and sending signals straight to my cock.

"You bet I am." I place a kiss on her nose and then take one of her hands in mine and lead her towards the ballroom doors. I know that we should say goodbye to everyone, but I think they will understand. Well, the ones that matter will understand, anyway.

We successfully make it out of the ballroom without being stopped. Once we are at the bottom of the stairs which will take us to our room for the night, I pick Stacey up so that I can carry her to our room. She squeals in response.

"There's no need to rush," she says playfully.

"Oh, I don't intend on rushing," I respond as I start to climb the stairs. Stacey nibbles on my ear lobe and I let a low growl escape my lips.

"Good, because I want to savour every moment. I never want to forget the night that I became Mrs Jake Waters." The sound of her taking my name is so fucking hot.

Her tongue starts to trail its way round to my mouth and it takes every ounce of willpower for me not to make love to her, here, on the hallway floor.

"I promise that there will be no forgetting tonight," I say as I finally reach the door to our room. I open the door and carry Stacey in, placing her on her feet when we get inside, closing the door behind me and locking it.

If anyone tries to disturb us tonight, then I am likely to lose my cool.

Stacey turns to face me and the look in her eyes is one that says she is hungry for me.

I walk towards her and she slowly starts to back away. She is luring me further into the room and I know that she is building up the anticipation between us. Her legs keep moving backwards until she is stood in front of the bed. I stop just in front of her and I signal for her to turn around, so that her back is to me. She does as I ask, and I move so that I am stood right behind her, but not touching her. I can hear her breathing quicken as she senses my close proximity.

I lower my head, so that my lips connect with her shoulder before I move her hair to one side and trail kisses all the way to her neck and then up to her ear.

"Are you ready to scream, baby," I whisper to her, mimicking the words from one of our previous night's together.

"Yes," she answers, breathless.

"You sure you're ready for me?"

"Born ready," she replies, cottoning on to the fact that I am building up memories of our previous trysts together before I completely shatter her world with what I am going to do her tonight. I allow my hands to rest on her hips as I pull her back, so she is flush against my chest.

"You're a bad girl, Mrs Waters."

"Only for you," she replies as she moans at the feel of my teeth on her ear lobe. Her hand reaches up and caresses the back of my neck. "If you don't get a move on, Waters, then I may have to think of another sexual revenge plan to inflict upon you."

I laugh at her words as I turn her around, so that she is facing me.

"Okay, okay. Although the thought of another one of those plans would be quite welcome," I reply, the image of her sat on the chair in our bedroom with her legs spread wide from her previous plan is a welcome sight.

"Pants off," she says with a raise of her eyebrows.

I smile and obey her wishes.

After all, what kind of man would I be to deny my new bride such a simple request?

CHAPTER NINETEEN

STACEY

I am in Jake's car, being driven back to the house, so that we can pack our things as we need to leave for our honeymoon in the next couple of hours.

As Jake drives us back home, I let my mind replay the events from yesterday. It was truly a wonderful day. Everything ran smoothly, and I think everyone enjoyed themselves. The ceremony was beautiful, the wedding breakfast was delicious, and the evening reception was so much fun. The amount of people that turned up to celebrate with us still amazes me.

I hum along to the radio, and I have to say that it would take something catastrophic to wipe the smile off of my face today.

As I stare at the scenery passing us by, I feel Jake place his hand on my knee. I look to his hand and my eyes fixate on his wedding ring. I feel a jolt of excitement rush through me at the fact that he is officially mine. I place my hand over his and rest my head against the seat as I turn to look at him.

"You okay over there?" I ask him.

"I'm better than okay," he replies with a smile.

At this point in time, I still have no idea where Jake is taking me on our honeymoon, so I decide to try and delve once more to see if he will tell me anything.

"So, what exactly do I need to pack for our trip?" I ask him, hoping that I'm not being too obvious. Jake chuckles and I know that he has seen right through my failed attempt of being sly.

"Clothes."

"Oh, ha ha, very funny, mister." I remove my hand from his and cross my arms over my chest. "I need to know what to pack, Jake. Do I need warm clothes? Do I need summery clothes? What types of evening dresses do I need?"

"You don't need warm clothes." I feel a smirk grace my lips at this little piece of information. "But that's the only clue that you're getting."

"You don't play fair."

"Trust me, you are going to love it. Now stop digging and get your fine ass out of the car." It is at this point that I realise that we have pulled onto the driveway of our house. I sigh and open the car door, getting out and making my way to the front door.

Jake comes behind me, unlocks the door and opens it for me. I walk in and run up to the bedroom, so that I can start sorting through the clothes that I want to take. I am immersed in the walk-in wardrobe when Jake comes waltzing in. In the few minutes that I have been in here, I have already picked out my evening dresses to wear.

"Jeez, you don't waste any time, do you?" Jake says as he eyes the pile of clothes that I have hung on the door.

"Well, I hardly think that the plane is going to wait for me to finish packing, so I need to get a move on. I suggest that you do the same, Waters," I say as I continue to rifle through my clothes.

"Yes, ma'am," Jake says as I see him salute me out of the corner of my eye. "I should have known that marrying you would make you more bossy," he says playfully.

"Damn straight. Now get a move on."

JAKE

I sit back and relax with a glass of scotch in my hand as Stacey sleeps peacefully next to me. We have been on the plane for a couple of hours and there are still a fair few to go before we reach our destination. Stacey still has no idea where we are going as I managed to keep it from her when we were checking in. I booked us seats in business class, so that we would be able to relax comfortably.

I am hoping that I made the right choice when I chose our honeymoon destination. I think that Stacey will love that we are going to the Maldives. It seemed perfect as it is remote with beautiful scenery, and it will give us a chance to be on our own, seeing as Stacey will be leaving in a few weeks for America. I sigh at the thought.

I understand that she needs to go, and I know that I haven't been that thrilled about it at times, but it is only because she is going to be gone for such a long time. I am already looking at scaling back my schedule, so that I can fly out as much as possible but running a multi-million-pound business doesn't allow for too many extended breaks. I am already toying with the idea of taking more of a back seat, but it is hard to fully convince myself to do that.

I have built my business up from nothing, so to just hand it over to someone else to run would be bloody difficult.

I run my hands through my hair as the idea rolls over in my mind. I haven't said anything to Stacey about my business yet as I know that she would try and discourage me. She is the one person that has never asked me to make more time for her. She is also the only person that I have considered doing it for, without her saying anything. She knows how important my career is, and I know that I need to come across as more supportive of hers. I need her to see that I am incredibly proud of her for what she has achieved. I just wish, selfishly, that her career didn't take her away from me quite so much.

I take her hand in mine and she stirs in her sleep. I look at the rings that don her finger, and I smile.

She is mine.

We belong together, and I know that we can get through anything that is thrown our way.

CHAPTER TWENTY

STACEY

This is the life.

I am sat outside our own secluded pad, with a cocktail in my hand and the sun beating down on me. It is absolutely glorious in the Maldives. Jake made absolutely the right choice when he chose this as our honeymoon destination.

My husband is led next to me, dozing on the lounger, and I watch as fish swim beneath us. Our resort is like something out of a fairy tale. I am so sad that this is our last day here. We have had the most amazing week.

We haven't done a lot other than enjoy each other's company, and I wouldn't have had it any other way. Jake has paid all of his attention to me, and it is exactly what I needed before I am whisked away from him in a few short weeks. It has been made even better by the fact that neither of us brought our mobile phones with us. We have been shut off from the world for a little while, and it is so peaceful.

Jake has made arrangements for us to eat our last meal together tonight, in the exact spot that I am sat in now. Just outside of our accommodation, so that we can enjoy the view for one last night. I sigh contentedly and take another sip of my cocktail.

I see Jake stir and I decide to spice up our last afternoon in this picturesque place. I put my cocktail down and quietly get off of my lounger before moving over to Jake. I put my legs either side of him and lower my face to his.

I see him smirking and I lightly trail my lips over his face. His hands move and rest on the tops of my thighs.

"Hey, handsome," I say in my most seductive voice.

"Mmm. Now this is how I think you should wake me up every day," Jake replies, opening his eyes.

"Play your cards right, Waters, and that just might happen," I say before placing my lips on his. I take my time as there is no need to rush anything. I slowly move my lips against his and let out a small whimper as his tongue merges with mine. Jake's hands stroke up and down my legs, causing goose-bumps to appear, and I shiver with delight as his fingers graze the inside of my thighs.

"Maybe we should move this into the bedroom?" I say, not wanting to be caught out by anybody.

"No one can see us here, Stace. That's the beauty of it being private and secluded," Jake replies as he brushes against my sex.

"We can't, Jake. What if one of the staff come round here?"

"They won't," he says as he continues to rub me through my bikini bottoms.

"You are making it very hard to resist you, Mr Waters."

"Then don't," he whispers as he captures my mouth with his. And I am afraid that any restraint that I have at the idea of having sex out here vanishes.

JAKE

I am waiting on our private balcony for Stacey to join me for dinner. It is our last night here and I have a gift to give her to make this night even more special.

The staff have set a table up out here, complete with candles. The atmosphere is romantic, just as I wanted it to be. There is the sound of the gentle waves in the background, but the tranquility around us is exactly what I was hoping for.

I take a sip of my beer and watch as Stacey emerges from inside our room. She is wearing her hair loose and she has gone with the natural look this evening. She truly is beautiful, as I tell her as often as I can without coming across as too much of a soppy sod.

She is wearing a floor length, red evening dress that has lace running down the sides, affording me a glimpse of her skin beneath. It also allows me to see that the cheeky minx isn't wearing any underwear.

I smirk as she sits down and picks up her wine glass that I filled for her a few moments ago.

"Mmm," she mumbles appreciatively as she takes a sip. "You know, I could literally stay here forever," she says, voicing thoughts that I had earlier.

"That could be arranged," I say with a wiggle of my brows.

"If only." She places her wine glass down and then the hotel staff appear with our evening meal. I have no idea what it is as the chef decided to keep the food a surprise from us on our last night here. The staff seem to love the fact that we are a newlywed couple, seeming to want to make our honeymoon even more special.

Our food is placed in front of us and then the staff leave us in peace. I lift the cover off of my plate and am greeted by the sight of some sort of fish and rice dish. It smells delicious.

"This looks good," Stacey says as she places her cover on the floor beside her. She picks up her fork and begins to eat. I decide that we should eat our meal before I give her the gift that I have for her.

We eat and chat between mouthfuls about the amazing week that we have had here.

"Can you believe that we have been married for a week tomorrow already?" she says to me.

"I know, it's flown by." Time always flies when you're enjoying yourself, and I am slightly dreading having to return to reality tomorrow.

We finish our food and it isn't long before the staff return to clear our plates and serve us our pudding. An exotic fruit cocktail is set before us, consisting of every tropical fruit that you can imagine.

"Thank you for bringing me here, Jake," Stacey says with a smile across her face.

"It has been my pleasure, Mrs Waters."

"Hmm, I love the way that sounds."

"Not as much as I do, I can assure you." This earns a chuckle from her and I think that now is the time for me to give her the gift that I have kept hidden for the last few weeks.

I sit forward and push my dessert to one side. Stacey pauses and puts her spoon down, frowning at me. I move her dessert away too and take her hands in mine.

"You okay?" she asks me.

"Yeah, I just... I have something for you." I let go of one of her hands to reach into my trouser pocket. I place the small ring box on the table between us and place her hand back in mine.

"What's that for?" she says, her curiosity peaking.

"I've had this for a few weeks now, but I have been waiting for the right time to give it to you." I remove my hands from hers and push the box towards her.

"Jake, you don't need to get me anything. You have done enough for me already."

"Just open it," I say as I sit back and await her reaction.

"You spoil me way too much," she says as she reaches for the box. She stares at it for a few moments and then slowly opens it.

"Oh my God," she exclaims as her hand comes rushing up to cover her mouth. Her wide eyes look back to me, and I see the unshed tears glistening. "Jake, how did you... Where..." Her voice fades off as emotion overwhelms her.

"It took me a while to find them, but I wasn't going to give up until I did. They were found in some back-street pawn shop a few miles from home. I told you that I would get them back for you." She looks flabbergasted as she takes her parents wedding rings out of the box and looks them over. "I hope you don't mind, but I had them cleaned before giving them to you."

"Mind? Of course I don't mind."

I stay quiet as I watch the emotions flicker across her face. She puts the rings back in the box and closes it before standing up and walking around to me. She bends down and places the most delicious kiss on my lips and I pull her onto my lap.

"You are the most kind-hearted man," she says between kissing me. "I don't deserve you." I nuzzle my nose against hers and then we sit there in contended silence.

Stacey rests her head on my chest and we look out to the ocean before us. It's like our own little slice of heaven here, and we will definitely be coming back.

And I am going to make sure that we make the most of our last night here...

CHAPTER TWENTY-ONE

STACEY

"Fucking asshole," I shout as Chloe updates me on the latest goings on since I have been away. I have only been back home an hour, and I am already wishing that I was a million miles away from here.

"Calm down, Stace," Chloe says down the phone, trying to get me to be rational.

"Calm down? How the hell am I supposed to do that when that asshole is trying to portray me to be some gold-digging whore?" I snap at her.

"Look, I'm doing damage control. Try not to worry. And for God's sake, don't look at the internet," Chloe warns me.

Yeah, like I am going to listen to that piece of advice.

"I will call you tomorrow. I will discredit this, Stacey. You just have to trust me." The line then goes dead and I hope that Chloe means what she says. She needs to get this shit sorted, and quick.

"What's going on?" Jake says as he enters the kitchen, clearly having heard me shouting.

I sigh and throw my phone onto the kitchen island.

"Fucking Charles."

"Charles? What about him?" Jake asks looking puzzled.

"He has only gone and sold a story about me—"

"He's done what?" Jake says, interrupting me.

"Yeah, that was my reaction too. I haven't actually read what he has said yet, but to quote Chloe, apparently he has said that I am gold-digger that cheated on him and left him heartbroken."

"Please tell me that you're joking?"

"Really, Jake?" I say a bit too sarcastically. "Do you really think that I would joke about this?"

"Of course not. Sorry."

"You don't need to apologise. I shouldn't be snapping at you."

"Where do I find the story?"

"Oh, it will be really simple to find, seeing as its fucking trending all over the internet." With this, Jake goes running from the room and I know that he is going to his office to look on his computer.

I stay where I am as I try to calm myself down. I think that I should wait and see Jake's reaction before I read the story for myself, so I busy myself in the kitchen making a coffee. I make Jake one too, although I'm sure we could both do with something stronger.

As I place the coffees on the island, Jake comes stalking back into the kitchen, his jaw set firm.

"I made you a drink," I say as I push his coffee towards him. He doesn't say anything as he takes a seat. I walk around and sit next to him, bracing myself for the answer to the question that I am about to ask. "What does it say, Jake?"

He lets out a puff of air before speaking and I can see that it is taking every ounce of his willpower not to lose his shit right now.

"It says what Chloe told you. But there are also pictures."

"Pictures? Of what?"

"You."

"Me?" I say, my voice rising a little bit higher.

"Yes, Stace. Pictures of you, in your underwear, all over the fucking internet." Jake looks at me and I can see the anger in his eyes. I close my mouth and literally want the ground to swallow me up.

Pictures of me, near enough naked.

Pictures that millions of people can see if they want to.

"The slimy son of a bitch has done a real good job of trying to grab a slice of your fame. And it appears to be working."

"Oh God." I don't know what to say. There is nothing that I can say. Charles has taken private pictures of me and posted them for the world to see.

"I need to see for myself," I say as I rise from the stool and make my way up to Jake's office.

I am in a daze as I sit at Jake's desk and type my name into the search engine on his computer. The page seems to take an age to load as I sit there, nervously anticipating what pictures have been made public.

The page loads and there is a link for some website that I have never heard of before. I click on the link and as the page comes into view, I see that my picture dominates the screen with the heading, 'The Author That Broke my Heart.' Next to the heading is a picture of Charles looking as smug as ever. I click on the heading and the page loads to the story that Charles has sold.

I read the story in silence as Jake enters the room and kneels down next to me. The story is complete and utter bollocks and it is quite clear that Charles is trying to make a quick buck out of this. The details are bordering on insane as he describes our sex life as the wildest that he has ever experienced.

If the situation wasn't so dire to my reputation, then I am sure that I would almost find this bullshit funny.

Almost.

I read to the end of the story and then there are two pictures of me. The one that I have already seen from the first page, which is of me posing in a T-shirt and a pair of knickers. That I can just about cope with, but the second picture is of me posing in a bra and panties as I strike a sexy pose. It was taken so long ago that I had forgotten about it. The only reason that I ever took it was to inject some much-needed variety into mine and Charles' sex life. That was obviously before I had lost all interest in him in that way.

I stare at the picture and all I want to do is go and see Charles and tell him what I think of him. I can't believe that he would sink so low.

I feel Jake's hand rub my back and I wrench my eyes away from the screen, so that I am looking at him. The hurt that I feel within me is more for Jake's sake than my own.

He doesn't deserve to see me posing for some other guy, even if it was before I ever met him.

He doesn't need to have pictures of his wife practically naked, plastered over the internet for other people to see.

Jake is a serious business man. What are his contacts going to think?

What are his employees going to think?

How the hell am I meant to face people after this?

"I'm so sorry," I say to him, my eyes looking to the floor in shame. Jake's hands come up and he places them on either side of my face.

"Look at me," he says, but I don't want to. "Stacey, look at me," he says, slower this time. I sigh and raise my eyes to meet his. "You have nothing to apologise to me for."

"Yes, I do," I whisper.

"No, you don't."

"Jake—" I don't have chance to say anything else as Jake cuts me off.

"Charles is the one to blame here. Not you. You have done nothing wrong. That wanker has violated your privacy and I am damn well going to make sure that he pays the price for doing that." Jake places a kiss on the end of my nose and then stands up.

He takes his mobile phone out of his pocket and starts to call someone as I sit there, waiting to see what he is doing.

"Tony... I need your help with something."

JAKE

"You need to shut this shit down and get those pictures taken off the internet," I say before I hang the phone up.

"Who was that?" Stacey asks me. She looks deflated as she stays seated in my office chair.

"That was my solicitor. He's going to put an injunction on Charles doing anything else, and he is also going to make sure that those damn pictures are removed." All I want to do is go and beat the shit out of Charles, but I know that he will be waiting for a reaction from us, so I'll be damned if I'm going to give the prick what he wants. "We are going to get this sorted, babe. He's not going to get away with it."

"I'm sorry," she says, repeating her words from a few moments ago.

"I'm so sorry," she says again as she breaks down and covers her face with her hands. I immediately go to her and scoop her up in my arms, carrying her out of my office and to our bedroom.

I enter the ensuite and set her down on her feet. "Now, we are going to enjoy our last day together before we both return to work tomorrow." I am going to make sure that she forgets about Charles fucking Montpellior's actions if it's the last thing I do.

I turn the shower on and then I start to get undressed. Stacey looks to me and frowns. I simply pull her towards me and place my lips on hers. I can taste the saltiness of her tears as our lips massage one another. I let my hands wander and I start to undress her.

Once we are both naked, I carry her into the shower and I take my time with her, wanting to rid her of the shitty welcome that we came home to. I press her back against the wall and position my cock at her opening. I slowly push into her, keeping our lips locked as she digs her fingers into my shoulders.

I ride her slowly, wanting her to feel nothing but me.

She moans into my mouth, but I don't break my lips from hers. She needs to know that I don't care what has happened previously.

She is my wife and I will fight for her.

I will make anyone that hurts her wish that they had never done so.

She is my life, and if you fuck with her, then you fuck with me.

And Charles Montpellior is going to wish that he had fucked with somebody else, because he will be ruined by the time that I am finished with him.

CHAPTER TWENTY-TWO

STACEY

I am sat in Chloe's office as she prattles on about the upcoming America tour, but all I can think about are the pictures that were on the internet. I am trying to focus, but it is incredibly difficult to do so.

"Stacey?" Chloe says, jolting me out of my thoughts. "Are you listening to me?" I shake my head at her. "Stacey, we have a lot to sort before we leave. I need you to focus."

"Yeah, because it's that simple," I snap at her. "You try focussing when half naked pictures of you are put on the bloody internet." I realise that I am being a bit of a bitch, but I am hoping to be excused in this instance.

"Stacey, the pictures were removed this morning."

"Yes, I know that, Chloe, but it still doesn't change the fact that people will have seen them." Jake's solicitor sprang into action quickly, and by eight o'clock this morning, the pictures had been deleted. An injunction has been put in place to prevent Charles from doing anything else. And the website that published the pictures has been widely discredited for the way in which the story was handled.

"Just remember, there is no such thing as bad publicity," Chloe says. She even has the nerve to smile at me as she says it.

"Are you being serious right now?"

"Look, I know that having a picture of you in your underwear on the internet isn't ideal, but I have taken calls all morning from magazines, radio stations and television shows for you to tell your side of the story. I currently have a bit of a bidding war going on for you to give an exclusive interview." She sounds so fucking happy about this outcome that I almost get up and march out of her office.

"Oh, well, as long as it brings in some revenue, then please, continue to make money off of my embarrassment," I reply sarcastically.

Chloe sighs and at least has the decency to look a little less happy.

"I'm just saying that something good came out of it."

"Pfft." I blow a lock of hair out of my eyes and avert my gaze from her. I am not in the mood to be discussing anything with her, but I know that I have to finalise everything for the book tour. "Let's just get this meeting over with, so that I can go home."

JAKE

"I have done everything that I can to try and keep this bastard at bay," Tony says as he sits opposite me at my desk. I drum my hands on the table as I listen to him give me a run-down of what he has managed to stop Charles doing.

"I appreciate it, but I need to get this asshole out of our lives for good."

"Don't do anything stupid, Jake. I know that you're angry, but you need to keep a lid on it."

Huh. Bet he wouldn't be this calm if it was his wife plastered all over the internet in just her underwear.

"In regards to why Charles would need to sell a story about your wife, I have a friend who is looking into it for me." I process his words. I have no doubt that he will find out the information that I want to know, but it still doesn't stop me from wanting to go and pay dear old Charles a visit.

The buzzer on my desk goes, interrupting our conversation.

"Yes, Valerie," I say after pressing the button to talk to her.

"Mrs Waters is here to see you, sir."

"Send her on in," I reply. The doors open a few seconds later and my wife enters, looking as hot as hell. She gives me a smile and walks over.

"Hi, handsome," she says. "I know that you are busy, but I just needed to see you," she continues, giving a nod to Tony to acknowledge him.

"Stacey, this is Tony, my solicitor. Tony, this is my wife, Stacey," I say, even though it is plainly obvious who she is.

"Mrs Waters," Tony says as he stands up and puts his hand out for her to shake.

"Hi," she responds. "I guess I have you to thank for getting those awful pictures of me taken off of the internet." To anyone else, she sounds like she is making a joke of the situation, however, I know how hurt she is deep down.

"No problem at all," Tony replies. "Listen, Jake, I need to get going, but I will be in touch the minute that I hear any news."

"Thanks, Tony." Tony then says goodbye to Stacey and leaves my office. "Come here you," I say, gesturing for Stacey to sit on my lap. She willingly obliges and puts her arms on my shoulders as she sits down. "How did your meeting with Chloe go?"

"Ugh. Well, she thinks that having half naked pictures of me on the internet is just fantastic. In fact, it is so fantastic that she has people bidding for me to give an exclusive interview about it." I don't fail to hear the sarcasm in her tone.

"Maybe it wouldn't hurt to tell your side of the story?" I say.

She lets out a loud sigh. "I guess not. I just wish that I didn't have to tell anything in the first place." She sounds so down about it all. I wish I could take the hurt away from her.

I place a kiss on the end of her nose and wrap my arms around her waist.

"Charles will get what's coming to him."

"What do you mean?" she asks, looking highly suspiciously at me.

"I mean that there is no way that I am letting him get away with this."

"Jake, I don't want you to get into trouble because of that asshole." I give a little chuckle at her words. She underestimates me at times.

"I won't be doing anything, so don't go worrying that beautiful mind of yours."

"Hmm," she replies, not sounding convinced at all. I have no intention of having my name associated with anything that may happen to Charles. I like to think that I'm too bloody clever to actually get caught doing anything. "Oh, I spoke to Lydia earlier and invited them for Christmas dinner with us, but they have already arranged to go to Paul's parents for the day. She did however say that they would be free on New Year's Eve."

"So, we get our first Christmas all to ourselves?"

"We sure do, babe."

STACEY

I am led on the sofa, surfing on the internet for a Christmas present to get Jake, when I hear the front door open and then close. I quickly shut the lid of the laptop down as I don't want Jake to have any clue of what I might be getting him. I know that I have left it a bit late, what with Christmas being next week and all, but there has been so much going on that I haven't really had the time to do any Christmas present shopping. We haven't even got the Christmas decorations up for goodness sake.

I place the laptop by the side of me as Jake walks into the room. His eyes find me on the sofa, and then without any warning, he runs over and launches himself on top of me. I give a squeal and cover my face with my hands. He soon moves my hands though and places a delicious kiss on my lips.

"Well, hello to you too," I say when we finally come up for air. "And what's put you in such a good mood?"

"Just the thought of coming home to my gorgeous wife. I don't need any other reason."

"Uh huh." I love his answer. "And you're sure that's all it is?"

"There may be one other thing. God, you know me far too well woman." I laugh at him.

"And what might this other thing be?" A mischievous smirk appears on his face, and I know from that look alone that he isn't going to tell me anything.

"You will just have to wait and see, Mrs Waters."

"You don't play fair," I say, pouting at him. He laughs and then pushes himself off of me, so he is standing up.

"Come on," he says, taking my hand in his to pull me up from the sofa.

"Where are we going?"

"We aren't going anywhere, but we are going to put up the Christmas decorations." He leads me to the hallway where I see several shopping bags filled with different decorations. "This Christmas is going to be the best one ever. Just you wait and see."

CHAPTER TWENTY-THREE

JAKE

I bid everyone a good Christmas as I leave the office. It is the day before Christmas eve, and I can honestly say that this is the first year that I am seriously looking forward to the Christmas break. I usually work through it, but there is no way that I am doing that this year.

I finally have someone I want to share the festive period with, and I am going to bloody well enjoy it.

I exit the Waters Industries building and dive into the limo which is waiting outside for me. Eric shuts the door behind me and then gets into the driver's seat a few seconds later.

"Good day?" he asks me as we set off.

"It wasn't too bad actually, but I am looking forward to the next week of not having to be here." I hear Eric laugh.

"Wouldn't be anything to do with that wife of yours, would it?"

"Whatever gave you that idea?" I banter back.

"I've never seen you look so animated over having time off over Christmas, and I've known you a bloody long time."

"Okay, fair enough," I say, holding my hands up in surrender. "My wife is *absolutely* the reason that I am in such a good mood."

"She sure is a special lady," he remarks, and I can't argue with him. She is special.

I look in the carrier bag that I put her Christmas present in this morning and I smile. I had her gift specially made, so that it's meaning is only relevant to us. She said that she didn't need a present, but of course I completely ignored her. Her argument was that we have everything that we could possibly need, but I ignored that too.

I watch out of the window as we drive back to my house. It doesn't take us long to get there as most people have already finished work by now.

We pull onto the driveway a few moments later and I exit the car, wishing Eric a Merry Christmas as I hand him his Christmas bonus. He thanks me and then I make my way up the steps to the front door.

I am about to open the front door when I see that there is a note stuck to it. I rip the note off and read.

Time to play a game of hide and seek. I will be waiting for you to find me...

A smirk crosses my face at Stacey's playful nature.

She certainly keeps me on my toes.

I open the front door and walk in to be greeted by complete and utter silence. The lights are all on, but apart from that there is no sign of life.

I close the front door and lock it behind me, placing my bags by the front door and I taking my coat off.

Let the game begin...

STACEY

I watch from across the road as Jake enters our house.

I am currently sat in the brand new Porsche that I bought for him as his Christmas present. I then left a note on the door to mislead him into thinking that I was in the house.

As I watch through the windows, I wait for Jake to make his way up the stairs to the second floor, so that I have time to move the car onto our drive, ready to surprise him. It takes a few minutes, but I eventually see him making his way up to the first floor. I start to feel a jolt of excitement go through me as I imagine what kind of thank you I am going to get from him when he sees this car.

About five minutes later, I see Jake making his way to the top floor.

That's my cue.

I start the car and pull onto our drive as quickly as possible. I cut the engine when I am positioned directly in front of the door to our house and clap my hands together at how well my plan is coming along. I honestly wasn't sure if I was going to be able to pull it off without him finding out, but I have, and I feel triumphant about that.

The next part is the worst bit as I make my way out of the car and sit myself on the car bonnet. I pull my coat tighter around me as the chilly winter air bites into my skin. Ideally, I wanted to be waiting for him on the bonnet of the car in just my underwear, but with recent events, I decided against that. Also, I didn't want to risk giving any of the neighbours a heart attack if they were to see me.

I just hope that Jake decides to look back outside again, and quickly.

It would be nice to be found before I develop any type of frostbite.

JAKE

Where the fucking hell is she?

I have searched the house and the garden from top to bottom, but there is no sign of her. I try ringing her mobile phone, but it keeps going to answerphone.

I rack my brains trying to think of where she could be hiding and pace the kitchen as I try to think of what she might be up to. Her car was on the drive, so she is definitely here.

I decide to re-trace my steps and I make my way to the front door. I unlock it and open it, and I freeze. My eyes roam over the Porsche that is parked on the driveway, with my wife sat on the bonnet.

"Merry Christmas, baby," she says, her mouth curving into the biggest grin that I have ever seen.

"What... Why..." I have no words as I stammer like an idiot, making Stacey chuckle.

"I'm guessing by your reaction that I did good with this choice of gift for you?" I walk forwards and make my way down the few steps from our front door to the driveway.

I come to a stop in front of the Porsche, my eyes still not quite believing what I am seeing.

"This is my gift?"

"Uh huh." The sight of my wife sat on top of a Porsche that she has bought for me is truly the sexiest sight that I have ever seen. I feel my dick harden in my trousers and I would love nothing more than to fuck her right here, right now.

"Wanna take her for a spin?" Stacey says as she jingles the keys in front of my face. I grab her hand and pull her towards me. She slides down the bonnet and laughs as I pick her up and twirl her around in my arms.

"Are you talking about the car or you?" I whisper in here ear in answer to her question.

"Car first, me later," she says as she runs her tongue along my jaw line. I groan and capture her mouth with mine. No one has ever done anything like this for me before.

I break my lips from hers and stare into her penetrating blue eyes.

"Thank you."

"My pleasure. Now, come on, let's see what she can really do." Stacey pushes me away from her gently and then she makes her way to the passenger seat and gets in.

I quickly go and lock the front door before getting into the driver's seat and switching the engine on.

"I fucking love you, Mrs Waters."

"I know," she replies with a cheeky wink. "Now drive." I salute her as I manoeuvre the car and pull off of the drive.

This woman can still surprise me, and I am the lucky bastard that got the chance to marry her.

Life is pretty damn awesome.

CHAPTER TWENTY-FOUR

STACEY

The last week has been absolutely incredible. Mine and Jake's first Christmas was perfect. We spent the entire time in our own little cocoon. Well, except for a couple of hours on boxing day when we popped round to Lydia and Paul's to give them their gifts, and of course to see our beautiful god-daughter.

Christmas morning was amazing as Jake presented me with the most beautiful gift. He had had a charm bracelet specially made for me, and each charm represents a part of our lives together. I love it and I haven't taken it off since he has given it to me.

I cooked Christmas dinner for us, we drank fine wine in the evening and just spent quality time together.

"Stace," I hear Jake shout, breaking into my thoughts. I put down the decorations that I am putting up for our New Year's Eve get together and go into the kitchen to see what he is calling me for.

"What's up?" I ask as I enter the kitchen. He seems to be frantically looking for something as he is opening cupboards and closing them again.

"I can't find the bloody... Ah, here it is," he says, more to himself than to me. I look to see what it is he was trying to find, but his hand is balled into a fist. He turns to face me, and I frown at him. He walks over to me and opens his hand, revealing the most gorgeous diamond necklace. I gasp.

"Turn around," he says in his dominant, commanding voice. I do as he asks, wrenching my eyes away from the sight of the diamonds.

"Lift your hair up," he whispers, his breath feathering against my cheek. I hold my hair into a ponytail as Jake proceeds to put the necklace on me. When he has finished, I let my hair go and turn back around to face him.

"Perfect," he exclaims.

"Jake, you shouldn't have," I say as I bring my hand up to the necklace and touch it with my fingers.

"Well, I did. You bought me a Porsche, I buy you a necklace."

"You already bought me a charm bracelet," I say with a raise of my eyebrows.

"And your point is what?" I roll my eyes at him and place a kiss on his lips.

The doorbell goes interrupting our moment together.

"I don't think that our guests would appreciate being left in the cold so that I can thank you properly. I guess I'll have to do it later."

"Minx." I laugh and wink at him as I go to answer the door.

When I open it, I almost have to shield my eyes. Martin is stood there in a fire-engine red shirt and white skinny jeans.

"Hey hey, pretty lady," he says, handing me a bottle of wine that he has brought with him.

"Hi, Mart," I reply as I usher him inside. "Go on through to the kitchen."

I close the door behind him and then do a quick detour to the lounge, so that I can quickly finish putting up the last few decorations. I survey my work and am pleased with the gold theme that I have gone for. Carrying the bottle of wine that Martin brought, I make my way into the kitchen to see that Jake is sat at the kitchen island, whilst Martin appears to be making himself a cocktail.

"Jake, you really should be a better host," I say playfully.

"Hey, I offered to get him a drink, but he asked me for a sex on the beach. Clearly beer or scotch is as far as my knowledge of alcohol goes." I swat him on the arm and walk round to Martin.

"Do you know what you're doing, Mart?" I ask as he shakes his cocktail to within an inch of its life.

"Sure I do. You underestimate me, Stacey Waters." Martin looks pretty pleased with himself, but when he starts to pour the drink into a glass, his triumphant smile turns into a bit of a grimace.

"It's green." Sex on the beach shouldn't be green.

"Hmm. Maybe it tastes better than it looks?" Martin says as he puts the cocktail shaker down and takes a sip of his drink. As soon as he tastes it, he puts the glass down and starts coughing and spluttering.

"I'm guessing that it tastes exactly how it looks?" Jake asks, trying not to laugh.

"Ugh. That is vile," Martin exclaims with his face screwed up in disgust. "Baby girl, help me out here." Martin knows that I can make a mean cocktail, so it was only a matter of time before he asked me to do it.

"Go and sit down and let the master get to work," I say cockily.

"No need to brag, Stace," Martin says as he takes a seat next to Jake. I swill the contents out of the cocktail shaker, carefully avoiding splashing anything onto my white dress. I am half way through making the cocktail when the doorbell goes again.

"I'll go," Jake says.

I continue to make Martin's drink and a few seconds later, Lydia comes barrelling into the kitchen.

"Hey, guys," she says.

"Hi, Lyd," Martin and I reply in unison.

"Want a sex on the beach?" I ask her as I start to pour Martin's drink.

"Oooo, yes, please. Why is it so quiet in here? Where's the music?" Before I can answer her, she disappears out of the kitchen.

Paul and Jake enter, and Jake gets Paul a beer. They are typical alpha males. No fancy cocktails needed for them. I pass Martin his drink and manage to say hello to Paul before loud music starts to play. Martin jumps at the sudden shock, nearly spilling his drink everywhere. Lydia comes bounding into the kitchen a few seconds later.

"Fucking hell, Lydia," Martin shouts. "You nearly gave me a heart attack when you put that music on." I love how dramatic he is.

"Shush you. Now come on, guys, is this a party or a wake?" she shouts as she begins to jig on the spot. Clearly, Lydia is going to make the most of being Amber-free tonight. I pour myself a glass of wine and it for a toast.

"To friends who have become family. May this next year be everything that you hope for," I shout above the music. Everyone comes over and clinks their glass or bottle against mine. "I love you guys."

"Woo hoo," Lydia answers. Jake gives me a wink as Lydia grabs my hand and motions for me to dance with her. It isn't long before Martin joins in, and it doesn't take much longer for us to start drinking shots.

It may only be the five of us, but we sure know how to party.

JAKE

Our New Year's Eve party finally ends at just gone three in the morning. Lydia and Paul left about half an hour ago and Martin is staying in one of our guest rooms.

"Night, baby girl," Martin says as he gives Stacey a kiss on the cheek.

"Night, Mart."

"Fabulous party, Jake," Martin says as he shakes my hand and then pulls me into a hug. I am now used to Martin, so his behaviour no longer shocks me. "Good night you ridiculously good-looking couple."

With that, Martin sashays out of the room. Stacey shakes her head and then starts to put some of the used glasses into the dishwasher. I walk up behind her and place my hand on hers, stopping her from doing anymore tidying up.

"This can wait until the morning," I say as I place my hands on her ass and lift her up. She wraps her legs around my waist and places her hands on my shoulders. "Your husband on the other hand can't." I raise one eyebrow at her suggestively, but I don't really need to. She knows exactly what I mean.

"Well in that case, lead the way, Waters."

CHAPTER TWENTY-FIVE

STACEY

I am awoken by the sound of my mobile phone vibrating on the bedside table. I groan and reach across to it, ready to tell whoever is phoning me to fuck off.

"Hello," I answer, not even bothering to open my eyes and see who it is that is calling me.

"Stacey," Chloe's voice booms through the speaker. I grab my head with my other hand as pain shoots through me.

"Jesus, Chloe, do you have to shout?" I whine down the phone at her.

"I'm not shouting," she insists, even though her voice appears louder than it did a minute ago. "Anyway, I will get straight to the point of why I am calling you this early on New Year's Day."

"What time is it?" I mumble, more to myself than to Chloe.

"It's just gone nine." I let out a groan as I realise that I have only had about three hours sleep. I prise my eyes open slowly as I allow the light to infiltrate them. "Stacey, are you listening to me?"

"Yes, yes, I'm listening." I stifle a yawn as I sit up a little and await whatever it is that Chloe wants to talk to me about.

"Well, I received an email a couple of days ago from a guy called Chance Chambers—" I snicker at the name, stopping Chloe from continuing with her news.

"Sorry," I say, not feeling in the least bit sorry at all. "Chance Chambers? Is this seriously someone's name?"

"Yes, Stacey, and it is the name of someone very important in the film industry."

"And why would that be relevant to me?" I ask.

"Are you honestly not getting where I am going with this?" Chloe asks as I sense a bit of annoyance in her tone. I hear her sigh before she continues to talk. "Chance is a big name on the Hollywood circuit, and he has emailed me to ask if you would like to meet him to discuss the possibility of turning your book into a film."

This piece of information makes me sit bolt upright in bed, despite the blinding hangover that is emerging.

"Holy shit," I exclaim, a little louder than I intended, and I feel Jake stir next to me.

"I know, this is exciting news, isn't it? Anyway," Chloe continues, clearly not wanting an answer to the question she just asked, "Chance wants to meet with you as soon as possible."

"Okay. Well, when does he want to meet?"

"Friday."

"As in this Friday coming?"

"Yes."

"I can do that. Can you send the details to me of where I need to meet him and at what time?"

"Uh..." I can sense Chloe's hesitancy through the phone.

"What is it, Chloe?"

"Well, I can email you over the details, that's no problem—"

"So why do you sound so worried?"

"Well, the meeting needs to take place at Chance's offices. In New York."

"What?" I screech loudly. *New York? On Friday?* "Chloe, I can't do that. There isn't enough time to sort everything out for me to leave that soon."

"Actually, there isn't much to sort. I have already booked the flight and accommodation. I have confirmed the meeting for two o'clock in the afternoon, New York time of course. All you really need to do is pack and be at the airport on time." She makes everything sound so bloody simple.

Does it not occur to her that I have a life outside of this book?

"You okay, babe?" I hear Jake mumble from beside me.

"Uh, I'm going to have to call you back," I say to Chloe before I hang up the phone. I shouldn't be rude like that, but I would rather break the news to Jake without having Chloe listening in the background.

I put my phone back on the bedside table and lie down, snuggling as close to Jake as I can get.

"How's your head?" I ask.

"Fine. Yours?"

"Pounding."

"Want me to get you some paracetamol?"

"Please." Jake places a kiss on the end of my nose and then hops out of the bed. He pulls on a pair of jogging bottoms and then leaves the bedroom. I sigh as I wonder how the hell I am going to break it to him about the phone call I just had with Chloe. I send her a quick text telling her that I will call her back within the next hour. I put the phone back down and prop myself up in bed.

Jake comes back a few moments later with a glass of water and the paracetamol in his hand.

"Thanks," I say as I take the tablets and swill them down with the ice-cold water. Jake takes his jogging bottoms off, climbs back into bed and lies on his side, so that he is facing me.

"Who was that on the phone?" he asks. A feeling of dread builds in my stomach at having to burst the happy bubble that we have been living in for the last two weeks.

"Chloe."

"It's New Year's Day. What the hell did she want?"

"Um..."

"Stace?" I place the glass of water on the bedside table and close my eyes as I reveal what Chloe phoned me about.

"She phoned to tell me that a producer is interested in turning my book into a film—"

"That's awesome," Jake says, interrupting me. I try to smile but I don't achieve the happy look that I was going for. "Why are you not more excited about this?"

"They want to meet with me on Friday... In New York." My eyes may be closed already but I squeeze them shut a little bit more as I wait for Jake's reaction.

"This Friday?" he asks me. I just nod. "I see." I choose this moment to open my eyes and look at him. He looks anything but pissed off, which leaves me frowning in response. "And you told Chloe that you would go, right?"

"I haven't told her anything yet. She can't just drop a bombshell like this on me and expect me to give her an answer straight away."

"You have to go, Stace. This opportunity is too big to turn down."

"Okay, who are you and what have you done with my husband?" I say, feeling a little confused by Jake's laid-back reaction. He laughs and moves so that he is sitting in front of me, on the bed. I cross my legs and he takes my hands in his.

"Babe, you need to call Chloe back and tell her that you will be there for that meeting. It might be short notice, but this chance might not come along again."

"But—"

"No buts. You deserve this." He leans forward and places a light kiss on my lips.

"Now give her a call," he says, nodding towards my phone. "Whilst you do that, I will go and make us a coffee." Before I can respond, Jake has put his jogging bottoms on and left the bedroom.

I am a little shell-shocked that he didn't seem irritated by the fact that I am going to be going away before the start of my book tour.

I pick my phone up and find Chloe's name in the phone book. I bite my bottom lip as I go back and forth between wanting to go and not wanting to leave Jake so soon.

Stacey, Jake will still be here when you get back. He's not going anywhere.
Now make the damn call!

I press the call button and wait for Chloe to answer the phone. She picks up after three rings.

"Hi, Stacey."

"Hi."

"Have you made a decision yet?" Chloe asks me. I can almost feel the tension radiating off of her down the phone.

"Yes."

"And?"

"I'm in."

"Really?" she asks, clearly unable to believe that I have agreed to this so easily. From her tone it is quite clear that she expected me to turn this opportunity down.

"Really. I guess we're gonna go and get my book onto the big screen."

CHAPTER TWENTY-SIX

STACEY

I frantically run through my check list of things to take to America with me seeing as I need to leave for the airport in the next hour. Chloe was unable to tell me how long we would actually be out there for. I guess it all depends on how my meeting with Chance Chambers goes. If it goes badly, then I will be coming home as soon as possible. If it goes well, then I may need to stay out there a while longer and attend more meetings.

I have no idea what goes into turning a book into a film, so it's safe to say that I will be winging it ever so slightly.

I have just finished going through my check list when Jake walks into the bedroom. I stop what I am doing and go over to him, flinging my arms around his neck and burying my face in his chest.

"Hey, what's this for?" he asks. "Not that I am complaining," he quickly adds. I smile against his chest.

"I'm just going to miss you so much." I promised myself that I wouldn't get emotional over leaving him, but that promise was one that I was definitely going to break. "And I'm a little scared."

"Scared? Why?" he asks as he rests his chin on the top of my head.

"What if this Chance guy doesn't like me, Jake? His name is huge in show business. What if we don't get along and it reflects on my book tour?"

"Stop," Jake says as he arches away from me slightly. I look up at him and he brushes a lock of hair away from my face. "This Chance guy would be a fool not to like you. Obviously, I don't want him to like you too much mind," he says with a wink. I smile and appreciate that he is trying to keep this conversation light. "He clearly sees the potential of adapting the book into a film, otherwise he wouldn't have asked for a meeting with you."

"I guess you're right," I say with a sigh.

"Of course I am," he replies, pulling me closer to him again. I rest my head back on his chest and just enjoy the feel of his arms around me.

"I wish you were going to be there with me," I whisper.

Jake is my rock, and although I like to think of myself as independent, he is the first person that I turn to when I need support. The fact that he isn't going to be there with me makes me feel miserable.

God, if I'm like this now, what the hell am I going to be like on my book tour? I wasn't this bad when I went away before. I need to get a grip.

"Do you want me to?" Jake asks, breaking my thoughts.

"Do I want you to what?" I mumble against his chest.

"Come with you." I fling my head back at his words and look into his eyes.

"I would love nothing more, but you have to work."

"You are my top priority, Stacey. Work doesn't even come close." His words melt my heart. He is always thinking about my needs over his.

"Just ignore me, I'm just being silly," I say, trying to downplay my comments from a few moments ago. "Hopefully I will only be gone for a few days anyway."

"As long as you're sure, because if you want me to go then I'll book my flight right now."

"No no, it's fine, honestly," I say as I break our embrace and busy myself with going over my check list one last time.

"Alright. I'm just going to make a quick phone call before I drive you to the airport."

"Okay," I answer, not looking at him. I know that if I look at him then I will start to get teary-eyed, and I have to let him think that I am okay.

I don't want to go away and have him worrying about me when I am just being stupid.

JAKE

Being silly my ass!

Stacey clearly thinks that I just bought her little performance in there.

I didn't.

I make my way down to my office, taking my passport and flight details out of the top drawer of my desk. I spoke to Chloe yesterday and got her to give me all of the information for Stacey's stay in America. I could have just asked Stacey, but I wanted to surprise her with the fact that I am going with her.

I packed a bag late last night whilst she was sleeping, and I hid it behind my office door. I put my relevant documents in the inside of my jacket pocket and go back up to the bedroom. As I enter, Stacey is zipping up her suitcase.

"You all done packing?" I ask her.

"Yes, I have checked my list three times, so if I have forgotten anything, then it is just tough."

"I'll take these down to the car," I say as I go over and pick up her suitcase. "What the hell have you got in here?" I ask as it feels like she has packed a ton of bloody bricks.

"Just the essentials," she answers innocently. I haul the suitcase out of the room and down the stairs, making my way to the car and putting her suitcase in the boot. I am not taking the Porsche for this trip. The four-by-four seemed like the most logical car to take, and good job too with what Stacey has packed. She comes sauntering out of the house a few seconds later with her handbag and another holdall. I take the bags off of her and place them in the boot, on top of her suitcase.

"You ready to get going?" I ask her.

"Yes." Stacey proceeds to get into the passenger seat and I run back into the house and grab my bag from my office. I do a double check of the house and make sure that everything is switched off. When I am satisfied, I make my way to the front door. I don't want Stacey to see my bag, so I parked the car with the boot facing the front door, hoping that she wouldn't see. In hindsight, I should have put my bag in the boot first, but in my haste to get things ready, I didn't think to do that.

I quickly put my bag in the boot and shut the door. I then lock the house and make my way round to the driver's seat. I get in and start the car, and I steel a quick glance at Stacey. She is concentrating on her phone and this satisfies me that she didn't see my put my bag in the boot. I put my seatbelt on and then we set off for the airport. Stacey turns the radio on a few seconds later and start singing along to the radio. It is taking all of my willpower not to tell her that I am going to America with her.

I just hope that she likes the surprise as much as I think she will.

STACEY

We get to the airport and I let Jake load my bags onto a trolley whilst I get my flight information out of my bag. He comes round to the passenger door a few moments later and opens it for me.

"You all set?" he asks me. I nod at him and exit the car. I lead the way into the airport with Jake following behind.

Chloe is already in America finalising everything for the meeting tomorrow. I am quite glad that she won't be accompanying me on the flight. As excited as I am about what may happen once I'm there, I wouldn't have needed Chloe going on about it the whole way there. At least this way I can gather my thoughts and try to plan out what I may say when I meet Chance Chambers.

I go to the check-in desk and give them my details. The woman behind the counter takes a few minutes checking everything and then she tells me to have a safe trip and gestures for me go to the waiting area. I thank her and make my way to the seating area as I prepare for the two hour wait I now have in store before my flight takes off. I choose a seat that is positioned next to giant windows that allow you to watch the planes as they land and take off. It is only when I turn around that I notice that Jake isn't behind me. I frown as I look to see where the hell he might have gone. I spot him a few moments later, minus my bags. He must have deposited them at the relevant area for my flight.

"I've put your bags through for you," he says as he sits down.

"Thanks," I say as I sit next to him.

"So, we have a couple of hours to kill before your flight takes off. Shall I go and get us a coffee?" Jake asks me.

"Yes, please."

"Okay, I won't be long."

JAKE

Stacey's flight has just been called for her to board, and I still haven't told her that I am going with her. I smirk as I follow her to her flight check-in point. She hands over her ticket and the guy checking the tickets wishes her a safe flight.

She moves out of the queue and then turns to me.

"I guess this is me," she says, her eyes misting over.

"Guess so."

"I'm going to miss you," she says as she puts her arms around me. I pull her close to me as I mask my amusement.

"Let me know when you get there."

"I will," she whispers before capturing my mouth in hers. I groan as her tongue delves into my mouth.

"I love you," I say when we come up for air.

"Love you too, handsome." I let go of her and watch as she walks away. She gives a little wave before disappearing around a corner to go and board her plane. I wave back and then smile to myself at how well my plan has worked.

I make my way to the desk and give them my flight information before I walk the same way that Stacey did only seconds ago.

I can't wait to see her face when I sit next to her on that plane.

STACEY

I put my handbag in the overhead compartment and then flop down in my seat, in business class. I am a little surprised that Chloe booked me a ticket in this compartment seeing as it must have cost a fortune, but I'm certainly not going to complain about it.

As I get myself settled by the window of the plane, I buckle my belt up and feel someone sit next to me. I roll my eyes as I hope that I don't have to make small talk with someone that I don't know. I take in a breath and lift my head up.

As I look out of the corner of my eye at the person sat next to me, I almost stop breathing.

My head whips round so fast that I crick my neck.

"Ouch," I say as my hand comes up to my neck and starts to massage the part that is now in pain.

"You okay?" Jake says as he struggles to stop himself from smiling at my reaction.

"Never mind me," I say in a high-pitched voice. "What the hell are you doing sitting next to me?"

"Oh, jeez, that is quite a welcome, Stace," he responds playfully.

"Cut out the banter, Waters," I say giving him my most stern look. I see his eyes blaze with desire.

"If you do that look again then we will most definitely be joining the mile-high club."

"Seriously, Jake. What are you doing on my flight?"

"Isn't it obvious? I'm going to America with you." My mouth drops at his answer. I know that I said I would have loved him to come with me, but I was just talking in jest.

"But... You have your company to run."

"And I can do that from America," he says with a shrug of his shoulders.

"When did you plan all of this?" I ask him, seeing as he has only had a few days to organise this.

"Since the moment that you told me that Chloe had booked you this meeting."

"And where exactly did you put your luggage? Have you already had it shipped over there?" I ask, sarcasm evident in my tone.

"My luggage was put through with yours. I put it in the car after I put all of your bags in the boot. Luckily for me, you took no notice of what I was doing." He smiles, and I find it hard not to grin back at him.

"You are—"

"Awesome? Incredible?"

"I was going to say sneaky, but I guess you are kind of awesome too," I say as I allow my smile to grow wider by the second.

"Good surprise?" he asks me as he leans closer and lets his lips hover in front of mine.

"The best," I whisper before I push my lips against his.

My husband has once again left me wondering if there will ever be any way in which he won't be able to surprise me.

CHAPTER TWENTY SEVEN

STACEY

And we have arrived in America!

Jake takes my hand as we get into a waiting car that will take us to our accommodation. He ushers me into the back seat and then follows behind me.

I feel overwhelming excitement at the fact that he is here to share this with me.

I felt so sad when I had to say goodbye to him at the airport, but his surprise of coming with me has put me on cloud nine.

I hold his hand as we journey to our hotel, watching the scenery pass us by and taking in the sights before me. New York is stunning. I have always wanted to come here, and to come for my book is just phenomenal.

Our car pulls up outside a grand hotel about twenty minutes later and as I exit the car, my mouth drops open. The lavish building is like nothing I have seen before. The whole place screams class and I suddenly feel very out of place. I know that Chloe wouldn't have booked us to stay somewhere as upscale as this, so I can only assume that our accommodation plans are solely down to Jake.

Jake leads me into the lobby whilst a bell boy gets our bags and welcomes us. I follow Jake to the reception desk and let him deal with the finer details of our stay. I look around me at the plush furnishings and the people that are dressed in designer attire. A few minutes pass and then we are on our way to the lifts which will take us to our room. The bell boy says that he will bring our luggage up and then he passes us over to a concierge who accompanies us in the lift and then leads us to our room. Jake tips him when we reach our room and then he opens the door using a key card.

Jake steps back and allows me to enter first and I suck in a breath at the grandeur of our room. Well, I say room, but what we actually appear to have is an entire apartment.

"Wow," I exclaim as I make my way to the huge windows that lead onto our own private balcony. I open the sliding doors and step outside to look at our view. High rise buildings can be seen in the distance, but below us is a massive garden area which is obviously part of the hotel. I place my hand on the concrete railings and just take in my surroundings.

I feel Jake come behind me and he places his hands either side of mine so that his chest is pressing against my back.

"Beautiful, isn't it?" he says in my ear. I just nod at him as I have no words right now. "I knew that you would love it here as soon as I saw it."

"Jake, this must have cost a fortune."

"And your point is?" I turn to face him and one of his eyebrows is raised in question.

"I just didn't expect it, that's all."

"Well, enjoy it."

"How can I not? I am staying in the most luxurious hotel that I have ever been in, and I am in America with my husband," I say in a seductive voice as I run my hands up Jake's chest. "I do have one request that you haven't fulfilled yet though…"

"Oh yeah? And what might that be?" Jake says, his breath feathering my face.

"Well, my husband is yet to fuck me in this luxurious hotel room in America," I say before licking my lips. Jake pushes back off of the railing and his hands grab my ass. He lifts me up and I wrap my legs around his waist, squealing with delight as I do. He then takes me back inside and lies me down on the rug in front of the huge windows.

"Far be it for me to not give you what you want," he says as he runs his tongue along my jaw line. I let my hands entwine in his hair and I give a gentle tug. He growls, and it makes my sex spring awake with desire.

"Pants off, Waters…"

―――

JAKE

Stacey is on the phone to Chloe as I lie in bed and wait for her to re-join me. I put my hands behind my head and stare at the ceiling as I replay the events of the last couple of hours. We haven't been here long, and Stacey and I have already had sex three times. She really is insatiable, and I fucking love it.

Her meeting with Chance is due to take place at nine tomorrow morning and I have taken the liberty of ordering in room service, so that we can stay in our room and relax. Deciding to come here was definitely one of my better choices.

Stacey disrupts me from my thoughts by sauntering her sweet ass back into the bedroom. She's wearing my shirt and nothing else. I smirk as she puts her phone on the bedside table and crawls across me.

"Hey, handsome," she says as she lies down on me and places her hands under her chin.

"Hello to you too. I ordered some food for us. It should be here soon."

"You mean we're not going out?"

"Hell no. I've got you all to myself until tomorrow morning and I intend to make the most of it." She giggles, and it makes my dick throb.

"This trip is turning out to be more fun than I thought."

"Yeah? Well, if you think this afternoon was fun, then you're in for a real treat this evening."

"Mmm," she murmurs as she places her soft lips on mine. Of course this is the moment when there is a knock at our door which interrupts us. Stacey pulls back from me and raises one eyebrow. "Better hold that thought, Waters. Looks like that is our room service."

"Remind me to bring food with me next time so that nothing disturbs us." She swats at me playfully before getting off of the bed and putting a pair of trousers on. I frown at the sudden loss of her naked flesh. "Don't worry, the trousers won't be staying on for long. I just don't think the bell boy will appreciate me answering the door half naked."

"If he's anything like me then it would make his fucking day. Actually, scrap that, it would make his fucking year."

"You're biased."

"And you're delusional," I reply as I hand her my wallet to tip the bell boy when he leaves. It always amazes me that she doesn't see how beautiful she really is. Never have I been with a woman who is so down-to-earth and not just hung up on her looks.

"Be back in a minute."

"If it's longer than a minute you're getting punished."

"In that case, I'll see you in two."

"Minx," I reply as she walks off laughing.

I sigh with contentment at what a lucky bastard I really am.

CHAPTER TWENTY-EIGHT

STACEY

I get back to the hotel after my meeting with Chance, and I make my way back up to mine and Jake's room. I feel deflated as the concierge presses the relevant floor button for me.

The meeting did not go as I had hoped.

It seems that Chance Chambers is actually a bit of a prick. Hot shot Hollywood director he may be, but gentleman he certainly isn't.

From the minute that I sat down, all he did was leer at me. It quickly became apparent that Chance is a man that gets what he wants. Unfortunately for him though, I am not someone who is willing to sit by and let him take the lead on things. He wanted to completely change the storyline of my book as, and I quote, "It isn't quite sexy enough." How I didn't pick up my glass of water and throw it at him, I really don't know.

Chloe was of course hooked on his every word, but I am sure that having her name linked to this is earning her a pretty penny, so of course she wants to do everything he said.

I rub my temples as I feel an impending headache coming on. All I want to do is climb into a hot bath and wash the meeting off of me.

The lift opens when it reaches my floor and I thank the concierge. He nods politely as I exit the lift and make my way to my room door. I use the key card to open it and I walk in, shutting the door behind me.

As I walk into the lounge area, I see that the table has been set for two, complete with candles and a massive bunch of roses in a vase set to one side. My heart melts as my husband comes walking into the room, dressed in his grey suit, which is of course my favourite.

"Hey, babe," he says as he comes over to me and pulls me into a hug. I take a deep breath as I inhale his scent. He smells divine and I feel some of the tension leaving my body. I mould myself against him as I try to put the events of the day out of my head. "How did your meeting go?"

"Ugh." Jake releases me and puts his hands on my shoulders, pushing me away from him slightly.

"What's wrong?" he asks, his brow furrowed.

"It was a disaster from start to finish."

"Want to tell me about it over dinner?"

"Sure."

JAKE

Stacey tells me all about her meeting with Chance over our meal. The more she tells me, the more pissed off I become. This Chance guy sounds like a complete asshole.

"I don't know what to do, Jake. I understand that this is a massive opportunity, but I don't think I can work with someone like Chance," she says with a sigh.

"If it doesn't feel right, then maybe you should go with your gut instinct."

"Yeah, maybe."

"Or maybe it will seem a bit better in the morning, once you have had some time to sleep on it."

"Hmm." She seems to go off in her own little world for a moment, so I re-fill her wine glass and wait until she is ready to talk again. "Anyway, I don't want to talk about it anymore. I just want to sink into a hot bath and not think about the book for a while."

"I can help you with that."

"Oh, I know you can," she says, some of the sparkle filtering back into her eyes.

I put my beer on the table and stand up. "I'll go and run the bath."

She smiles at me and it takes all of my restraint not to tear her clothes off of her and take her straight to bed. I leave the room before I do exactly that and make my way to the bathroom. I run the bath and put plenty of bubbles in, as I know Stacey likes to be surrounded by bloody bubbles when she's relaxing.

I hear her come to the doorway as I finish running the bath and she is already naked. My dick springs to attention on sight. Fucking beautiful. She sashays her way to the bath tub, making sure to brush against me as she does.

"Are you going to join me?" she asks as she sinks down into the bath tub. In answer to her question, I start to strip my clothes off. She eyes my body appreciatively as I uncover it piece by piece. Her eyes are transfixed as I take off my trousers and boxers, allowing my erection to spring free.

I get into the bath tub and sit opposite her. There is plenty of room as the tub is ridiculously big. Stacey's eyes meet mine and all I can see in hers is heat. Heat for me, and heat for us.

Our sex life is off the fucking charts and I don't think there will ever be a day when I don't want to devour her.

I feel her foot slide up the inside of my leg as she slowly moves it towards my cock. I lie my head back and close my eyes as she rubs her foot against the inside of my thigh. As I enjoy the sensations that she is inflicting upon me, she quickly removes her foot and straddles me.

I open my eyes as she lowers herself down on me, slowly. Her eyelids look heavy as she starts to ride me up and down. I place my hands on her hips and explore her nipples with my tongue. As I suck and nip at her, she starts to ride me faster.

I move one of my hands from her hip and place my thumb on her clit. This elicits a loud cry of pleasure from her and I start to move my thumb in circles. I am so close to release, but I make myself wait for her. I speed up the movement of my thumb and I know that when I hear her whisper the words, "Oh God," that she is close to climax.

She arches her back and I suck her nipple a bit harder, wanting her to experience as many sensations as possible.

"I'm there, Jake, I'm coming." With these few words, I let go of my release at the same time as she does. We climax together and ride out our pleasure until we are both spent.

Stacey collapses on top of me and I hold her whilst we get our panting under control.

"God, I needed that," she says as she moves off of me and sits back at the opposite end of the bath tub.

"Glad to be of service," I say with a wink.

"I don't ever want to lose what we have, Jake," she replies, taking the conversation to a more serious level. I frown at her as I wonder where this line of thinking is coming from.

"What makes you say that?"

"I just... I don't want us to become one of those couples who ever stop trying, you know?"

"There is nothing in this world that would stop me trying with you, Stacey."

"I hope not," she says as she lowers her eyes to stare at the water.

"Hey," I say as move towards her. "Look at me." She does, and her eyes are clouded with unshed tears.

Where the hell is this reaction coming from?

"I will *never* give up on you. You are stuck with me, babe," I say, trying to make light of the seriousness. She tries to force a smile, but it doesn't reach her eyes. "What's brought all of this on?"

"I don't know. I just love you so much, I couldn't bear the thought of anything breaking us."

"Nothing will. You have my word." She must know that by now we can get through anything. This turn of conversation is making me feel a little uneasy and I don't want anything to ruin our time here together.

"Come on," I say as I get out of the bath and wrap a towel around my waist. "Let's go and watch a crap film and make out like a couple of horny teenagers."

She laughs and chucks some bubbles my way. "You're a real cheese at times, Waters."

"Hey, I can't be charming all the time." I hold a towel out for Stacey to step into as she gets out of the bath.

"Even when you're being cheesy you do it with charm."

"I must be doing something right seeing as you married me." She wraps the towel around herself and then kisses me on the cheek.

"Yes I did. Don't ever change."

"I don't intend to."

"Good. Now let's go pick out that crappy film that you mentioned."

CHAPTER TWENTY-NINE

STACEY

"I've had Chance Chambers on the phone, Stacey. Why haven't you bitten his arm off yet about the film offer?" Chloe asks in an accusing manner.

"I don't want to do it, Chloe." I have thought about nothing else since I woke up this morning and I have come to the conclusion that Chance is not the right person to turn my book into a film.

"Why ever not?" She sounds horrified.

"It just doesn't feel right."

"Doesn't feel right? Are you crazy?" Her voice has gone up an octave, making me pull the phone away from my ear slightly.

"It's my book, Chloe, and I'm not just going to give the film rights to Chance because he is the first person that has shown an interest."

"He's the *only* person that has shown an interest." Chloe sounds exasperated, but I am not backing down on this one.

"Look, I came here, I met with him, and I don't like him. I don't like what he wants to do with the story, and I don't want to work with him. End of discussion as far as I am concerned."

"But—"

"I have already booked a flight home for later today. Just tell Chance that I don't have time to concentrate on a film at the moment."

"I can't tell him that."

"Okay then, tell him that I think he is a prick."

"Stacey!" she scolds me like I'm being a naughty child.

"It's not going to happen, Chloe. I'll see you back in the UK." With that I hang the phone up and turn it off. I know she will try and call me back, but I don't have the energy to argue with her.

I feel so tired.

I just want to go home.

"You all packed?" Jake asks me as he walks back into the bedroom. I put my phone in my handbag and am so grateful that he managed to book us flights back home in a couple of hours.

"Yep."

"Was that Chloe on the phone?"

"Yep."

"I take it she wasn't too happy?"

"Nope."

"Are you going to be more forth coming with your answers, or am I being treated to one word answers all day?" he says, teasingly.

"Let's just say that she isn't too happy with my decision. And let's also say that, at this moment in time, I couldn't give a toss."

"Fair enough," Jake says with a chuckle. "You ready to get out of here?"

"Hell yes. I can't wait to get back home."

"Are you sure that you don't want to stay and explore the city for a few days?"

"No." For some reason, I don't have any interest in staying here right now. "I will be back here in a couple of weeks. I can explore then if I want to." I pick up my handbag and am about to pick up my suitcase when Jake stops me.

"I'll get that."

"Jake, it's on wheels for God's sake. I can pull a damn suitcase along."

"I know you can, but I'm here and I'm doing it. Is that a problem, Mrs Waters?"

"Ass."

"Yours will be mine later," he says, repeating words that he has spoken to me before. I feel a shiver make its way down my back at his answer. It brings up feelings in me from our earlier moments together.

"We'll see about that…"

"Yeah?" he asks sounding intrigued. I smirk at him.

"We have a flight to catch," I reply, completely changing the subject.

"Tease," I hear him mutter behind me as I walk out of the bedroom and head for the door to our room.

"You love it." I hear him chuckle as I head out into the hallway.

"Yes I fucking do."

JAKE

I'm a little bit worried and confused. Stacey is acting slightly off, and I can't put my finger on why. She didn't want to do the film and that's fine, but she has been all over the place the last few days. I just thought that it was nerves from coming out here and meeting a film producer, but there's something else going on.

I know her, and I know that something isn't right.

She was so excited about coming to America, but now she can't wait to get back home. I offered for us to stay on for a few days and treat it as a mini holiday, but she wasn't interested.

Maybe all this book stuff is getting too much for her?

Maybe she just genuinely misses being at home?

Maybe she has had enough of being around me?

Shut the fuck up, Waters.

This isn't about you.

I shake my head as I rid myself of the thought that she wouldn't want me here. She would have said so if she didn't. She smiles at me as I follow her into our waiting car and it immediately makes me dispel any doubt in my mind that I may have had about coming here.

I'm not the problem. I would know about it if I was.

No, there is something else going on in that mind of hers.

She settles back for the car journey to the airport and rests her head on my shoulder. I place a kiss on the top of her head and take her hand in mine. I hear her sigh and I rest my head on top of hers.

I can only hope that she will talk to me when we get back home.

CHAPTER THIRTY

STACEY

We have been home now for the last hour, and I can honestly say that I am so glad that I am back here. I may have only been gone for a few days, and Jake may have come with me and booked us a gorgeous place to stay in, but I don't want to be anywhere else.

I am unpacking mine and Jake's things when Jake comes into the bedroom, his mobile phone in hand.

"Everything okay?" I ask him.

"I don't know. I just had a call from the office and it seems that my help is needed. Do you mind if I go and check out what's going on?"

"Of course not. Why would I mind?"

"No reason," he replies with a forced smile.

"Hmm, I'm not buying it, Waters," I say as I walk towards him. He sighs and holds my gaze as I come to a stop in front of him.

"It's just... You don't seem like you have been yourself over the last few days."

"You're right," I reply, shocking the hell out of him. I don't think that he expected me to agree with him. "I haven't been feeling like myself."

"And the reason for that is?"

"I don't know," I answer honestly with a shrug of my shoulders. "I can't explain it, but I suppose I feel kind of restless, you know? Almost as if there is something bugging me, but I can't quite put my finger on it."

"Okay," Jake says slowly.

"I know that doesn't make much sense. Maybe I'm just tired, and the fact that the meeting with Chance didn't go as well as I had hoped might have something to do with it?"

Jake pulls me against him and wraps his arms around me.

"You're not restless of me, are you?" he asks tentatively.

I pull back from him and fixate my eyes on his whilst placing my hands on my hips.

"Jake Waters, that has got to be one of the most ridiculous questions that you have ever asked me." Jake has the decency to look a little sheepish at this point. "If I was restless of you then you would damn well know about it." I don't intend my words to sound so harsh, but my emotions are all over the place. Jake holds his hands up, almost as if he is surrendering.

"Okay, forget I asked," he says with a slight grin on his face.

"I will. Now, get going before you manage to ask me another daft question." He salutes at me and then disappears from the room.

"I will be as quick as I can," he shouts as he walks along the hallway, and I huff as I turn my attention back to the task of un-packing.

JAKE

I don't like lying to Stacey about where I am going, but I didn't want to worry her by saying that I was paying Charles a visit.

I have just been informed by my solicitor, Tony, that Charles is sat in some back-street bar, by himself. Tony also informed me that this back-street bar isn't somewhere that I am likely to be seen by anyone important, so my 'chance' encounter of running into Charles should go unseen.

I know that Stacey would go mad if she was to find out that I was doing this, but I need to see him. I need to say a few things to him, and I need him to know that if he ever tries to mess with Stacey again, then I will make his life miserable. Well, more miserable than it is already.

Tony managed to find out a few things about Charles Montpellior that, so far, Charles has managed to keep hidden from everyone. I am planning on using this information as my bargaining chip in exchange for Charles leaving Stacey the hell alone.

I pull up outside the bar and turn the car off. I exit and put my phone in my pocket. The bar looks awful from the outside. It is so run down that you would think that it was shut.

I make my way to the door and push it open. As I walk in the smell of musty cigarettes hits my nose and I fight the urge not to screw it up in distaste. My feet almost stick to the rug on the floor as I let my eyes roam around until I find Charles. It doesn't take me long to spot him, seeing as there are only two other people in here.

Charles is sat on a stool at the bar, his head hanging down and a pint of lager in his hand. I make my way over and stand next to him, ordering a drink from the old guy behind the bar. I opt for a beer that comes in a bottle as I wouldn't trust drinking out of any of the glasses in here.

Charles turns to look at me as the old guy hands me my beer. I pass over a five pound note and tell him to keep the change. The old guy doesn't even smile or say thank you. He just takes the money and makes his way to the other end of the bar and starts to watch a small television that is situated on the wall.

"What are you doing here?" Charles asks me, clearly shocked that I have just rocked up next to him in this dive.

"I could ask you the same thing. I wouldn't have thought that this would be your kind of place," I reply as I look straight ahead.

"I don't have to explain myself to you," he answers, sounding pissed off.

I smile to myself.

I am going to enjoy the next few minutes of this conversation.

I take a sip of my beer and I place it back on the bar. I turn to face Charles and am a little shocked at his gaunt appearance. If it was anyone else then I might feel sorry for them, but this is Charles. He has hurt the one person that I care about more than anything in the world. I despise him.

"I'm not quite sure what to make of this Charles. One day you're sipping champagne at one of my functions, and the next you're drinking a flat lager from a backstreet dive."

"Yeah, well, sometimes life doesn't pan out as it should."

"You're right there. In fact, your life has gone to shit since Stacey left you, hasn't it?" I say as I take another sip of my beer.

Charles looks at me with a frown on his face. "I don't know what you're talking about."

"Oh, I think you do."

"What do you want, Jake?" he asks, defensively.

"I want to know why you sold a story about Stacey." I know why, but I need to see if he is going to tell me the truth.

"I don't want to talk about that bitch. You're welcome to her." I feel my hackles rise at the use of the word bitch in reference to my wife. My hands curl into fists and I fight the urge to smack him off of his bar stool.

"It might be a good idea for you to not call my wife a bitch. I told you once before that if you disrespected her, then you disrespected me. You don't want to disrespect me, Charles," I say, my tone laced with warning.

I can see the war going on inside Charles' head as I stare him down. A war that he must quickly decide that I am prepared to start, seeing as he is starting to look nervous. "Why don't you just tell me why you sold a story about *my wife.*"

I see Charles physically gulp. "I needed the money."

"And why do you need the money?" I can see that Charles really doesn't want to answer this, but I want this asshole to squirm. I want this asshole to show some remorse over his treatment of Stacey.

"I'm fucking broke, okay? There, now you have the answer, you can fuck off and leave me alone." He clearly thinks that I am finished with him, but he couldn't be further from the truth.

"I'll go as soon as I'm finished, which I'm not, just so we're clear." I take another sip of beer before I forge ahead with what I came here to say.

"You must be loving this," he says as I wait to see where he is going with this comment. "I bet you have always wanted to see me fail. Well, here you go, this is it. This is me fucking failing." He holds his hands out either side of him in defeat.

"Believe me, Charles, I couldn't give a toss what happens to you. If you hadn't of involved my wife in the press, then I wouldn't have come near you, but you did and here I am."

"The story isn't even relevant anymore, so why the hell do you care so much?"

"I care because you put private information out there about her. I care because you put private pictures of her all over the internet. I care because I fucking love her, and I would do *anything* for her."

"Why?" he scoffs. "She's just going to leave you like she did me when you're no use to her." I laugh at him. I actually fucking laugh.

"I'm not even going to respond to the bullshit that just came out of your mouth."

"Well, it's true. She had everything with me, and she threw it all away."

"Everything? Really?" God, this guy is an absolute moron. "You know, that resentment you're holding on to is why you are in the mess that you are in right now."

"Resentment?"

"Yeah. You're pissed that your life fell apart the day that Stacey left you. Look at yourself, Charles. You're sat in some run-down shitty bar, you are about to lose your business and probably your house too. Your mother has disowned you, leaving you with no-one. And there is no-one to blame but yourself."

"How the hell do you know all of that?" he asks looking shocked that I have just revealed some of his inner turmoil.

"I have contacts. Just like I also know that you have whittled away money on prostitutes over the past few months. And just like I know that you have picked up a nasty little drug habit which has fuelled your money problems." Charles hangs his head down in shame. "I also know that you would sell your soul to stop people finding out any of this information."

His head snaps up and he finally seems to see that I have an agenda here.

"What do you want, Jake?" I lower myself down slightly, so that I am eye level with him.

"I want you to give a full, public apology to Stacey about what you did. You are also going to say that you made up everything that you said about her in the story that you sold. You will say that you were bitter over your split and you now realise how childish your actions were."

"And how am I meant to do that?"

"By contacting a fucking magazine or newspaper and having them publish your apology."

He scoffs at my answer. "And what if they won't publish it?"

"Then you better be prepared for me to bring your shitty existence into the public eye." I don't waver from looking at him. He needs to understand that I will go through with this. He seems to get the gist pretty quickly as he nods his head in response. "You are also going to get rid of every single photo that you have of my wife."

He nods again. "And you are never going to speak about her again, or to her for that matter. If you see her in the street, then you look the other way. You are not worthy of speaking to her, do I make myself clear?" I can hear the venom in my voice and it doesn't take more than a few seconds for Charles to answer me.

"Yes."

"Good," I reply as I take another swig of beer. "I guess we have nothing else to talk about." I place my left-over beer in front of Charles. "You can finish that. Let's hope that you stick to your word, because if I have to come and speak to you again then I can assure you that it won't be ending this amicably if I do."

"I get it, Jake."

"Just remember that I will be keeping an eye out for your apology." With that I walk away and out of the run-down bar. I get back in my car and start the engine.

Today is the one and only time that I have lied to Stacey about what I am doing. I feel terrible for doing it, but I don't want her worrying.

It is my job to protect her and keep her safe, and that is exactly what I shall continue to do for the rest of my life.

CHAPTER THIRTY-ONE

STACEY

Shocked is an understatement right now. I have been back from America for a week, and I am sat at the kitchen island, staring at the front page of the newspaper with wide eyes.

I have read the article in front of me over and over again, and all I feel is confusion.

There, in black and white before me, is an apology from Charles about the story that he previously sold about me.

I am flabbergasted as to why he has done this. The whole article is dedicated to how Charles fabricated the story of me, and it expresses his deepest regret at making private pictures of me public. Chloe has been ringing me non-stop to let me know that she has been inundated with offers for me to be interviewed. I never got the chance to set the record straight last time, so I guess my silence has made reporters want my side of the story even more. I told Chloe that I needed some time to think about what I wanted to do.

I don't relish the thought of laying my life bare for some stranger, just so other strangers can read about it. I may write books, but at least the characters are made up. If I go and give an interview about Charles' apology, then essentially, I am giving up my privacy on the matter. I am not sure if I am ready to do that.

"Morning, gorgeous," Jake says, startling me. I jump and place my hand over my heart. "Sorry, didn't mean to scare you."

"No, it's fine."

"Why do you look like you have seen a ghost?" he asks me.

"Um, there's something that you need to see." Jake had been having a lie-in, so he doesn't have a clue about the newspaper article yet. He frowns as he walks over to me and ruffles his hair with his hands. I simply push the newspaper towards him and stay silent as I let him read what it says. I watch for his reaction, but he is keeping a straight face.

"Huh," he says when he has finished reading. He pushes the newspaper away from him and then busies himself making a coffee.

Okay, that was not the reaction that I was expecting.

I patiently wait for him to finish making his drink and join me back at the kitchen island. When he takes his seat next to me, I turn so that my body is facing him. He takes a sip of his drink and I see him look at me out of the corner of his eye.

It is at this point that the penny drops.

He had something to do with this.

"Jake Waters, what did you do?" I say, narrowing my gaze on him. He looks at me and tries to put on an innocent face, but I don't buy it. I fold my arms across my chest and wait. He sighs and eventually turns to face me, so that our knees are touching.

"I didn't do anything," he says as he looks to the floor.

"Pfft. Seriously? That's the line that you're going with?" I ask incredulously. He looks back up at me and my heart starts to flutter at the way he holds my gaze. His eyes are smouldering. I am a complete sucker for those caramel pools of his. "I don't need to know the ins and outs, Jake, I just need to know that nothing is going to come back and bite you in the ass."

His eyes widen at my words. He was obviously expecting me to be mad with him.

"I promise you that nothing will come back on me." I stare at him for a few moments. Jake's jaw is set firm as he waits to see what I will do next. I don't have the energy or the inclination to argue about this. And to be honest, I don't want to argue about it. I actually feel a little thrill at the fact that Jake got Charles to apologise. I know that Jake is a man of many talents, but I would never have thought that he could get Charles to retract everything he said about me.

I stand up, keeping my arms crossed, and I place a kiss on Jake's lips. When I pull away, he looks as shocked as hell.

"Thank you," is all I say to him. His mouth drops open and I smirk. I then exit the kitchen and make my way to our bedroom, so that I can take a shower.

I strip my clothes off and leave them in a trail to the ensuite. I turn the shower on and step underneath the hot water. Jake enters the ensuite a few minutes later and pops his head around the shower door.

"Can I join you?" he asks tentatively.

"Sure." Jake's head disappears as he gets undressed. He must strip in record time as he saunters into the shower seconds later. I pick up the shower gel and start to wash myself.

"Um, am I missing something here?" Jake asks.

"What do you mean?" I respond as I continue to wash myself.

"Are you not mad with me?"

I stop what I am doing and let the water cascade down my back as I step towards him.

"How can I be mad with you when all you do is try to protect me?"

"I—" I place my finger on his lips to stop him from talking.

I put my other hand on the back of his neck and pull his face down to mine, letting my tongue slide along his lips. He groans but I'm not finished talking to him yet.

"Just know that I would do the same for you, if the roles were reversed." I don't get the chance to say anything else as Jake's mouth crashes down on mine.

It doesn't take long for me to be pushed against the wall, with Jake inside me.

I shout his name as he pounds into me.

He owns me.

Heart, body and mind, he owns me.

———

JAKE

My wife is the most amazing woman to have graced this earth.

    She understands me.

    She gets me.

    She would do the same for me.

    She is absolute fucking perfection.

CHAPTER THIRTY-TWO

STACEY

There are now only two days until I leave for America. I am currently sat in Danish waiting for Martin and Lydia to join me. It has been so long since the three of us hung out together, and I miss it. I know that all of our lives are changing, but sometimes I yearn for the simpler days when we were all able to meet up more regularly.

The waitress brings the drinks over that I ordered ready for when Lydia and Martin arrive. She is depositing them on the table when Martin comes waltzing in.

"Baby girl," he screeches as he bounds over to me. The waitress jumps at the loudness that is Martin. I stand up and hug Martin as he reaches me and wraps his arms around me. I almost feel like I am going to cry. My emotions are still up in the air, but they are bound to be seeing as I am going away for six months in two days' time.

I rapidly blink the tears away as I pull back from Martin.

"Oh, honey, why so sad?" Martin pouts, making me laugh, which is just what I needed at this point.

"Oh, just ignore me. I've been a bit emotional recently," I say as I let go of him and sit back down at the table. Martin sits beside me, and I push his drink towards him.

"Hardly surprising what with everything that you have going on," Martin says as he takes a sip of his latte.

"I know, but I don't want to talk about me. I want to hear all about you." At this point Martin breaks out into a massive grin and does a little giggle. I know that look and I know that there is a guy causing it.

"What's his name?" I ask.

"How do you know that the reason I am smiling is down to a guy?"

"Please," I say sarcastically. "I have known you for too long to not know that a guy is making you smile like the cat that got the cream."

"Oh, I got the cream alright."

"Eww," I say as I laugh at his response. "TMI, Martin!"

"No such thing as TMI, baby girl." Martin has no shame. I love how care-free he can be.

"So, come on, I want details," I say as I eagerly wait for him to update me on his life.

"Gosh, I don't quite know where to start."

"From the beginning would be good."

"Oh, bloody funny, ha ha," he retorts.

"Guys," I hear Lydia shout from across the room. She comes hurrying over and I stand up to give her a hug. She almost knocks me on my ass as she bashes into me, her arms going around me like a vice grip. I feel Martin's hand on my back as he helps to steady me. I mouth "Thank you" at him over Lydia's shoulder and he gives me a thumbs up.

"I bloody missed you, lady," Lydia says as I hear her sniffle.

"Oh God, don't cry, Lyd. You'll set me off if you do."

"Sorry," she says as she releases her arms from around me. "I just... I can't believe that it's been so long since I saw you."

"Lyd, it's been three days since I last saw you," I say as she makes her way to sit opposite me. I lower myself into my seat once again and point to Lydia's coffee to indicate that it is hers.

"Well, three days is a long time when I used to see you nearly every day." She takes a tissue out of her pocket and dabs underneath her eyes. She cried like this the other day too. It's not like Lydia to be so emotional. The only time she has ever been like this is when she has been...

"Oh my God. Are you pregnant?" I blurt out before I can stop myself. I hear Martin gasp beside me.

"Shhh," Lydia hisses at me quietly.

"You are, aren't you?" I say as I try to contain my excitement. Lydia looks from me to Martin and then back to me again. The slight nod of her head is all it takes for me to squeal with delight at her news. I jump up and go round to her. Martin stands up too and we both engulf her in a hug, making her laugh. We stay like that for a few moments as all three of us soak up the joy that we are feeling.

"Okay, guys, that's enough. People will be staring at us," Lydia scolds.

"Who gives a shit if they stare," Martin says, ever his sassy self.

"Just sit down, you," Lydia says, giving Martin a stern look. He looks at me and I nod for him to sit down, and I do the same. I remember Lydia's pregnancy hormones from before, and I don't wish to awaken them just yet.

"Lydia, this is so exciting. I can't believe you're having another little jellybean," I say as I refer to the name that she used for Amber whilst she was carrying her.

"I know, but you have to keep it quiet as we're waiting for the three month check before we tell people." Lydia must see my eyes widen slightly at her request to keep it quiet. She immediately cottons on to why I might be freaking out slightly. "You can tell Jake though," she adds with a wink.

"Phew," I say out loud.

"So, come on," Martin says. "When did you find out?"

"Just a few days ago. We have been trying as I didn't want much of an age gap between Amber and her sibling."

"I bet Paul is thrilled," I say knowing that Paul loves kids and is great with Amber.

"Yeah, he's pretty excited. Although, I don't think that he is looking forward to the hormones and the labour." I laugh as I remember how Lydia was during labour. "I have said that I will try not to threaten to castrate him this time, but when you're in that much pain you can't promise anything." She takes a sip of her drink and then places it back on the table. "I guess I might as well ask now... Will you be my birthing partner again, Stace?"

"I would love to, but are you sure that you want me there a second time?"

"Paul has practically begged me to ask you. Apparently, you have a calming effect on me," she says with a swish of her hand. "Honestly, I wasn't that bad the first time."

I decide not to answer her, but I grin instead. She does a double take as she looks at me.

"What?" she asks, innocently.

"Nothing." The three of us all burst out laughing and we spend the remainder of the afternoon chatting and immersing ourselves in each other's lives.

It hits me that I am not going to have this for the next six months.

I am going to miss out on seeing Lydia's bump grow.

I am going to miss out on seeing Amber grow up.

I am going to miss out on watching Martin's new romance blossoming.

Six months didn't sound too bad back when I first heard about touring America, but now it sounds like forever.

JAKE

TWO DAYS LATER

Saying goodbye to Stacey at the airport this morning was fucking depressing. I can't believe that I won't get to be with her for the next few months. She left me her schedule for whilst she will be gone, which sees her promoting her book all over America. What with her flitting from state to state and my work being more hectic than ever, I just don't know when we are going to get the chance to visit one another.

I know some might think six months is nothing, but it's almost too fucking long for me.

I enter our house after driving back from the airport, and the place already feels empty. I never expected to become a guy that pines after their woman, but I can honestly say that I am already missing her.

I know that we can talk on the phone and FaceTime, but it's not the same as actually being with her. She still hasn't been completely herself and I just hope that the stress of being away from everyone, and touring all over the place, doesn't make her feel worse...

CHAPTER THIRTY-THREE

STACEY

ONE MONTH LATER

I flop down on my bed at the end of a very long day. I have just finished a book signing that lasted for five hours. The queue of people wanting to have their book signed was so big that we have had to add an extra date on near the end of the tour, to come back here.

I'm not sure how I managed to get through the day though as I have been feeling off since the moment that I woke up. A dull ache in my stomach has had me second guessing the lasagne that I ate last night. Or it could just be that I feel homesick and this is a side effect of it, and the tour is far from over.

So far, I have been to Los Angeles and Las Vegas, and I am currently in New York, staying in the exact hotel that Jake booked for us when we came out here at the end of January. I haven't spoken to Jake for two days, what with the time difference and our work schedules clashing. I have managed to speak to Lydia and Martin a few times, but I miss being able to just pop and see them or meet up for a coffee.

I sigh as I take my phone out of my handbag and prop myself against the headboard, so that I can try and get through to Jake. I kick my shoes off and drop them off of the side of the bed before I get comfortable. I find Jake's name and press the call button. It rings four or five times and I pray that he will answer the phone. It rings a couple more times, and just when I think that it is going to go to voicemail, he answers.

"Hi, babe," he says, his masculine tones floating down the line to me. I close my eyes with relief that I have heard his voice.

"Hi, handsome."

"It's so good to hear your voice," he says, mirroring my thoughts. "How's it going out there?"

"It's okay. Today was ridiculously busy. In fact, it was so busy that they have added an extra date at the end of my tour to come back here." I hear Jake groan at this piece of information and I can completely understand. I made the same groan when Chloe first told me.

"More dates?"

"Just one. I told Chloe that she wasn't to add anything else. I would have told her not to add this one, but she had promoted the extra date before she even told me about it."

"Typical Chloe," Jake remarks. Chloe has always been a bit sneaky when it comes to making me bend to her will.

"Yeah, well, I don't think that she will pull that stunt again in a hurry after I had a go at her about it." I get that she wants to make this book as successful as possible, and I do too, but not at the expense of my personal life.

I know now that Jake supports me in anything that I do, but I think six months is long enough to be away from my home life without having extra pressure put on me to extend my tour. "Anyway, I don't want to talk about the tour for the moment. How have things been at home?"

"To put it simply, work is crazy and being at home without you sucks."

"Only five months to go," I say, trying to put a good spin on it seeing as a month has already passed, but I fail miserably.

"Oh, I know how long it is. I'm marking each day off of the fucking calendar." I laugh at him as I picture his frustration at seeing how many days are left until I return home.

"Have you seen Amber at all?" I ask, the image of my god-daughter filling my mind.

"Yeah, I went round there last night for a couple of drinks." I picture, what I call my family, spending the evening without me and it brings a pain to my chest.

"Did you have a nice time?" I say as tears prick the backs of my eyes. Jake goes silent for a moment before answering.

"It wasn't the same without you there." I don't try to stop the tears from falling this time. I do try to keep my sobs silent, but I fail in that attempt. "Don't cry, babe."

"I'm sorry, I just miss you all so much."

"I know, but it's killing me hearing you so upset and me not being able to do anything." I can hear the pain in his voice and I try to calm myself down for his sake.

"I'm just being silly. I'll be okay in a minute." I take a tissue out of the box on the bedside table and wipe my eyes, probably smearing mascara everywhere whilst I do so.

"Are you still struggling?" Jake asks me, his voice becoming softer. I know that he is referring to my emotional ups and downs, he doesn't need to expand on his question.

"A bit," I say, sugar-coating my answer. I have been struggling more than a bit, but I don't need Jake to worry any more than he probably already is.

"Why don't you ask Chloe for a break, so you can come home for a few days?"

"I can't. It's too late to change any of the dates now," I say with a sigh. "Anyway, even if I could, it would only mean that the dates would be re-scheduled for another time." I turn so that I am led on my side and as I do, I feel a sharp pain shoot through the bottom of my belly.

"Ouch," I say out loud, cursing myself as I do.

"Why are you saying ouch?"

"I just had a..." I don't get to finish my sentence as another sharp pain comes just as quickly as the first one. I clutch my belly as I screw my eyes up from the pain.

"Stace? Stacey?" I can hear Jake trying to talk to me, but another pain strikes, rendering me speechless. I try to breath in and out slowly to help ease some of the pain, but it doesn't work.

Another sharp shooting courses through me and I cry out in pain. I try to sit up and I drop the phone on the bed.

"STACEY?" I hear Jake shout from the phone, but I can't talk to him. I stand up and try to make my way to the bathroom, but I freeze as I look down.

"Oh God," I whisper as I see blood trickling down the inside of my legs.

I try to think but another pain quickly shoots through me, making me drop to my knees.

Get your phone, Stacey.

You need to call an ambulance.

I can feel sweat start to trickle down my neck as panic threatens to overtake me.

Get your fucking phone!

I cry out as another pain hits and I take a deep breath as I reach over and grab my phone off of the bed.

"STACEY!" Jake is still shouting. Oh God, he's going to be going out of his fucking mind. I try to focus on my phone and I press the loudspeaker button. Jake's voice booms through the receiver and it takes all of my effort to answer him.

"I'm here," I say, panting.

"Oh thank God. What the fuck is going on?" He sounds frantic.

"I don't know," I cry as the pain starts to work its way down the entire bottom half of my body. "I'm bleeding, Jake. I'm bleeding."

"Bleeding? What? How? Why are you bleeding?"

"I don't know. I need a doc..." I don't get to finish my sentence as a blinding pain hits and I pass out.

CHAPTER THIRTY-FOUR

STACEY

I am led in a hospital bed and I am completely numb.

I feel nothing.

I stare at the ceiling as I try to process what the doctor has just told me.

"I am so sorry, Mrs Waters," I hear the doctor say, but I don't acknowledge him. "I'll come back in a little while to check on you." I still don't say a word.

I have no words to say.

Nothing can be said to make this outcome any better.

Nothing can repair what I have managed to lose.

I hear the door to my room click shut and I am alone.

———

JAKE

My fucking heart is beating so fast.

I run through the airport like a man possessed as I go to hail a taxi to take me to Stacey. I have no idea what has happened. All I know is that she is in hospital and I need to get to her.

I jump into an available taxi and tell them to take me to the hospital. It seems to be taking forever for me to get to her.

My mind has been replaying my phone call with Stacey over and over. One minute she was fine and the next she's telling me that she's bleeding.

Fucking bleeding.

Then when the line went quiet, my heart plummeted. I felt like I had died for a few seconds before I sprang into action and called Chloe. From that point on, everything is a bit of a blur.

Whilst Chloe went to check on Stacey, I was booking flights to New York. Chloe couldn't get Stacey to answer her hotel room door, so she called for a concierge to help. That seemed to take a fucking age, but by this time I had locked up the house and was in my car ready to drive to the airport. I didn't bring any bags with me, all I brought was my phone, passport, wallet and set of keys. I didn't even think about clothes or anything. My mind was just on getting to my wife.

I placed the phone on handsfree as I started to drive the car. When Chloe finally managed to get into Stacey's room, my heart sank even lower. All it took was for Chloe to gasp and I knew there was something seriously wrong.

As I replay Chloe telling me that she needed to call an ambulance, I feel sick.

I have never felt so helpless in all of my life.

I put my foot down on the accelerator and I made it to the airport in record time. Luckily, I didn't get stopped by any police, but then again, I wouldn't have given a fuck if I had. I was thousands of miles away from Stacey, and I had no idea what had happened to her.

I still don't know what's happened to her.

The only thing I know is the hospital that she is in, and the floor and room number.

The taxi eventually pulls up outside the hospital and I throw a load of cash at the driver as I exit the car and run into the building. I thank God that I had money left from our last trip to America together, meaning I didn't have to fuck about trying to get any.

I find the lifts and barrel into one that is just about to close. There are two other people in here that look at me with wide eyes. I take no notice of them as I press the number three for the level that Stacey is on.

My jaw ticks as the lifts seems to be going at a snail's pace.

When the doors open on level three, I burst out of them and run straight to the nurses' desk. I tell the nurse at the desk that I am here to see my wife and she directs me to the room number that I have been given. I follow her directions and I go screeching around the corner until I get to room number nineteen.

My hand goes to the handle and I fling the door open, taking in deep mouthfuls of air as I do.

The sight before me breaks my heart.

My wife is led on her back and her head turns to look at who has just entered the room.

Her eyes are devoid of any emotion, until she registers that it is me that has just burst in here.

"Jake?" she says in a whisper.

"Yeah, I'm here, babe." I shut the door behind me and I go to her. I take her hand in mine and place my other hand on her cheek.

"You're here," she says, still whispering.

"Of course I'm here. I got the first flight out that I could." I search her eyes for anything that might give away what has happened to her, but all I see are her tears beginning to fall. I put my arms around her as she sobs. I've seen Stacey cry before, but never have I seen her break like this. I hold her as panic consumes me.

What the hell has happened to her?

"I'm so sorry," she says quietly, repeating the words over and over again.

Sorry?

What has she got to be sorry for?

I don't want to push her, but I need to know what's going on.

"Stacey, what's happened?" I can hear the quiver in my voice as I ask the question.

"I..." I hear her take a deep breath and then she gently moves back from me, so that she is looking at me. "Jake..."

"Yeah?" My eyes frantically search hers as I see her struggling to form words. I take hold of her hands again and will her to find the strength to speak. "Stace, you can tell me."

"I lost our baby." She says the words so quietly that I almost think that I have misheard her. I look into her eyes and the sadness there tells me that I heard her correctly.

Lost our baby?

Our baby?

I feel my eyes fill with tears as Stacey places one of her hands on my cheek. "I had a miscarriage, Jake."

I take in a deep breath as I process her words. She strokes my cheek with her thumb and I know that she is trying to be brave for me. I know that she is breaking inside, but she is trying to hold it together now that she has told me.

I move, so that I can lie on the bed with her. She shifts over and allows me to do so.

I don't speak.

I don't have any words right now.

All I want to do is hold her. And that is what I do. I take her in my arms and I hold her.

"I didn't even know that I was pregnant," she whispers as she starts to cry again. The sound of her hurting, and the hurt that I feel inside of me, is like nothing that I have experienced before.

I couldn't protect her from this.

I couldn't protect our baby from this.

I let myself cry along with Stacey.

We cry for the pain that we are being put through right now.

We cry for each other.

We cry for a baby that we didn't know existed.

And we cry for the little life that we have lost.

CHAPTER THIRTY-FIVE

JAKE

Four days have passed since Stacey miscarried.

She was allowed to leave the hospital yesterday.

We can't go back home yet as the doctor wants to see Stacey in a few days' time. We are currently led in bed, watching a film on the television that is on the wall opposite us.

Stacey is led next to me, with her arm around my waist and her head on my chest. I have my arm around her shoulders and my other hand is entwined with hers.

An unexpected knock at the door has me gently disentangling myself from her, so that I can go and see who it is.

"I'll get rid of whoever it is," I say to her, but she doesn't respond. She continues to look blankly at the television screen.

It pains me to see her looking so despondent and so withdrawn from life, but I'm not going to push her.

It's still only been four days and that is no time at all when we are both dealing with this kind of loss.

I wearily walk to the door, rubbing my neck as I do, but when I open it, I wish that I hadn't bothered.

"Chloe," I greet her, not offering for her to come in. I appreciate that she got Stacey to the hospital on that awful night, but apart from that, her face is one that I would like to see less of.

"Hi, Jake. Can I come in for a few minutes?" she asks, nerves in her voice. She is fidgeting on the spot and wringing her hands together.

"I don't think that now is the best time. Stacey is in bed and she needs to rest."

"I know that she does, but this won't take long." She looks so worried that I almost feel sorry for her. I move to one side and usher her in. She enters and comes to a stop in front of the dining table. I close the door and sigh as I turn to look at her.

"So, what's this about, Chloe?" I ask, my tone stern.

"Um, is Stacey not able to come and join us?"

"I told you, she needs her rest. If there is anything you need to discuss then you can speak to me." I fold my arms across my chest and wait to hear what she has to say.

"Oh, right, yes, well… It's a bit of a sensitive matter, you see."

"Sensitive? You mean, more sensitive than what we are going through right now?" I can't help the sarcasm or the venom in my tone.

Chloe has the decency to look mortified as she starts to colour red.

"I'm sorry, I didn't mean to speak out of turn," Chloe says as she looks at the floor.

"Just get to the point of why you are here, Chloe," I respond with a sigh.

"Right. Well, I've um… I've had my boss on the phone and he wants to know when the book tour is going to resume." Chloe doesn't look up at me until she has finished speaking, but when she does her eyes widen. The look on my face must say it all. I don't think that I have ever disliked someone so much in my life, but right now she fits that bill.

My teeth are gritted together, my jaw clenched tight. My brain sifts through the possible answers that I could give her, each one ruder than the next, but I am saved the trouble of responding by the voice to my left.

"It's not," I hear Stacey say as I look to the doorway of the bedroom and see her standing there, arms folded around her. My heart goes out to her at having to deal with this on top of losing our baby.

Chloe's head whips round to look at Stacey. I shift and put my hands in my trouser pockets as I wait to see what Chloe is going to say. If she upsets my wife further, then I have no qualms about dragging her ass out of this room.

"Stacey, I thought that you were resting?" Chloe says as she wrings her hands together.

"I was, but then I heard you in here and I thought I should come and speak to you myself. And in answer to your question, there is no more book tour." My eyes widen at Stacey's answer, and Chloe's mouth has dropped open. I keep quiet as this isn't my decision to make.

"But you can't do that," Chloe exclaims.

"I can and I am."

"Stacey, I know that you are going through something horrific right now—"

"No, you don't," Stacey says cutting Chloe off. Chloe clamps her mouth shut. "Have you ever suffered a miscarriage, Chloe?" Stacey's voice doesn't waver.

"No."

"Exactly. You have no idea what it feels like, so there is no way that you can comprehend the way that I am feeling right now."

"I'm sorry," Chloe says, but she clearly isn't done with trying to persuade Stacey to carry on with the tour. "But you might feel different in a few days' time."

I clench my fists in my trouser pockets as I struggle not to interrupt. All Chloe cares about is her fucking commission for this tour. She has no idea who my wife really is.

"I won't, so you can call your boss and tell him that it's over."

"Stacey—"

"No, Chloe," Stacey responds, raising her voice slightly. "As soon as I have been cleared by the doctor here, I am going back home and that is where I will be staying."

"But what about all of the sponsors? What about your fans?"

"Fuck the sponsors. I don't give a shit about the money, Chloe. And as for my fans, hopefully they will understand why I can't carry on with this tour, and if they don't, well, I really don't give a shit about that either at this moment in time."

"But... But..."

"I think it's time for you to go, Chloe," I say, needing to get her out of here.

I need to be alone with my wife.

I look to Stacey for confirmation that she wants me to get Chloe out of here and she gives a slight nod of her head.

"Goodbye, Chloe," Stacey says as she turns and disappears back into the bedroom. Chloe looks absolutely frantic as she is clearly having difficulty processing what my wife has just said.

She turns to me with a pleading look in her eyes. "Jake, please talk to her."

"No," I say firmly. "It's Stacey's decision to make and I am not going to interfere."

"But... But she can't give up on her dream," Chloe responds, looking panicked.

"That's the part that you aren't quite getting. I don't think that this is her dream anymore."

STACEY

I listen from the bedroom as I hear Chloe pleading with Jake to get me to reconsider. I could almost laugh at how pathetic her begging sounds.

I climb back onto the bed and prop myself up against the headboard. Jake comes into the bedroom a few moments later and sits on the edge of the bed, facing me.

"Thanks for getting rid of her," I say with a sad smile on my face.

"No problem." He reaches out to me and brushes a lock of hair from my face. "Can I get you anything? A drink or something to eat?"

"No, thank you."

"Babe, you haven't eaten for three days. You need to make sure that you are looking after yourself." I can see the worry in his eyes, but I can't bring myself to put any food in my mouth.

"I don't need food, Jake. I just need you."

"And you've got me. I'm not going anywhere." I close my eyes as I feel tears re-emerge.

I take a few deep breaths as I try to push the tears away. I am aware that Jake and I haven't really spoken about the baby that we lost, but I think that now is the time to do it.

I open my eyes and look at his handsome features. He really is my world, but I need to see if he feels the same way about me after what has happened.

I would hate to think that he is staying with me out of pity.

"Jake, I think it's time that we talked." I see him gulp and he gives a slight nod of his head. I don't need to tell him what we need to talk about, he already knows where I am going with this line of conversation.

"As long as you're ready." He is always thinking about me and how I am feeling, but I need to know how he is feeling as well. It's unfair of me to clam up and not be there for him.

"I am." I lean forward and take his hands in mine. "I need to say some things to you and I need you to let me finish before you respond." He nods at me, his eyes searching mine. "I know that I have shut myself down over the last few days and I am sorry if that has made you feel any worse."

I can see that he wants to answer me, but he respects my wishes and keeps quiet. "I just... I need you to know that I truly had no idea that I was pregnant. If I had of done, then I would never have come on this book tour. I keep thinking that, if only I had been at home with you, then maybe I wouldn't have—"

"Don't," Jake says, interrupting me, his voice firm but quiet.

I feel more tears spring to the backs of my eyes and I take a deep breath as I know that he doesn't want me to finish my sentence. I do anyway.

"Lost our baby." He goes to speak again but I place a finger on his lips. "Let me finish," I whisper, keeping my finger there for the time being. "I know that it was only a few months ago that I said I wasn't ready for a family yet, but I promise you that I would have been ready for this baby. I promise that I would never intentionally do anything to put a child of ours at risk."

Tears start to fall from my eyes and Jake hands me a tissue from the bedside table. I take it and dab my eyes, but I need to keep going. "I also know that, as much as you might love me now, there may come a time when you resent me." His brow furrows at this but it has been bugging me for the best part of the last twenty-four hours.

"There may come a day when you think that this is all my fault and that might be the day that you decide that you no longer want to be with me." The thought alone has my heart breaking a little bit more. I see Jake clamp his jaw tight and I know that he is struggling with hearing what I am saying. "If that day comes, I want you to know that I will understand. I don't want you to think that you have to stay with me out of duty because we are married."

"Stacey, stop." I ignore his request and I continue to speak.

"I'm so sorry that I couldn't keep our baby safe. I'm so sorry that I couldn't do the one thing a mother should do and keep our baby protected," I say as I start to sob loudly. "I'm so sorry, Jake." Clearly, this is the point where Jake has had enough as he takes my face in his hands and looks me straight in the eye.

"Stacey Waters, this was not your fault. Do you hear me?" I shake my head at him as I close my eyes and let the tears flow. I can't stand to see the pain on his face. I can hardly look at myself, so I don't know how he is being so caring towards me.

"Look at me." I don't. "Stacey, look at me," he says a little more forcefully this time.

I take a deep breath and open my eyes, even though it pains me to do so as I look into his tear-filled caramel pools.

"Miscarriages happen for all sorts of reasons. It has nothing to do with you being unable to keep a baby safe." I hear his words, but they only cause me to cry harder.

"Jake—"

"No. You have said your bit and now it's my turn." He clears his throat. "What has happened has been fucking heart-breaking. I have never felt anything like this in my life, and neither have you. I know that you had no idea that you were pregnant. I know that you would have cancelled this tour if you had found out that you were before it began. And I know that, when the time is right, you are going to be an amazing mother to our children."

His voice breaks slightly at this point and I let out a loud cry.

He is hurting just as much as me and I have been too wrapped up in my own grief to see that he needs my support too.

"As for me resenting you, that is never going to happen. I would never blame you for this. It happens, and unfortunately it has happened to us." I bring my hands up and place them on his which are still caressing the sides of my face. "We are going to get through this, and we are going to get through it together. We will never get over it, but we will work through it. And we will never forget the little life that was taken away from us too soon." I don't know how he is still speaking. His words are so beautiful even in our time of turmoil.

"I fucking love you, Stacey, and that is never going to change." I let go of his hands and wrap my arms around his neck, burying my face in his neck. His arms go around me, and he holds me close to him.

We both cry and let our emotions overtake any part of us that was trying to remain strong.

"I love you too," I manage to say between sobs.

I don't know if I could have gotten through this without Jake.

I hate the pain that we are both going through, but I have to be thankful that we have each other.

We may not have our baby, but we have us.

I make a promise to the little life that was lost that we will never forget about them.

I will always hold a special place in my heart for them.

And I know that Jake will do the same.

CHAPTER THIRTY-SIX

JAKE

We arrived back in the UK a couple of hours ago and have just gotten back to our house.

"You go on in and I'll bring the bags," I say to Stacey. She gives me a smile and proceeds to unlock the front door.

After our heart to heart the other day, things have been slowly getting better. We may still be grieving but being able to communicate has helped a little.

I take the bags out of the car and take them into the house, leaving them in the hallway and closing the front door behind me.

I go through to the kitchen where Stacey is making us both a coffee, as I knew that she would be. I go behind her and wrap my arms around her, clasping them together in front of her stomach. She leans back into me and I inhale her scent. Her hand comes up and finds the nape of my neck. She turns her head and places the softest kiss on my lips. When she pulls away, she has the most beautiful grin on her face.

"If you want a drink, Waters, then you need to give me some room," she says, teasingly. It's refreshing to see that some of her playful nature is starting to seep back in. I chuckle and release her, giving her nose a kiss as I do.

I make my way to the kitchen island as I watch her make the drinks. My mind wanders to a phone call I received yesterday before we left for the airport. I haven't told Stacey about it yet, but I intend to, now that we are back home.

She brings the drinks over and then sits down next to me.

"I need to talk to you about something," I say as I turn to face her.

"Okay. What's up, Waters?"

"I received a phone call yesterday from a guy called Lance Roberts."

"Okay." She looks confused and I guess that is because she has no idea who Lance Roberts is.

"Lance Roberts is an up and coming businessman who is causing waves in the financial world."

"Right. So why is he calling you?" she asks as she takes a sip of her coffee.

"Well, he wants to meet with me and discuss the possibility of buying my company." In hindsight, I should have told her that part when she wasn't taking a sip of her drink. She coughs and splutters at my unexpected news.

"What?" she screeches when she is able to talk. "Jake, you can't sell your company."

"Why not?" I say with a shrug of my shoulders.

"You have worked so hard to make the company what it is today. Why would you want to give that up?" she asks as she is struggling to comprehend why I would ever sell my business.

"Because some things in life are more important than owning a company." I see her eyes soften at my words. I don't need to expand on my answer, she knows what I am referring to.

"I love that you don't let your life revolve around your work. I love that you feel the need to be here for me, but you don't need to sell your company in order to do that."

"What I if I want to sell it?"

"Do you really?" she asks with a raise of her eyebrows.

"I might do."

"Jake," she says as she takes my hands in hers. "If you want to sell your company, then I won't stop you. But you need to be doing it for the right reasons. I get that you might feel that this is the best decision in the short term, but you need to think about the long term."

"After what we have been through, Stace, I don't want to spend time away from you because of work. Work is not as important to me anymore." I mean every word that I say. Work is at the bottom of my priority list now, something that I never thought would ever happen.

"I just think you need to think long and hard about this before you make any final decisions."

"I will. I'm meeting with Lance on Monday morning, so I have the weekend to mull it over." Stacey nods at me and then her eyes start to sparkle. I watch her, intrigued by her reaction.

"What if I was to come and work at Waters Industries?" she says, completely throwing me. "Would that help you make your decision?"

"You want to come and work for me?" I ask, shock evident in my voice.

"Why not?" she says with a shrug of her shoulders.

"What about your writing career?" I ask. I know that she will return to it one day.

"I can still write and have a job, you know?"

"Yeah, but what about when you need to go and promote your future books?" I don't think that she has fully thought this idea through.

"I won't be going anywhere. I have already decided to write under a false name."

"Seriously?" She has completely floored me.

"Yeah. I don't want an agent hounding me to do this and that. I don't want to be beholden to deadlines. I think that it's best for me to write at my own pace and then self-publish when I am ready." She says all of this with ease and I see no hint of stress over her decision. "Plus, if I write under a false name, then no one will know that it is actually me."

She makes a fucking good point, but I don't want her to feel that she has to come and work for me in order for me to keep my company. "I think that we should start a trial run on Monday. If at the end of the week neither of us are happy with me working at Waters Industries, then I'll quit."

"You'll quit?" I say as a smile creeps onto my face.

"Yeah. It's not going to hurt to try it and see how it goes." She finishes drinking her coffee and places the cup in front of her. I laugh and pull her towards me, holding her close against me.

"You are the most amazing woman, Mrs Waters."

"I do try," she responds playfully.

"I love you."

"I love you too, handsome."

STACEY

I go up to the bedroom after having my fantastic idea of working with Jake, and I sit on the edge of the bed as I call Lydia.

"Hey, babes," she says as she picks up the phone.

"Hi, Lyd."

"How are you?" she asks me straight away.

"I'm okay," I answer quickly. I do feel better than I have done in the last week, but it's going to take me a long time to recover from losing a baby.

"How's that gorgeous god-daughter of mine?" I ask her, changing the subject. Lydia pauses for a moment before answering.

"She's good. She misses her Auntie Stacey though."

"Well, you can tell her that Auntie Stacey will be round to see her tomorrow."

"Really? You're coming back tomorrow?"

"Actually, we got back to the UK a couple of hours ago. I would have come round tonight but I feel wiped from the travelling." I hear Lydia sniffle. "What's wrong?" I ask, concern growing for her.

"I'm just so glad that you're back."

"Okay," I answer as it dawns on me that Lydia's pregnancy hormones must be in full force.

"I'm sorry, I don't mean to get upset. I just can't seem to help my emotions these days." I feel a slight pang that I was experiencing those emotions only a few weeks ago. I quickly push the pang to one side.

"How is the jellybean doing?" I ask, wanting Lydia to know that I am okay with discussing her pregnancy. She goes quiet and I know that she is worried about broaching the subject of babies with me. "It's okay, Lyd," I say, trying to reassure her.

"No, it's not, babes. I didn't want to get upset, but I am so sorry." I feel a lone tear fall down my cheek and I wipe it away.

"I know," I whisper as the pain resurfaces.

"Oh God, Stace, I am so bloody tactless sometimes."

"Don't worry, Lyd, it's fine." I don't want my friends to pussy-foot around me. In some way that would make it worse. I brace myself for the words that I am about to speak. "In fact, it's quite nice that I can talk about my baby with you." I hear her intake of breath on the other end of the phone at the mention of the child that I lost. "I know that I never got to meet my child, but it doesn't mean that I have to forget about the life that was taken from me."

"Oh, Stace, of course you don't."

"And it doesn't mean that I am going to lose my shit if you talk about your babies with me. Your babies are an important part of my life too." I let a few more tears slip down my cheeks, a mixture of happy and sad tears.

"And you are important to all of us." I smile at her words and realise that I am going to be okay, and I am going to remember my lost child forever. "Did you have a name picked out?" Lydia asks me.

"Actually, Jake and I decided on a name the other day." I smile as the memory of our conversation comes into my mind. A memory that I shall cherish forever as it gave our baby their name.

"Do you want to tell me?" Lydia asks tentatively.

"She was called Paris."

"Oh, that is a beautiful name."

"Yeah." Jake and I decided on the name that I lost when I married Jake. We both thought that Paris was the perfect choice.

"Stacey?"

"Yeah?"

"I love you, girl."

"I love you too, Lyd."

CHAPTER THIRTY-SEVEN

JAKE

My wife and I stroll into Waters Industries on Monday morning, hand in hand. We make our way to my office and greet Valerie on arrival.

"Oh hello, dear," Valerie says to Stacey with a smile.

"Morning, Valerie."

"Valerie, as of today Stacey will be working here," I inform her. Her eyes widen as she looks from Stacey to me.

"Oh," she says, clearly shocked but recovering herself quickly. "Welcome to the firm, Mrs Waters."

"It's okay, you can still call me Stacey," Stacey tells Valerie with a wink.

"I have a meeting today with Lance Roberts," I say.

"Yes, it's still scheduled for one o'clock."

"Could you call him and let him know that I will no longer be needing to meet with him."

"Of course," Valerie answers. I look to Stacey and she frowns at me.

"Thank you. I will be running through things with Stacey this morning so there are to be no interruptions," I say, not taking my eyes off of Stacey.

"Very well, Mr Waters." At this point I lead Stacey into my office and shut the door behind us.

"Are you going to tell me why you cancelled the meeting with Lance?" Stacey asks me, her arms folded across her chest.

"I changed my mind about selling," I say with a shrug of my shoulders.

"Just like that?"

"Just like that," I confirm.

"How come?" she asks, needing me to spell it out for her.

"I no longer need to sell, seeing as you will be helping me run this place." Her eyes widen at my suggestion.

"Jake, I can't run this place with you."

"Why not?"

"Far be it from me to point out the obvious, but I have no idea what I am doing."

"You'll learn." She scoffs, and I chuckle at her reaction.

"And what if at the end of the week we decide that this isn't going to work?" She is challenging me, but I already have my answer for her.

"It'll work," I reply as I walk over to my desk and take a seat behind it. Stacey watches me, still flabbergasted by this turn of events. "So, are you ready to get to work, Mrs Waters?"

She shakes her head at me, but a smile starts to form on her lips. "You're crazy."

"Crazy for you, yes."

She laughs as she walks over and takes a seat opposite me, on the other side of my desk.

"So, I think that we should start by going over the various departments and then we can decide which ones are suited to us individually. That way, you will control the ones that you feel most comfortable with." I turn on my laptop and pick up a few papers lying on my desk, but I stop when I feel Stacey staring at me. I look to her and see that she is still smiling.

"You have this all figured out already, don't you?"

"Of course I do. I don't own a multi-million-pound company for nothing, babe."

"I guess not," she says as she crosses her legs and settles back for her first morning of working with me. "Okay, Waters, let's get started."

STACEY

It only takes Jake and I until lunchtime to decide which departments I will be running. Of course my first choice was the event planning department. I smile as I knock on Martin's office door and wait for him to answer.

"Come in," I hear him shout through the door. I open it and can see that he is bent over his desk, concentrating on some paperwork.

"Hi, Mart," I say as I close the door behind me. His head whips up and his face breaks into a grin as he sees me.

"Baby girl," he says as he stands up and makes his way over to me and gives me a hug. I saw Martin on Saturday, but I didn't mention the fact that I would be starting work here today.

"What are you doing here? Did you bring sushi?" he says as he looks to my hands to see if I have any bags.

"No, I didn't have time to get any today."

"Oh, well, never mind. Just don't forget to bring it next time," he says with a wink.

"I won't, but I don't think that you should be talking to your new boss in that way," I say, teasingly. He freezes and gives me a suspicious look.

"My new boss?" he says, his eyebrows raised.

"Yep. As of this morning, I started working for Waters Industries. And as of half an hour ago, I took over the running of the event planning department."

"Are you shitting me?"

"No," I say, laughing. "I'm not shitting you as you so eloquently put it."

"You're my boss now?"

"Uh, yeah," I say, now feeling slightly nervous that this may make things awkward. I don't want anything to disrupt mine and Martin's friendship. "But I can give this department back to Jake if it's going to make things awkward," I add quickly. Before I can say anything else, Martin throws his arms around me with a squeal.

"Oh my God, baby girl, this is going to be so much fun."

"Really?" I ask, a little surprised seeing as I thought that he was disappointed when I first told him.

"Are you kidding me? This is fabulous. Not only do I get to have a great new boss, but I also get to see you nearly every day." I feel the excitement coming off of him in waves and it makes my own excitement accelerate.

"Phew, for a minute there I thought that you were annoyed."

"No way. Don't get me wrong, Jake has been a good boss, but I have a feeling that you are going to be even better."

"Well, what can I say, I obviously have a charm that Jake doesn't."

"Hmm, I wouldn't go that far. Your husband is charm personified." I laugh as Martin leads me to his desk and gestures for me to sit down.

"I can't argue with you on that one."

"I didn't think that you would. Anyway," Martin says with a wave of his hands, "You need to tell me how this came about, baby girl, and you need to tell me now. There are only fifty-seven minutes left of my lunch hour and I need every detail."

"I'm sure that your new boss could stretch to a bit of a longer lunch today. Just for celebratory purposes of course," I say with a wink.

"Well, in that case, sushi bar?" Martin asks as he jumps up from his seat.

"You read my mind."

CHAPTER THIRTY-EIGHT

JAKE

SEVEN YEARS LATER

My wife is still the most beautiful woman that I have ever seen.

As I sit in our back garden, I watch her playing with our two daughters and I feel like the luckiest man alive. Each of their squeals of laughter pulls at my heart.

I take a sip of my beer and smile. As I watch the girls disappear inside the ridiculously big playhouse I got for them last week, Stacey saunters towards me. I am mesmerised by the sight of her, even after eight years together.

She owns me, and fuck does it feel good.

I drink in her appearance and my cock starts to twitch. She's wearing a white vest top, denim shorts and flip flops. That's it. Nothing dressy or fancy, but I can honestly say that she has never looked hotter. Her long dark hair hangs down in waves, framing her face. It seems to take forever for her to reach me, but when she does, she places her hands on either side of my chair and leans down so that we are eye-level. My dick reacts as her cleavage is now on display, due to her being bent over slightly.

I run my eyes back up to her face and am met with her mouth smirking at me.

"Having a good look, are we?" she asks playfully. Her eyes sparkle with mischief.

"I'm just thanking my lucky stars that my wife is so hot," I reply giving her my heart-stopping grin that I know makes her go weak at the knees. She chuckles, and the sound is like music to my ears.

"Oh, you're good, Waters." She moves her face closer to mine. "Even after all this time, you still have the power to make me swoon." Her lips cover mine before I can respond, her tongue delving into my waiting mouth. I accept her, hungrily.

I don't think that I will ever get to the point where this woman no longer excites me.

She is the reason that I breath.

She is the one who brought meaning to my life.

She is the one who penetrated my heart.

I shuffle forwards on my seat and move my hands to her waist, so that I can pull her against me. She lets out a squeal as her body collides with mine. Her hands move to my shoulders, her moans making me want to do naughty things to her.

"Mummy, will you leave Daddy alone so that we can play tea parties?" says the little voice of Esme from behind her mother's back. Stacey springs away from me, giggling. She steps to one side, allowing me a view of my daughter.

I laugh as Esme stands there with her hands on her hips, frowning. She looks just like a miniature version of her mother.

"What's so funny, Daddy?" she asks me.

"Nothing, sweetheart. You just remind me of Mummy, *a lot*." I catch Stacey's eye and she is grinning at me.

"Esme!" cries Charlotte from inside the playhouse. "Esme!" Esme rolls her eyes and starts to make her way back to the playhouse. As Esme disappears from view, I look to Stacey who is watching me with interest.

"Everything okay over there?" I ask her, my brows pulling together at the look on her face. She holds my gaze for a few moments, neither of us speak, and I start to feel a bit nervous at her lack of speech.

I watch her as her gaze drifts over to the playhouse and then back to me.

Just when I think that I can't take the suspense any longer, she speaks.

"How many kids did you think that we were going to have, Jake?" she asks, making me wonder where this line of questioning is coming from.

"I don't know," I answer with a shrug of my shoulders. "Before you, I had never considered having any." She stares at me intently and I feel like she is waiting for me to say more. I rack my brains, trying to figure out what is running through that beautiful mind of hers, but I am at a loss.

"Okay," she says slowly, her eyes holding mine firm. "And now that you have me, and the girls, would you say that's enough?"

"Of course it is," I say as I stand up and face her. She looks up at me and her eyes glaze over. "What's going on, Stace? Where is all of this coming from?"

I can feel her heart pounding as I stand close to her. Actually, I am pretty sure that mine is doing the same thing. "You and the girls are all that I need. I love each of you more than you will ever know. You three are my life." A tear slips from her eye and I wipe it away with my thumb.

"Well," she whispers through her tears. "You better make room for one more in that heart of yours, Waters." I freeze, holding her face in my hands as I search her eyes for confirmation of what I think she is telling me.

"Are you?" I ask, shock evident in my voice.

"Yes, Jake. I'm pregnant." She looks a little nervous as she answers, but she has no need to be. Before she knows what is happening, I pick her up in my arms and twirl her around. She squeals with delight and there is a smile on my face that I am positive can never be erased.

I set her down a few moments later, seeing tears of joy running down her soft cheeks. I kiss her gently, conveying all of my emotions in just one kiss.

"Happy?" she asks me, when I break my lips from hers, her smile mirroring mine.

As I stare into her beautiful, heartfelt eyes, I am overcome with what this woman has done to my life. I hear the girls giggling from inside their playhouse and it makes my heart melt.

Before I found Stacey, I didn't think that I could ever love so fiercely and unconditionally.

She came into my life and turned it upside down.

She belongs with me.

She gave me a family.

She completes me.

Not only do I get to share my life with her, but I also run my company with her.

Since she came to work at Waters Industries, business has blossomed more than I could ever have hoped for. On top of working and raising a family, she still writes and is doing extremely well from being an anonymous writer. She stuck to her word about no more book tours, and I know that she loves the secretiveness of who she is behind the pages of the books that she writes.

I am so proud of her, and I am proud of us as a whole.

I wipe her tear stained cheeks with my thumbs and place a kiss on the end of her nose.

There is only one word that I need to say to her in response.

"Perfect."

THE END

BONUS CHAPTER

AT FIRST GLANCE

JAKE

As my eyes lock with hers across the dance floor, I feel my dick pulse with desire. The woman looking back at me is the most beautiful woman that I have ever seen. Long, dark brown hair frames her face, and her piercing blue eyes sparkle.

She is leaning against the bar, her hip jutting out slightly, allowing me to see the slight curve of her body. She is wearing a black dress that grazes the skin just above her knees.

Most women here are dressed with everything on display, nothing left to the imagination, but not her. She has retained her modesty whilst looking as sexy as sin. My heart speeds up a little as she licks her full lips, her tongue darting back into her mouth just as quickly as it came out. I give a slight nod of my head to acknowledge her, to which she quickly averts her eyes and turns her attention to the red-headed woman stood next to her.

As she feigns her interest in me, I can't help but smile.

"Dude," Paul says as he hands me a beer having just returned from the bar. I take my beer from him and take a generous swig.

"Cheers," I reply when I have finished drinking.

"I tell you what, there are some fine-looking woman in here tonight," Paul says, his eyes sweeping over the dance floor.

"There sure are," I reply, but my comment is aimed at one woman, and one woman only.

My eyes go back to her as she starts to sway her hips in time to the music. I watch as she starts to attract the attention of the men around her, even if she doesn't mean to. My jaw clenches as one guy goes up to her. This is not something that would usually annoy me, but the fact that this guy has grabbed her around the waist and is trying to bump and grind with her pisses me off.

I know that I have no right to be pissed off, but I can't help it. She shouldn't be treated like a piece of meat. I am fully aware that I have been appreciating her form, but at least I haven't tried to maul her in public.

I take a few steps forward and see that she has just turned and pushed the guy away from her. She doesn't look happy, and I can't say that I blame her. The next thing I see is the guy holding his hands up as he backs away. He goes back to his mates with his tail between his legs, and it helps to ease some of the tension that I was feeling only seconds ago. I hope to God that she doesn't shoot me down when I try to speak to her.

I would regret it if I didn't try and talk to her.

I don't normally act on impulse, but for her, I am willing to do just that.

I am halfway across the dance floor when I get stopped by some woman who throws her arms around my neck and starts to gyrate on me. I politely try to tell this woman that I am not interested, but my words fall on deaf ears.

As I try to disentangle myself from her, my eyes once again lock with the beauty stood at the bar. She gives me a small smile which I presume means that she finds my predicament amusing.

It takes a few more seconds to free myself from the woman trying to hump my leg, and then she is prowling towards her next unsuspecting victim.

I breathe a sigh of relief and continue towards the bar area. I keep walking until I am stood next to the lady with the captivating blue eyes. I signal to the bar staff that I require a drink and a woman quickly makes her way over to me. I order a bottle of beer and wait. I have no idea why I don't speak to the beauty next to me, it is what I came over her to do, but I guess I really want to see if she will speak first. I wouldn't want to make her feel uncomfortable in any way.

The time seems to pass by in slow motion, when in reality it has only been seconds.

My drink is placed in front of me and I hand over the money for it. I take a sip and turn, so I can lean back against the bar counter. The woman is still next to me, and as I turn, my arm brushes against hers. I can feel her whole body still from the contact, which I am hoping is a good sign.

I act like nothing has happened, even though I feel the tingle race up my arm as I take another sip of my drink.

I almost break into a grin when I see, out of the corner of my eye, that the woman next to me has turned and mimicked my position, elbows resting on the bar counter, slightly bent back. Her red-headed friend seems to have disappeared for the time being.

Now or never, Waters.

Take the plunge and speak or continue to be a pussy and say nothing.

I clear my throat and turn my head to find her looking at me. Her eyes are even more mesmerising up close. They twinkle with mischief as she lets her gaze drop to my lips.

Fuck.

I don't want to go in too hard here, so I go for the gentle approach.

"Hi." *Oh fuck me, what was that?*

Gentle approach? I might as well have sent Paul over here to tell her that I fancy her, like some kind of teenage boy would do. I want to smack myself for the weak opener, but my irritation soon disappears when I hear her laugh. My dick responds with a twitch, and it almost stands to attention when she leans in and her lips graze my ear.

"Hi," she says, her breath heating my skin. She moves back slightly, allowing me a look at her face. Fucking gorgeous.

"May I get you a drink?" I ask her.

"No, I'm good thanks."

I nod at her and rack my brains for where to go with the conversation next. I almost become flustered as I am lost for words.

Jake fucking Waters, lost for words.

This is a first for me.

I don't have time to worry about it thought as she laces her fingers through mine and guides me to the dance floor, pulling me to the edge near the DJ booth and away from the bar. She nestles us behind a couple of others dancing and turns to face me, moving her body to the beat of the music.

Her eyes never leave mine, intensifying the moment.

"Are you not going to dance?" she asks me after a few seconds, a slight frown appearing on her face. Instead of answering her with words, I smile and move closer to her. I see her breath hitch as I place my hands on her hips. Justin Timberlake "My Love" starts to pump through the sound system and I pull her against my body.

As we dance together, our bodies moulding as one, I find myself hoping that this woman doesn't have a man in her life. And if she does, then I will just have to do whatever it takes to make her mine. I have never had such a strong attraction to someone before.

Her appearance may be gorgeous, but as I look into her eyes, I get the feeling that her soul is more beautiful than any part of her exterior. I may be going out on a whim here, but I will do what I can to spend the night with her.

A night which will blow her mind.

A night in which I will let my guard down.

A night that I will make sure neither of us forget.

And a night that I will make as perfect as possible.

ABOUT THE AUTHOR

Lindsey lives in South West, England, with her partner and two children. She works within a family run business, and she began her writing career in 2013. She finds the time to write in-between working and raising a family.

Lindsey's love of reading inspired her to create her own book series. Her favourite book genre is romance, but her interests span over several genre's including mystery, suspense and crime.

To keep up to date with book news, you can find Lindsey on social media and you can also check out Lindsey's website where you can find all of her books:

https://lindseypowellauthor.wordpress.com

- facebook.com/lindseypowellperfect
- twitter.com/Lindsey_perfect
- instagram.com/lindseypowellperfect
- bookbub.com/authors/lindsey-powell
- goodreads.com/lpow21
- amazon.com/author/lindseypowell

AUTHOR ACKNOWLEDGEMENTS

I just want to say thank you for reading The Complete Perfect Series.

I hope you enjoyed the characters and the rollercoaster that their romance took them on.

I just want to say a quick thank you to my usual crew who continue to support me and help me believe that I can keep doing this. I love all of you ladies.

And if you enjoyed this series, I would love it if you could leave me a review on Amazon, Goodreads or Bookbub (or all three!).

I have plenty more coming your way, so stay tuned.

Until next time,

Much love,

Lindsey.

Printed in Great Britain
by Amazon